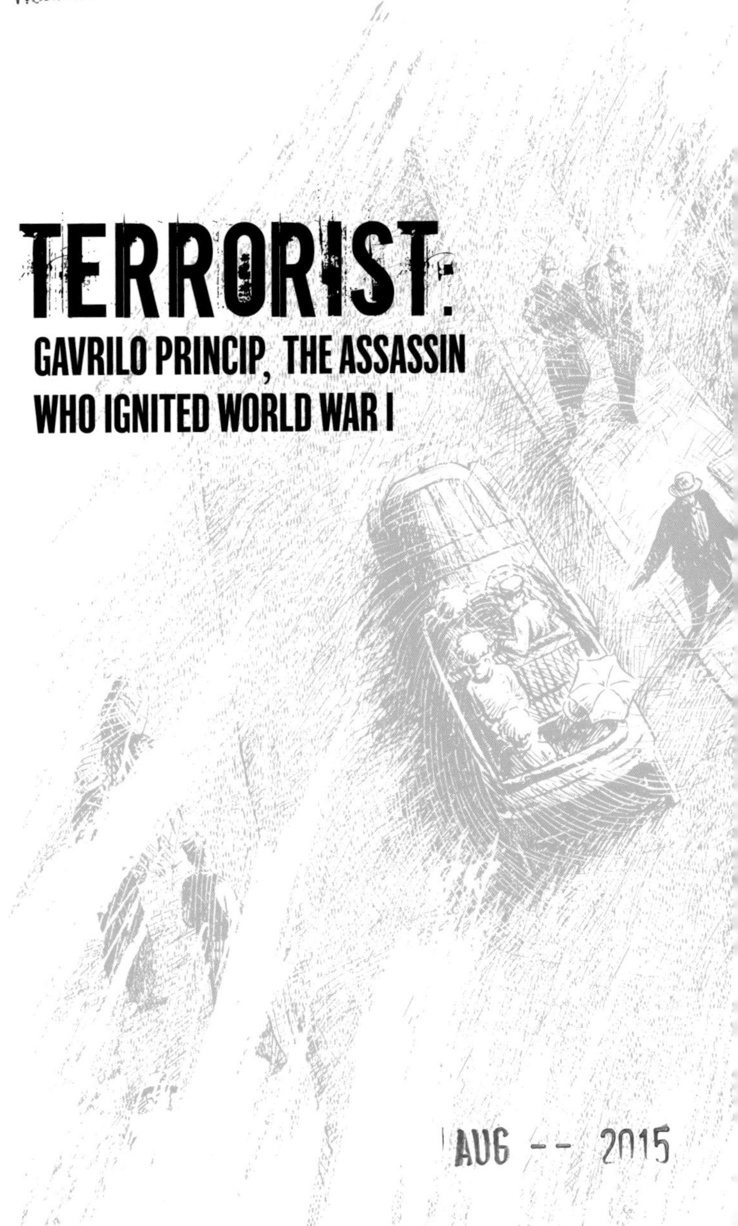

TERRORIST:

GAVRILO PRINCIP, THE ASSASSIN WHO IGNITED WORLD WAR I

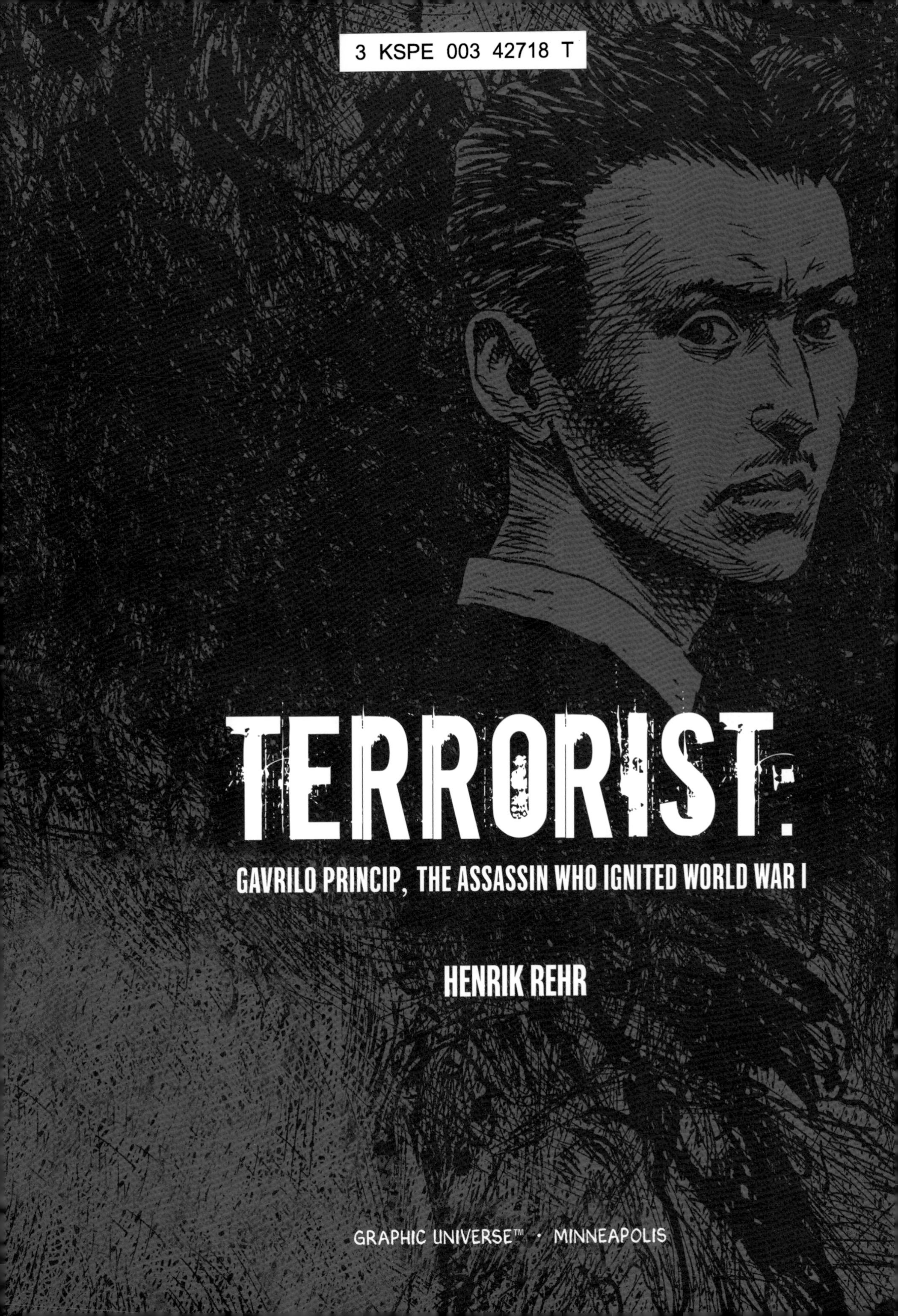

TERRORIST:

GAVRILO PRINCIP, THE ASSASSIN WHO IGNITED WORLD WAR I

HENRIK REHR

GRAPHIC UNIVERSE™ • MINNEAPOLIS

THE AUTHOR THANKS ALLAN HAVERHOLM, PAW MATHIASEN, KRISTIAN REHR, BOB MECOY, ALAIN DAVID AND THE FRIENDLY TEAM AT THE NEW YORK PUBLIC LIBRARY, WITHOUT WHOM THIS BOOK WOULD NOT HAVE HAPPENED.

STORY AND ART BY HENRIK REHR

FIRST AMERICAN EDITION PUBLISHED IN 2015 BY GRAPHIC UNIVERSE™.
PUBLISHED BY ARRANGEMENT WITH FUTUROPOLIS.

GAVRILO PRINCIP: L'HOMME QUI CHANGEA LE SIÈCLE BY HENRIK REHR
COPYRIGHT © FUTUROPOLIS, PARIS, 2014
COPYRIGHT © 2015 BY LERNER PUBLISHING GROUP, INC., FOR THE US EDITION

GRAPHIC UNIVERSE™ IS A TRADEMARK OF LERNER PUBLISHING GROUP, INC.

GRAPHIC UNIVERSE™
A DIVISION OF LERNER PUBLISHING GROUP, INC.
241 FIRST AVENUE NORTH
MINNEAPOLIS, MN 55401 USA

FOR READING LEVELS AND MORE INFORMATION, LOOK UP THIS TITLE AT WWW.LERNERBOOKS.COM.

LIBRARY OF CONGRESS CATALOGING-IN-PUBLICATION DATA

REHR, HENRIK.
    [GAVRILO PRINCIP, L'HOMME QUI CHANGEA LE SIÈCLE. ENGLISH]
    TERRORIST : GAVRILO PRINCIP, THE ASSASSIN WHO IGNITED WORLD WAR I / WRITTEN AND ILLUSTRATED BY HENRIK REHR. — FIRST AMERICAN EDITION.
        PAGES   CM
    SUMMARY: FICTIONAL ACCOUNT OF THE LIFE OF THE YOUNG SERBIAN TERRORIST, GAVRILO PRINCIP, WHO TOUCHED OFF WORLD WAR I IN 1914 BY ASSASSINATING THE ARCHDUKE FRANZ FERDINAND.
        ISBN 978-1-4677-7279-2 (LIB. BDG. : ALK. PAPER) — ISBN 978-1-4677-7284-6 (PBK.) — ISBN 978-1-4677-7285-3 (EB PDF)
        1. GRAPHIC NOVELS. [1. GRAPHIC NOVELS. 2. PRINCIP, GAVRILO, 1894-1918—FICTION. 3. ASSASSINS—FICTION. 4. SERBS—BOSNIA AND HERCEGOVINA—FICTION. 5. WORLD WAR, 1914-1918—FICTION.] I. TITLE.
    PZ7.7.R45GAV 2015
    741.5'944—DC23   2014021939

MANUFACTURED IN THE UNITED STATES OF AMERICA
1 — BP — 12/31/14

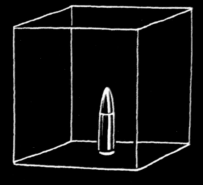

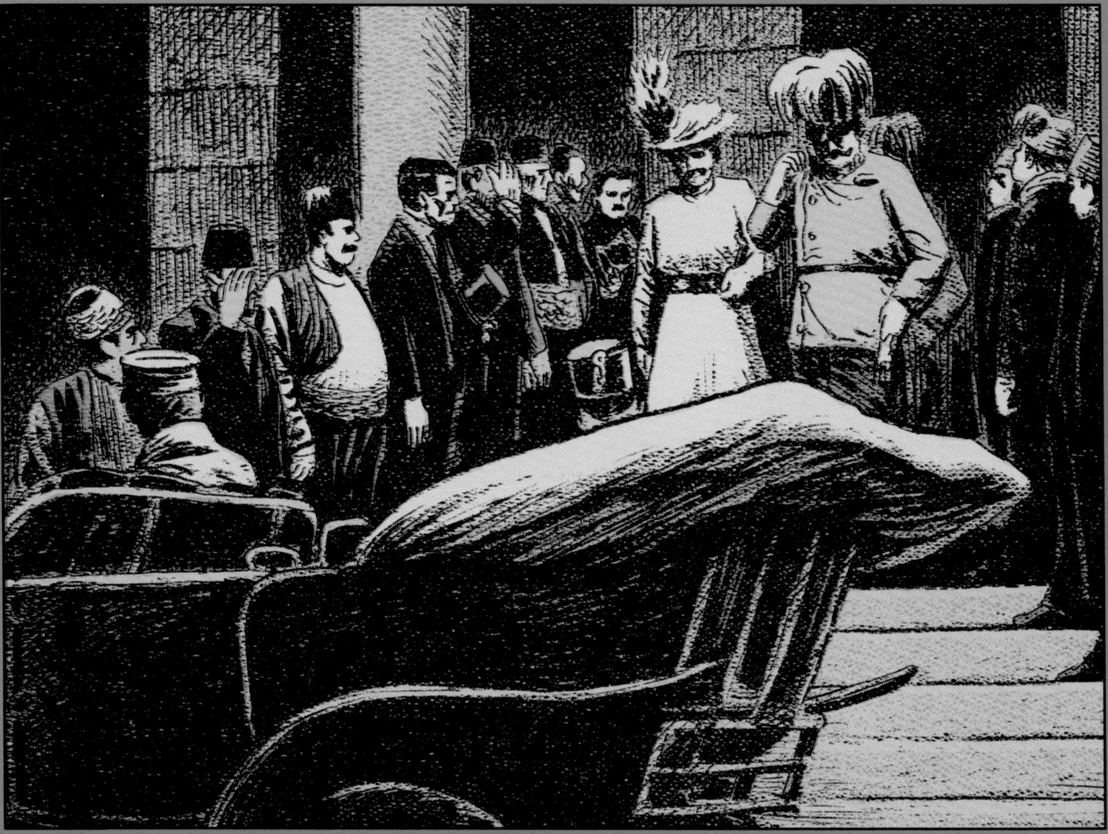

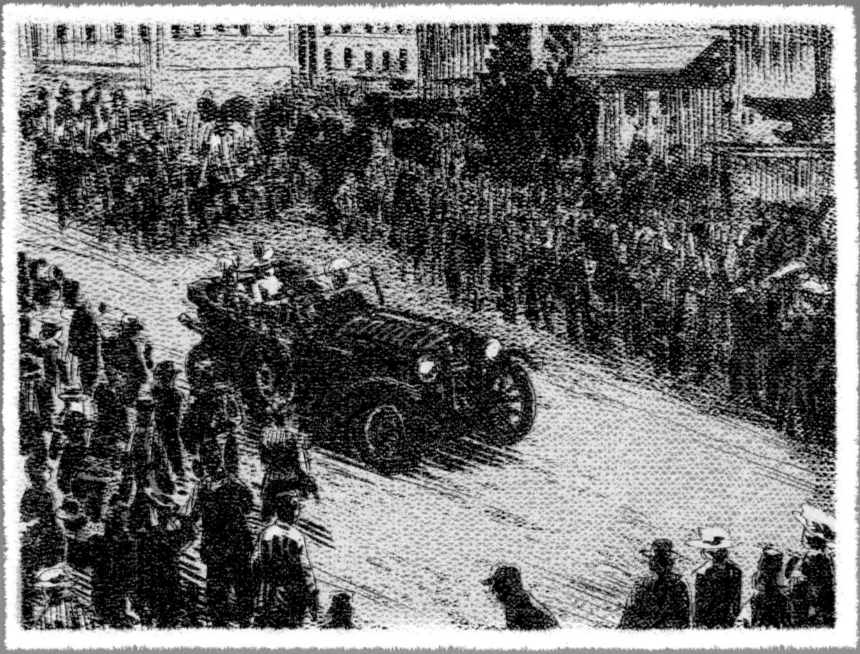

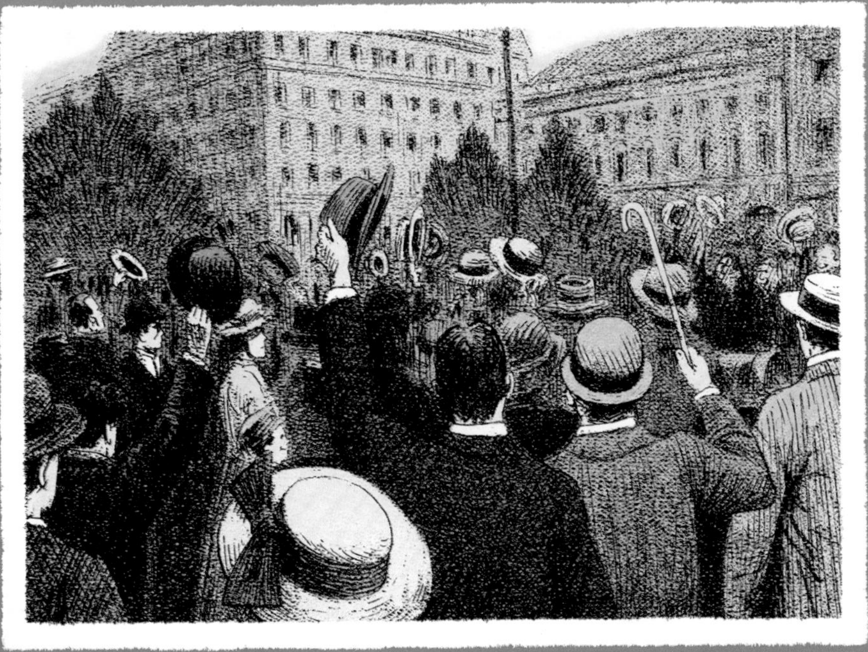

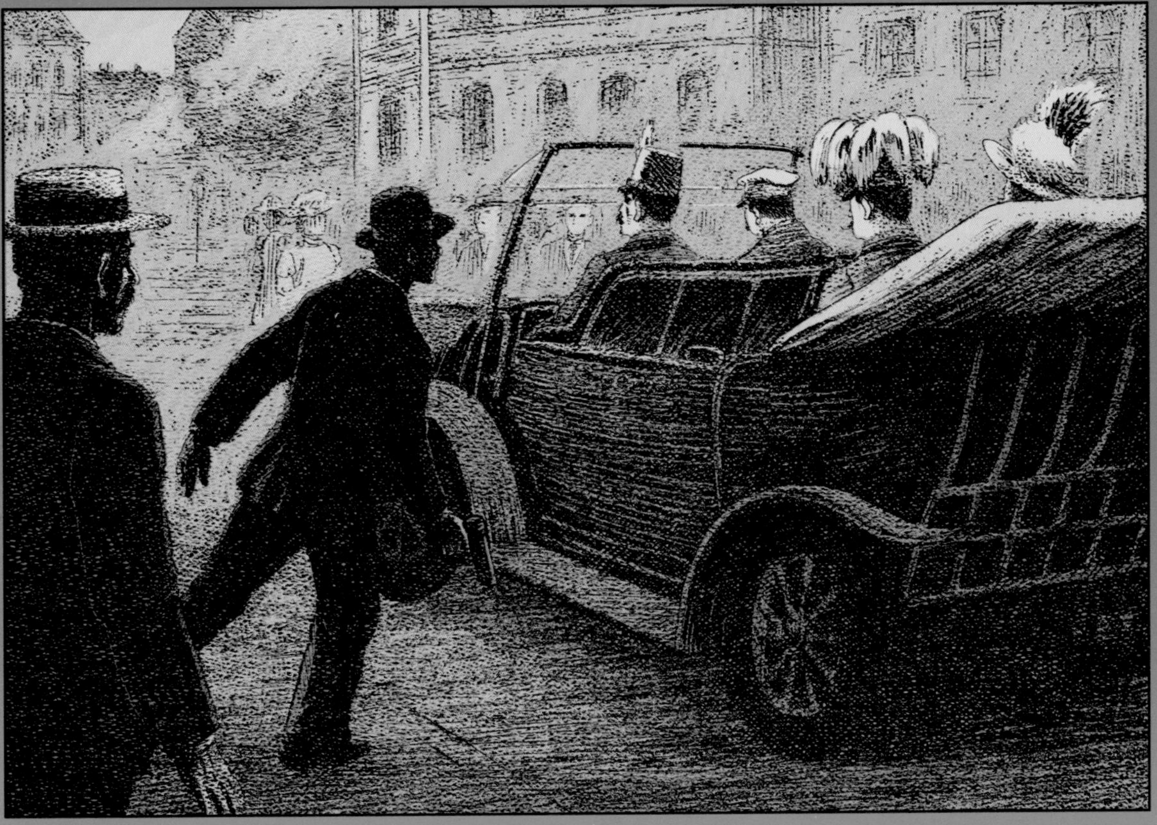

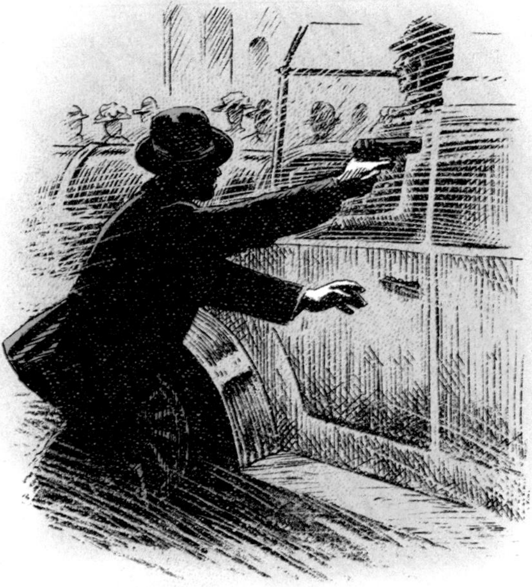

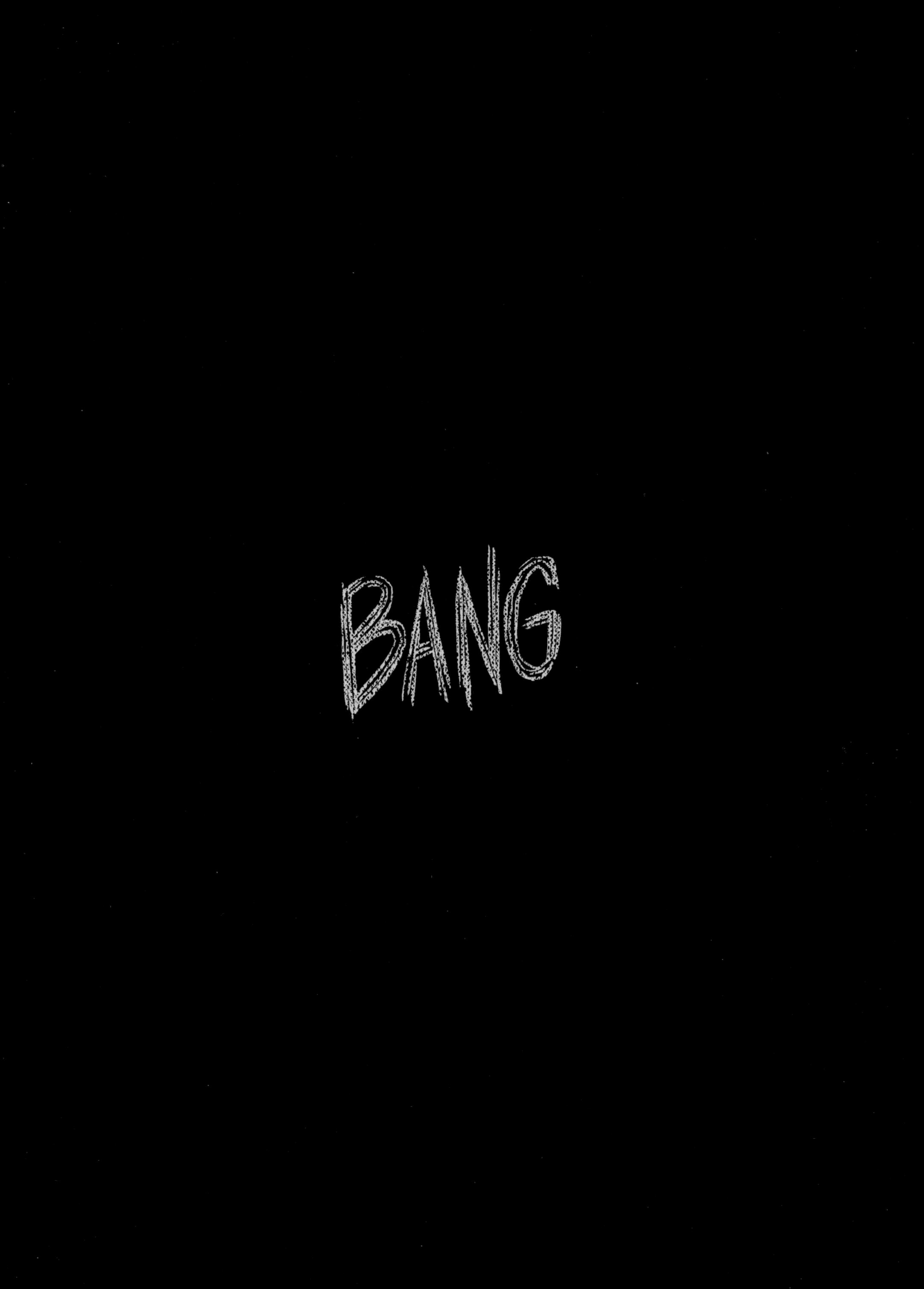
BANG

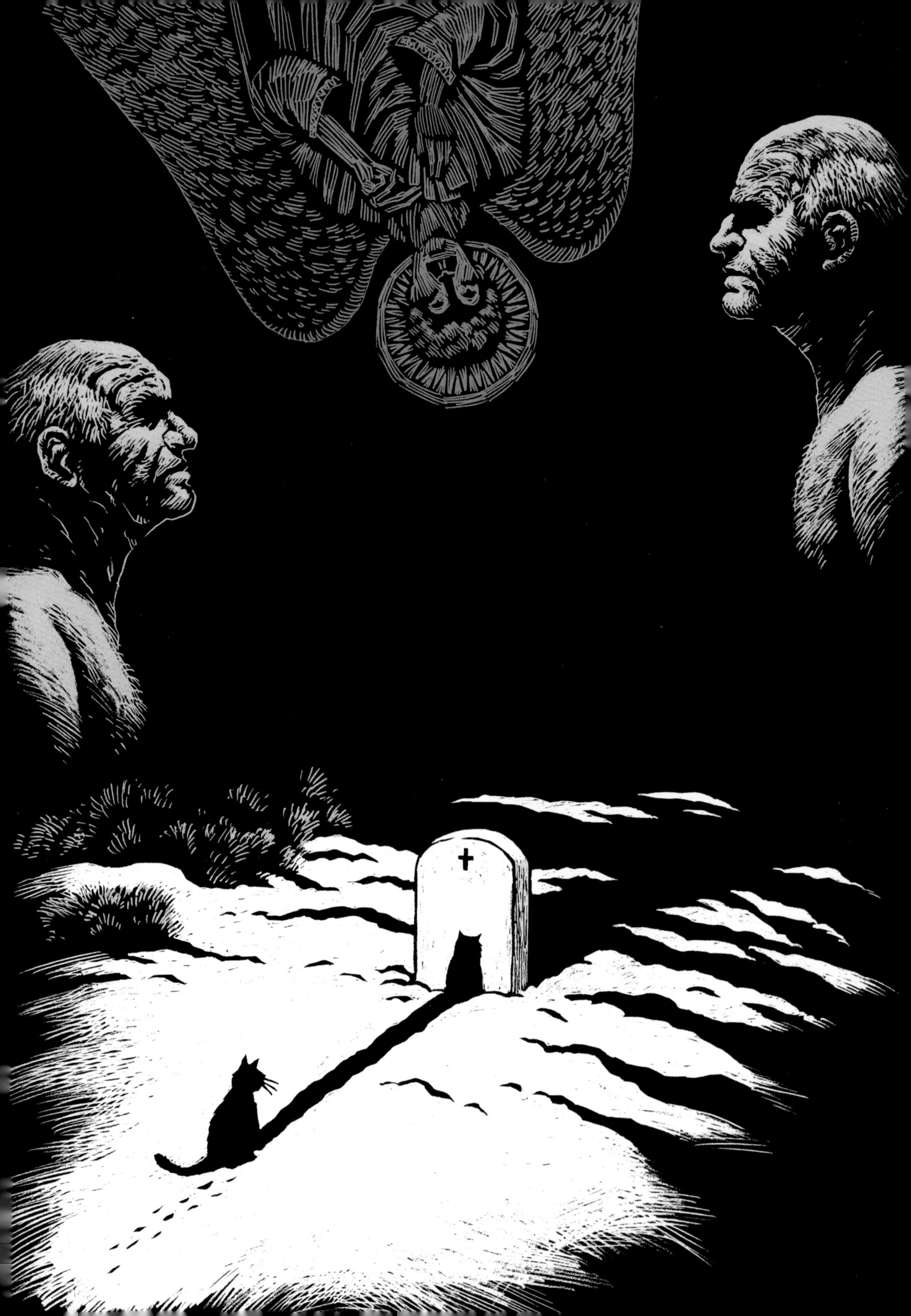

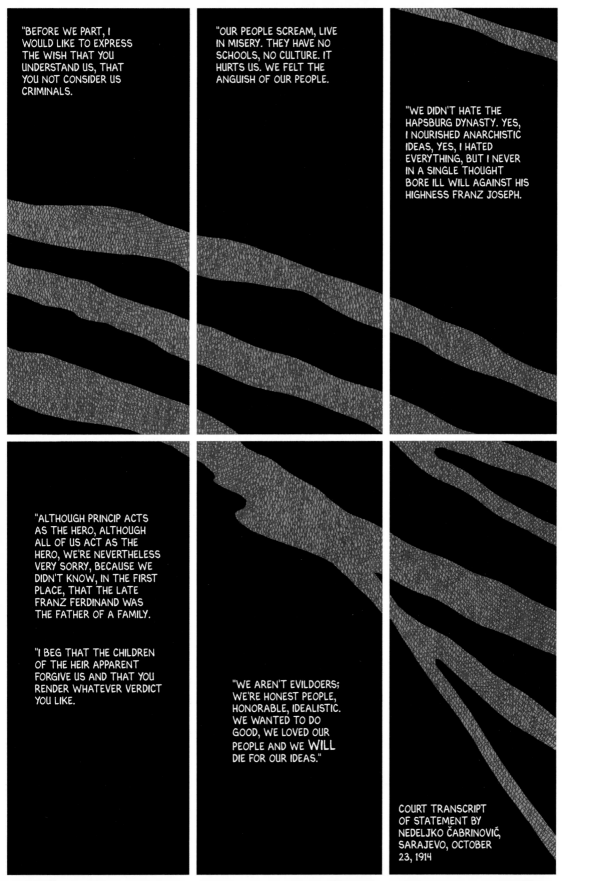

"BEFORE WE PART, I WOULD LIKE TO EXPRESS THE WISH THAT YOU UNDERSTAND US, THAT YOU NOT CONSIDER US CRIMINALS.

"OUR PEOPLE SCREAM, LIVE IN MISERY. THEY HAVE NO SCHOOLS, NO CULTURE. IT HURTS US. WE FELT THE ANGUISH OF OUR PEOPLE.

"WE DIDN'T HATE THE HAPSBURG DYNASTY. YES, I NOURISHED ANARCHISTIC IDEAS, YES, I HATED EVERYTHING, BUT I NEVER IN A SINGLE THOUGHT BORE ILL WILL AGAINST HIS HIGHNESS FRANZ JOSEPH.

"ALTHOUGH PRINCIP ACTS AS THE HERO, ALTHOUGH ALL OF US ACT AS THE HERO, WE'RE NEVERTHELESS VERY SORRY, BECAUSE WE DIDN'T KNOW, IN THE FIRST PLACE, THAT THE LATE FRANZ FERDINAND WAS THE FATHER OF A FAMILY.

"I BEG THAT THE CHILDREN OF THE HEIR APPARENT FORGIVE US AND THAT YOU RENDER WHATEVER VERDICT YOU LIKE.

"WE AREN'T EVILDOERS; WE'RE HONEST PEOPLE, HONORABLE, IDEALISTIC. WE WANTED TO DO GOOD, WE LOVED OUR PEOPLE AND WE WILL DIE FOR OUR IDEAS."

COURT TRANSCRIPT OF STATEMENT BY NEDELJKO ČABRINOVIĆ, SARAJEVO, OCTOBER 23, 1914

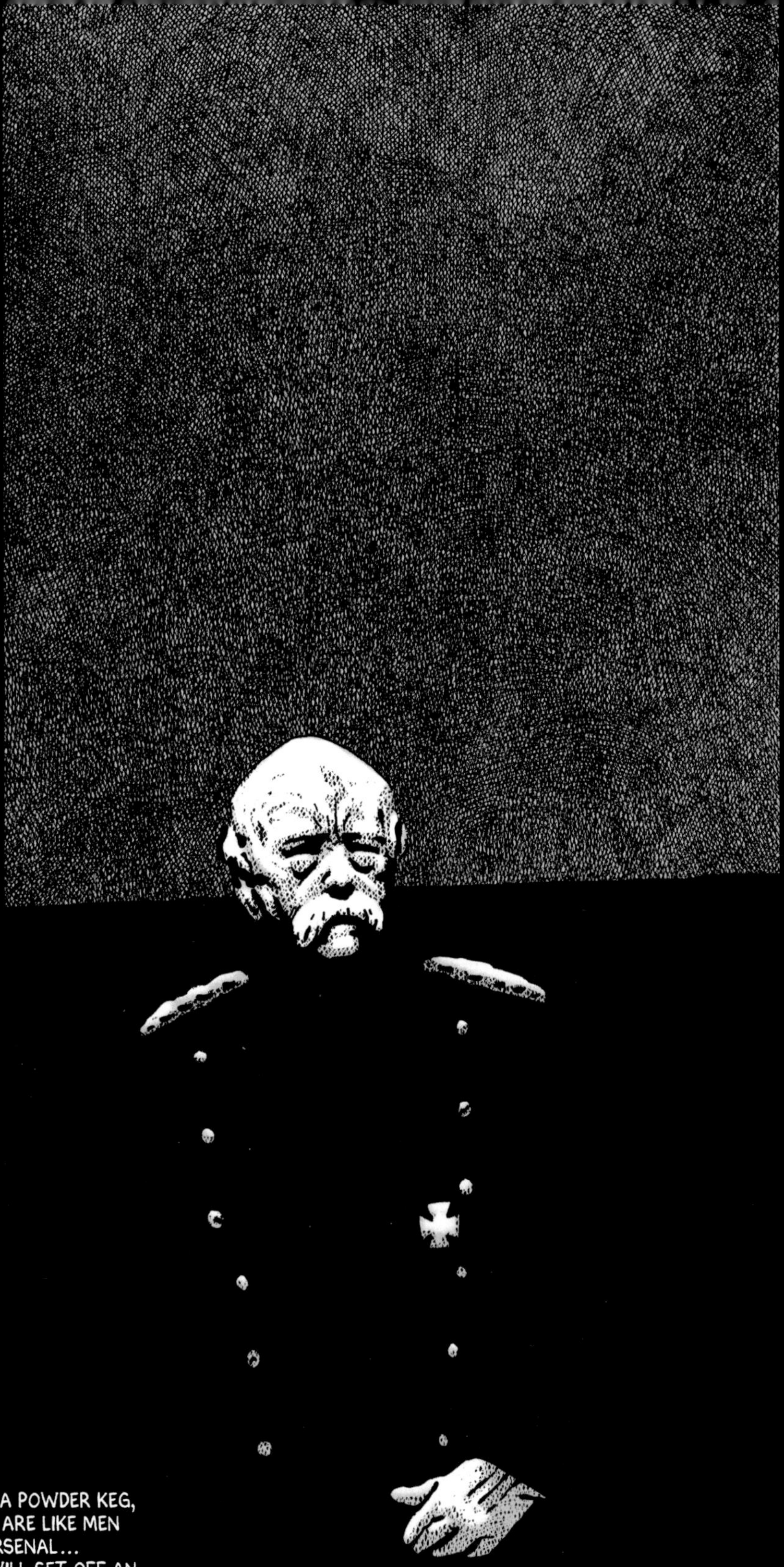

"EUROPE TODAY IS A POWDER KEG,
AND THE LEADERS ARE LIKE MEN
SMOKING IN AN ARSENAL...
A SINGLE SPARK WILL SET OFF AN
EXPLOSION THAT WILL CONSUME US ALL...
I CAN'T TELL YOU WHEN THAT EXPLOSION
WILL OCCUR, BUT I CAN TELL YOU WHERE...
SOME DAMNED FOOLISH THING IN THE
BALKANS WILL SET IT OFF."

—OTTO VON BISMARCK,
GERMAN CHANCELLOR, 1862–1890

THE TRUTH IS WRITTEN IN WATER.

THIS IS A TRUE STORY.

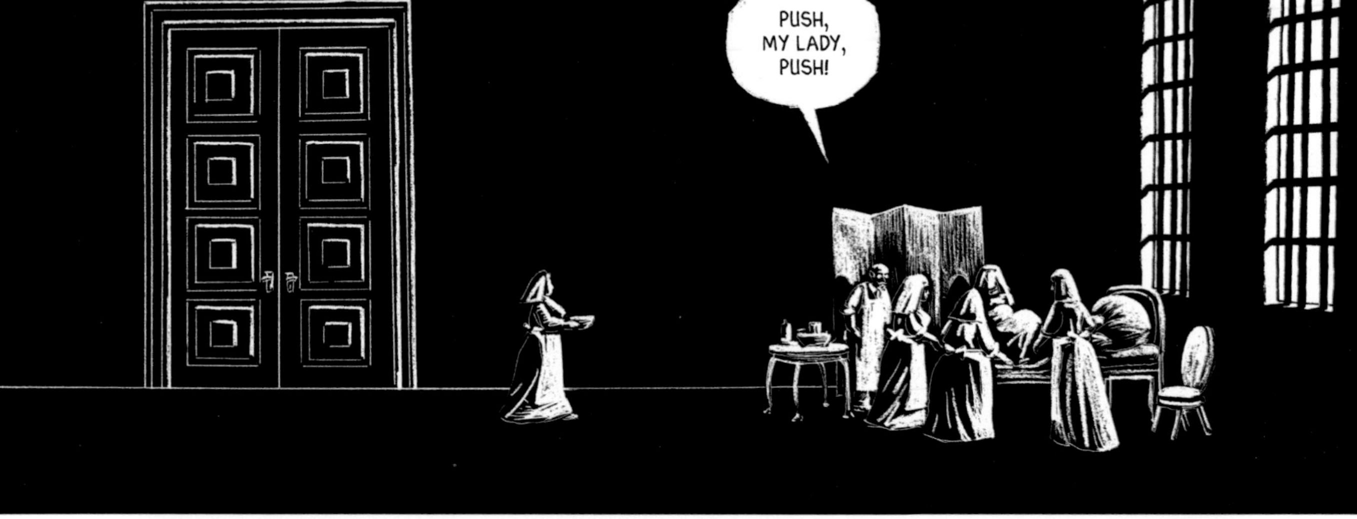
PUSH, MY LADY, PUSH!

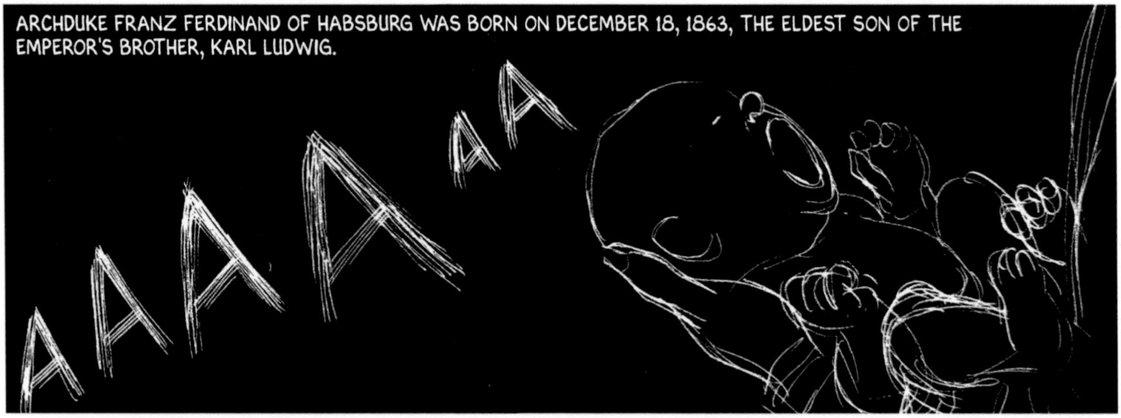
ARCHDUKE FRANZ FERDINAND OF HABSBURG WAS BORN ON DECEMBER 18, 1863, THE ELDEST SON OF THE EMPEROR'S BROTHER, KARL LUDWIG.
AAAAAA

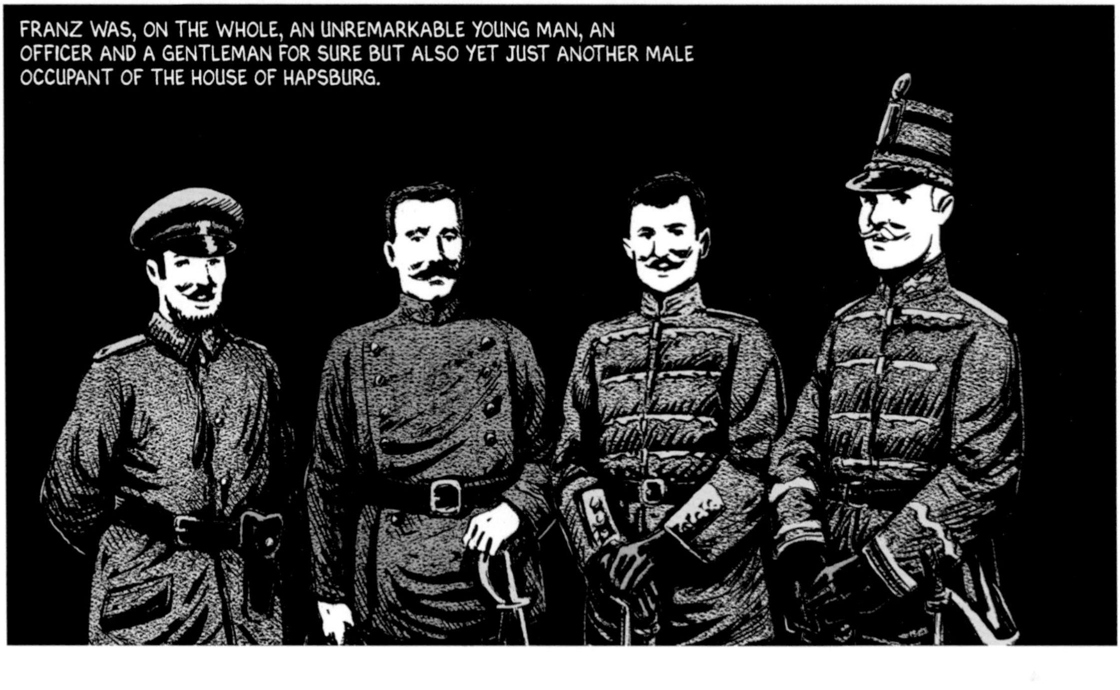
FRANZ WAS, ON THE WHOLE, AN UNREMARKABLE YOUNG MAN, AN OFFICER AND A GENTLEMAN FOR SURE BUT ALSO YET JUST ANOTHER MALE OCCUPANT OF THE HOUSE OF HAPSBURG.

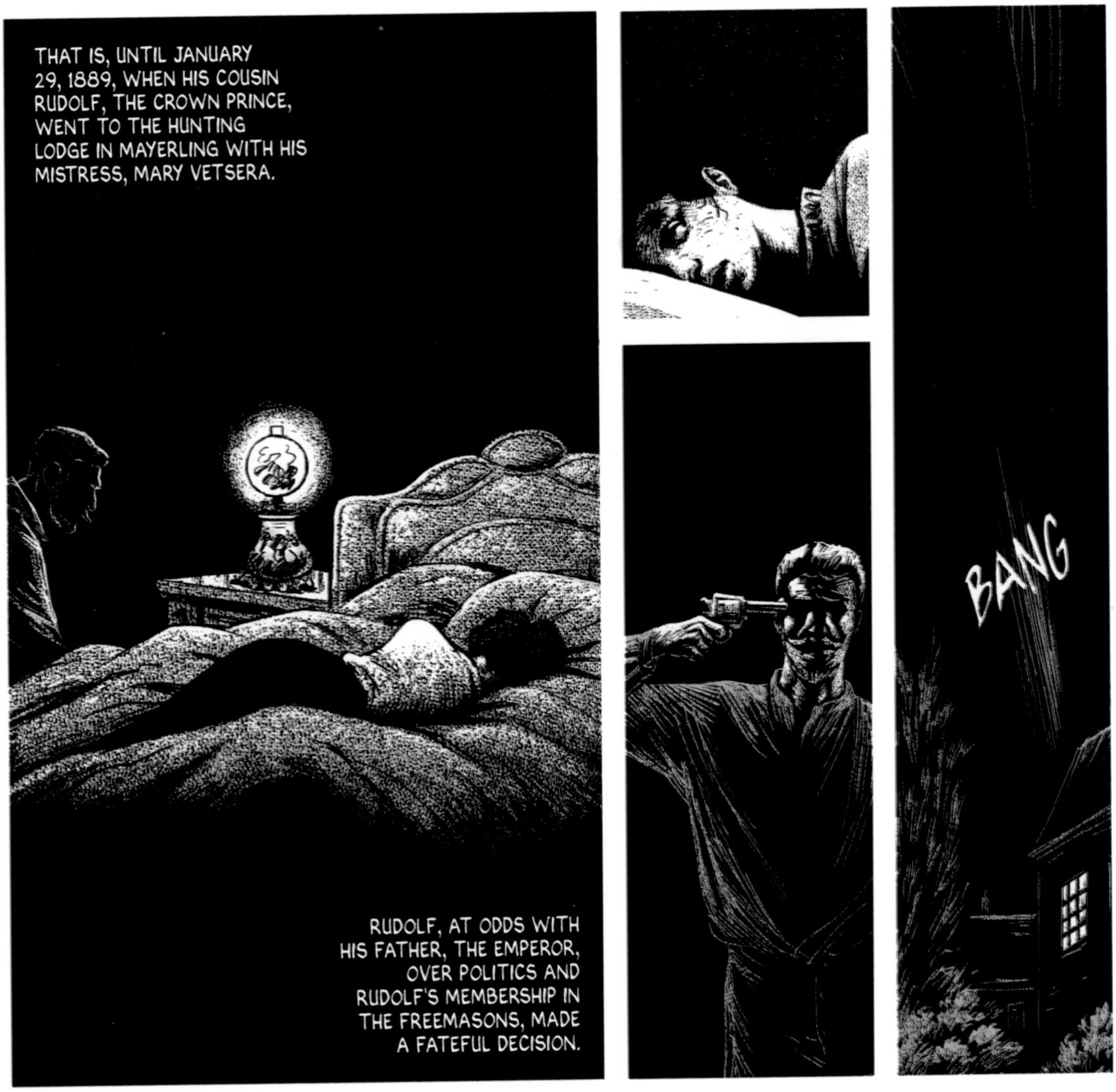
THAT IS, UNTIL JANUARY 29, 1889, WHEN HIS COUSIN RUDOLF, THE CROWN PRINCE, WENT TO THE HUNTING LODGE IN MAYERLING WITH HIS MISTRESS, MARY VETSERA.
RUDOLF, AT ODDS WITH HIS FATHER, THE EMPEROR, OVER POLITICS AND RUDOLF'S MEMBERSHIP IN THE FREEMASONS, MADE A FATEFUL DECISION.
BANG

SUDDENLY, FRANZ FERDINAND WAS THE HEIR APPARENT TO THE THRONE OF AUSTRIA-HUNGARY.

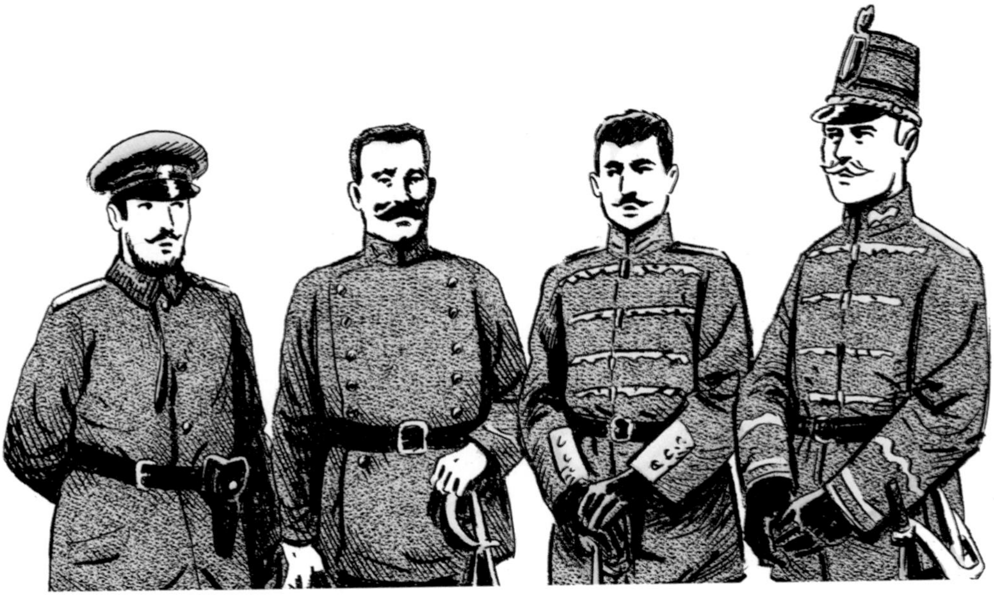

"KRAJINA'S LIKE A BLOOD-SOAKED RAG.
BLOOD IS OUR FARE AT NOON, BLOOD STILL IN THE EVENING.
ON EVERY LIP THE TASTE OF BLOOD.
NEVER A PEACEFUL DAY, NEVER ANY REST."

—SERBIAN FOLK SONG

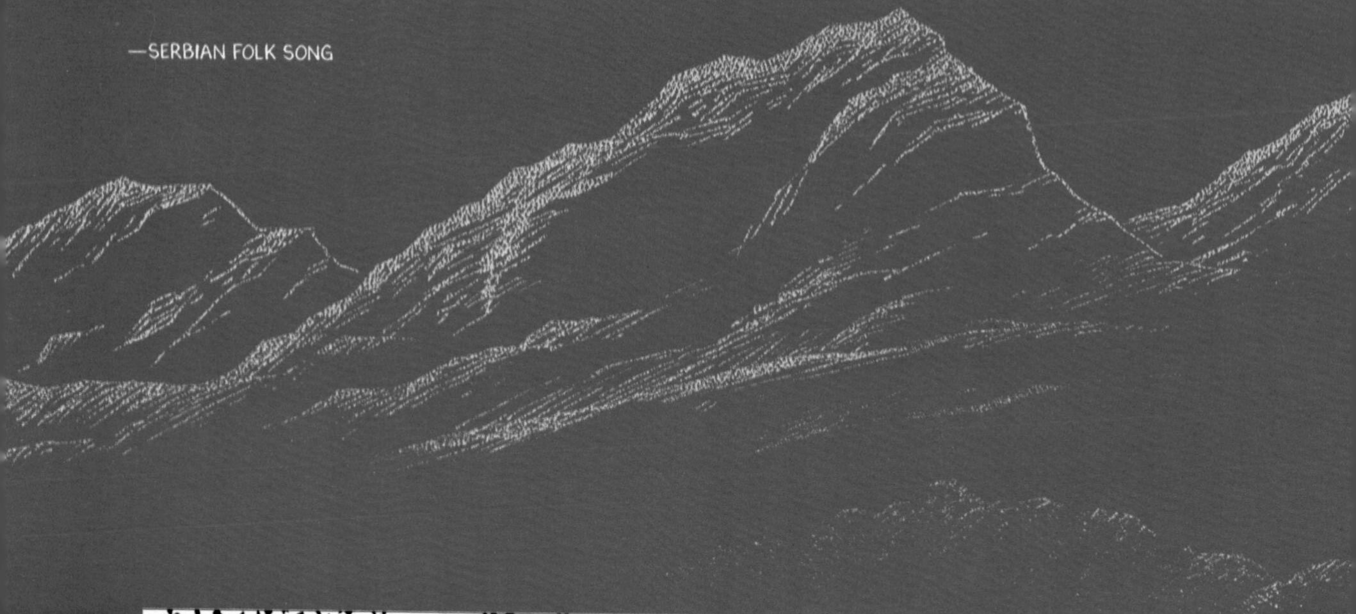

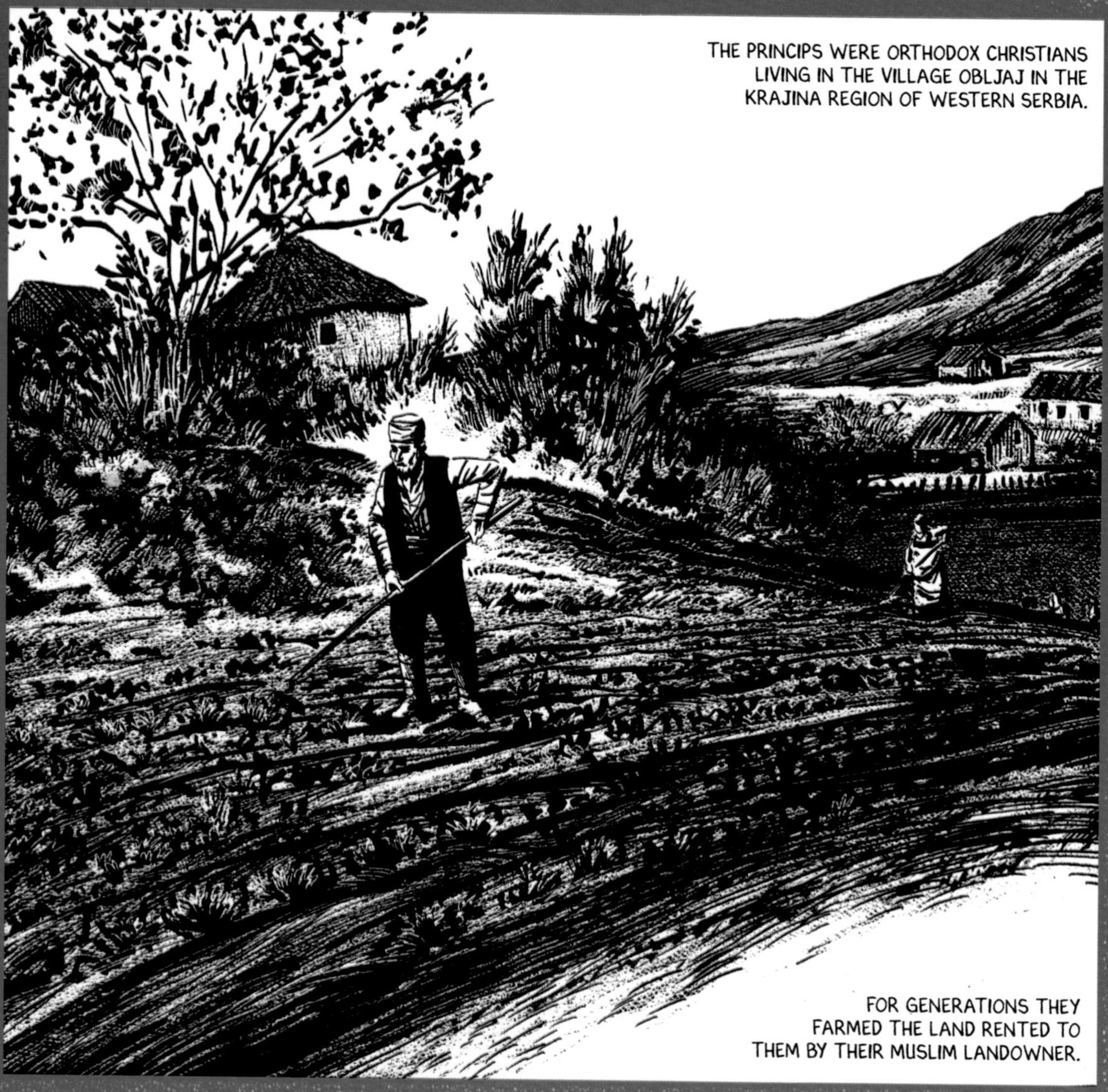
THE PRINCIPS WERE ORTHODOX CHRISTIANS LIVING IN THE VILLAGE OBLJAJ IN THE KRAJINA REGION OF WESTERN SERBIA.
FOR GENERATIONS THEY FARMED THE LAND RENTED TO THEM BY THEIR MUSLIM LANDOWNER.

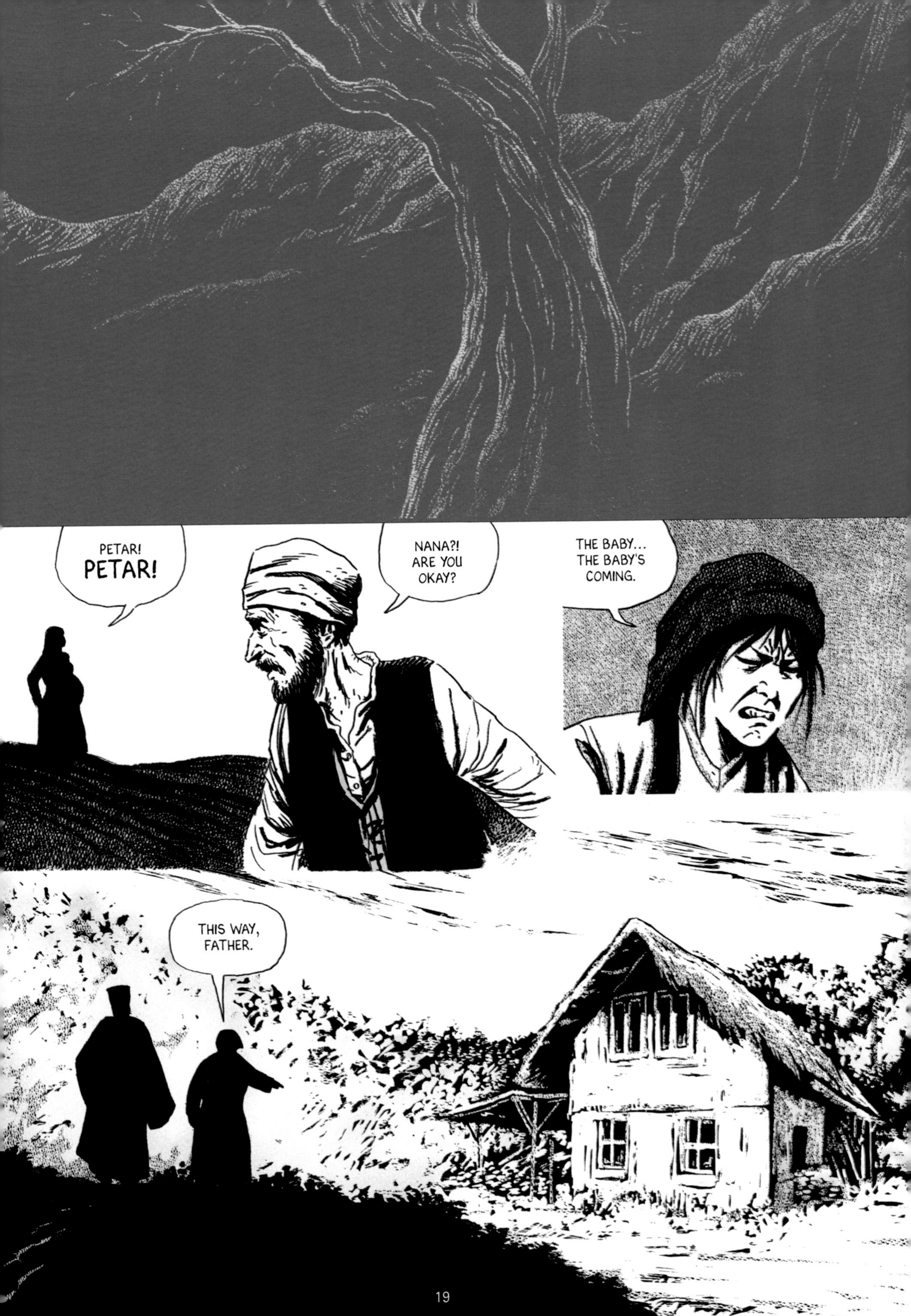
PETAR!
PETAR!
NANA?! ARE YOU OKAY?
THE BABY... THE BABY'S COMING.
THIS WAY, FATHER.

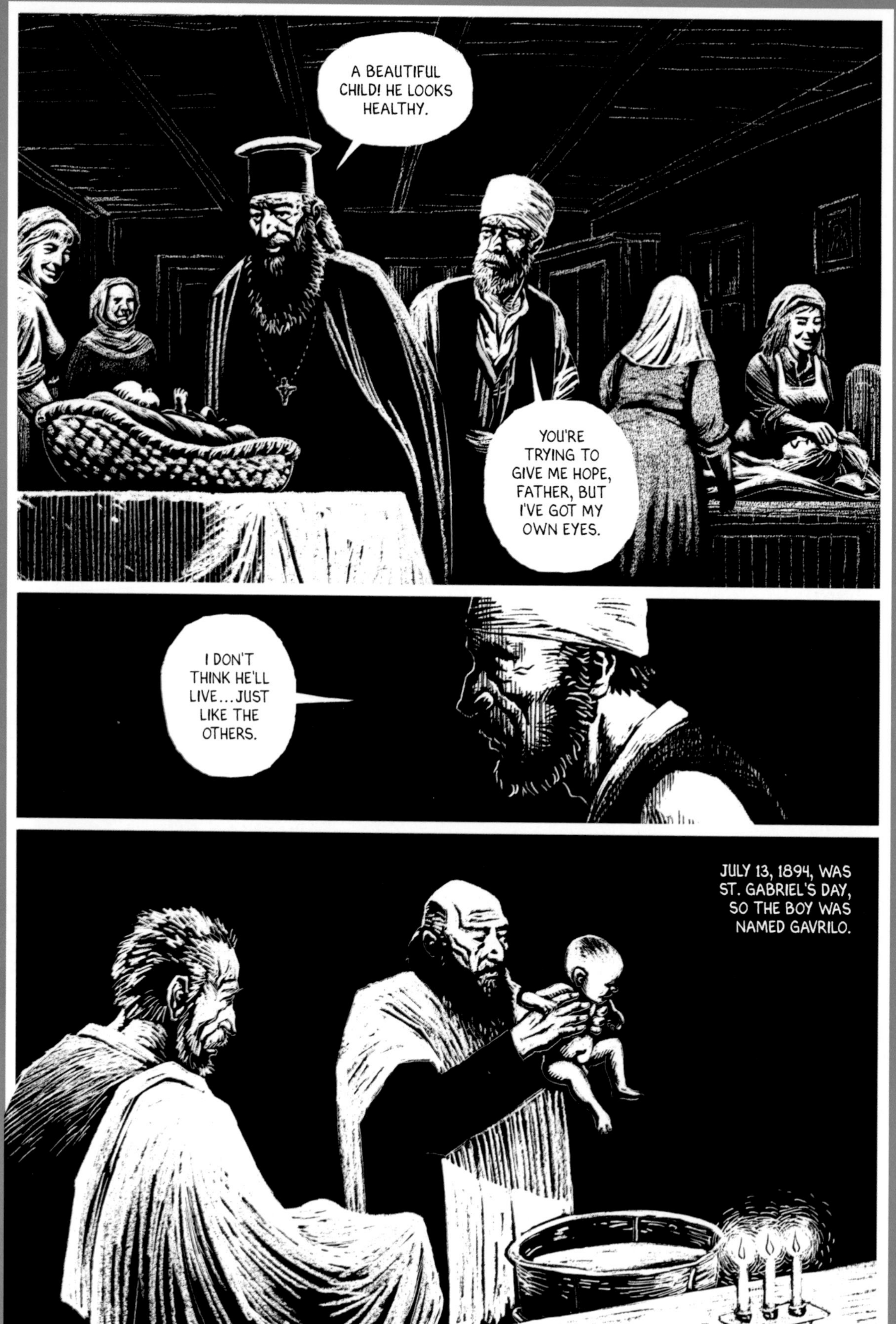
A BEAUTIFUL CHILD! HE LOOKS HEALTHY.
YOU'RE TRYING TO GIVE ME HOPE, FATHER, BUT I'VE GOT MY OWN EYES.
I DON'T THINK HE'LL LIVE... JUST LIKE THE OTHERS.
JULY 13, 1894, WAS ST. GABRIEL'S DAY, SO THE BOY WAS NAMED GAVRILO.

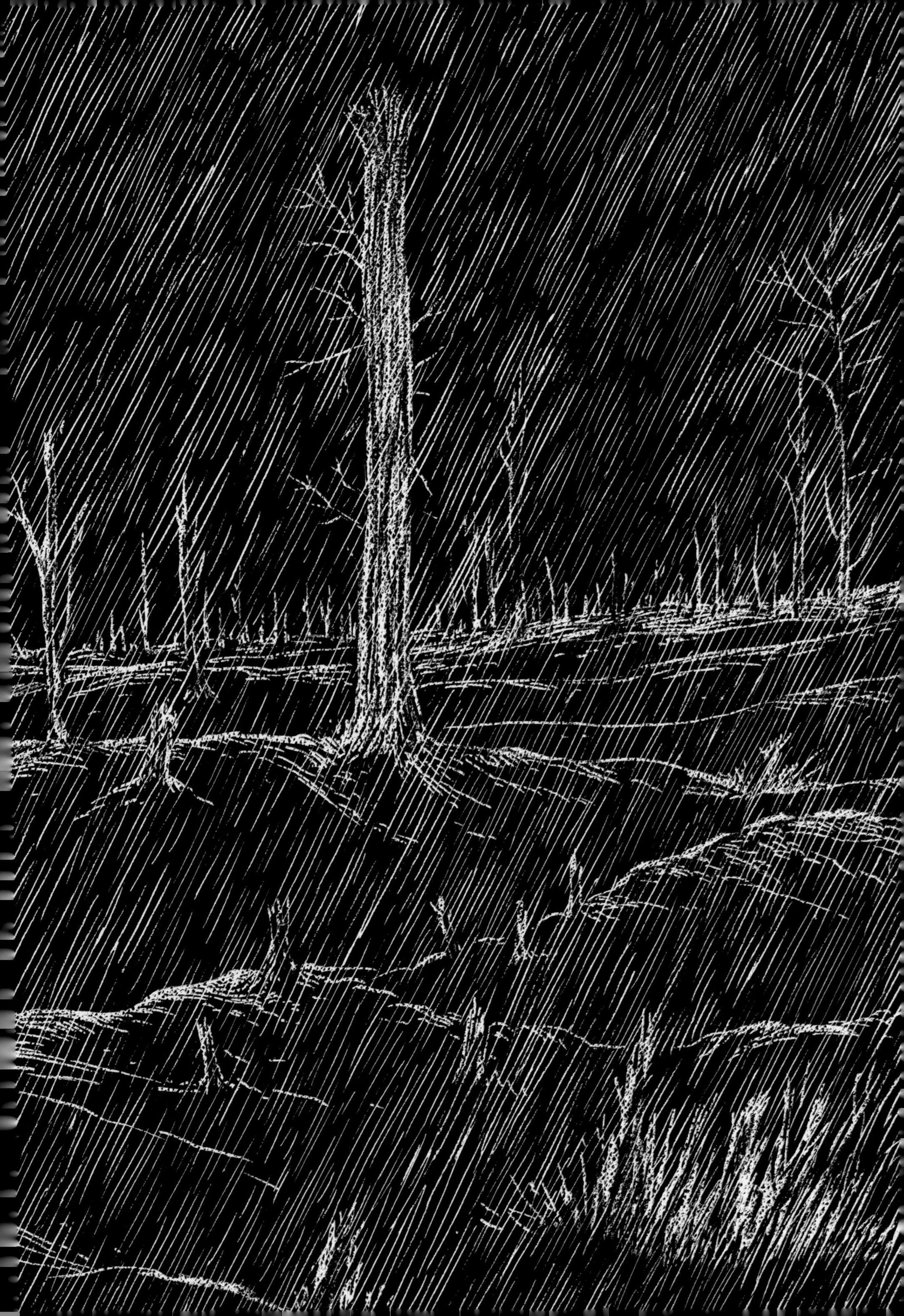

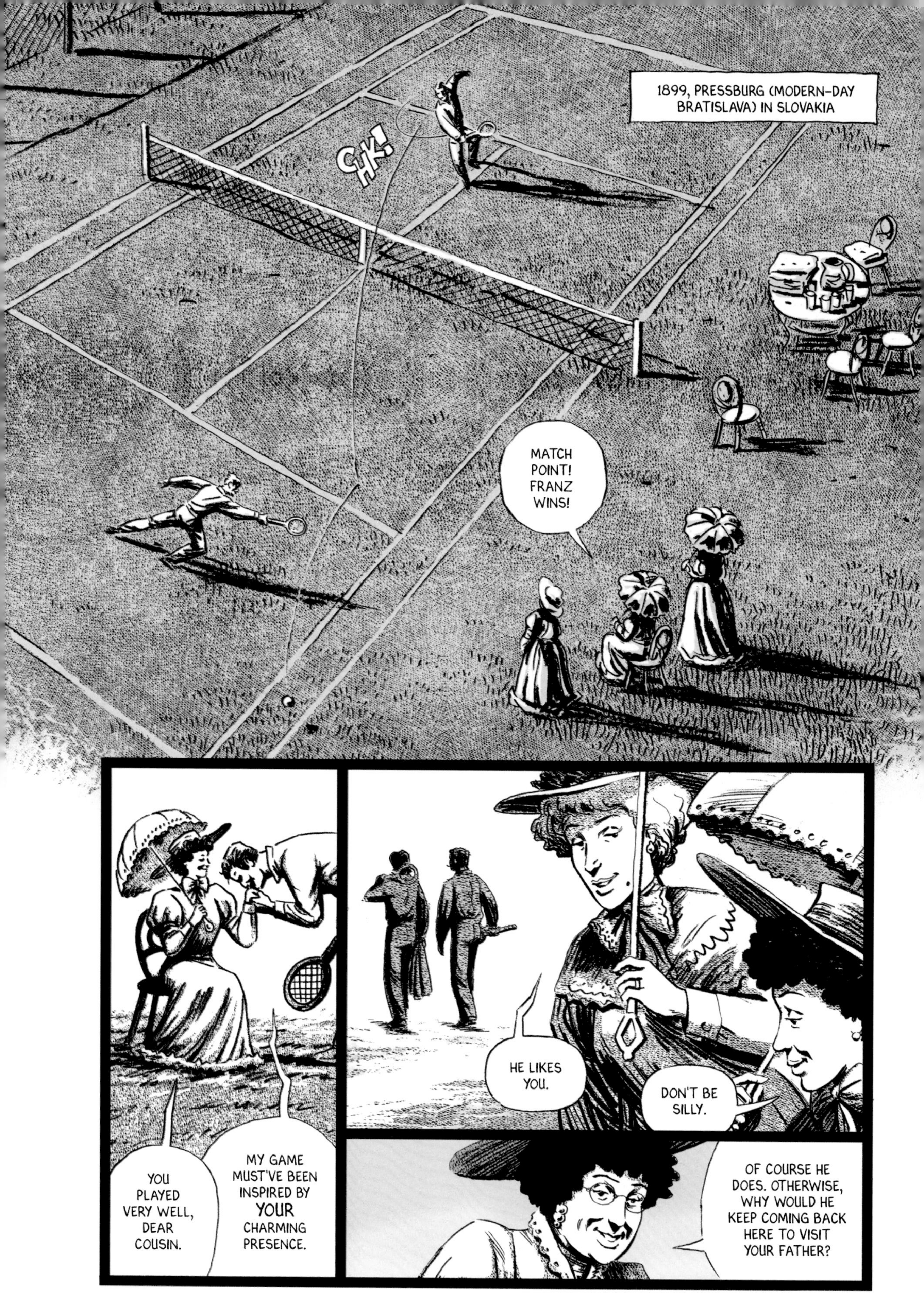
1899, PRESSBURG (MODERN-DAY BRATISLAVA) IN SLOVAKIA
CHK!
MATCH POINT! FRANZ WINS!
YOU PLAYED VERY WELL, DEAR COUSIN.
MY GAME MUST'VE BEEN INSPIRED BY YOUR CHARMING PRESENCE.
HE LIKES YOU.
DON'T BE SILLY.
OF COURSE HE DOES. OTHERWISE, WHY WOULD HE KEEP COMING BACK HERE TO VISIT YOUR FATHER?

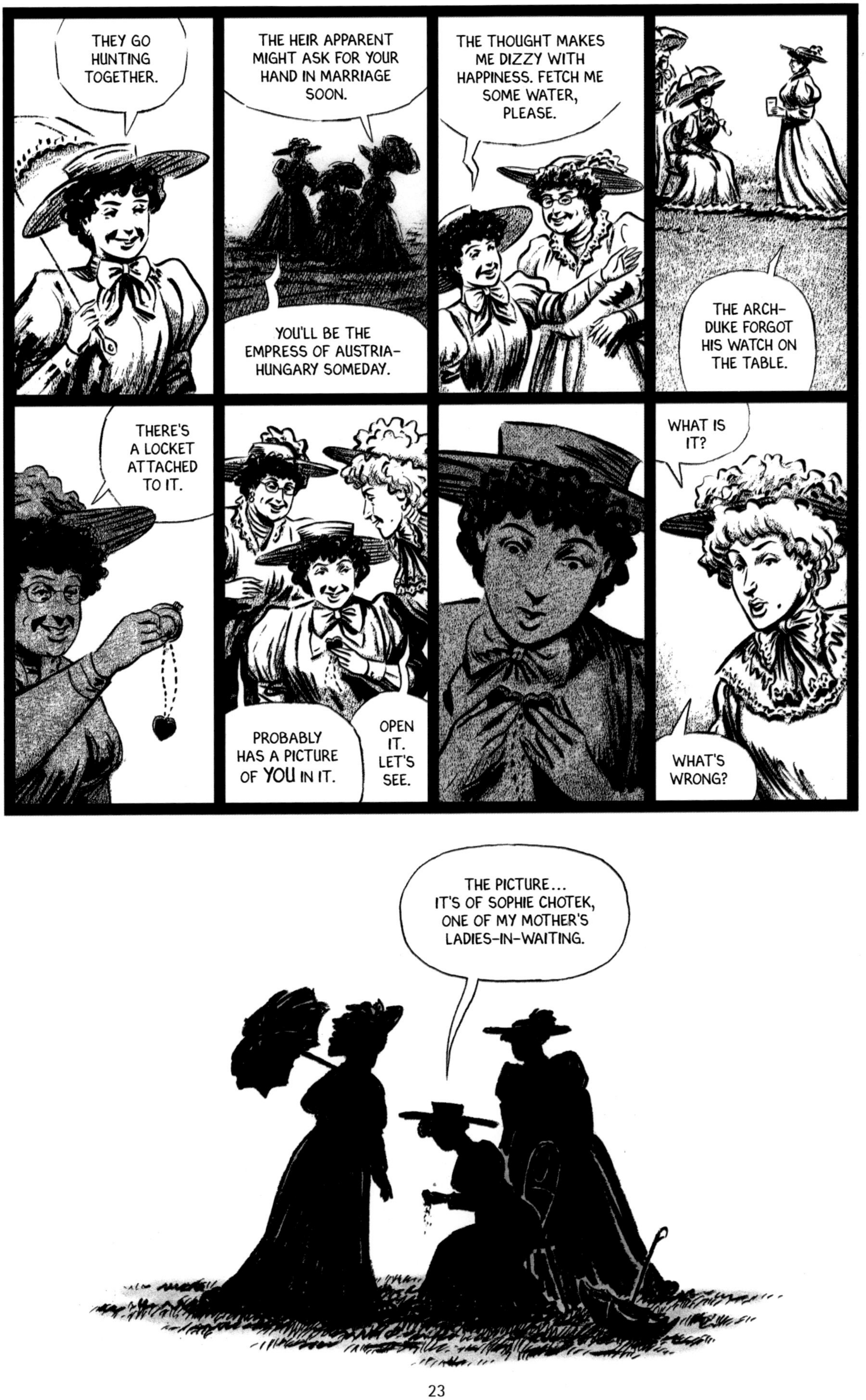
THEY GO HUNTING TOGETHER.
THE HEIR APPARENT MIGHT ASK FOR YOUR HAND IN MARRIAGE SOON.
YOU'LL BE THE EMPRESS OF AUSTRIA-HUNGARY SOMEDAY.
THE THOUGHT MAKES ME DIZZY WITH HAPPINESS. FETCH ME SOME WATER, PLEASE.
THE ARCH-DUKE FORGOT HIS WATCH ON THE TABLE.
THERE'S A LOCKET ATTACHED TO IT.
PROBABLY HAS A PICTURE OF YOU IN IT.
OPEN IT. LET'S SEE.
WHAT IS IT?
WHAT'S WRONG?
THE PICTURE... IT'S OF SOPHIE CHOTEK, ONE OF MY MOTHER'S LADIES-IN-WAITING.

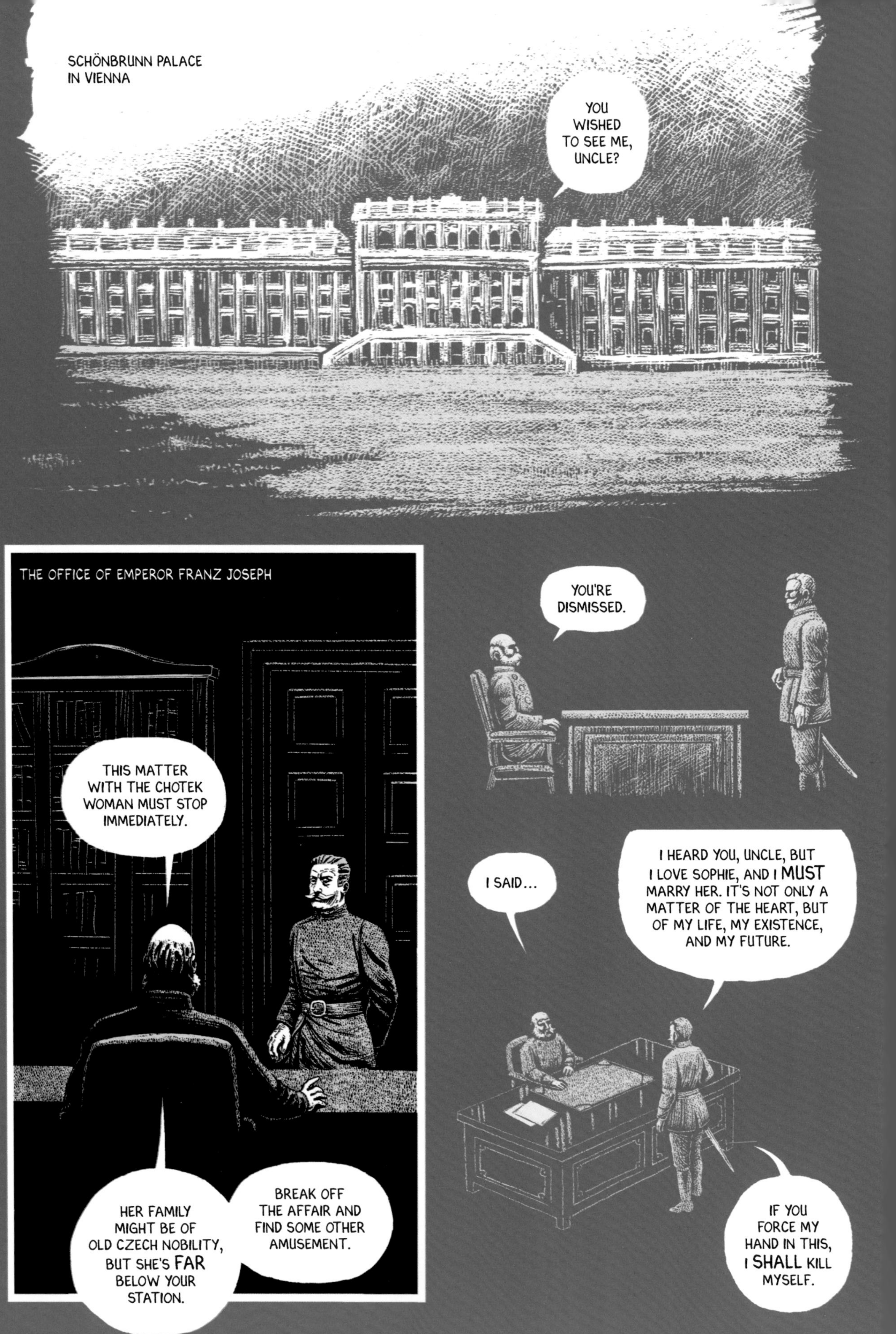
SCHÖNBRUNN PALACE IN VIENNA
YOU WISHED TO SEE ME, UNCLE?
THE OFFICE OF EMPEROR FRANZ JOSEPH
THIS MATTER WITH THE CHOTEK WOMAN MUST STOP IMMEDIATELY.
HER FAMILY MIGHT BE OF OLD CZECH NOBILITY, BUT SHE'S FAR BELOW YOUR STATION.
BREAK OFF THE AFFAIR AND FIND SOME OTHER AMUSEMENT.
YOU'RE DISMISSED.
I SAID...
I HEARD YOU, UNCLE, BUT I LOVE SOPHIE, AND I MUST MARRY HER. IT'S NOT ONLY A MATTER OF THE HEART, BUT OF MY LIFE, MY EXISTENCE, AND MY FUTURE.
IF YOU FORCE MY HAND IN THIS, I SHALL KILL MYSELF.

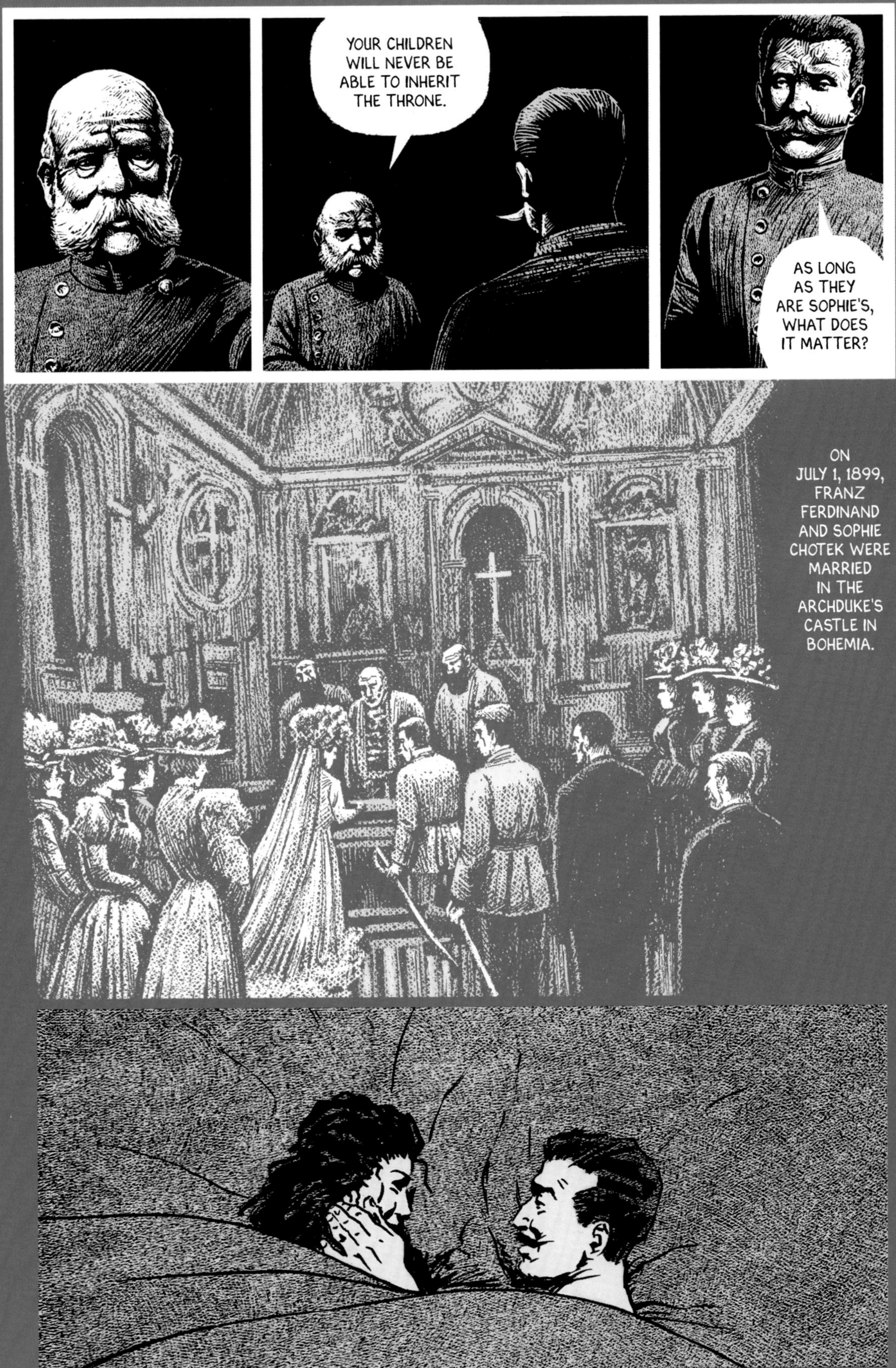
YOUR CHILDREN WILL NEVER BE ABLE TO INHERIT THE THRONE.
AS LONG AS THEY ARE SOPHIE'S, WHAT DOES IT MATTER?
ON JULY 1, 1899, FRANZ FERDINAND AND SOPHIE CHOTEK WERE MARRIED IN THE ARCHDUKE'S CASTLE IN BOHEMIA.

IN THE NINETEENTH CENTURY THE OTTOMAN EMPIRE'S HOLD ON THE BALKANS HAD BEGUN TO WEAKEN. WITH THE TREATY OF BERLIN IN 1878, SERBIA, MONTENEGRO, ROMANIA, AND BULGARIA GAINED THEIR INDEPENDENCE AFTER FIVE HUNDRED YEARS OF MUSLIM RULE.

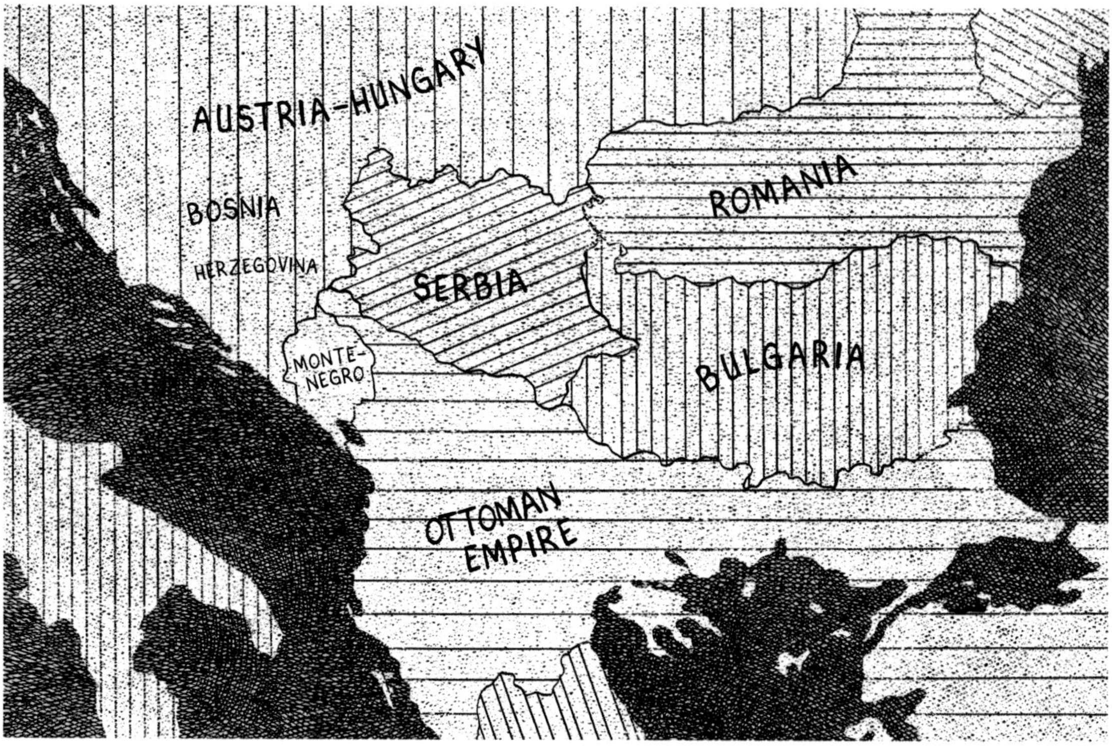

AUSTRIA-HUNGARY
BOSNIA
HERZEGOVINA
SERBIA
MONTE-NEGRO
ROMANIA
BULGARIA
OTTOMAN EMPIRE

SLOVENIA AND CROATIA CONTINUED TO BE GOVERNED BY AUSTRIA-HUNGARY, WHICH ALSO TOOK CONTROL OF BOSNIA-HERZEGOVINA, ALTHOUGH THE PEOPLE OF THE LATTER STILL TECHNICALLY WERE TURKISH CITIZENS.

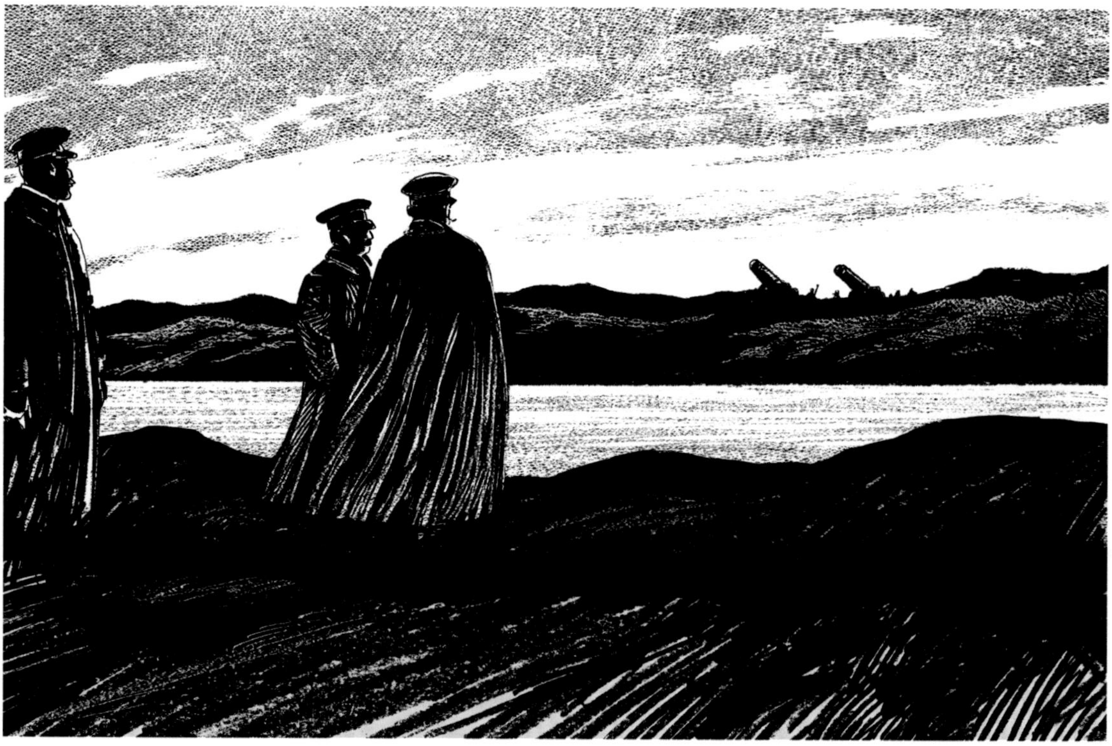

INSPIRED BY ITALY'S EXAMPLE, DREAMS OF UNIFICATION OF ALL THE SOUTHERN SLAVS BEGAN TO ARISE IN THE REGION. BY THE TURN OF THE CENTURY, IT WAS OBVIOUS TO BOTH THE TURKS AND THE AUSTRIANS THAT SERBIA WAS A FORCE TO BE RECKONED WITH.

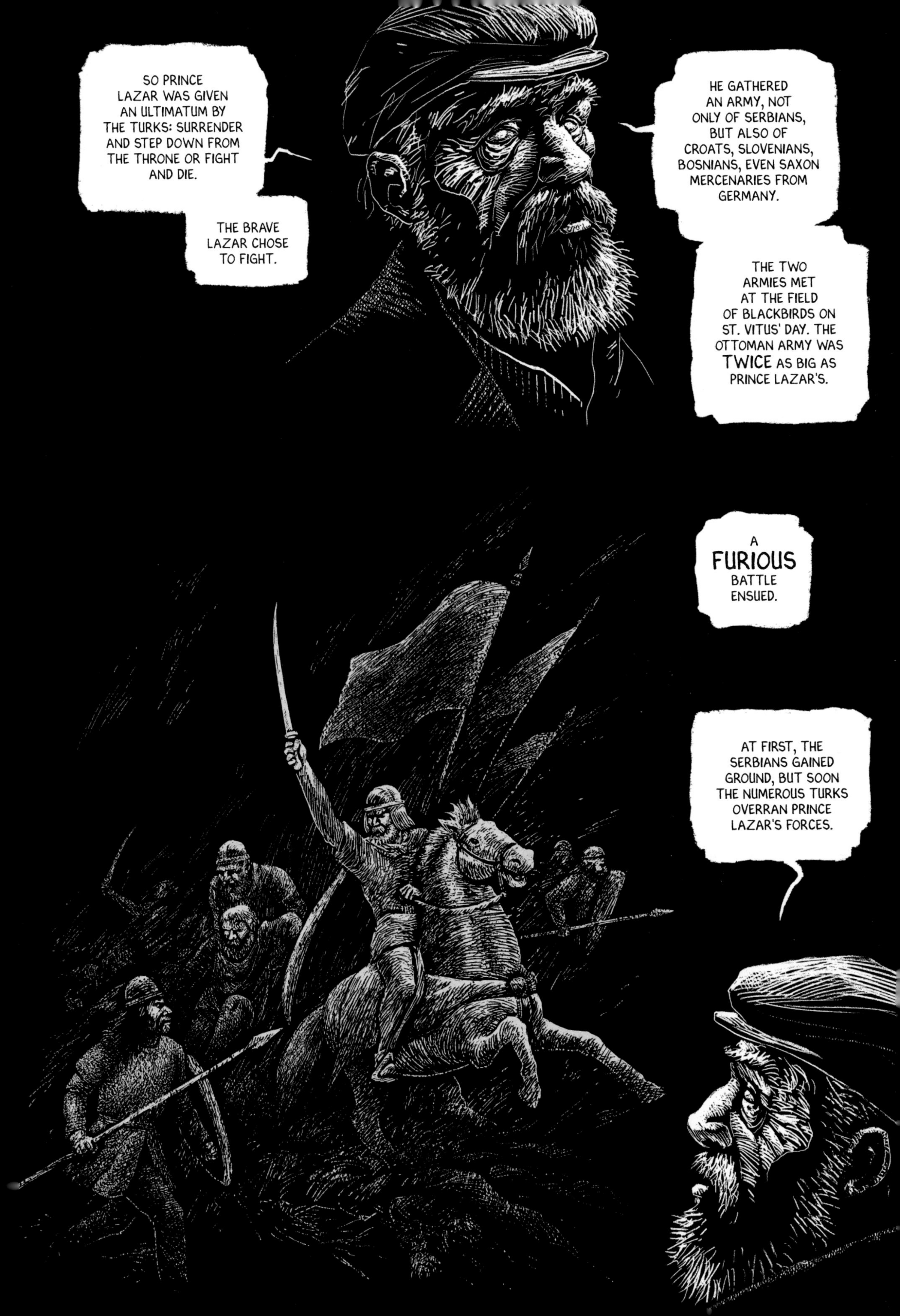
SO PRINCE LAZAR WAS GIVEN AN ULTIMATUM BY THE TURKS: SURRENDER AND STEP DOWN FROM THE THRONE OR FIGHT AND DIE.
THE BRAVE LAZAR CHOSE TO FIGHT.
HE GATHERED AN ARMY, NOT ONLY OF SERBIANS, BUT ALSO OF CROATS, SLOVENIANS, BOSNIANS, EVEN SAXON MERCENARIES FROM GERMANY.
THE TWO ARMIES MET AT THE FIELD OF BLACKBIRDS ON ST. VITUS' DAY. THE OTTOMAN ARMY WAS TWICE AS BIG AS PRINCE LAZAR'S.
A FURIOUS BATTLE ENSUED.
AT FIRST, THE SERBIANS GAINED GROUND, BUT SOON THE NUMEROUS TURKS OVERRAN PRINCE LAZAR'S FORCES.

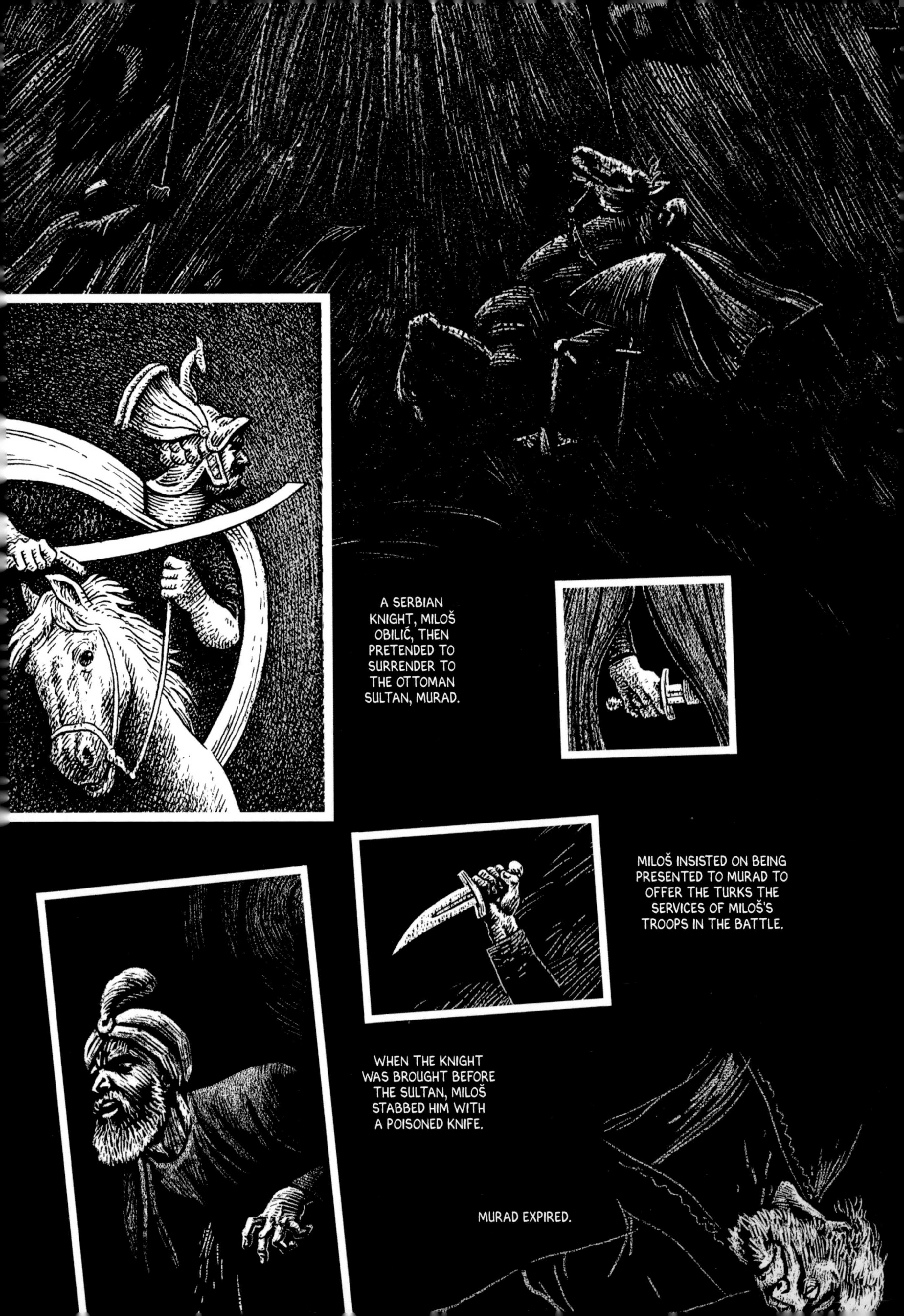
A SERBIAN KNIGHT, MILOŠ OBILIĆ, THEN PRETENDED TO SURRENDER TO THE OTTOMAN SULTAN, MURAD.
MILOŠ INSISTED ON BEING PRESENTED TO MURAD TO OFFER THE TURKS THE SERVICES OF MILOŠ'S TROOPS IN THE BATTLE.
WHEN THE KNIGHT WAS BROUGHT BEFORE THE SULTAN, MILOŠ STABBED HIM WITH A POISONED KNIFE.
MURAD EXPIRED.

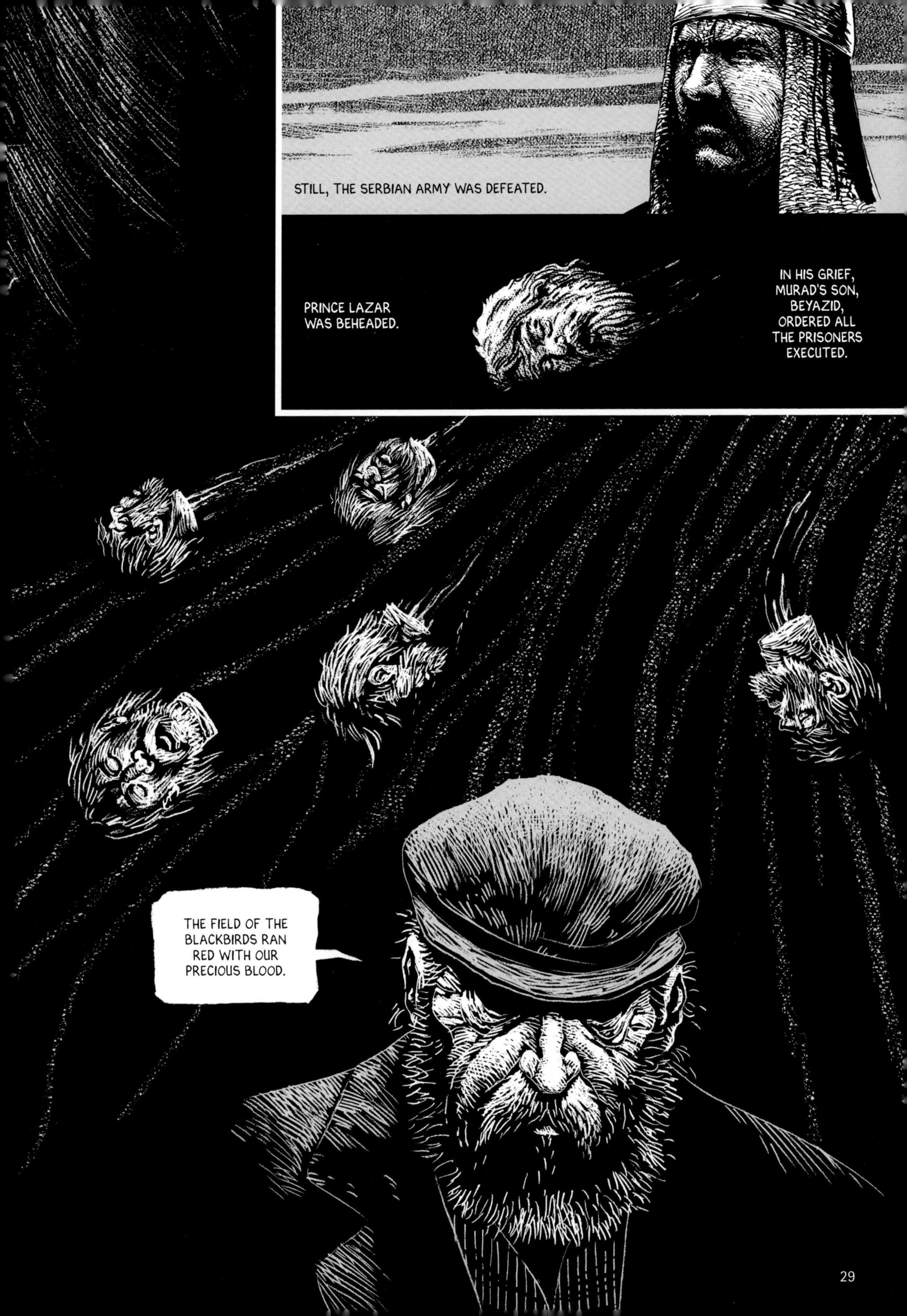
STILL, THE SERBIAN ARMY WAS DEFEATED.
PRINCE LAZAR WAS BEHEADED.
IN HIS GRIEF, MURAD'S SON, BEYAZID, ORDERED ALL THE PRISONERS EXECUTED.
THE FIELD OF THE BLACKBIRDS RAN RED WITH OUR PRECIOUS BLOOD.

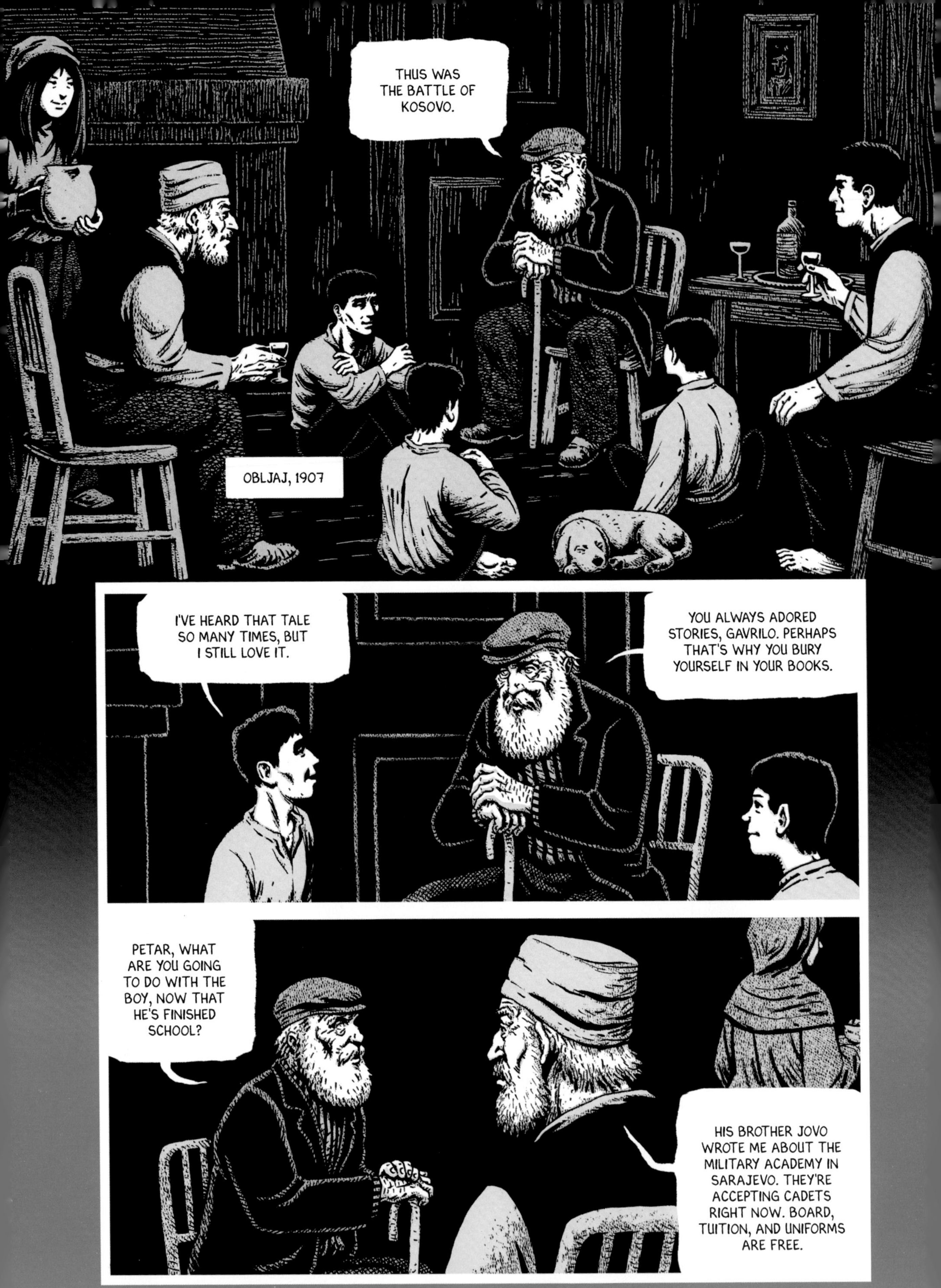
THUS WAS THE BATTLE OF KOSOVO.
OBLJAJ, 1907
I'VE HEARD THAT TALE SO MANY TIMES, BUT I STILL LOVE IT.
YOU ALWAYS ADORED STORIES, GAVRILO. PERHAPS THAT'S WHY YOU BURY YOURSELF IN YOUR BOOKS.
PETAR, WHAT ARE YOU GOING TO DO WITH THE BOY, NOW THAT HE'S FINISHED SCHOOL?
HIS BROTHER JOVO WROTE ME ABOUT THE MILITARY ACADEMY IN SARAJEVO. THEY'RE ACCEPTING CADETS RIGHT NOW. BOARD, TUITION, AND UNIFORMS ARE FREE.

I'LL TAKE GAVRILO OVER THE MOUNTAINS TO THE RAILWAY STATION NEXT WEEK.

A WISE DECISION. HE HAS NO CHANCE OF MAKING A DECENT LIVING IN THIS GODFORSAKEN VALLEY.

GAVRO, COME HERE.

BE CAREFUL IN THE CITY, BOY. TOWNSPEOPLE ARE VERY DIFFERENT FROM THE GENTLE FOLKS YOU'VE GROWN UP WITH HERE.

AND NEVER, **NEVER** FORGET WHO YOU ARE. SARAJEVO'S FULL OF MUSLIMS, AUSTRIANS, CROATS, WHAT HAVE YOU. BE A SERB ABOVE ALL ELSE.

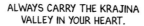

ALWAYS CARRY THE KRAJINA VALLEY IN YOUR HEART.

ALWAYS.

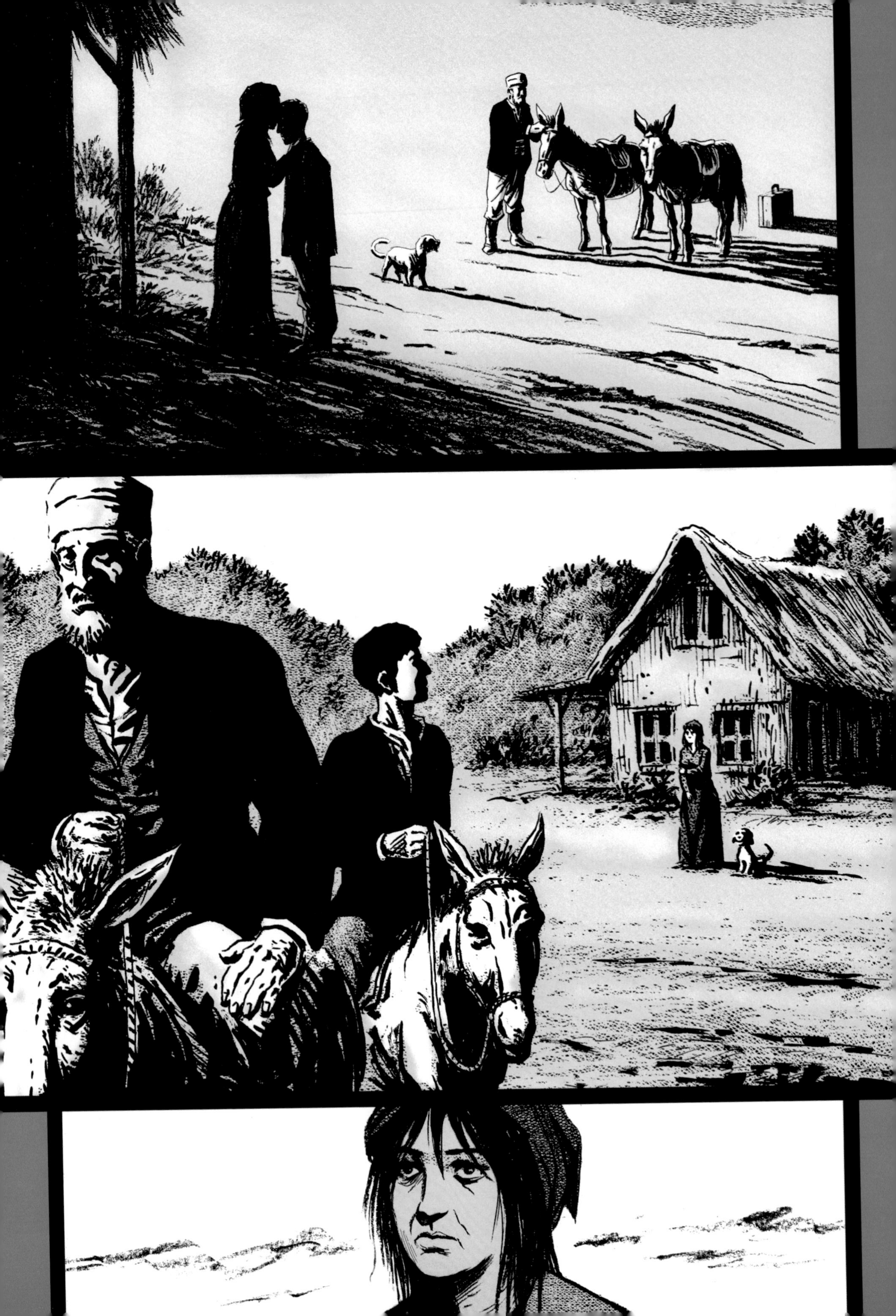

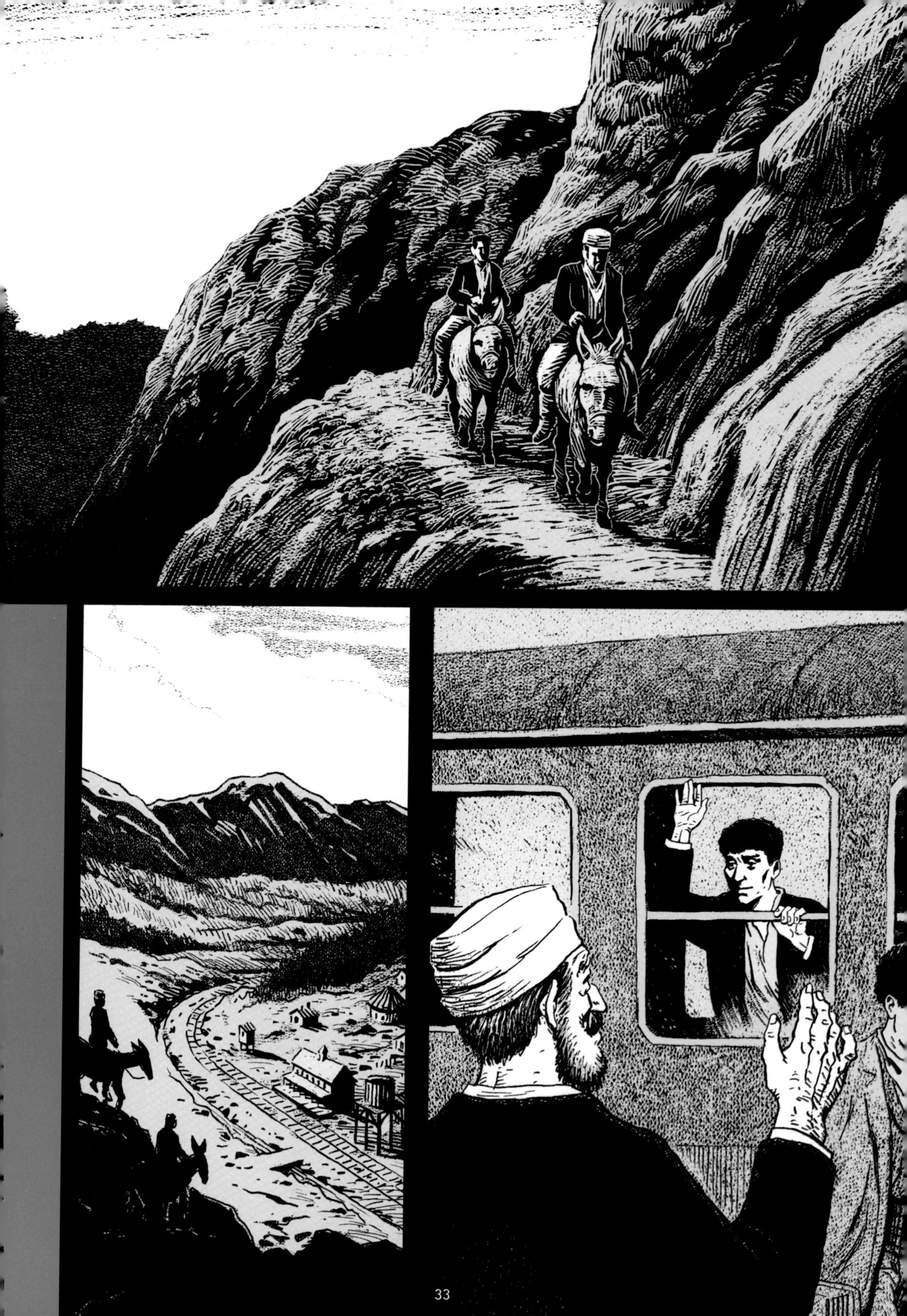

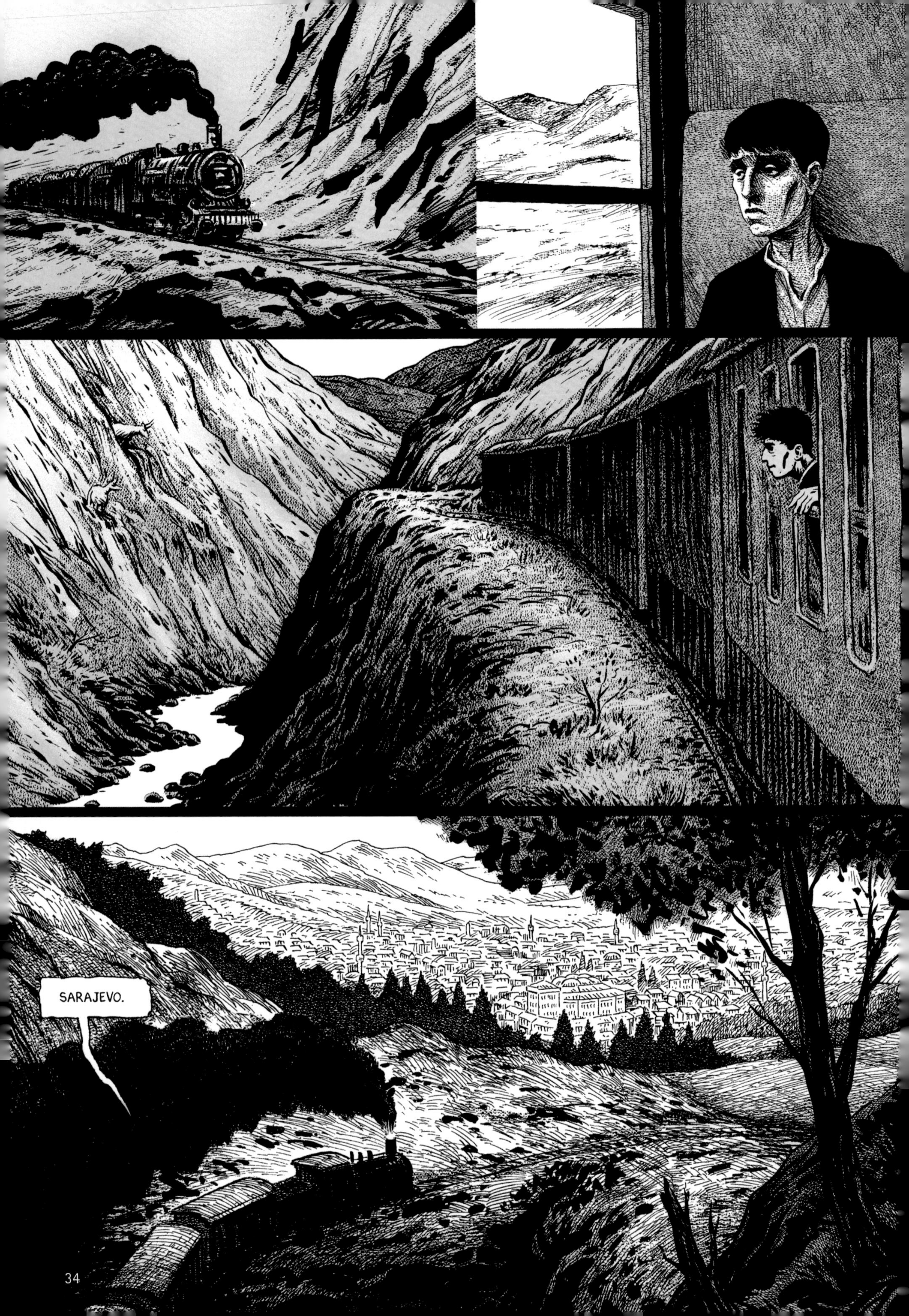
SARAJEVO.

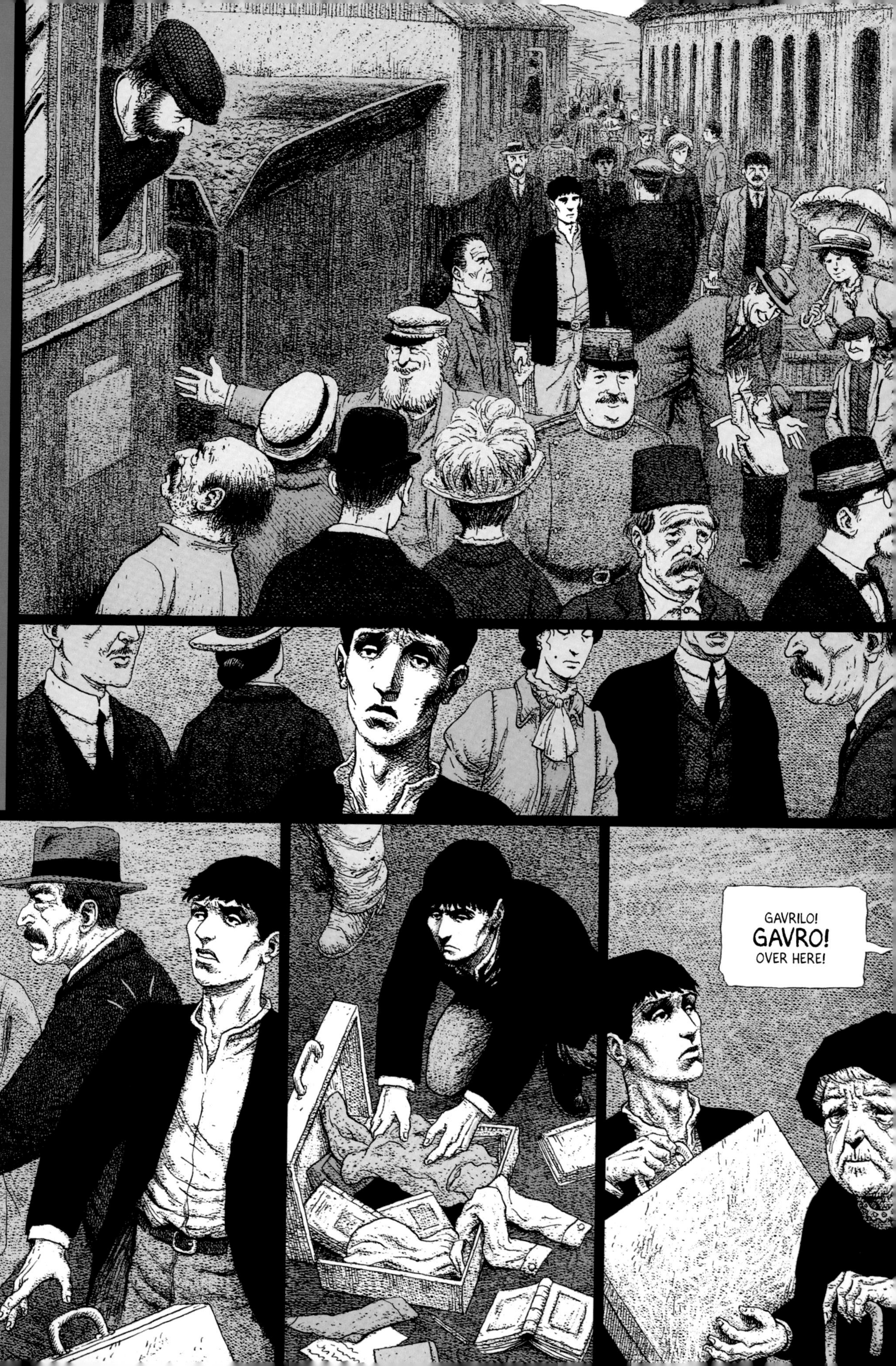
GAVRILO! GAVRO! OVER HERE!

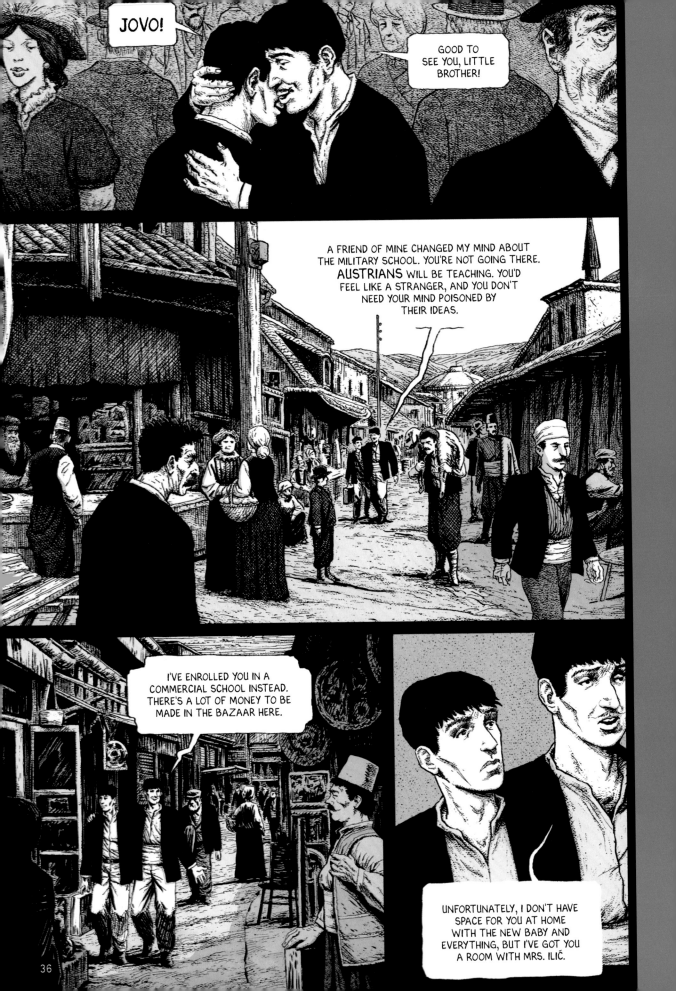

JOVO!

GOOD TO SEE YOU, LITTLE BROTHER!

A FRIEND OF MINE CHANGED MY MIND ABOUT THE MILITARY SCHOOL. YOU'RE NOT GOING THERE. AUSTRIANS WILL BE TEACHING. YOU'D FEEL LIKE A STRANGER, AND YOU DON'T NEED YOUR MIND POISONED BY THEIR IDEAS.

I'VE ENROLLED YOU IN A COMMERCIAL SCHOOL INSTEAD. THERE'S A LOT OF MONEY TO BE MADE IN THE BAZAAR HERE.

UNFORTUNATELY, I DON'T HAVE SPACE FOR YOU AT HOME WITH THE NEW BABY AND EVERYTHING, BUT I'VE GOT YOU A ROOM WITH MRS. ILIĆ.

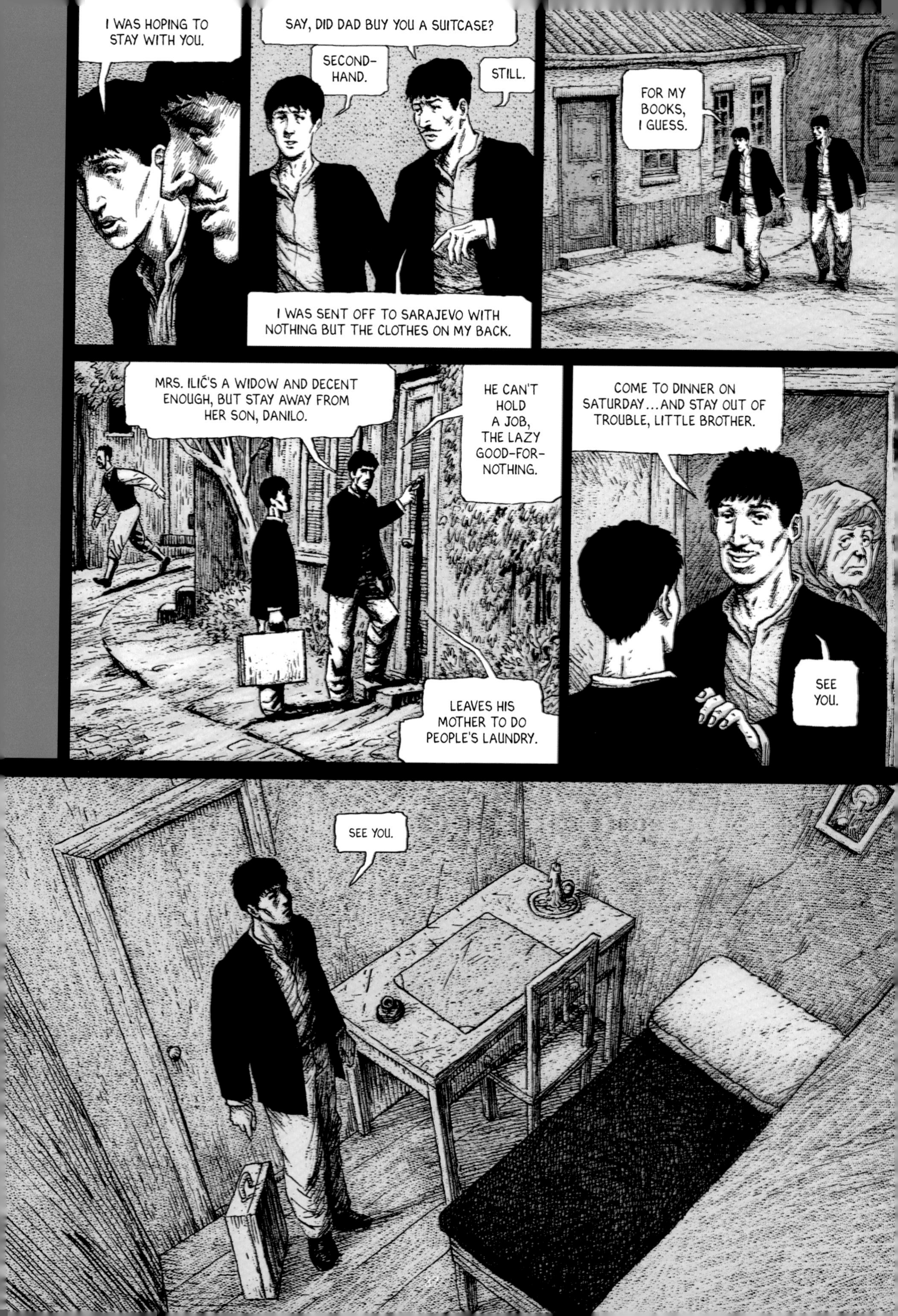
I WAS HOPING TO STAY WITH YOU.
SAY, DID DAD BUY YOU A SUITCASE?
SECOND-HAND.
STILL.
I WAS SENT OFF TO SARAJEVO WITH NOTHING BUT THE CLOTHES ON MY BACK.
FOR MY BOOKS, I GUESS.
MRS. ILIĆ'S A WIDOW AND DECENT ENOUGH, BUT STAY AWAY FROM HER SON, DANILO.
HE CAN'T HOLD A JOB, THE LAZY GOOD-FOR-NOTHING.
LEAVES HIS MOTHER TO DO PEOPLE'S LAUNDRY.
COME TO DINNER ON SATURDAY...AND STAY OUT OF TROUBLE, LITTLE BROTHER.
SEE YOU.
SEE YOU.

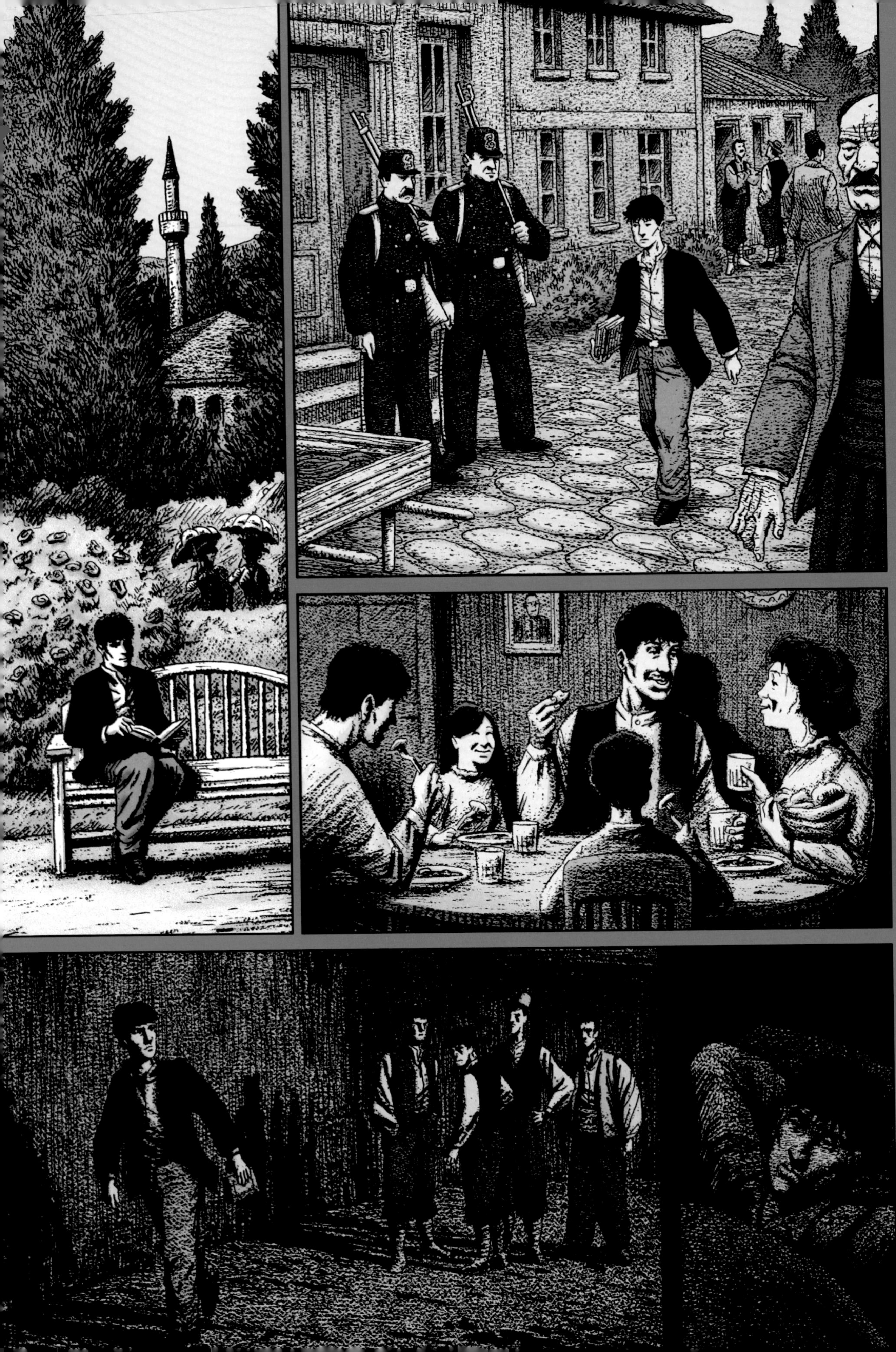

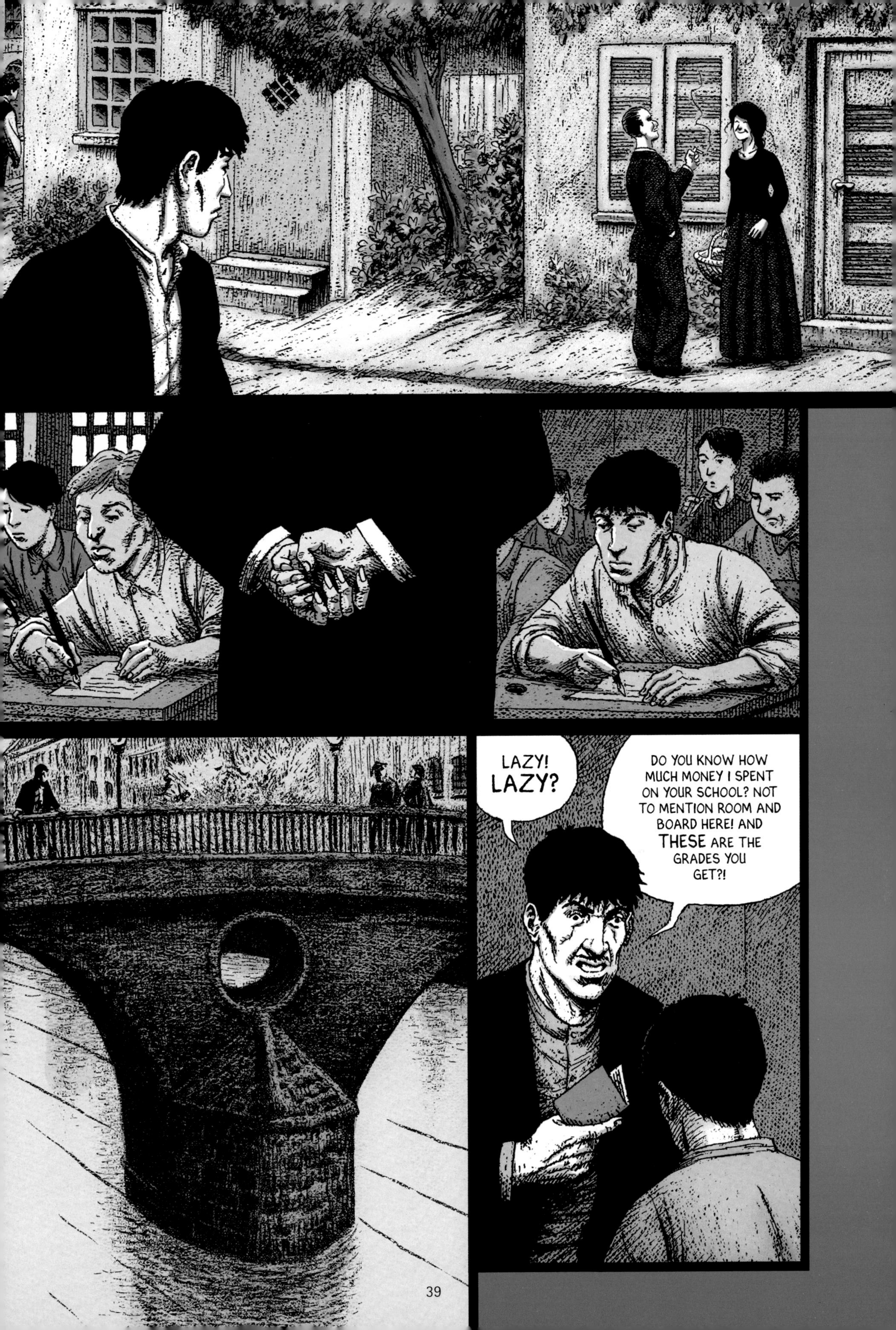
LAZY! LAZY?
DO YOU KNOW HOW MUCH MONEY I SPENT ON YOUR SCHOOL? NOT TO MENTION ROOM AND BOARD HERE! AND THESE ARE THE GRADES YOU GET?!

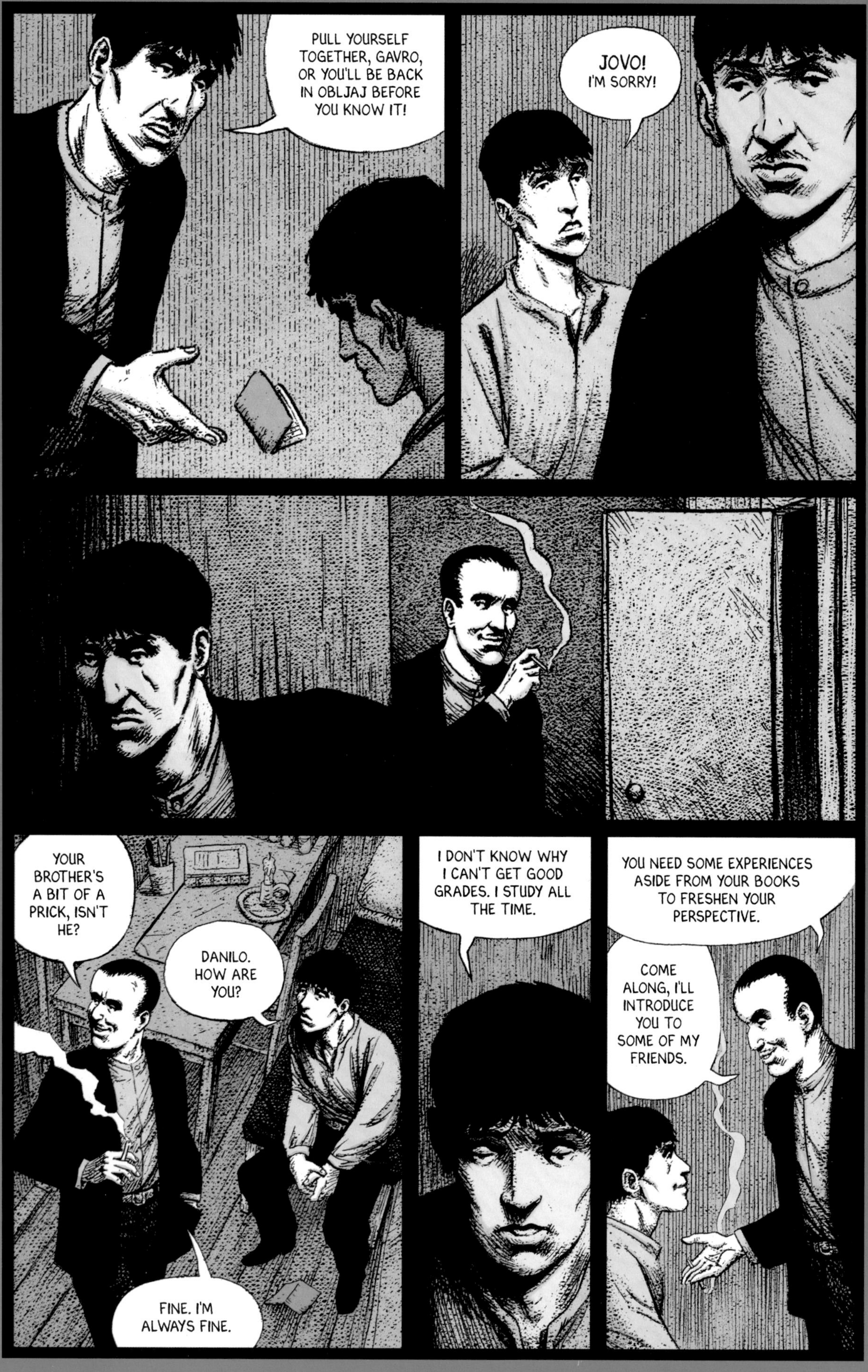
PULL YOURSELF TOGETHER, GAVRO, OR YOU'LL BE BACK IN OBLJAJ BEFORE YOU KNOW IT!
JOVO! I'M SORRY!
YOUR BROTHER'S A BIT OF A PRICK, ISN'T HE?
DANILO. HOW ARE YOU?
FINE. I'M ALWAYS FINE.
I DON'T KNOW WHY I CAN'T GET GOOD GRADES. I STUDY ALL THE TIME.
YOU NEED SOME EXPERIENCES ASIDE FROM YOUR BOOKS TO FRESHEN YOUR PERSPECTIVE.
COME ALONG, I'LL INTRODUCE YOU TO SOME OF MY FRIENDS.

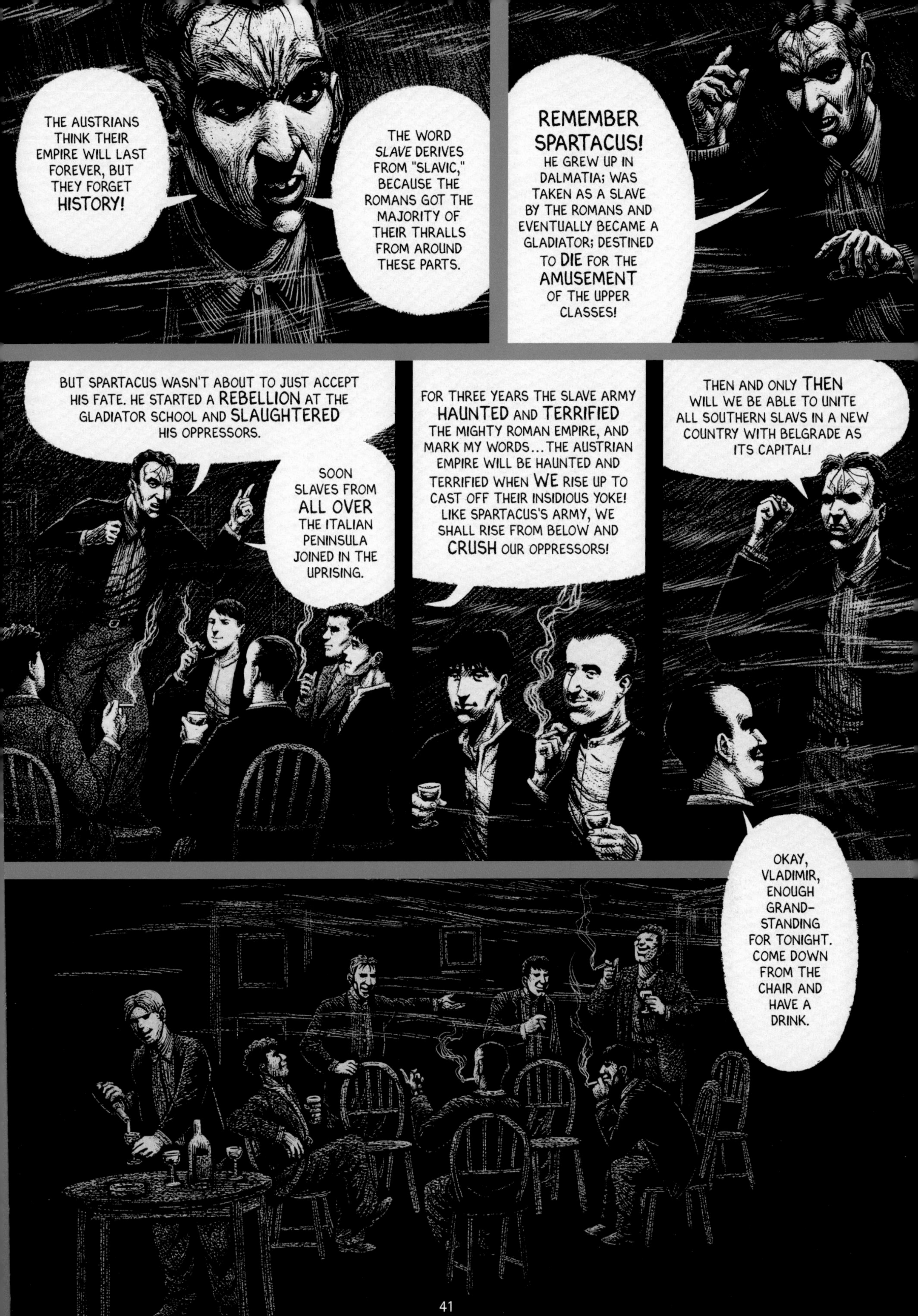

THE AUSTRIANS THINK THEIR EMPIRE WILL LAST FOREVER, BUT THEY FORGET HISTORY!
THE WORD *SLAVE* DERIVES FROM "SLAVIC," BECAUSE THE ROMANS GOT THE MAJORITY OF THEIR THRALLS FROM AROUND THESE PARTS.
REMEMBER SPARTACUS! HE GREW UP IN DALMATIA; WAS TAKEN AS A SLAVE BY THE ROMANS AND EVENTUALLY BECAME A GLADIATOR; DESTINED TO DIE FOR THE AMUSEMENT OF THE UPPER CLASSES!
BUT SPARTACUS WASN'T ABOUT TO JUST ACCEPT HIS FATE. HE STARTED A REBELLION AT THE GLADIATOR SCHOOL AND SLAUGHTERED HIS OPPRESSORS.
SOON SLAVES FROM ALL OVER THE ITALIAN PENINSULA JOINED IN THE UPRISING.
FOR THREE YEARS THE SLAVE ARMY HAUNTED AND TERRIFIED THE MIGHTY ROMAN EMPIRE, AND MARK MY WORDS... THE AUSTRIAN EMPIRE WILL BE HAUNTED AND TERRIFIED WHEN WE RISE UP TO CAST OFF THEIR INSIDIOUS YOKE! LIKE SPARTACUS'S ARMY, WE SHALL RISE FROM BELOW AND CRUSH OUR OPPRESSORS!
THEN AND ONLY THEN WILL WE BE ABLE TO UNITE ALL SOUTHERN SLAVS IN A NEW COUNTRY WITH BELGRADE AS ITS CAPITAL!
OKAY, VLADIMIR, ENOUGH GRAND-STANDING FOR TONIGHT. COME DOWN FROM THE CHAIR AND HAVE A DRINK.

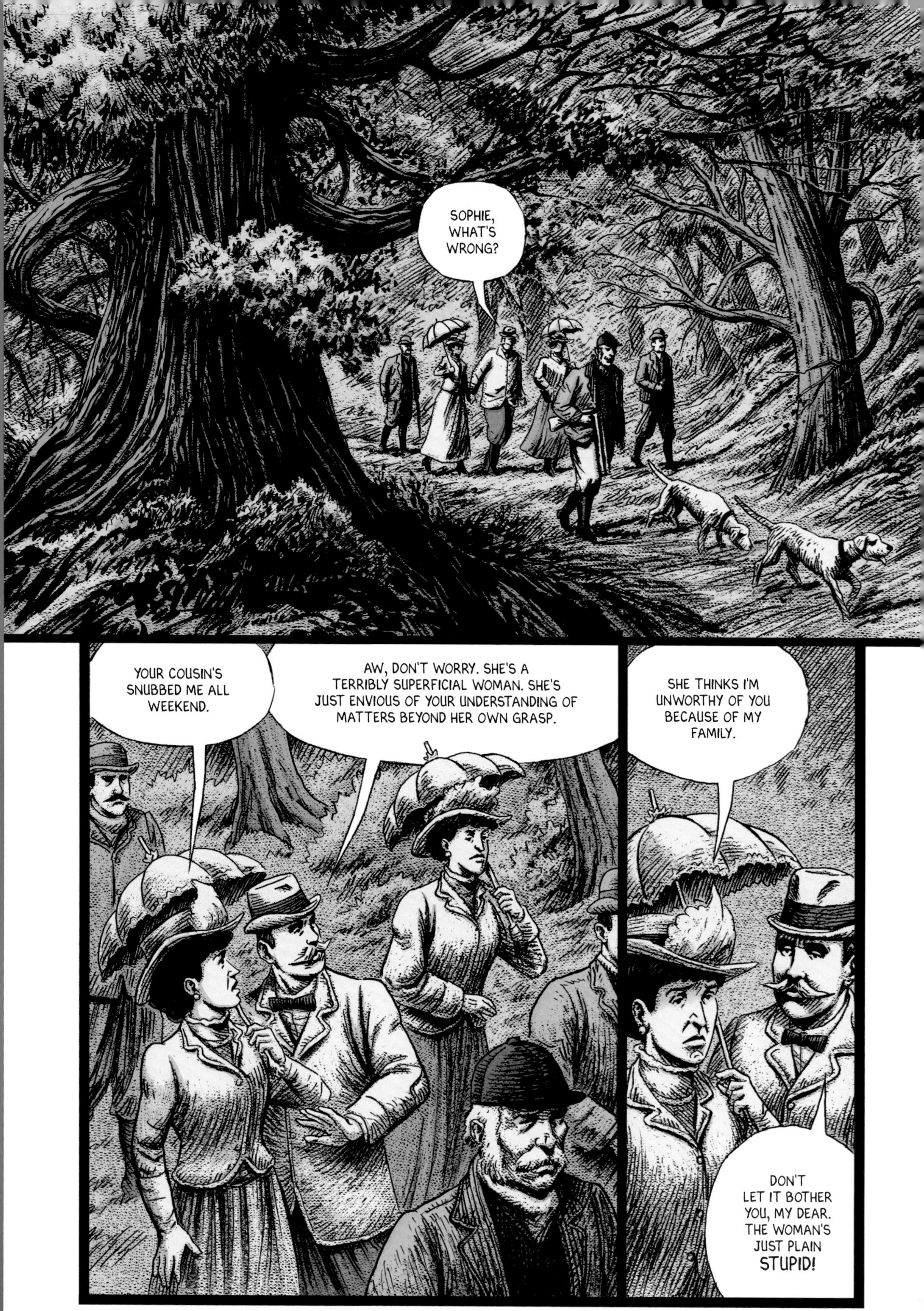
SOPHIE, WHAT'S WRONG?
YOUR COUSIN'S SNUBBED ME ALL WEEKEND.
AW, DON'T WORRY. SHE'S A TERRIBLY SUPERFICIAL WOMAN. SHE'S JUST ENVIOUS OF YOUR UNDERSTANDING OF MATTERS BEYOND HER OWN GRASP.
SHE THINKS I'M UNWORTHY OF YOU BECAUSE OF MY FAMILY.
DON'T LET IT BOTHER YOU, MY DEAR. THE WOMAN'S JUST PLAIN **STUPID!**

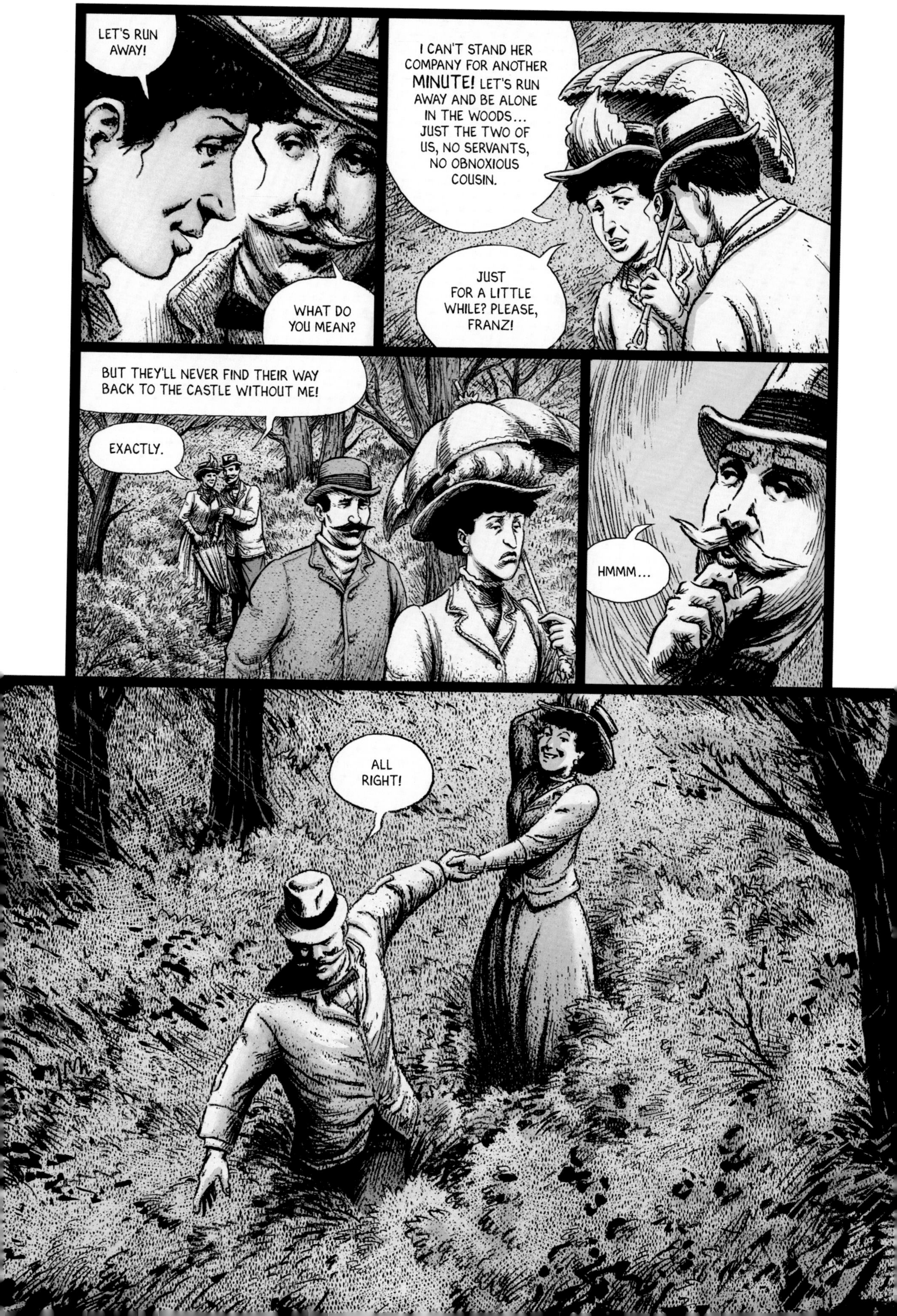
LET'S RUN AWAY!
WHAT DO YOU MEAN?
I CAN'T STAND HER COMPANY FOR ANOTHER MINUTE! LET'S RUN AWAY AND BE ALONE IN THE WOODS... JUST THE TWO OF US, NO SERVANTS, NO OBNOXIOUS COUSIN.
JUST FOR A LITTLE WHILE? PLEASE, FRANZ!
BUT THEY'LL NEVER FIND THEIR WAY BACK TO THE CASTLE WITHOUT ME!
EXACTLY.
HMMM...
ALL RIGHT!

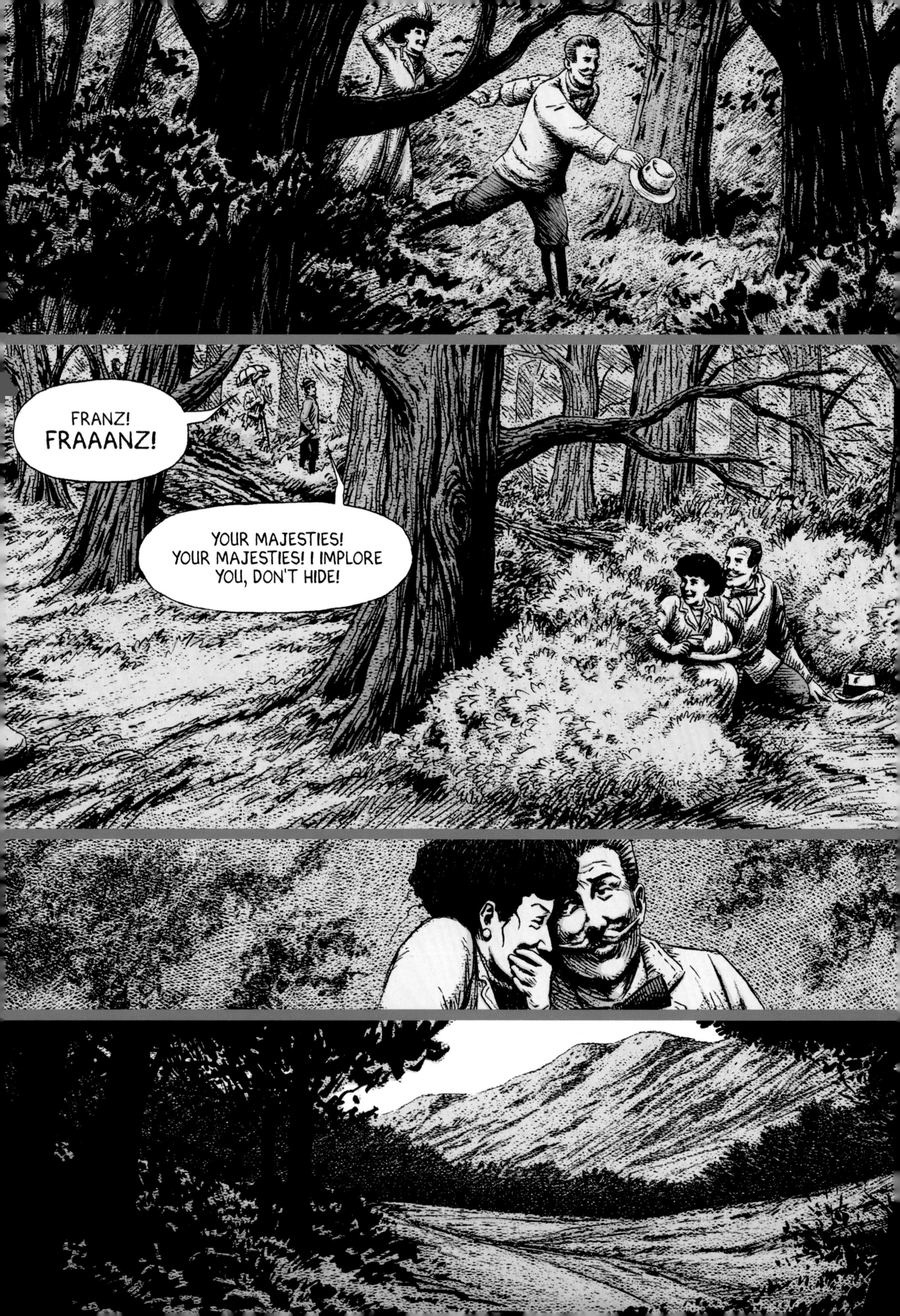
FRANZ!
FRAAANZ!
YOUR MAJESTIES! YOUR MAJESTIES! I IMPLORE YOU, DON'T HIDE!

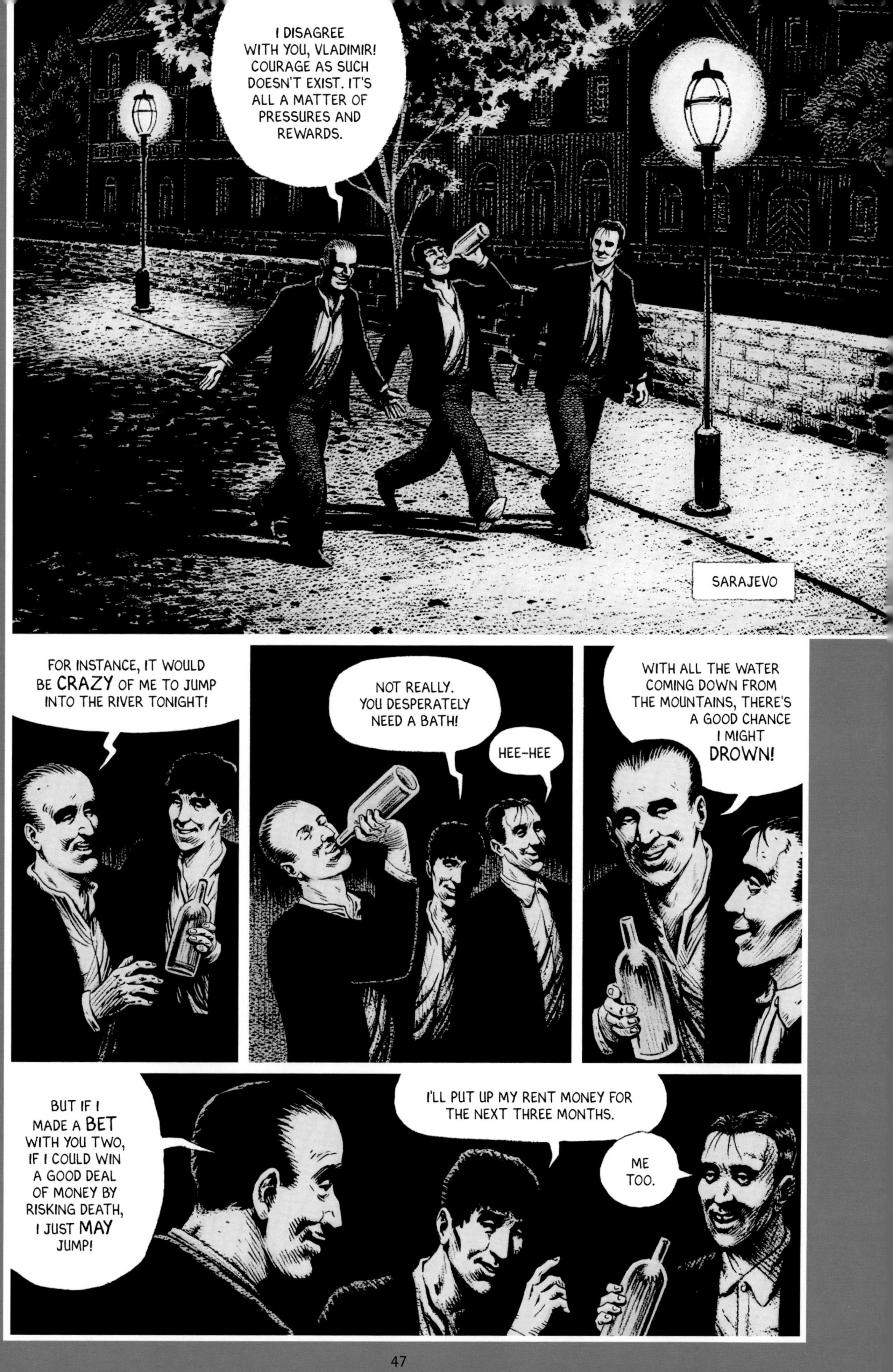
I DISAGREE WITH YOU, VLADIMIR! COURAGE AS SUCH DOESN'T EXIST. IT'S ALL A MATTER OF PRESSURES AND REWARDS.
SARAJEVO
FOR INSTANCE, IT WOULD BE CRAZY OF ME TO JUMP INTO THE RIVER TONIGHT!
NOT REALLY. YOU DESPERATELY NEED A BATH!
HEE-HEE
WITH ALL THE WATER COMING DOWN FROM THE MOUNTAINS, THERE'S A GOOD CHANCE I MIGHT DROWN!
BUT IF I MADE A BET WITH YOU TWO, IF I COULD WIN A GOOD DEAL OF MONEY BY RISKING DEATH, I JUST MAY JUMP!
I'LL PUT UP MY RENT MONEY FOR THE NEXT THREE MONTHS.
ME TOO.

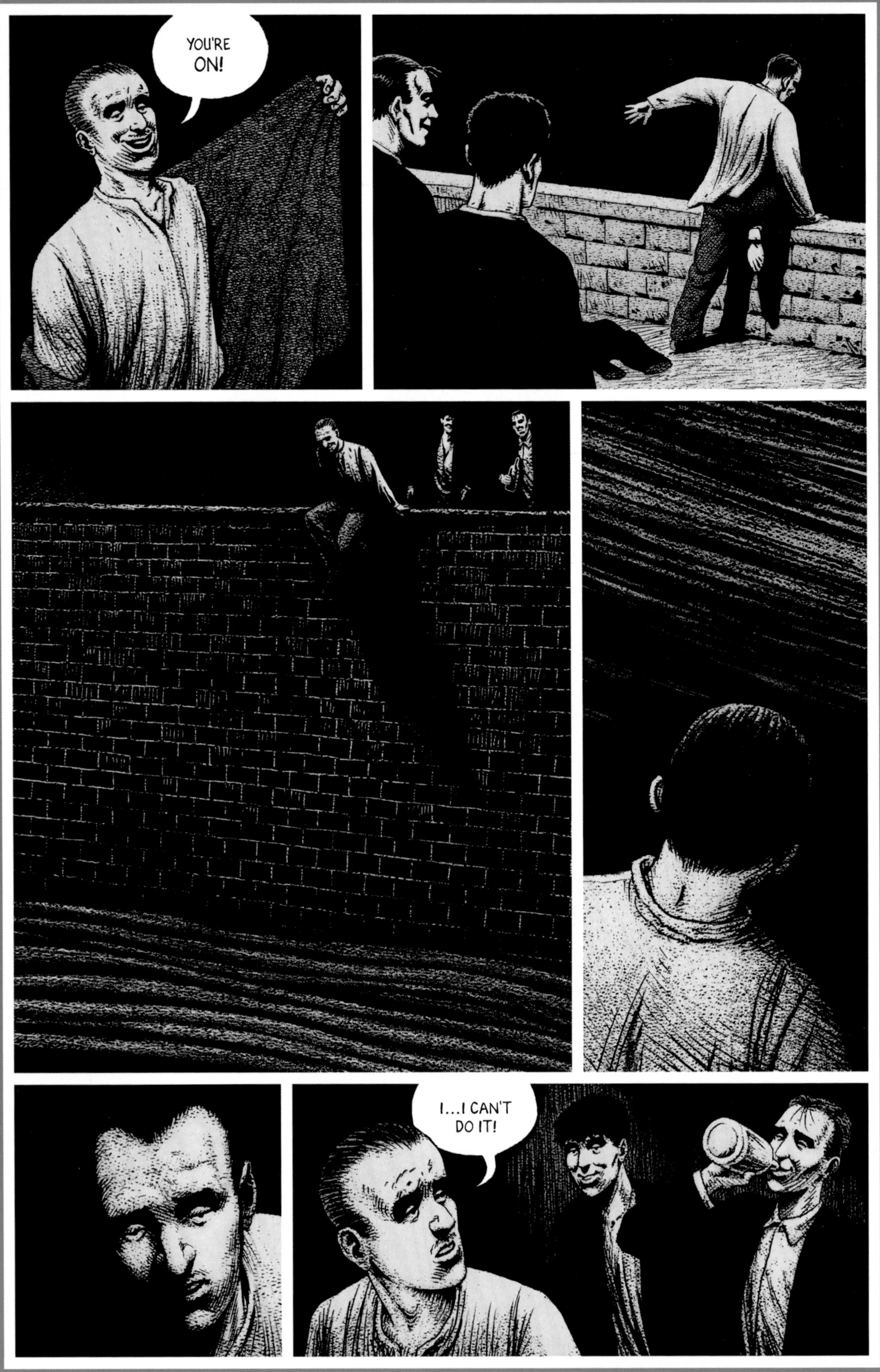
YOU'RE ON!
I...I CAN'T DO IT!

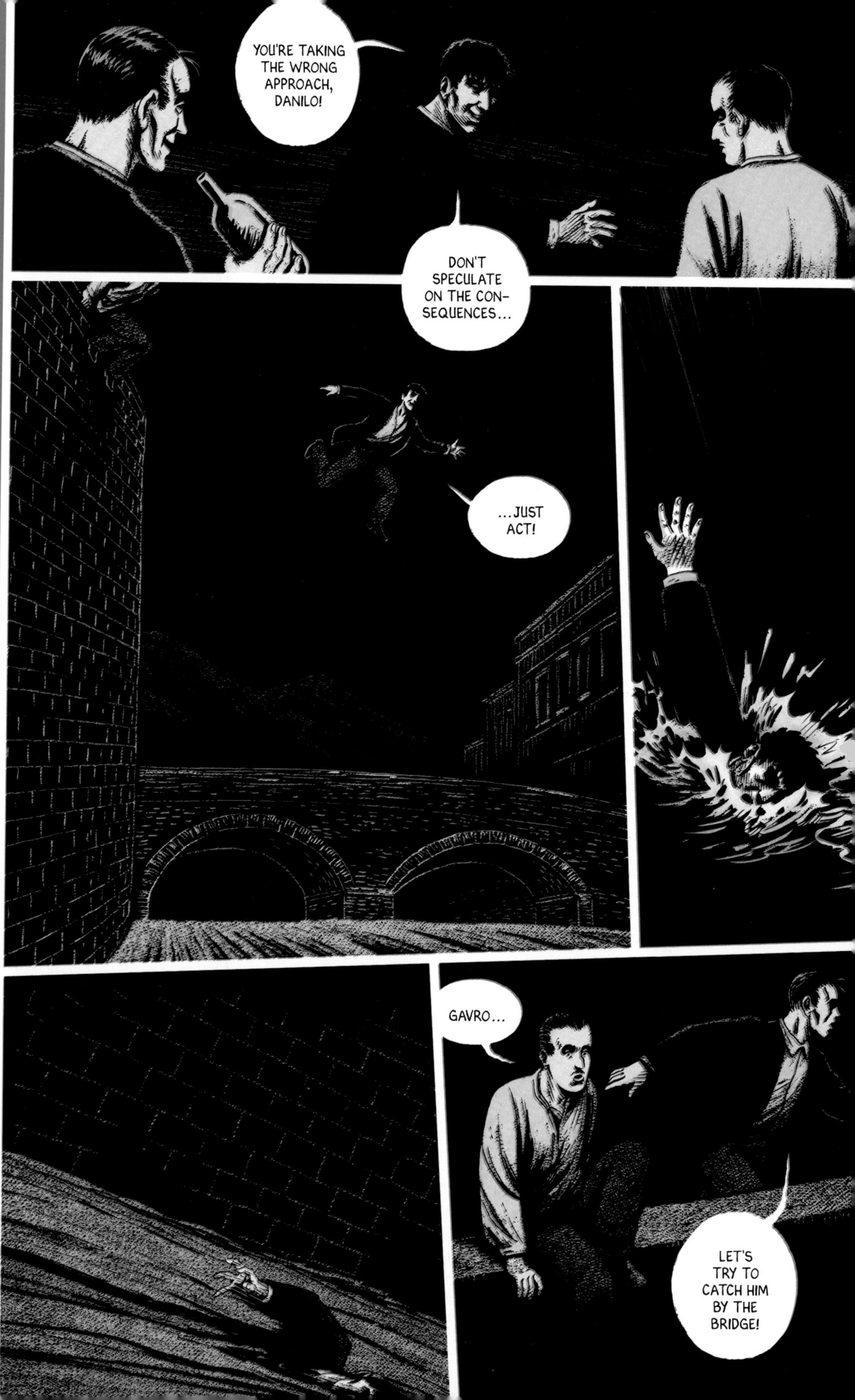
YOU'RE TAKING THE WRONG APPROACH, DANILO!
DON'T SPECULATE ON THE CON-SEQUENCES...
...JUST ACT!
GAVRO...
LET'S TRY TO CATCH HIM BY THE BRIDGE!

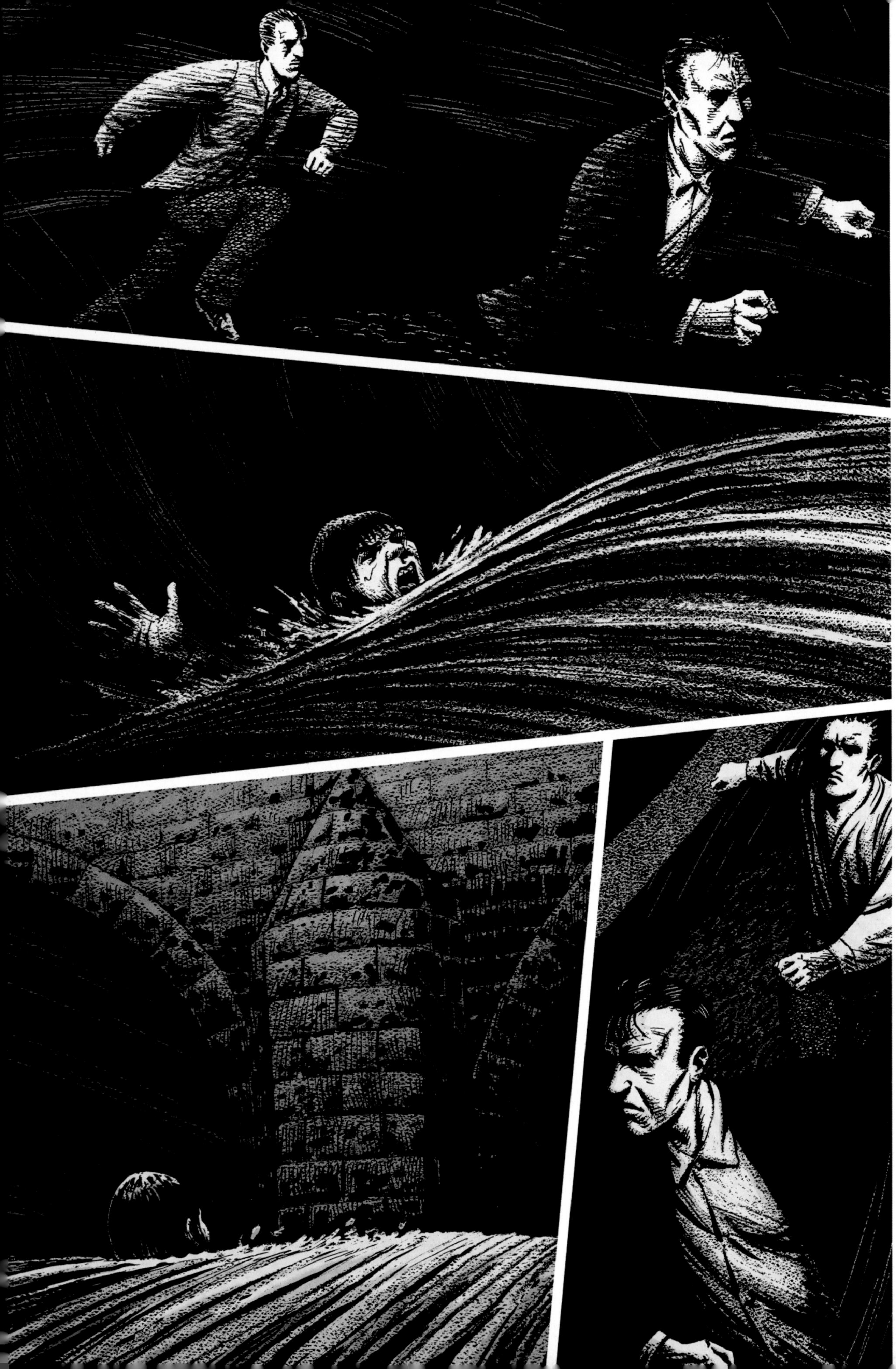

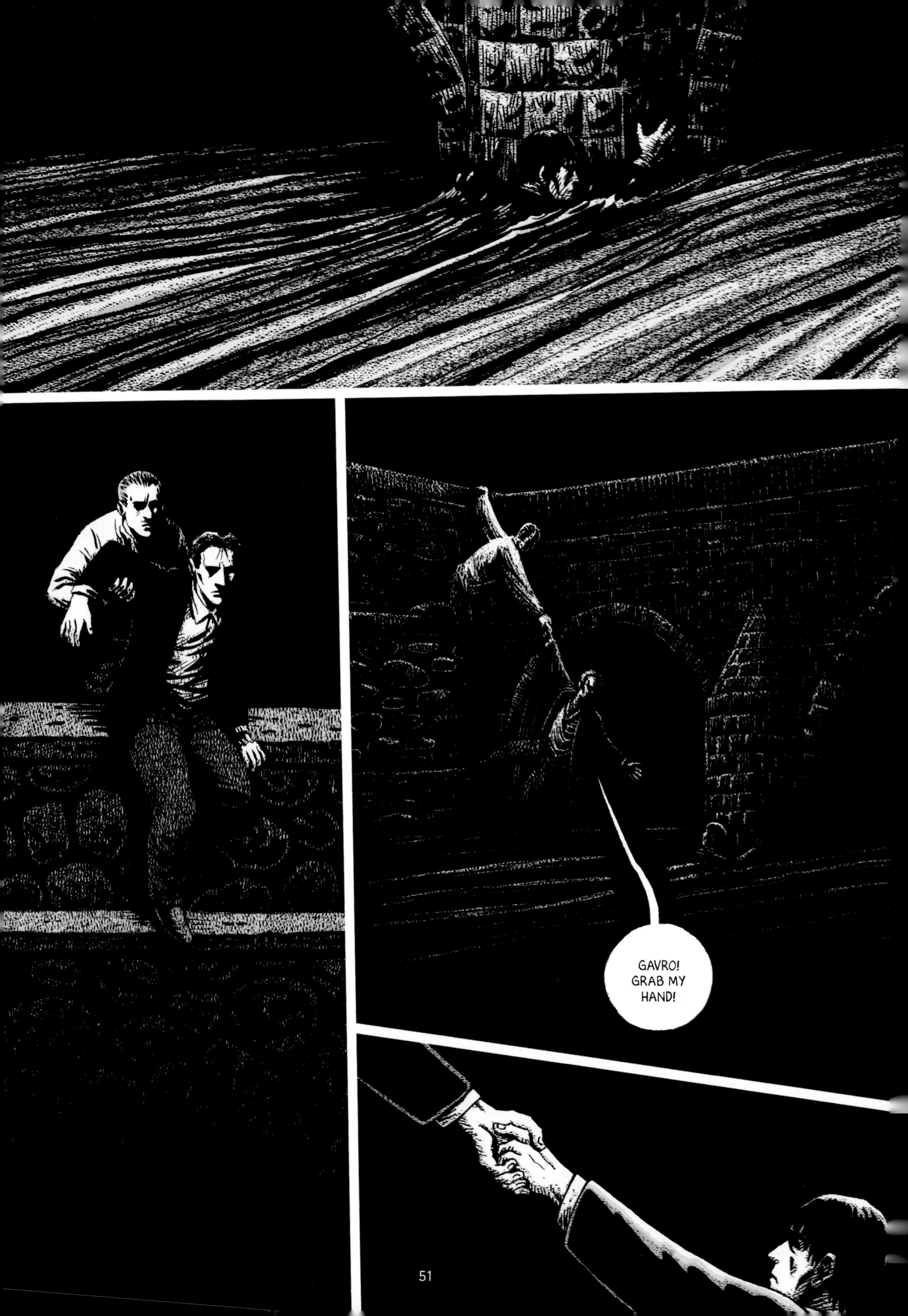
GAVRO!
GRAB MY
HAND!

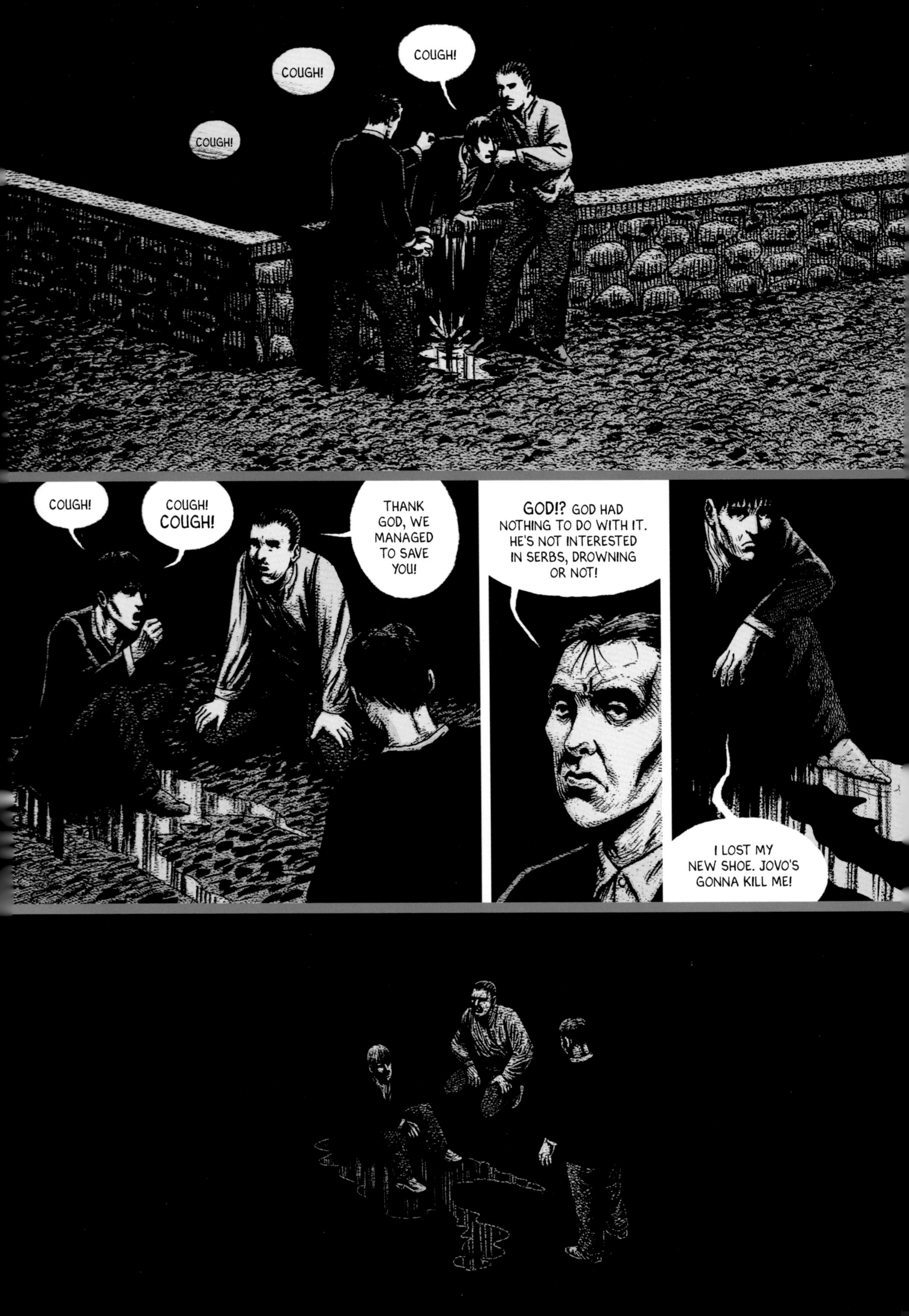
COUGH!
COUGH!
COUGH!
COUGH!
COUGH! COUGH!
THANK GOD, WE MANAGED TO SAVE YOU!
GOD!? GOD HAD NOTHING TO DO WITH IT. HE'S NOT INTERESTED IN SERBS, DROWNING OR NOT!
I LOST MY NEW SHOE. JOVO'S GONNA KILL ME!

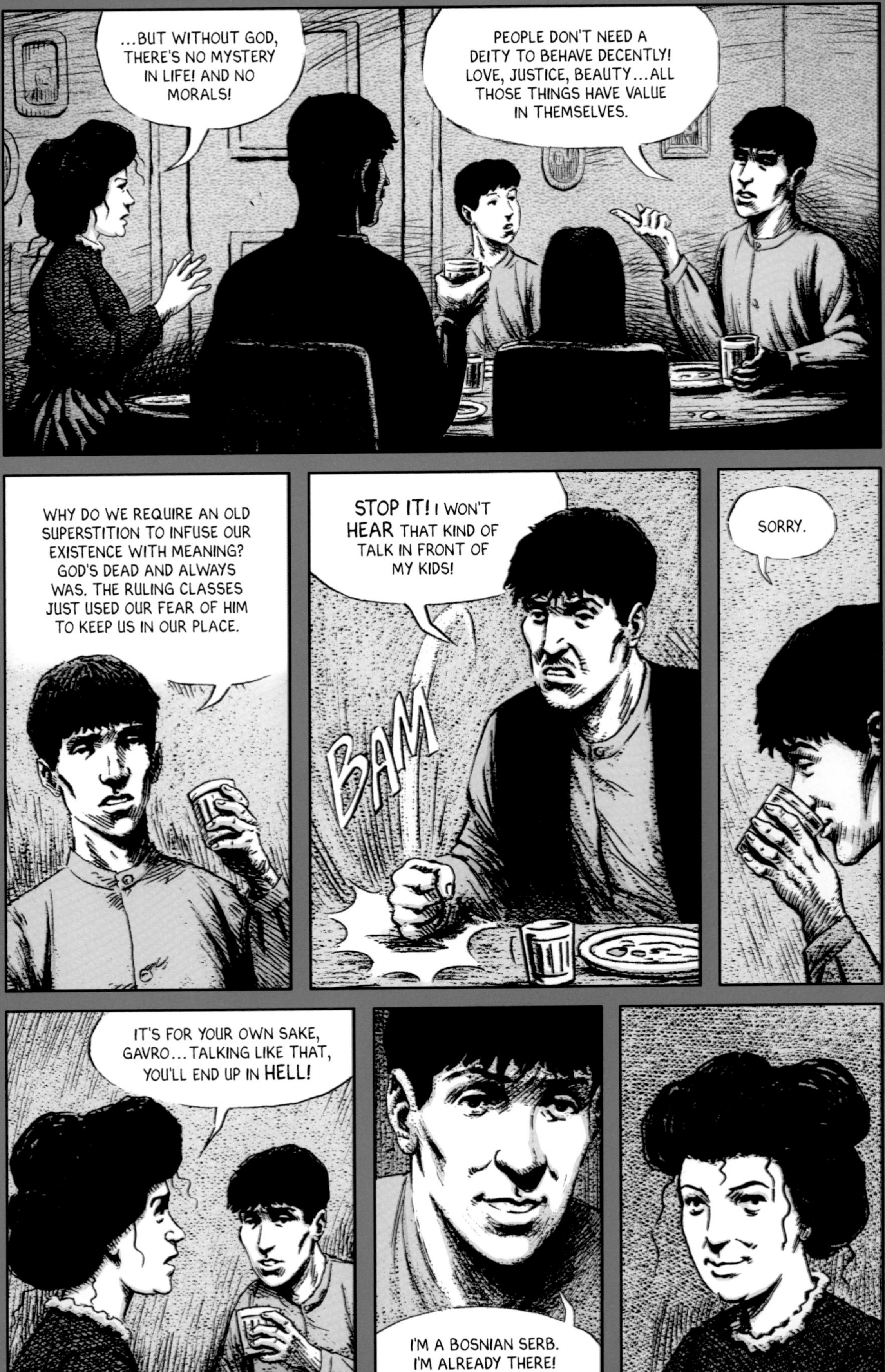
...BUT WITHOUT GOD, THERE'S NO MYSTERY IN LIFE! AND NO MORALS!
PEOPLE DON'T NEED A DEITY TO BEHAVE DECENTLY! LOVE, JUSTICE, BEAUTY... ALL THOSE THINGS HAVE VALUE IN THEMSELVES.
WHY DO WE REQUIRE AN OLD SUPERSTITION TO INFUSE OUR EXISTENCE WITH MEANING? GOD'S DEAD AND ALWAYS WAS. THE RULING CLASSES JUST USED OUR FEAR OF HIM TO KEEP US IN OUR PLACE.
STOP IT! I WON'T HEAR THAT KIND OF TALK IN FRONT OF MY KIDS!
BAM
SORRY.
IT'S FOR YOUR OWN SAKE, GAVRO... TALKING LIKE THAT, YOU'LL END UP IN HELL!
I'M A BOSNIAN SERB. I'M ALREADY THERE!

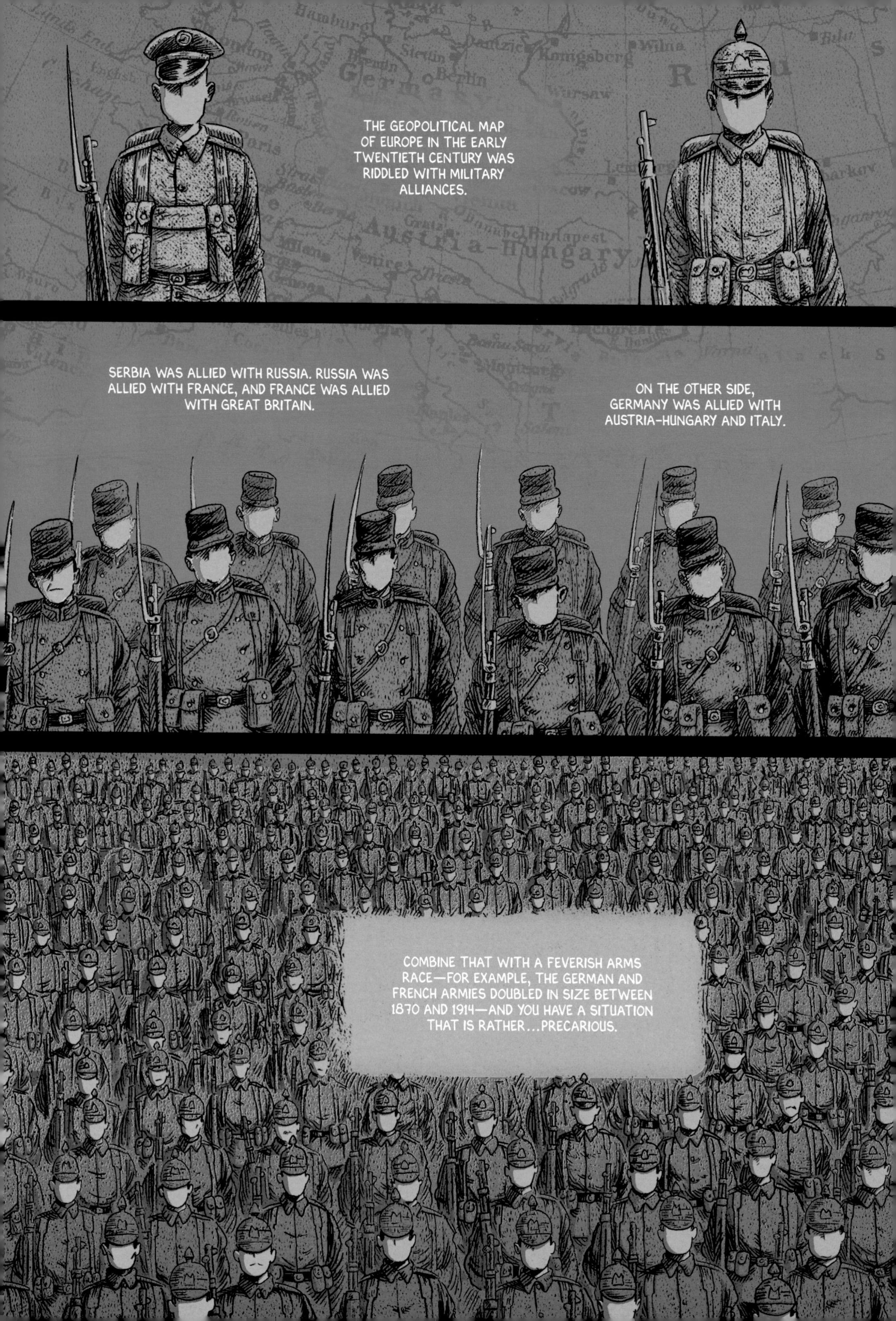
THE GEOPOLITICAL MAP OF EUROPE IN THE EARLY TWENTIETH CENTURY WAS RIDDLED WITH MILITARY ALLIANCES.
SERBIA WAS ALLIED WITH RUSSIA. RUSSIA WAS ALLIED WITH FRANCE, AND FRANCE WAS ALLIED WITH GREAT BRITAIN.
ON THE OTHER SIDE, GERMANY WAS ALLIED WITH AUSTRIA-HUNGARY AND ITALY.
COMBINE THAT WITH A FEVERISH ARMS RACE—FOR EXAMPLE, THE GERMAN AND FRENCH ARMIES DOUBLED IN SIZE BETWEEN 1870 AND 1914—AND YOU HAVE A SITUATION THAT IS RATHER...PRECARIOUS.

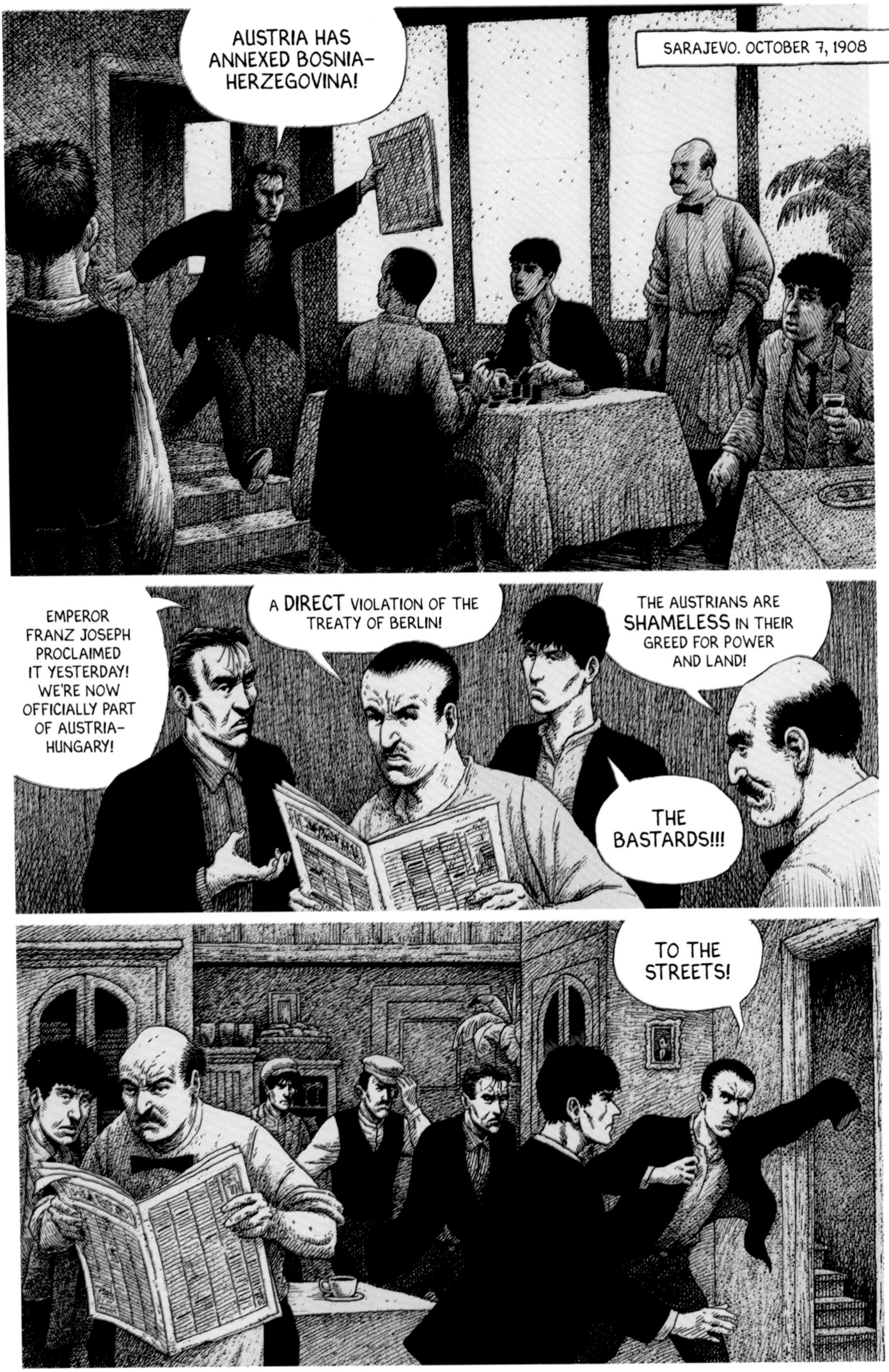
AUSTRIA HAS ANNEXED BOSNIA-HERZEGOVINA!
SARAJEVO. OCTOBER 7, 1908
EMPEROR FRANZ JOSEPH PROCLAIMED IT YESTERDAY! WE'RE NOW OFFICIALLY PART OF AUSTRIA-HUNGARY!
A DIRECT VIOLATION OF THE TREATY OF BERLIN!
THE AUSTRIANS ARE SHAMELESS IN THEIR GREED FOR POWER AND LAND!
THE BASTARDS!!!
TO THE STREETS!

THE AUSTRIAN PROCLAMATION OF THE ANNEXATION OF BOSNIA-HERZEGOVINA CAUSED AN UPROAR IN SERBIA.

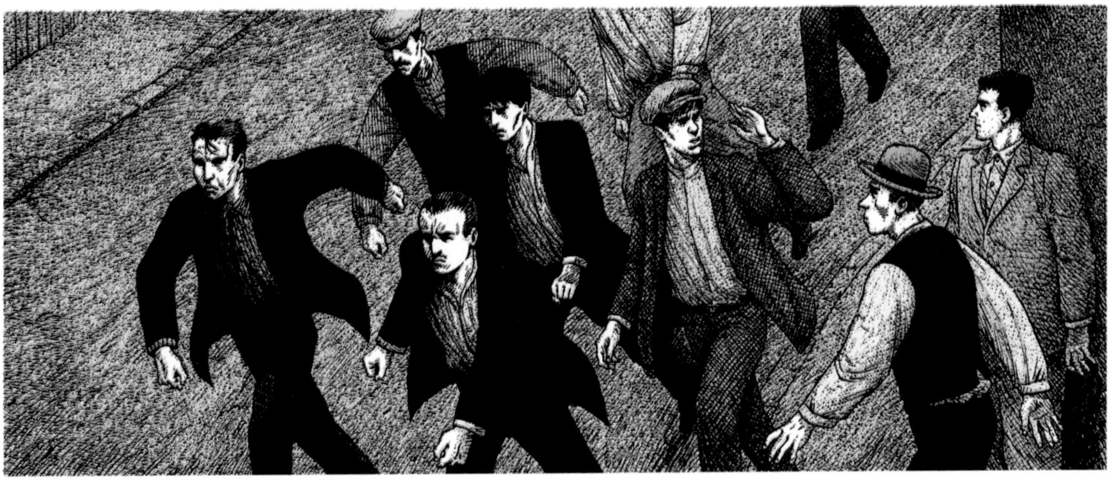

LARGE DEMONSTRATIONS TOOK PLACE IN BELGRADE. THE MILITARY RESERVES OF SERBIA WERE CALLED UP FOR A POSSIBLE WAR.

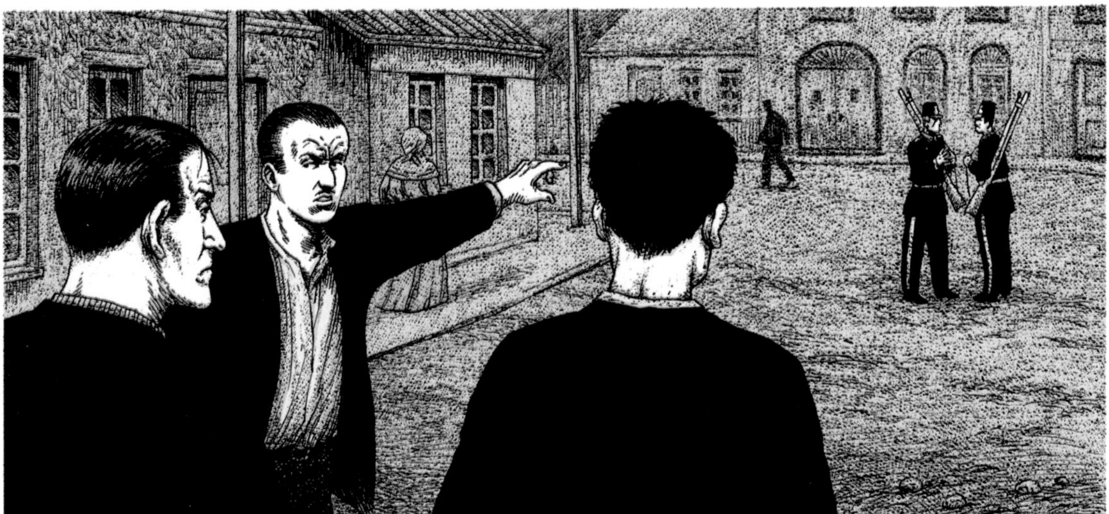

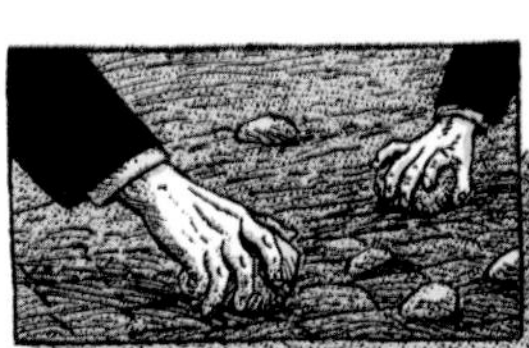

THE SERBIAN GOVERNMENT DEMANDED COMPENSATION FROM AUSTRIA-HUNGARY, CERTAIN THAT RUSSIA, THE SERB'S LONGTIME ALLY, WOULD BACK THEIR CLAIM.

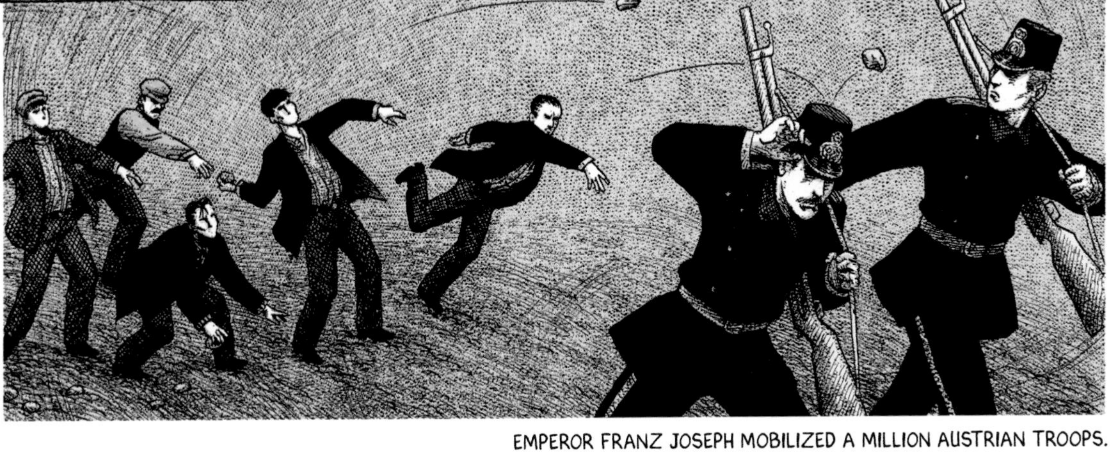

EMPEROR FRANZ JOSEPH MOBILIZED A MILLION AUSTRIAN TROOPS.

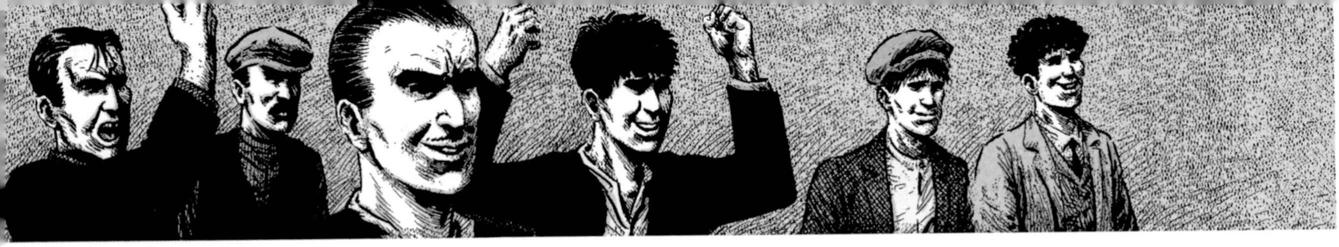

"BETTER SAFE THAN SORRY, THIS WAR'S BOUND TO COME SOONER OR LATER."

—COMMENT BY EMPEROR FRANZ JOSEPH TO HIS STAFF

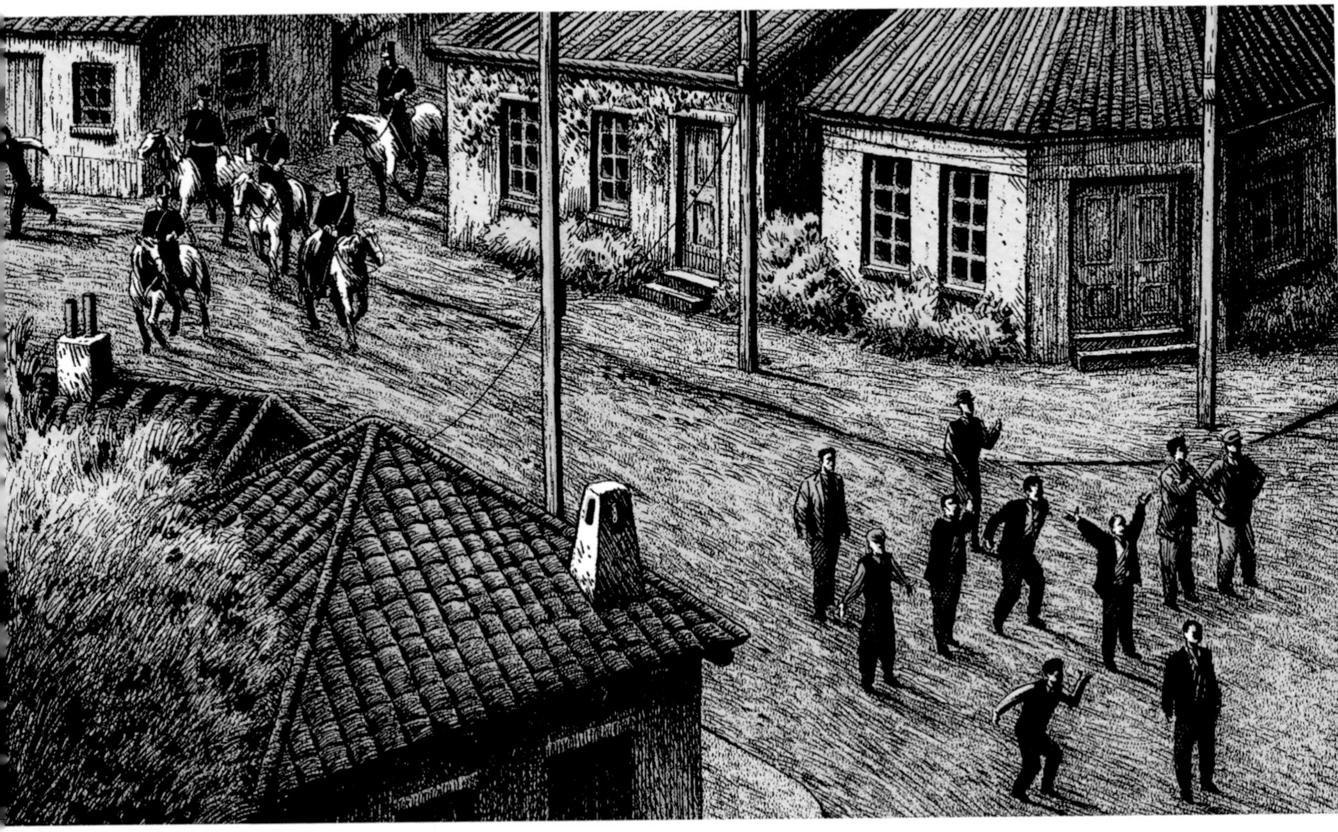

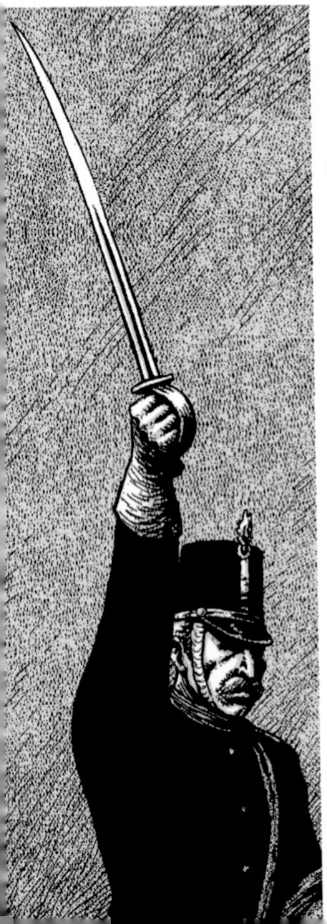

"STOP AGITATING FOR WAR. IT WOULD BE SPLENDID, INDEED VERY TEMPTING, TO CUT THE SERBS TO PIECES, BUT TO ACQUIRE SUCH CHEAP LAURELS COULD RESULT IN A EUROPEAN CONFLAGRATION IN WHICH WE WOULD BE FIGHTING ON TWO FRONTS WITHOUT ANY HOPE OF OVERALL SUCCESS."

—EXCERPT FROM LETTER BY FRANZ FERDINAND TO THE HEAD OF HIS MILITARY CHANCELLERY

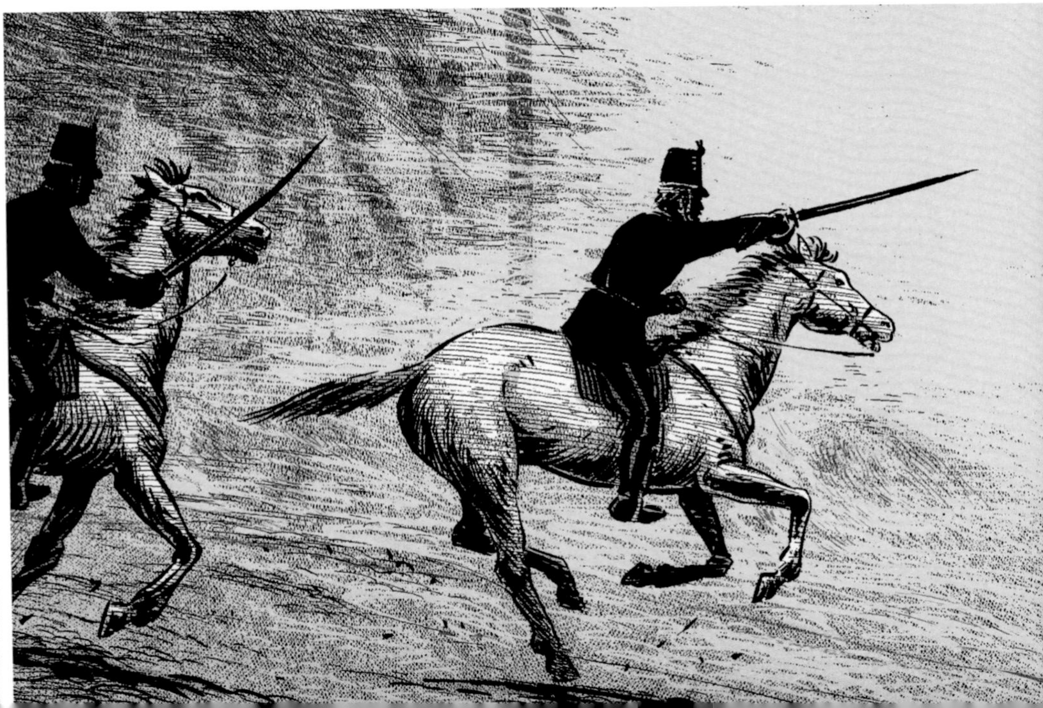

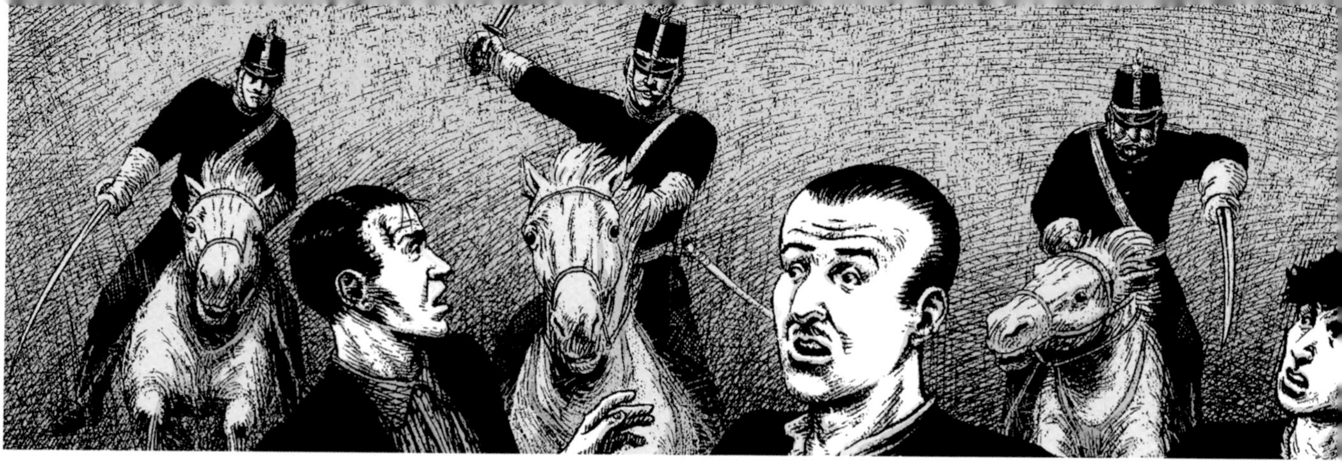

BELGRADE SAW THE CREATION OF NARODNA ODBRANA OR "DEFENSE OF THE PEOPLE," AN ORGANIZATION SET UP TO INFLAME THE NATIONAL CONSCIOUSNESS.

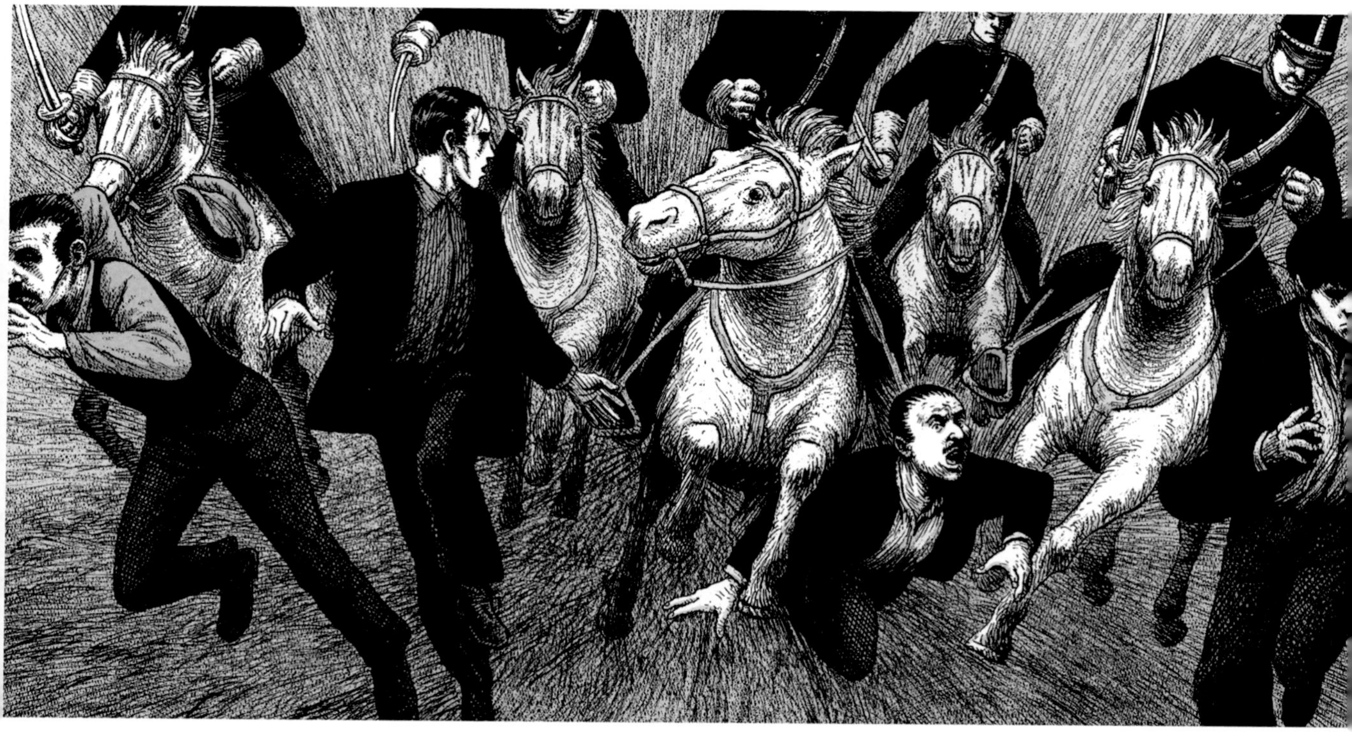

"THE NARODNA ODBRANA PROCLAIMS TO THE PEOPLE OF SERBIA THAT AUSTRIA IS OUR FIRST AND GREATEST ENEMY. JUST AS ONCE THE TURKS ATTACKED US FROM THE SOUTH, SO AUSTRIA ATTACKS US TODAY FROM THE NORTH. IF THE NARODNA ODBRANA PREACHES THE NECESSITY OF FIGHTING AUSTRIA, SHE PREACHES THE SACRED TRUTH OF OUR NATIONAL POSITION."

—EXCERPT FROM NARODNA ODBRANA'S MANIFESTO

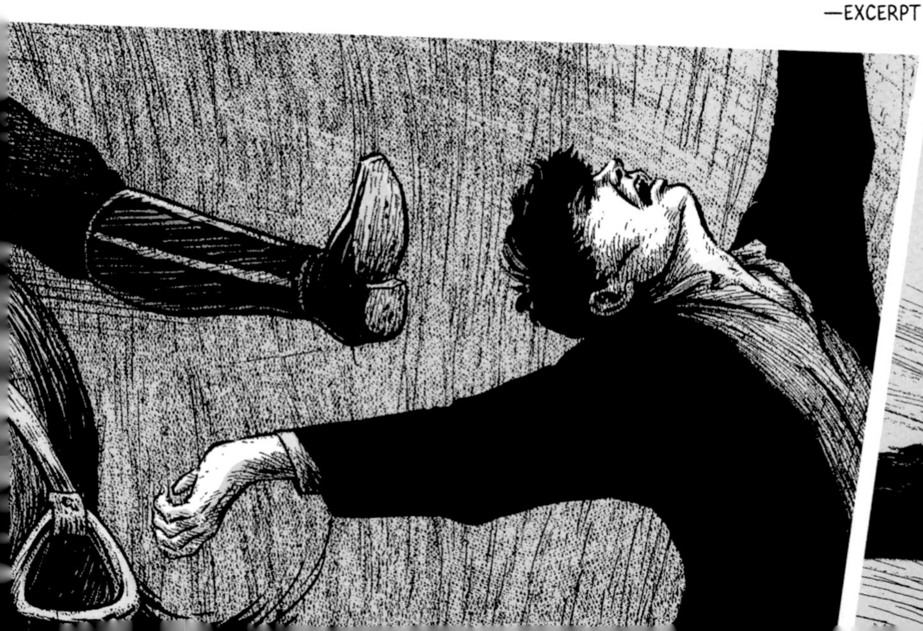

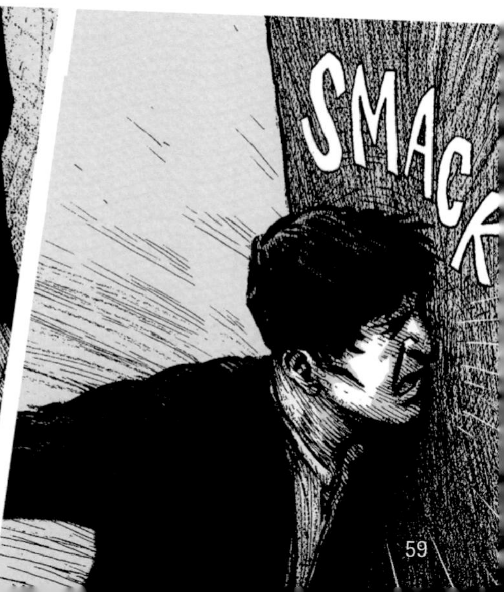
SMACK

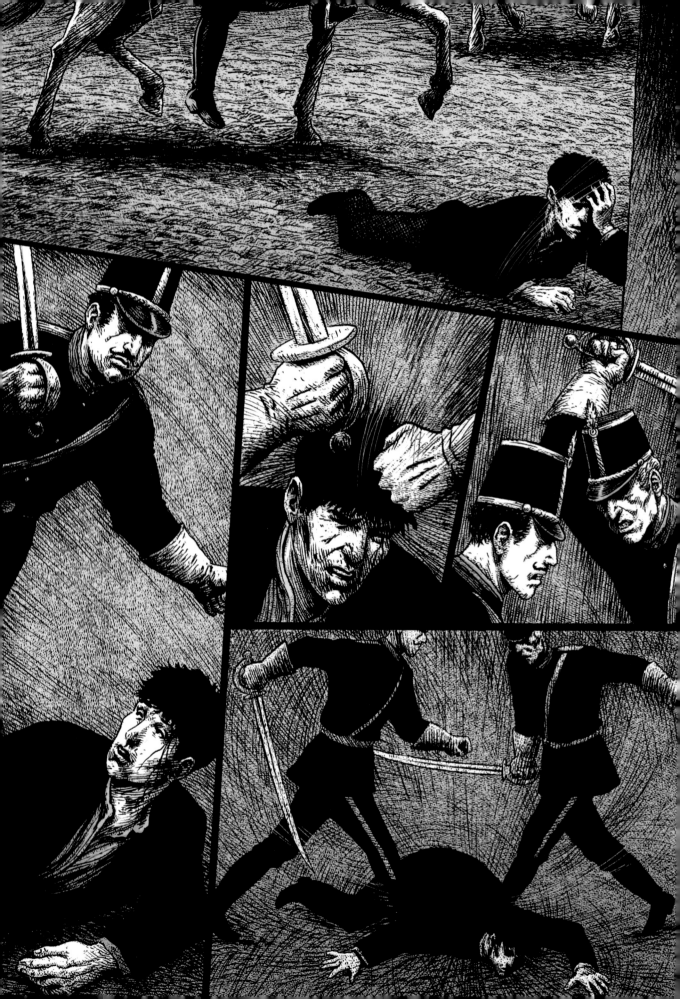

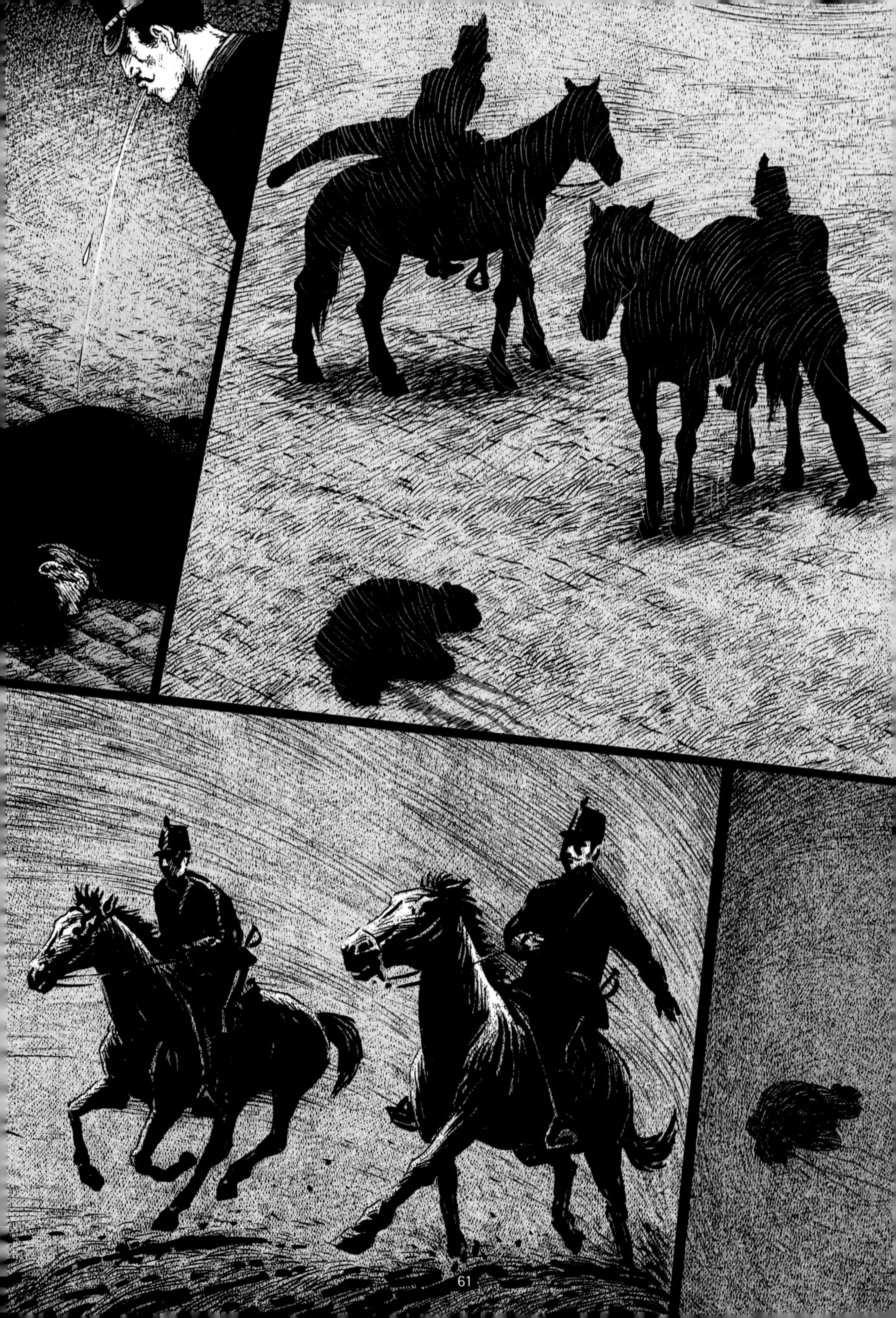

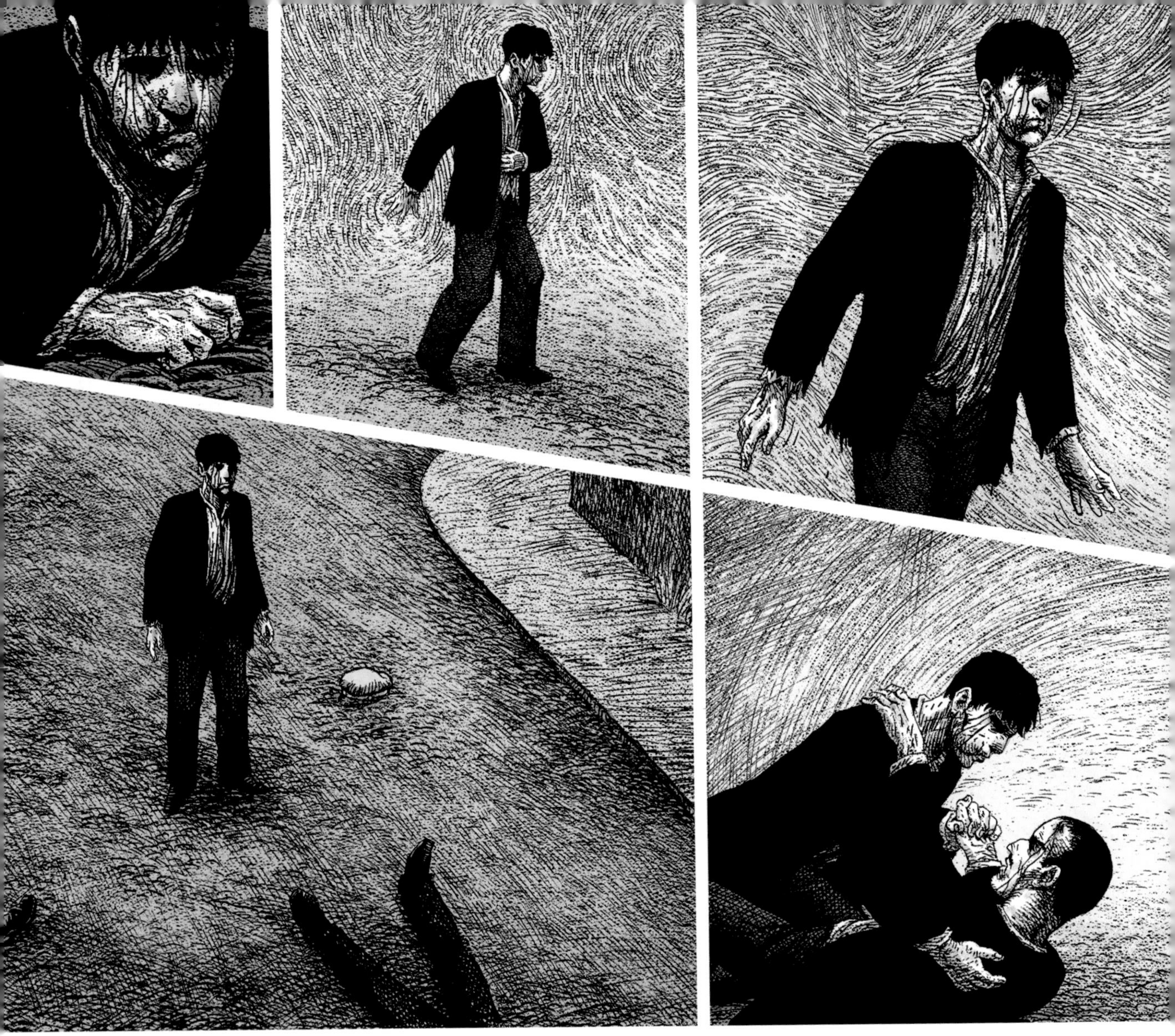

IN THE END, THE WAR WAS AVERTED. GERMANY PUT CONSIDERABLE POLITICAL PRESSURE ON THE CZAR, WHO THEN ANNOUNCED THAT RUSSIA ACCEPTED THE AUSTRIAN ANNEXATION OF BOSNIA-HERZEGOVINA.

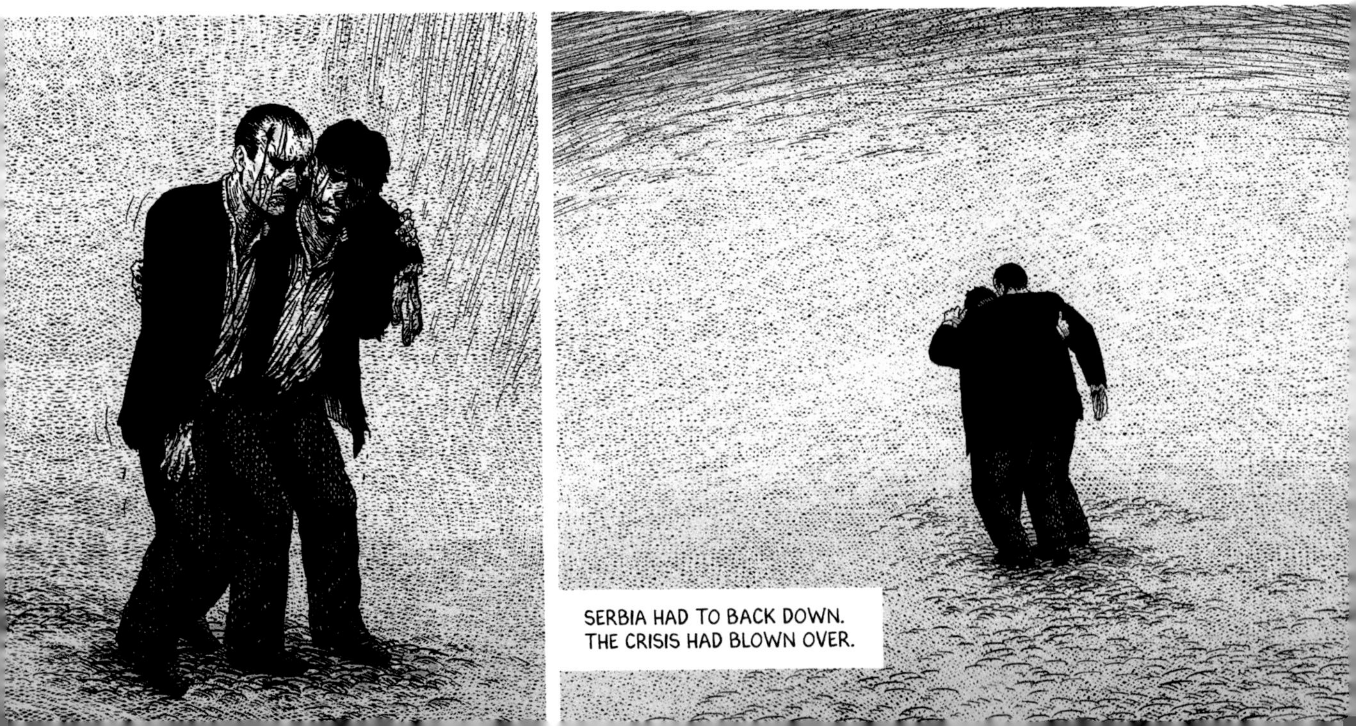
SERBIA HAD TO BACK DOWN.
THE CRISIS HAD BLOWN OVER.

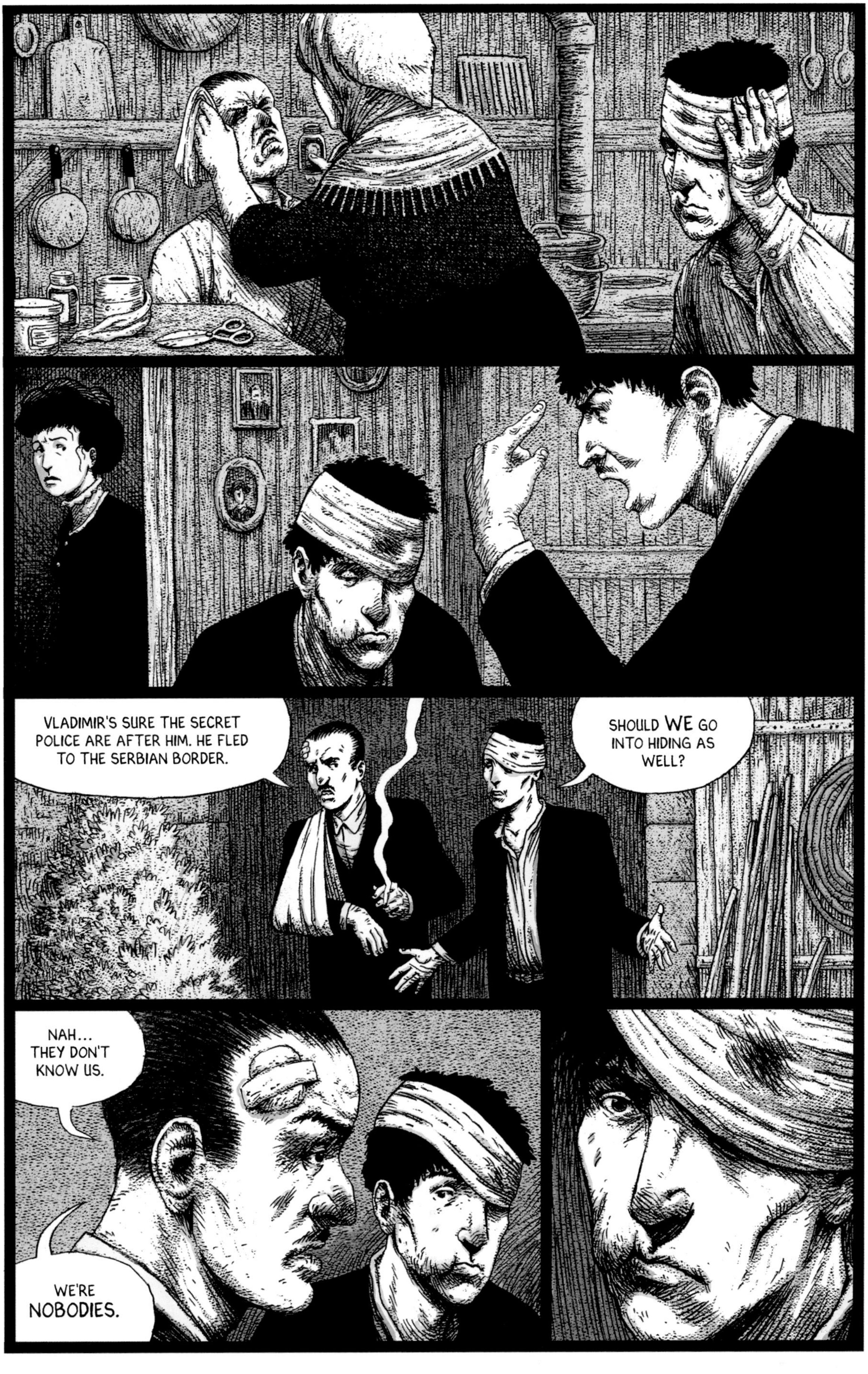
VLADIMIR'S SURE THE SECRET POLICE ARE AFTER HIM. HE FLED TO THE SERBIAN BORDER.
SHOULD WE GO INTO HIDING AS WELL?
NAH... THEY DON'T KNOW US.
WE'RE NOBODIES.

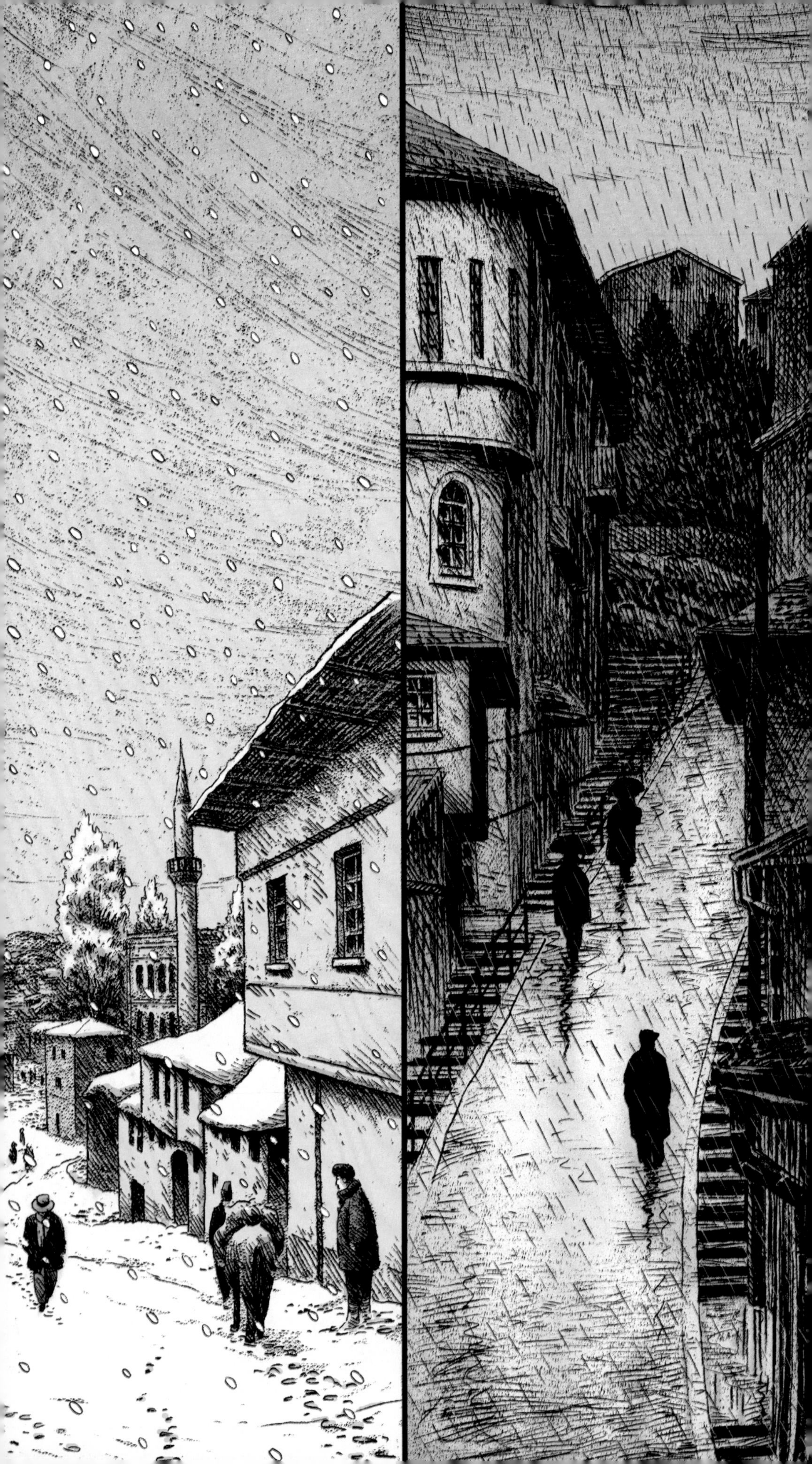

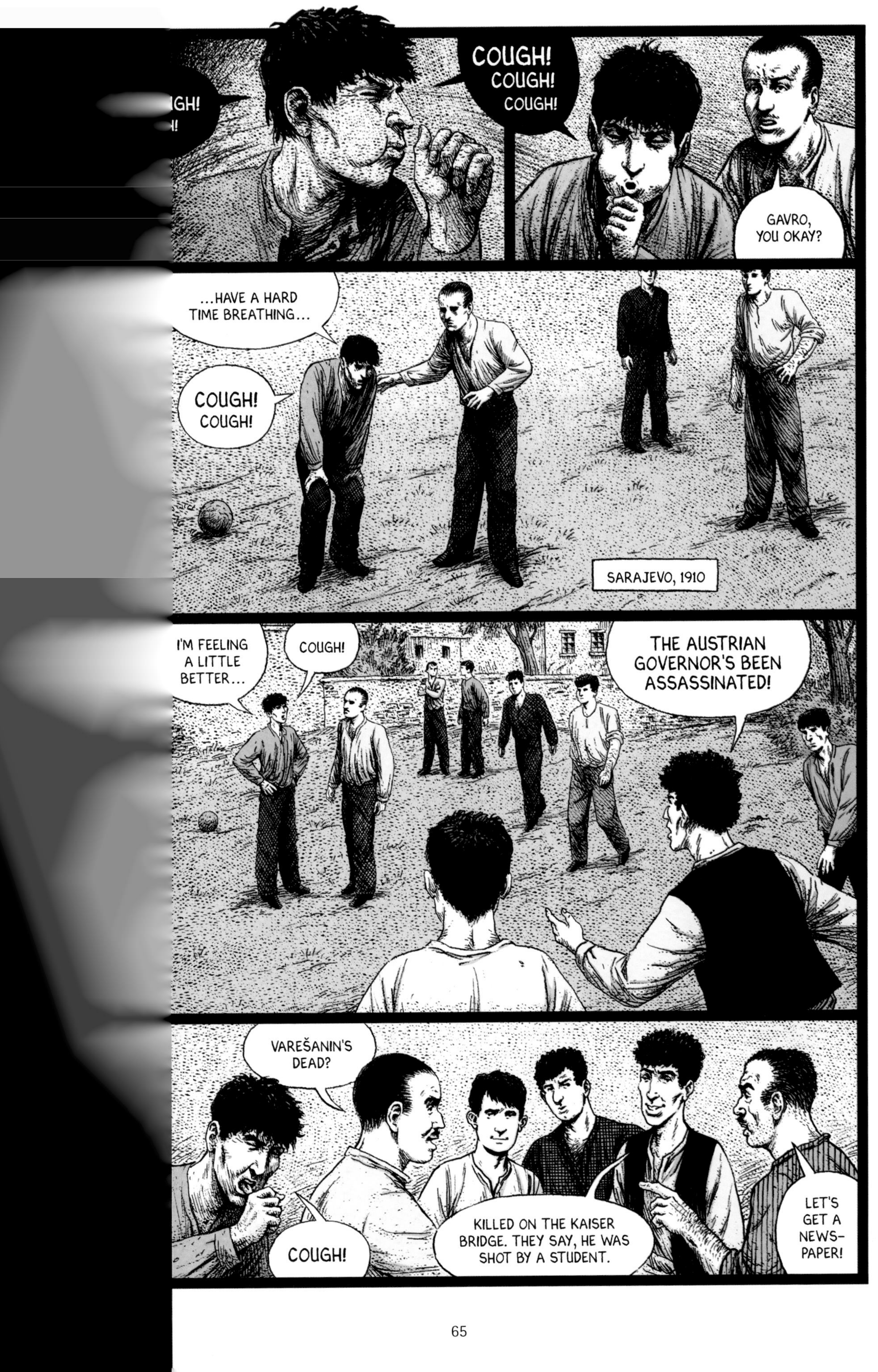
COUGH!
COUGH!
COUGH!
GAVRO, YOU OKAY?
...HAVE A HARD TIME BREATHING...
COUGH! COUGH!
SARAJEVO, 1910
I'M FEELING A LITTLE BETTER...
COUGH!
THE AUSTRIAN GOVERNOR'S BEEN ASSASSINATED!
VAREŠANIN'S DEAD?
COUGH!
KILLED ON THE KAISER BRIDGE. THEY SAY, HE WAS SHOT BY A STUDENT.
LET'S GET A NEWS-PAPER!

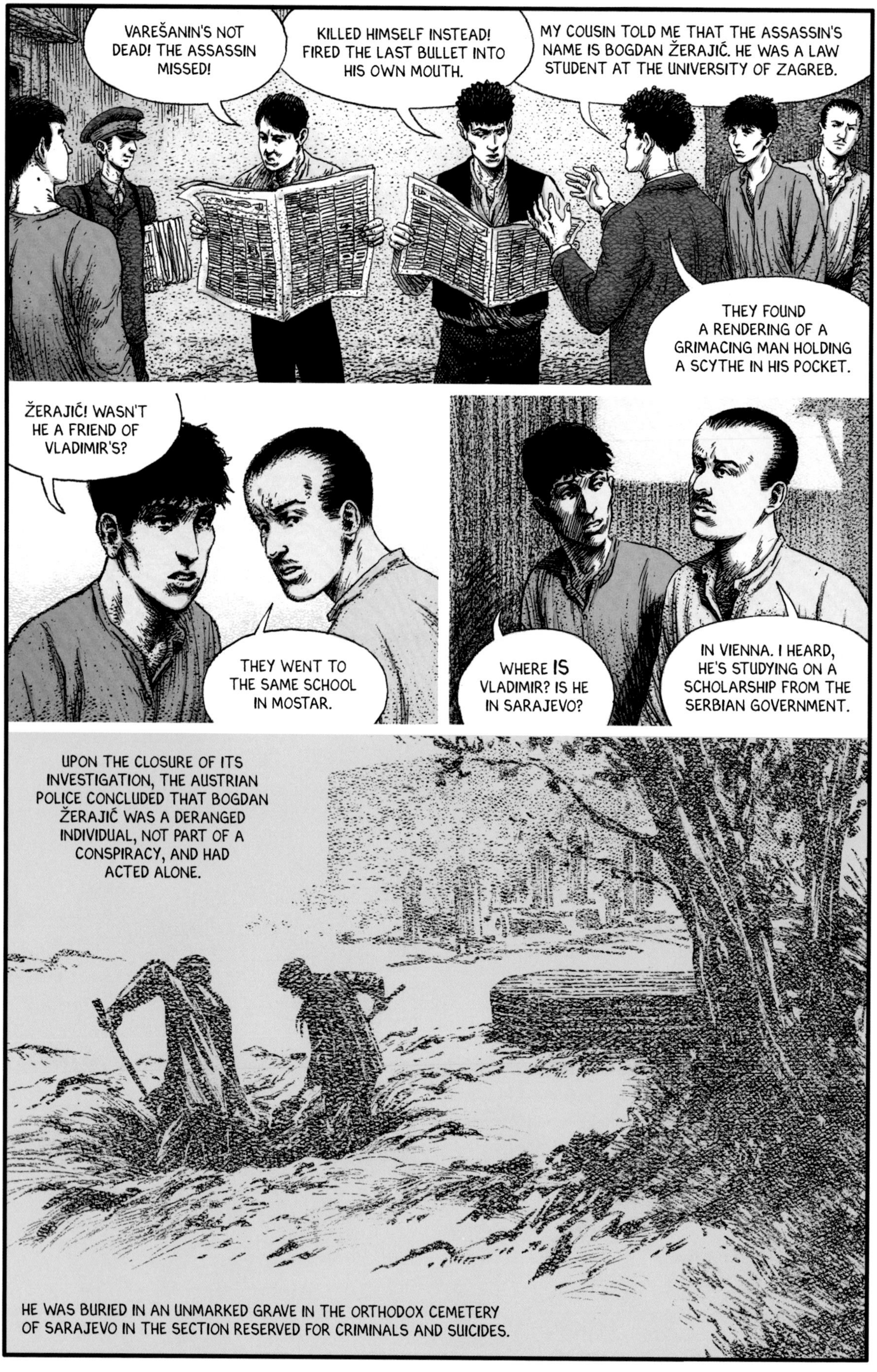
VAREŠANIN'S NOT DEAD! THE ASSASSIN MISSED!
KILLED HIMSELF INSTEAD! FIRED THE LAST BULLET INTO HIS OWN MOUTH.
MY COUSIN TOLD ME THAT THE ASSASSIN'S NAME IS BOGDAN ŽERAJIĆ. HE WAS A LAW STUDENT AT THE UNIVERSITY OF ZAGREB.
THEY FOUND A RENDERING OF A GRIMACING MAN HOLDING A SCYTHE IN HIS POCKET.
ŽERAJIĆ! WASN'T HE A FRIEND OF VLADIMIR'S?
THEY WENT TO THE SAME SCHOOL IN MOSTAR.
WHERE IS VLADIMIR? IS HE IN SARAJEVO?
IN VIENNA. I HEARD, HE'S STUDYING ON A SCHOLARSHIP FROM THE SERBIAN GOVERNMENT.
UPON THE CLOSURE OF ITS INVESTIGATION, THE AUSTRIAN POLICE CONCLUDED THAT BOGDAN ŽERAJIĆ WAS A DERANGED INDIVIDUAL, NOT PART OF A CONSPIRACY, AND HAD ACTED ALONE.
HE WAS BURIED IN AN UNMARKED GRAVE IN THE ORTHODOX CEMETERY OF SARAJEVO IN THE SECTION RESERVED FOR CRIMINALS AND SUICIDES.

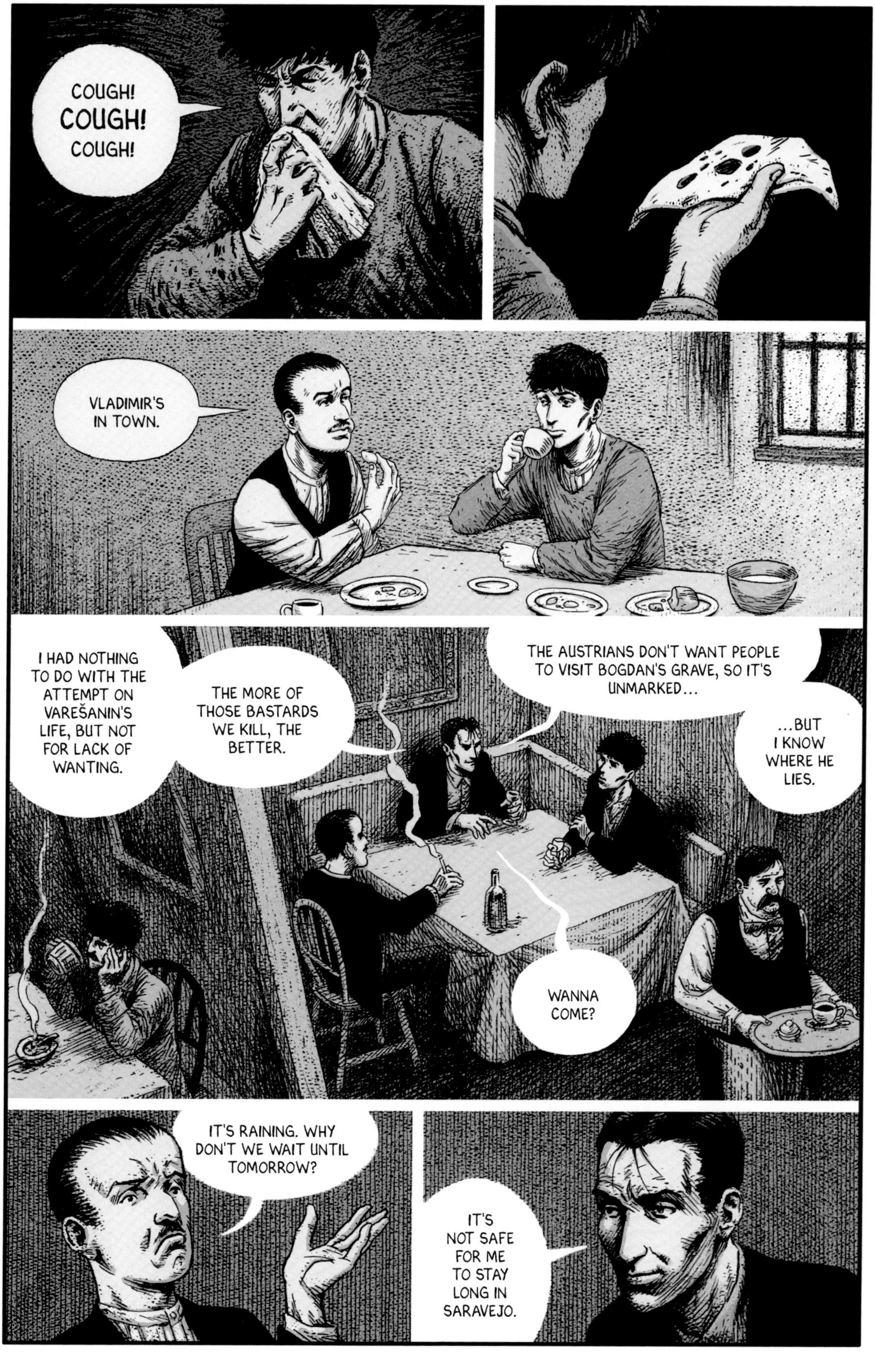
COUGH! COUGH! COUGH!
VLADIMIR'S IN TOWN.
I HAD NOTHING TO DO WITH THE ATTEMPT ON VAREŠANIN'S LIFE, BUT NOT FOR LACK OF WANTING.
THE MORE OF THOSE BASTARDS WE KILL, THE BETTER.
THE AUSTRIANS DON'T WANT PEOPLE TO VISIT BOGDAN'S GRAVE, SO IT'S UNMARKED...
...BUT I KNOW WHERE HE LIES.
WANNA COME?
IT'S RAINING. WHY DON'T WE WAIT UNTIL TOMORROW?
IT'S NOT SAFE FOR ME TO STAY LONG IN SARAVEJO.

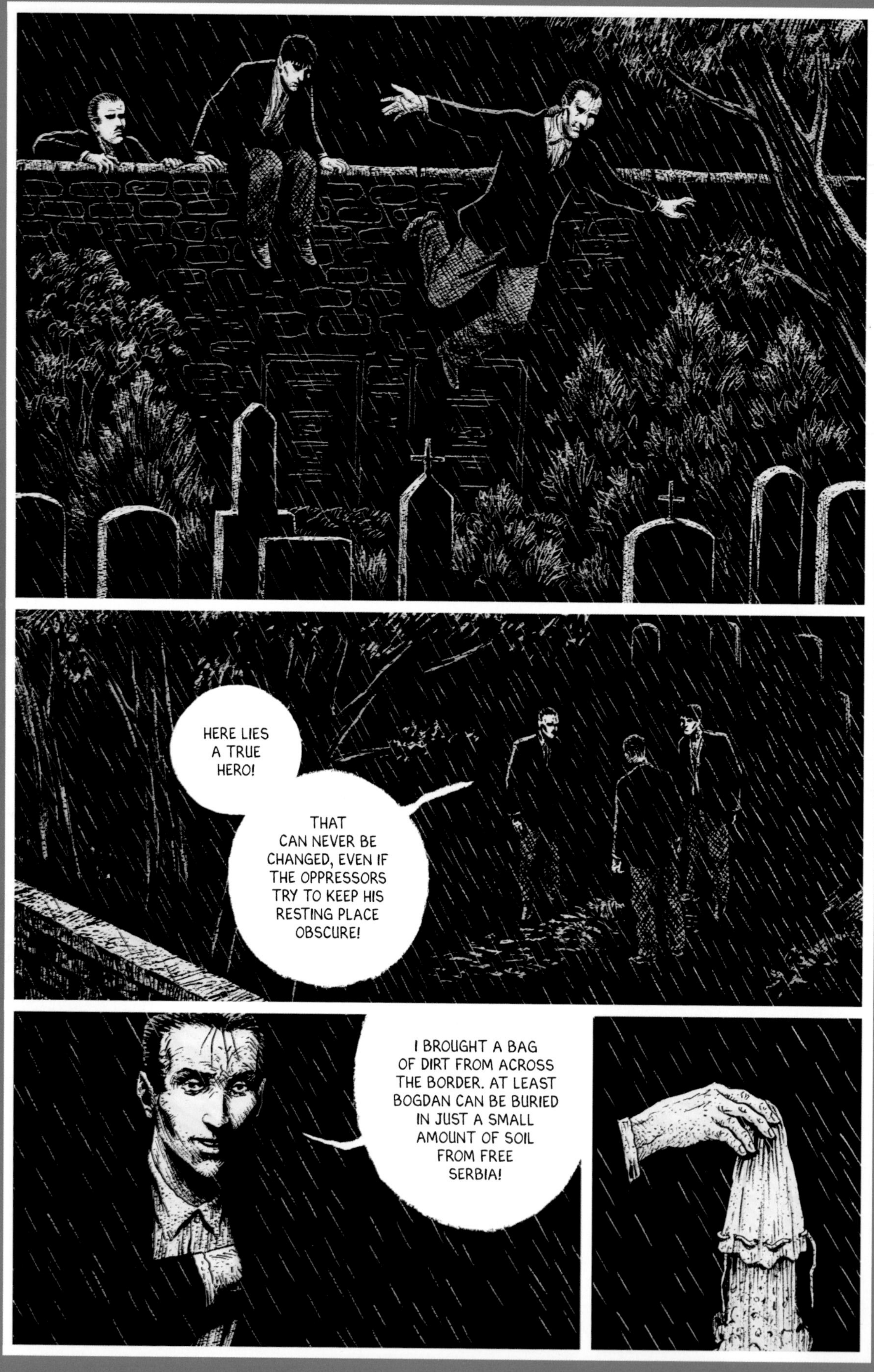
HERE LIES A TRUE HERO!
THAT CAN NEVER BE CHANGED, EVEN IF THE OPPRESSORS TRY TO KEEP HIS RESTING PLACE OBSCURE!
I BROUGHT A BAG OF DIRT FROM ACROSS THE BORDER. AT LEAST BOGDAN CAN BE BURIED IN JUST A SMALL AMOUNT OF SOIL FROM FREE SERBIA!

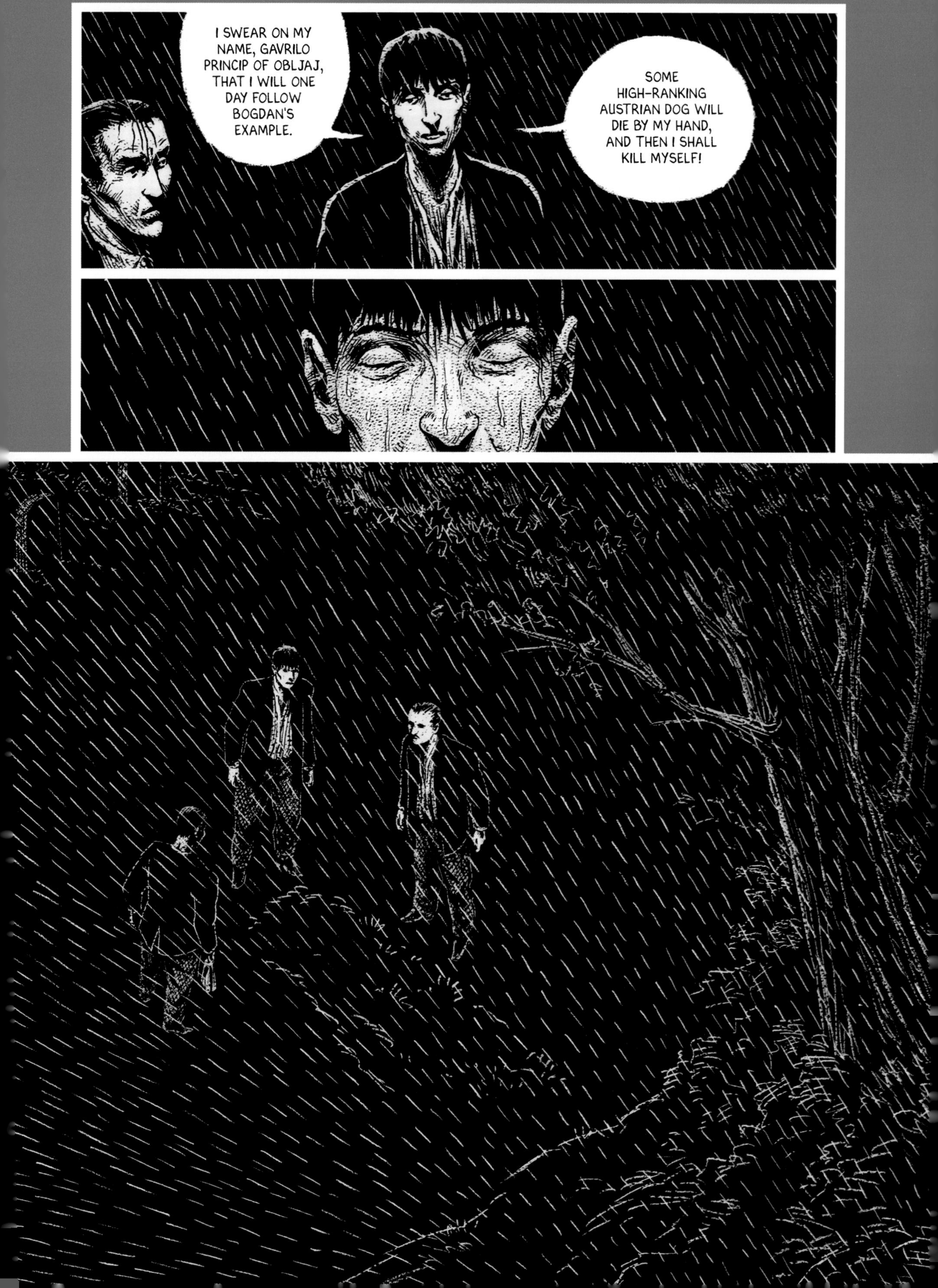
I SWEAR ON MY NAME, GAVRILO PRINCIP OF OBLJAJ, THAT I WILL ONE DAY FOLLOW BOGDAN'S EXAMPLE.
SOME HIGH-RANKING AUSTRIAN DOG WILL DIE BY MY HAND, AND THEN I SHALL KILL MYSELF!

"EVERYONE KNOWS THE EVIL INFLUENCE OF LAZINESS. WORK RELIEVES A MAN. BUT THERE IS WORK AND WORK. THERE IS THE WORK OF THE FREE INDIVIDUAL WHICH MAKES HIM FEEL A PART OF THE IMMENSE WHOLE. AND THEN THERE IS THAT OF A SLAVE WHICH DEGRADES."

—PETER KROPOTKIN, ANARCHIST
PHILOSOPHER, 1886

"IF THE BOURGEOISIE REALLY WANTS TO PERFORM ONE LAST SERVICE FOR HUMANITY; IF ITS LOVE FOR REAL, COMPLETE WORLDWIDE FREEDOM IS SINCERE; IF IT WISHES, IN A WORD, TO QUIT BEING REACTIONARY, THEN THERE IS ONLY ONE THING LEFT FOR IT TO DO: TO DIE GRACEFULLY, AS QUICKLY AS POSSIBLE."

—MIKHAIL BAKUNIN, ANARCHIST
PHILOSOPHER, 1870

COUGH!
COUGH!

"THE CHASM BETWEEN THE MODERN MILLIONAIRE WHO SQUANDERS THE PRODUCE OF HUMAN LABOR IN A GORGEOUS AND VAIN LUXURY, AND THE PAUPER REDUCED TO A MISERABLE AND INSECURE EXISTENCE, IS GROWING WIDER AND WIDER, SO AS TO BREAK THE VERY UNITY OF SOCIETY."

—PETER KROPOTKIN, ANARCHIST
PHILOSOPHER, 1887

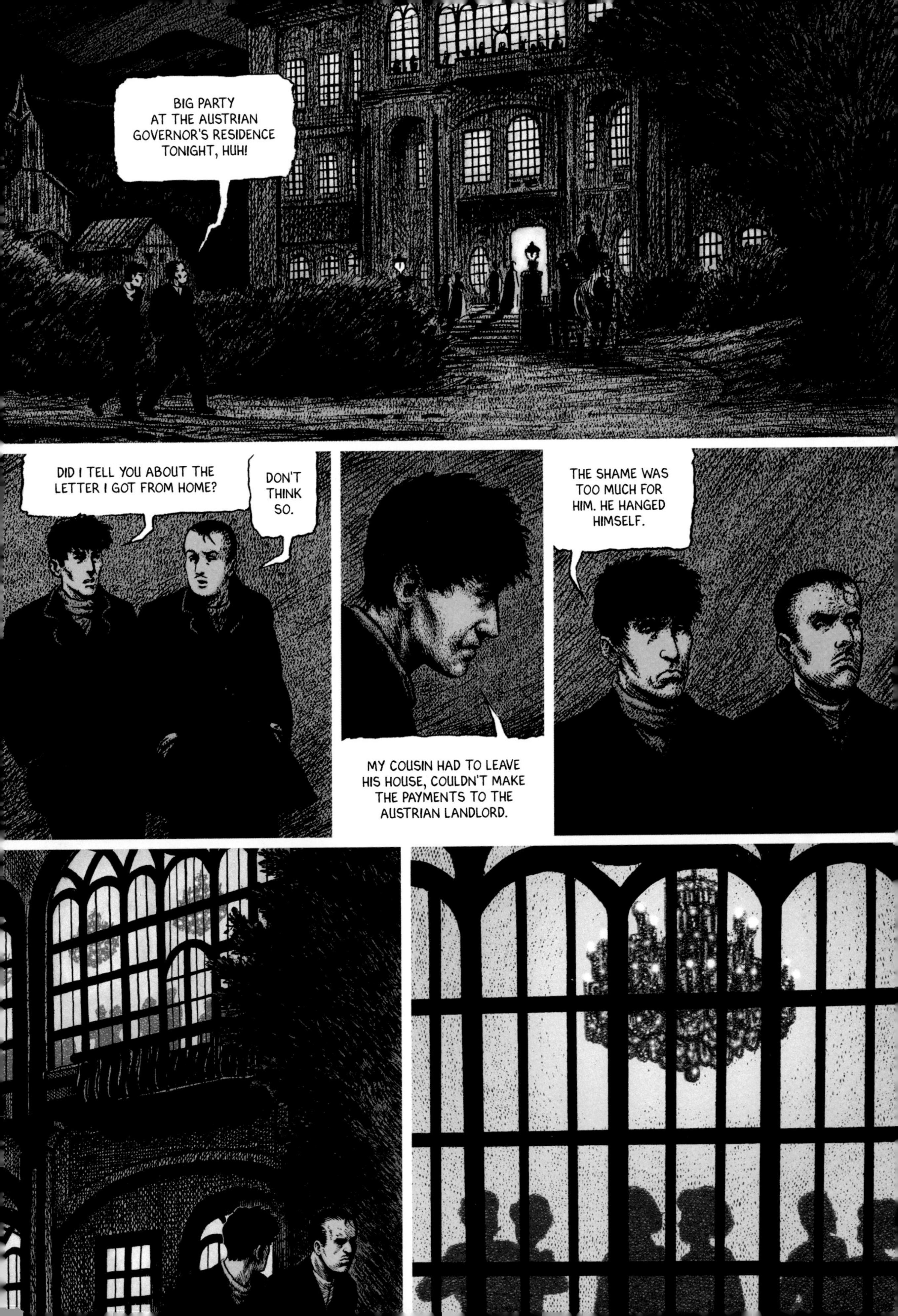
BIG PARTY AT THE AUSTRIAN GOVERNOR'S RESIDENCE TONIGHT, HUH!
DID I TELL YOU ABOUT THE LETTER I GOT FROM HOME?
DON'T THINK SO.
MY COUSIN HAD TO LEAVE HIS HOUSE, COULDN'T MAKE THE PAYMENTS TO THE AUSTRIAN LANDLORD.
THE SHAME WAS TOO MUCH FOR HIM. HE HANGED HIMSELF.

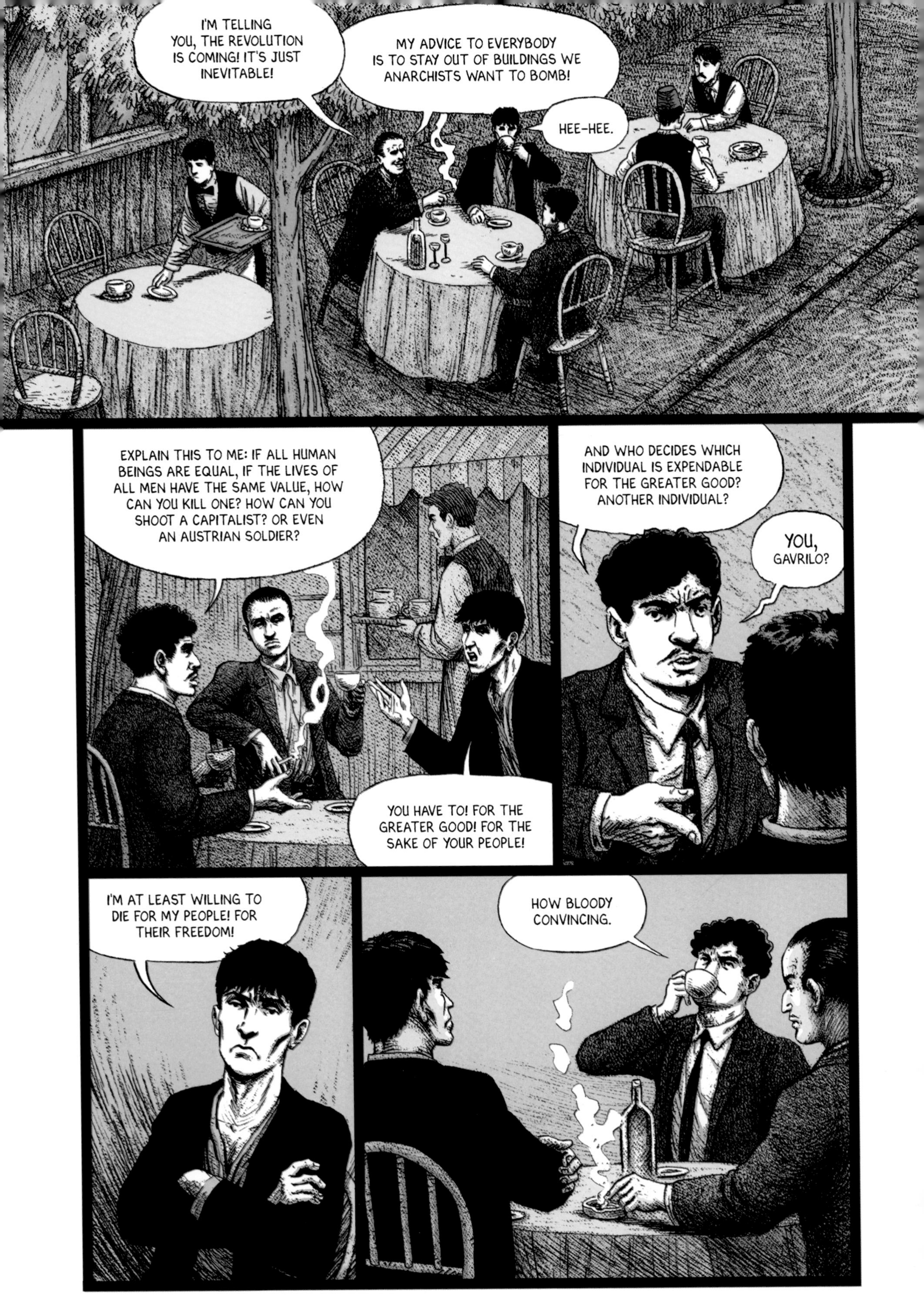
I'M TELLING YOU, THE REVOLUTION IS COMING! IT'S JUST INEVITABLE!
MY ADVICE TO EVERYBODY IS TO STAY OUT OF BUILDINGS WE ANARCHISTS WANT TO BOMB!
HEE-HEE.
EXPLAIN THIS TO ME: IF ALL HUMAN BEINGS ARE EQUAL, IF THE LIVES OF ALL MEN HAVE THE SAME VALUE, HOW CAN YOU KILL ONE? HOW CAN YOU SHOOT A CAPITALIST? OR EVEN AN AUSTRIAN SOLDIER?
YOU HAVE TO! FOR THE GREATER GOOD! FOR THE SAKE OF YOUR PEOPLE!
AND WHO DECIDES WHICH INDIVIDUAL IS EXPENDABLE FOR THE GREATER GOOD? ANOTHER INDIVIDUAL?
YOU, GAVRILO?
I'M AT LEAST WILLING TO DIE FOR MY PEOPLE! FOR THEIR FREEDOM!
HOW BLOODY CONVINCING.

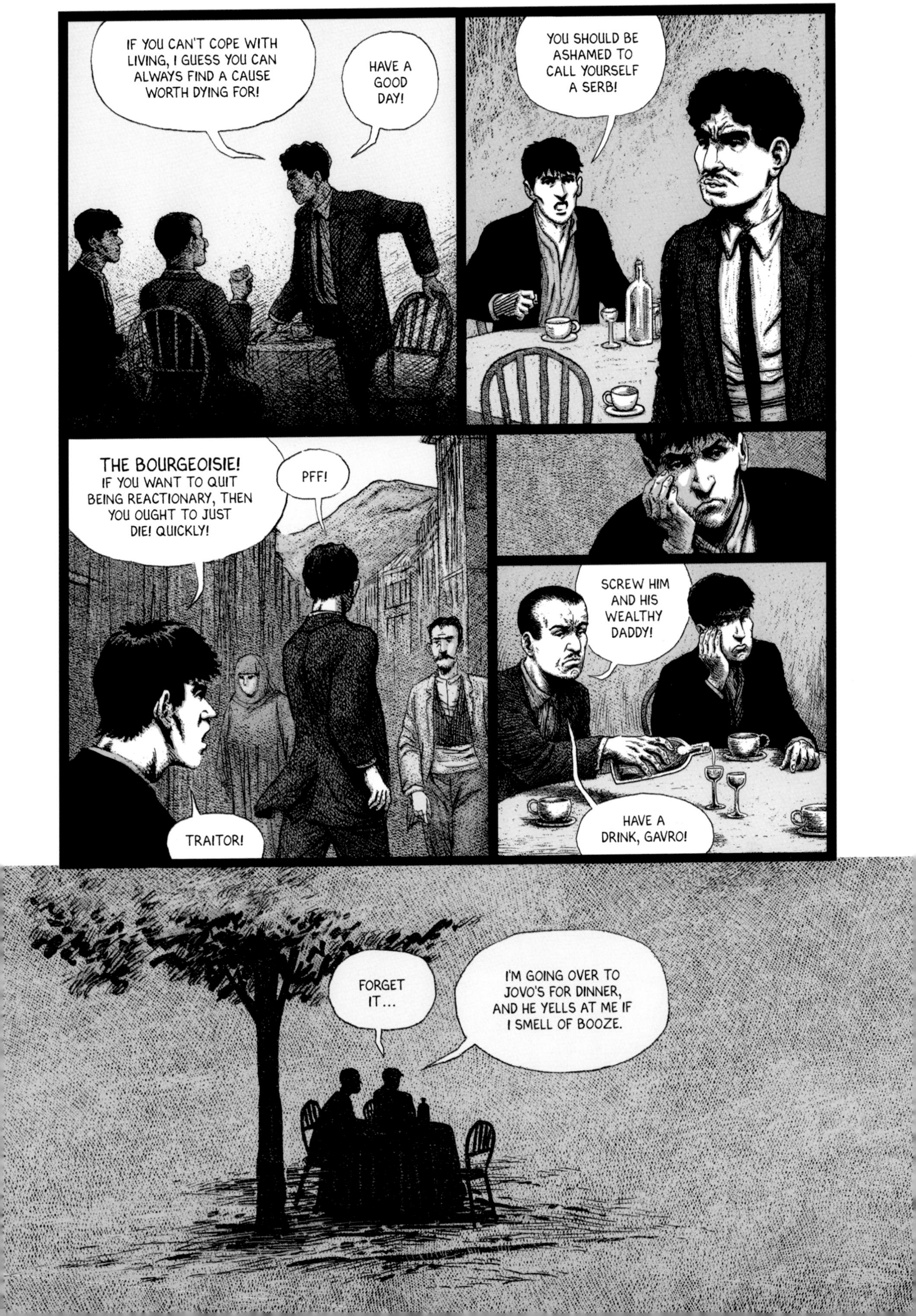
IF YOU CAN'T COPE WITH LIVING, I GUESS YOU CAN ALWAYS FIND A CAUSE WORTH DYING FOR!
HAVE A GOOD DAY!
YOU SHOULD BE ASHAMED TO CALL YOURSELF A SERB!
THE BOURGEOISIE! IF YOU WANT TO QUIT BEING REACTIONARY, THEN YOU OUGHT TO JUST DIE! QUICKLY!
PFF!
TRAITOR!
SCREW HIM AND HIS WEALTHY DADDY!
HAVE A DRINK, GAVRO!
FORGET IT...
I'M GOING OVER TO JOVO'S FOR DINNER, AND HE YELLS AT ME IF I SMELL OF BOOZE.

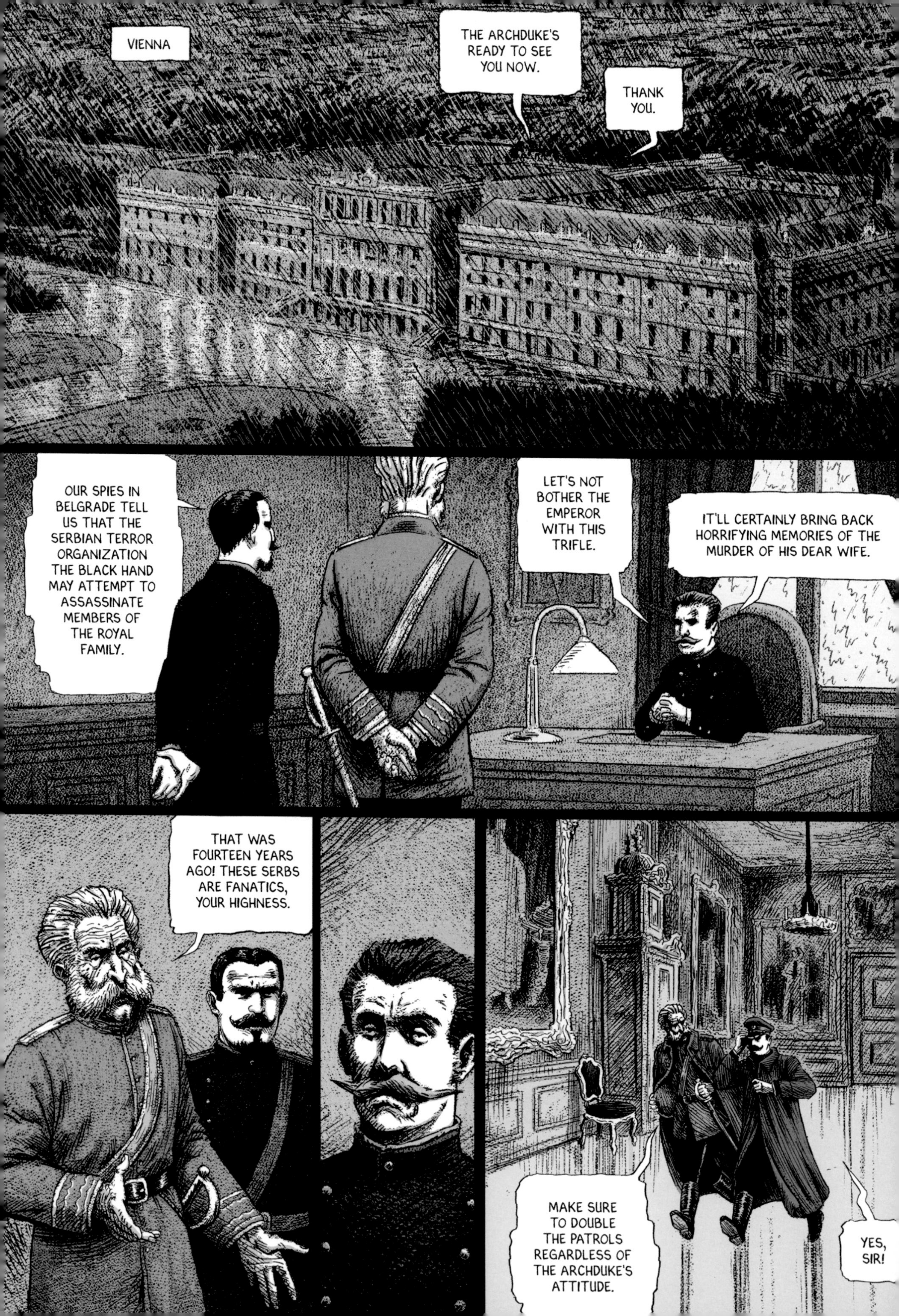
VIENNA
THE ARCHDUKE'S READY TO SEE YOU NOW.
THANK YOU.
OUR SPIES IN BELGRADE TELL US THAT THE SERBIAN TERROR ORGANIZATION THE BLACK HAND MAY ATTEMPT TO ASSASSINATE MEMBERS OF THE ROYAL FAMILY.
LET'S NOT BOTHER THE EMPEROR WITH THIS TRIFLE.
IT'LL CERTAINLY BRING BACK HORRIFYING MEMORIES OF THE MURDER OF HIS DEAR WIFE.
THAT WAS FOURTEEN YEARS AGO! THESE SERBS ARE FANATICS, YOUR HIGHNESS.
MAKE SURE TO DOUBLE THE PATROLS REGARDLESS OF THE ARCHDUKE'S ATTITUDE.
YES, SIR!

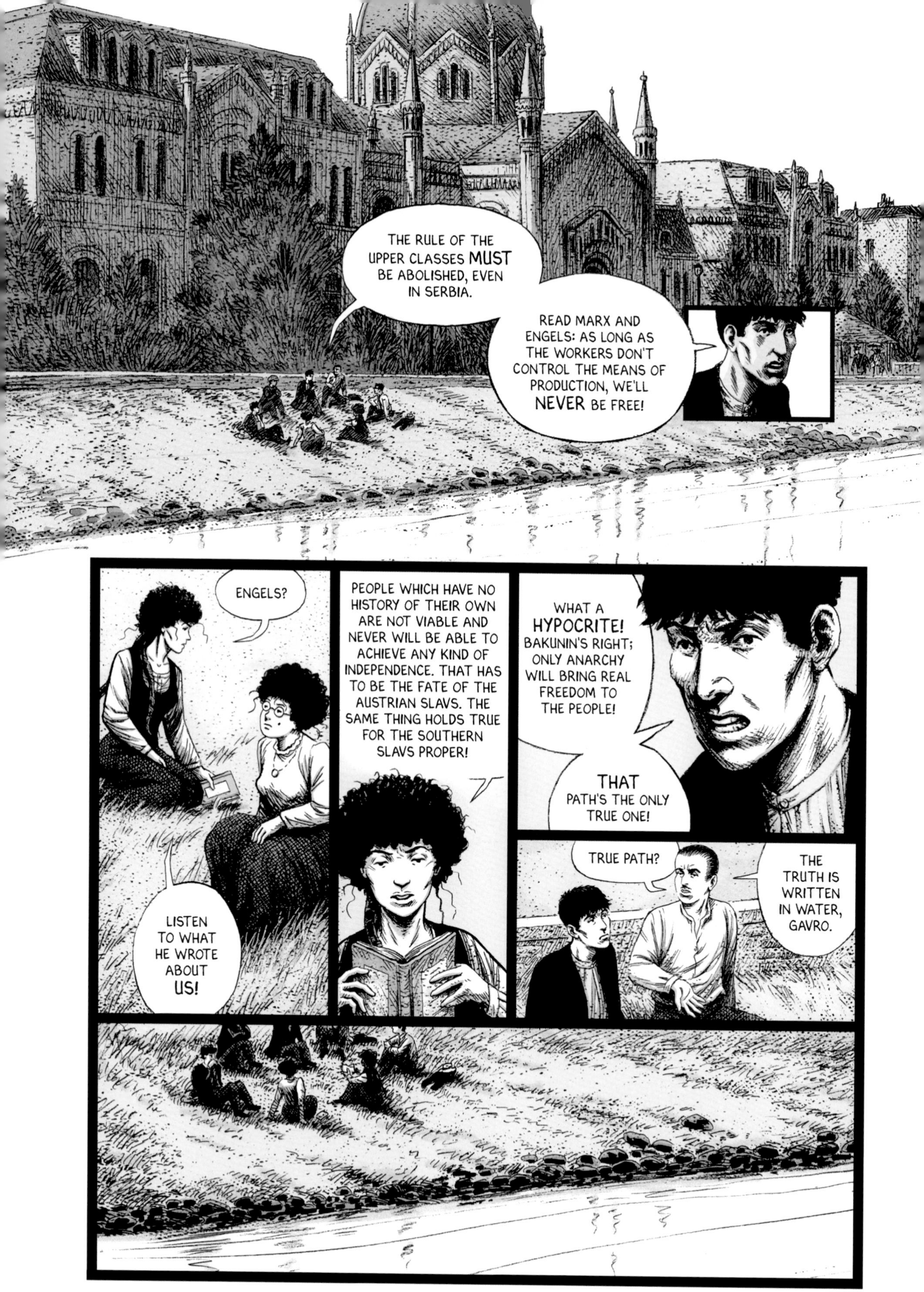
THE RULE OF THE UPPER CLASSES MUST BE ABOLISHED, EVEN IN SERBIA.
READ MARX AND ENGELS: AS LONG AS THE WORKERS DON'T CONTROL THE MEANS OF PRODUCTION, WE'LL NEVER BE FREE!
ENGELS?
LISTEN TO WHAT HE WROTE ABOUT US!
PEOPLE WHICH HAVE NO HISTORY OF THEIR OWN ARE NOT VIABLE AND NEVER WILL BE ABLE TO ACHIEVE ANY KIND OF INDEPENDENCE. THAT HAS TO BE THE FATE OF THE AUSTRIAN SLAVS. THE SAME THING HOLDS TRUE FOR THE SOUTHERN SLAVS PROPER!
WHAT A HYPOCRITE! BAKUNIN'S RIGHT; ONLY ANARCHY WILL BRING REAL FREEDOM TO THE PEOPLE!
THAT PATH'S THE ONLY TRUE ONE!
TRUE PATH?
THE TRUTH IS WRITTEN IN WATER, GAVRO.

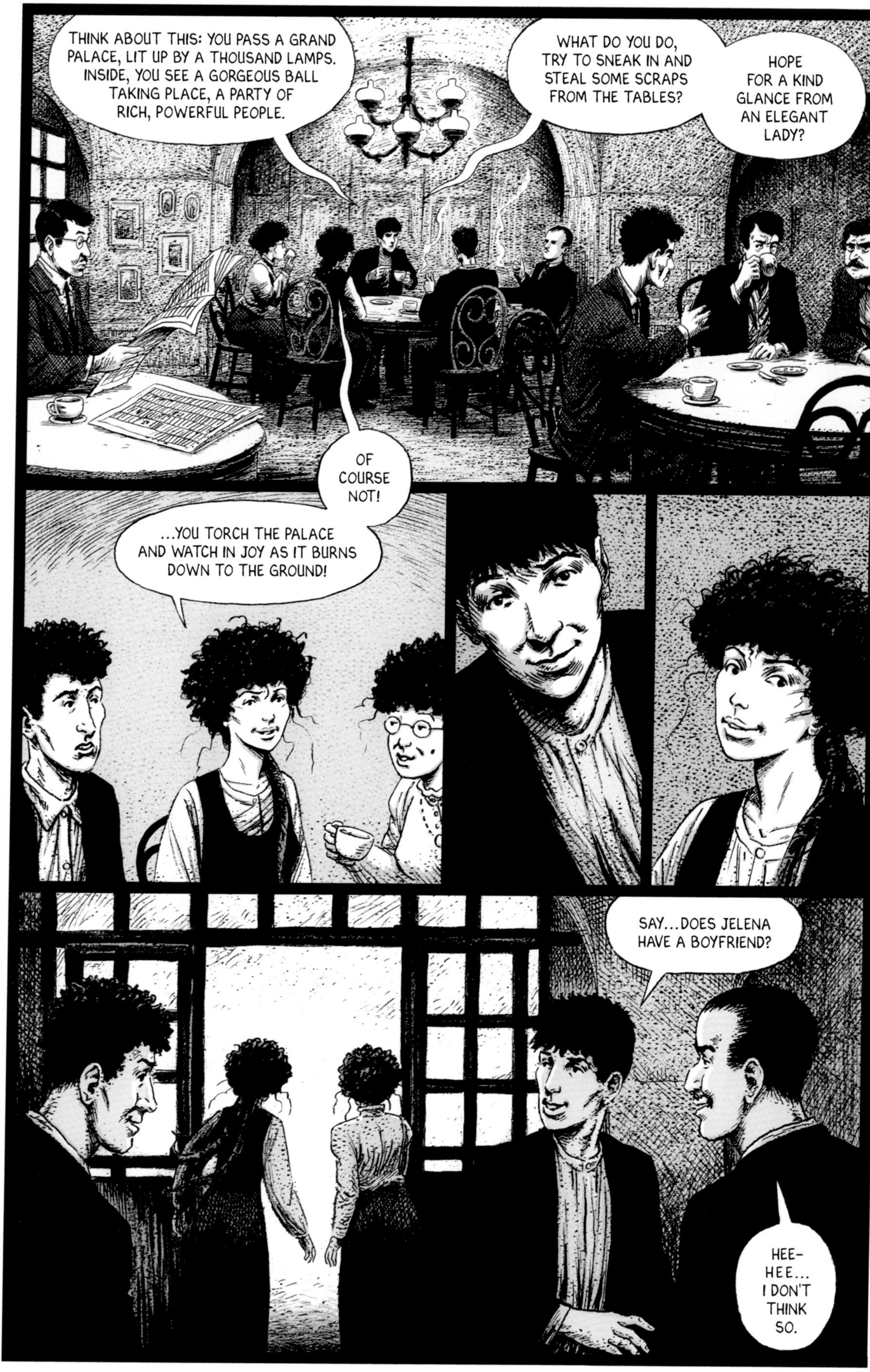
THINK ABOUT THIS: YOU PASS A GRAND PALACE, LIT UP BY A THOUSAND LAMPS. INSIDE, YOU SEE A GORGEOUS BALL TAKING PLACE, A PARTY OF RICH, POWERFUL PEOPLE.
WHAT DO YOU DO, TRY TO SNEAK IN AND STEAL SOME SCRAPS FROM THE TABLES?
HOPE FOR A KIND GLANCE FROM AN ELEGANT LADY?
OF COURSE NOT!
...YOU TORCH THE PALACE AND WATCH IN JOY AS IT BURNS DOWN TO THE GROUND!
SAY...DOES JELENA HAVE A BOYFRIEND?
HEE-HEE... I DON'T THINK SO.

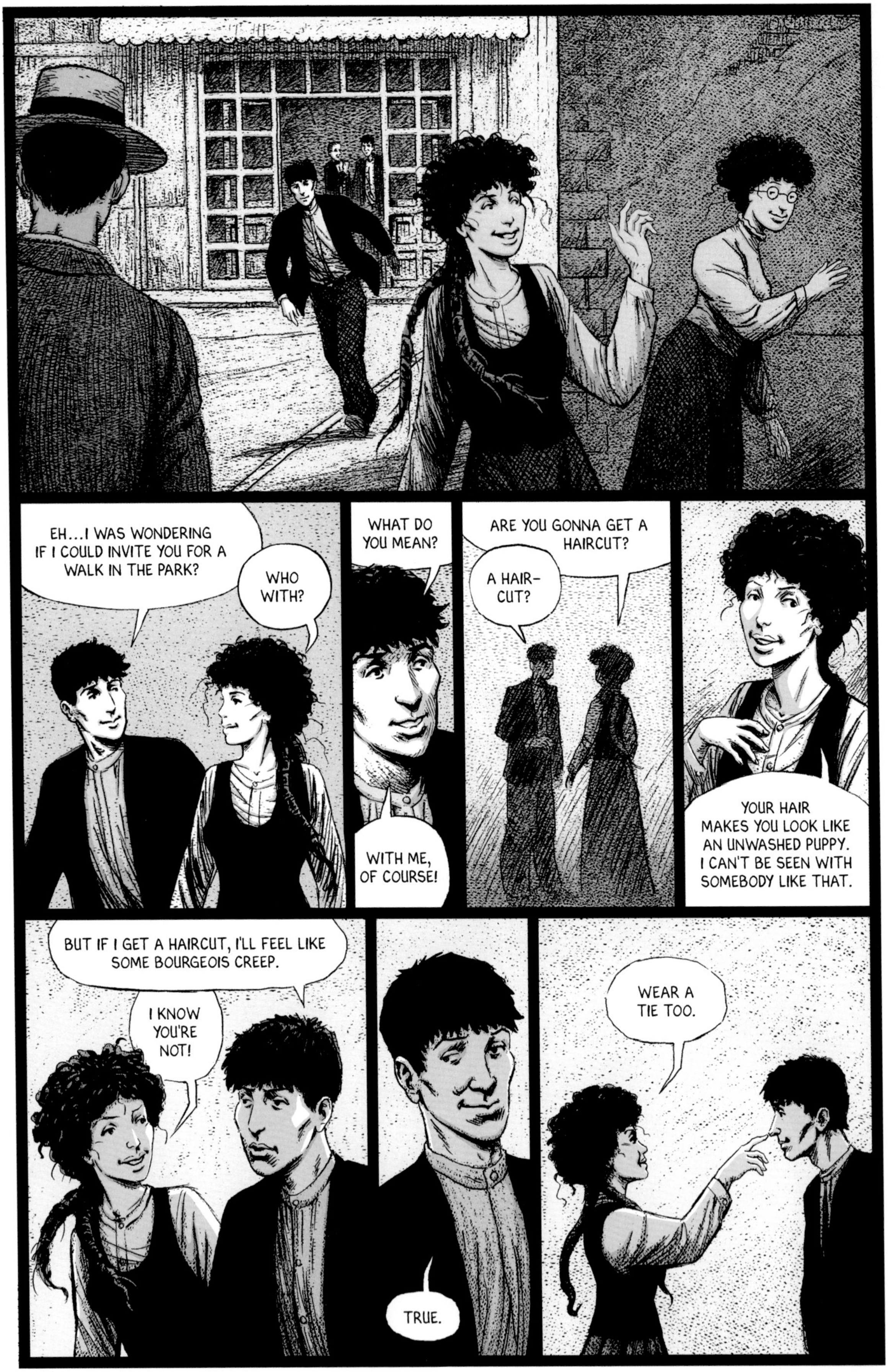

EH...I WAS WONDERING IF I COULD INVITE YOU FOR A WALK IN THE PARK?
WHO WITH?
WHAT DO YOU MEAN?
WITH ME, OF COURSE!
ARE YOU GONNA GET A HAIRCUT?
A HAIR-CUT?
YOUR HAIR MAKES YOU LOOK LIKE AN UNWASHED PUPPY. I CAN'T BE SEEN WITH SOMEBODY LIKE THAT.
BUT IF I GET A HAIRCUT, I'LL FEEL LIKE SOME BOURGEOIS CREEP.
I KNOW YOU'RE NOT!
TRUE.
WEAR A TIE TOO.

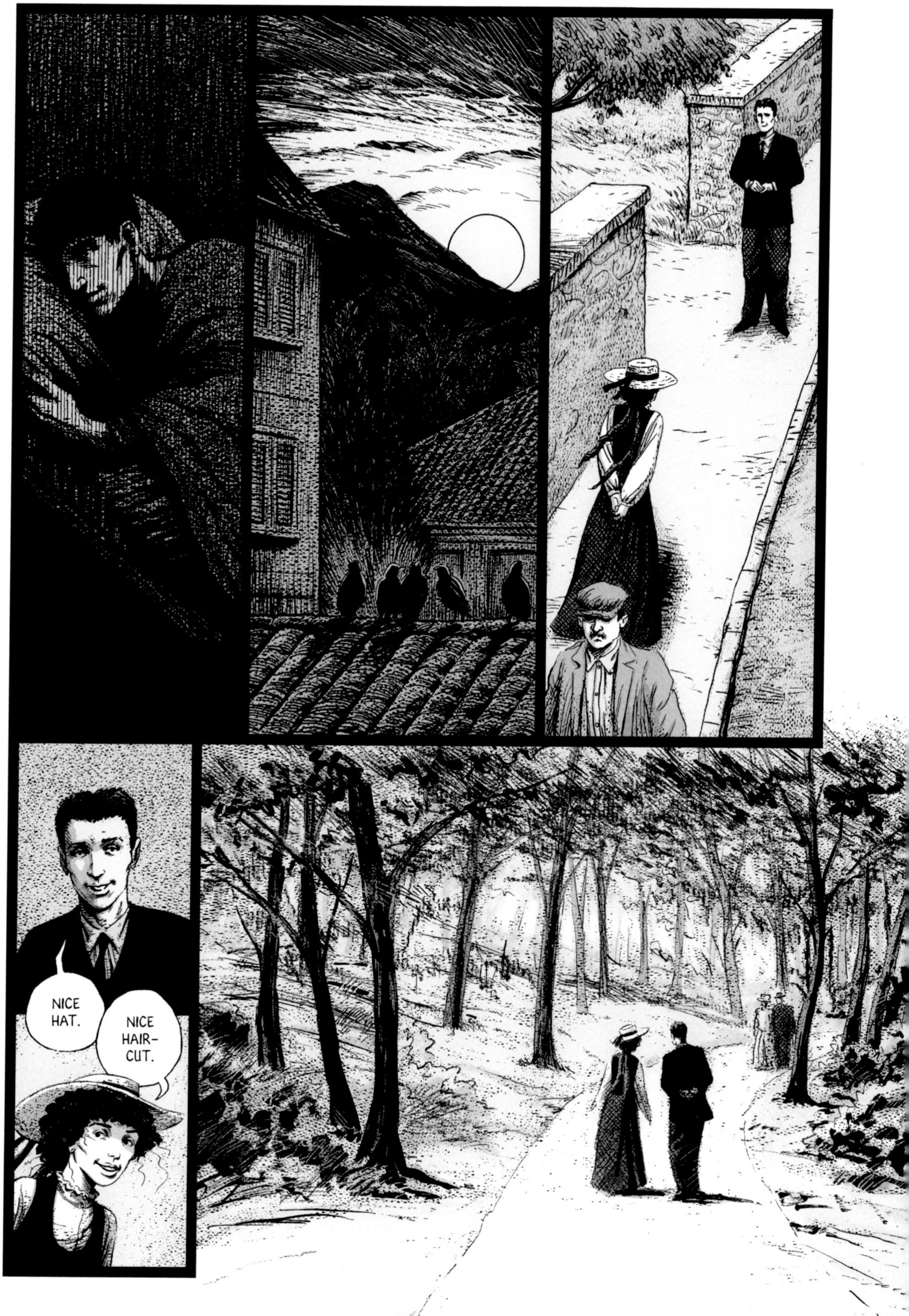
NICE HAT.
NICE HAIR-CUT.

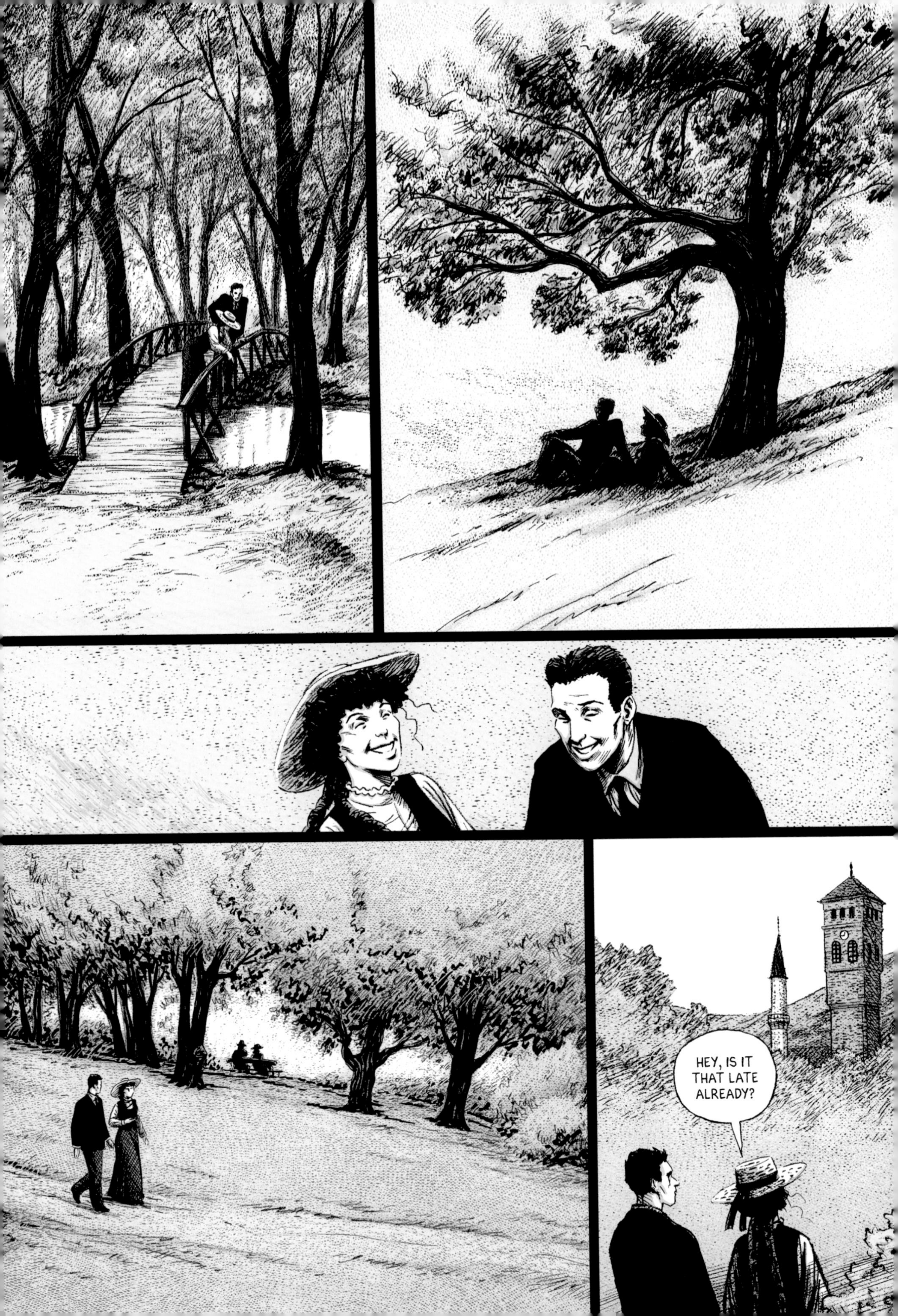
HEY, IS IT THAT LATE ALREADY?

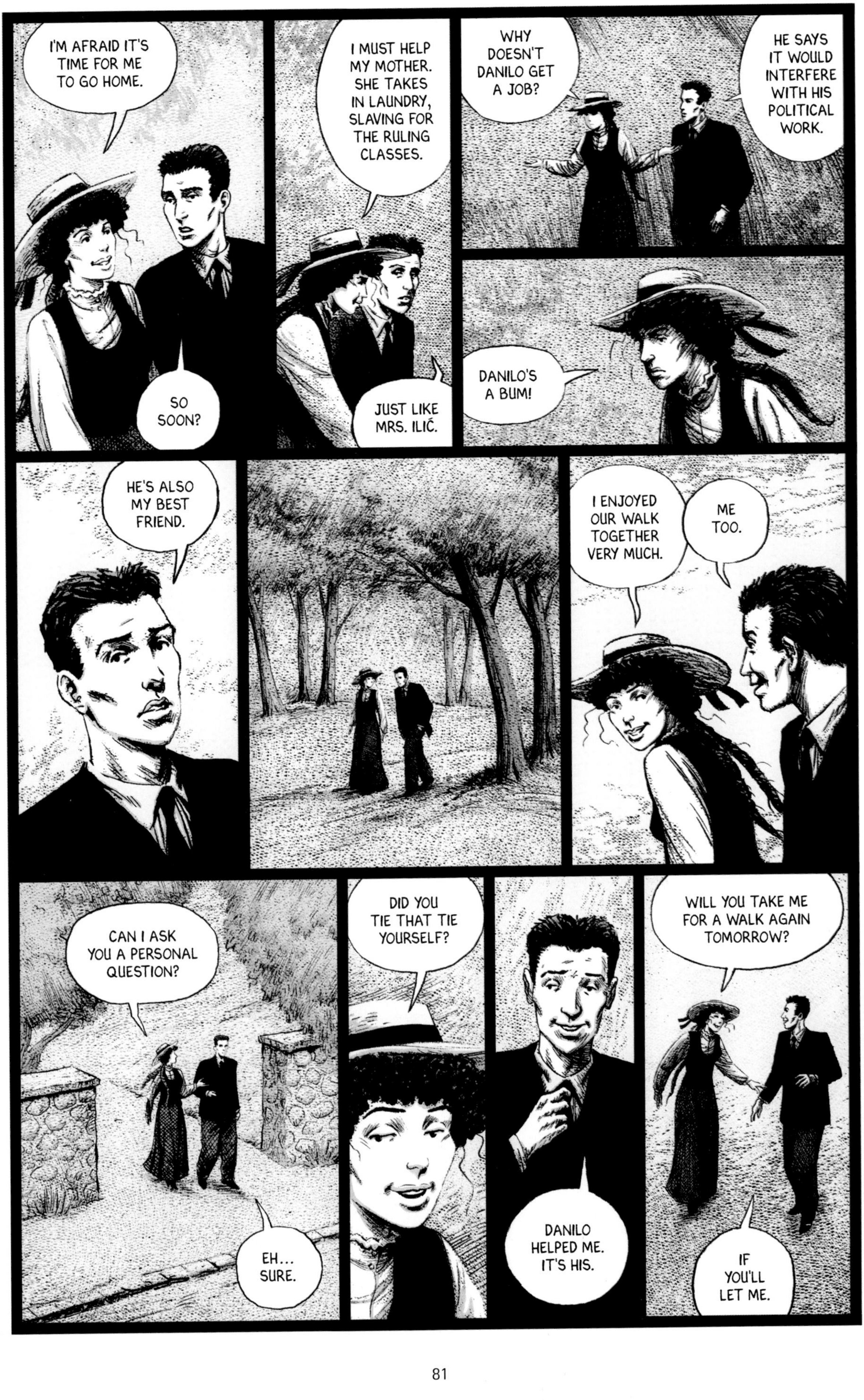
I'M AFRAID IT'S TIME FOR ME TO GO HOME.
SO SOON?
I MUST HELP MY MOTHER. SHE TAKES IN LAUNDRY, SLAVING FOR THE RULING CLASSES.
JUST LIKE MRS. ILIĆ.
WHY DOESN'T DANILO GET A JOB?
HE SAYS IT WOULD INTERFERE WITH HIS POLITICAL WORK.
DANILO'S A BUM!
HE'S ALSO MY BEST FRIEND.
I ENJOYED OUR WALK TOGETHER VERY MUCH.
ME TOO.
CAN I ASK YOU A PERSONAL QUESTION?
EH... SURE.
DID YOU TIE THAT TIE YOURSELF?
DANILO HELPED ME. IT'S HIS.
WILL YOU TAKE ME FOR A WALK AGAIN TOMORROW?
IF YOU'LL LET ME.

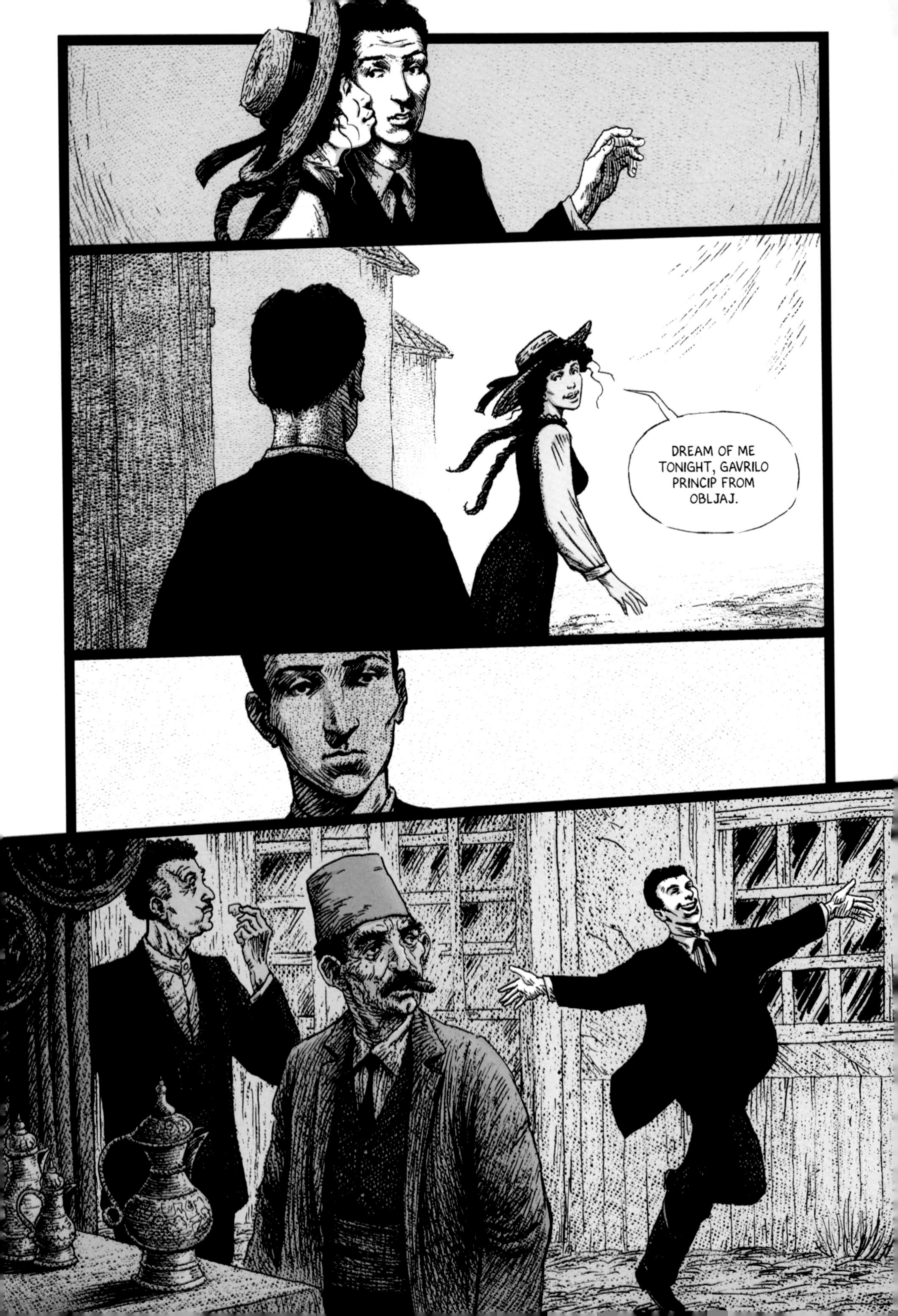
DREAM OF ME TONIGHT, GAVRILO PRINCIP FROM OBLJAJ.

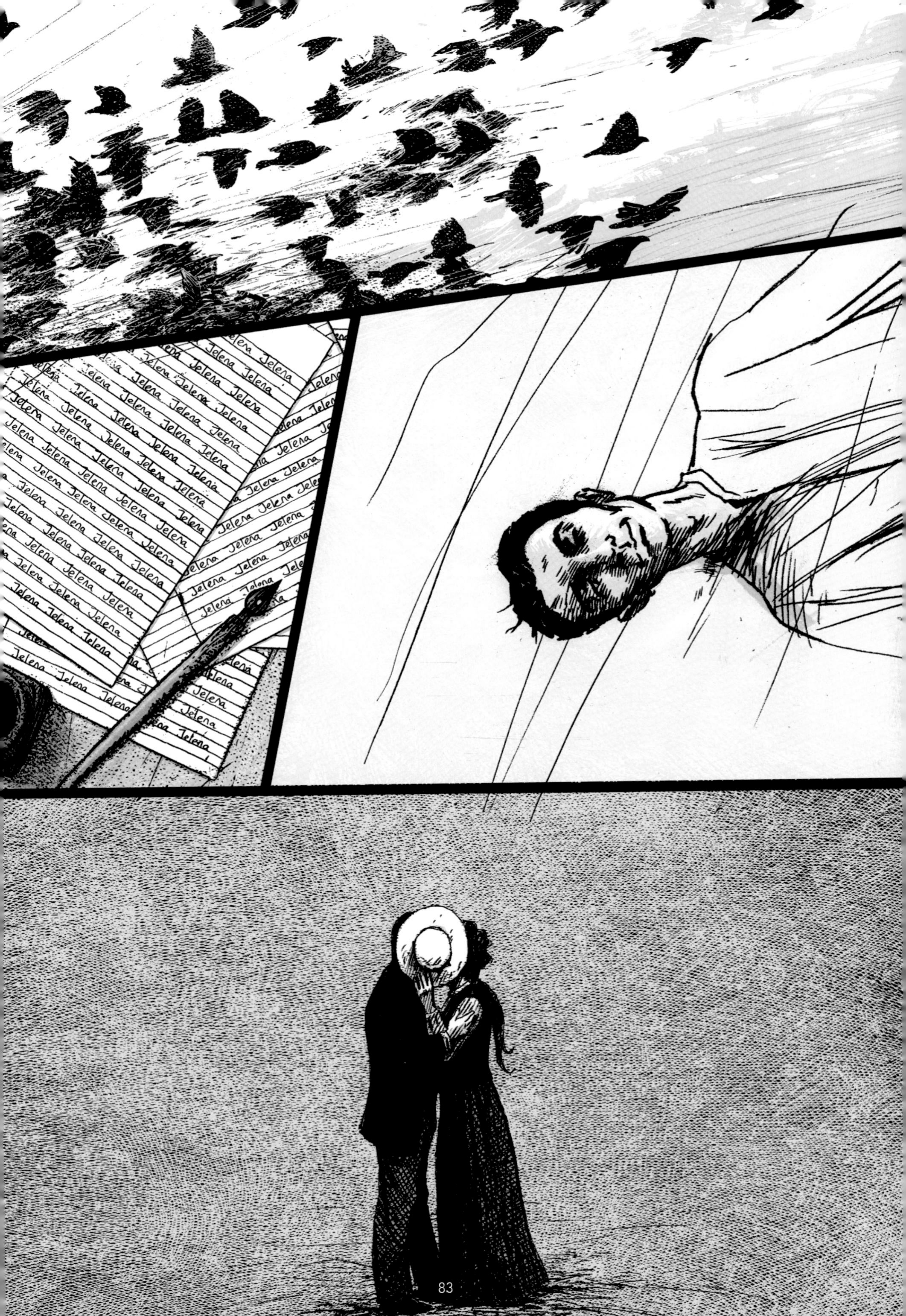
Jelena Jelena Jelena

IN BELGRADE, THE CAPITAL OF SERBIA

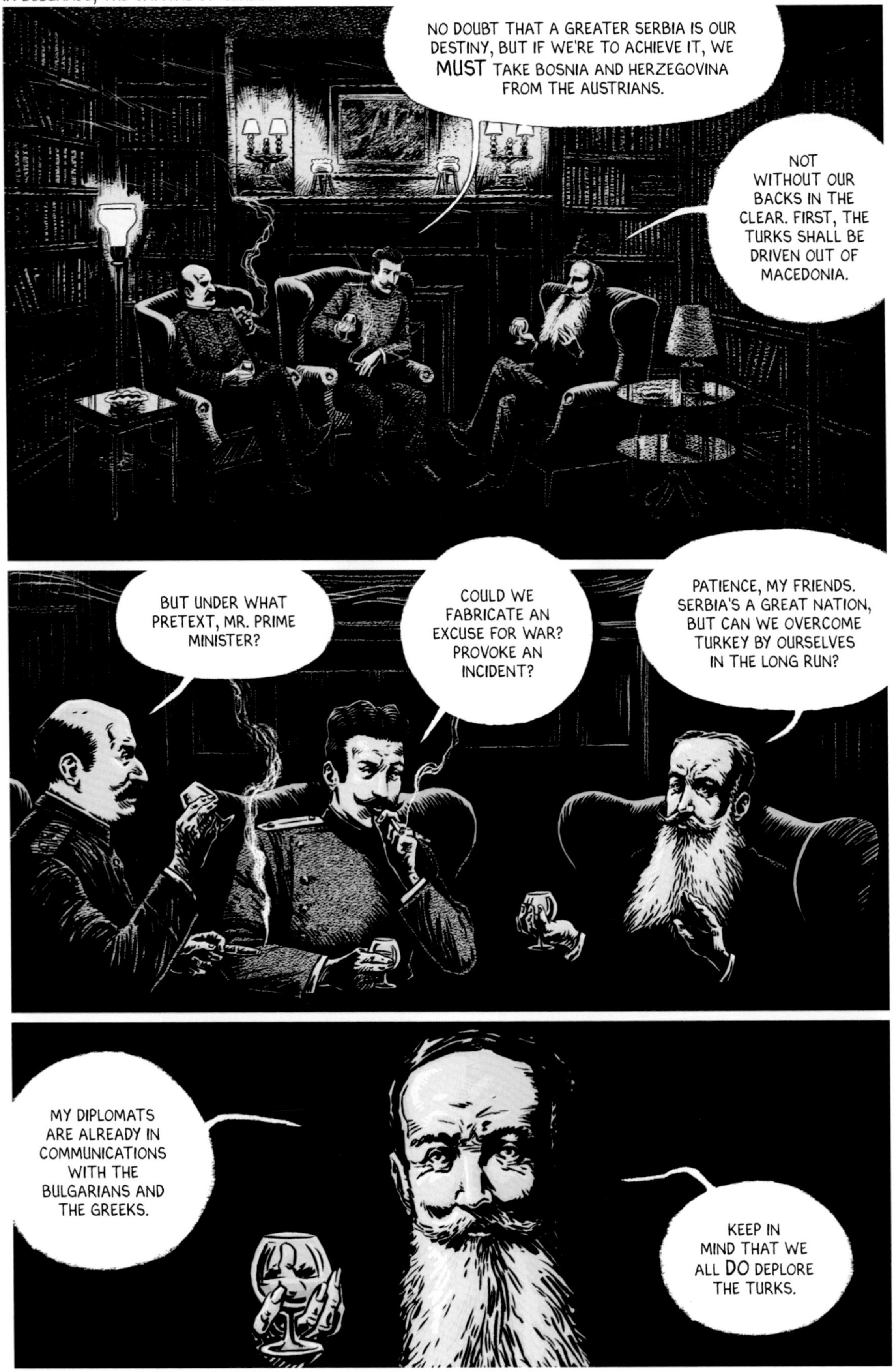
NO DOUBT THAT A GREATER SERBIA IS OUR DESTINY, BUT IF WE'RE TO ACHIEVE IT, WE MUST TAKE BOSNIA AND HERZEGOVINA FROM THE AUSTRIANS.
NOT WITHOUT OUR BACKS IN THE CLEAR. FIRST, THE TURKS SHALL BE DRIVEN OUT OF MACEDONIA.
BUT UNDER WHAT PRETEXT, MR. PRIME MINISTER?
COULD WE FABRICATE AN EXCUSE FOR WAR? PROVOKE AN INCIDENT?
PATIENCE, MY FRIENDS. SERBIA'S A GREAT NATION, BUT CAN WE OVERCOME TURKEY BY OURSELVES IN THE LONG RUN?
MY DIPLOMATS ARE ALREADY IN COMMUNICATIONS WITH THE BULGARIANS AND THE GREEKS.
KEEP IN MIND THAT WE ALL DO DEPLORE THE TURKS.

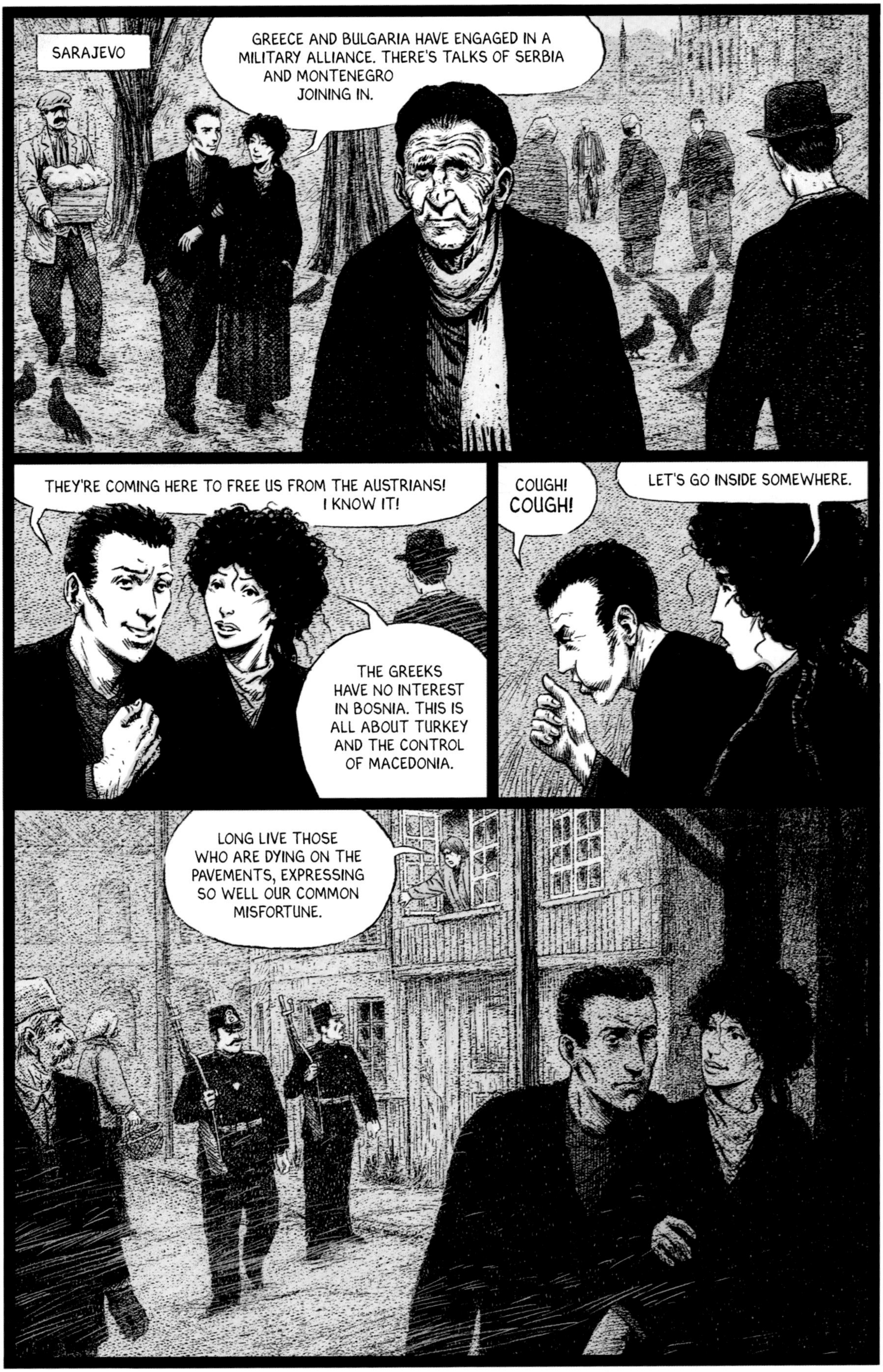
SARAJEVO
GREECE AND BULGARIA HAVE ENGAGED IN A MILITARY ALLIANCE. THERE'S TALKS OF SERBIA AND MONTENEGRO JOINING IN.
THEY'RE COMING HERE TO FREE US FROM THE AUSTRIANS! I KNOW IT!
THE GREEKS HAVE NO INTEREST IN BOSNIA. THIS IS ALL ABOUT TURKEY AND THE CONTROL OF MACEDONIA.
COUGH! COUGH!
LET'S GO INSIDE SOMEWHERE.
LONG LIVE THOSE WHO ARE DYING ON THE PAVEMENTS, EXPRESSING SO WELL OUR COMMON MISFORTUNE.

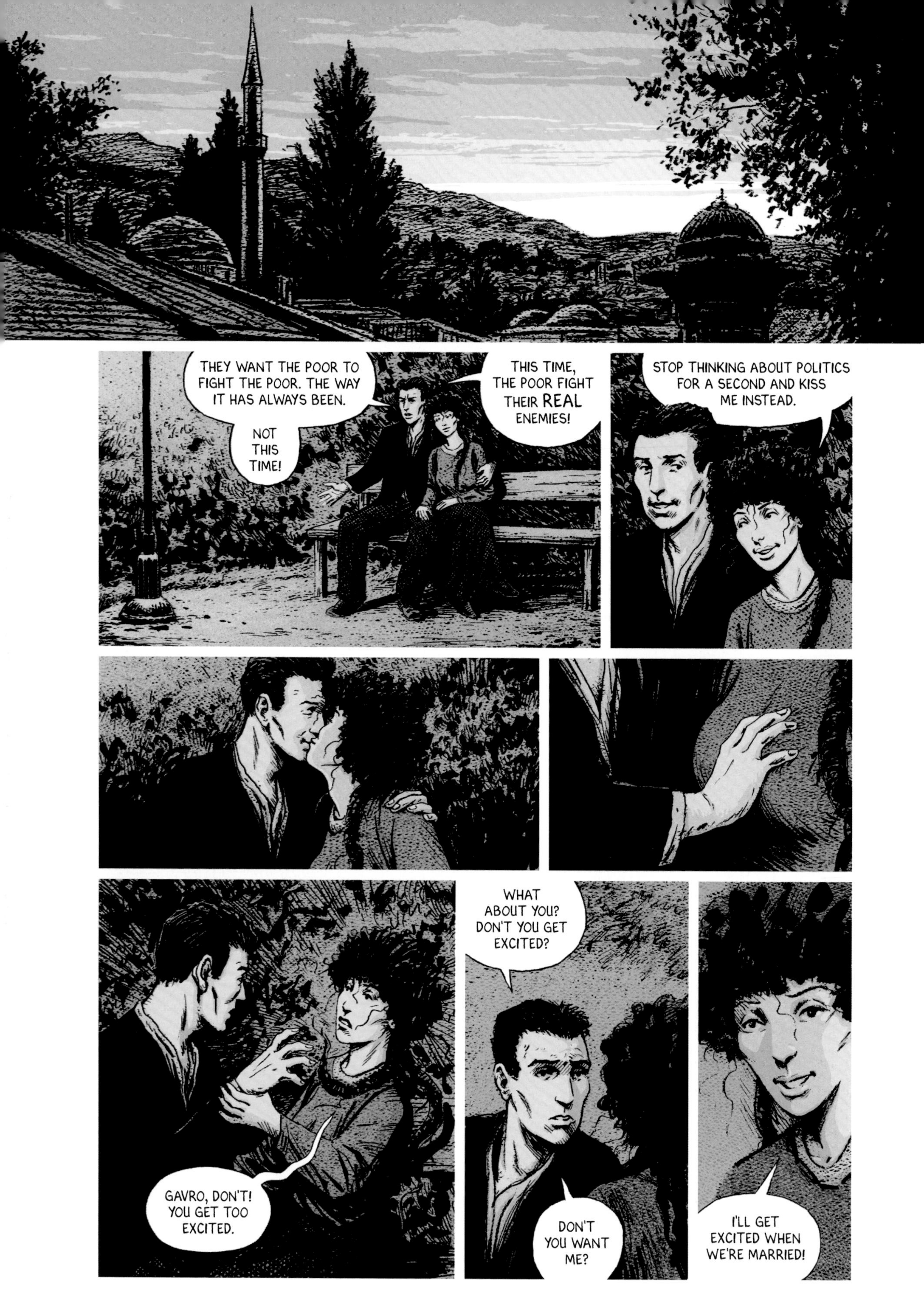
THEY WANT THE POOR TO FIGHT THE POOR. THE WAY IT HAS ALWAYS BEEN.
NOT THIS TIME!
THIS TIME, THE POOR FIGHT THEIR REAL ENEMIES!
STOP THINKING ABOUT POLITICS FOR A SECOND AND KISS ME INSTEAD.
GAVRO, DON'T! YOU GET TOO EXCITED.
WHAT ABOUT YOU? DON'T YOU GET EXCITED?
DON'T YOU WANT ME?
I'LL GET EXCITED WHEN WE'RE MARRIED!

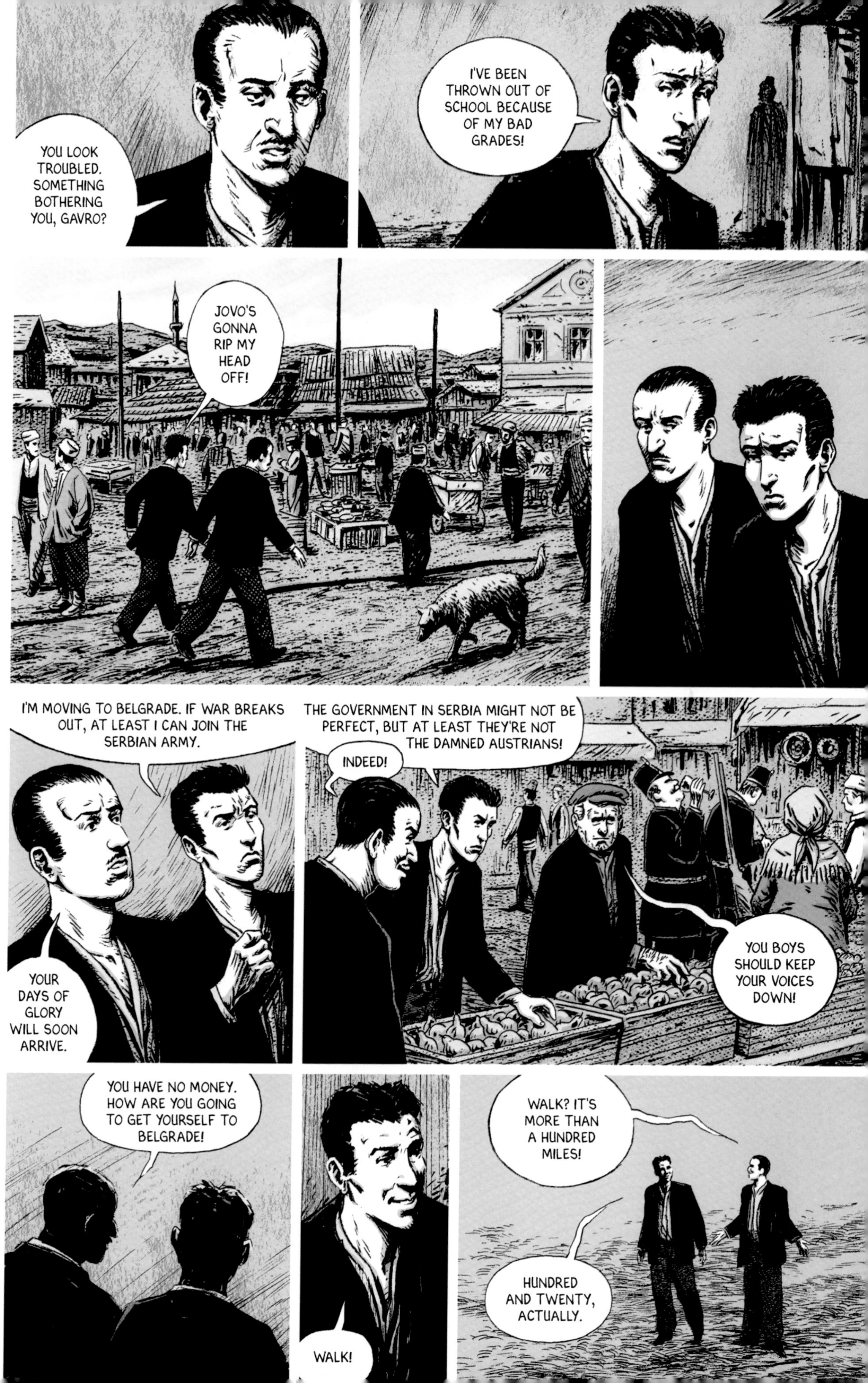
YOU LOOK TROUBLED. SOMETHING BOTHERING YOU, GAVRO?
I'VE BEEN THROWN OUT OF SCHOOL BECAUSE OF MY BAD GRADES!
JOVO'S GONNA RIP MY HEAD OFF!
I'M MOVING TO BELGRADE. IF WAR BREAKS OUT, AT LEAST I CAN JOIN THE SERBIAN ARMY.
YOUR DAYS OF GLORY WILL SOON ARRIVE.
THE GOVERNMENT IN SERBIA MIGHT NOT BE PERFECT, BUT AT LEAST THEY'RE NOT THE DAMNED AUSTRIANS!
INDEED!
YOU BOYS SHOULD KEEP YOUR VOICES DOWN!
YOU HAVE NO MONEY. HOW ARE YOU GOING TO GET YOURSELF TO BELGRADE!
WALK!
WALK? IT'S MORE THAN A HUNDRED MILES!
HUNDRED AND TWENTY, ACTUALLY.

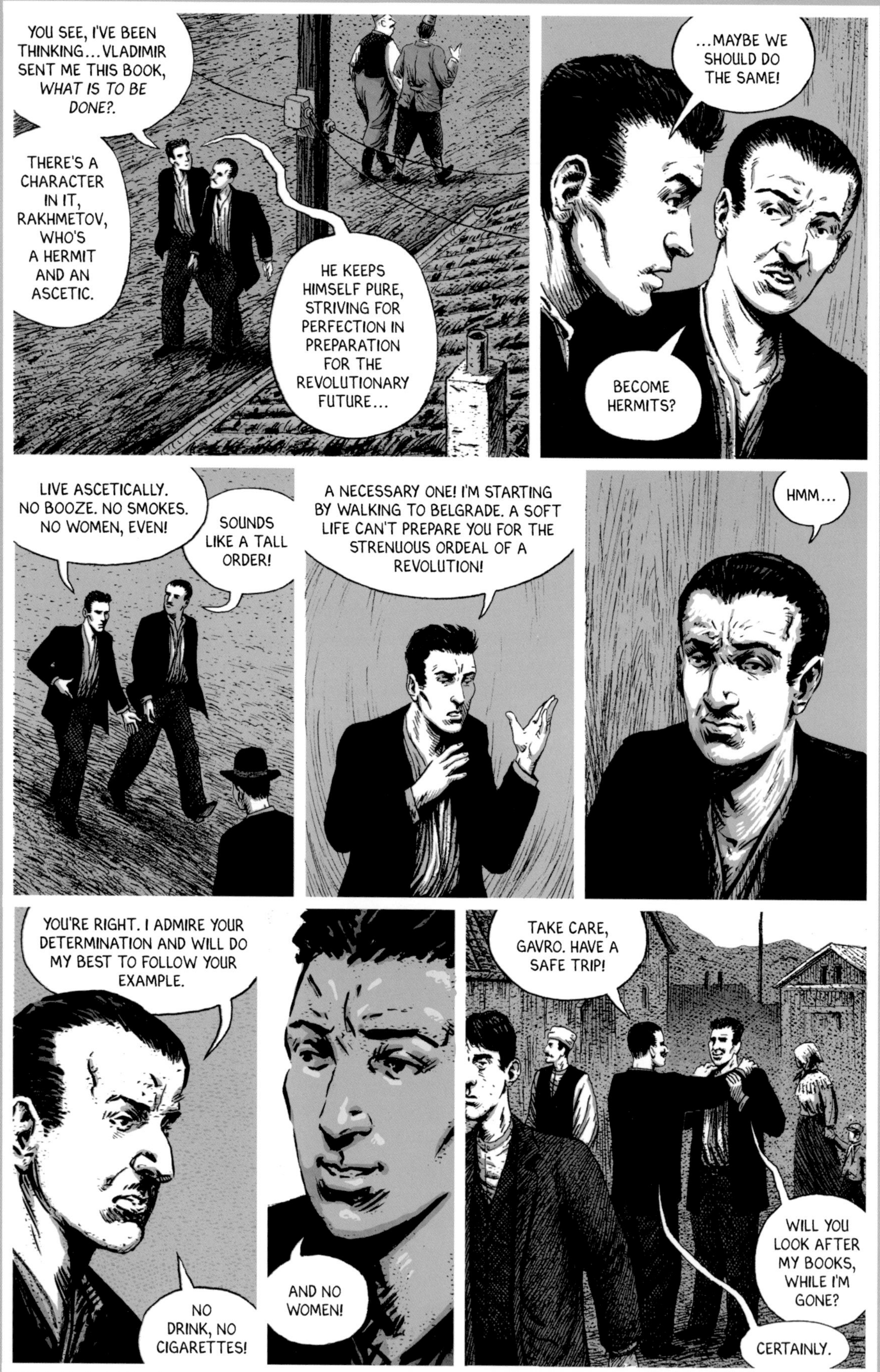

YOU SEE, I'VE BEEN THINKING... VLADIMIR SENT ME THIS BOOK, *WHAT IS TO BE DONE?*.
THERE'S A CHARACTER IN IT, RAKHMETOV, WHO'S A HERMIT AND AN ASCETIC.
HE KEEPS HIMSELF PURE, STRIVING FOR PERFECTION IN PREPARATION FOR THE REVOLUTIONARY FUTURE...
...MAYBE WE SHOULD DO THE SAME!
BECOME HERMITS?
LIVE ASCETICALLY. NO BOOZE. NO SMOKES. NO WOMEN, EVEN!
SOUNDS LIKE A TALL ORDER!
A NECESSARY ONE! I'M STARTING BY WALKING TO BELGRADE. A SOFT LIFE CAN'T PREPARE YOU FOR THE STRENUOUS ORDEAL OF A REVOLUTION!
HMM...
YOU'RE RIGHT. I ADMIRE YOUR DETERMINATION AND WILL DO MY BEST TO FOLLOW YOUR EXAMPLE.
NO DRINK, NO CIGARETTES!
AND NO WOMEN!
TAKE CARE, GAVRO. HAVE A SAFE TRIP!
WILL YOU LOOK AFTER MY BOOKS, WHILE I'M GONE?
CERTAINLY.

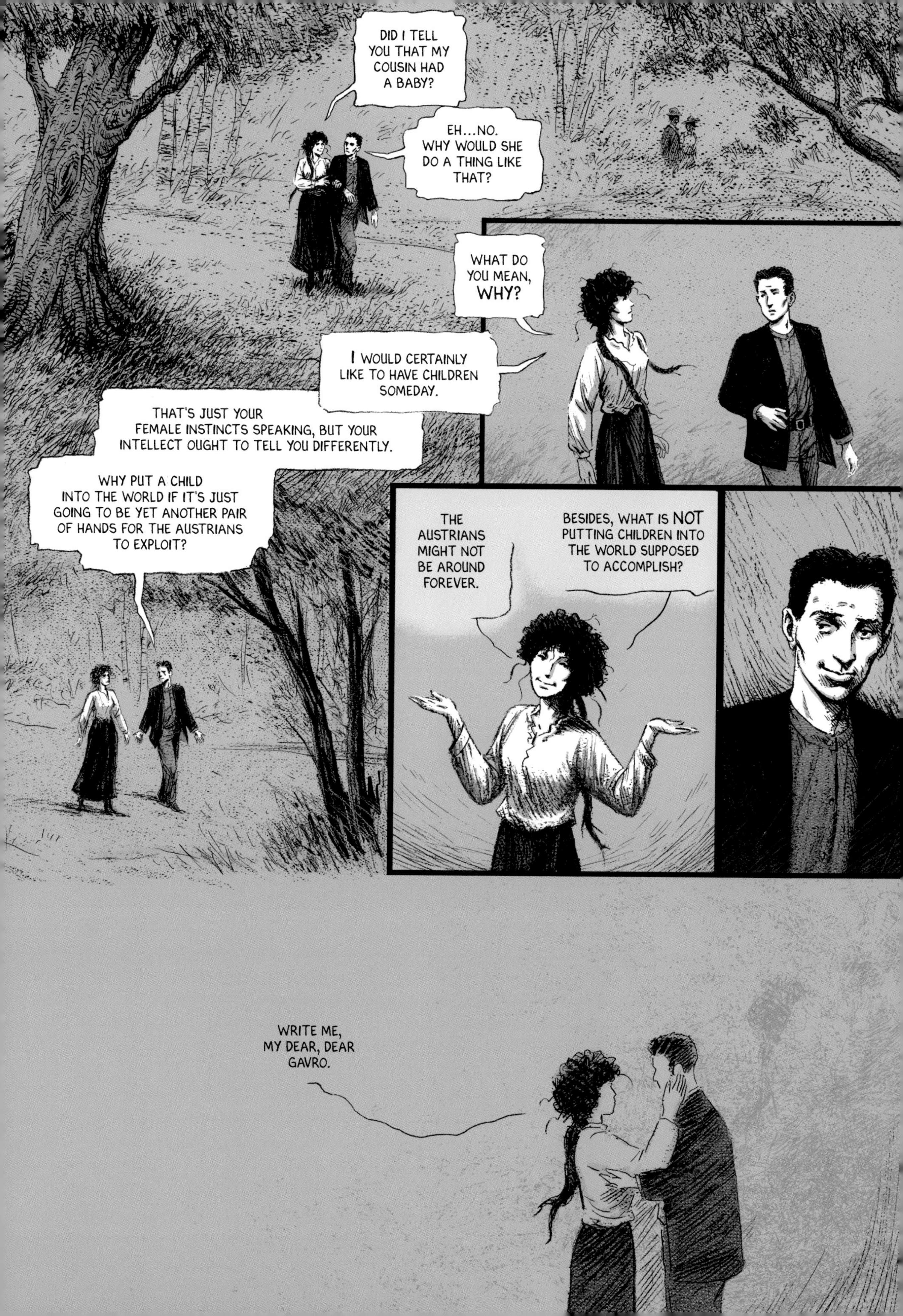
DID I TELL YOU THAT MY COUSIN HAD A BABY?
EH...NO. WHY WOULD SHE DO A THING LIKE THAT?
WHAT DO YOU MEAN, **WHY?**
I WOULD CERTAINLY LIKE TO HAVE CHILDREN SOMEDAY.
THAT'S JUST YOUR FEMALE INSTINCTS SPEAKING, BUT YOUR INTELLECT OUGHT TO TELL YOU DIFFERENTLY.
WHY PUT A CHILD INTO THE WORLD IF IT'S JUST GOING TO BE YET ANOTHER PAIR OF HANDS FOR THE AUSTRIANS TO EXPLOIT?
THE AUSTRIANS MIGHT NOT BE AROUND FOREVER.
BESIDES, WHAT IS **NOT** PUTTING CHILDREN INTO THE WORLD SUPPOSED TO ACCOMPLISH?
WRITE ME, MY DEAR, DEAR GAVRO.

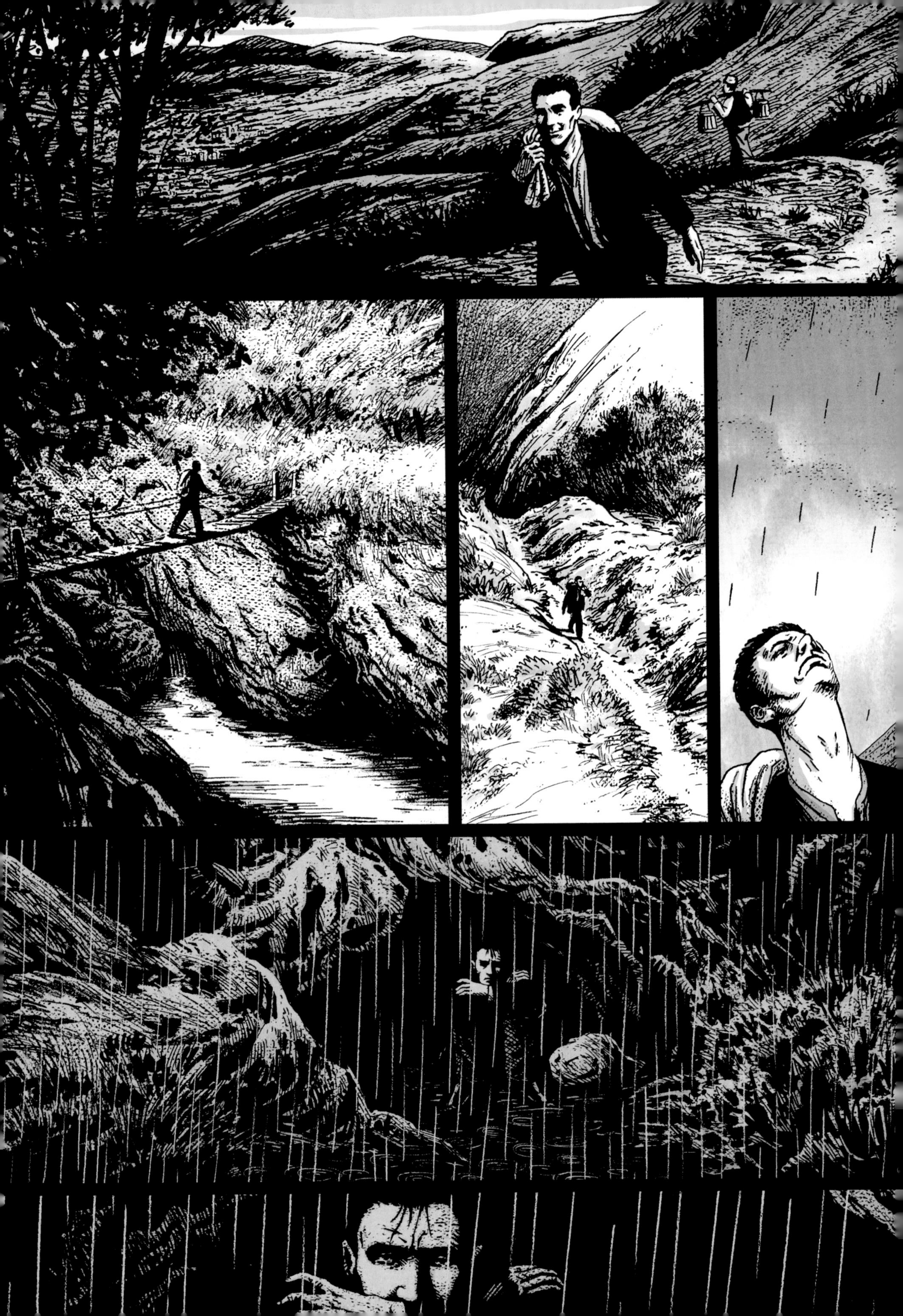

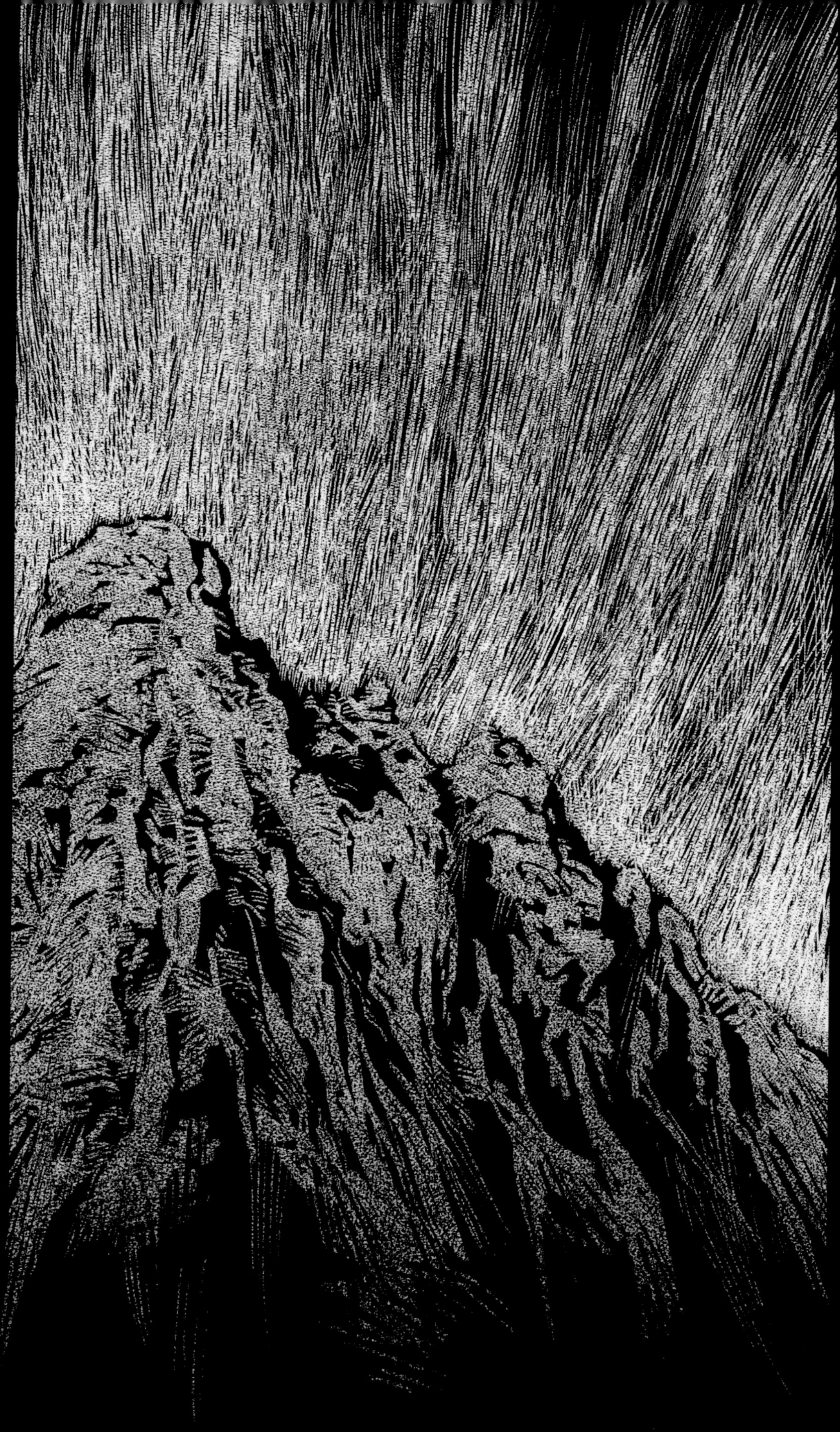

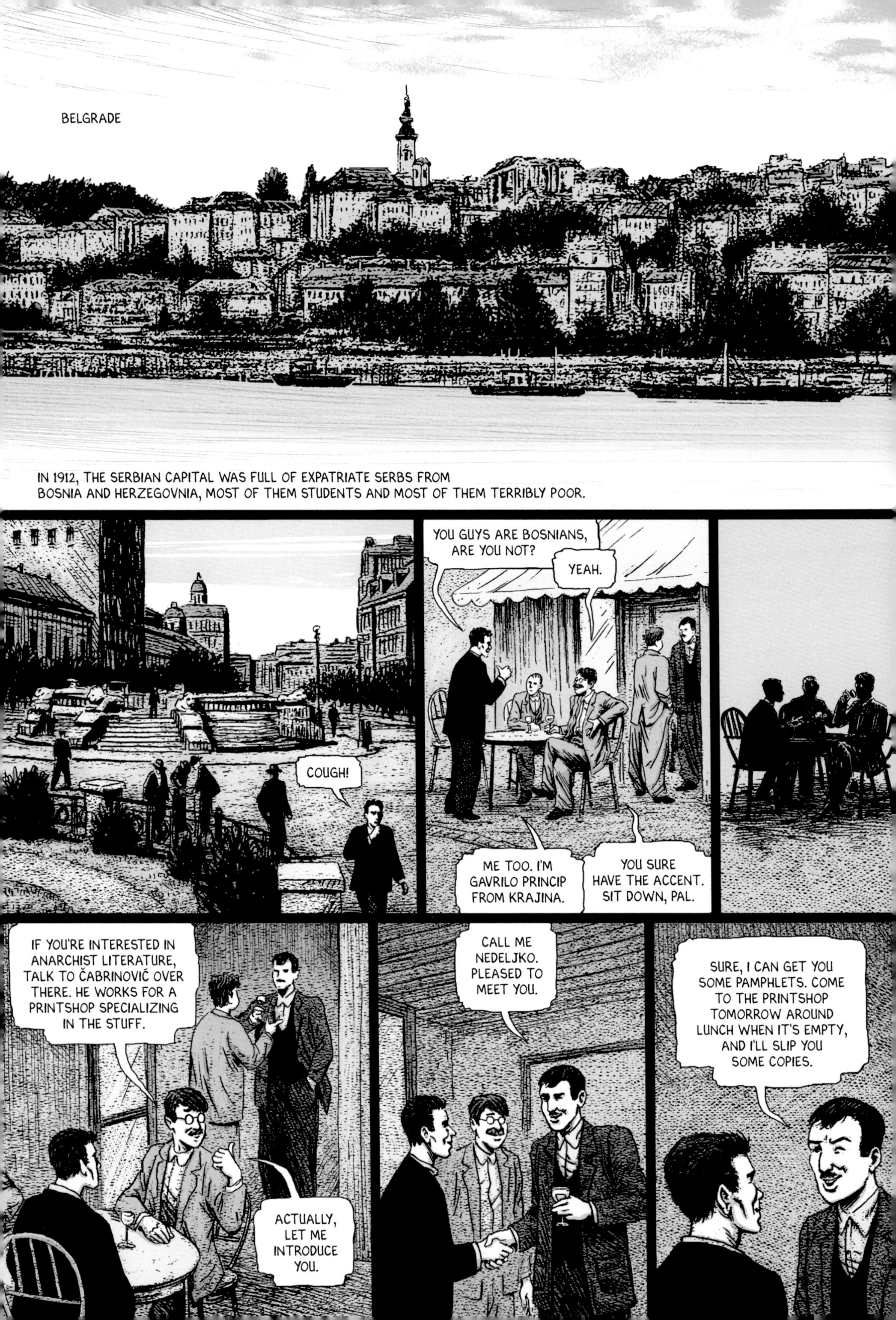

BELGRADE
IN 1912, THE SERBIAN CAPITAL WAS FULL OF EXPATRIATE SERBS FROM BOSNIA AND HERZEGOVNIA, MOST OF THEM STUDENTS AND MOST OF THEM TERRIBLY POOR.
COUGH!
YOU GUYS ARE BOSNIANS, ARE YOU NOT?
YEAH.
ME TOO. I'M GAVRILO PRINCIP FROM KRAJINA.
YOU SURE HAVE THE ACCENT. SIT DOWN, PAL.
IF YOU'RE INTERESTED IN ANARCHIST LITERATURE, TALK TO ČABRINOVIĆ OVER THERE. HE WORKS FOR A PRINTSHOP SPECIALIZING IN THE STUFF.
ACTUALLY, LET ME INTRODUCE YOU.
CALL ME NEDELJKO. PLEASED TO MEET YOU.
SURE, I CAN GET YOU SOME PAMPHLETS. COME TO THE PRINTSHOP TOMORROW AROUND LUNCH WHEN IT'S EMPTY, AND I'LL SLIP YOU SOME COPIES.

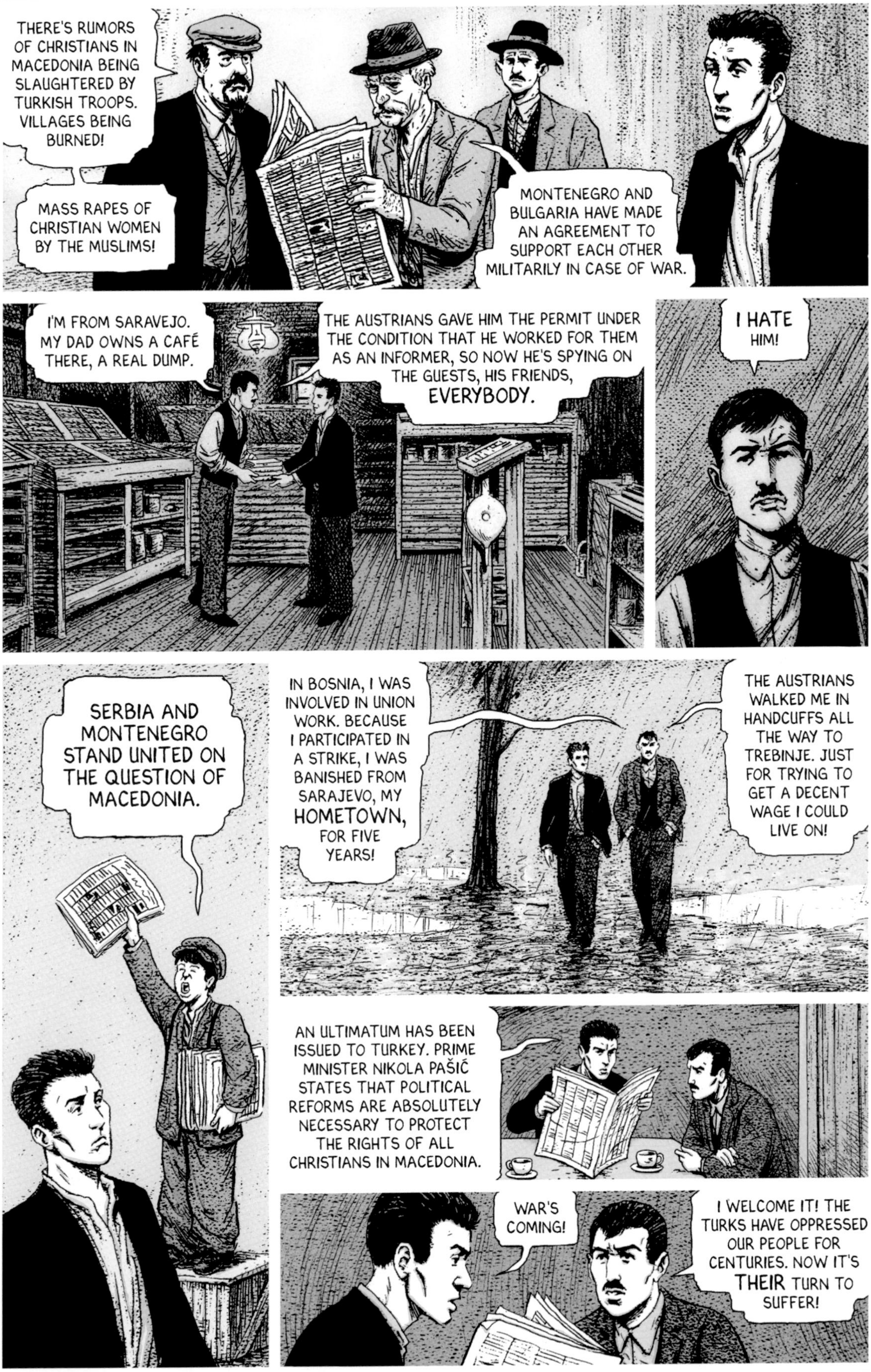
THERE'S RUMORS OF CHRISTIANS IN MACEDONIA BEING SLAUGHTERED BY TURKISH TROOPS. VILLAGES BEING BURNED!
MASS RAPES OF CHRISTIAN WOMEN BY THE MUSLIMS!
MONTENEGRO AND BULGARIA HAVE MADE AN AGREEMENT TO SUPPORT EACH OTHER MILITARILY IN CASE OF WAR.
I'M FROM SARAVEJO. MY DAD OWNS A CAFÉ THERE, A REAL DUMP.
THE AUSTRIANS GAVE HIM THE PERMIT UNDER THE CONDITION THAT HE WORKED FOR THEM AS AN INFORMER, SO NOW HE'S SPYING ON THE GUESTS, HIS FRIENDS, EVERYBODY.
I HATE HIM!
SERBIA AND MONTENEGRO STAND UNITED ON THE QUESTION OF MACEDONIA.
IN BOSNIA, I WAS INVOLVED IN UNION WORK. BECAUSE I PARTICIPATED IN A STRIKE, I WAS BANISHED FROM SARAJEVO, MY HOMETOWN, FOR FIVE YEARS!
THE AUSTRIANS WALKED ME IN HANDCUFFS ALL THE WAY TO TREBINJE. JUST FOR TRYING TO GET A DECENT WAGE I COULD LIVE ON!
AN ULTIMATUM HAS BEEN ISSUED TO TURKEY. PRIME MINISTER NIKOLA PAŠIĆ STATES THAT POLITICAL REFORMS ARE ABSOLUTELY NECESSARY TO PROTECT THE RIGHTS OF ALL CHRISTIANS IN MACEDONIA.
WAR'S COMING!
I WELCOME IT! THE TURKS HAVE OPPRESSED OUR PEOPLE FOR CENTURIES. NOW IT'S THEIR TURN TO SUFFER!

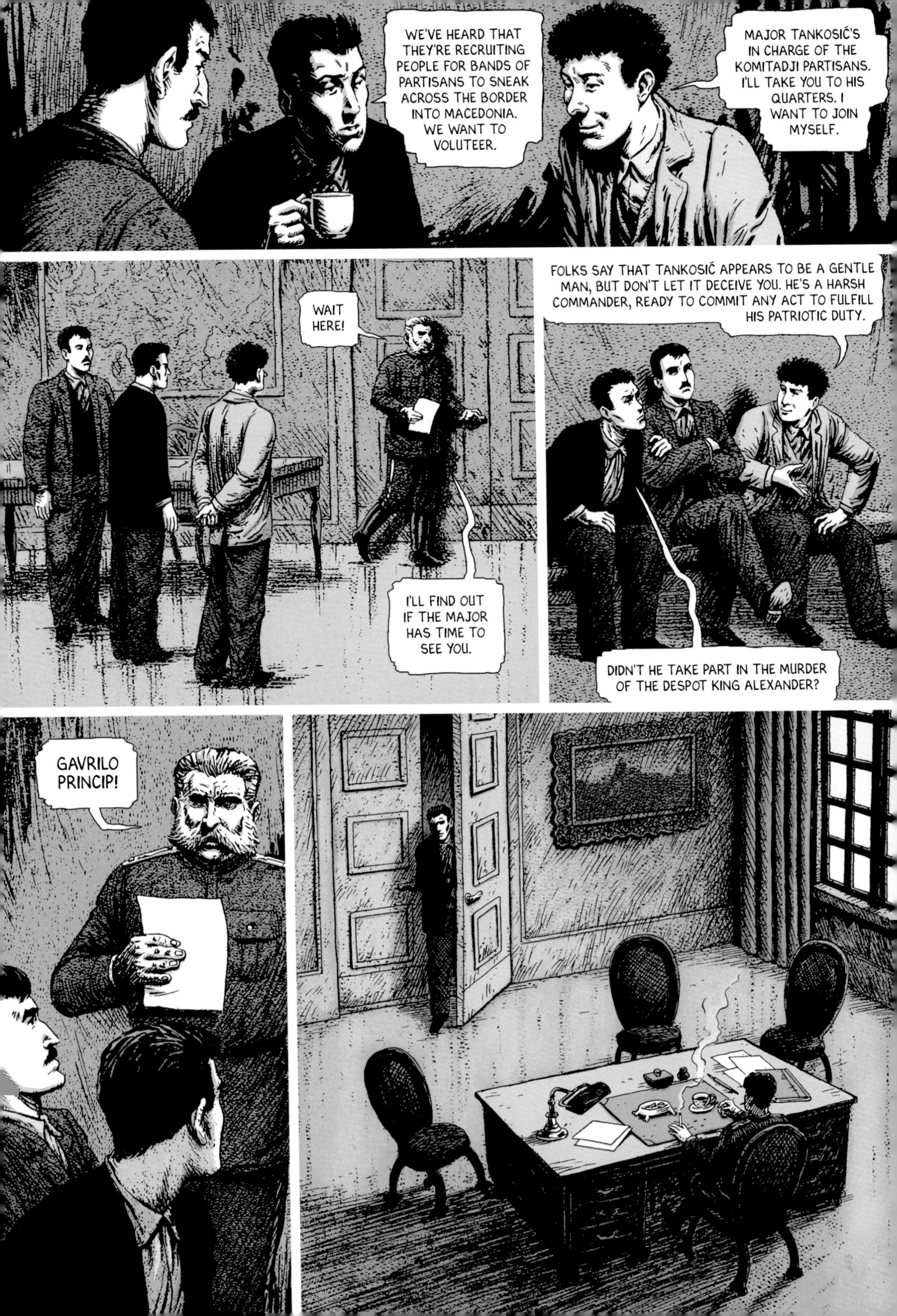
WE'VE HEARD THAT THEY'RE RECRUITING PEOPLE FOR BANDS OF PARTISANS TO SNEAK ACROSS THE BORDER INTO MACEDONIA. WE WANT TO VOLUTEER.
MAJOR TANKOSIĆ'S IN CHARGE OF THE KOMITADJI PARTISANS. I'LL TAKE YOU TO HIS QUARTERS. I WANT TO JOIN MYSELF.
WAIT HERE!
I'LL FIND OUT IF THE MAJOR HAS TIME TO SEE YOU.
FOLKS SAY THAT TANKOSIĆ APPEARS TO BE A GENTLE MAN, BUT DON'T LET IT DECEIVE YOU. HE'S A HARSH COMMANDER, READY TO COMMIT ANY ACT TO FULFILL HIS PATRIOTIC DUTY.
DIDN'T HE TAKE PART IN THE MURDER OF THE DESPOT KING ALEXANDER?
GAVRILO PRINCIP!

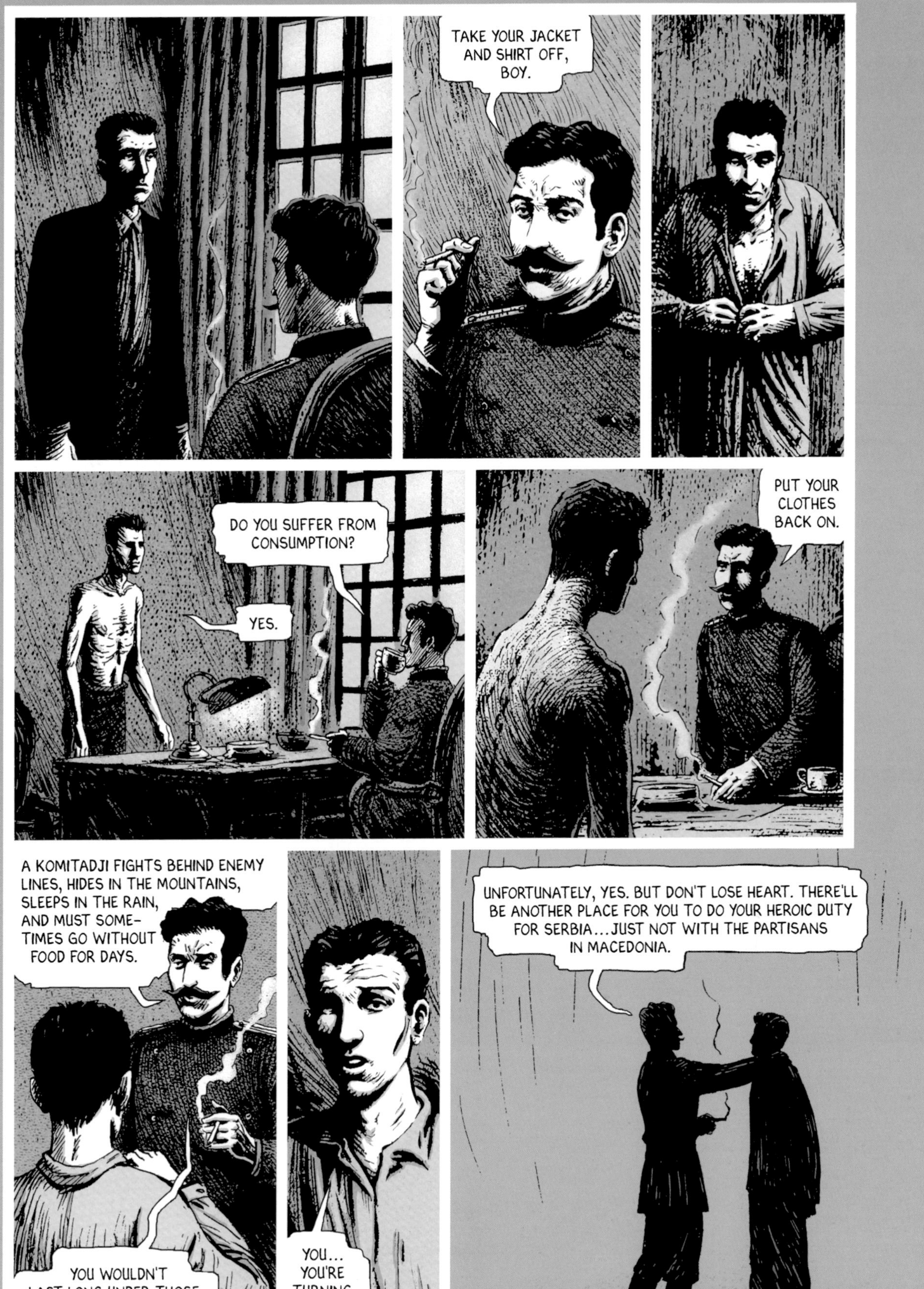
TAKE YOUR JACKET AND SHIRT OFF, BOY.
DO YOU SUFFER FROM CONSUMPTION?
YES.
PUT YOUR CLOTHES BACK ON.
A KOMITADJI FIGHTS BEHIND ENEMY LINES, HIDES IN THE MOUNTAINS, SLEEPS IN THE RAIN, AND MUST SOME-TIMES GO WITHOUT FOOD FOR DAYS.
YOU WOULDN'T LAST LONG UNDER THOSE CIRCUMSTANCES, I'M AFRAID.
YOU... YOU'RE TURNING ME DOWN?
UNFORTUNATELY, YES. BUT DON'T LOSE HEART. THERE'LL BE ANOTHER PLACE FOR YOU TO DO YOUR HEROIC DUTY FOR SERBIA...JUST NOT WITH THE PARTISANS IN MACEDONIA.

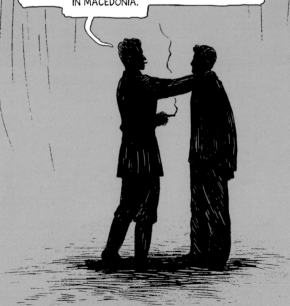

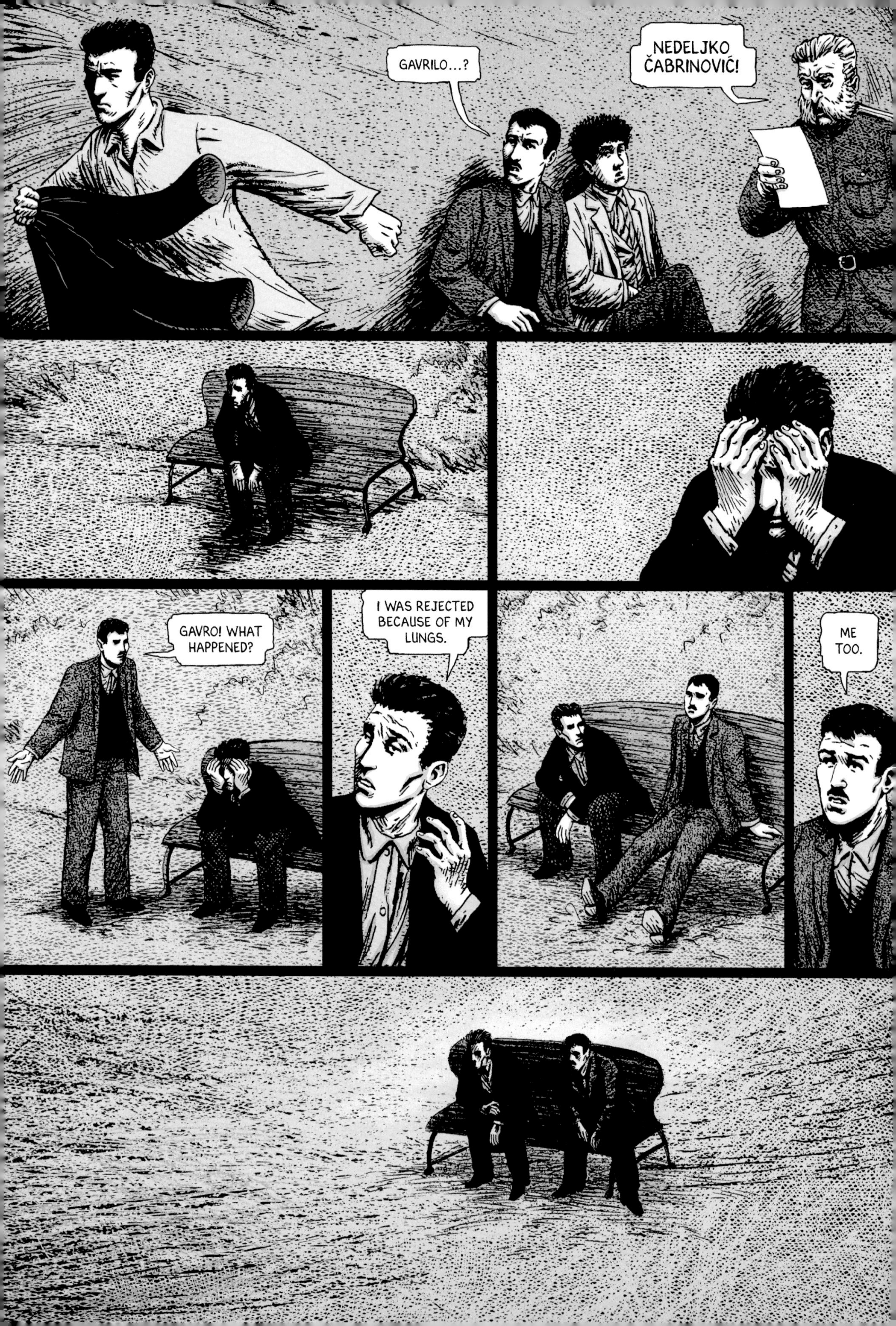
GAVRILO...?
NEDELJKO ČABRINOVIĆ!
GAVRO! WHAT HAPPENED?
I WAS REJECTED BECAUSE OF MY LUNGS.
ME TOO.

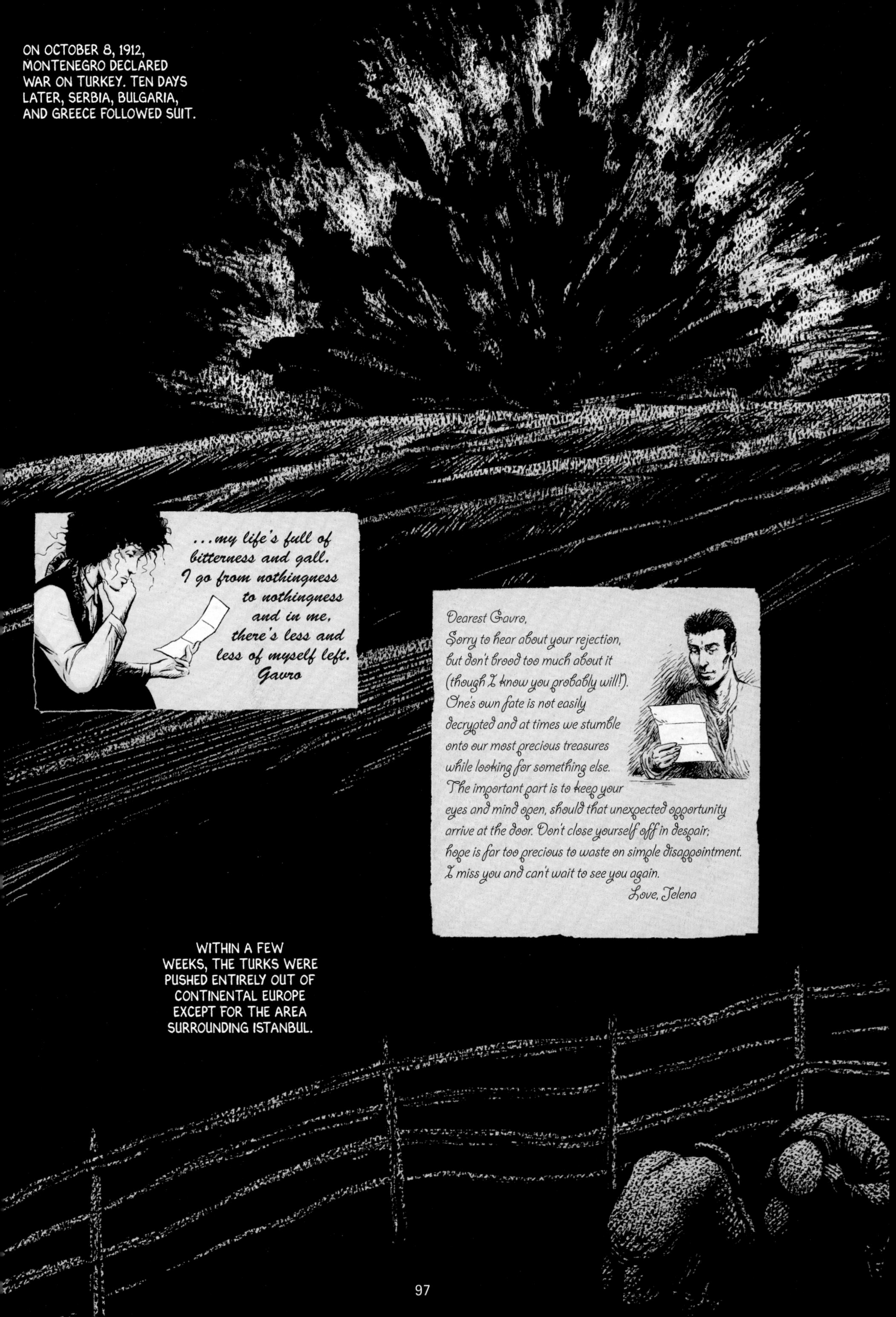
ON OCTOBER 8, 1912, MONTENEGRO DECLARED WAR ON TURKEY. TEN DAYS LATER, SERBIA, BULGARIA, AND GREECE FOLLOWED SUIT.
...my life's full of bitterness and gall. I go from nothingness to nothingness and in me, there's less and less of myself left. Gavro
Dearest Gavro,
Sorry to hear about your rejection, but don't brood too much about it (though I know you probably will!). One's own fate is not easily decrypted and at times we stumble onto our most precious treasures while looking for something else. The important part is to keep your eyes and mind open, should that unexpected opportunity arrive at the door. Don't close yourself off in despair; hope is far too precious to waste on simple disappointment. I miss you and can't wait to see you again.
Love, Jelena
WITHIN A FEW WEEKS, THE TURKS WERE PUSHED ENTIRELY OUT OF CONTINENTAL EUROPE EXCEPT FOR THE AREA SURROUNDING ISTANBUL.

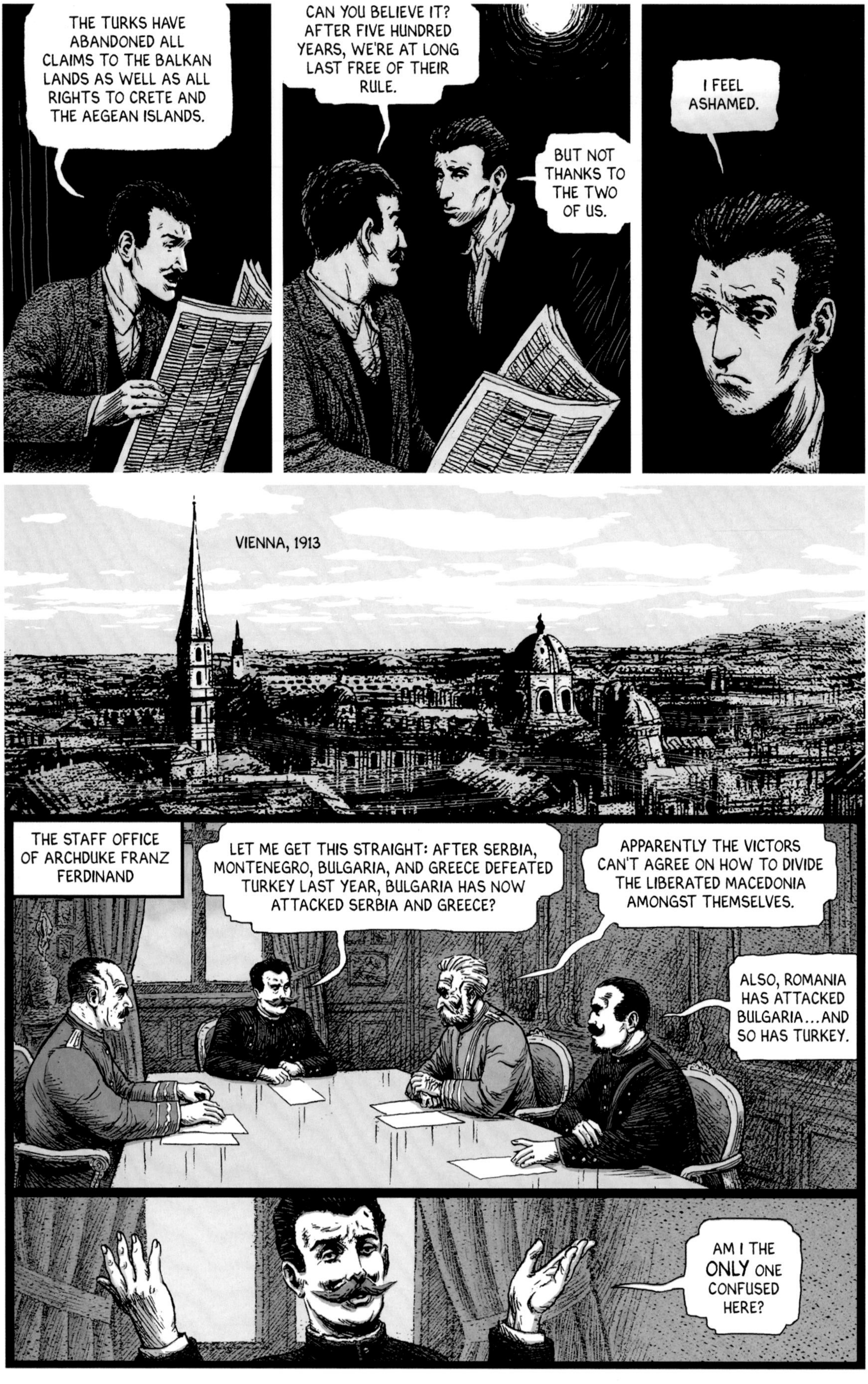
THE TURKS HAVE ABANDONED ALL CLAIMS TO THE BALKAN LANDS AS WELL AS ALL RIGHTS TO CRETE AND THE AEGEAN ISLANDS.
CAN YOU BELIEVE IT? AFTER FIVE HUNDRED YEARS, WE'RE AT LONG LAST FREE OF THEIR RULE.
BUT NOT THANKS TO THE TWO OF US.
I FEEL ASHAMED.
VIENNA, 1913
THE STAFF OFFICE OF ARCHDUKE FRANZ FERDINAND
LET ME GET THIS STRAIGHT: AFTER SERBIA, MONTENEGRO, BULGARIA, AND GREECE DEFEATED TURKEY LAST YEAR, BULGARIA HAS NOW ATTACKED SERBIA AND GREECE?
APPARENTLY THE VICTORS CAN'T AGREE ON HOW TO DIVIDE THE LIBERATED MACEDONIA AMONGST THEMSELVES.
ALSO, ROMANIA HAS ATTACKED BULGARIA...AND SO HAS TURKEY.
AM I THE ONLY ONE CONFUSED HERE?

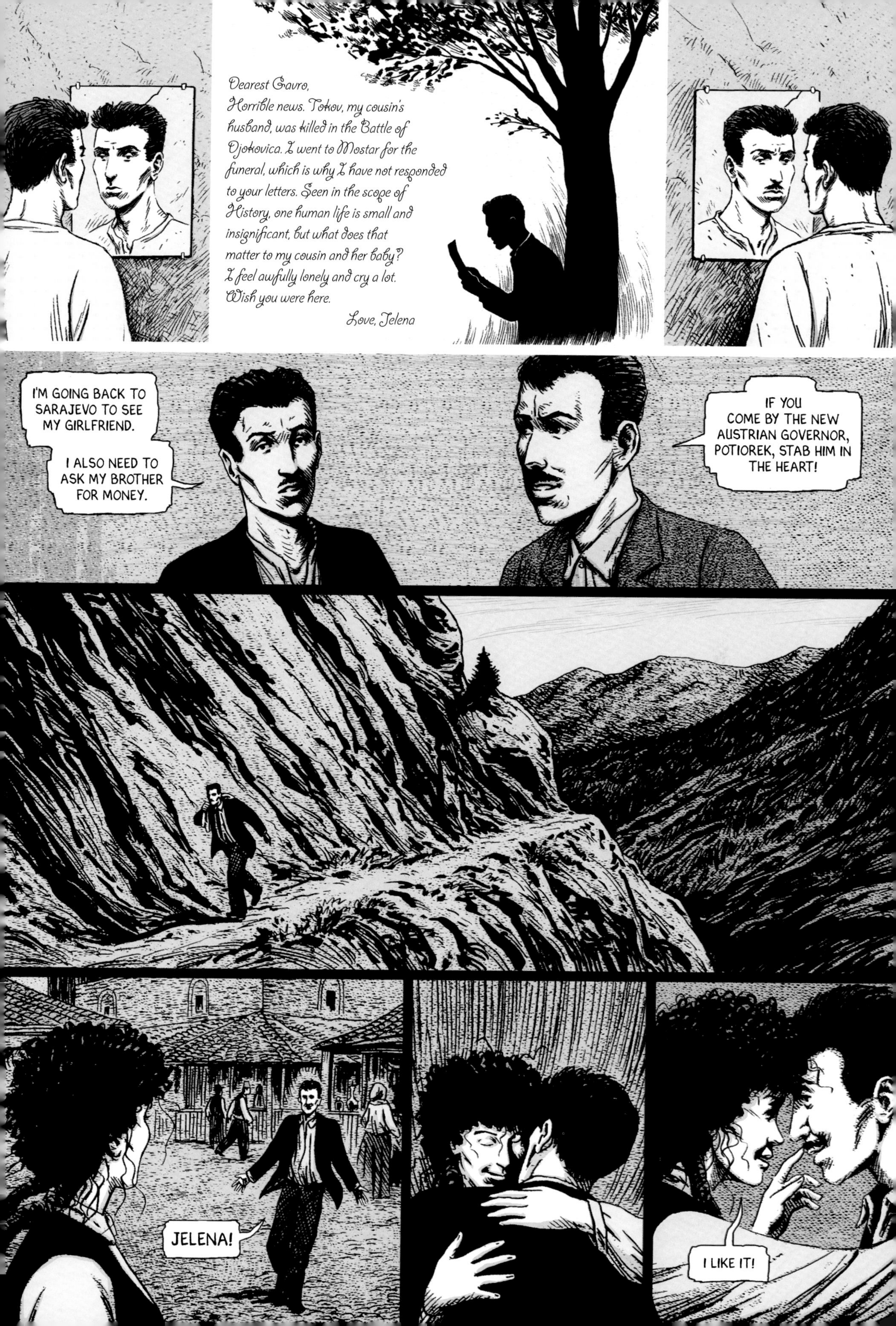

Dearest Gavro,
Horrible news. Tokov, my cousin's husband, was killed in the Battle of Djokovica. I went to Mostar for the funeral, which is why I have not responded to your letters. Seen in the scope of History, one human life is small and insignificant, but what does that matter to my cousin and her baby? I feel awfully lonely and cry a lot. Wish you were here.
Love, Jelena
I'M GOING BACK TO SARAJEVO TO SEE MY GIRLFRIEND.
I ALSO NEED TO ASK MY BROTHER FOR MONEY.
IF YOU COME BY THE NEW AUSTRIAN GOVERNOR, POTIOREK, STAB HIM IN THE HEART!
JELENA!
I LIKE IT!

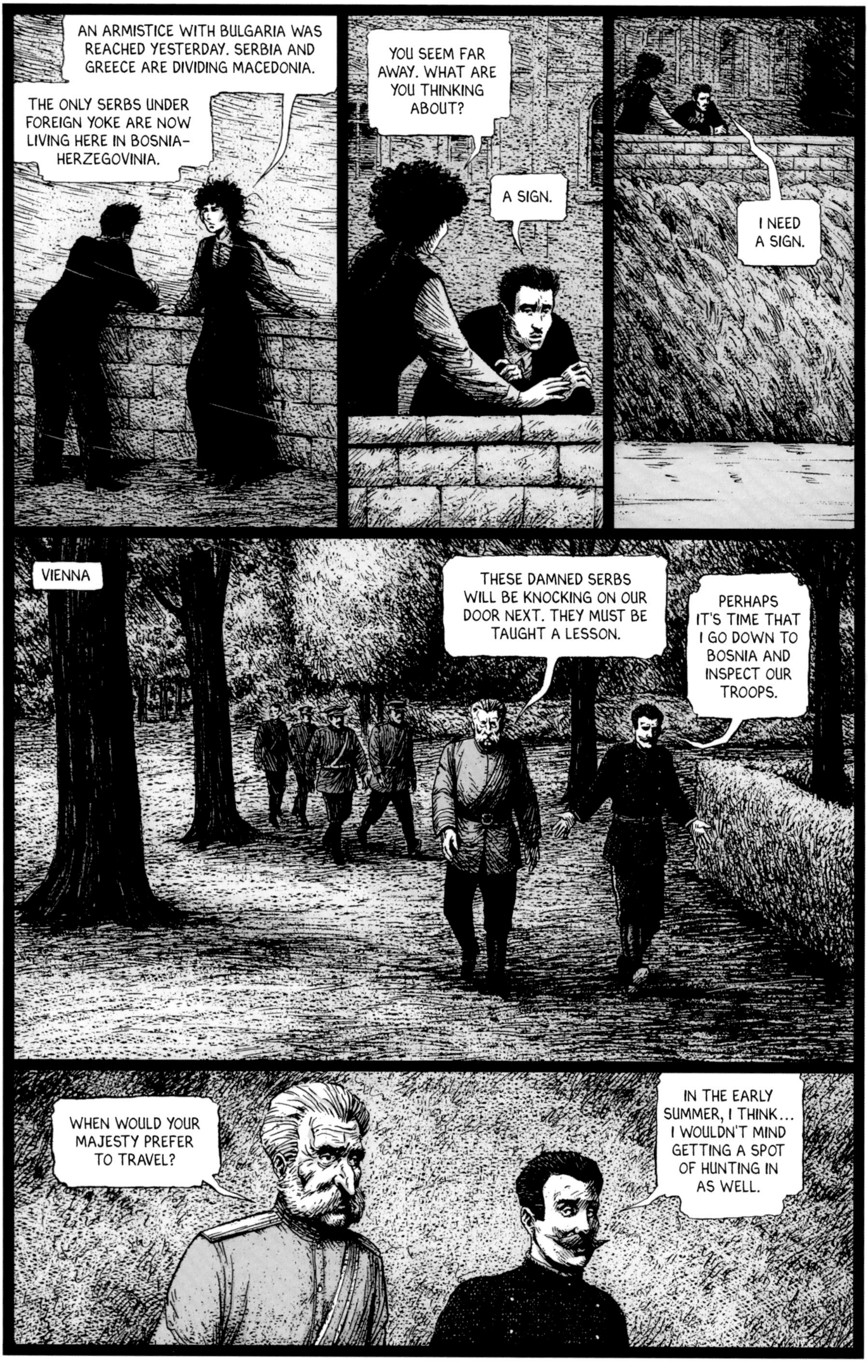
AN ARMISTICE WITH BULGARIA WAS REACHED YESTERDAY. SERBIA AND GREECE ARE DIVIDING MACEDONIA.
THE ONLY SERBS UNDER FOREIGN YOKE ARE NOW LIVING HERE IN BOSNIA-HERZEGOVINIA.
YOU SEEM FAR AWAY. WHAT ARE YOU THINKING ABOUT?
A SIGN.
I NEED A SIGN.
VIENNA
THESE DAMNED SERBS WILL BE KNOCKING ON OUR DOOR NEXT. THEY MUST BE TAUGHT A LESSON.
PERHAPS IT'S TIME THAT I GO DOWN TO BOSNIA AND INSPECT OUR TROOPS.
WHEN WOULD YOUR MAJESTY PREFER TO TRAVEL?
IN THE EARLY SUMMER, I THINK... I WOULDN'T MIND GETTING A SPOT OF HUNTING IN AS WELL.

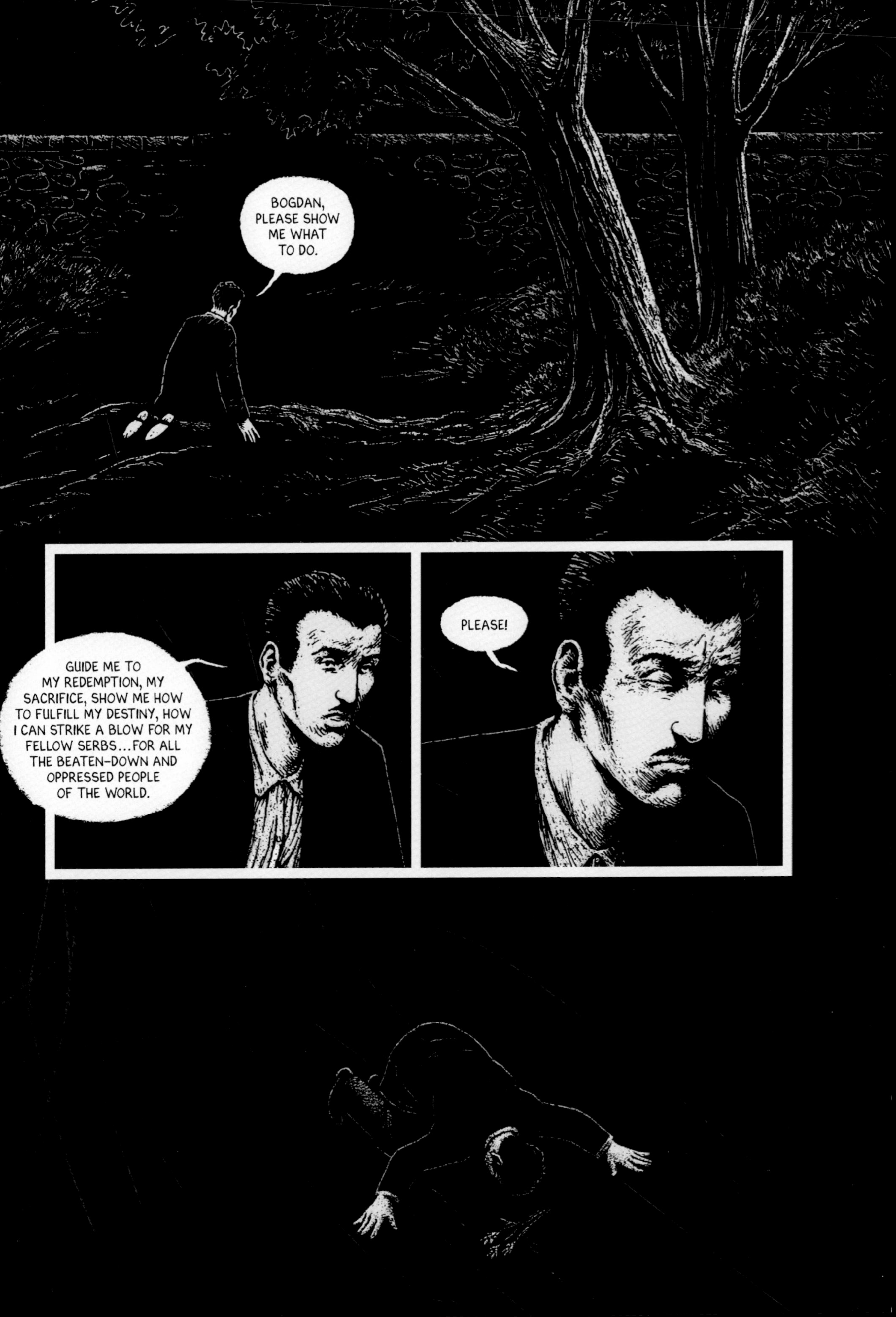
BOGDAN, PLEASE SHOW ME WHAT TO DO.
GUIDE ME TO MY REDEMPTION, MY SACRIFICE, SHOW ME HOW TO FULFILL MY DESTINY, HOW I CAN STRIKE A BLOW FOR MY FELLOW SERBS...FOR ALL THE BEATEN-DOWN AND OPPRESSED PEOPLE OF THE WORLD.
PLEASE!

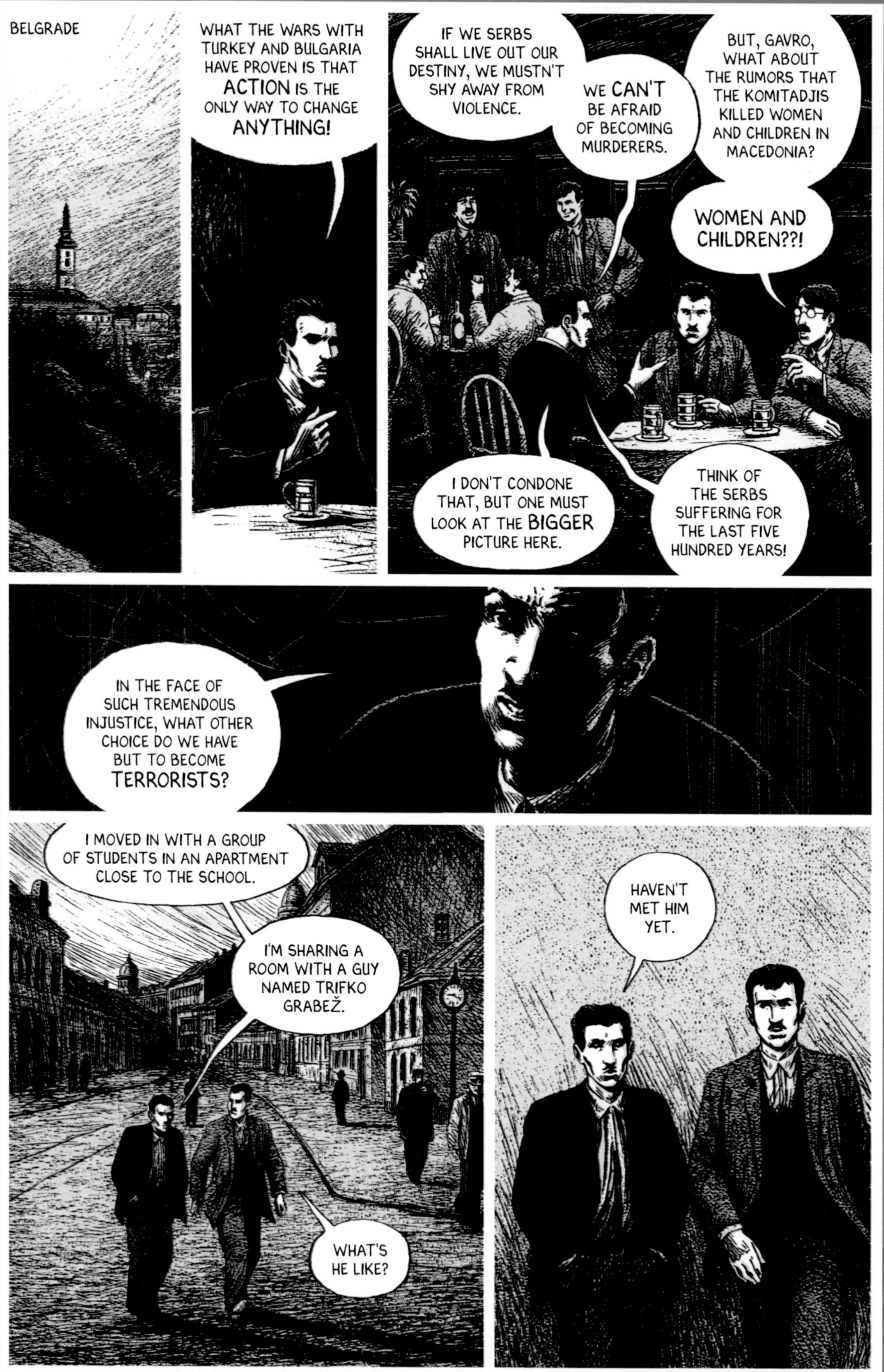
BELGRADE
WHAT THE WARS WITH TURKEY AND BULGARIA HAVE PROVEN IS THAT ACTION IS THE ONLY WAY TO CHANGE ANYTHING!
IF WE SERBS SHALL LIVE OUT OUR DESTINY, WE MUSTN'T SHY AWAY FROM VIOLENCE.
WE CAN'T BE AFRAID OF BECOMING MURDERERS.
BUT, GAVRO, WHAT ABOUT THE RUMORS THAT THE KOMITADJIS KILLED WOMEN AND CHILDREN IN MACEDONIA?
WOMEN AND CHILDREN??!
I DON'T CONDONE THAT, BUT ONE MUST LOOK AT THE BIGGER PICTURE HERE.
THINK OF THE SERBS SUFFERING FOR THE LAST FIVE HUNDRED YEARS!
IN THE FACE OF SUCH TREMENDOUS INJUSTICE, WHAT OTHER CHOICE DO WE HAVE BUT TO BECOME TERRORISTS?
I MOVED IN WITH A GROUP OF STUDENTS IN AN APARTMENT CLOSE TO THE SCHOOL.
I'M SHARING A ROOM WITH A GUY NAMED TRIFKO GRABEŽ.
WHAT'S HE LIKE?
HAVEN'T MET HIM YET.

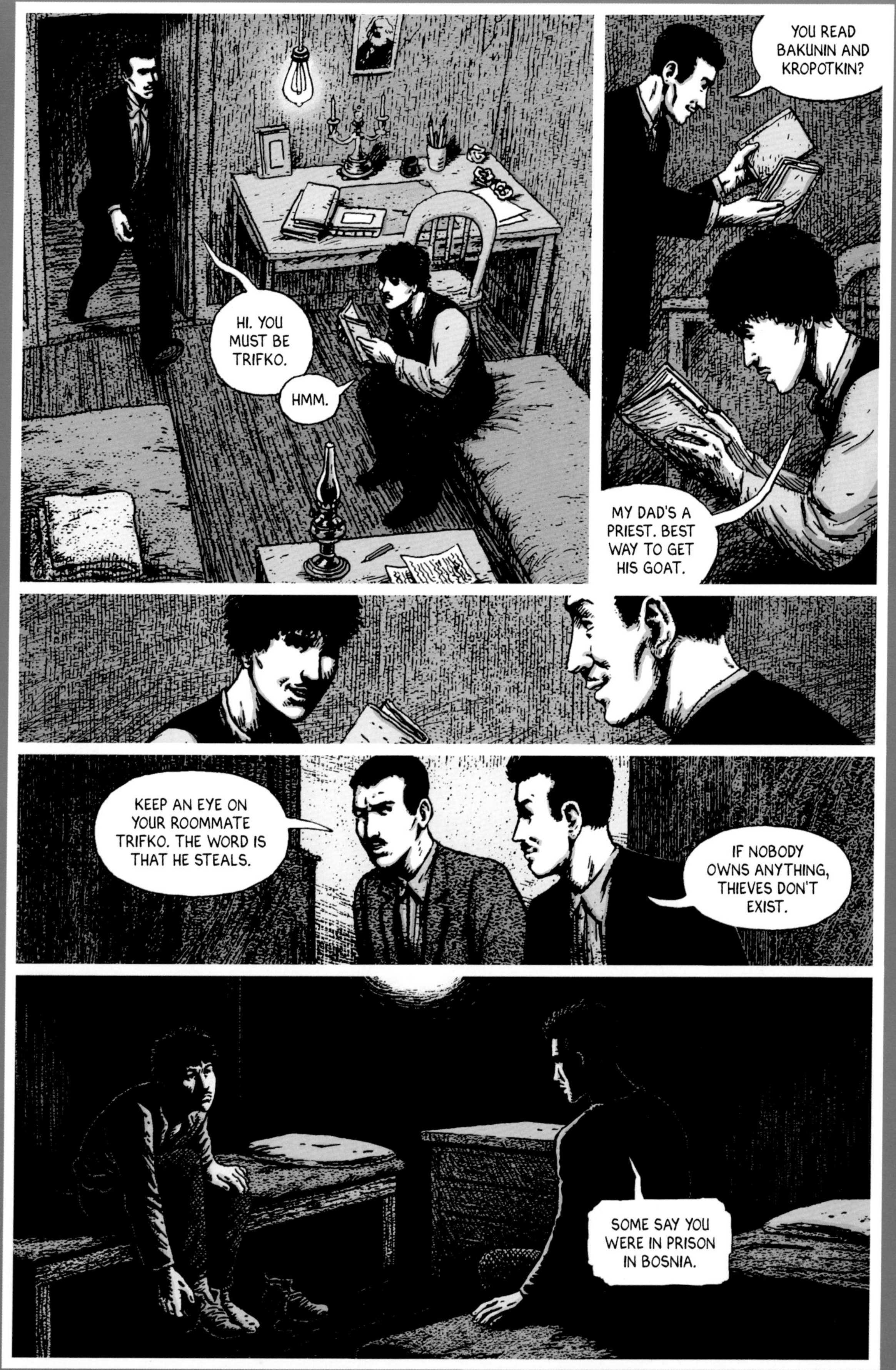
HI. YOU MUST BE TRIFKO.
HMM.
YOU READ BAKUNIN AND KROPOTKIN?
MY DAD'S A PRIEST. BEST WAY TO GET HIS GOAT.
KEEP AN EYE ON YOUR ROOMMATE TRIFKO. THE WORD IS THAT HE STEALS.
IF NOBODY OWNS ANYTHING, THIEVES DON'T EXIST.
SOME SAY YOU WERE IN PRISON IN BOSNIA.

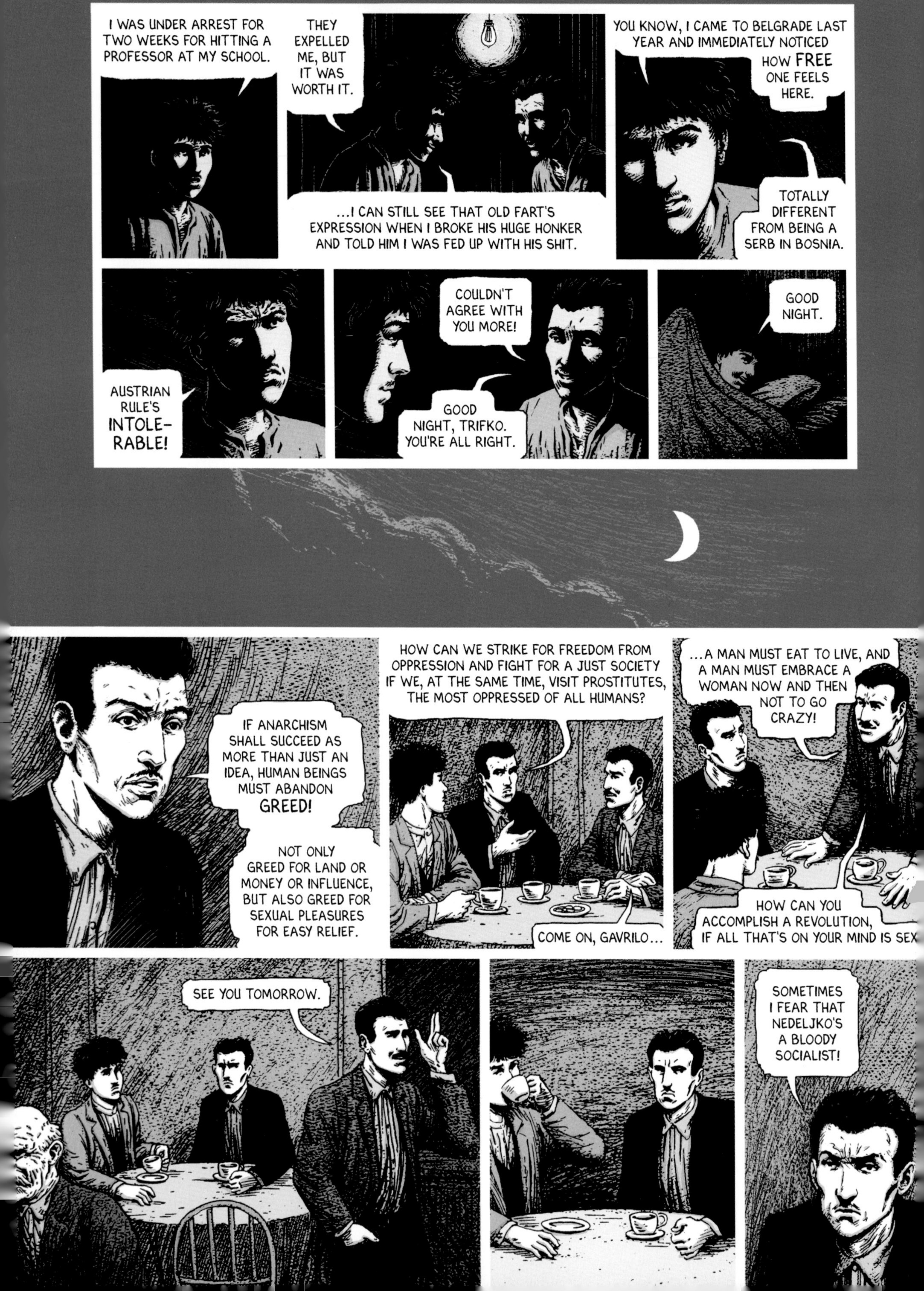

I WAS UNDER ARREST FOR TWO WEEKS FOR HITTING A PROFESSOR AT MY SCHOOL.
THEY EXPELLED ME, BUT IT WAS WORTH IT.
...I CAN STILL SEE THAT OLD FART'S EXPRESSION WHEN I BROKE HIS HUGE HONKER AND TOLD HIM I WAS FED UP WITH HIS SHIT.
YOU KNOW, I CAME TO BELGRADE LAST YEAR AND IMMEDIATELY NOTICED HOW FREE ONE FEELS HERE.
TOTALLY DIFFERENT FROM BEING A SERB IN BOSNIA.
AUSTRIAN RULE'S INTOLE-RABLE!
COULDN'T AGREE WITH YOU MORE!
GOOD NIGHT, TRIFKO. YOU'RE ALL RIGHT.
GOOD NIGHT.
IF ANARCHISM SHALL SUCCEED AS MORE THAN JUST AN IDEA, HUMAN BEINGS MUST ABANDON GREED!
NOT ONLY GREED FOR LAND OR MONEY OR INFLUENCE, BUT ALSO GREED FOR SEXUAL PLEASURES FOR EASY RELIEF.
HOW CAN WE STRIKE FOR FREEDOM FROM OPPRESSION AND FIGHT FOR A JUST SOCIETY IF WE, AT THE SAME TIME, VISIT PROSTITUTES, THE MOST OPPRESSED OF ALL HUMANS?
COME ON, GAVRILO...
...A MAN MUST EAT TO LIVE, AND A MAN MUST EMBRACE A WOMAN NOW AND THEN NOT TO GO CRAZY!
HOW CAN YOU ACCOMPLISH A REVOLUTION, IF ALL THAT'S ON YOUR MIND IS SEX
SEE YOU TOMORROW.
SOMETIMES I FEAR THAT NEDELJKO'S A BLOODY SOCIALIST!

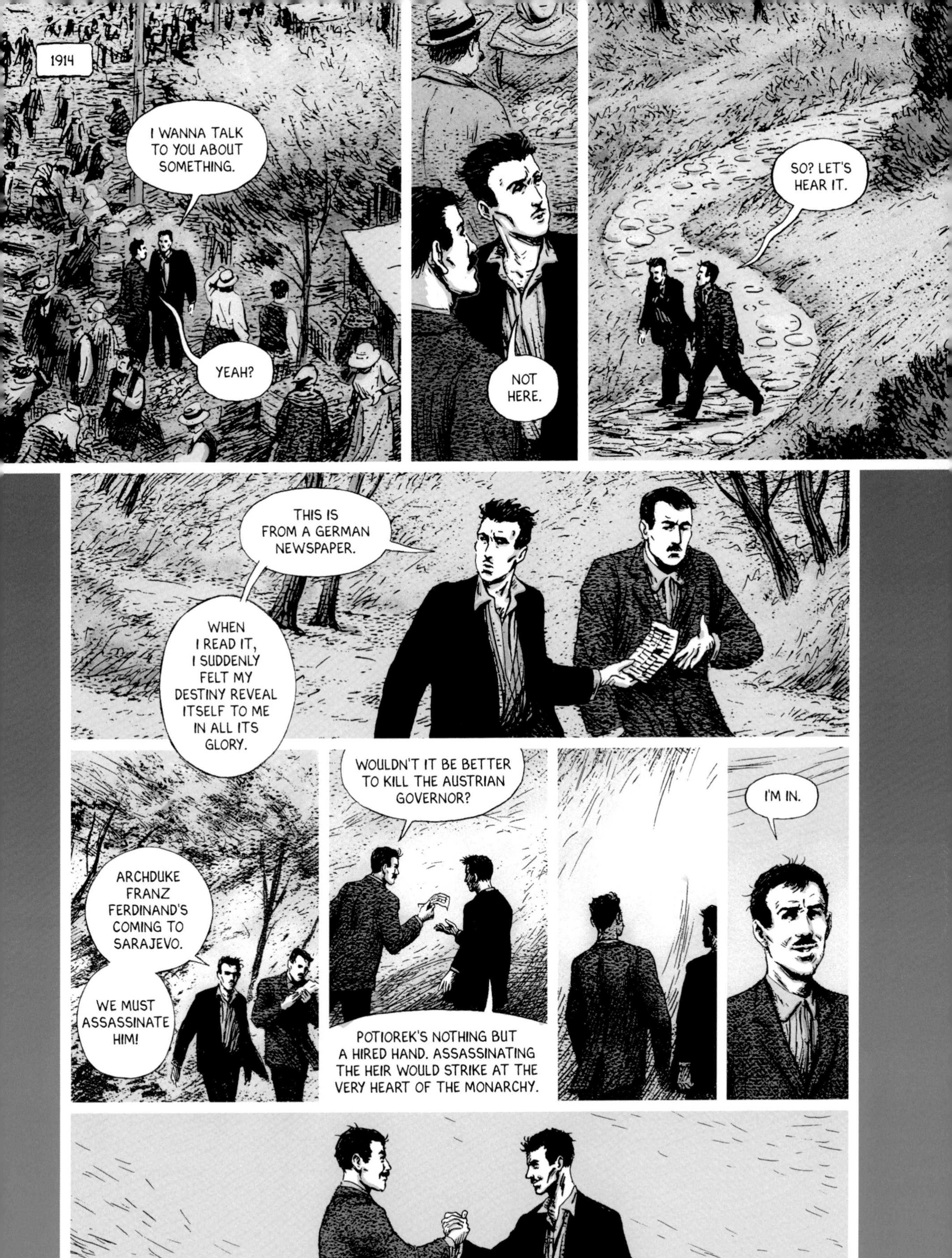
1914
I WANNA TALK TO YOU ABOUT SOMETHING.
YEAH?
NOT HERE.
SO? LET'S HEAR IT.
THIS IS FROM A GERMAN NEWSPAPER.
WHEN I READ IT, I SUDDENLY FELT MY DESTINY REVEAL ITSELF TO ME IN ALL ITS GLORY.
ARCHDUKE FRANZ FERDINAND'S COMING TO SARAJEVO.
WE MUST ASSASSINATE HIM!
WOULDN'T IT BE BETTER TO KILL THE AUSTRIAN GOVERNOR?
POTIOREK'S NOTHING BUT A HIRED HAND. ASSASSINATING THE HEIR WOULD STRIKE AT THE VERY HEART OF THE MONARCHY.
I'M IN.

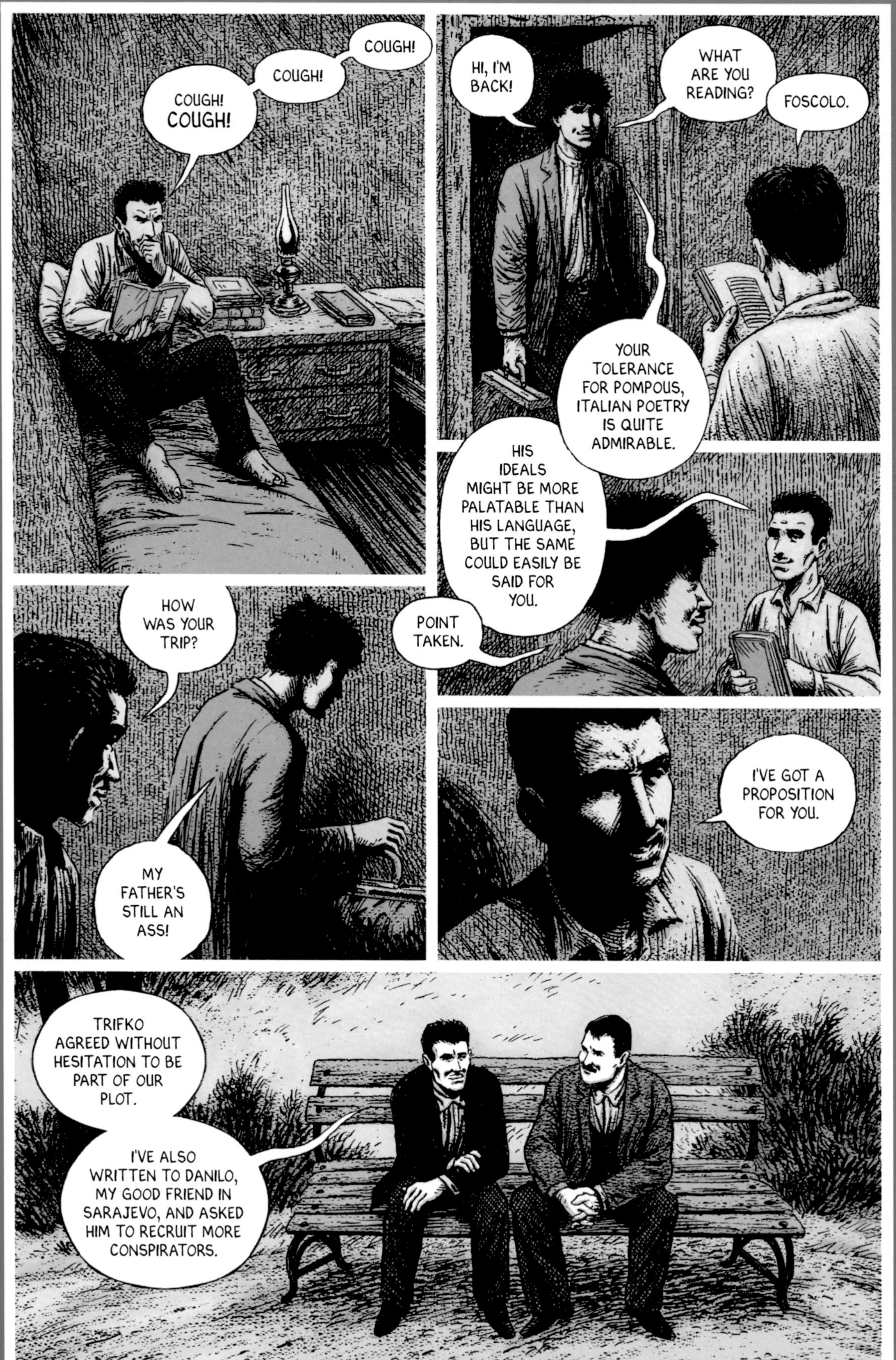
COUGH! COUGH!
COUGH!
COUGH!
HI, I'M BACK!
WHAT ARE YOU READING?
FOSCOLO.
YOUR TOLERANCE FOR POMPOUS, ITALIAN POETRY IS QUITE ADMIRABLE.
HIS IDEALS MIGHT BE MORE PALATABLE THAN HIS LANGUAGE, BUT THE SAME COULD EASILY BE SAID FOR YOU.
POINT TAKEN.
HOW WAS YOUR TRIP?
MY FATHER'S STILL AN ASS!
I'VE GOT A PROPOSITION FOR YOU.
TRIFKO AGREED WITHOUT HESITATION TO BE PART OF OUR PLOT.
I'VE ALSO WRITTEN TO DANILO, MY GOOD FRIEND IN SARAJEVO, AND ASKED HIM TO RECRUIT MORE CONSPIRATORS.

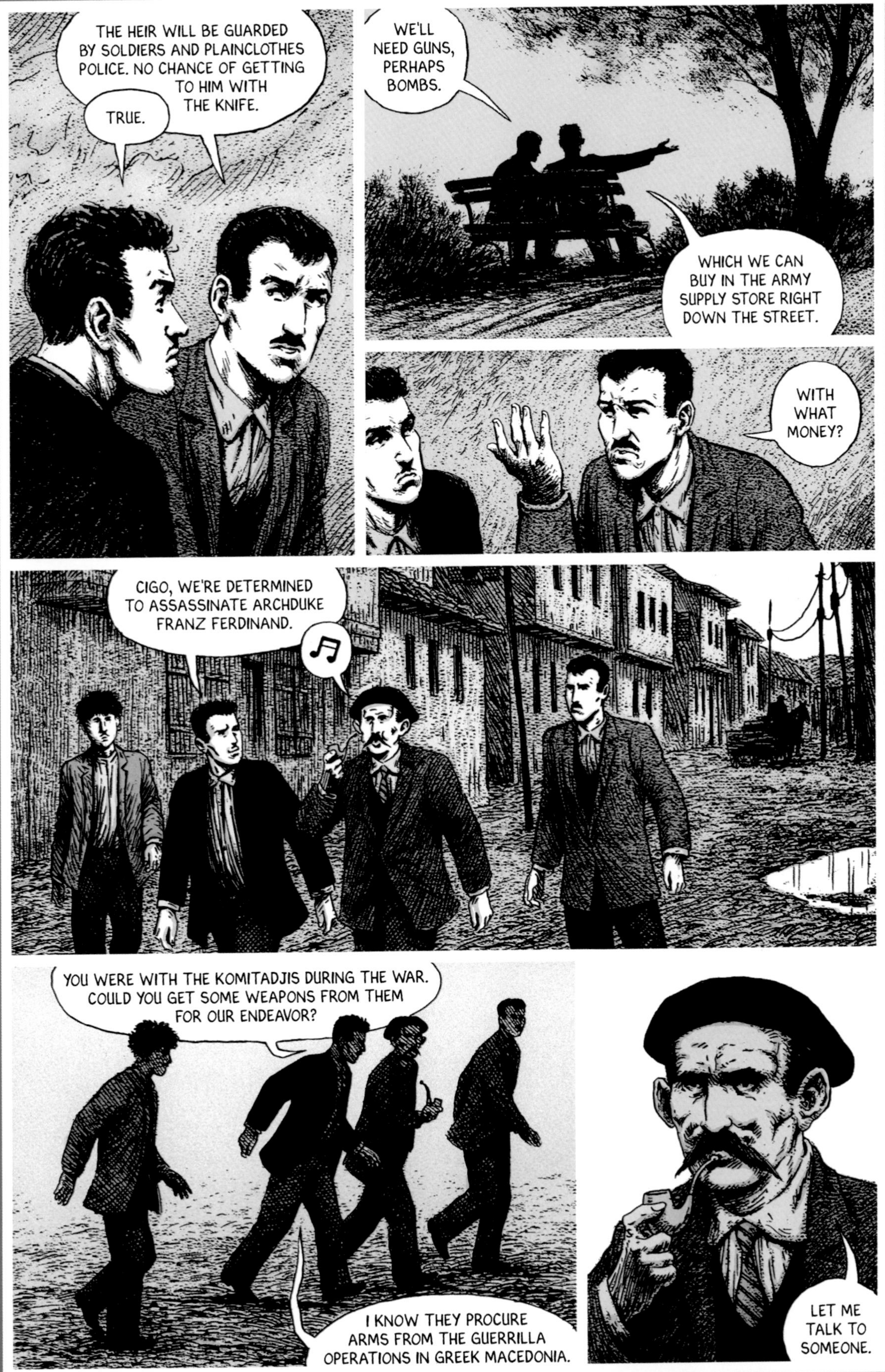
THE HEIR WILL BE GUARDED BY SOLDIERS AND PLAINCLOTHES POLICE. NO CHANCE OF GETTING TO HIM WITH THE KNIFE.
TRUE.
WE'LL NEED GUNS, PERHAPS BOMBS.
WHICH WE CAN BUY IN THE ARMY SUPPLY STORE RIGHT DOWN THE STREET.
WITH WHAT MONEY?
CIGO, WE'RE DETERMINED TO ASSASSINATE ARCHDUKE FRANZ FERDINAND.
YOU WERE WITH THE KOMITADJIS DURING THE WAR. COULD YOU GET SOME WEAPONS FROM THEM FOR OUR ENDEAVOR?
I KNOW THEY PROCURE ARMS FROM THE GUERRILLA OPERATIONS IN GREEK MACEDONIA.
LET ME TALK TO SOMEONE.

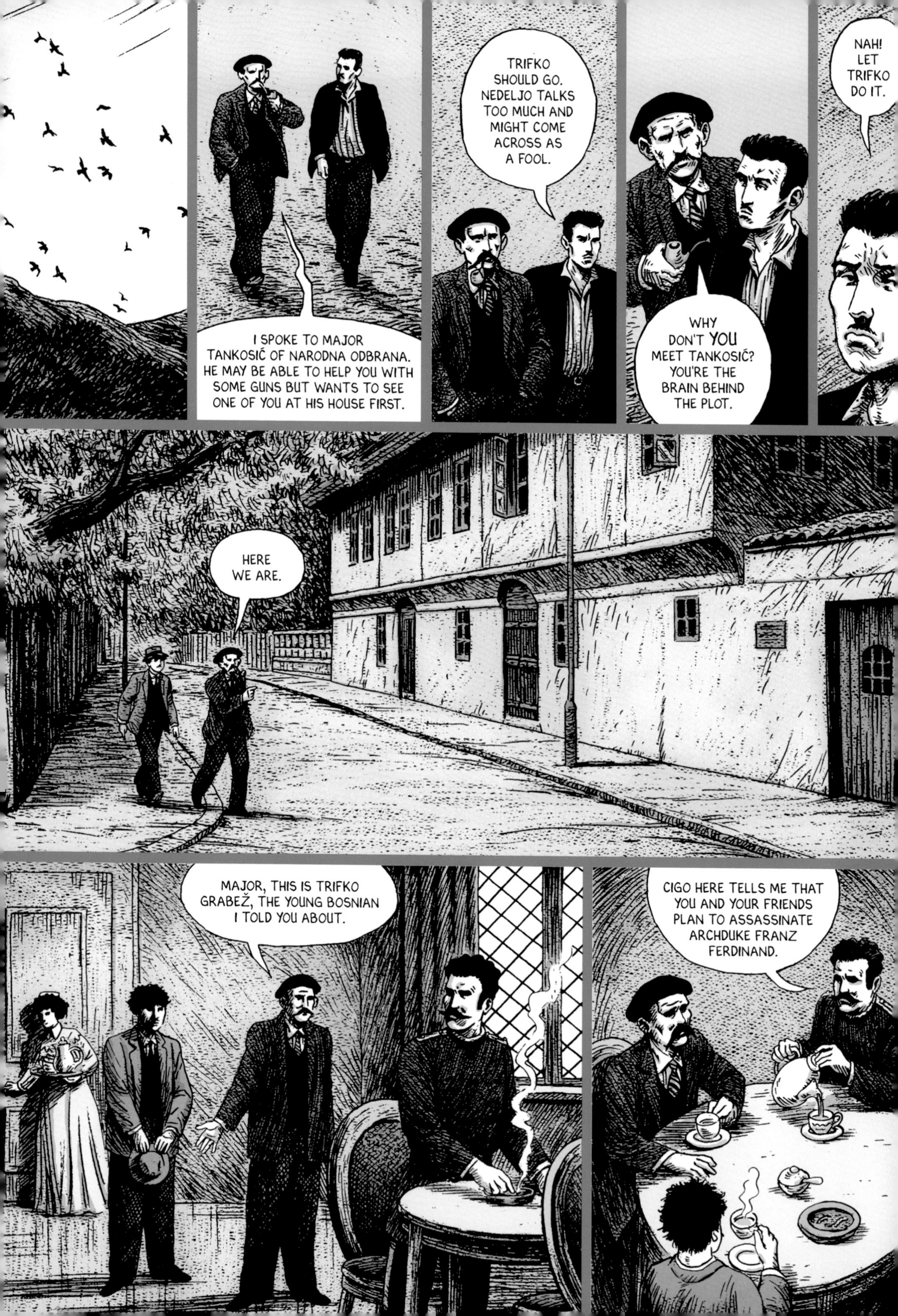
I SPOKE TO MAJOR TANKOSIĆ OF NARODNA ODBRANA. HE MAY BE ABLE TO HELP YOU WITH SOME GUNS BUT WANTS TO SEE ONE OF YOU AT HIS HOUSE FIRST.
TRIFKO SHOULD GO. NEDELJO TALKS TOO MUCH AND MIGHT COME ACROSS AS A FOOL.
WHY DON'T YOU MEET TANKOSIĆ? YOU'RE THE BRAIN BEHIND THE PLOT.
NAH! LET TRIFKO DO IT.
HERE WE ARE.
MAJOR, THIS IS TRIFKO GRABEŽ, THE YOUNG BOSNIAN I TOLD YOU ABOUT.
CIGO HERE TELLS ME THAT YOU AND YOUR FRIENDS PLAN TO ASSASSINATE ARCHDUKE FRANZ FERDINAND.

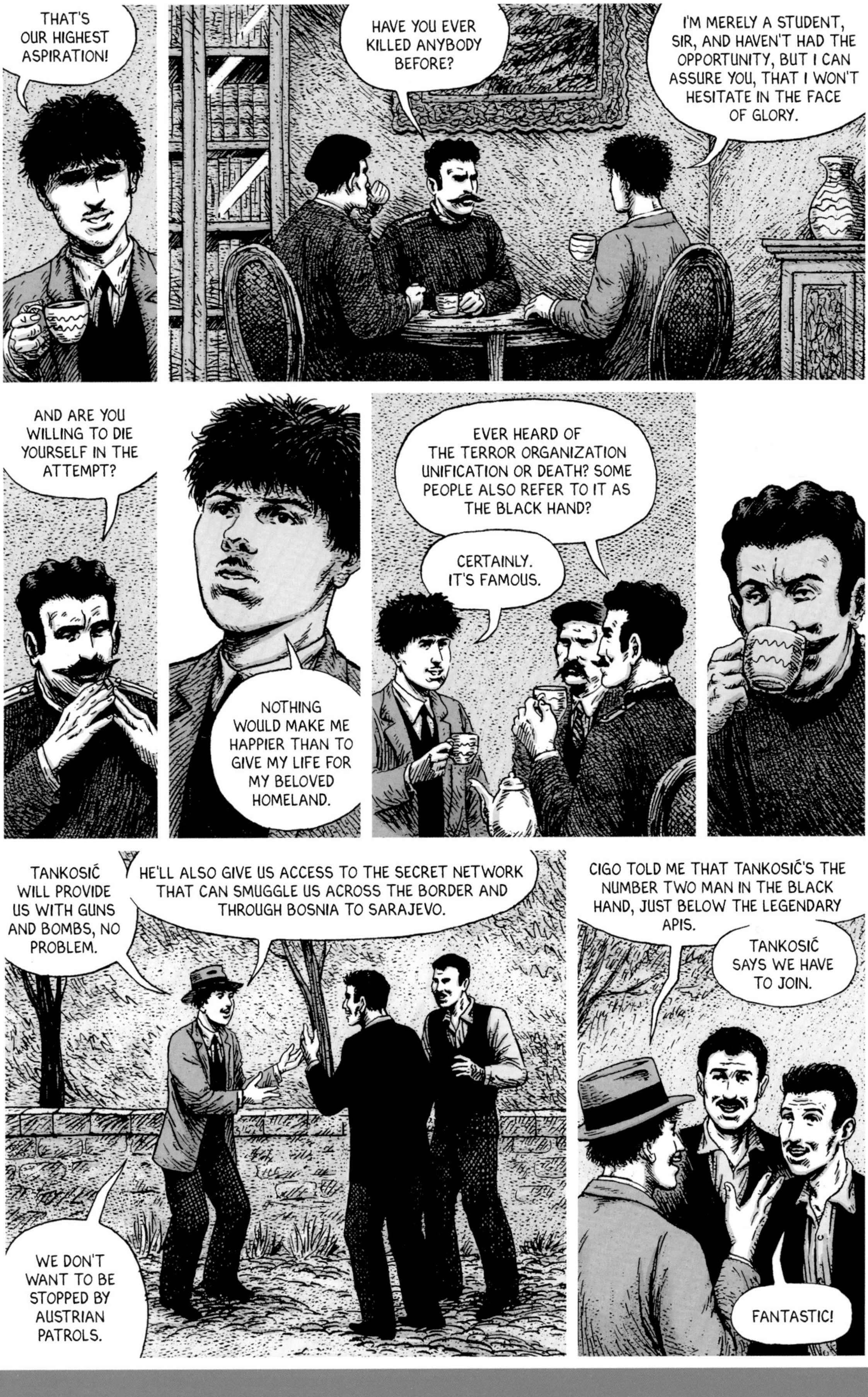
THAT'S OUR HIGHEST ASPIRATION!
HAVE YOU EVER KILLED ANYBODY BEFORE?
I'M MERELY A STUDENT, SIR, AND HAVEN'T HAD THE OPPORTUNITY, BUT I CAN ASSURE YOU, THAT I WON'T HESITATE IN THE FACE OF GLORY.
AND ARE YOU WILLING TO DIE YOURSELF IN THE ATTEMPT?
NOTHING WOULD MAKE ME HAPPIER THAN TO GIVE MY LIFE FOR MY BELOVED HOMELAND.
EVER HEARD OF THE TERROR ORGANIZATION UNIFICATION OR DEATH? SOME PEOPLE ALSO REFER TO IT AS THE BLACK HAND?
CERTAINLY. IT'S FAMOUS.
TANKOSIĆ WILL PROVIDE US WITH GUNS AND BOMBS, NO PROBLEM.
HE'LL ALSO GIVE US ACCESS TO THE SECRET NETWORK THAT CAN SMUGGLE US ACROSS THE BORDER AND THROUGH BOSNIA TO SARAJEVO.
WE DON'T WANT TO BE STOPPED BY AUSTRIAN PATROLS.
CIGO TOLD ME THAT TANKOSIĆ'S THE NUMBER TWO MAN IN THE BLACK HAND, JUST BELOW THE LEGENDARY APIS.
TANKOSIĆ SAYS WE HAVE TO JOIN.
FANTASTIC!

I, IN JOINING UNIFICATION OR DEATH, SWEAR BY THE SUN THAT WARMS ME, BY THE EARTH THAT NOURISHES ME, BEFORE GOD, BY THE BLOOD OF OUR ANCESTORS, ON MY HONOR, AND ON MY LIFE, THAT I'LL FROM THIS MOMENT UNTIL MY DEATH BE FAITHFUL TO THE LAWS OF THIS ORGANIZATION, AND THAT I'LL ALWAYS BE READY TO MAKE ANY SACRIFICE FOR IT.

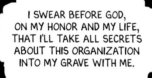

I SWEAR BEFORE GOD, ON MY HONOR AND MY LIFE, THAT I'LL TAKE ALL SECRETS ABOUT THIS ORGANIZATION INTO MY GRAVE WITH ME.

TAKE THESE BOYS OUT TO THE WOODS AND TEACH THEM HOW TO SHOOT.

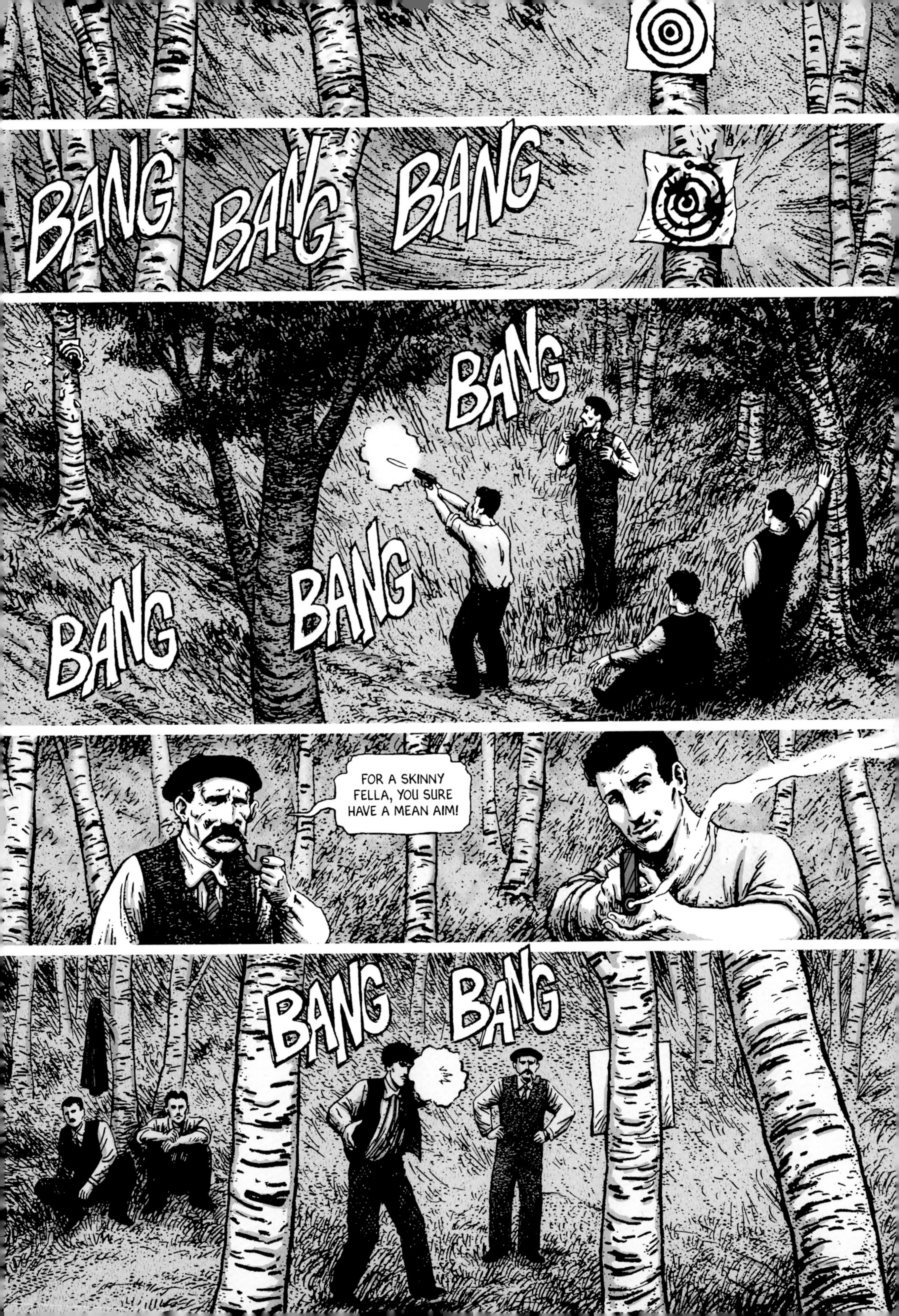
BANG BANG BANG
BANG
BANG
BANG
FOR A SKINNY FELLA, YOU SURE HAVE A MEAN AIM!
BANG BANG

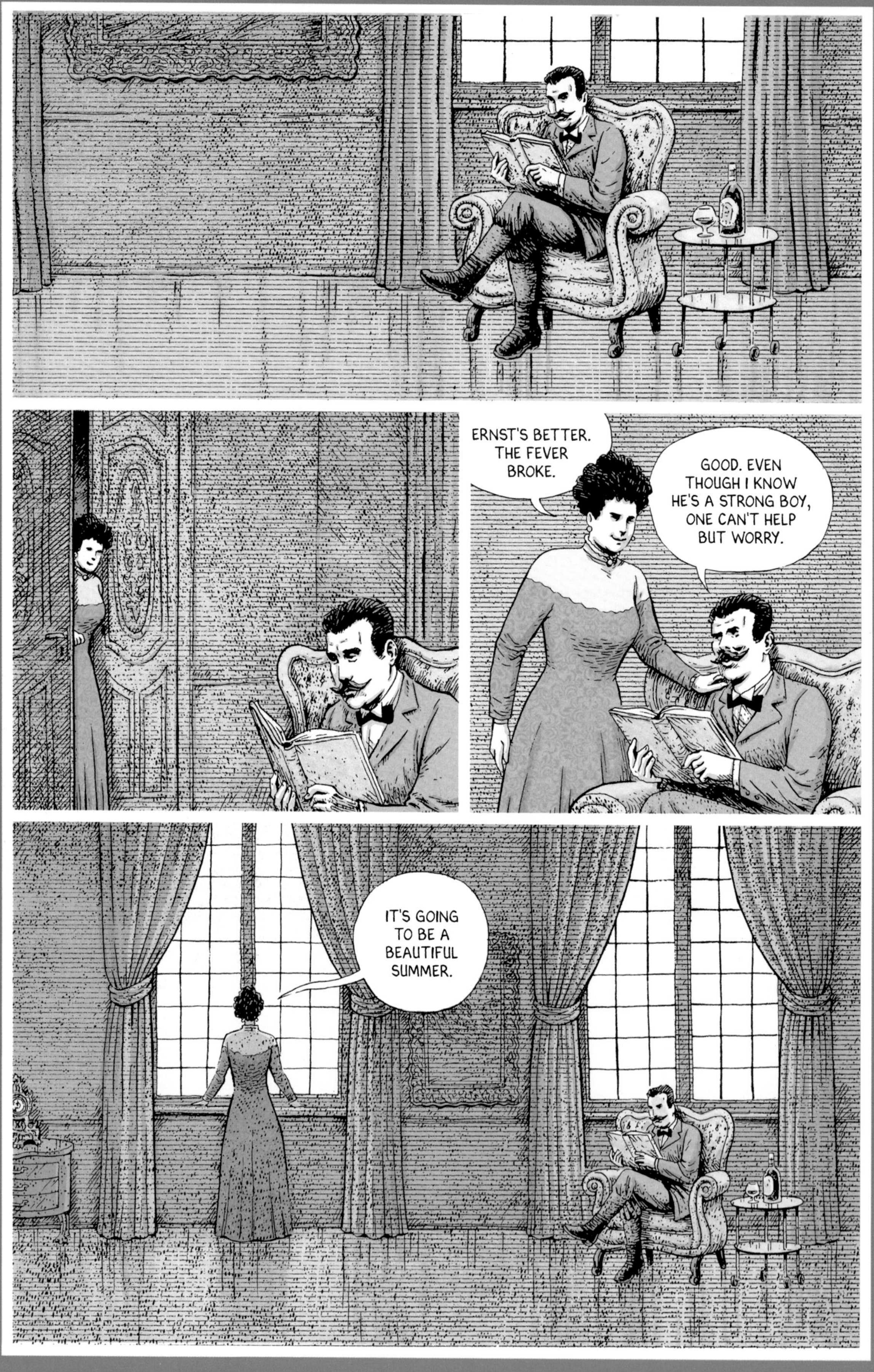
ERNST'S BETTER. THE FEVER BROKE.
GOOD. EVEN THOUGH I KNOW HE'S A STRONG BOY, ONE CAN'T HELP BUT WORRY.
IT'S GOING TO BE A BEAUTIFUL SUMMER.

I GOT YOUR STUFF.

FOUR BROWNINGS, LOADED WITH SEVEN SHOTS EACH, FOUR EXTRA MAGAZINES, ALSO LOADED, AND SIX BOMBS.

THE BOMBS ARE EASY TO OPERATE. JUST UNSCREW THE SAFETY CAP, KNOCK THE BOMB AGAINST SOMETHING HARD, AND IT'LL EXPLODE TEN SECONDS LATER.

MAKE SURE YOU'RE NOT CAUGHT, EVEN BY THE SERBIAN POLICE, WITH THESE WEAPONS ON YOU.

WE KNOW.

TOMORROW YOU'LL BOARD THE STEAMER TO ŠABAC.

ONCE YOU GET THERE, FIND CAPTAIN POPOVIČ OF THE FRONTIER GENDARMERIE AND GIVE HIM THIS CARD WITH MY INITIALS ON IT. HE'LL GET YOU SMUGGLED INTO BOSNIA.

HERE'S SOME MONEY FOR THE TRIP.

BUT THIS IS TOTALLY INADEQUATE!

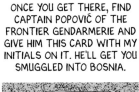

IT'S ALL I CAN GIVE YOU.

IMPROVISE, THAT'S WHAT I USED TO DO WITH THE KOMITADJIS IN THE MACEDONAN MOUNTAINS.

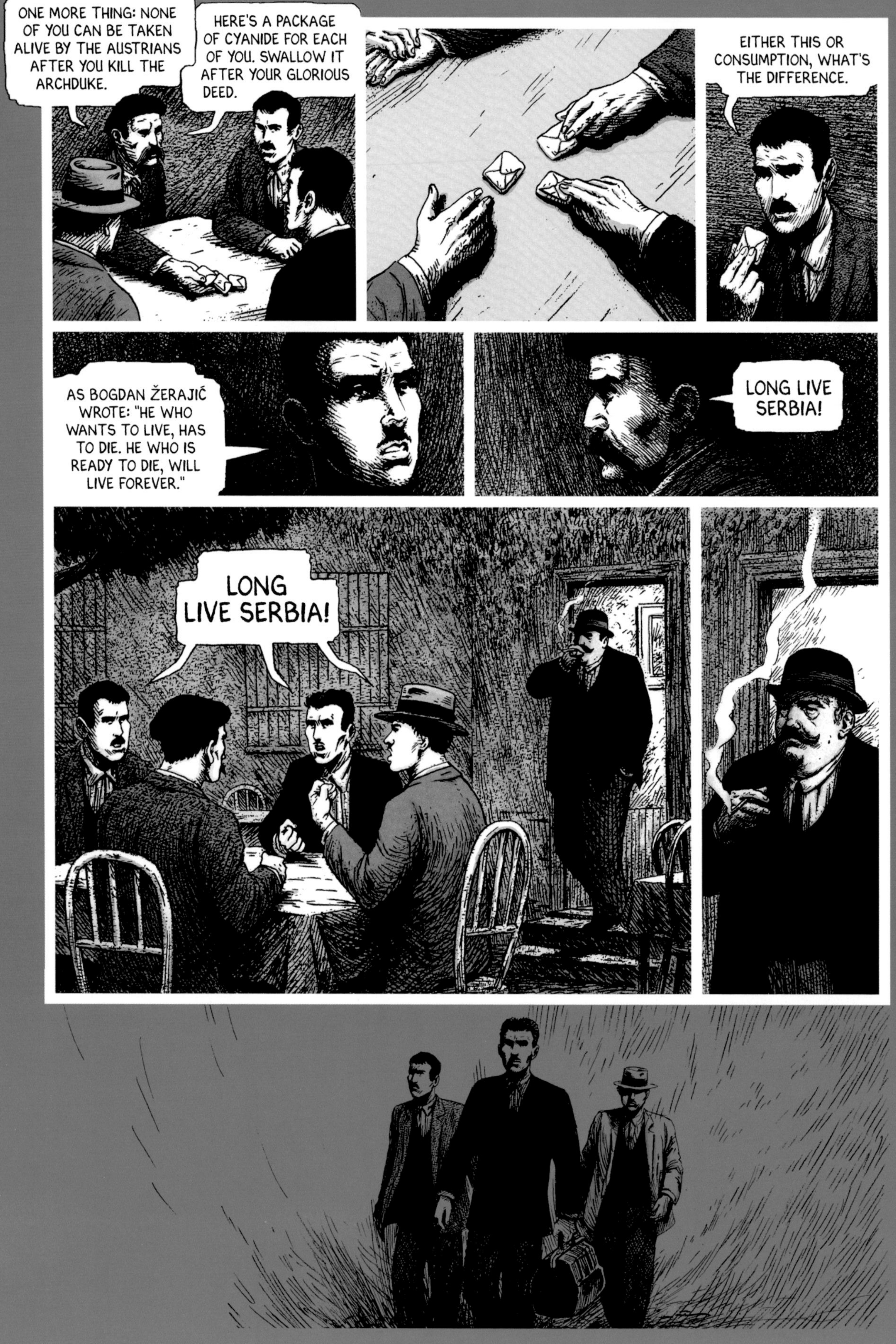

ONE MORE THING: NONE OF YOU CAN BE TAKEN ALIVE BY THE AUSTRIANS AFTER YOU KILL THE ARCHDUKE.
HERE'S A PACKAGE OF CYANIDE FOR EACH OF YOU. SWALLOW IT AFTER YOUR GLORIOUS DEED.
EITHER THIS OR CONSUMPTION, WHAT'S THE DIFFERENCE.
AS BOGDAN ŽERAJIĆ WROTE: "HE WHO WANTS TO LIVE, HAS TO DIE. HE WHO IS READY TO DIE, WILL LIVE FOREVER."
LONG LIVE SERBIA!
LONG LIVE SERBIA!

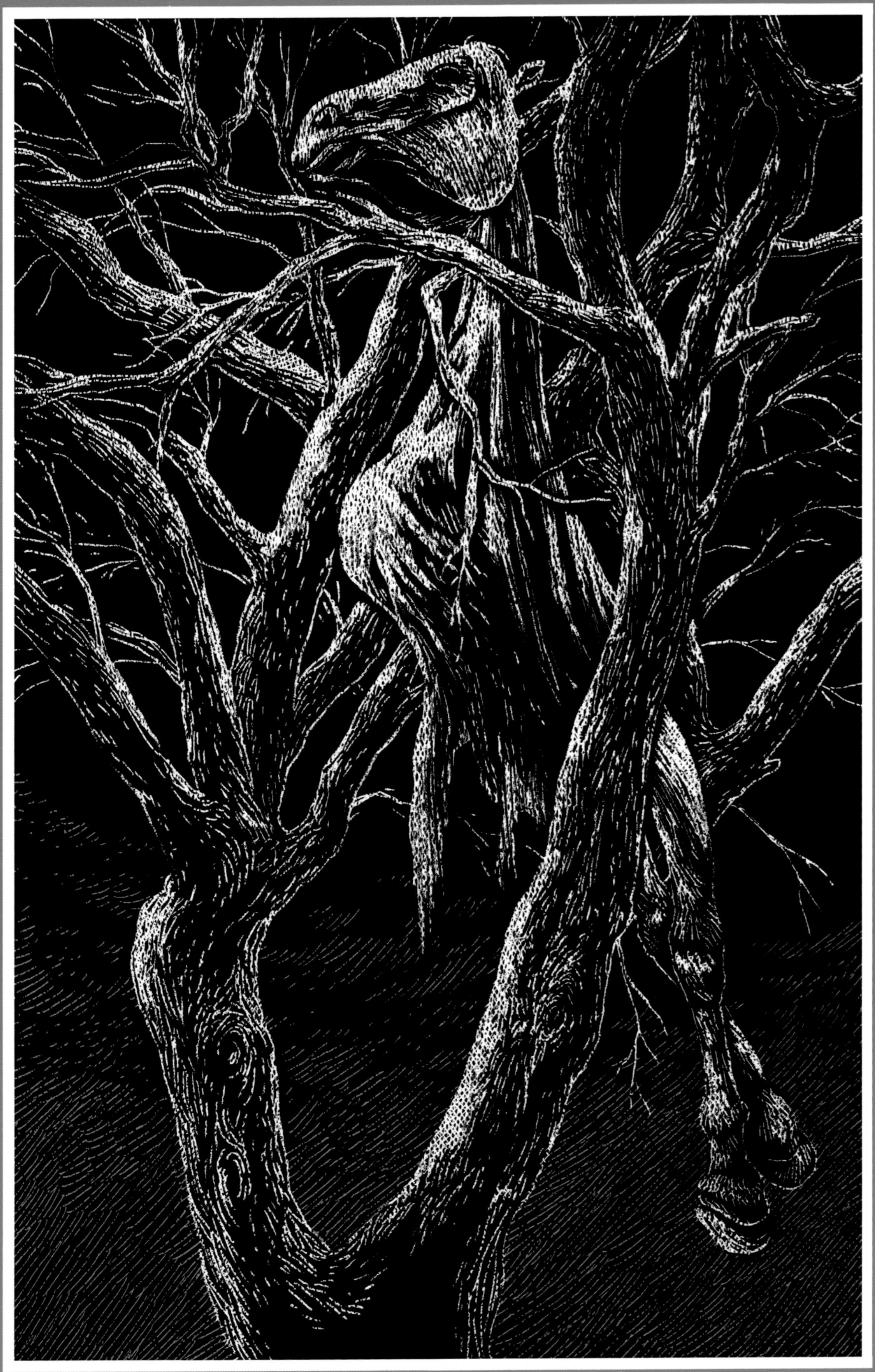

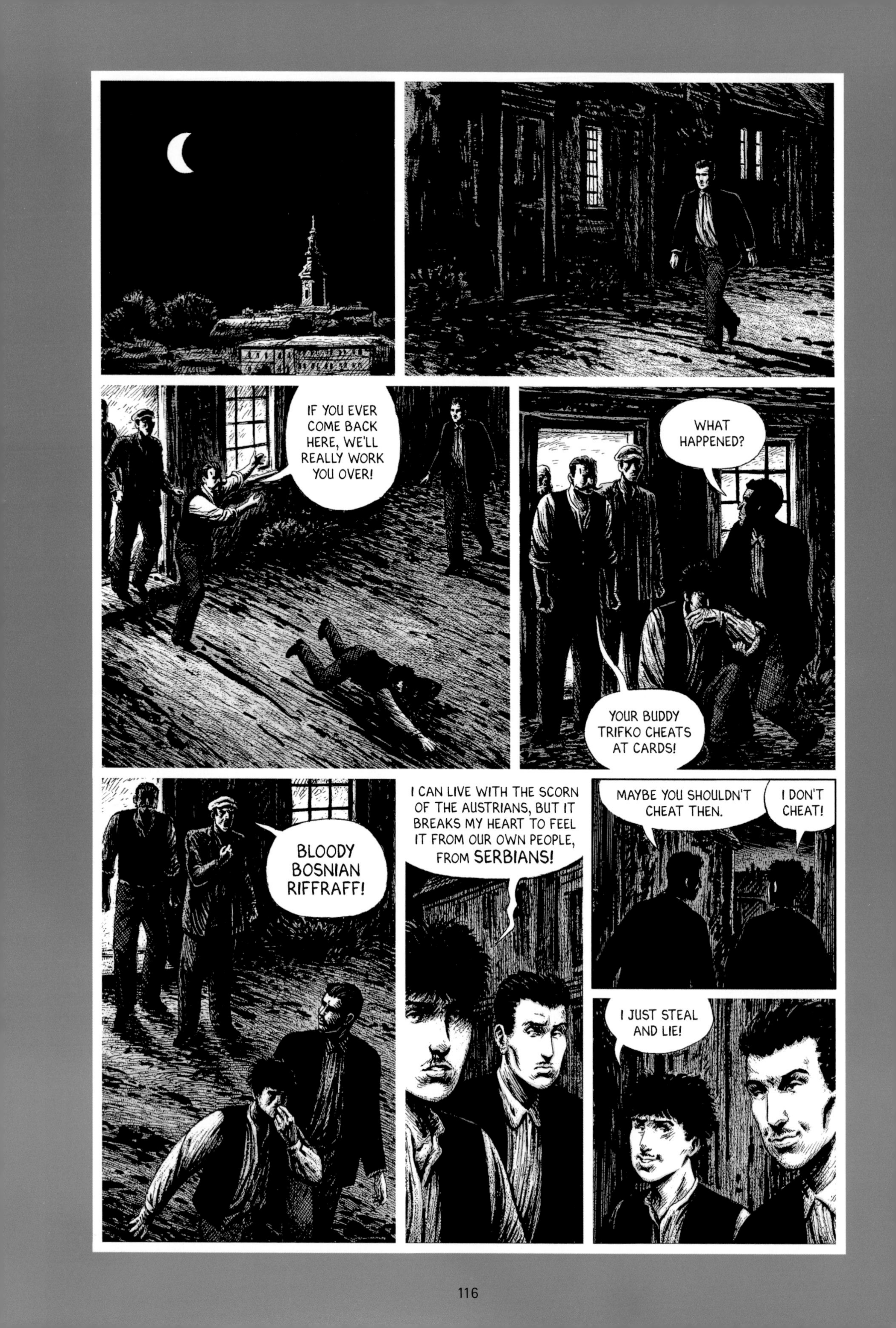
IF YOU EVER COME BACK HERE, WE'LL REALLY WORK YOU OVER!
WHAT HAPPENED?
YOUR BUDDY TRIFKO CHEATS AT CARDS!
BLOODY BOSNIAN RIFFRAFF!
I CAN LIVE WITH THE SCORN OF THE AUSTRIANS, BUT IT BREAKS MY HEART TO FEEL IT FROM OUR OWN PEOPLE, FROM SERBIANS!
MAYBE YOU SHOULDN'T CHEAT THEN.
I DON'T CHEAT!
I JUST STEAL AND LIE!

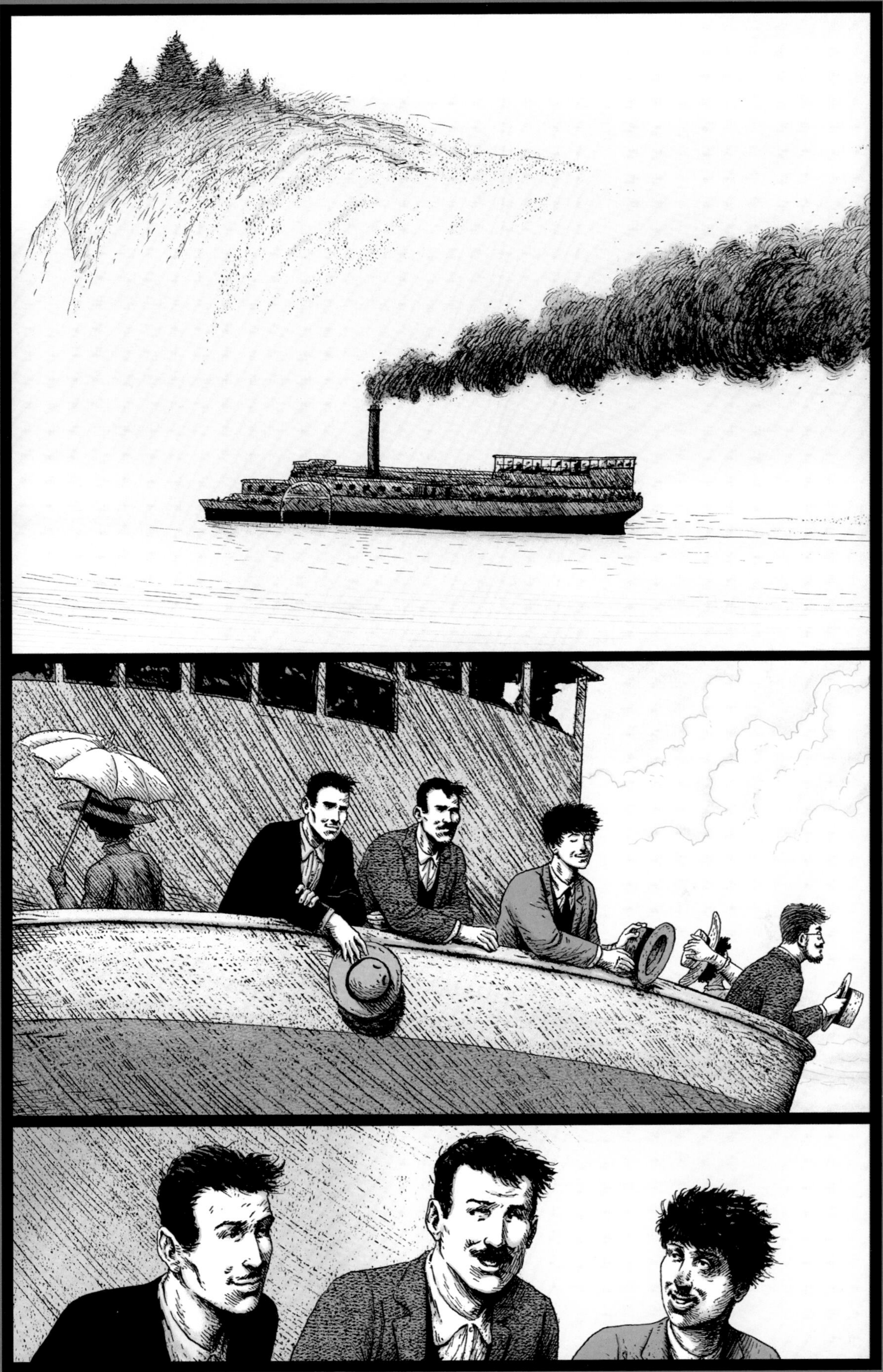

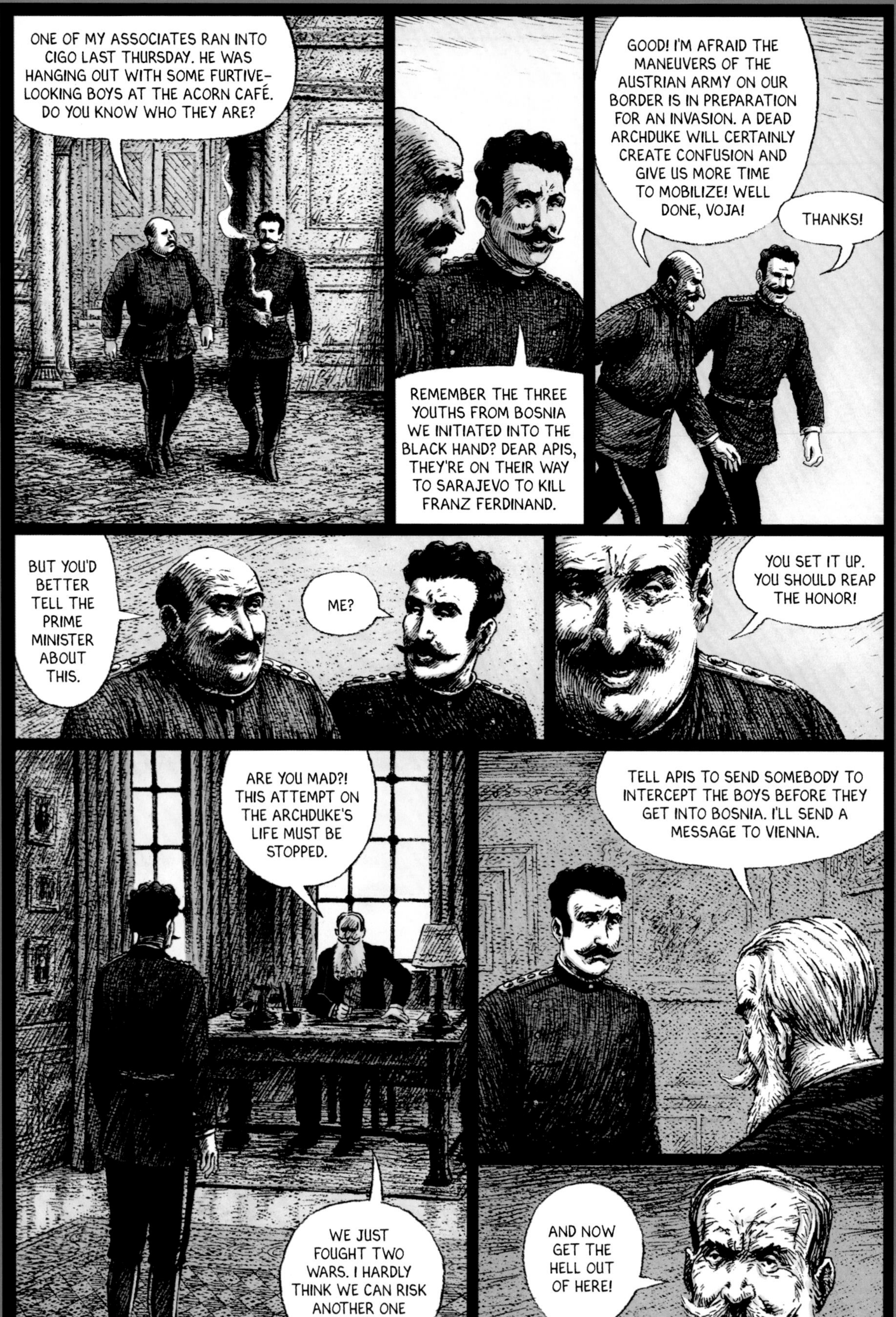

ONE OF MY ASSOCIATES RAN INTO CIGO LAST THURSDAY. HE WAS HANGING OUT WITH SOME FURTIVE-LOOKING BOYS AT THE ACORN CAFÉ. DO YOU KNOW WHO THEY ARE?
REMEMBER THE THREE YOUTHS FROM BOSNIA WE INITIATED INTO THE BLACK HAND? DEAR APIS, THEY'RE ON THEIR WAY TO SARAJEVO TO KILL FRANZ FERDINAND.
GOOD! I'M AFRAID THE MANEUVERS OF THE AUSTRIAN ARMY ON OUR BORDER IS IN PREPARATION FOR AN INVASION. A DEAD ARCHDUKE WILL CERTAINLY CREATE CONFUSION AND GIVE US MORE TIME TO MOBILIZE! WELL DONE, VOJA!
THANKS!
BUT YOU'D BETTER TELL THE PRIME MINISTER ABOUT THIS.
ME?
YOU SET IT UP. YOU SHOULD REAP THE HONOR!
ARE YOU MAD?! THIS ATTEMPT ON THE ARCHDUKE'S LIFE MUST BE STOPPED.
WE JUST FOUGHT TWO WARS. I HARDLY THINK WE CAN RISK ANOTHER ONE RIGHT AWAY.
TELL APIS TO SEND SOMEBODY TO INTERCEPT THE BOYS BEFORE THEY GET INTO BOSNIA. I'LL SEND A MESSAGE TO VIENNA.
AND NOW GET THE HELL OUT OF HERE!

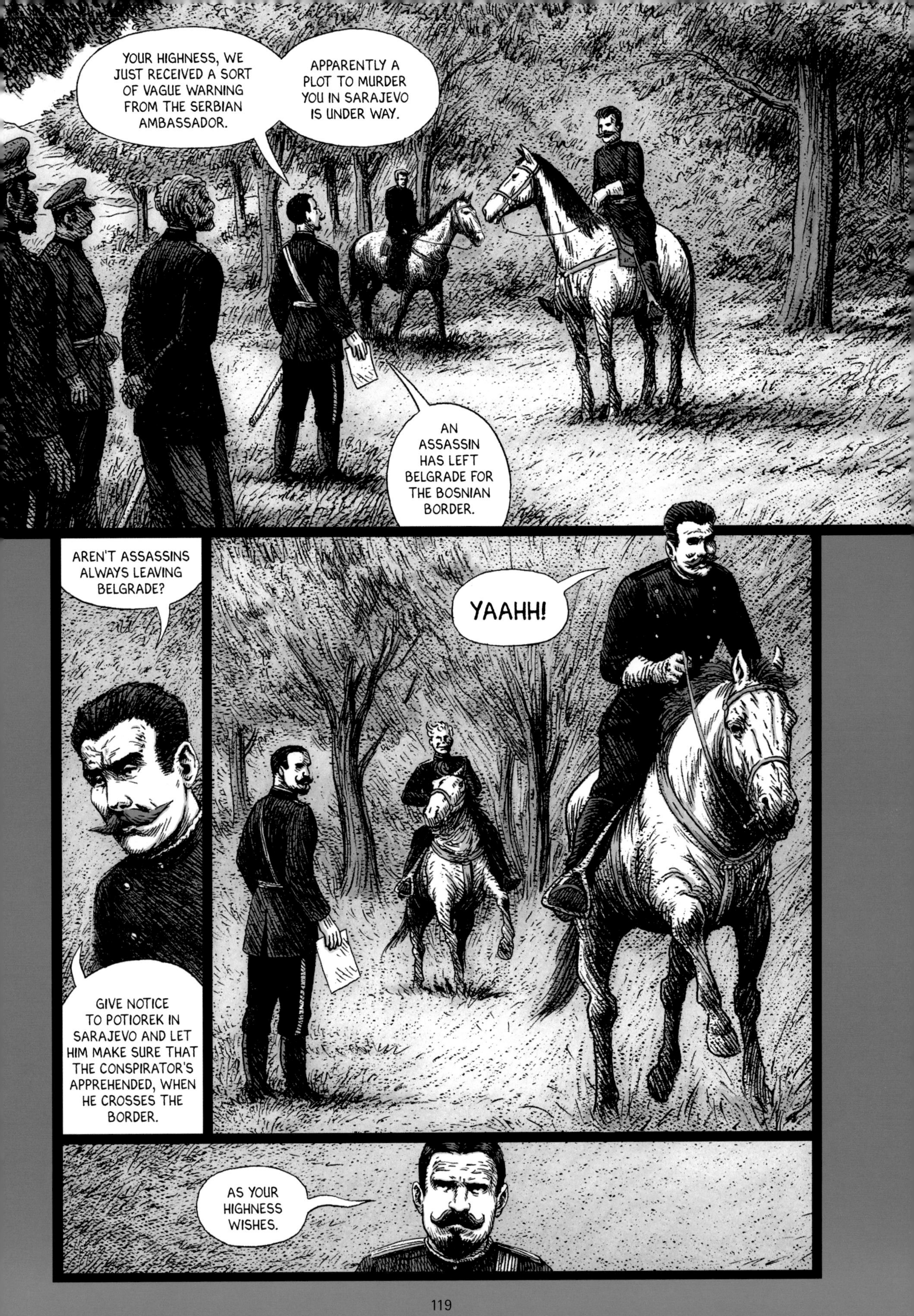
YOUR HIGHNESS, WE JUST RECEIVED A SORT OF VAGUE WARNING FROM THE SERBIAN AMBASSADOR.
APPARENTLY A PLOT TO MURDER YOU IN SARAJEVO IS UNDER WAY.
AN ASSASSIN HAS LEFT BELGRADE FOR THE BOSNIAN BORDER.
AREN'T ASSASSINS ALWAYS LEAVING BELGRADE?
GIVE NOTICE TO POTIOREK IN SARAJEVO AND LET HIM MAKE SURE THAT THE CONSPIRATOR'S APPREHENDED, WHEN HE CROSSES THE BORDER.
YAAHH!
AS YOUR HIGHNESS WISHES.

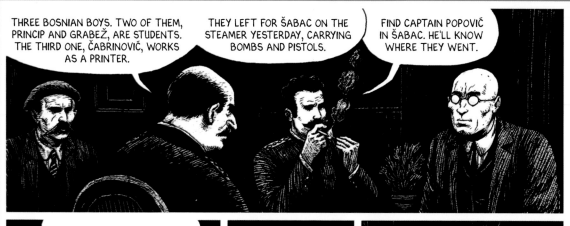

THREE BOSNIAN BOYS. TWO OF THEM, PRINCIP AND GRABEŽ, ARE STUDENTS. THE THIRD ONE, ČABRINOVIĆ, WORKS AS A PRINTER.

THEY LEFT FOR ŠABAC ON THE STEAMER YESTERDAY, CARRYING BOMBS AND PISTOLS.

FIND CAPTAIN POPOVIĆ IN ŠABAC. HE'LL KNOW WHERE THEY WENT.

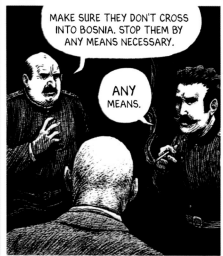

MAKE SURE THEY DON'T CROSS INTO BOSNIA. STOP THEM BY ANY MEANS NECESSARY.

ANY MEANS.

YOU'RE SENDING HIM OUT TO KILL GAVRILO AND HIS FRIENDS? AFTER VOJA HERE APPROVED THEIR MISSION?

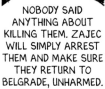

NOBODY SAID ANYTHING ABOUT KILLING THEM. ZAJEC WILL SIMPLY ARREST THEM AND MAKE SURE THEY RETURN TO BELGRADE, UNHARMED.

LET'S HOPE SO.

CAPTAIN POPOVIĆ?

CAN I HELP YOU?

A MUTUAL FRIEND TOLD ME TO GIVE YOU THIS. WE NEED TO CROSS THE DRINA INTO BOSNIA. SECRETLY.

THE TRAIN? WE HAVE VERY LITTLE MONEY.

I'LL MAKE A WARRANT STATING THAT YOU'RE CUSTOMS OFFICIALS. IT'LL GIVE YOU A SUBSTANTIAL REDUCTION ON THE TICKET PRICES.

TAKE THE TRAIN DOWN TO LOZNICA AND SHOW THIS NOTE TO CAPTAIN PRVANOVIĆ IN THE GENDARMERIE THERE. HE'LL TAKE YOU ACROSS WHERE HE THINKS BEST.

ACROSS THE BORDER IN BOSNIA

CAPTAIN! A DISPATCH FROM GOVERNOR POTIOREK HIMSELF.

APPARENTLY, AN ASSASSIN IS TRYING TO CROSS THE BORDER. GIVE INSTRUCTIONS TO THE BORDER GUARDS TO CHECK ALL PAPERS MORE CAREFULLY. AND SEND OUT EXTRA PATROLS AT NIGHT.

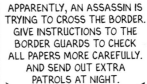

YES, SIR!

CATCHING THIS GUY JUST MIGHT GET ME OUT OF THIS HELLHOLE AND BACK TO SALZBURG.

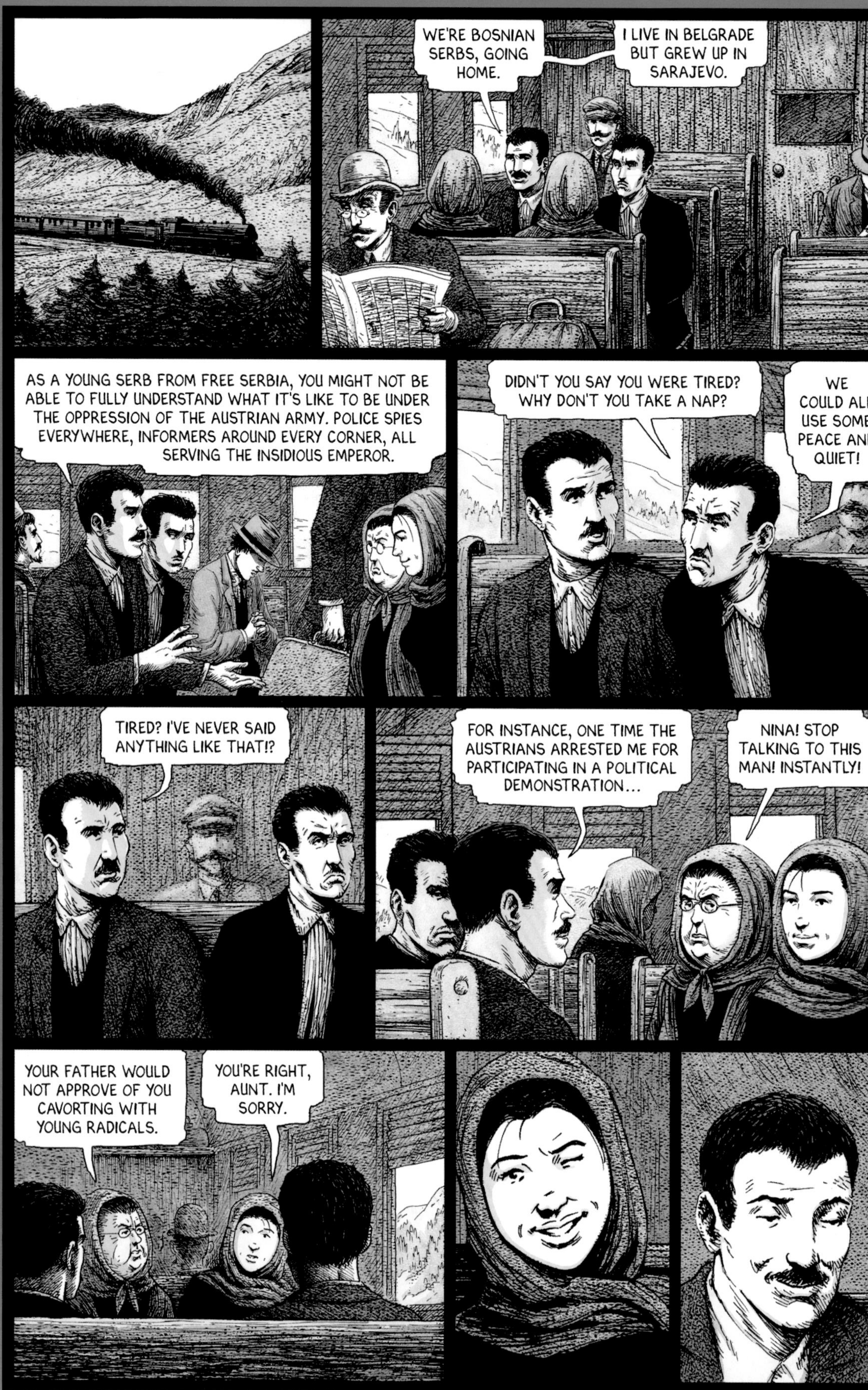
WE'RE BOSNIAN SERBS, GOING HOME.
I LIVE IN BELGRADE BUT GREW UP IN SARAJEVO.
AS A YOUNG SERB FROM FREE SERBIA, YOU MIGHT NOT BE ABLE TO FULLY UNDERSTAND WHAT IT'S LIKE TO BE UNDER THE OPPRESSION OF THE AUSTRIAN ARMY. POLICE SPIES EVERYWHERE, INFORMERS AROUND EVERY CORNER, ALL SERVING THE INSIDIOUS EMPEROR.
DIDN'T YOU SAY YOU WERE TIRED? WHY DON'T YOU TAKE A NAP?
WE COULD ALL USE SOME PEACE AND QUIET!
TIRED? I'VE NEVER SAID ANYTHING LIKE THAT!?
FOR INSTANCE, ONE TIME THE AUSTRIANS ARRESTED ME FOR PARTICIPATING IN A POLITICAL DEMONSTRATION…
NINA! STOP TALKING TO THIS MAN! INSTANTLY!
YOUR FATHER WOULD NOT APPROVE OF YOU CAVORTING WITH YOUNG RADICALS.
YOU'RE RIGHT, AUNT. I'M SORRY.

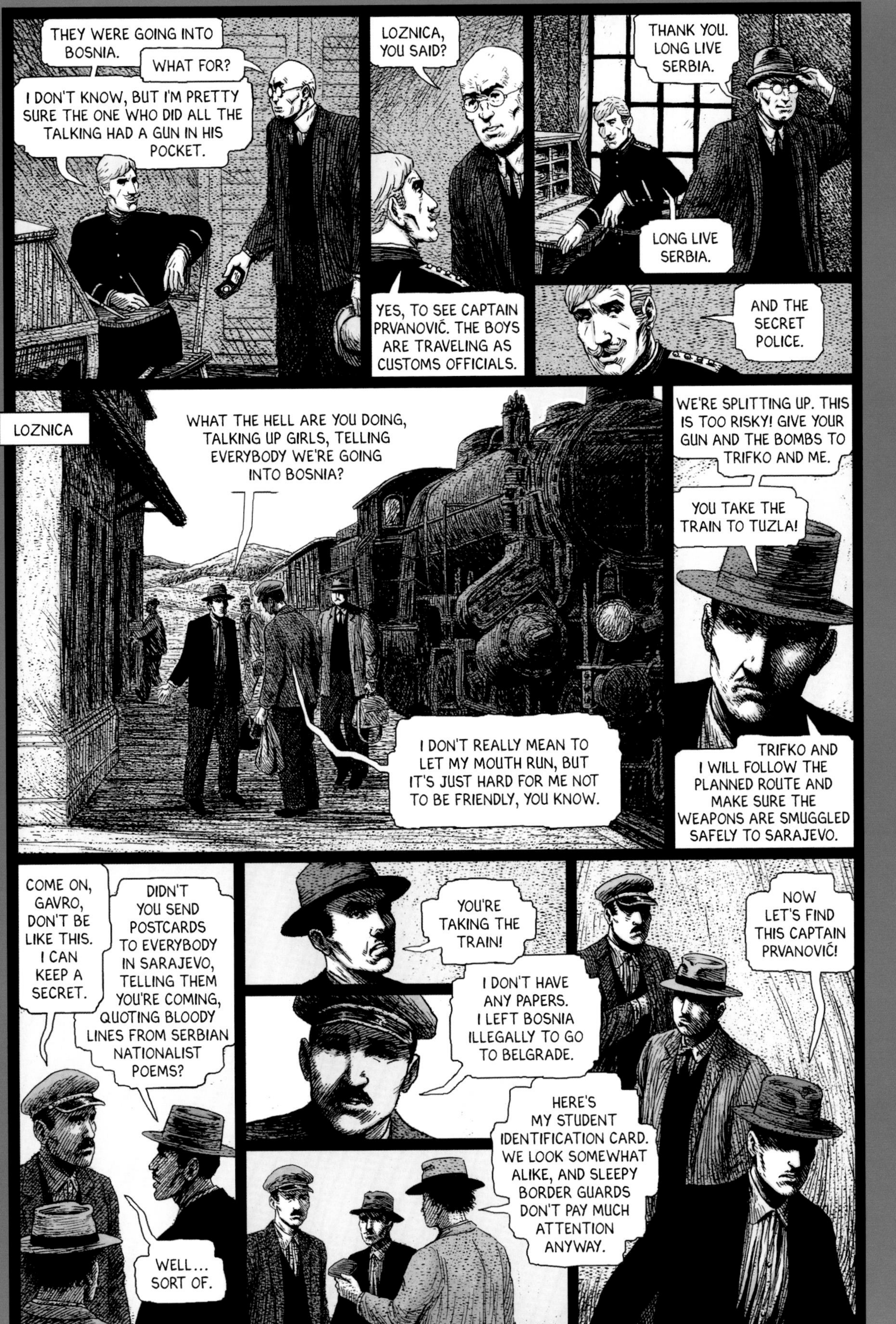
THEY WERE GOING INTO BOSNIA.
WHAT FOR?
I DON'T KNOW, BUT I'M PRETTY SURE THE ONE WHO DID ALL THE TALKING HAD A GUN IN HIS POCKET.
LOZNICA, YOU SAID?
YES, TO SEE CAPTAIN PRVANOVIĆ. THE BOYS ARE TRAVELING AS CUSTOMS OFFICIALS.
THANK YOU. LONG LIVE SERBIA.
LONG LIVE SERBIA.
AND THE SECRET POLICE.
LOZNICA
WHAT THE HELL ARE YOU DOING, TALKING UP GIRLS, TELLING EVERYBODY WE'RE GOING INTO BOSNIA?
I DON'T REALLY MEAN TO LET MY MOUTH RUN, BUT IT'S JUST HARD FOR ME NOT TO BE FRIENDLY, YOU KNOW.
WE'RE SPLITTING UP. THIS IS TOO RISKY! GIVE YOUR GUN AND THE BOMBS TO TRIFKO AND ME.
YOU TAKE THE TRAIN TO TUZLA!
TRIFKO AND I WILL FOLLOW THE PLANNED ROUTE AND MAKE SURE THE WEAPONS ARE SMUGGLED SAFELY TO SARAJEVO.
COME ON, GAVRO, DON'T BE LIKE THIS. I CAN KEEP A SECRET.
DIDN'T YOU SEND POSTCARDS TO EVERYBODY IN SARAJEVO, TELLING THEM YOU'RE COMING, QUOTING BLOODY LINES FROM SERBIAN NATIONALIST POEMS?
WELL... SORT OF.
YOU'RE TAKING THE TRAIN!
I DON'T HAVE ANY PAPERS. I LEFT BOSNIA ILLEGALLY TO GO TO BELGRADE.
HERE'S MY STUDENT IDENTIFICATION CARD. WE LOOK SOMEWHAT ALIKE, AND SLEEPY BORDER GUARDS DON'T PAY MUCH ATTENTION ANYWAY.
NOW LET'S FIND THIS CAPTAIN PRVANOVIĆ!

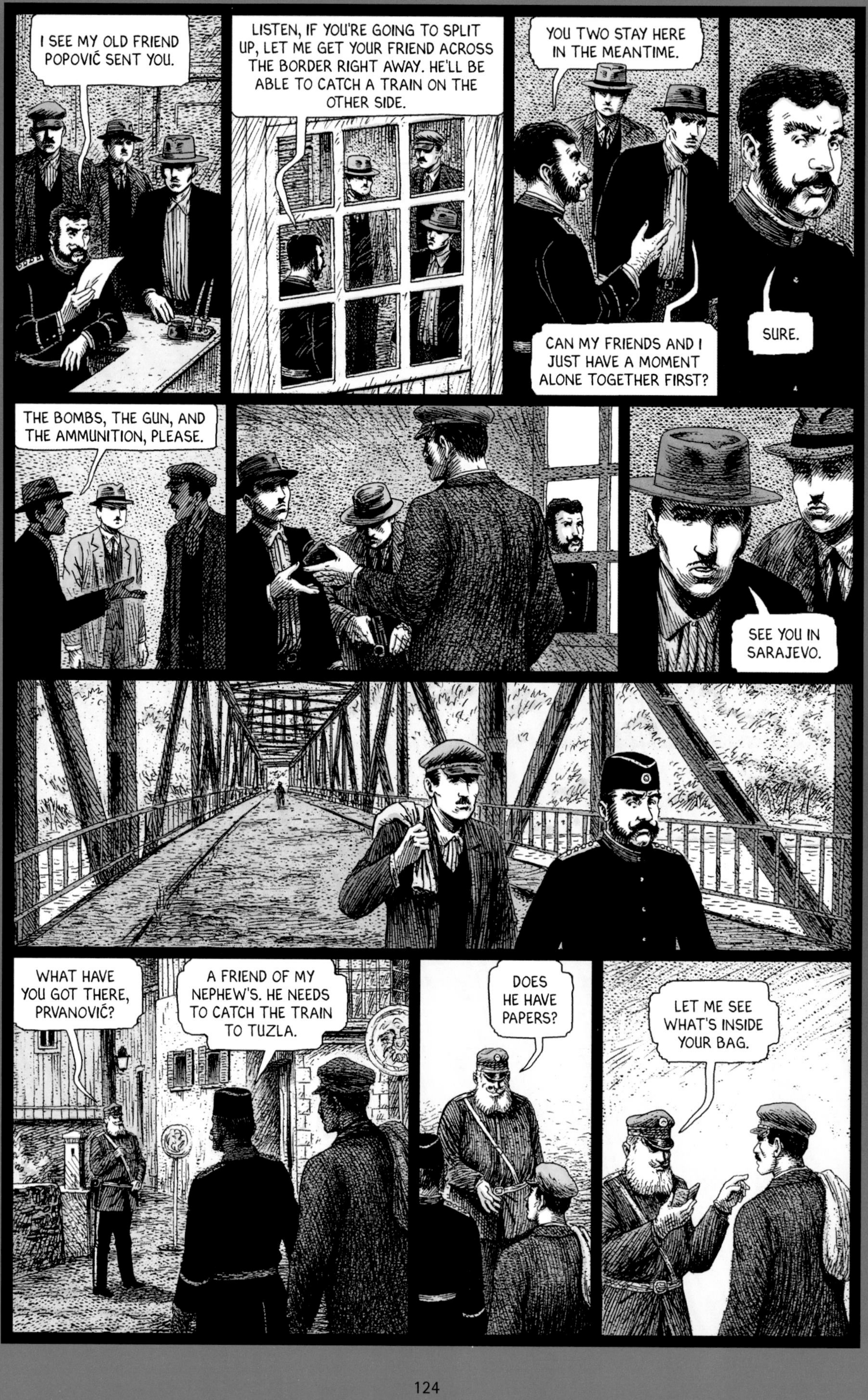
I SEE MY OLD FRIEND POPOVIĆ SENT YOU.
LISTEN, IF YOU'RE GOING TO SPLIT UP, LET ME GET YOUR FRIEND ACROSS THE BORDER RIGHT AWAY. HE'LL BE ABLE TO CATCH A TRAIN ON THE OTHER SIDE.
YOU TWO STAY HERE IN THE MEANTIME.
CAN MY FRIENDS AND I JUST HAVE A MOMENT ALONE TOGETHER FIRST?
SURE.
THE BOMBS, THE GUN, AND THE AMMUNITION, PLEASE.
SEE YOU IN SARAJEVO.
WHAT HAVE YOU GOT THERE, PRVANOVIĆ?
A FRIEND OF MY NEPHEW'S. HE NEEDS TO CATCH THE TRAIN TO TUZLA.
DOES HE HAVE PAPERS?
LET ME SEE WHAT'S INSIDE YOUR BAG.

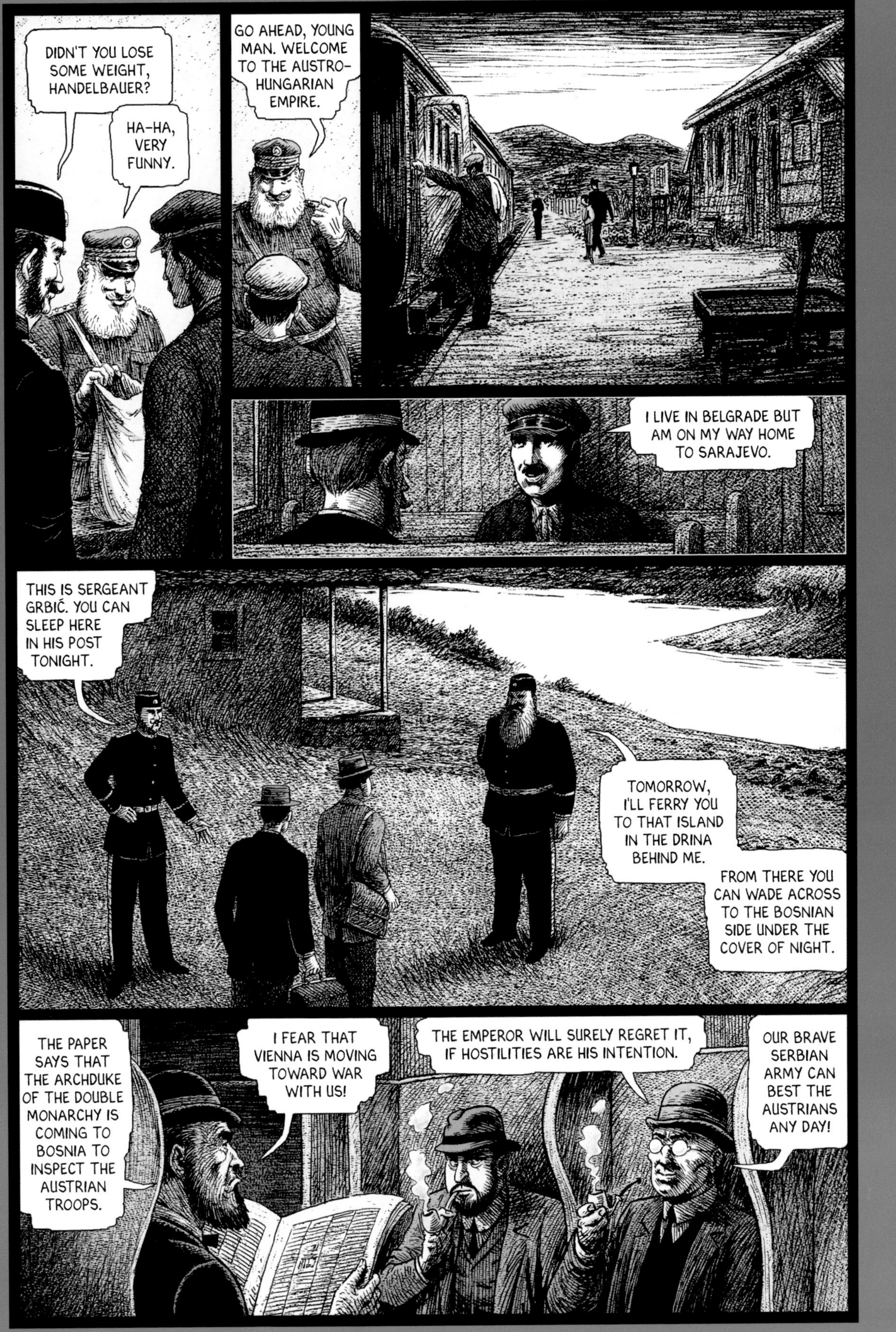
DIDN'T YOU LOSE SOME WEIGHT, HANDELBAUER?
HA-HA, VERY FUNNY.
GO AHEAD, YOUNG MAN. WELCOME TO THE AUSTRO-HUNGARIAN EMPIRE.
I LIVE IN BELGRADE BUT AM ON MY WAY HOME TO SARAJEVO.
THIS IS SERGEANT GRBIĆ. YOU CAN SLEEP HERE IN HIS POST TONIGHT.
TOMORROW, I'LL FERRY YOU TO THAT ISLAND IN THE DRINA BEHIND ME.
FROM THERE YOU CAN WADE ACROSS TO THE BOSNIAN SIDE UNDER THE COVER OF NIGHT.
THE PAPER SAYS THAT THE ARCHDUKE OF THE DOUBLE MONARCHY IS COMING TO BOSNIA TO INSPECT THE AUSTRIAN TROOPS.
I FEAR THAT VIENNA IS MOVING TOWARD WAR WITH US!
THE EMPEROR WILL SURELY REGRET IT, IF HOSTILITIES ARE HIS INTENTION.
OUR BRAVE SERBIAN ARMY CAN BEST THE AUSTRIANS ANY DAY!

I HAD A NIGHTMARE LAST NIGHT.

YEAH?

I WAS ON THE OCEAN IN A LITTLE BOAT, ALL ALONE.

IT WAS DARK, IN THE MIDDLE OF THE NIGHT, AND A FIERCE WIND WAS BLOWING.

I KEPT HEARING OUR CHILDREN CALLING FOR HELP, SHOUTING THAT THEY WERE DROWNING, BUT I COULDN'T SEE THEM.

SO I JUMPED INTO THE BLACK WATER. IT WAS TERRIBLY COLD.

LIKE ICE.

I WENT DOWN FAST.

LARGE FISH SWAM BY ME.

I COULD FEEL THEIR SLIMY BODIES AGAINST MY SKIN.

WHEN I REACHED THE BOTTOM, I SAW YOU. YOU WERE CARRYING THE CHILDREN IN YOUR ARMS.

THEY WERE PALE WITH THEIR EYES CLOSED, AND I WAS CERTAIN THEY WERE DEAD.

AN INCREDIBLE SADNESS OVERWHELMED ME. BUT YOU SMILED AND SAID "DON'T WORRY, THEY'RE ONLY SLEEPING."

AND HOLDING OUT MY HAND, YOU LED US ALL OUT OF THE WATER AND TO THE SAFETY OF THE SHORE.

DAWN HAD BROKE AS WE WALKED UP UNTO THE BEACH, AND THE CHILDREN WOKE UP. ERNST WAS INSTANTLY HUNGRY THE WAY HE ALWAYS IS IN THE MORNING.

YOU DON'T NEED TO WORRY ABOUT ME, DEAR. I BEAT THE TUBERCULOSIS SIXTEEN YEARS AGO, AND THE ASTHMA ISN'T REALLY BOTHERING ME THESE DAYS.

I KNOW.

I THANK GOD FOR HIS SMALL MERCIES EVERY DAY.

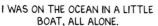

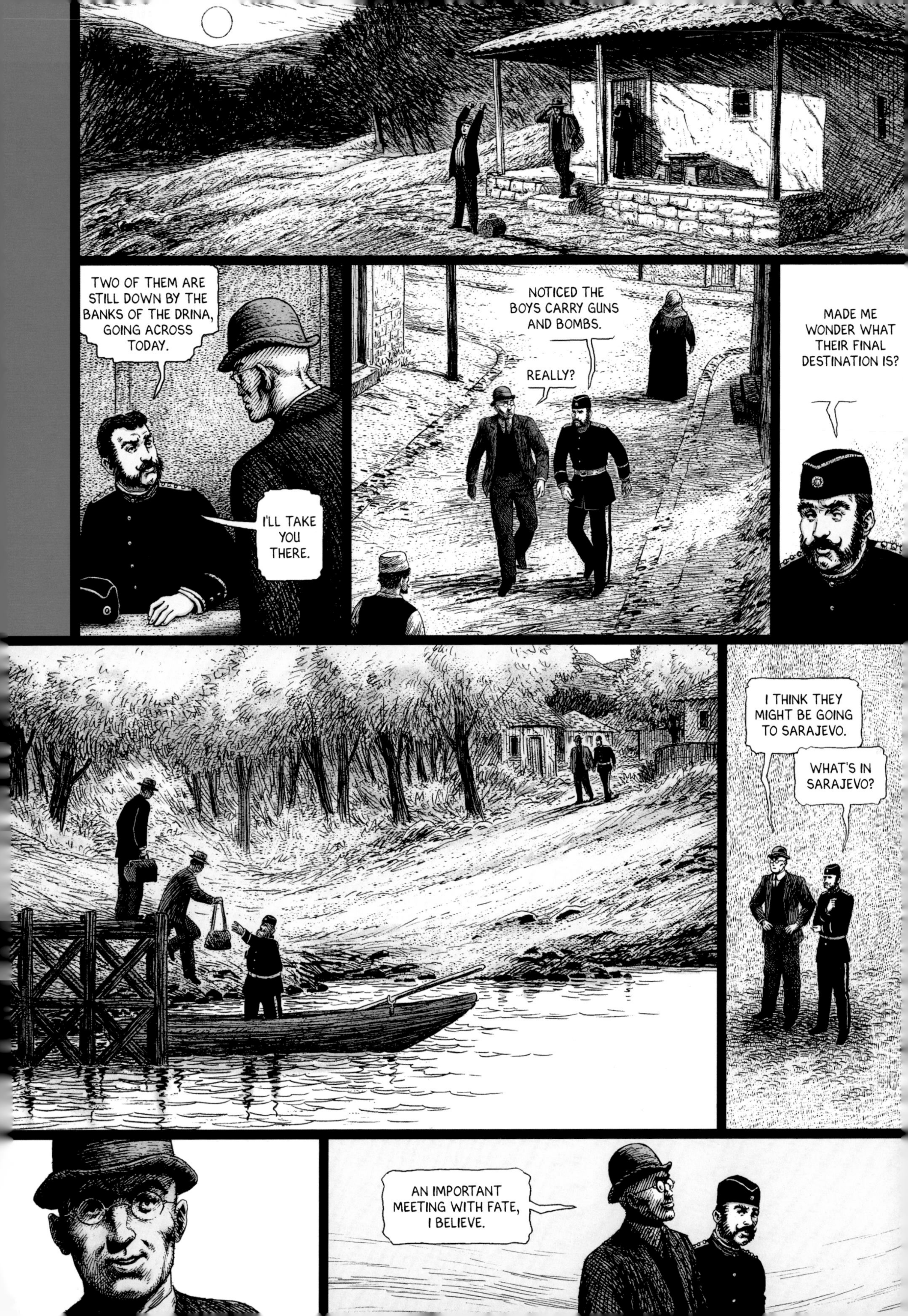

TWO OF THEM ARE STILL DOWN BY THE BANKS OF THE DRINA, GOING ACROSS TODAY.
I'LL TAKE YOU THERE.
NOTICED THE BOYS CARRY GUNS AND BOMBS.
REALLY?
MADE ME WONDER WHAT THEIR FINAL DESTINATION IS?
I THINK THEY MIGHT BE GOING TO SARAJEVO.
WHAT'S IN SARAJEVO?
AN IMPORTANT MEETING WITH FATE, I BELIEVE.

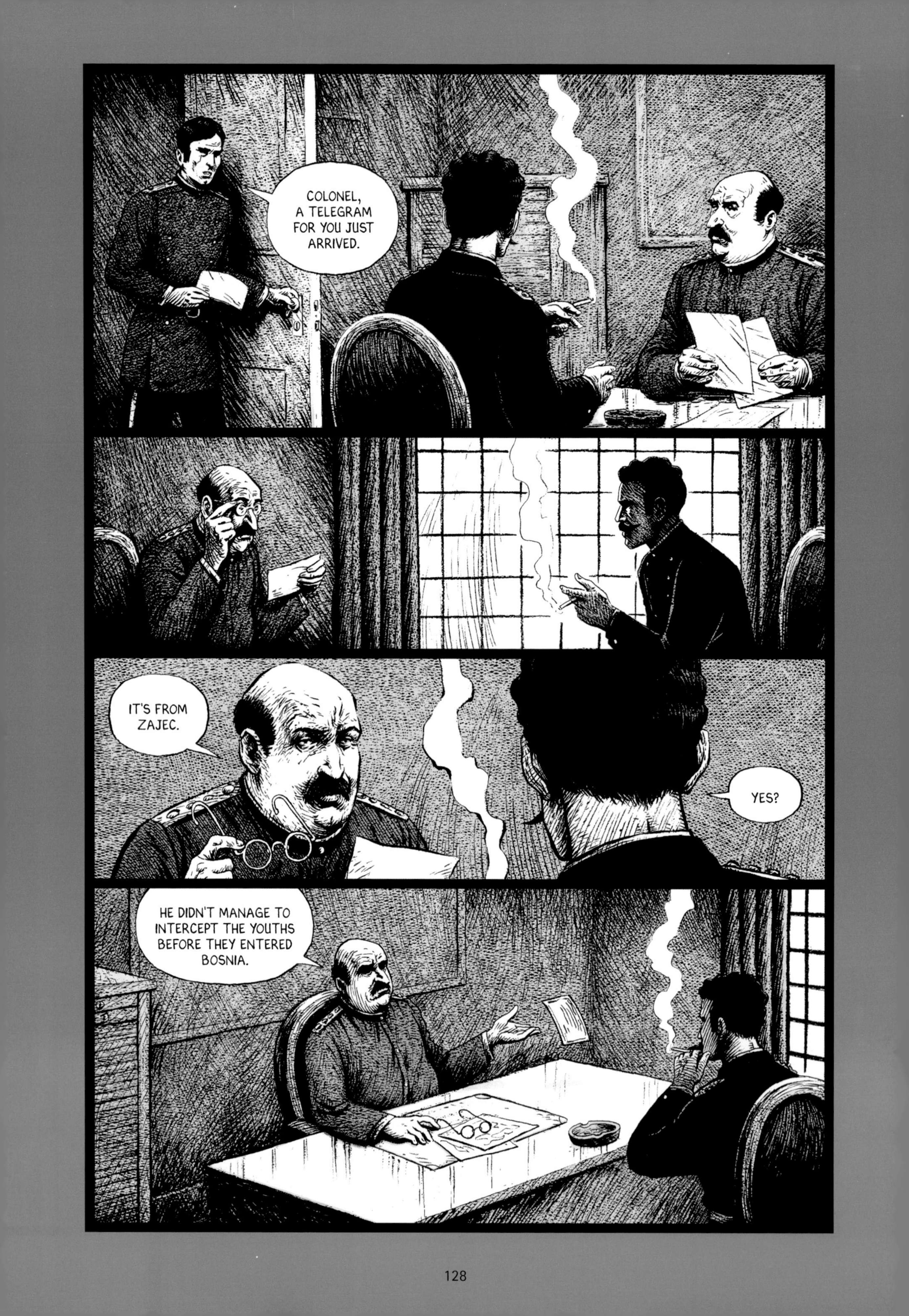
COLONEL, A TELEGRAM FOR YOU JUST ARRIVED.
IT'S FROM ZAJEC.
YES?
HE DIDN'T MANAGE TO INTERCEPT THE YOUTHS BEFORE THEY ENTERED BOSNIA.

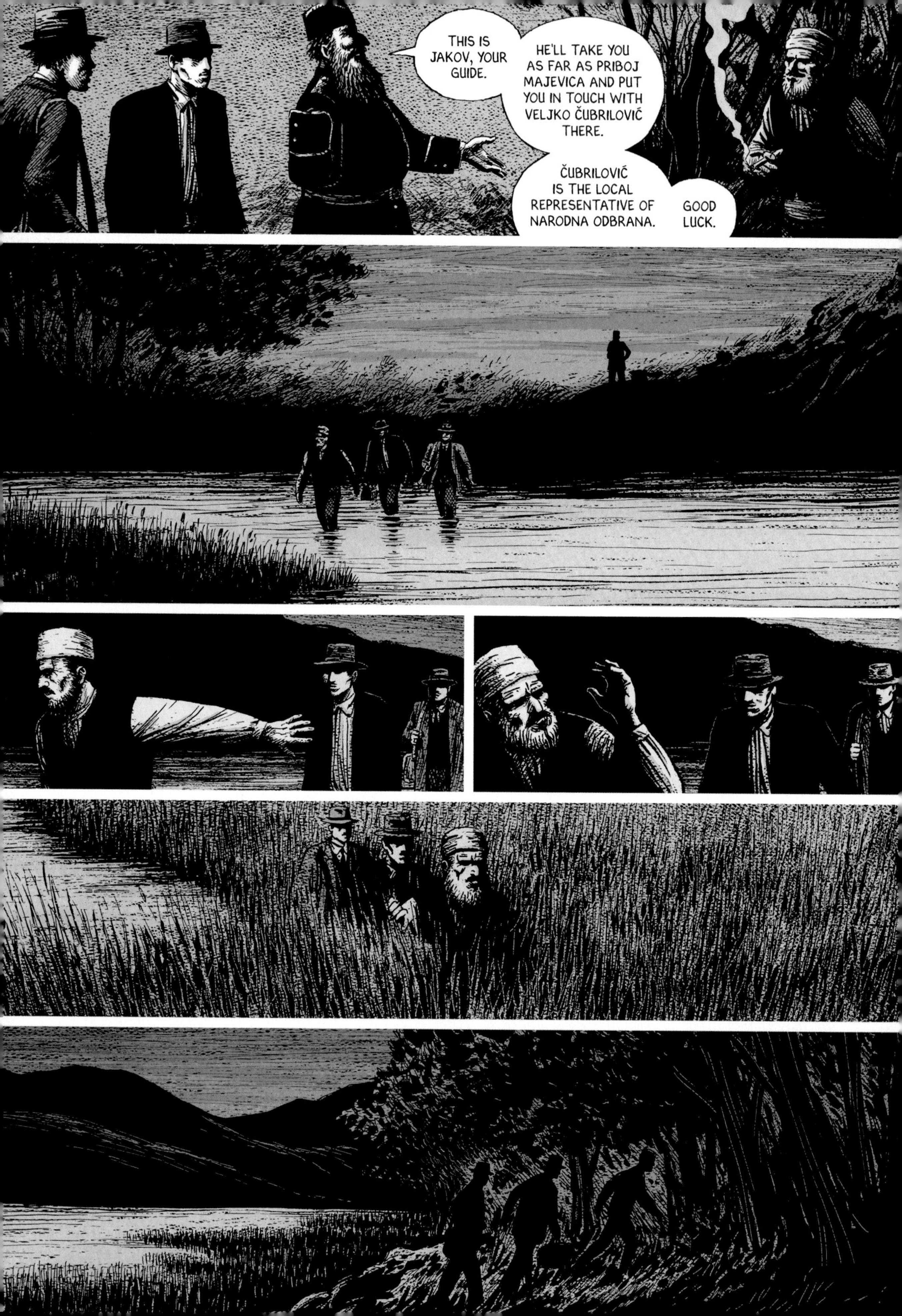
THIS IS JAKOV, YOUR GUIDE.
HE'LL TAKE YOU AS FAR AS PRIBOJ MAJEVICA AND PUT YOU IN TOUCH WITH VELJKO ČUBRILOVIĆ THERE.
ČUBRILOVIĆ IS THE LOCAL REPRESENTATIVE OF NARODNA ODBRANA.
GOOD LUCK.

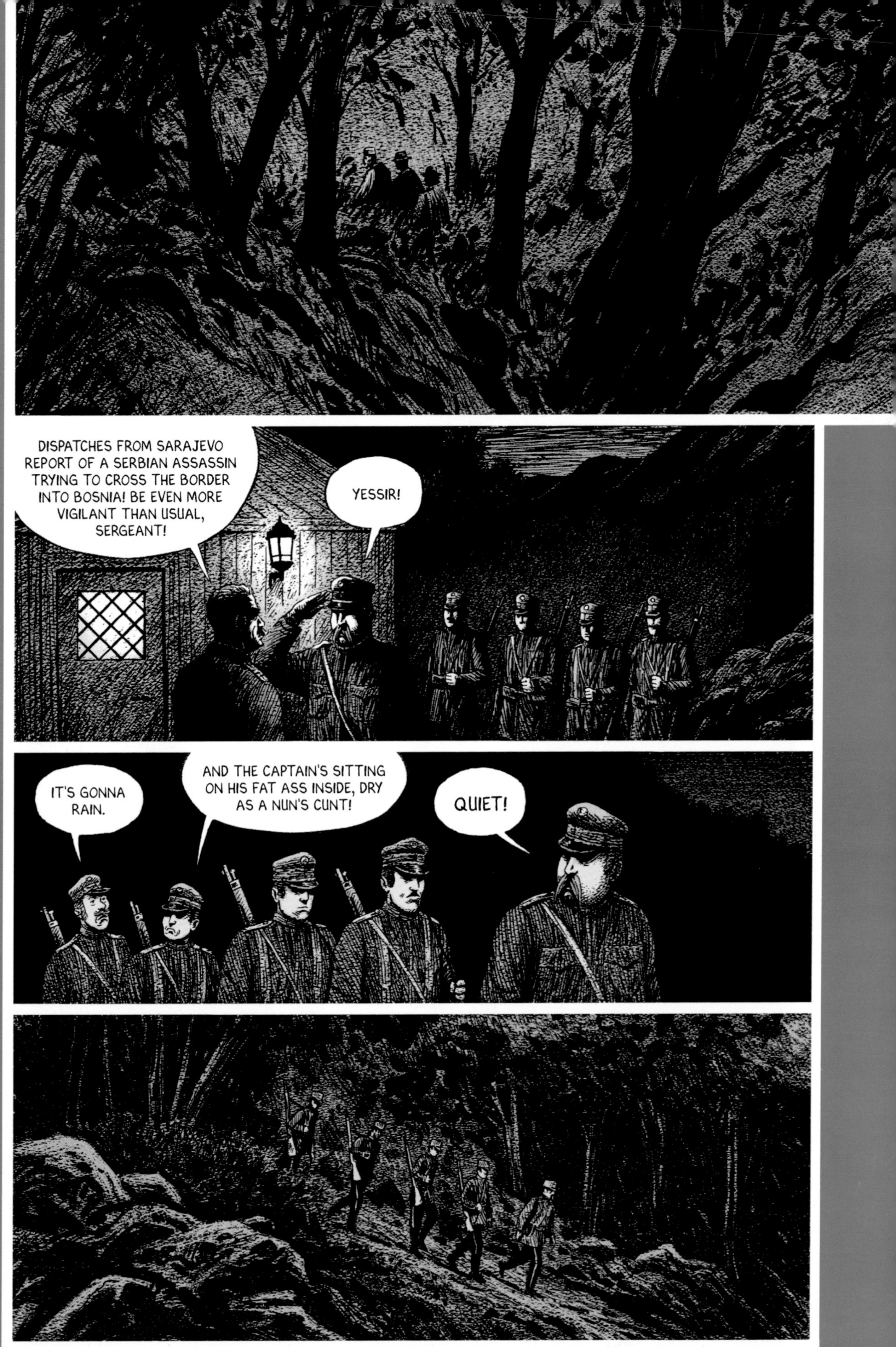
DISPATCHES FROM SARAJEVO REPORT OF A SERBIAN ASSASSIN TRYING TO CROSS THE BORDER INTO BOSNIA! BE EVEN MORE VIGILANT THAN USUAL, SERGEANT!
YESSIR!
IT'S GONNA RAIN.
AND THE CAPTAIN'S SITTING ON HIS FAT ASS INSIDE, DRY AS A NUN'S CUNT!
QUIET!

...I'M RECONCILED WITH THAT, AT PEACE WITH BOTH THE DEED AND MY OWN DEATH, BUT...

A GIRL I WAS SEEING IN BELGRADE, ANA, BEGGED ME NOT TO GO. NOT THAT SHE KNEW ANYTHING ABOUT OUR PLAN, BUT SHE MUST HAVE SENSED SOMETHING IN MY DEMEANOR...I...

WELL, SHE SAID SHE LOVED ME.

AND YOU? HOW DO YOU FEEL ABOUT HER?

HOW DO YOU KNOW THAT YOU LOVE SOMEBODY, GAVRO?

WHEN, FOR ONCE, YOUR OWN SELF IS NOT THE MOST IMPORTANT THING IN THE WORLD.

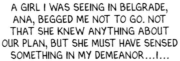

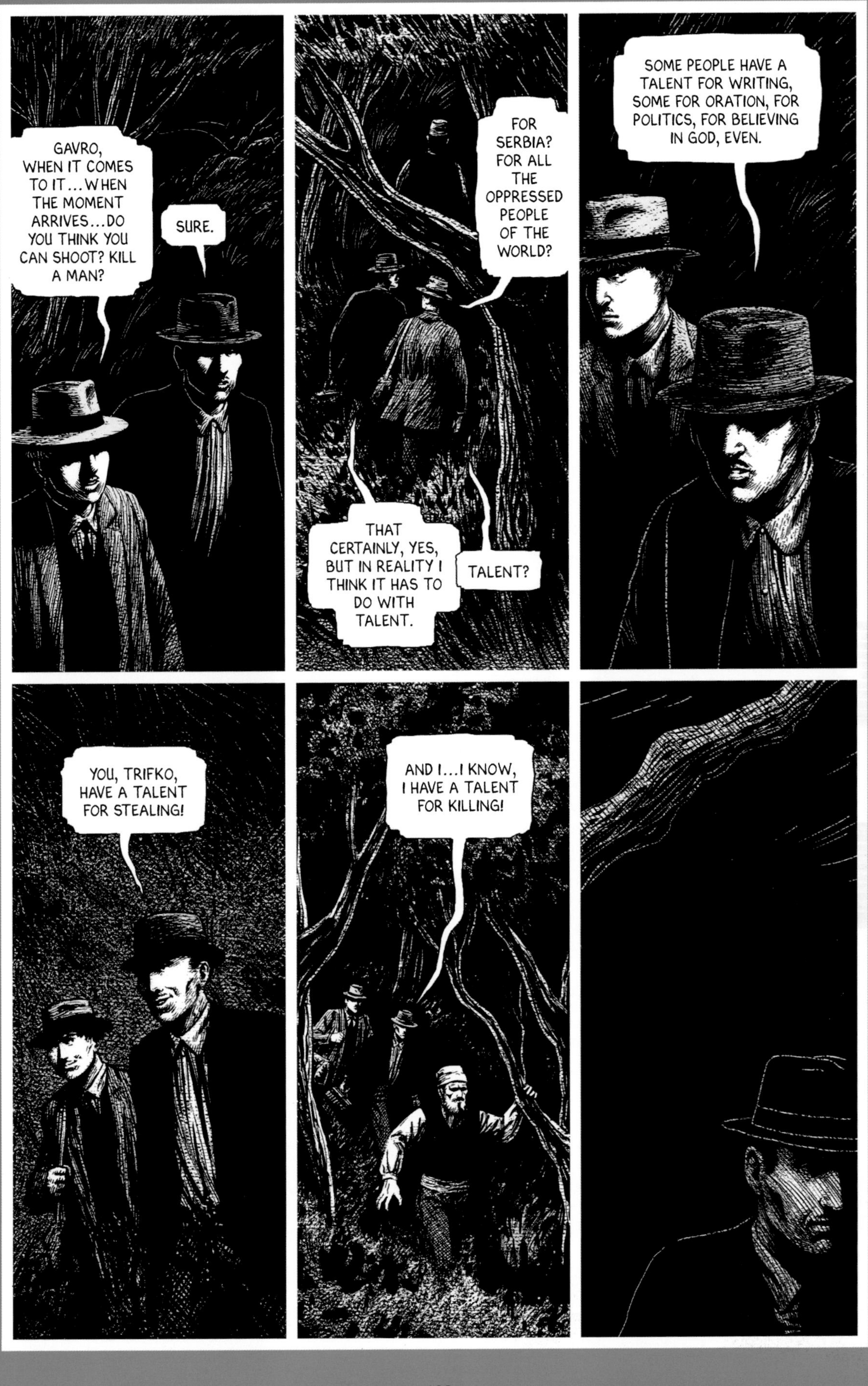
GAVRO, WHEN IT COMES TO IT... WHEN THE MOMENT ARRIVES...DO YOU THINK YOU CAN SHOOT? KILL A MAN?
SURE.
FOR SERBIA? FOR ALL THE OPPRESSED PEOPLE OF THE WORLD?
THAT CERTAINLY, YES, BUT IN REALITY I THINK IT HAS TO DO WITH TALENT.
TALENT?
SOME PEOPLE HAVE A TALENT FOR WRITING, SOME FOR ORATION, FOR POLITICS, FOR BELIEVING IN GOD, EVEN.
YOU, TRIFKO, HAVE A TALENT FOR STEALING!
AND I...I KNOW, I HAVE A TALENT FOR KILLING!

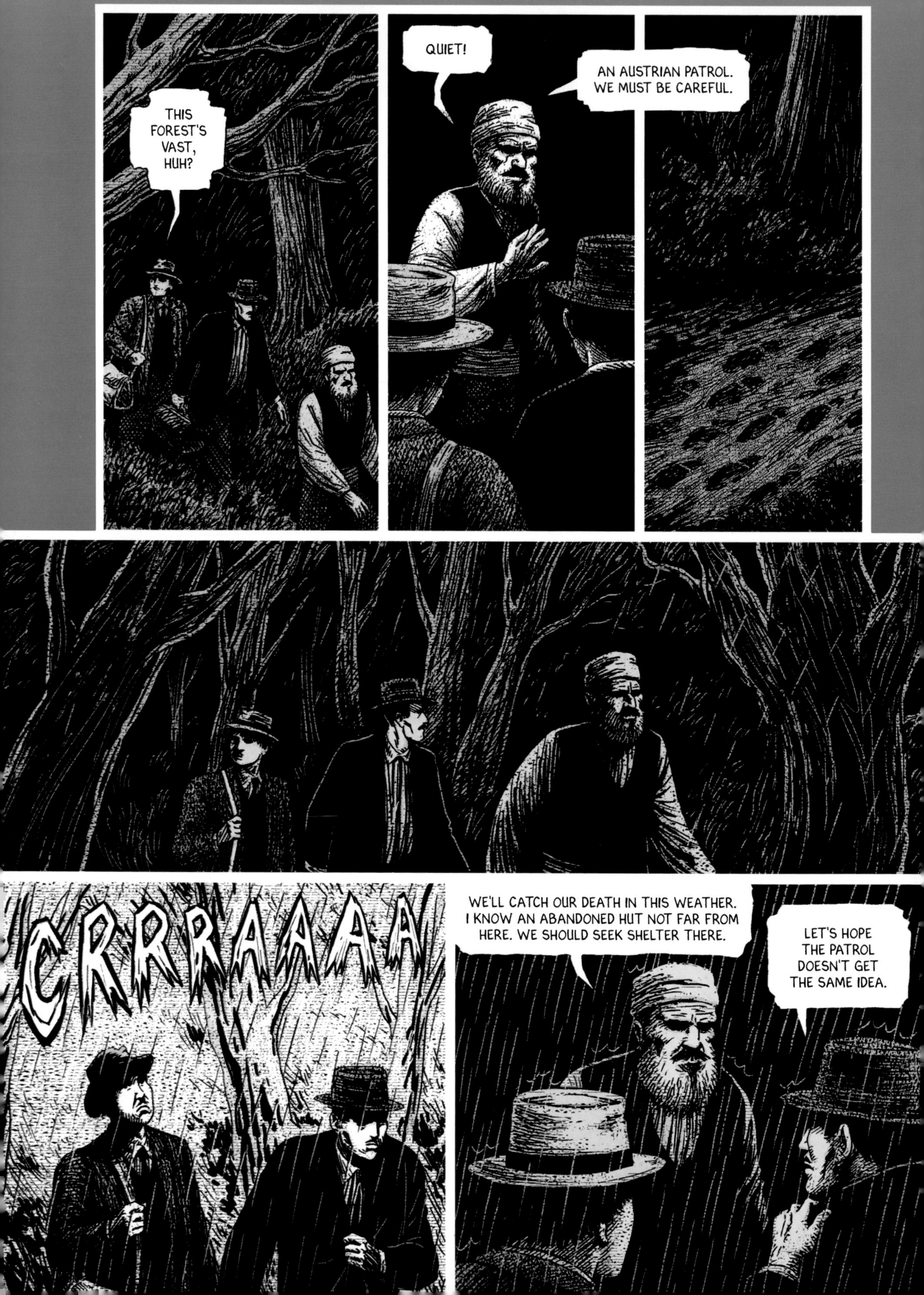
THIS FOREST'S VAST, HUH?
QUIET!
AN AUSTRIAN PATROL. WE MUST BE CAREFUL.
CRRRAAAA
WE'LL CATCH OUR DEATH IN THIS WEATHER. I KNOW AN ABANDONED HUT NOT FAR FROM HERE. WE SHOULD SEEK SHELTER THERE.
LET'S HOPE THE PATROL DOESN'T GET THE SAME IDEA.

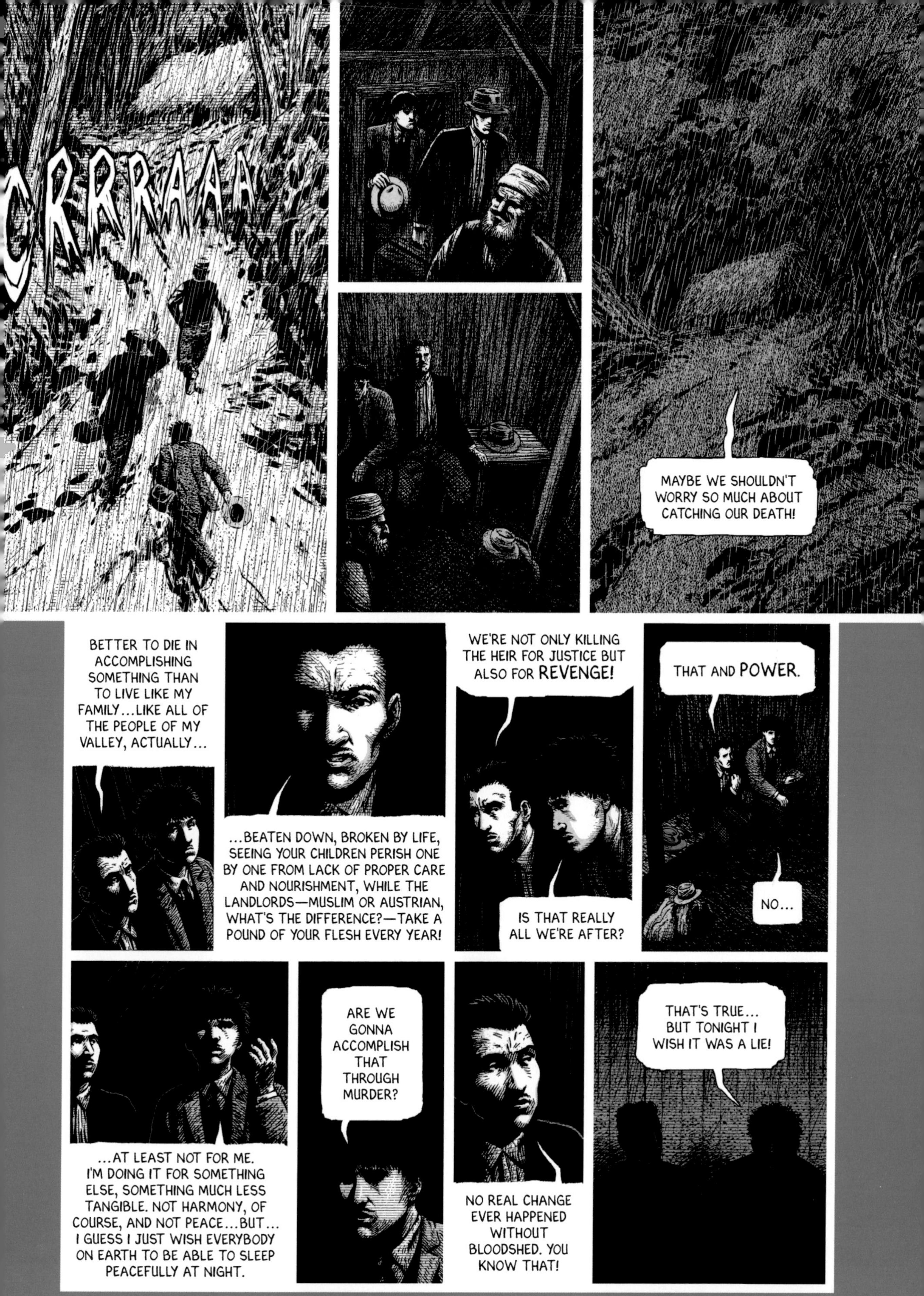
CRRRAAA
MAYBE WE SHOULDN'T WORRY SO MUCH ABOUT CATCHING OUR DEATH!
BETTER TO DIE IN ACCOMPLISHING SOMETHING THAN TO LIVE LIKE MY FAMILY...LIKE ALL OF THE PEOPLE OF MY VALLEY, ACTUALLY...
...BEATEN DOWN, BROKEN BY LIFE, SEEING YOUR CHILDREN PERISH ONE BY ONE FROM LACK OF PROPER CARE AND NOURISHMENT, WHILE THE LANDLORDS—MUSLIM OR AUSTRIAN, WHAT'S THE DIFFERENCE?—TAKE A POUND OF YOUR FLESH EVERY YEAR!
WE'RE NOT ONLY KILLING THE HEIR FOR JUSTICE BUT ALSO FOR REVENGE!
IS THAT REALLY ALL WE'RE AFTER?
THAT AND POWER.
NO...
...AT LEAST NOT FOR ME. I'M DOING IT FOR SOMETHING ELSE, SOMETHING MUCH LESS TANGIBLE. NOT HARMONY, OF COURSE, AND NOT PEACE...BUT... I GUESS I JUST WISH EVERYBODY ON EARTH TO BE ABLE TO SLEEP PEACEFULLY AT NIGHT.
ARE WE GONNA ACCOMPLISH THAT THROUGH MURDER?
NO REAL CHANGE EVER HAPPENED WITHOUT BLOODSHED. YOU KNOW THAT!
THAT'S TRUE... BUT TONIGHT I WISH IT WAS A LIE!

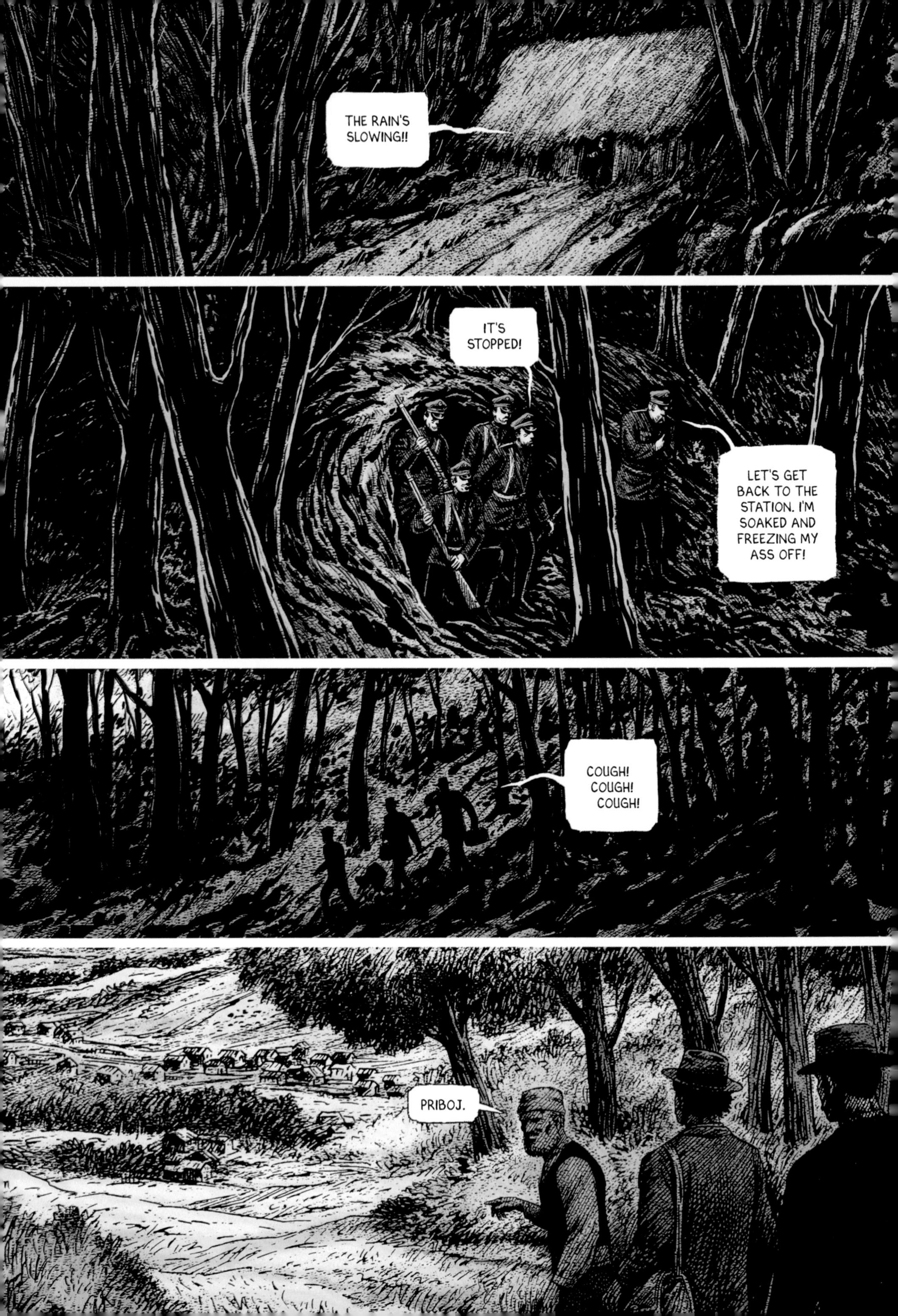
THE RAIN'S SLOWING!!
IT'S STOPPED!
LET'S GET BACK TO THE STATION. I'M SOAKED AND FREEZING MY ASS OFF!
COUGH! COUGH! COUGH!
PRIBOJ.

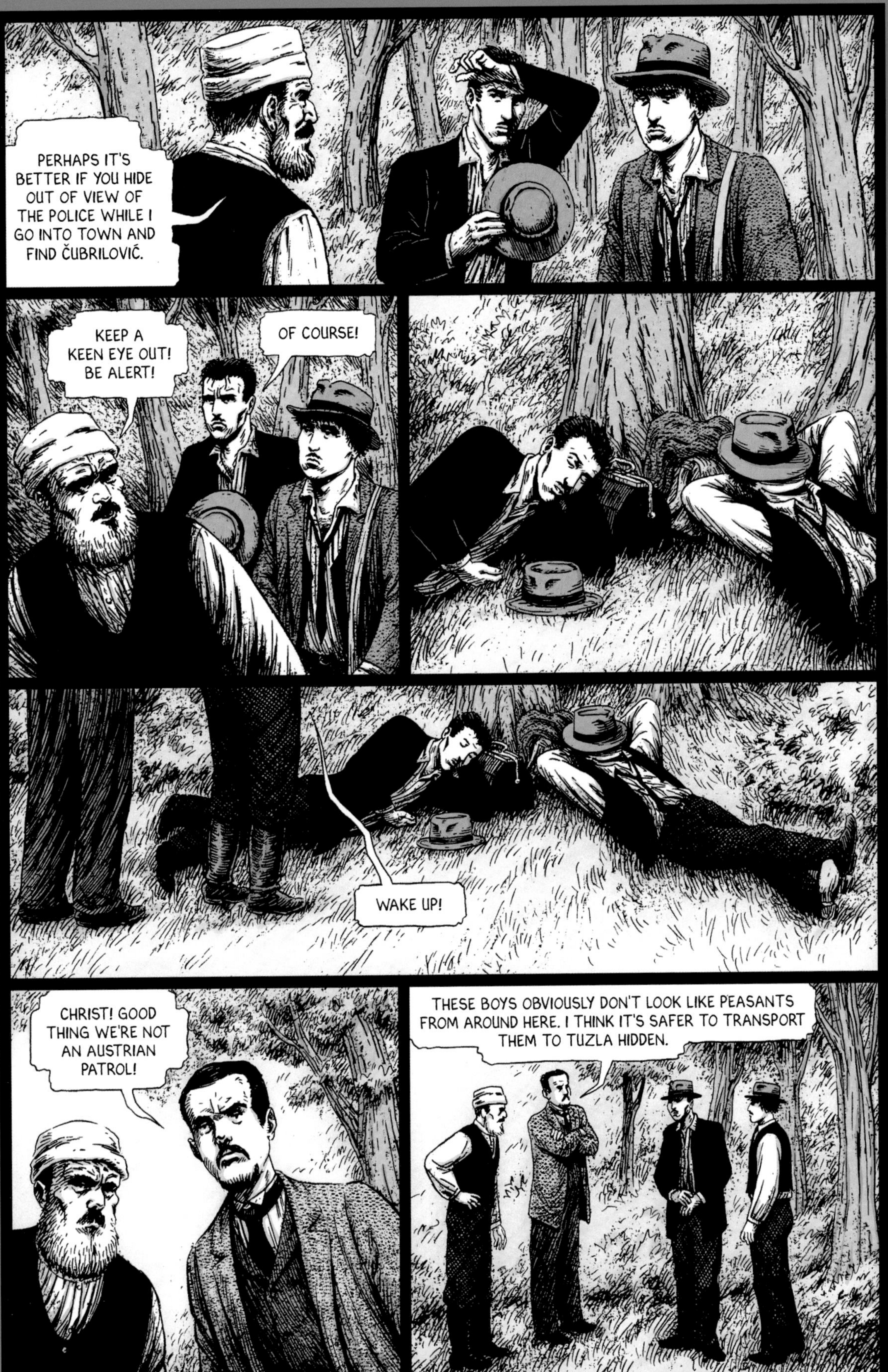
PERHAPS IT'S BETTER IF YOU HIDE OUT OF VIEW OF THE POLICE WHILE I GO INTO TOWN AND FIND ČUBRILOVIĆ.
KEEP A KEEN EYE OUT! BE ALERT!
OF COURSE!
WAKE UP!
CHRIST! GOOD THING WE'RE NOT AN AUSTRIAN PATROL!
THESE BOYS OBVIOUSLY DON'T LOOK LIKE PEASANTS FROM AROUND HERE. I THINK IT'S SAFER TO TRANSPORT THEM TO TUZLA HIDDEN.

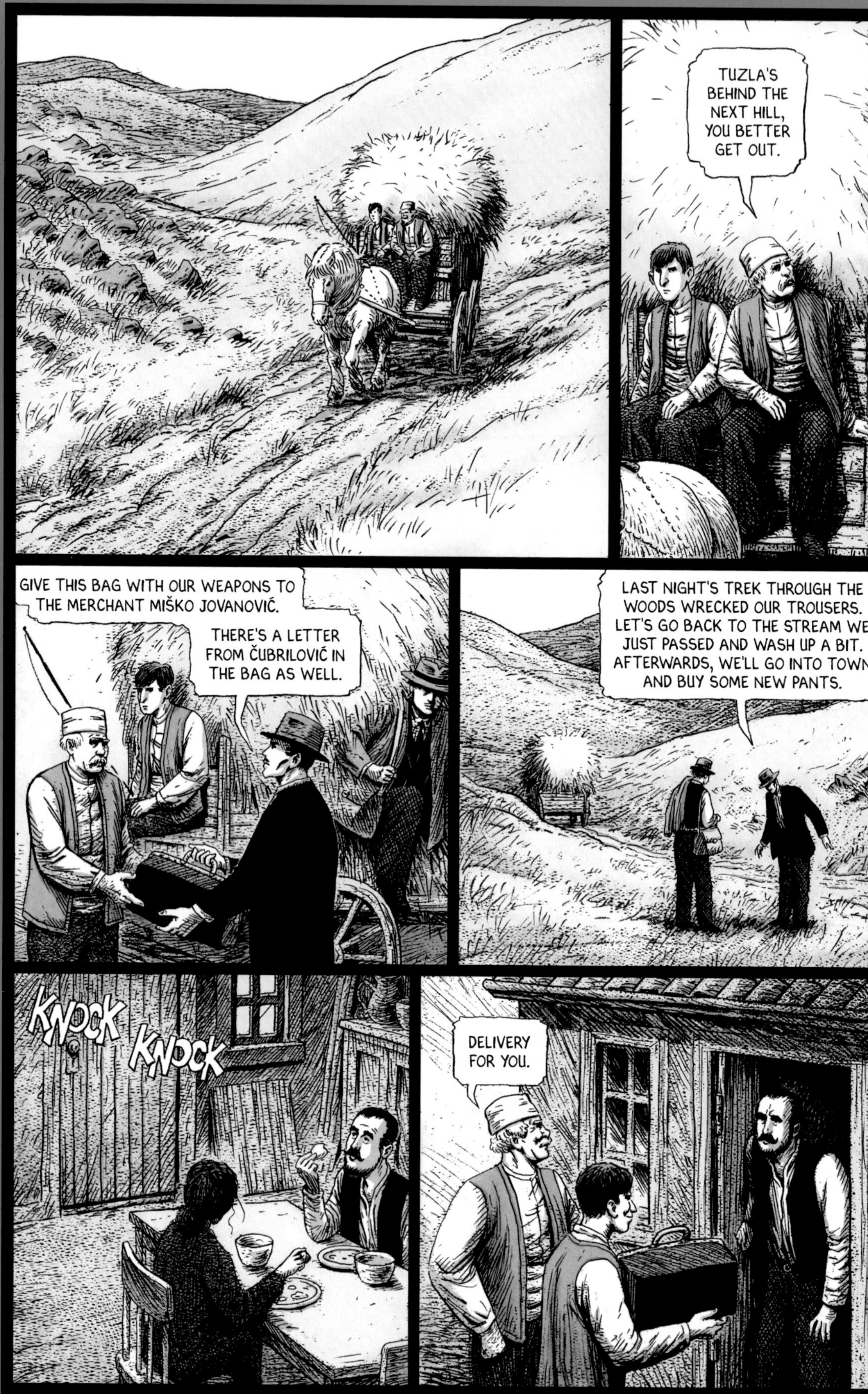
TUZLA'S BEHIND THE NEXT HILL, YOU BETTER GET OUT.
GIVE THIS BAG WITH OUR WEAPONS TO THE MERCHANT MIŠKO JOVANOVIĆ.
THERE'S A LETTER FROM ČUBRILOVIĆ IN THE BAG AS WELL.
LAST NIGHT'S TREK THROUGH THE WOODS WRECKED OUR TROUSERS. LET'S GO BACK TO THE STREAM WE JUST PASSED AND WASH UP A BIT. AFTERWARDS, WE'LL GO INTO TOWN AND BUY SOME NEW PANTS.
KNOCK KNOCK
DELIVERY FOR YOU.

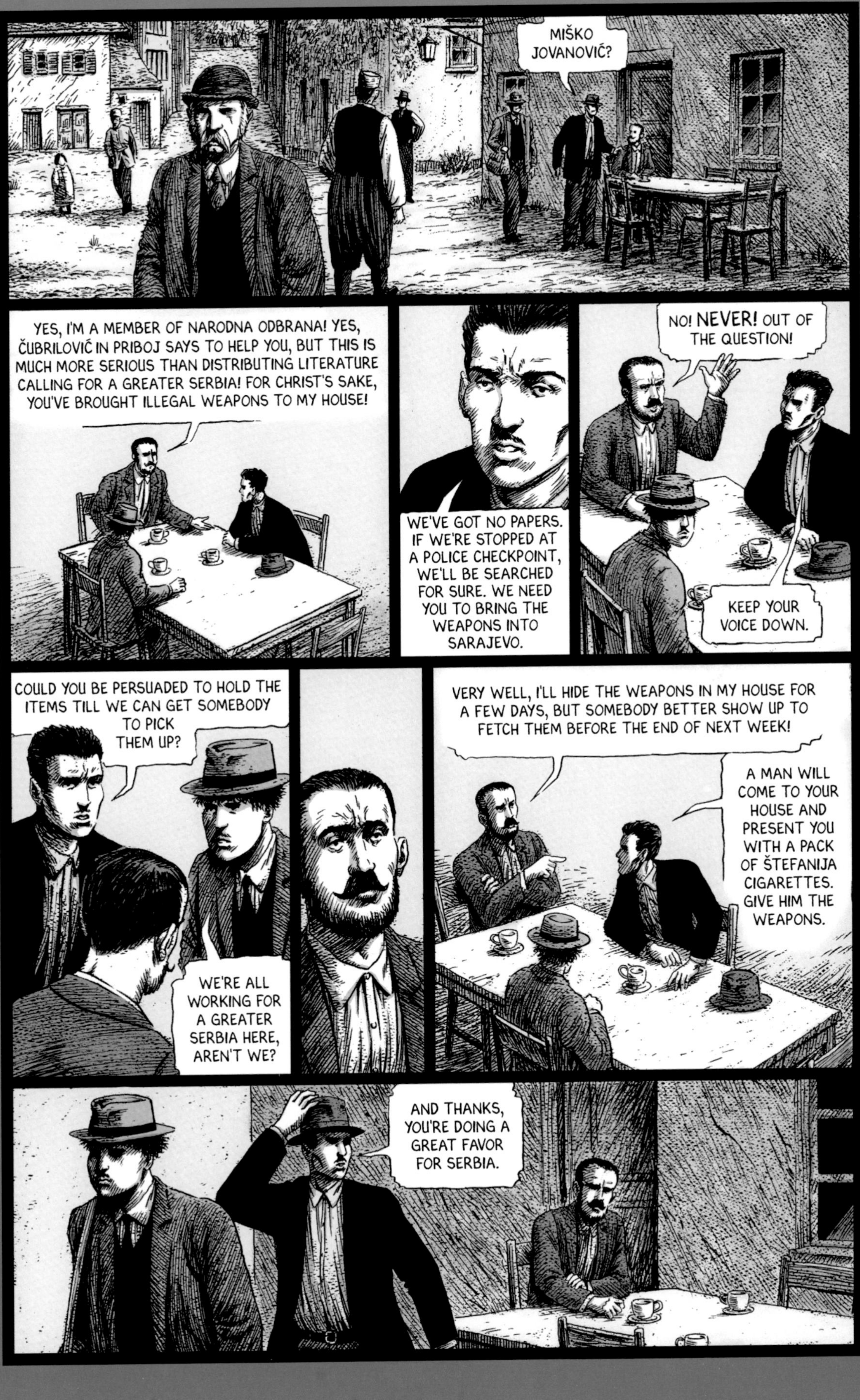
MIŠKO JOVANOVIĆ?
YES, I'M A MEMBER OF NARODNA ODBRANA! YES, ČUBRILOVIĆ IN PRIBOJ SAYS TO HELP YOU, BUT THIS IS MUCH MORE SERIOUS THAN DISTRIBUTING LITERATURE CALLING FOR A GREATER SERBIA! FOR CHRIST'S SAKE, YOU'VE BROUGHT ILLEGAL WEAPONS TO MY HOUSE!
WE'VE GOT NO PAPERS. IF WE'RE STOPPED AT A POLICE CHECKPOINT, WE'LL BE SEARCHED FOR SURE. WE NEED YOU TO BRING THE WEAPONS INTO SARAJEVO.
NO! NEVER! OUT OF THE QUESTION!
KEEP YOUR VOICE DOWN.
COULD YOU BE PERSUADED TO HOLD THE ITEMS TILL WE CAN GET SOMEBODY TO PICK THEM UP?
WE'RE ALL WORKING FOR A GREATER SERBIA HERE, AREN'T WE?
VERY WELL, I'LL HIDE THE WEAPONS IN MY HOUSE FOR A FEW DAYS, BUT SOMEBODY BETTER SHOW UP TO FETCH THEM BEFORE THE END OF NEXT WEEK!
A MAN WILL COME TO YOUR HOUSE AND PRESENT YOU WITH A PACK OF ŠTEFANIJA CIGARETTES. GIVE HIM THE WEAPONS.
AND THANKS, YOU'RE DOING A GREAT FAVOR FOR SERBIA.

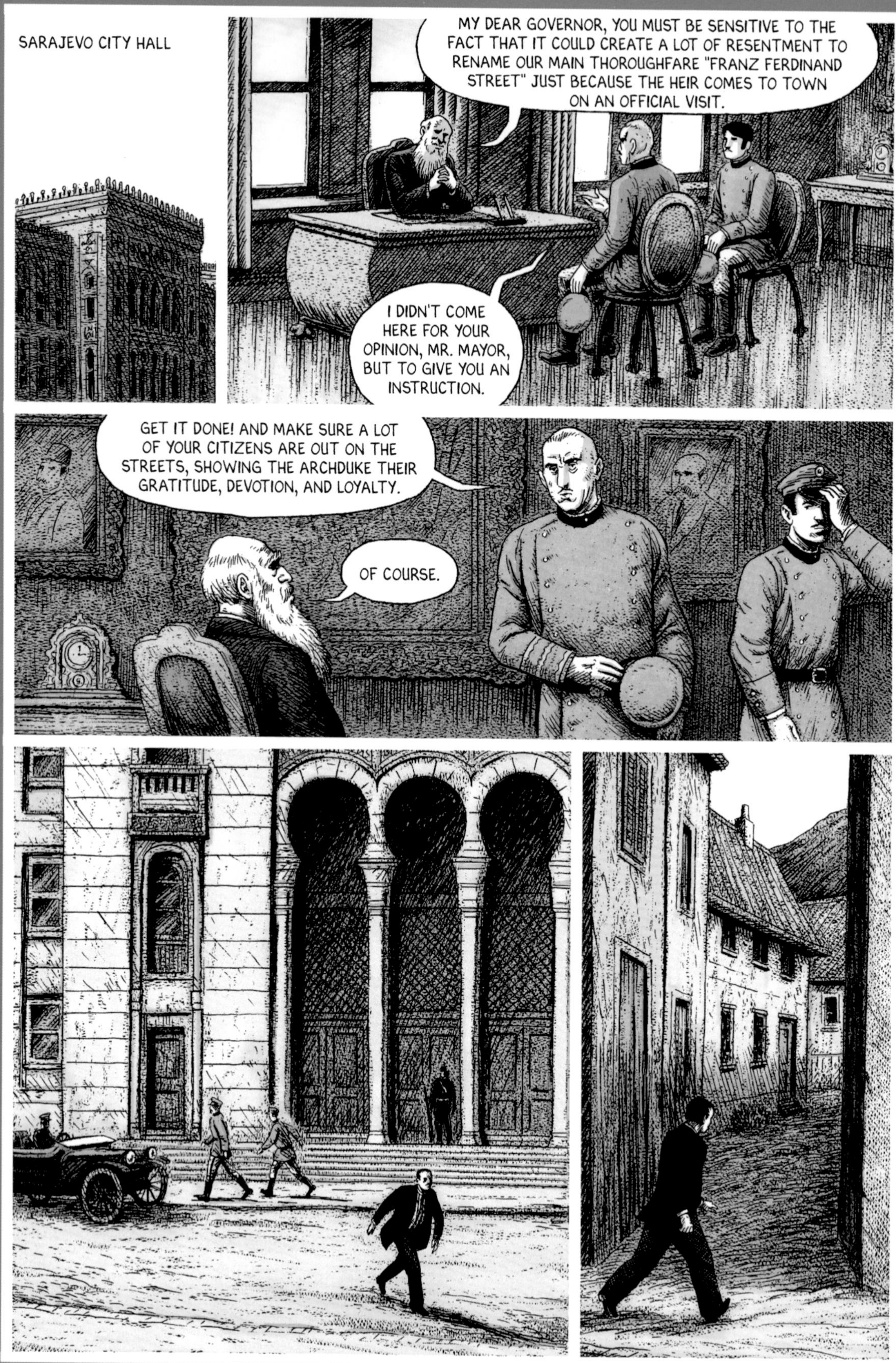
SARAJEVO CITY HALL
MY DEAR GOVERNOR, YOU MUST BE SENSITIVE TO THE FACT THAT IT COULD CREATE A LOT OF RESENTMENT TO RENAME OUR MAIN THOROUGHFARE "FRANZ FERDINAND STREET" JUST BECAUSE THE HEIR COMES TO TOWN ON AN OFFICIAL VISIT.
I DIDN'T COME HERE FOR YOUR OPINION, MR. MAYOR, BUT TO GIVE YOU AN INSTRUCTION.
GET IT DONE! AND MAKE SURE A LOT OF YOUR CITIZENS ARE OUT ON THE STREETS, SHOWING THE ARCHDUKE THEIR GRATITUDE, DEVOTION, AND LOYALTY.
OF COURSE.

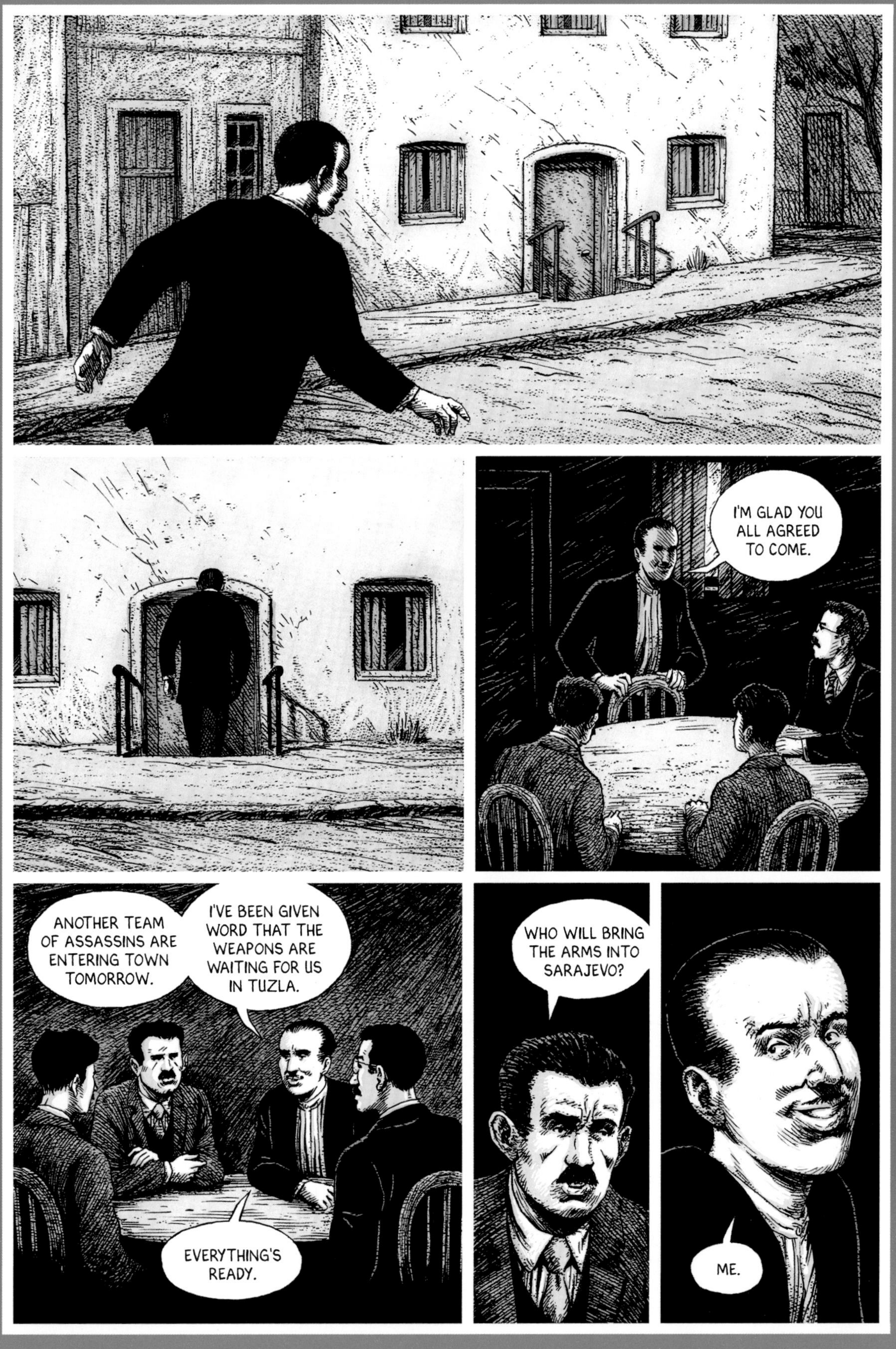
I'M GLAD YOU ALL AGREED TO COME.
ANOTHER TEAM OF ASSASSINS ARE ENTERING TOWN TOMORROW.
I'VE BEEN GIVEN WORD THAT THE WEAPONS ARE WAITING FOR US IN TUZLA.
EVERYTHING'S READY.
WHO WILL BRING THE ARMS INTO SARAJEVO?
ME.

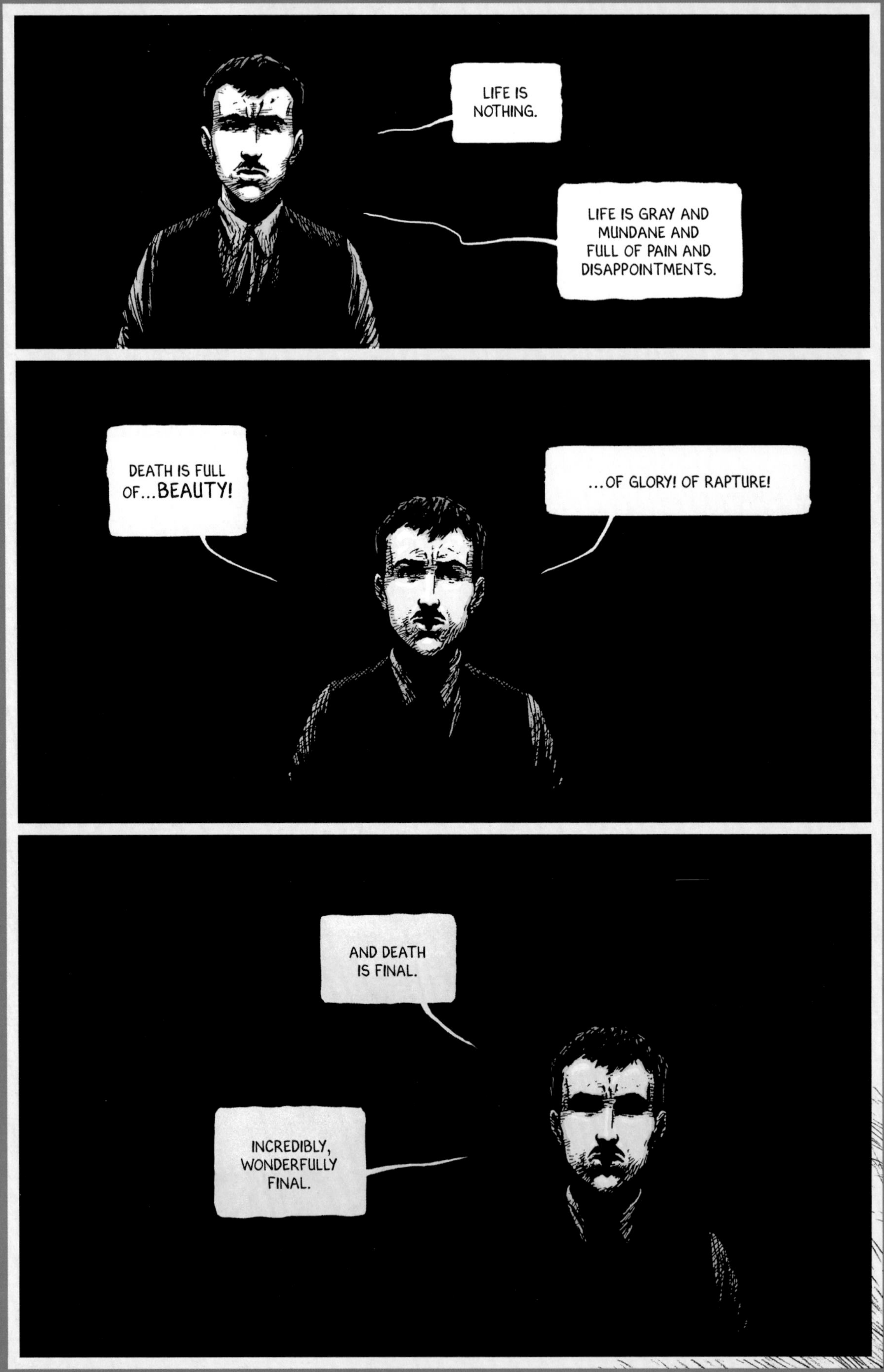
LIFE IS NOTHING.
LIFE IS GRAY AND MUNDANE AND FULL OF PAIN AND DISAPPOINTMENTS.
DEATH IS FULL OF...BEAUTY!
...OF GLORY! OF RAPTURE!
AND DEATH IS FINAL.
INCREDIBLY, WONDERFULLY FINAL.

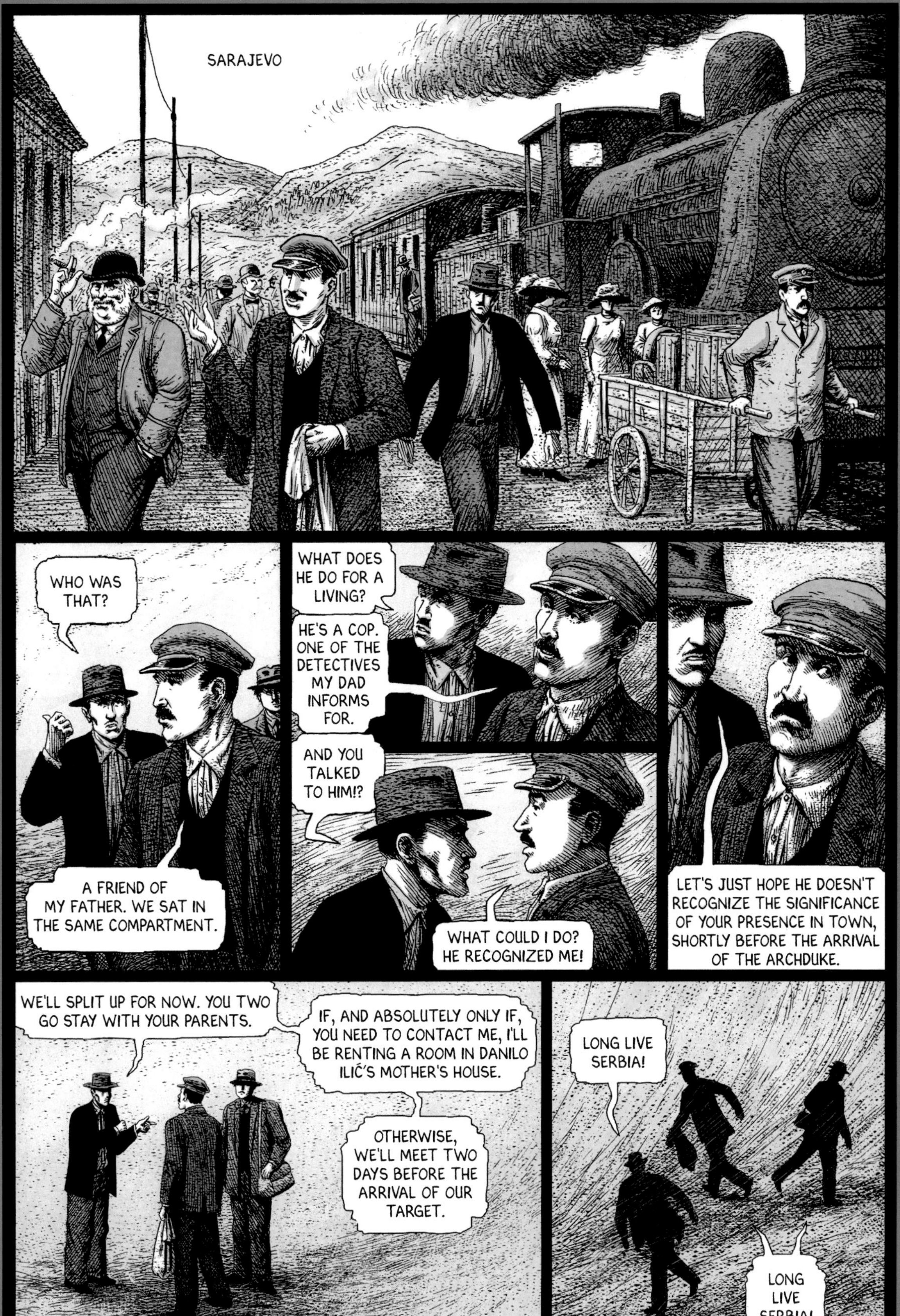
SARAJEVO
WHO WAS THAT?
A FRIEND OF MY FATHER. WE SAT IN THE SAME COMPARTMENT.
WHAT DOES HE DO FOR A LIVING?
HE'S A COP. ONE OF THE DETECTIVES MY DAD INFORMS FOR.
AND YOU TALKED TO HIM!?
WHAT COULD I DO? HE RECOGNIZED ME!
LET'S JUST HOPE HE DOESN'T RECOGNIZE THE SIGNIFICANCE OF YOUR PRESENCE IN TOWN, SHORTLY BEFORE THE ARRIVAL OF THE ARCHDUKE.
WE'LL SPLIT UP FOR NOW. YOU TWO GO STAY WITH YOUR PARENTS.
IF, AND ABSOLUTELY ONLY IF, YOU NEED TO CONTACT ME, I'LL BE RENTING A ROOM IN DANILO ILIĆ'S MOTHER'S HOUSE.
OTHERWISE, WE'LL MEET TWO DAYS BEFORE THE ARRIVAL OF OUR TARGET.
LONG LIVE SERBIA!
LONG LIVE SERBIA!

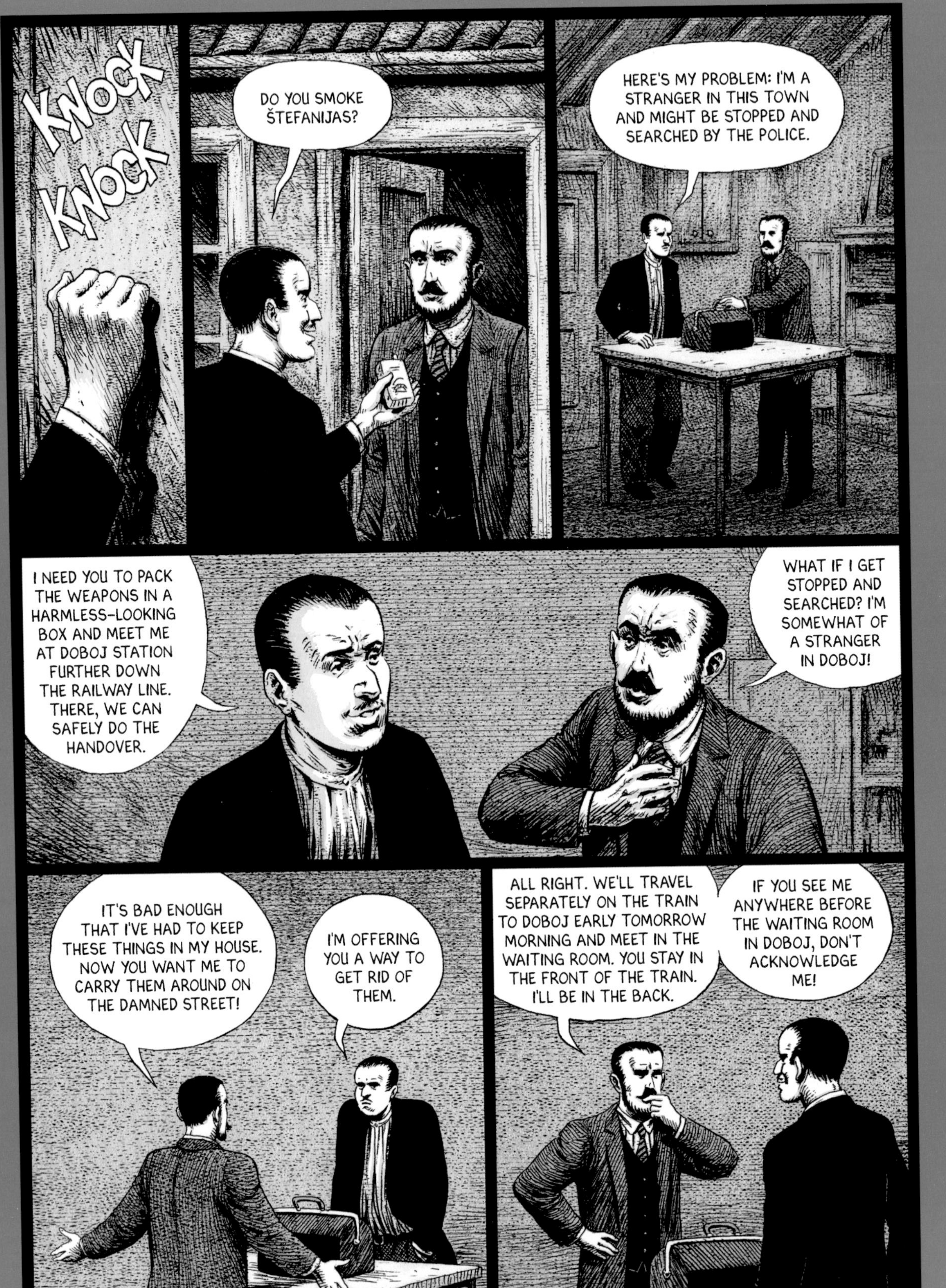
KNOCK KNOCK
DO YOU SMOKE ŠTEFANIJAS?
HERE'S MY PROBLEM: I'M A STRANGER IN THIS TOWN AND MIGHT BE STOPPED AND SEARCHED BY THE POLICE.
I NEED YOU TO PACK THE WEAPONS IN A HARMLESS-LOOKING BOX AND MEET ME AT DOBOJ STATION FURTHER DOWN THE RAILWAY LINE. THERE, WE CAN SAFELY DO THE HANDOVER.
WHAT IF I GET STOPPED AND SEARCHED? I'M SOMEWHAT OF A STRANGER IN DOBOJ!
IT'S BAD ENOUGH THAT I'VE HAD TO KEEP THESE THINGS IN MY HOUSE. NOW YOU WANT ME TO CARRY THEM AROUND ON THE DAMNED STREET!
I'M OFFERING YOU A WAY TO GET RID OF THEM.
ALL RIGHT. WE'LL TRAVEL SEPARATELY ON THE TRAIN TO DOBOJ EARLY TOMORROW MORNING AND MEET IN THE WAITING ROOM. YOU STAY IN THE FRONT OF THE TRAIN. I'LL BE IN THE BACK.
IF YOU SEE ME ANYWHERE BEFORE THE WAITING ROOM IN DOBOJ, DON'T ACKNOWLEDGE ME!

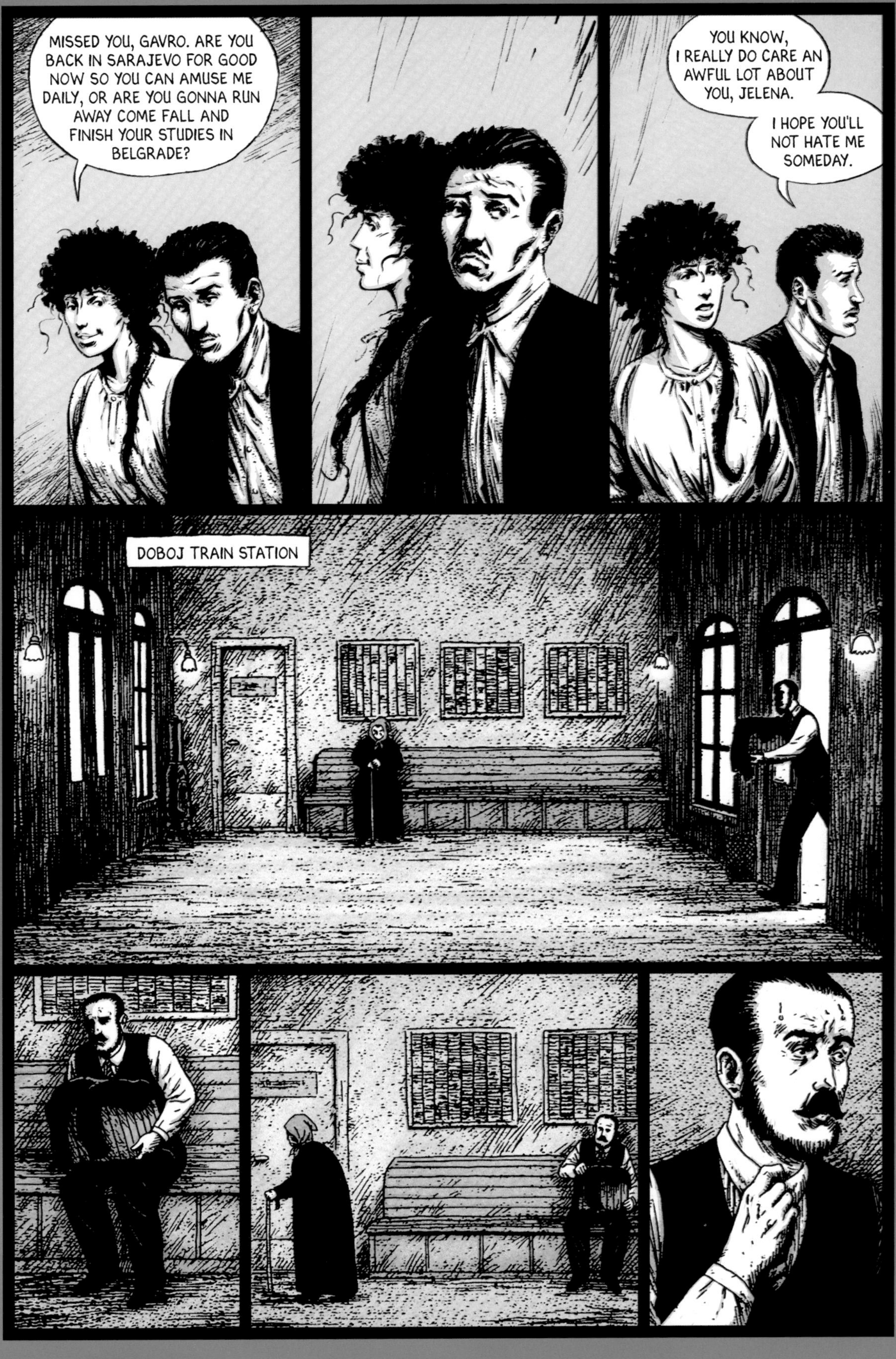
MISSED YOU, GAVRO. ARE YOU BACK IN SARAJEVO FOR GOOD NOW SO YOU CAN AMUSE ME DAILY, OR ARE YOU GONNA RUN AWAY COME FALL AND FINISH YOUR STUDIES IN BELGRADE?
YOU KNOW, I REALLY DO CARE AN AWFUL LOT ABOUT YOU, JELENA.
I HOPE YOU'LL NOT HATE ME SOMEDAY.
DOBOJ TRAIN STATION

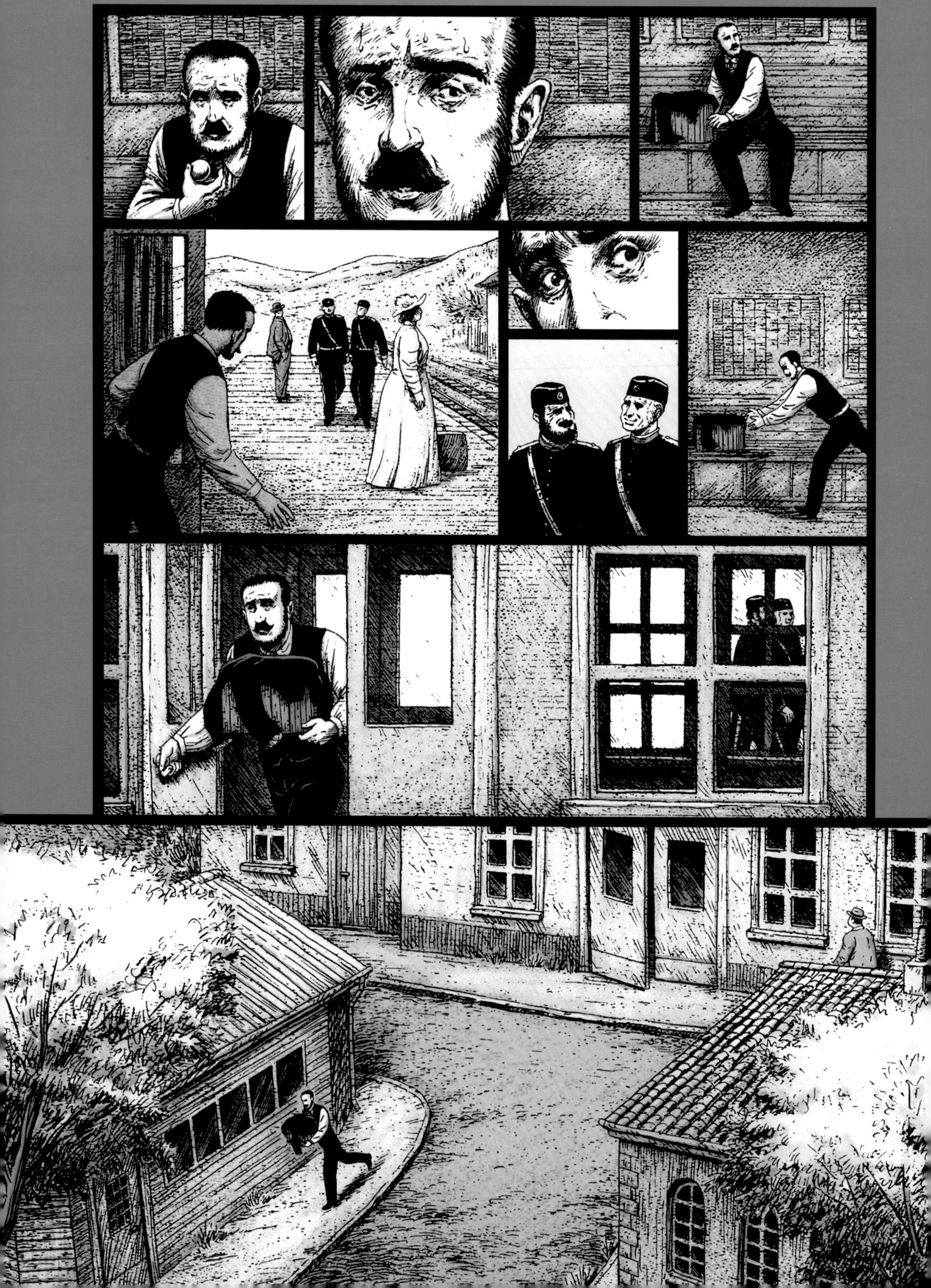

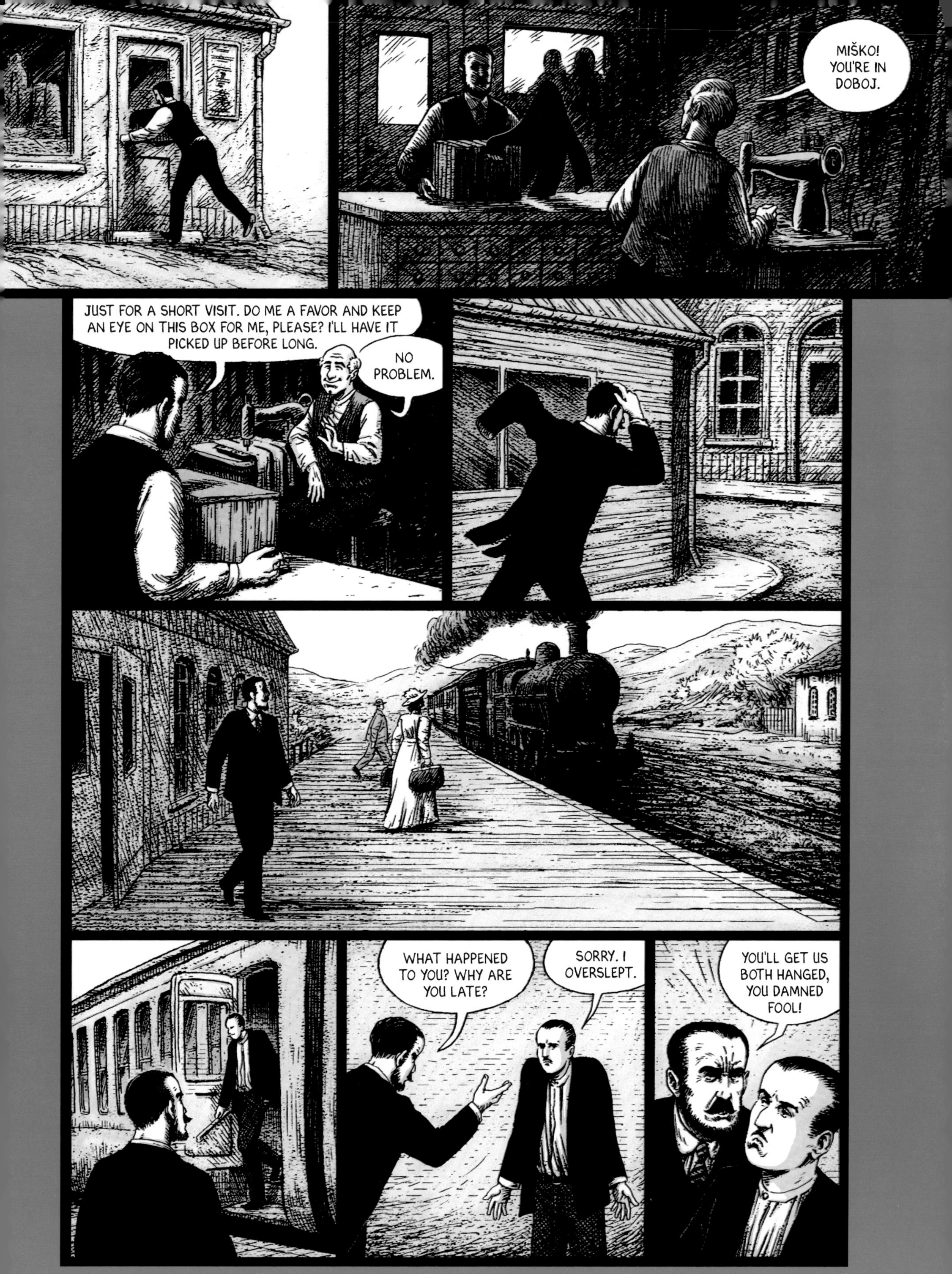
MIŠKO! YOU'RE IN DOBOJ.
JUST FOR A SHORT VISIT. DO ME A FAVOR AND KEEP AN EYE ON THIS BOX FOR ME, PLEASE? I'LL HAVE IT PICKED UP BEFORE LONG.
NO PROBLEM.
WHAT HAPPENED TO YOU? WHY ARE YOU LATE?
SORRY. I OVERSLEPT.
YOU'LL GET US BOTH HANGED, YOU DAMNED FOOL!

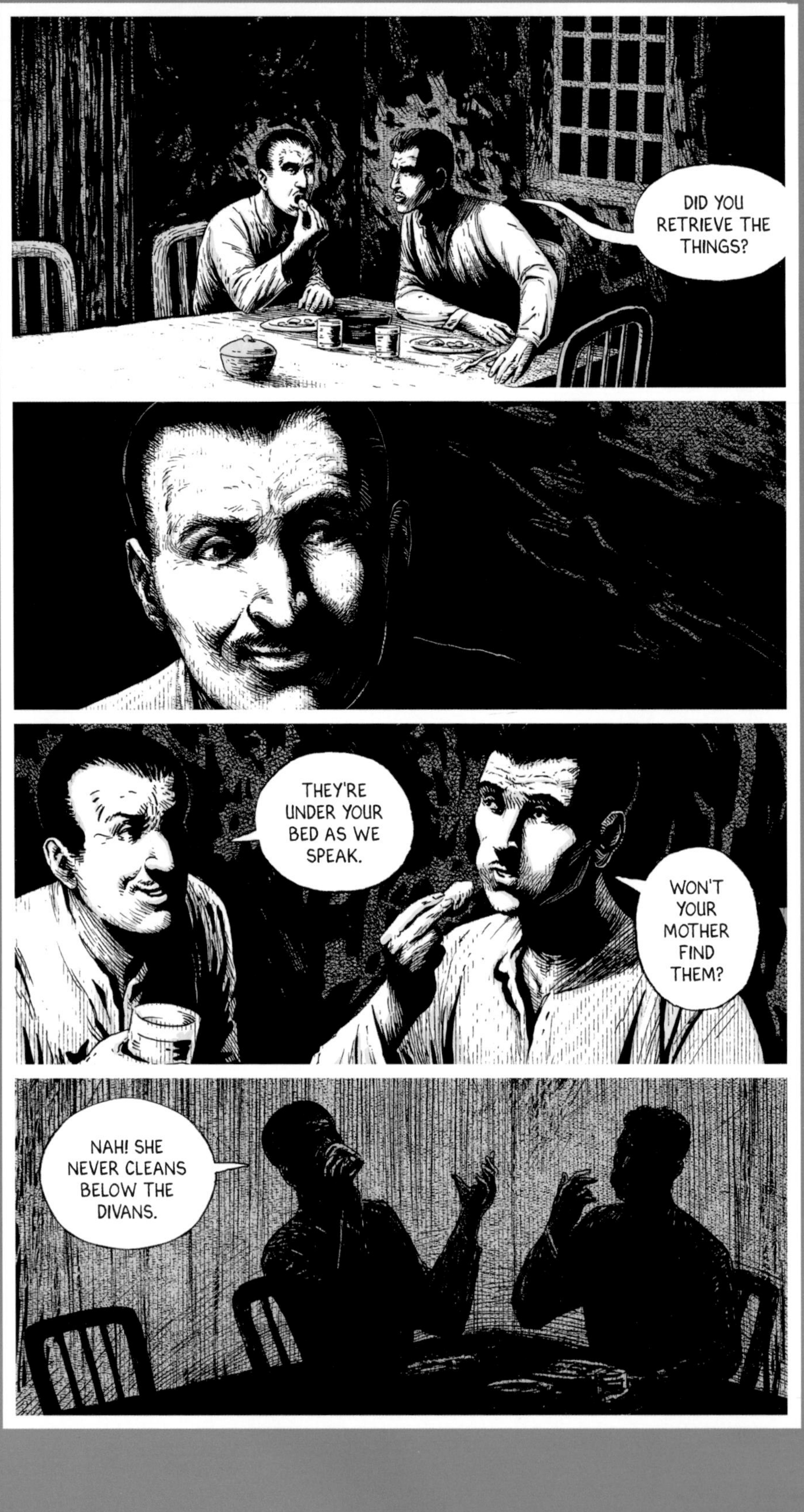
DID YOU RETRIEVE THE THINGS?
THEY'RE UNDER YOUR BED AS WE SPEAK.
WON'T YOUR MOTHER FIND THEM?
NAH! SHE NEVER CLEANS BELOW THE DIVANS.

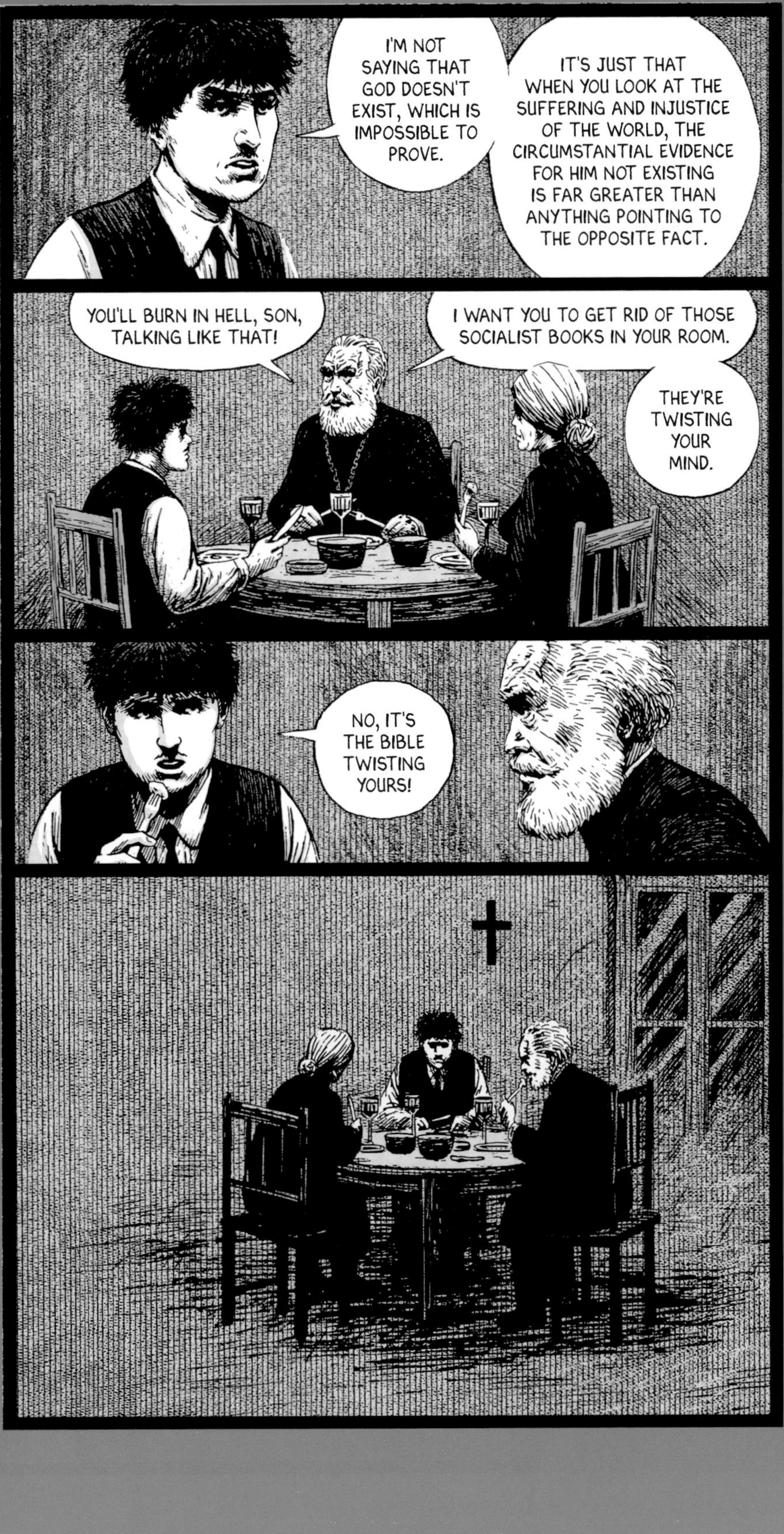
I'M NOT SAYING THAT GOD DOESN'T EXIST, WHICH IS IMPOSSIBLE TO PROVE.
IT'S JUST THAT WHEN YOU LOOK AT THE SUFFERING AND INJUSTICE OF THE WORLD, THE CIRCUMSTANTIAL EVIDENCE FOR HIM NOT EXISTING IS FAR GREATER THAN ANYTHING POINTING TO THE OPPOSITE FACT.
YOU'LL BURN IN HELL, SON, TALKING LIKE THAT!
I WANT YOU TO GET RID OF THOSE SOCIALIST BOOKS IN YOUR ROOM.
THEY'RE TWISTING YOUR MIND.
NO, IT'S THE BIBLE TWISTING YOURS!

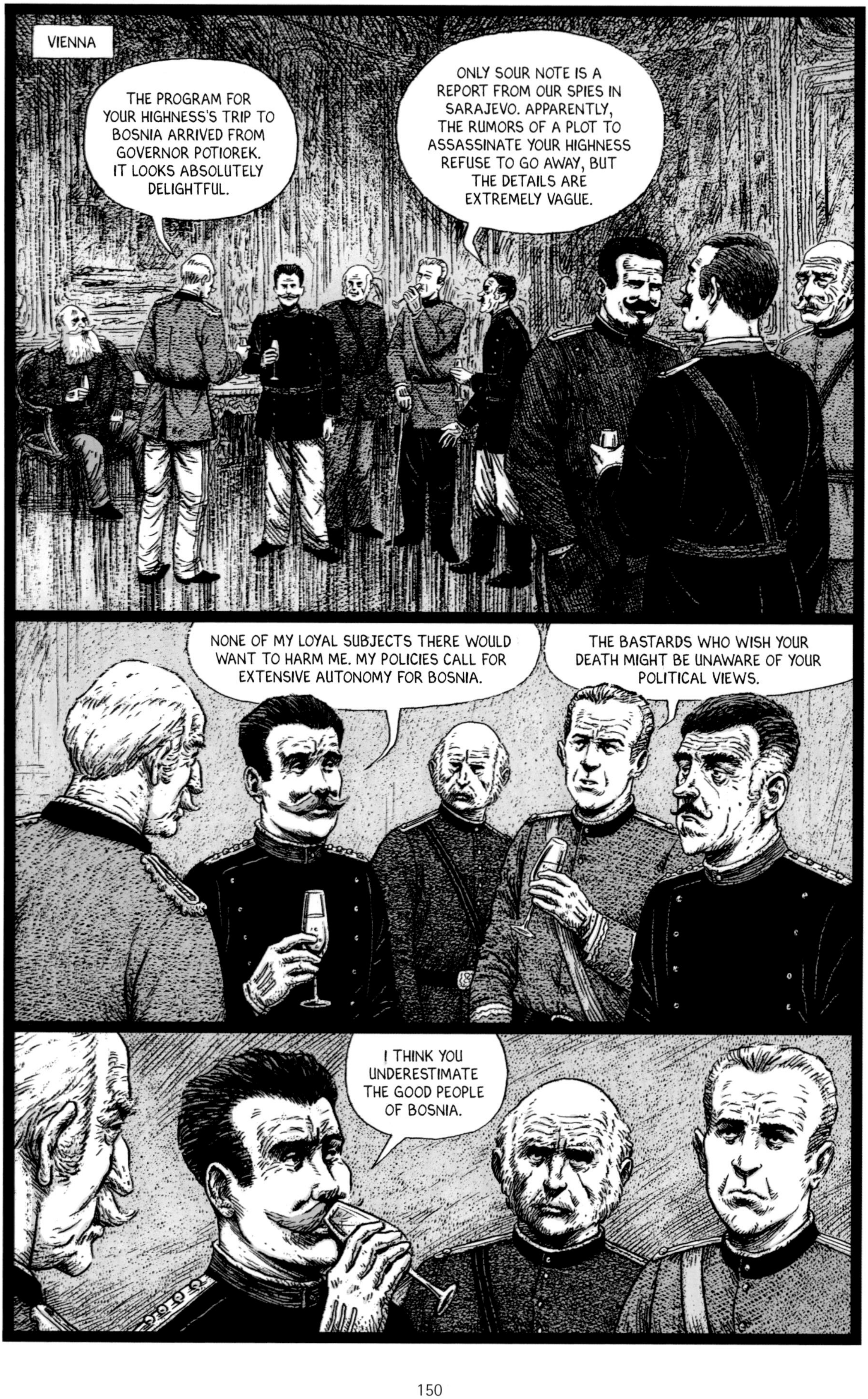
VIENNA
THE PROGRAM FOR YOUR HIGHNESS'S TRIP TO BOSNIA ARRIVED FROM GOVERNOR POTIOREK. IT LOOKS ABSOLUTELY DELIGHTFUL.
ONLY SOUR NOTE IS A REPORT FROM OUR SPIES IN SARAJEVO. APPARENTLY, THE RUMORS OF A PLOT TO ASSASSINATE YOUR HIGHNESS REFUSE TO GO AWAY, BUT THE DETAILS ARE EXTREMELY VAGUE.
NONE OF MY LOYAL SUBJECTS THERE WOULD WANT TO HARM ME. MY POLICIES CALL FOR EXTENSIVE AUTONOMY FOR BOSNIA.
THE BASTARDS WHO WISH YOUR DEATH MIGHT BE UNAWARE OF YOUR POLITICAL VIEWS.
I THINK YOU UNDERESTIMATE THE GOOD PEOPLE OF BOSNIA.

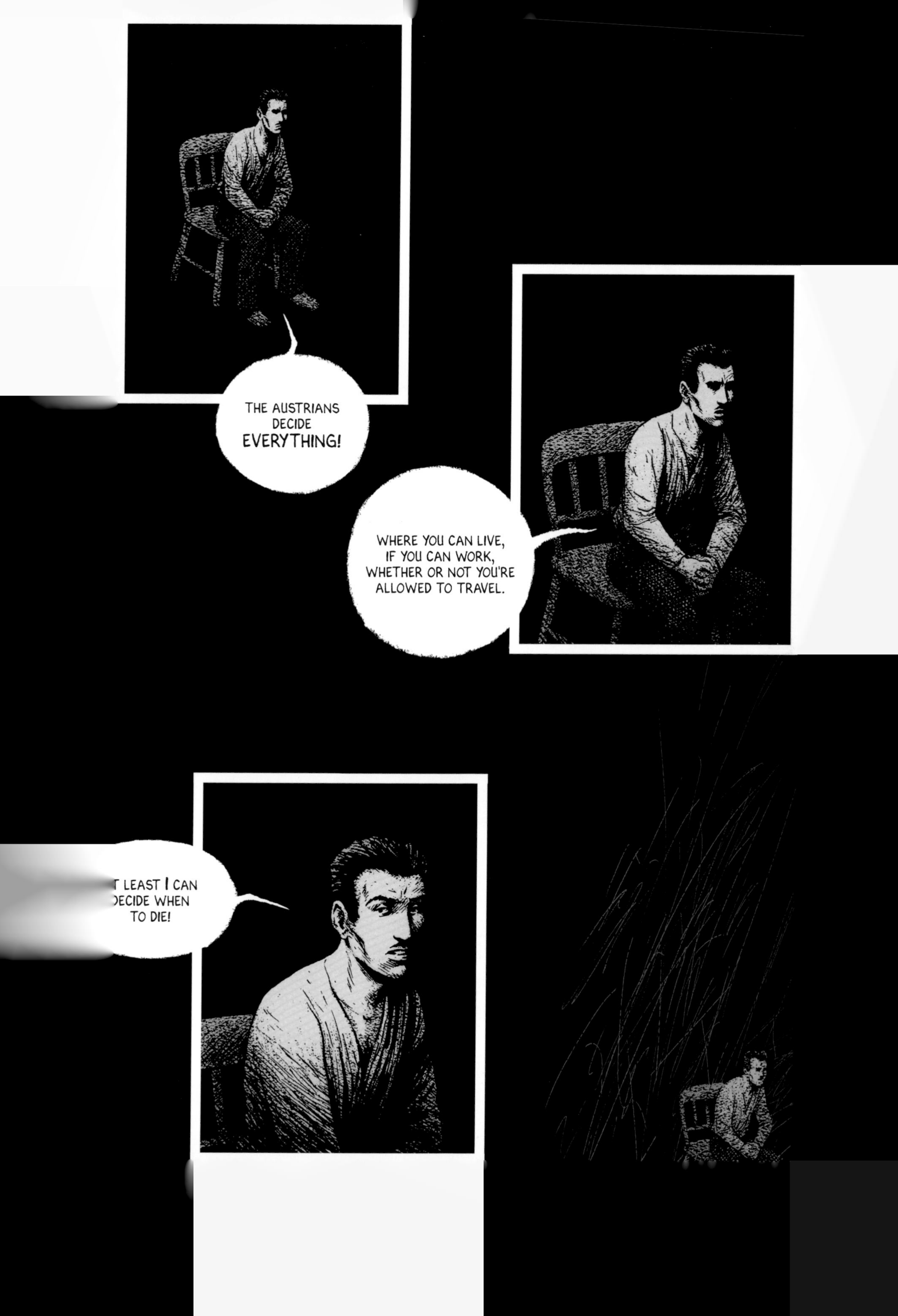
THE AUSTRIANS DECIDE EVERYTHING!
WHERE YOU CAN LIVE, IF YOU CAN WORK, WHETHER OR NOT YOU'RE ALLOWED TO TRAVEL.
T LEAST I CAN ECIDE WHEN TO DIE!

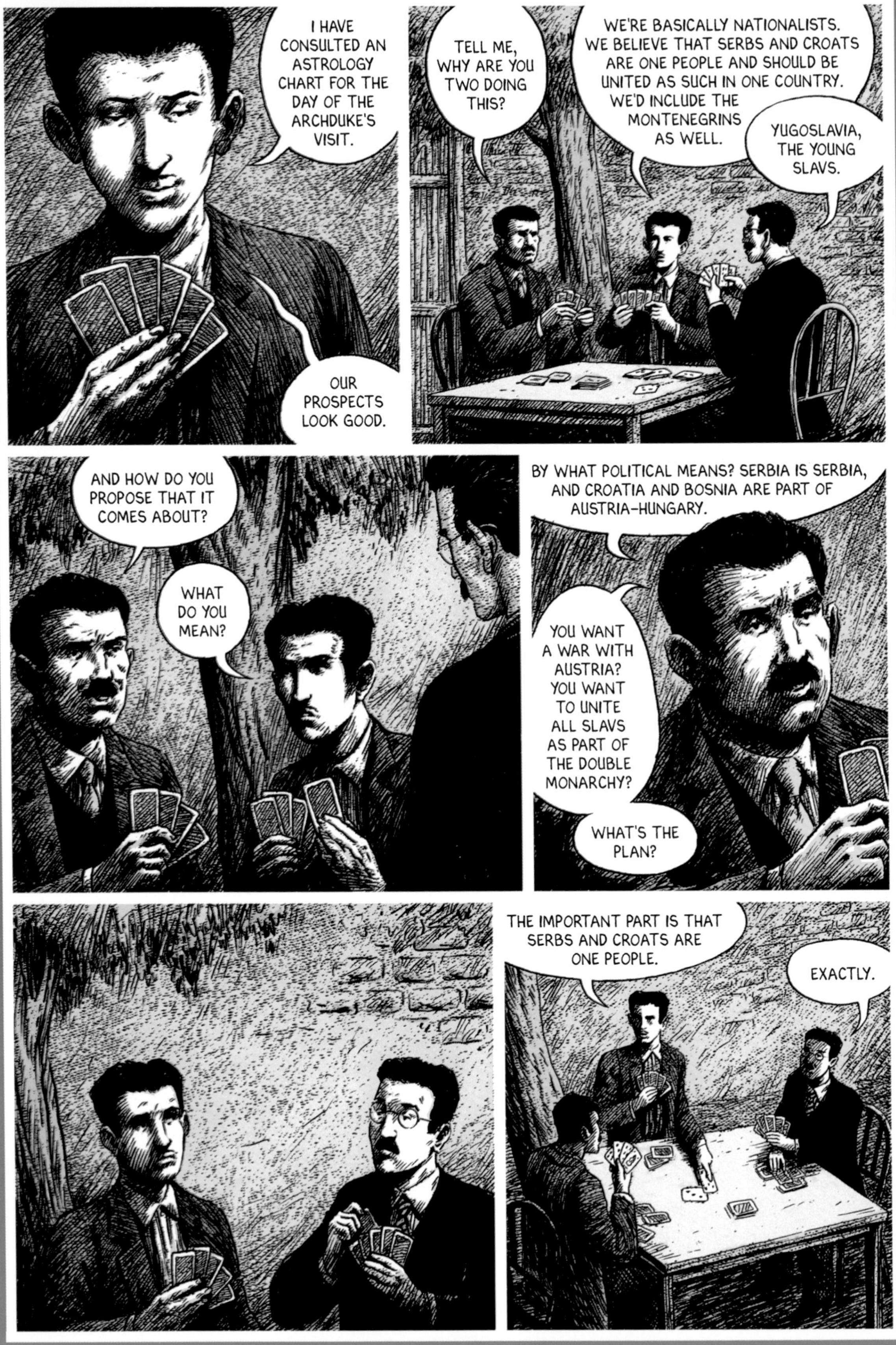
I HAVE CONSULTED AN ASTROLOGY CHART FOR THE DAY OF THE ARCHDUKE'S VISIT.
OUR PROSPECTS LOOK GOOD.
TELL ME, WHY ARE YOU TWO DOING THIS?
WE'RE BASICALLY NATIONALISTS. WE BELIEVE THAT SERBS AND CROATS ARE ONE PEOPLE AND SHOULD BE UNITED AS SUCH IN ONE COUNTRY. WE'D INCLUDE THE MONTENEGRINS AS WELL.
YUGOSLAVIA, THE YOUNG SLAVS.
AND HOW DO YOU PROPOSE THAT IT COMES ABOUT?
WHAT DO YOU MEAN?
BY WHAT POLITICAL MEANS? SERBIA IS SERBIA, AND CROATIA AND BOSNIA ARE PART OF AUSTRIA-HUNGARY.
YOU WANT A WAR WITH AUSTRIA? YOU WANT TO UNITE ALL SLAVS AS PART OF THE DOUBLE MONARCHY?
WHAT'S THE PLAN?
THE IMPORTANT PART IS THAT SERBS AND CROATS ARE ONE PEOPLE.
EXACTLY.

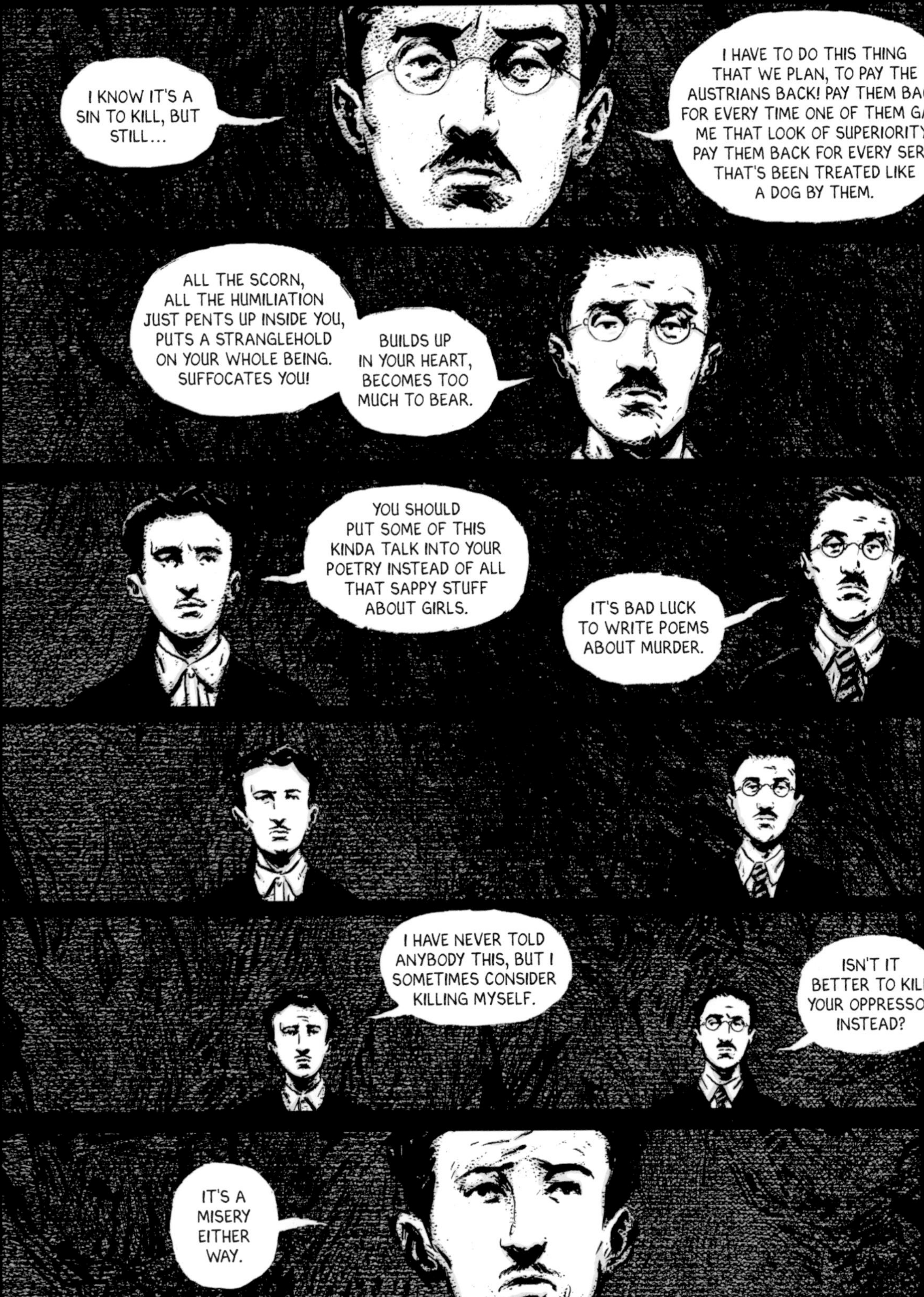
I KNOW IT'S A SIN TO KILL, BUT STILL...
I HAVE TO DO THIS THING THAT WE PLAN, TO PAY THE AUSTRIANS BACK! PAY THEM BACK FOR EVERY TIME ONE OF THEM GAVE ME THAT LOOK OF SUPERIORITY. PAY THEM BACK FOR EVERY SERB THAT'S BEEN TREATED LIKE A DOG BY THEM.
ALL THE SCORN, ALL THE HUMILIATION JUST PENTS UP INSIDE YOU, PUTS A STRANGLEHOLD ON YOUR WHOLE BEING. SUFFOCATES YOU!
BUILDS UP IN YOUR HEART, BECOMES TOO MUCH TO BEAR.
YOU SHOULD PUT SOME OF THIS KINDA TALK INTO YOUR POETRY INSTEAD OF ALL THAT SAPPY STUFF ABOUT GIRLS.
IT'S BAD LUCK TO WRITE POEMS ABOUT MURDER.
I HAVE NEVER TOLD ANYBODY THIS, BUT I SOMETIMES CONSIDER KILLING MYSELF.
ISN'T IT BETTER TO KILL YOUR OPPRESSOR INSTEAD?
IT'S A MISERY EITHER WAY.

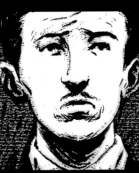

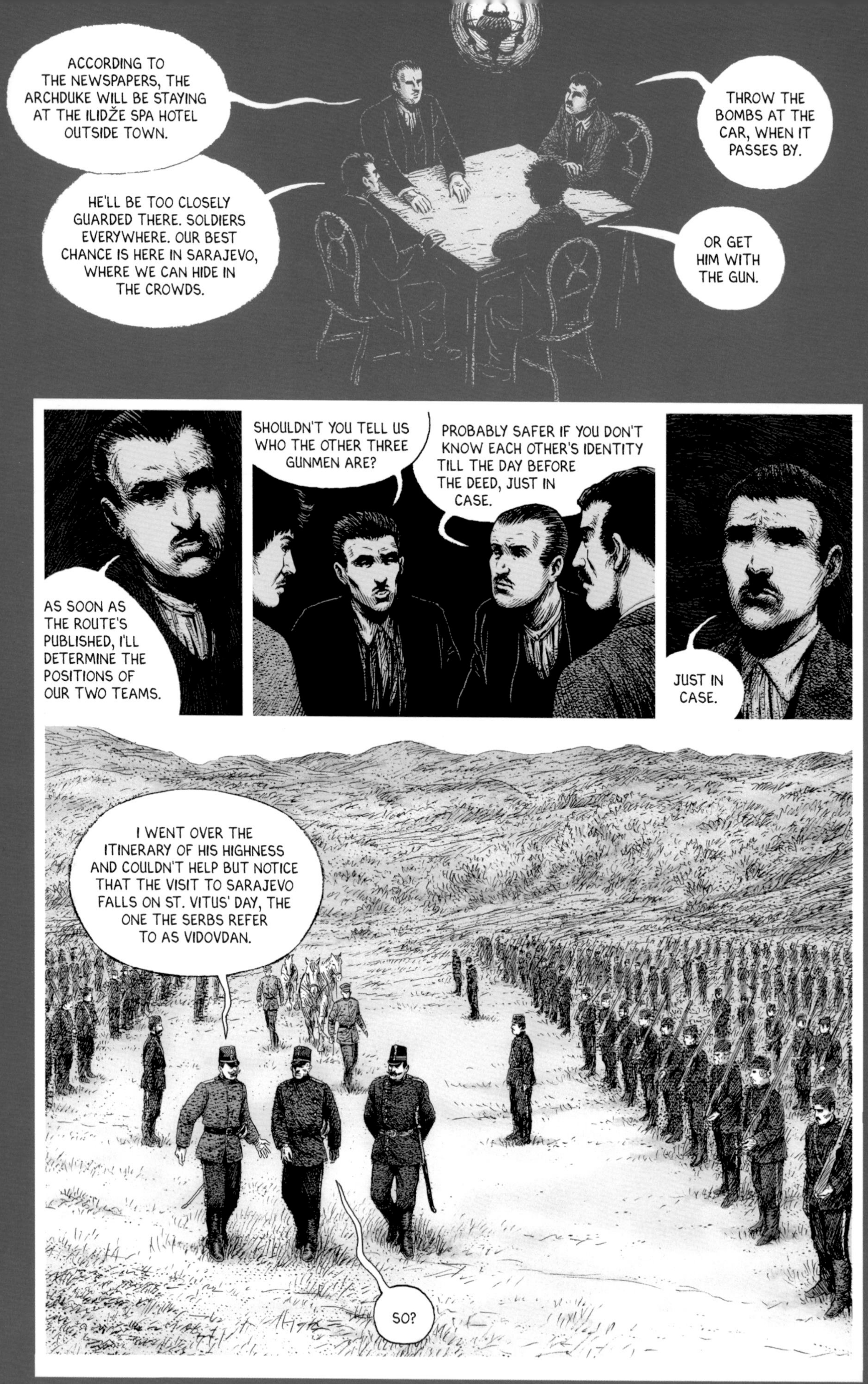
ACCORDING TO THE NEWSPAPERS, THE ARCHDUKE WILL BE STAYING AT THE ILIDŽE SPA HOTEL OUTSIDE TOWN.
THROW THE BOMBS AT THE CAR, WHEN IT PASSES BY.
HE'LL BE TOO CLOSELY GUARDED THERE. SOLDIERS EVERYWHERE. OUR BEST CHANCE IS HERE IN SARAJEVO, WHERE WE CAN HIDE IN THE CROWDS.
OR GET HIM WITH THE GUN.
AS SOON AS THE ROUTE'S PUBLISHED, I'LL DETERMINE THE POSITIONS OF OUR TWO TEAMS.
SHOULDN'T YOU TELL US WHO THE OTHER THREE GUNMEN ARE?
PROBABLY SAFER IF YOU DON'T KNOW EACH OTHER'S IDENTITY TILL THE DAY BEFORE THE DEED, JUST IN CASE.
JUST IN CASE.
I WENT OVER THE ITINERARY OF HIS HIGHNESS AND COULDN'T HELP BUT NOTICE THAT THE VISIT TO SARAJEVO FALLS ON ST. VITUS' DAY, THE ONE THE SERBS REFER TO AS VIDOVDAN.
SO?

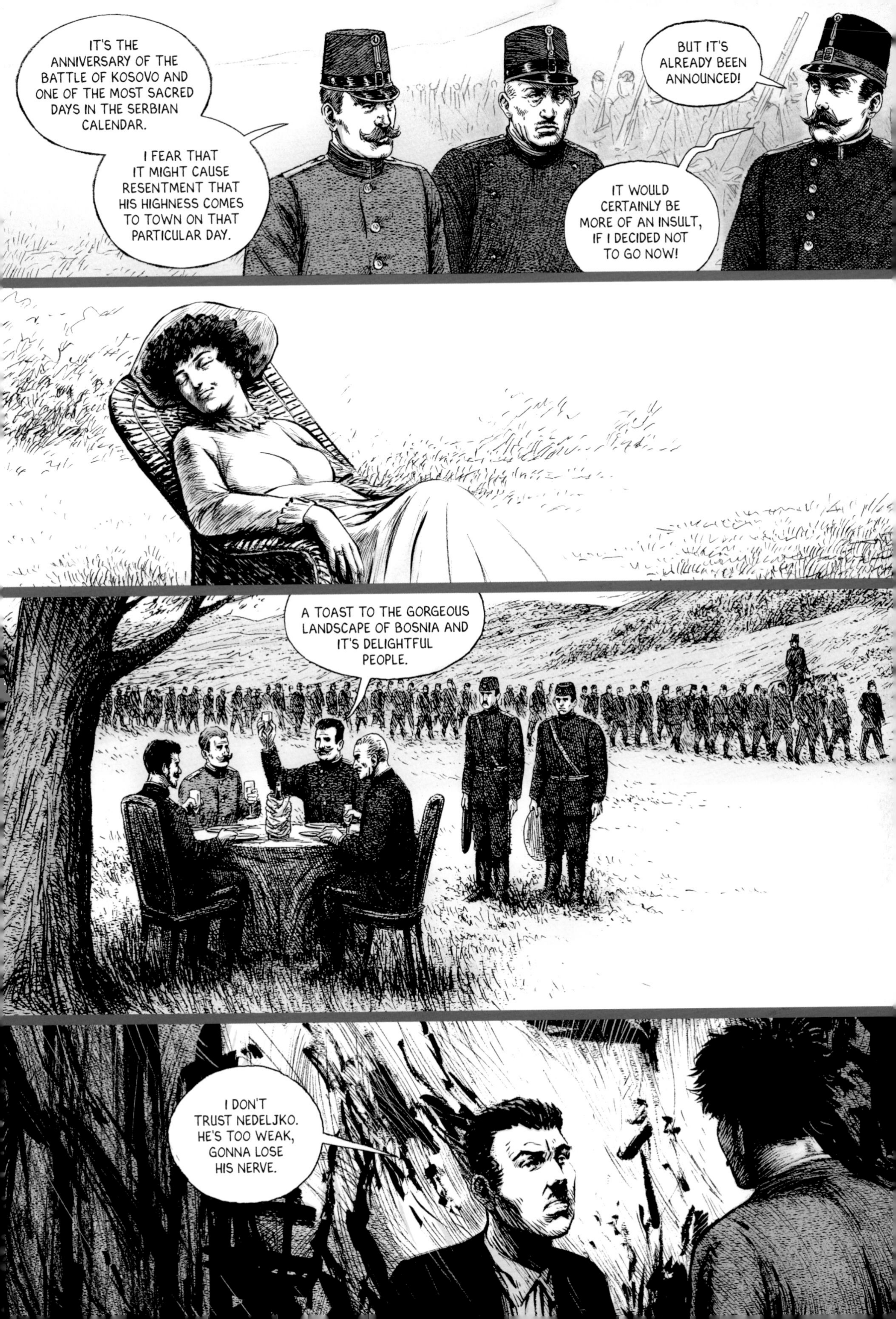
IT'S THE ANNIVERSARY OF THE BATTLE OF KOSOVO AND ONE OF THE MOST SACRED DAYS IN THE SERBIAN CALENDAR.
I FEAR THAT IT MIGHT CAUSE RESENTMENT THAT HIS HIGHNESS COMES TO TOWN ON THAT PARTICULAR DAY.
BUT IT'S ALREADY BEEN ANNOUNCED!
IT WOULD CERTAINLY BE MORE OF AN INSULT, IF I DECIDED NOT TO GO NOW!
A TOAST TO THE GORGEOUS LANDSCAPE OF BOSNIA AND IT'S DELIGHTFUL PEOPLE.
I DON'T TRUST NEDELJKO. HE'S TOO WEAK, GONNA LOSE HIS NERVE.

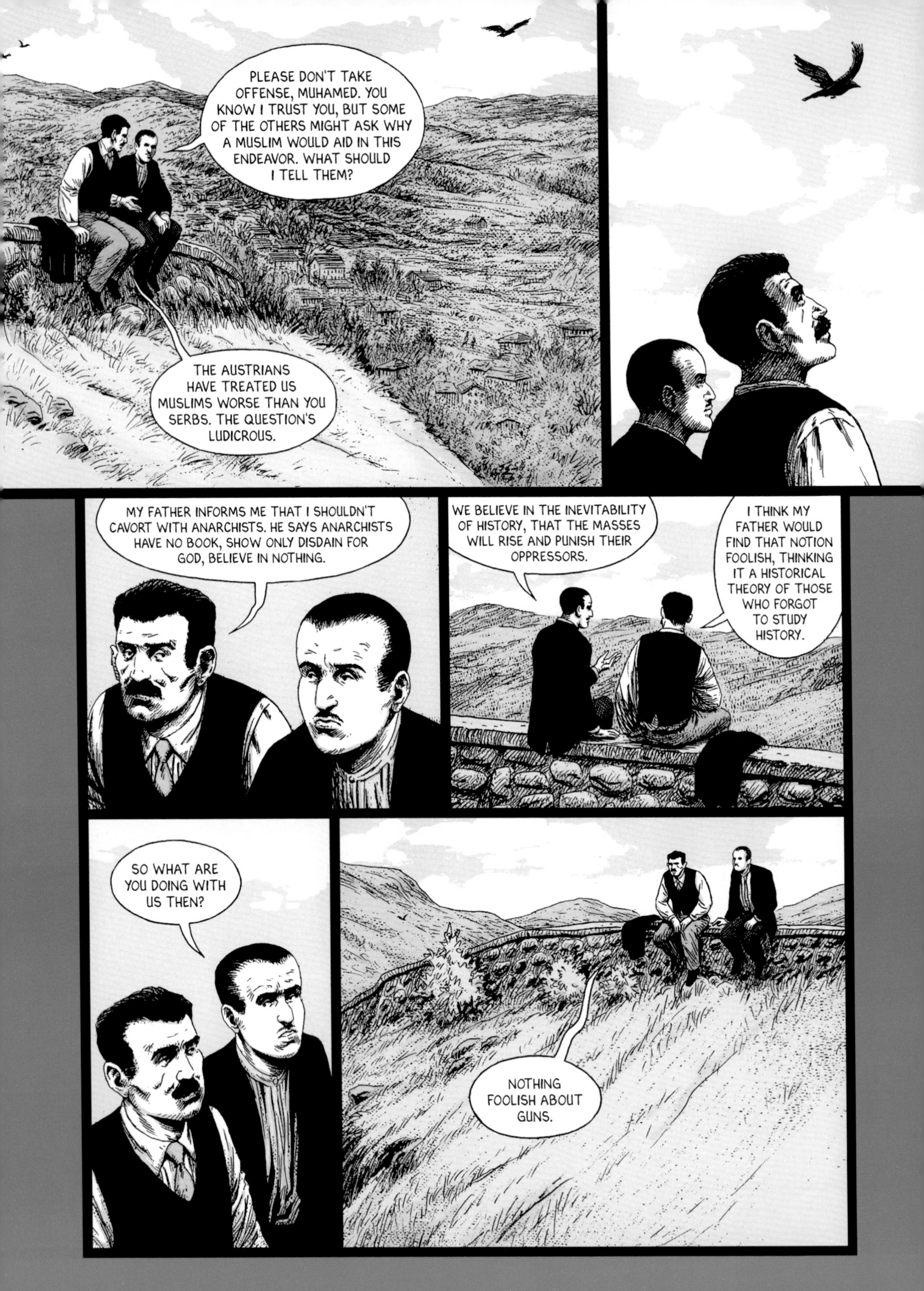
PLEASE DON'T TAKE OFFENSE, MUHAMED. YOU KNOW I TRUST YOU, BUT SOME OF THE OTHERS MIGHT ASK WHY A MUSLIM WOULD AID IN THIS ENDEAVOR. WHAT SHOULD I TELL THEM?
THE AUSTRIANS HAVE TREATED US MUSLIMS WORSE THAN YOU SERBS. THE QUESTION'S LUDICROUS.
MY FATHER INFORMS ME THAT I SHOULDN'T CAVORT WITH ANARCHISTS. HE SAYS ANARCHISTS HAVE NO BOOK, SHOW ONLY DISDAIN FOR GOD, BELIEVE IN NOTHING.
WE BELIEVE IN THE INEVITABILITY OF HISTORY, THAT THE MASSES WILL RISE AND PUNISH THEIR OPPRESSORS.
I THINK MY FATHER WOULD FIND THAT NOTION FOOLISH, THINKING IT A HISTORICAL THEORY OF THOSE WHO FORGOT TO STUDY HISTORY.
SO WHAT ARE YOU DOING WITH US THEN?
NOTHING FOOLISH ABOUT GUNS.

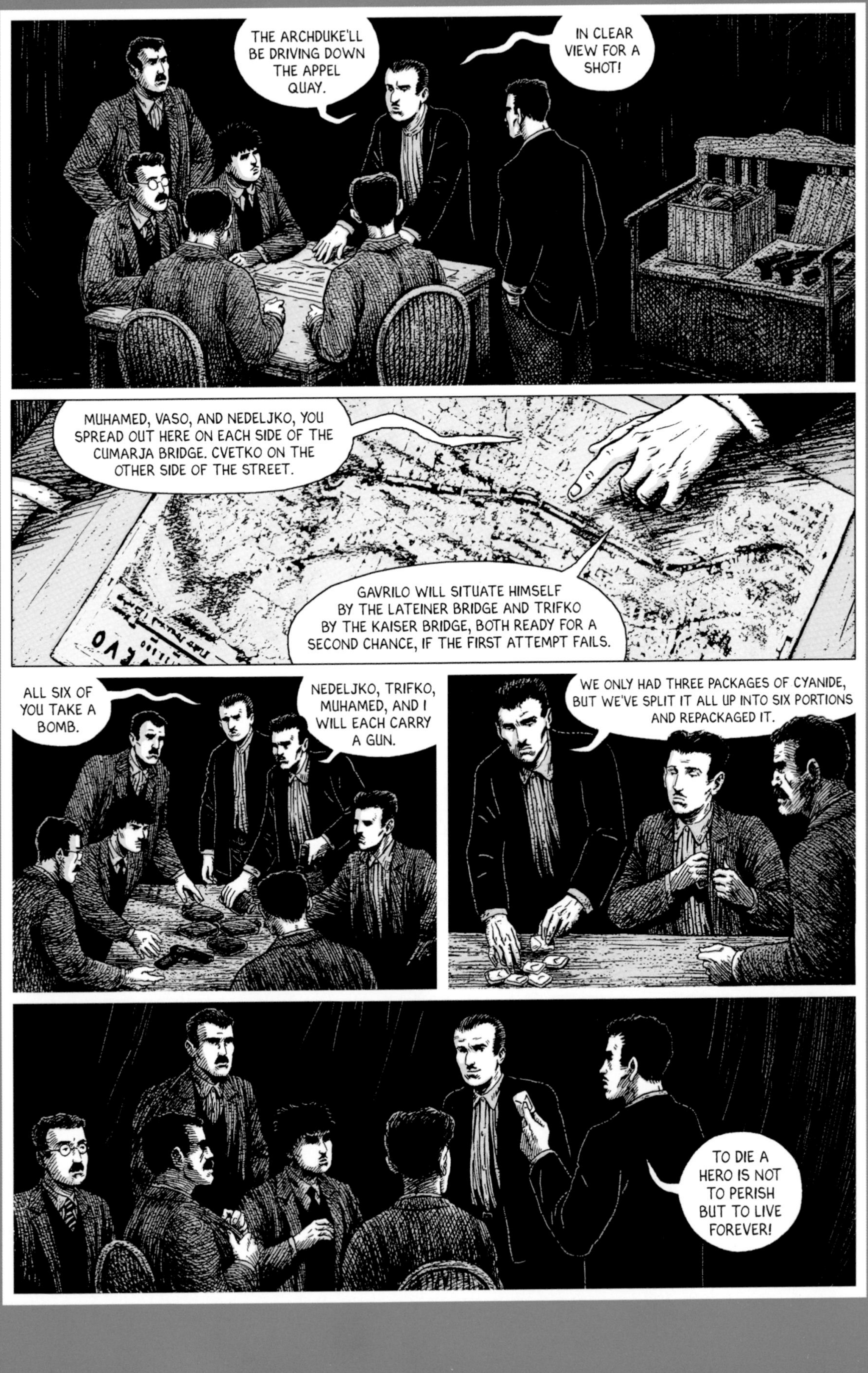
THE ARCHDUKE'LL BE DRIVING DOWN THE APPEL QUAY.
IN CLEAR VIEW FOR A SHOT!
MUHAMED, VASO, AND NEDELJKO, YOU SPREAD OUT HERE ON EACH SIDE OF THE CUMARJA BRIDGE. CVETKO ON THE OTHER SIDE OF THE STREET.
GAVRILO WILL SITUATE HIMSELF BY THE LATEINER BRIDGE AND TRIFKO BY THE KAISER BRIDGE, BOTH READY FOR A SECOND CHANCE, IF THE FIRST ATTEMPT FAILS.
ALL SIX OF YOU TAKE A BOMB.
NEDELJKO, TRIFKO, MUHAMED, AND I WILL EACH CARRY A GUN.
WE ONLY HAD THREE PACKAGES OF CYANIDE, BUT WE'VE SPLIT IT ALL UP INTO SIX PORTIONS AND REPACKAGED IT.
TO DIE A HERO IS NOT TO PERISH BUT TO LIVE FOREVER!

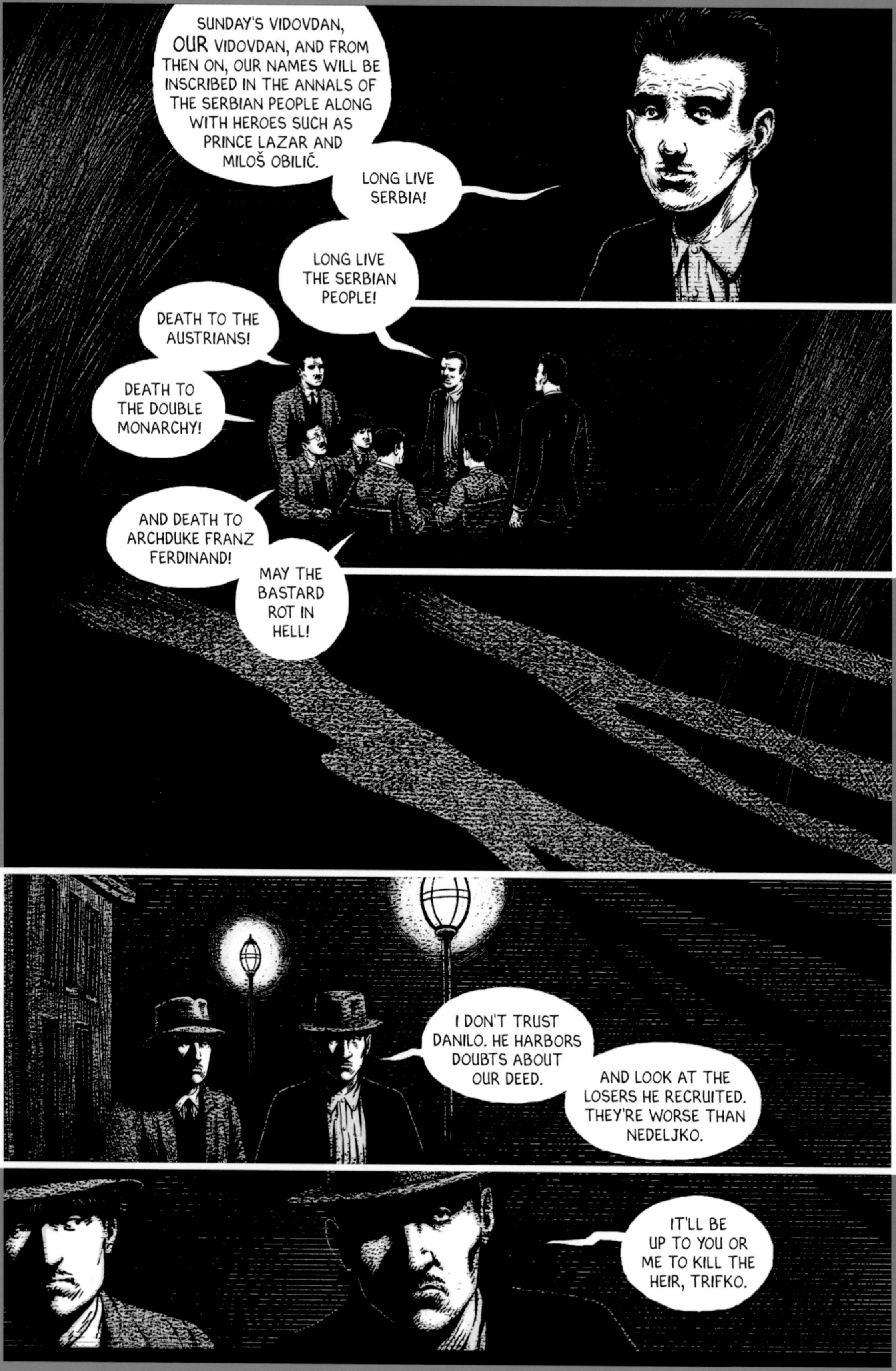
SUNDAY'S VIDOVDAN, OUR VIDOVDAN, AND FROM THEN ON, OUR NAMES WILL BE INSCRIBED IN THE ANNALS OF THE SERBIAN PEOPLE ALONG WITH HEROES SUCH AS PRINCE LAZAR AND MILOŠ OBILIĆ.
LONG LIVE SERBIA!
LONG LIVE THE SERBIAN PEOPLE!
DEATH TO THE AUSTRIANS!
DEATH TO THE DOUBLE MONARCHY!
AND DEATH TO ARCHDUKE FRANZ FERDINAND!
MAY THE BASTARD ROT IN HELL!
I DON'T TRUST DANILO. HE HARBORS DOUBTS ABOUT OUR DEED.
AND LOOK AT THE LOSERS HE RECRUITED. THEY'RE WORSE THAN NEDELJKO.
IT'LL BE UP TO YOU OR ME TO KILL THE HEIR, TRIFKO.

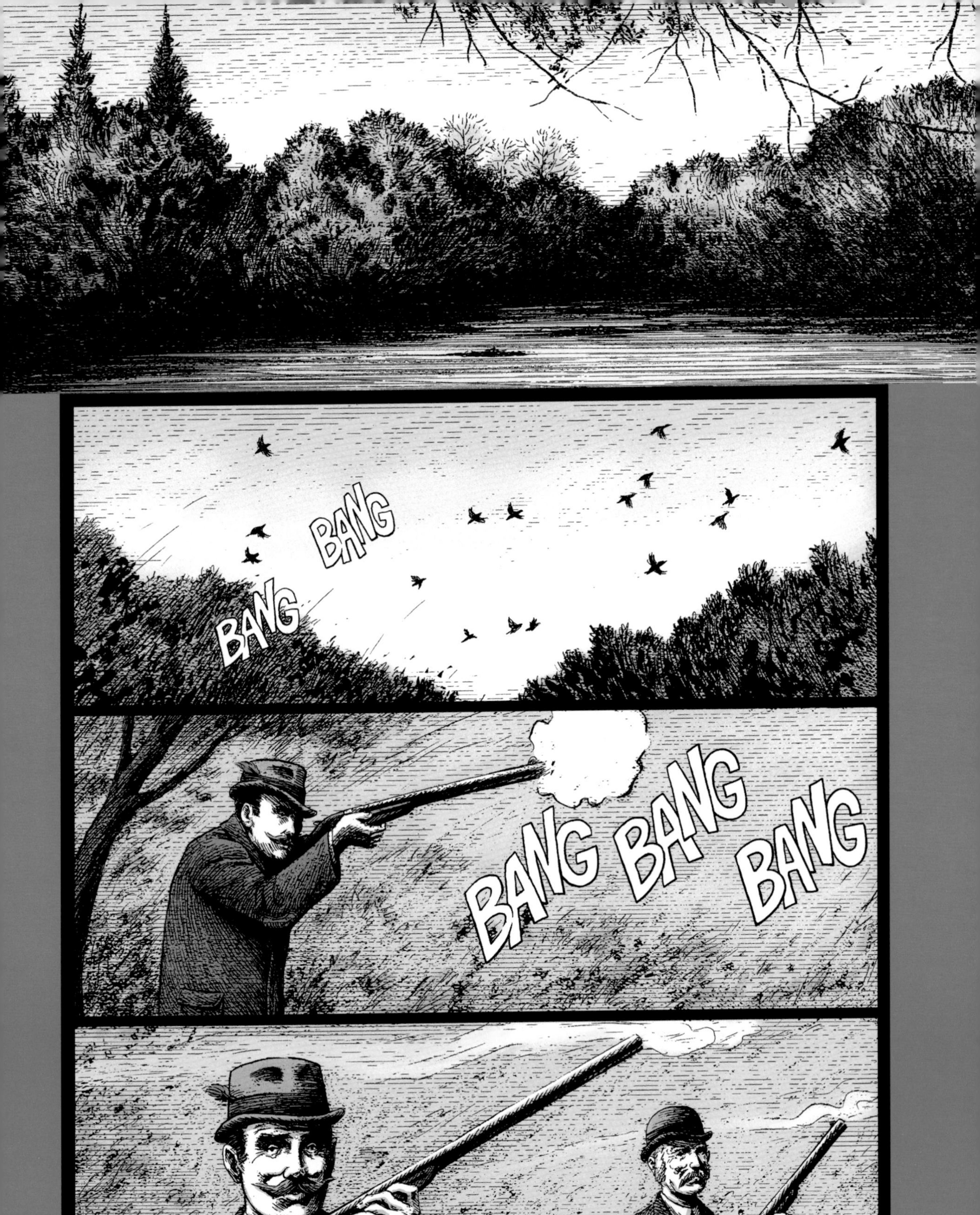
BANG
BANG
BANG
BANG
BANG

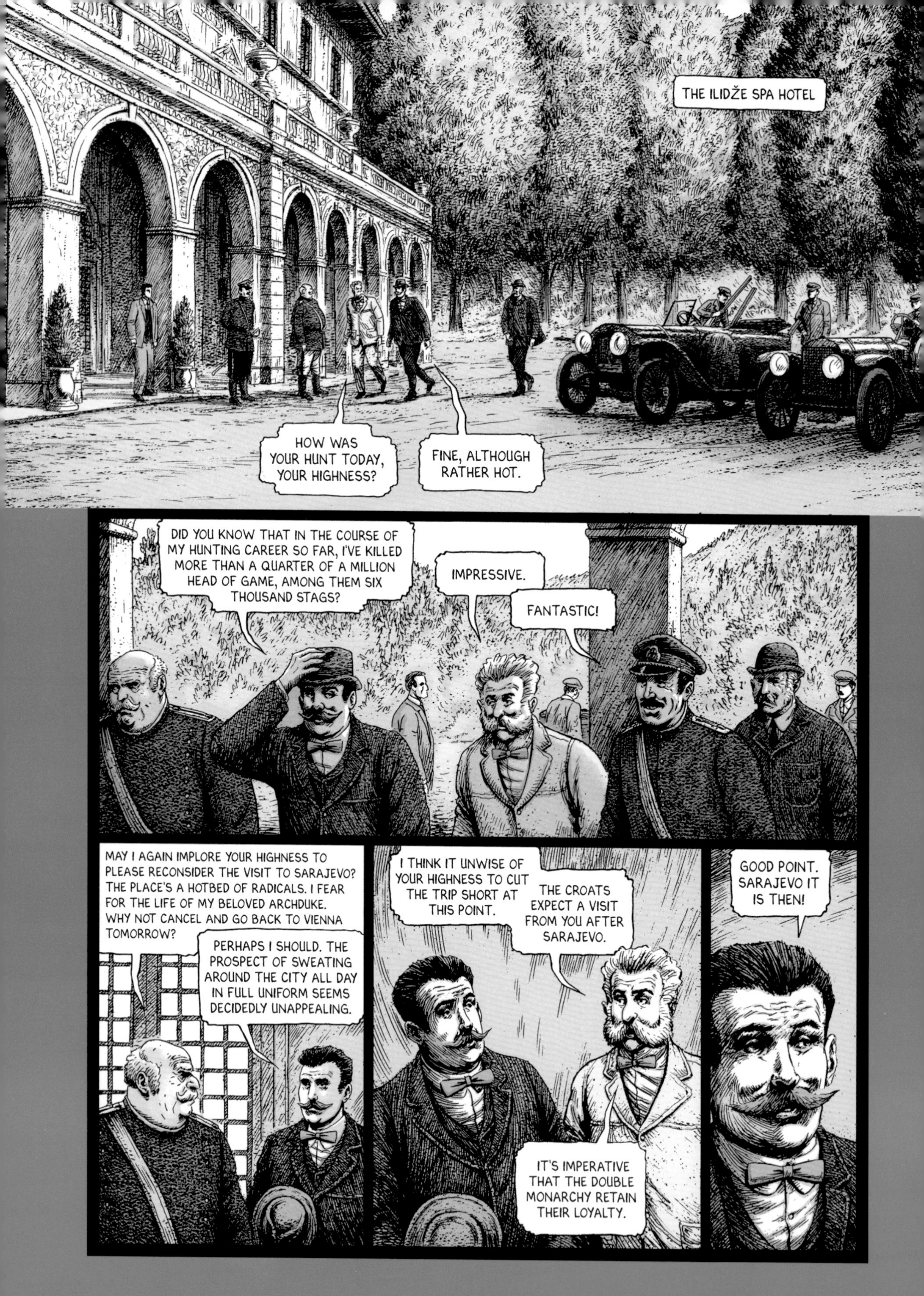
THE ILIDŽE SPA HOTEL
HOW WAS YOUR HUNT TODAY, YOUR HIGHNESS?
FINE, ALTHOUGH RATHER HOT.
DID YOU KNOW THAT IN THE COURSE OF MY HUNTING CAREER SO FAR, I'VE KILLED MORE THAN A QUARTER OF A MILLION HEAD OF GAME, AMONG THEM SIX THOUSAND STAGS?
IMPRESSIVE.
FANTASTIC!
MAY I AGAIN IMPLORE YOUR HIGHNESS TO PLEASE RECONSIDER THE VISIT TO SARAJEVO? THE PLACE'S A HOTBED OF RADICALS. I FEAR FOR THE LIFE OF MY BELOVED ARCHDUKE. WHY NOT CANCEL AND GO BACK TO VIENNA TOMORROW?
PERHAPS I SHOULD. THE PROSPECT OF SWEATING AROUND THE CITY ALL DAY IN FULL UNIFORM SEEMS DECIDEDLY UNAPPEALING.
I THINK IT UNWISE OF YOUR HIGHNESS TO CUT THE TRIP SHORT AT THIS POINT.
THE CROATS EXPECT A VISIT FROM YOU AFTER SARAJEVO.
IT'S IMPERATIVE THAT THE DOUBLE MONARCHY RETAIN THEIR LOYALTY.
GOOD POINT. SARAJEVO IT IS THEN!

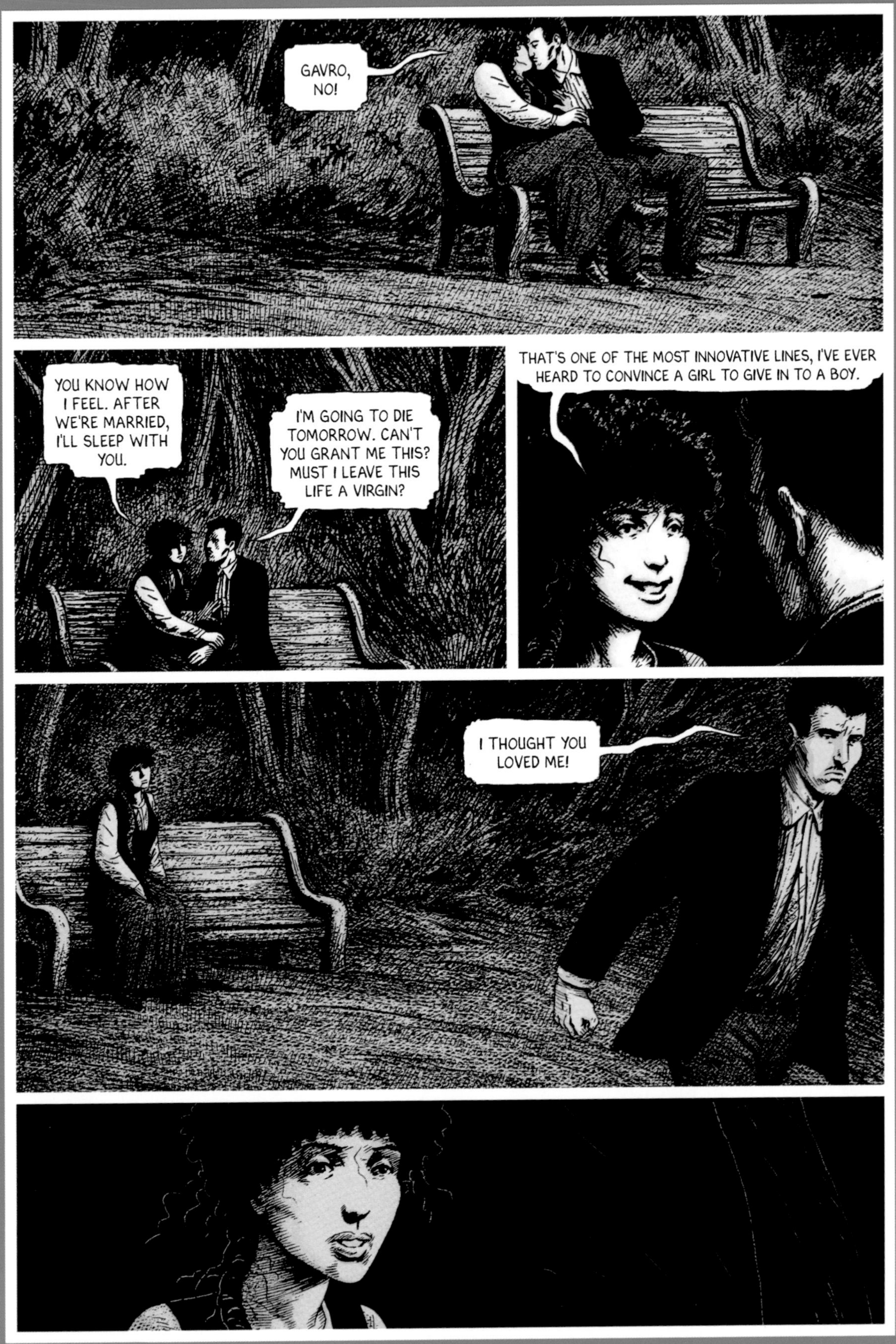
GAVRO, NO!
YOU KNOW HOW I FEEL. AFTER WE'RE MARRIED, I'LL SLEEP WITH YOU.
I'M GOING TO DIE TOMORROW. CAN'T YOU GRANT ME THIS? MUST I LEAVE THIS LIFE A VIRGIN?
THAT'S ONE OF THE MOST INNOVATIVE LINES, I'VE EVER HEARD TO CONVINCE A GIRL TO GIVE IN TO A BOY.
I THOUGHT YOU LOVED ME!

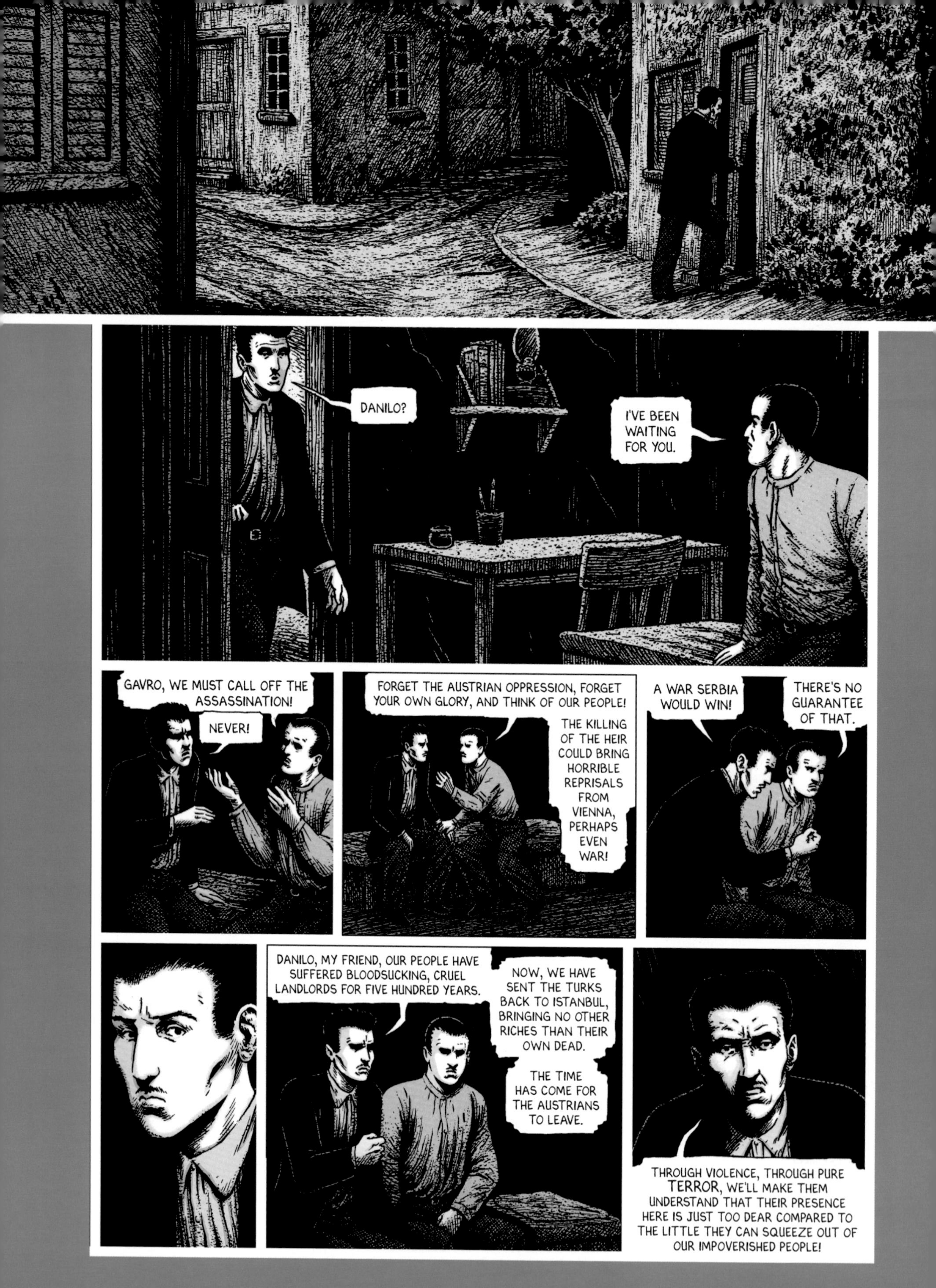
DANILO?
I'VE BEEN WAITING FOR YOU.
GAVRO, WE MUST CALL OFF THE ASSASSINATION!
NEVER!
FORGET THE AUSTRIAN OPPRESSION, FORGET YOUR OWN GLORY, AND THINK OF OUR PEOPLE!
THE KILLING OF THE HEIR COULD BRING HORRIBLE REPRISALS FROM VIENNA, PERHAPS EVEN WAR!
A WAR SERBIA WOULD WIN!
THERE'S NO GUARANTEE OF THAT.
DANILO, MY FRIEND, OUR PEOPLE HAVE SUFFERED BLOODSUCKING, CRUEL LANDLORDS FOR FIVE HUNDRED YEARS.
NOW, WE HAVE SENT THE TURKS BACK TO ISTANBUL, BRINGING NO OTHER RICHES THAN THEIR OWN DEAD.
THE TIME HAS COME FOR THE AUSTRIANS TO LEAVE.
THROUGH VIOLENCE, THROUGH PURE TERROR, WE'LL MAKE THEM UNDERSTAND THAT THEIR PRESENCE HERE IS JUST TOO DEAR COMPARED TO THE LITTLE THEY CAN SQUEEZE OUT OF OUR IMPOVERISHED PEOPLE!

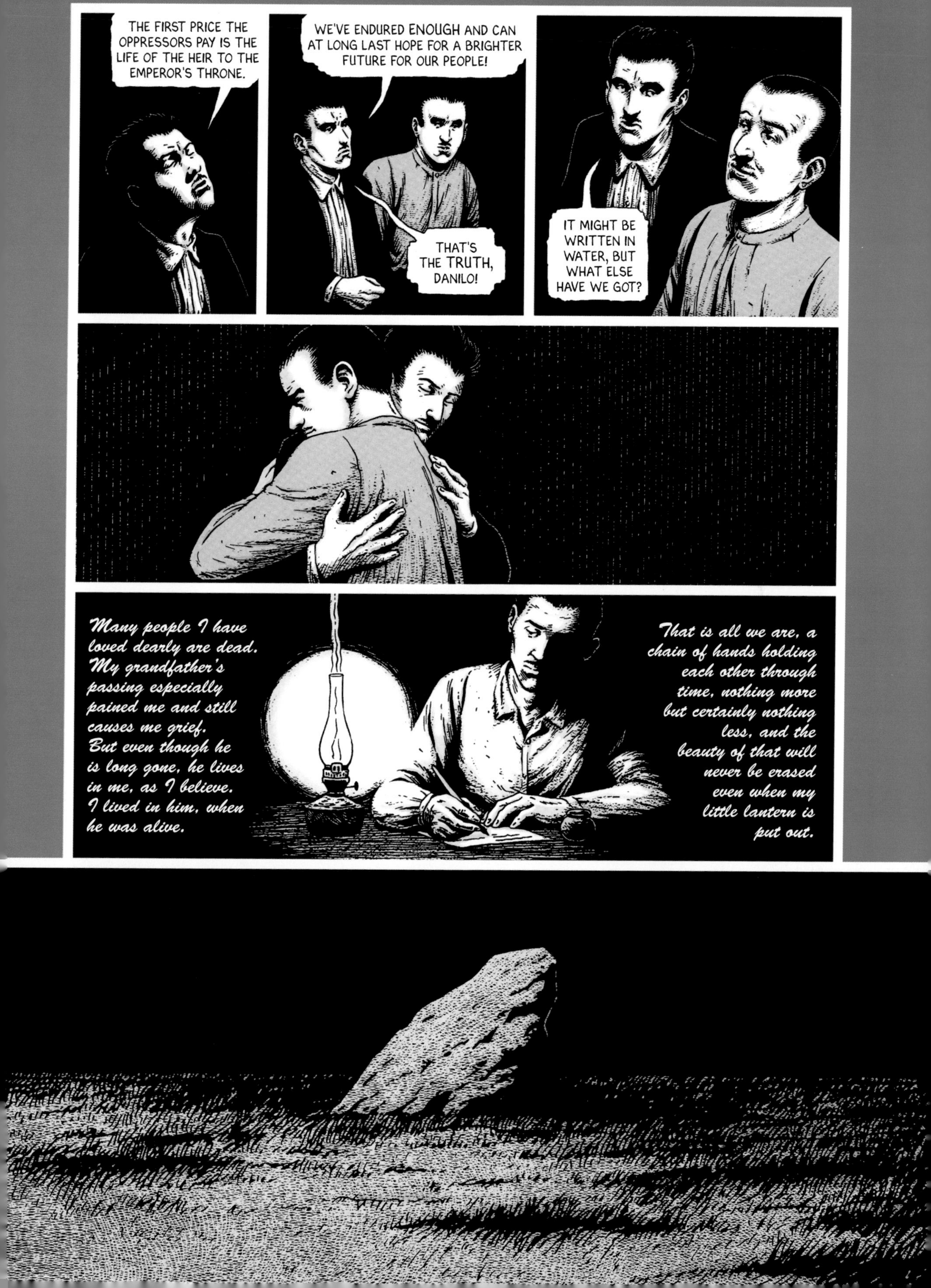
THE FIRST PRICE THE OPPRESSORS PAY IS THE LIFE OF THE HEIR TO THE EMPEROR'S THRONE.
WE'VE ENDURED ENOUGH AND CAN AT LONG LAST HOPE FOR A BRIGHTER FUTURE FOR OUR PEOPLE!
THAT'S THE TRUTH, DANILO!
IT MIGHT BE WRITTEN IN WATER, BUT WHAT ELSE HAVE WE GOT?
Many people I have loved dearly are dead. My grandfather's passing especially pained me and still causes me grief. But even though he is long gone, he lives in me, as I believe. I lived in him, when he was alive.
That is all we are, a chain of hands holding each other through time, nothing more but certainly nothing less, and the beauty of that will never be erased even when my little lantern is put out.

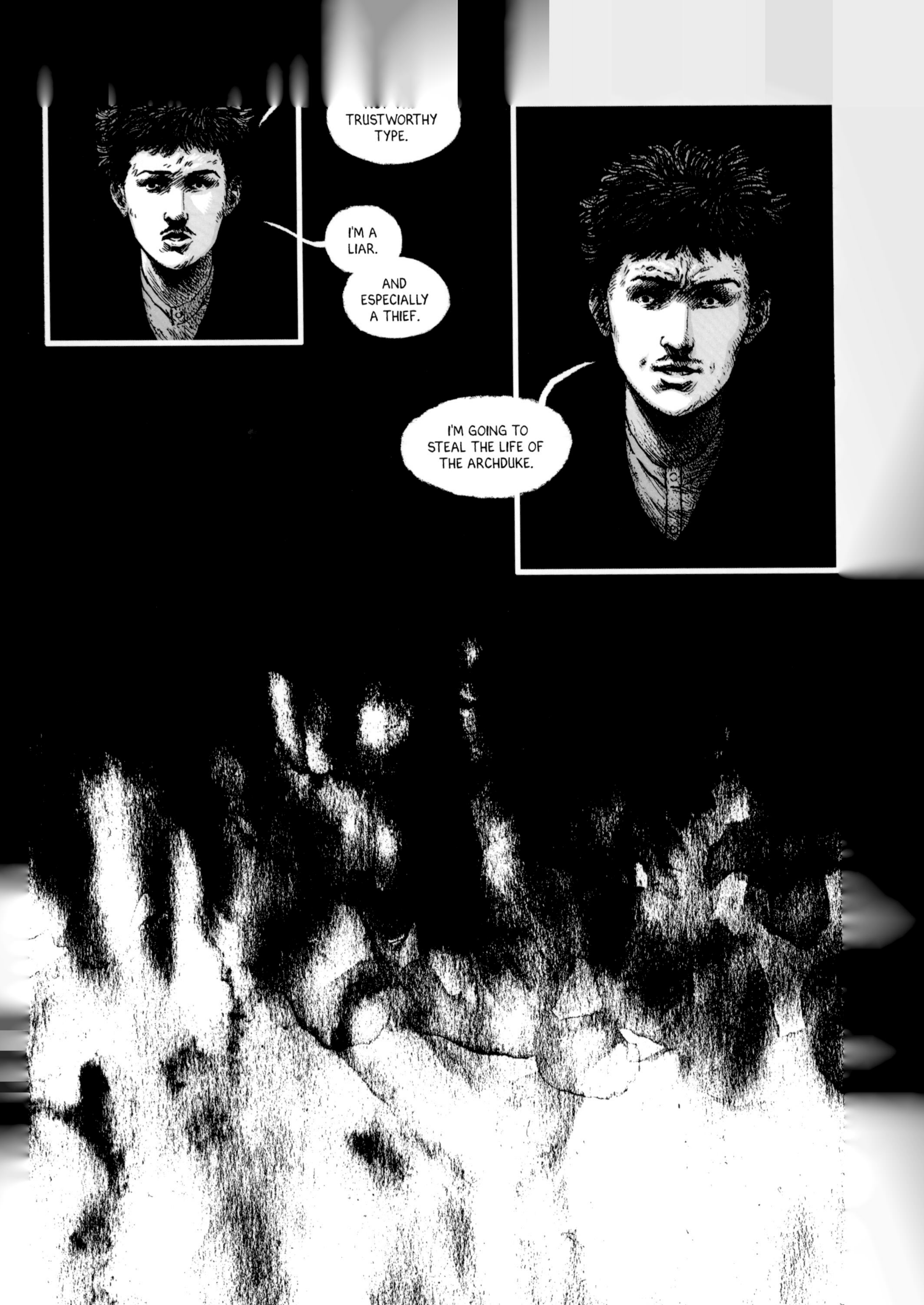
TRUSTWORTHY TYPE.
I'M A LIAR.
AND ESPECIALLY A THIEF.
I'M GOING TO STEAL THE LIFE OF THE ARCHDUKE.

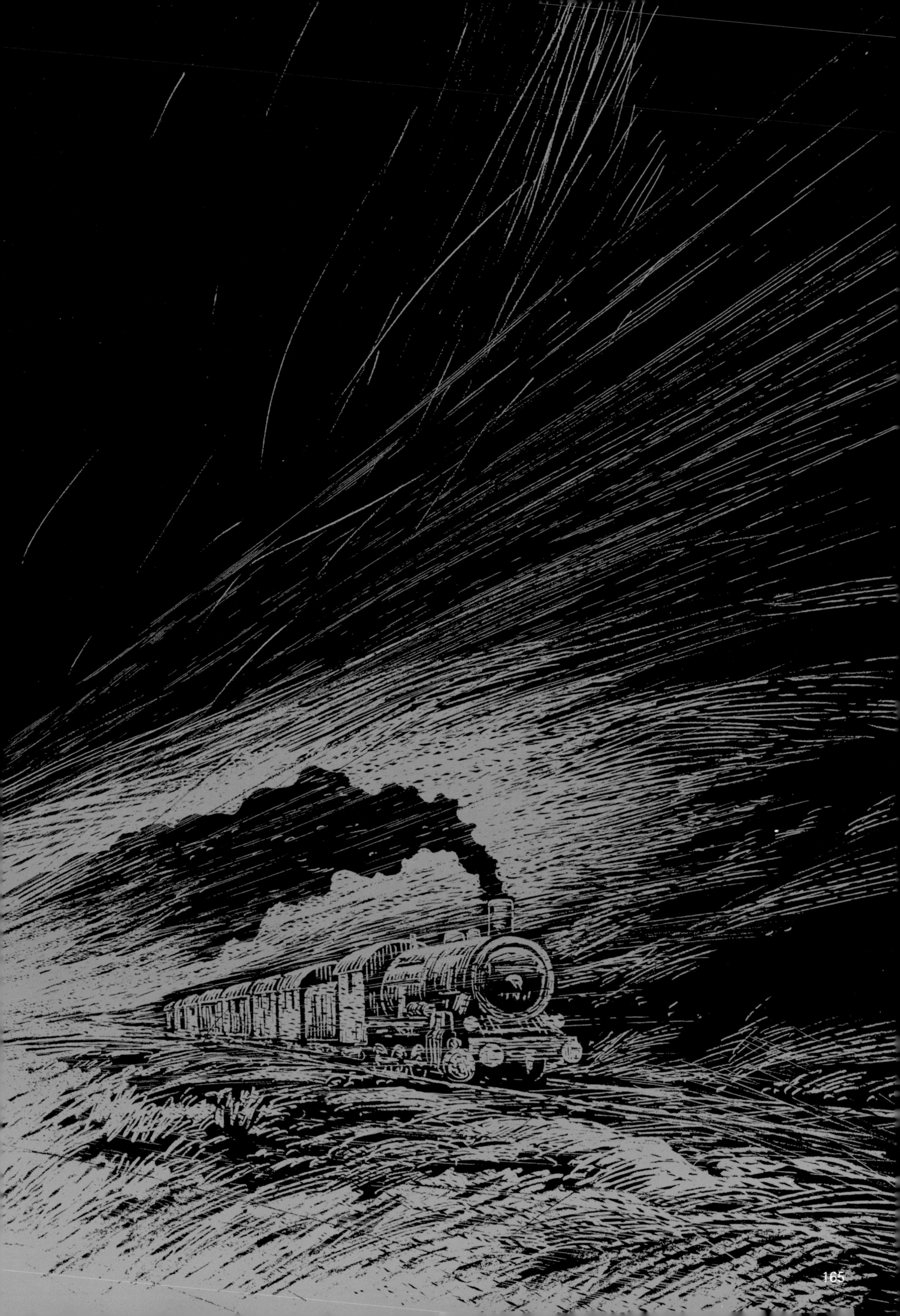

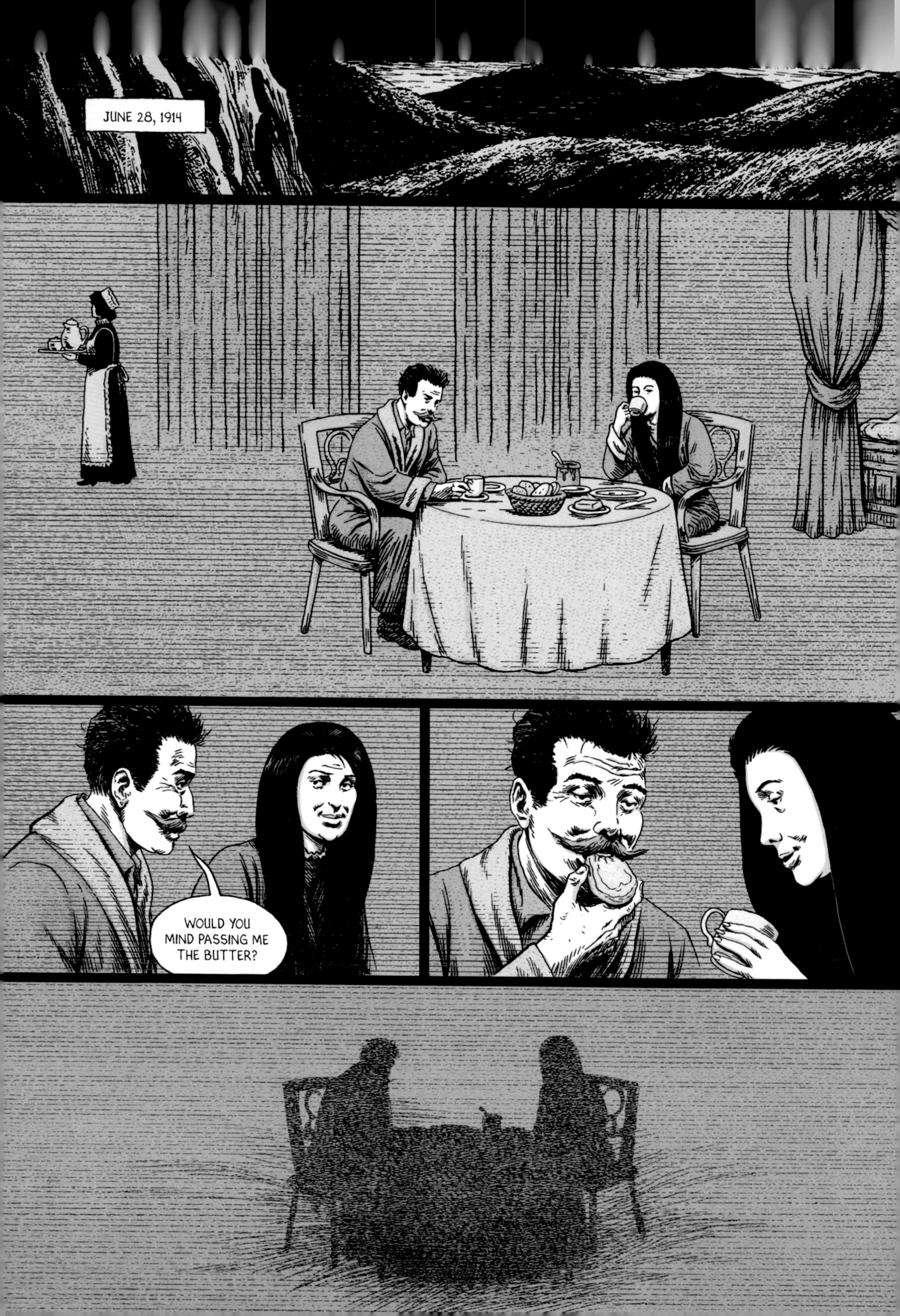
JUNE 28, 1914
WOULD YOU MIND PASSING ME THE BUTTER?

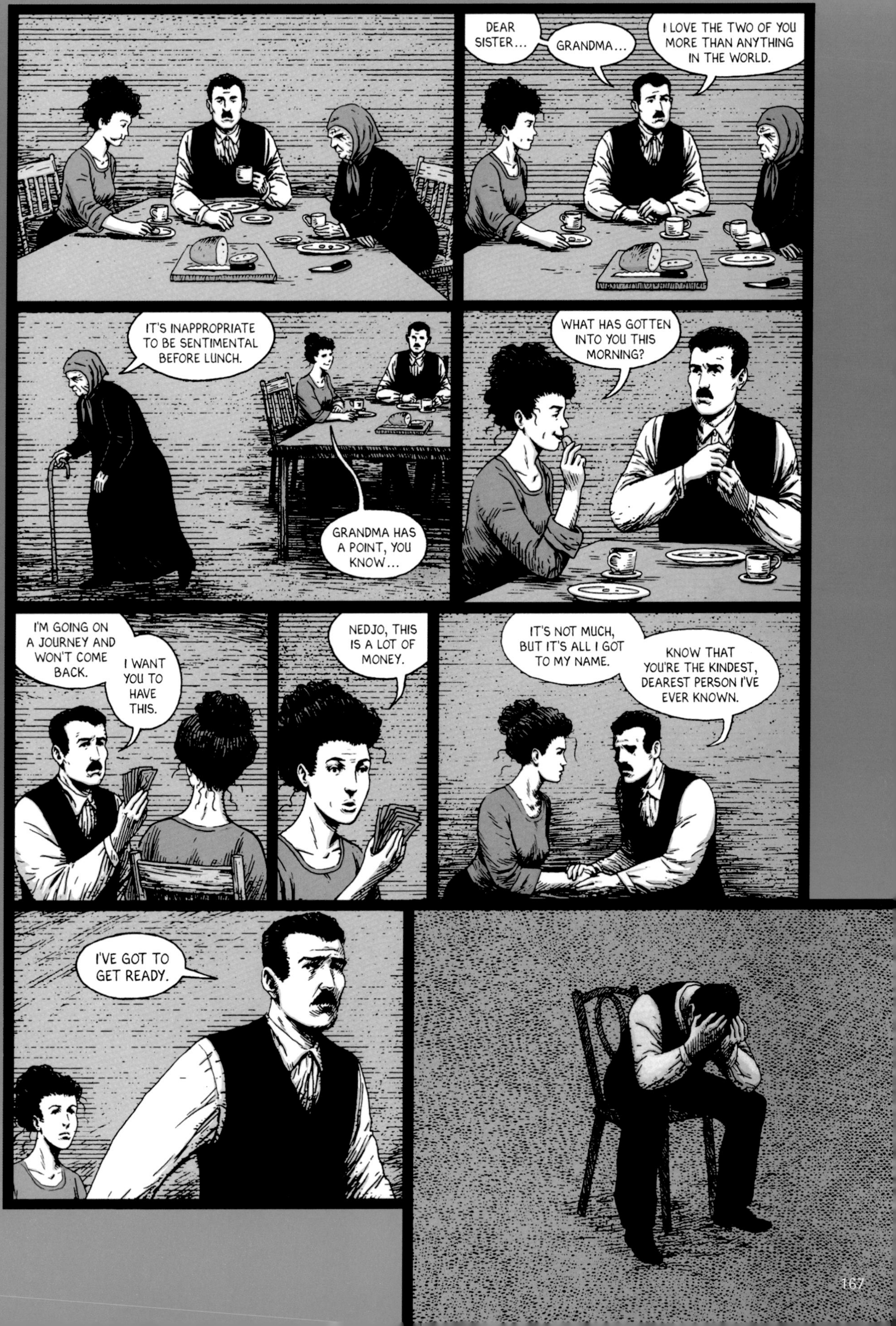
DEAR SISTER...
GRANDMA...
I LOVE THE TWO OF YOU MORE THAN ANYTHING IN THE WORLD.
IT'S INAPPROPRIATE TO BE SENTIMENTAL BEFORE LUNCH.
GRANDMA HAS A POINT, YOU KNOW...
WHAT HAS GOTTEN INTO YOU THIS MORNING?
I'M GOING ON A JOURNEY AND WON'T COME BACK.
I WANT YOU TO HAVE THIS.
NEDJO, THIS IS A LOT OF MONEY.
IT'S NOT MUCH, BUT IT'S ALL I GOT TO MY NAME.
KNOW THAT YOU'RE THE KINDEST, DEAREST PERSON I'VE EVER KNOWN.
I'VE GOT TO GET READY.

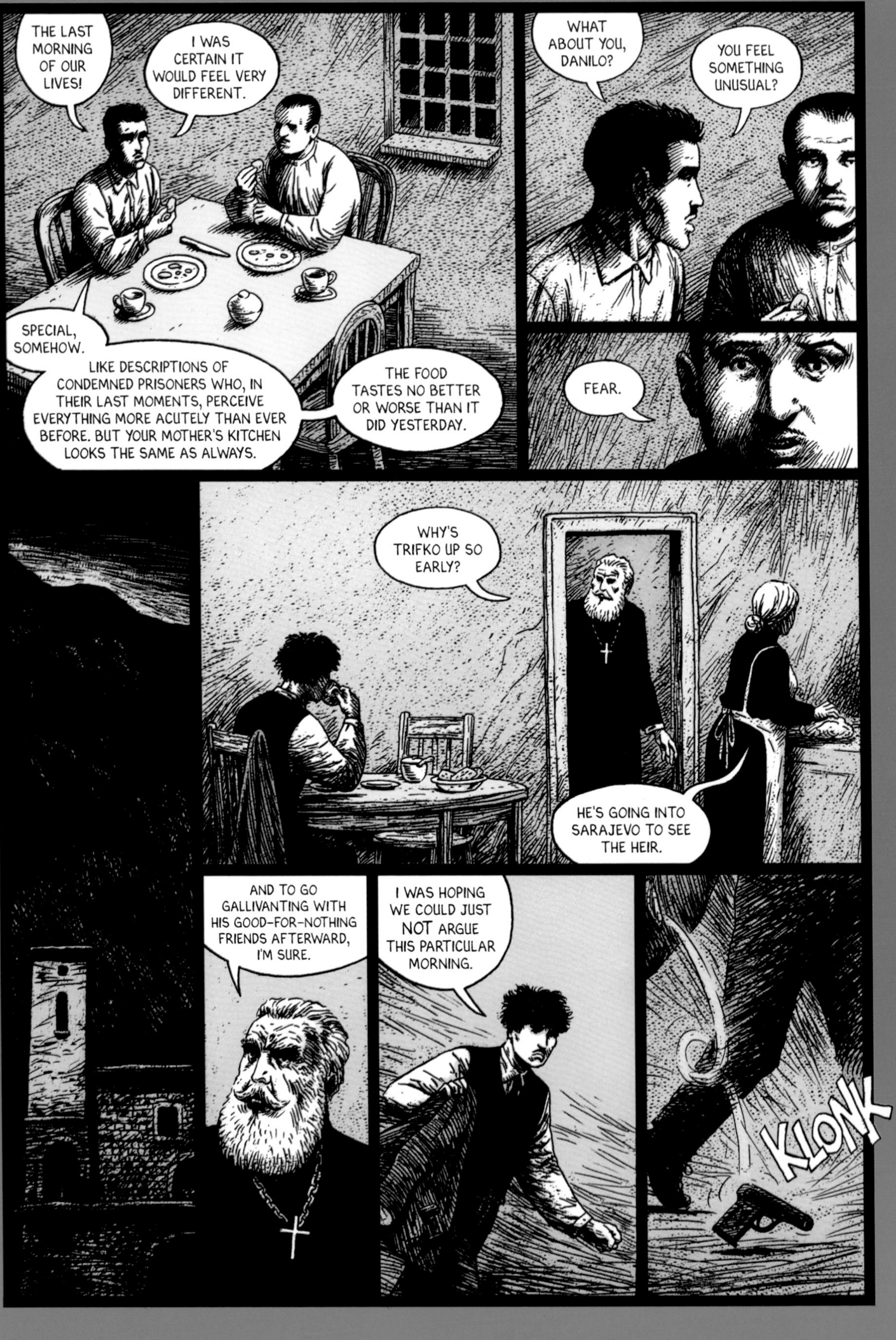

THE LAST MORNING OF OUR LIVES!
I WAS CERTAIN IT WOULD FEEL VERY DIFFERENT.
SPECIAL, SOMEHOW.
LIKE DESCRIPTIONS OF CONDEMNED PRISONERS WHO, IN THEIR LAST MOMENTS, PERCEIVE EVERYTHING MORE ACUTELY THAN EVER BEFORE. BUT YOUR MOTHER'S KITCHEN LOOKS THE SAME AS ALWAYS.
THE FOOD TASTES NO BETTER OR WORSE THAN IT DID YESTERDAY.
WHAT ABOUT YOU, DANILO?
YOU FEEL SOMETHING UNUSUAL?
FEAR.
WHY'S TRIFKO UP SO EARLY?
HE'S GOING INTO SARAJEVO TO SEE THE HEIR.
AND TO GO GALLIVANTING WITH HIS GOOD-FOR-NOTHING FRIENDS AFTERWARD, I'M SURE.
I WAS HOPING WE COULD JUST NOT ARGUE THIS PARTICULAR MORNING.
KLONK

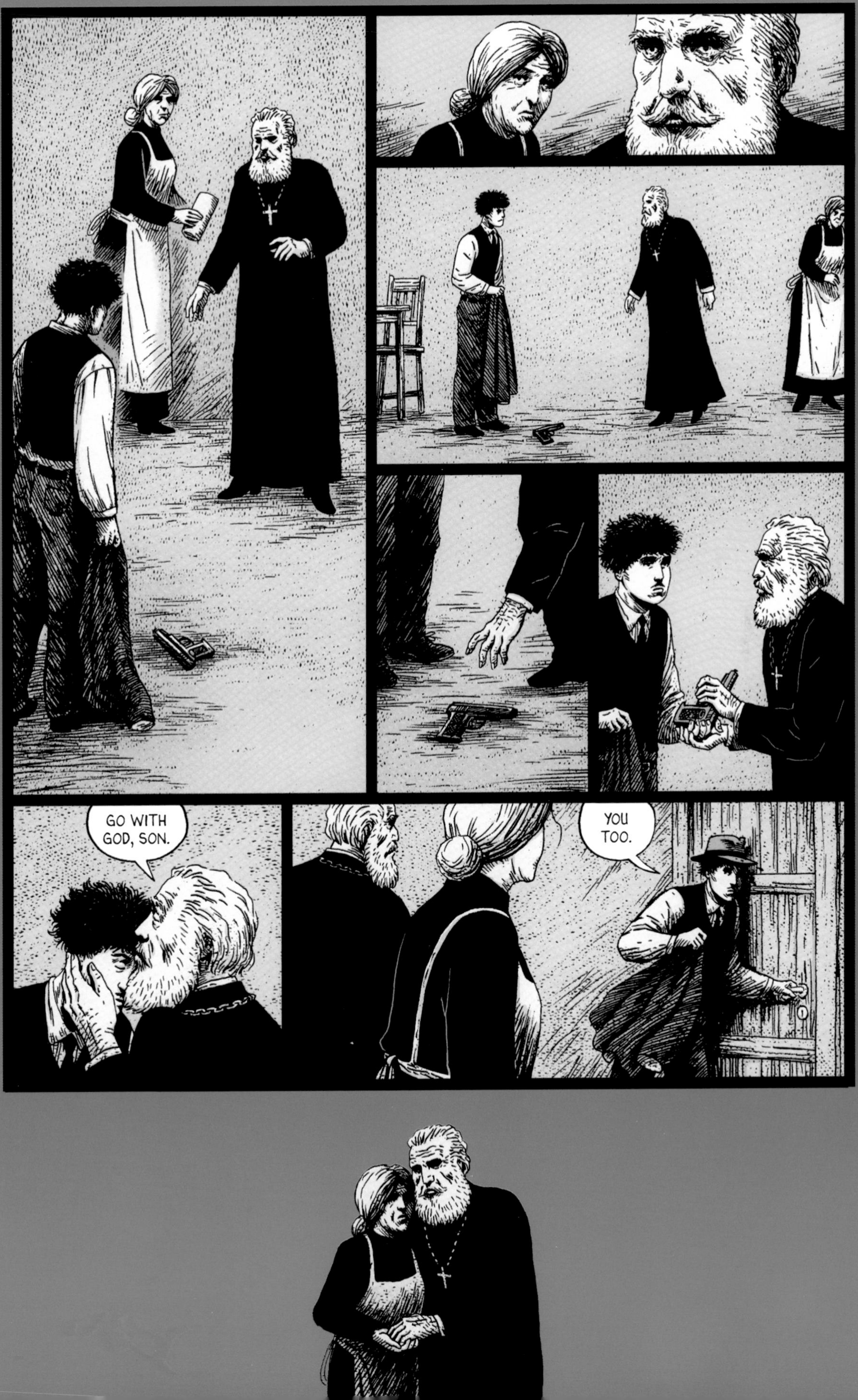
GO WITH GOD, SON.
YOU TOO.

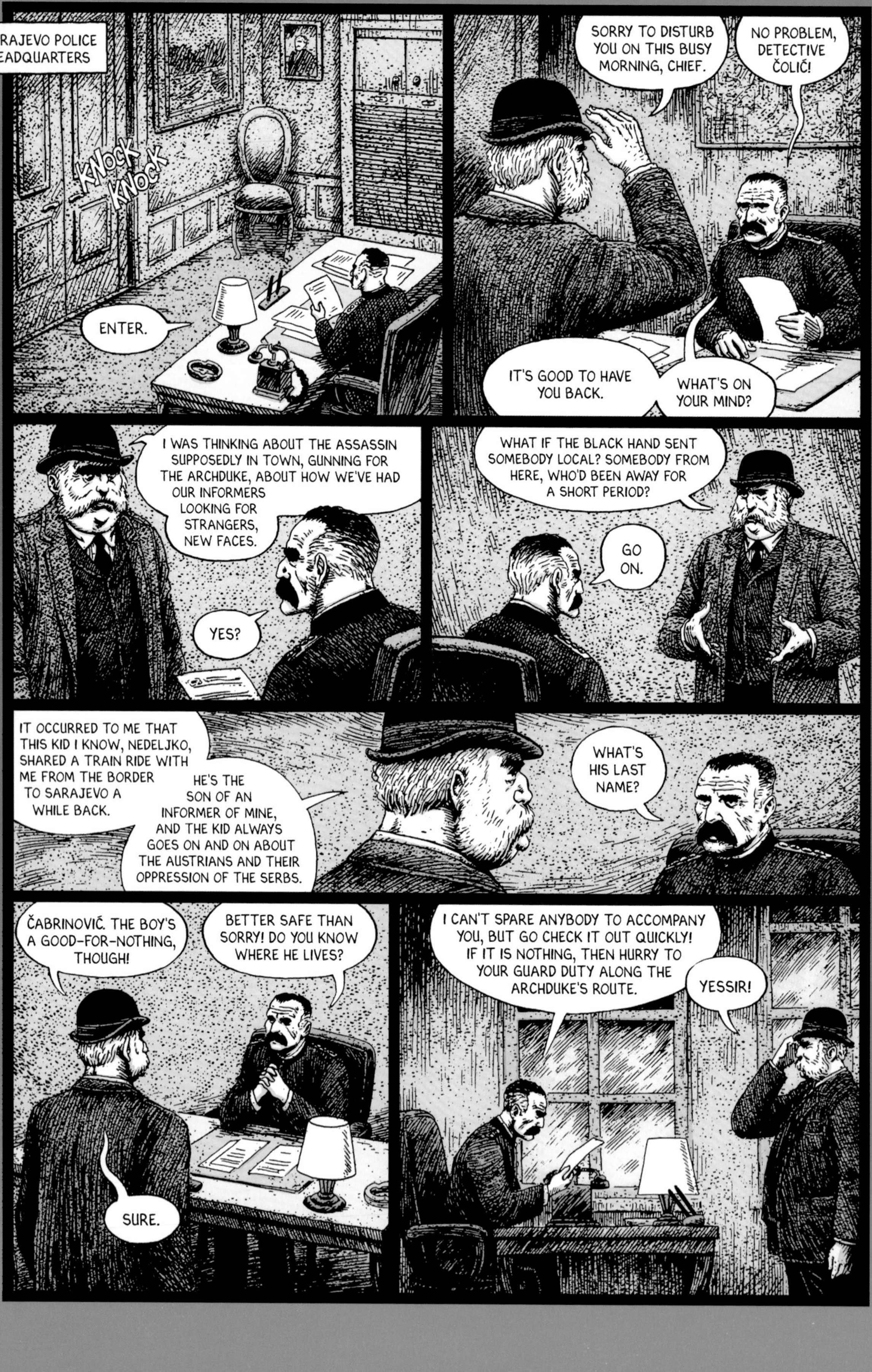
SARAJEVO POLICE HEADQUARTERS
KNOCK KNOCK
ENTER.
SORRY TO DISTURB YOU ON THIS BUSY MORNING, CHIEF.
NO PROBLEM, DETECTIVE ČOLIĆ!
IT'S GOOD TO HAVE YOU BACK.
WHAT'S ON YOUR MIND?
I WAS THINKING ABOUT THE ASSASSIN SUPPOSEDLY IN TOWN, GUNNING FOR THE ARCHDUKE, ABOUT HOW WE'VE HAD OUR INFORMERS LOOKING FOR STRANGERS, NEW FACES.
YES?
WHAT IF THE BLACK HAND SENT SOMEBODY LOCAL? SOMEBODY FROM HERE, WHO'D BEEN AWAY FOR A SHORT PERIOD?
GO ON.
IT OCCURRED TO ME THAT THIS KID I KNOW, NEDELJKO, SHARED A TRAIN RIDE WITH ME FROM THE BORDER TO SARAJEVO A WHILE BACK.
HE'S THE SON OF AN INFORMER OF MINE, AND THE KID ALWAYS GOES ON AND ON ABOUT THE AUSTRIANS AND THEIR OPPRESSION OF THE SERBS.
WHAT'S HIS LAST NAME?
ČABRINOVIĆ. THE BOY'S A GOOD-FOR-NOTHING, THOUGH!
BETTER SAFE THAN SORRY! DO YOU KNOW WHERE HE LIVES?
SURE.
I CAN'T SPARE ANYBODY TO ACCOMPANY YOU, BUT GO CHECK IT OUT QUICKLY! IF IT IS NOTHING, THEN HURRY TO YOUR GUARD DUTY ALONG THE ARCHDUKE'S ROUTE.
YESSIR!

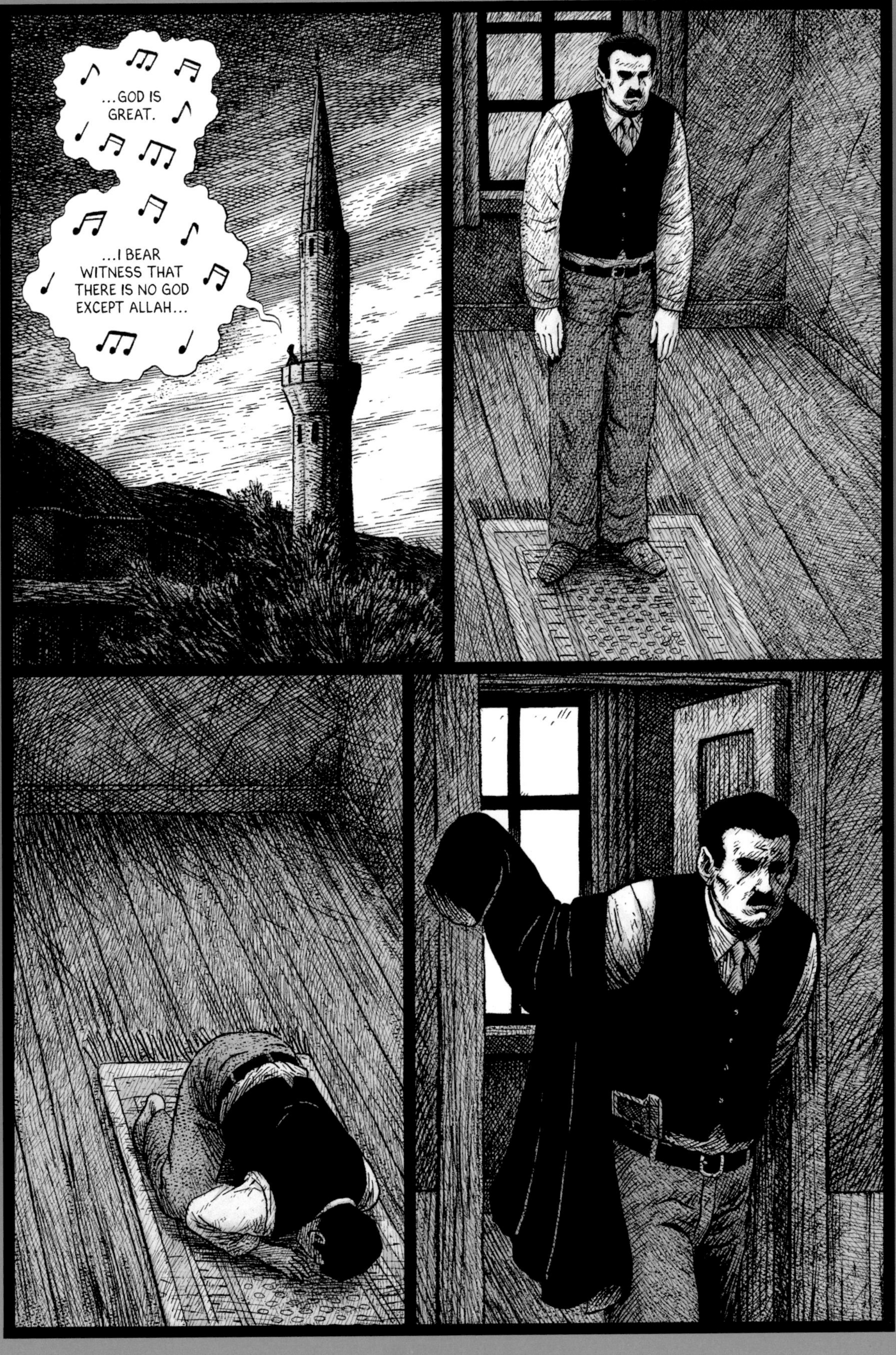
...GOD IS GREAT.
...I BEAR WITNESS THAT THERE IS NO GOD EXCEPT ALLAH...

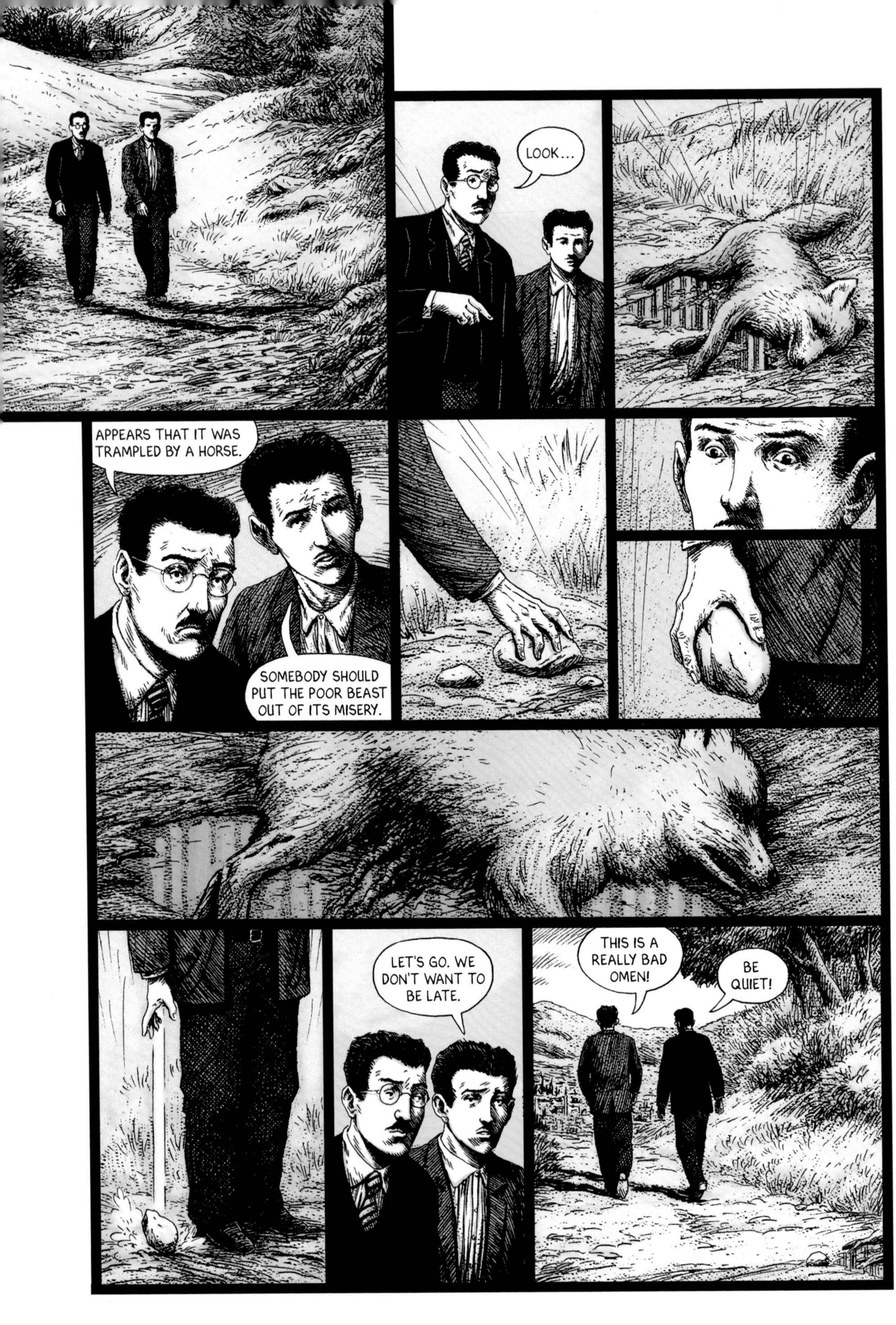
LOOK...
APPEARS THAT IT WAS TRAMPLED BY A HORSE.
SOMEBODY SHOULD PUT THE POOR BEAST OUT OF ITS MISERY.
LET'S GO. WE DON'T WANT TO BE LATE.
THIS IS A REALLY BAD OMEN!
BE QUIET!

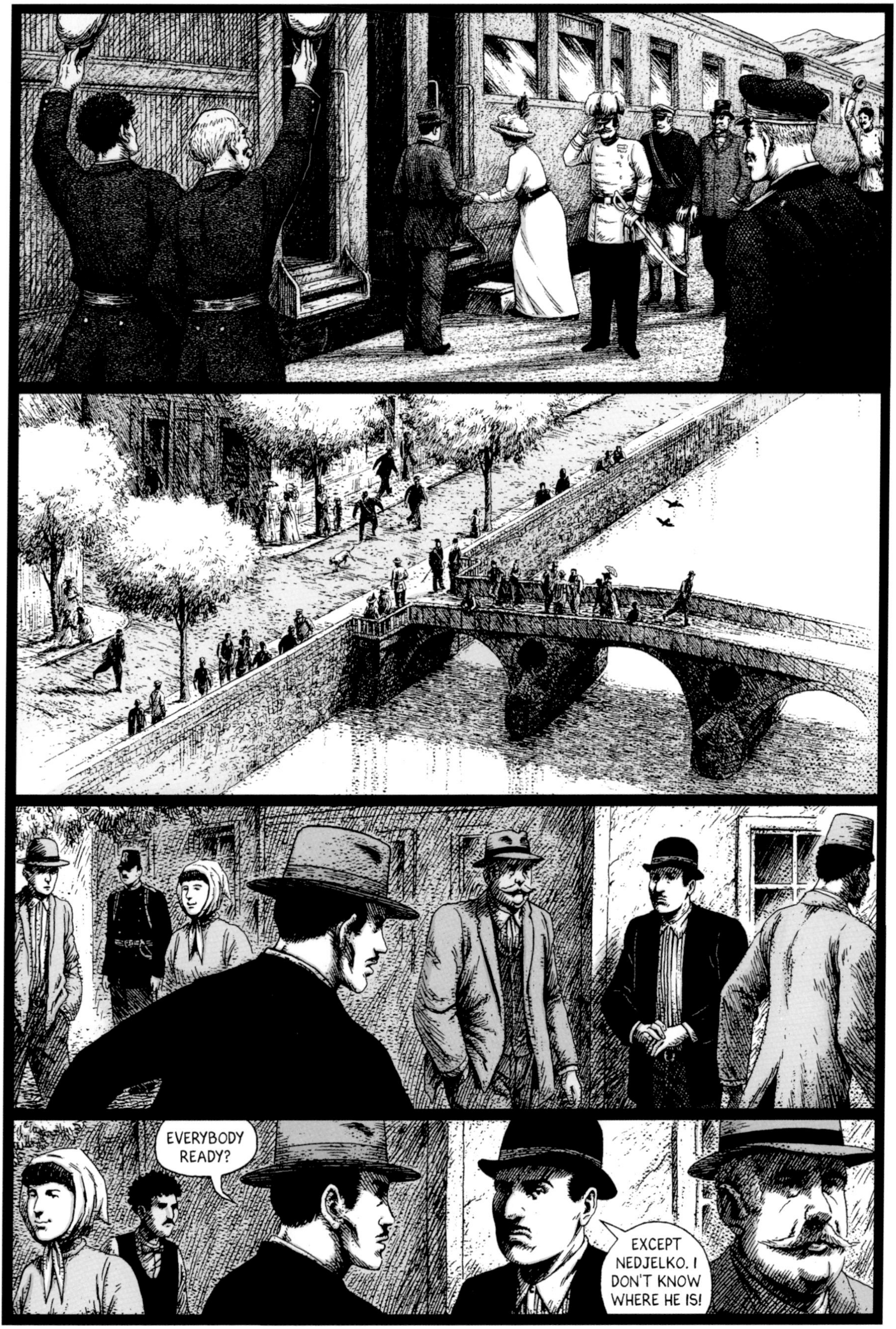
EVERYBODY READY?
EXCEPT NEDJELKO. I DON'T KNOW WHERE HE IS!

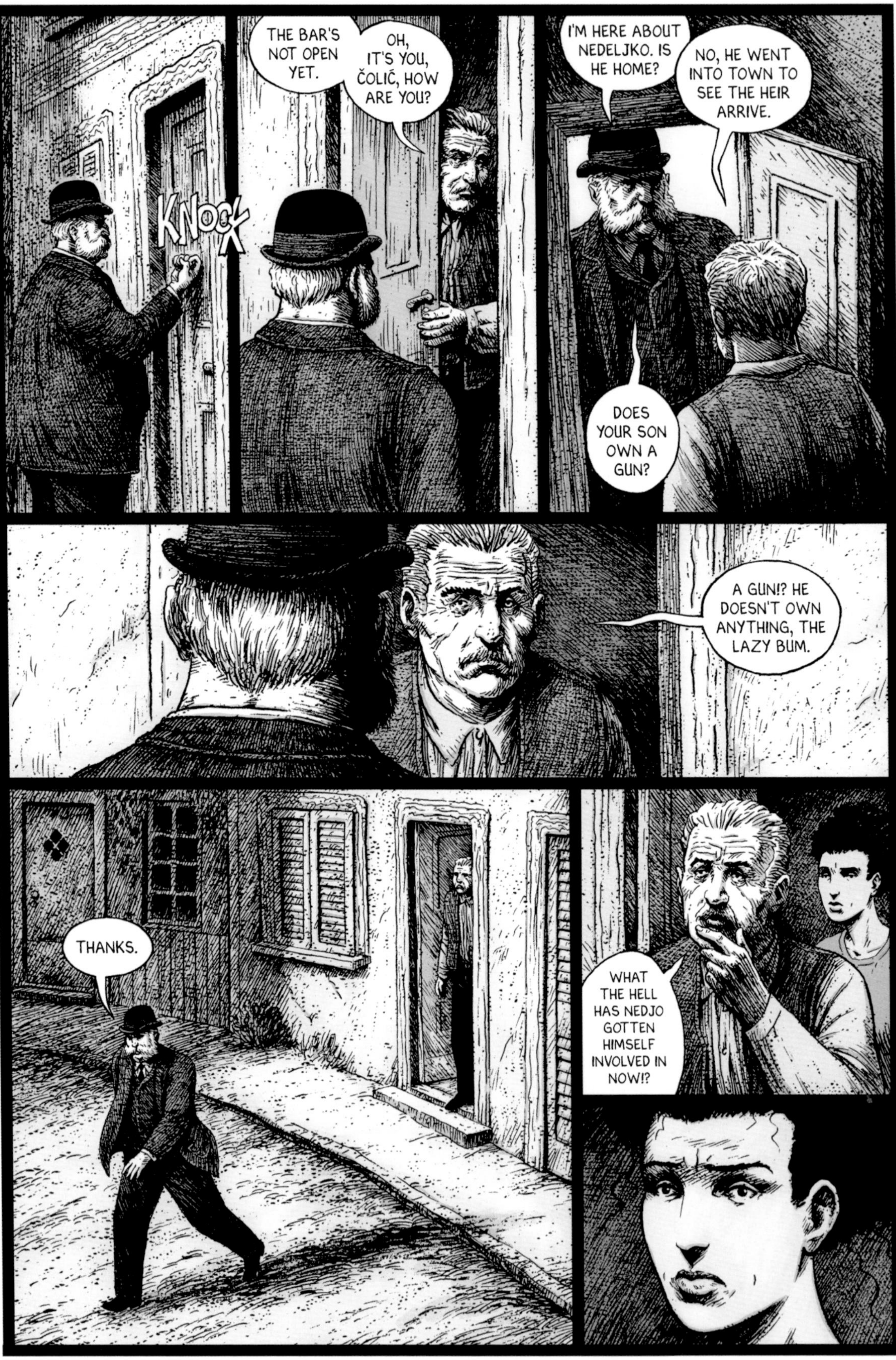
KNOCK
THE BAR'S NOT OPEN YET.
OH, IT'S YOU, ČOLIĆ, HOW ARE YOU?
I'M HERE ABOUT NEDELJKO. IS HE HOME?
NO, HE WENT INTO TOWN TO SEE THE HEIR ARRIVE.
DOES YOUR SON OWN A GUN?
A GUN!? HE DOESN'T OWN ANYTHING, THE LAZY BUM.
THANKS.
WHAT THE HELL HAS NEDJO GOTTEN HIMSELF INVOLVED IN NOW!?

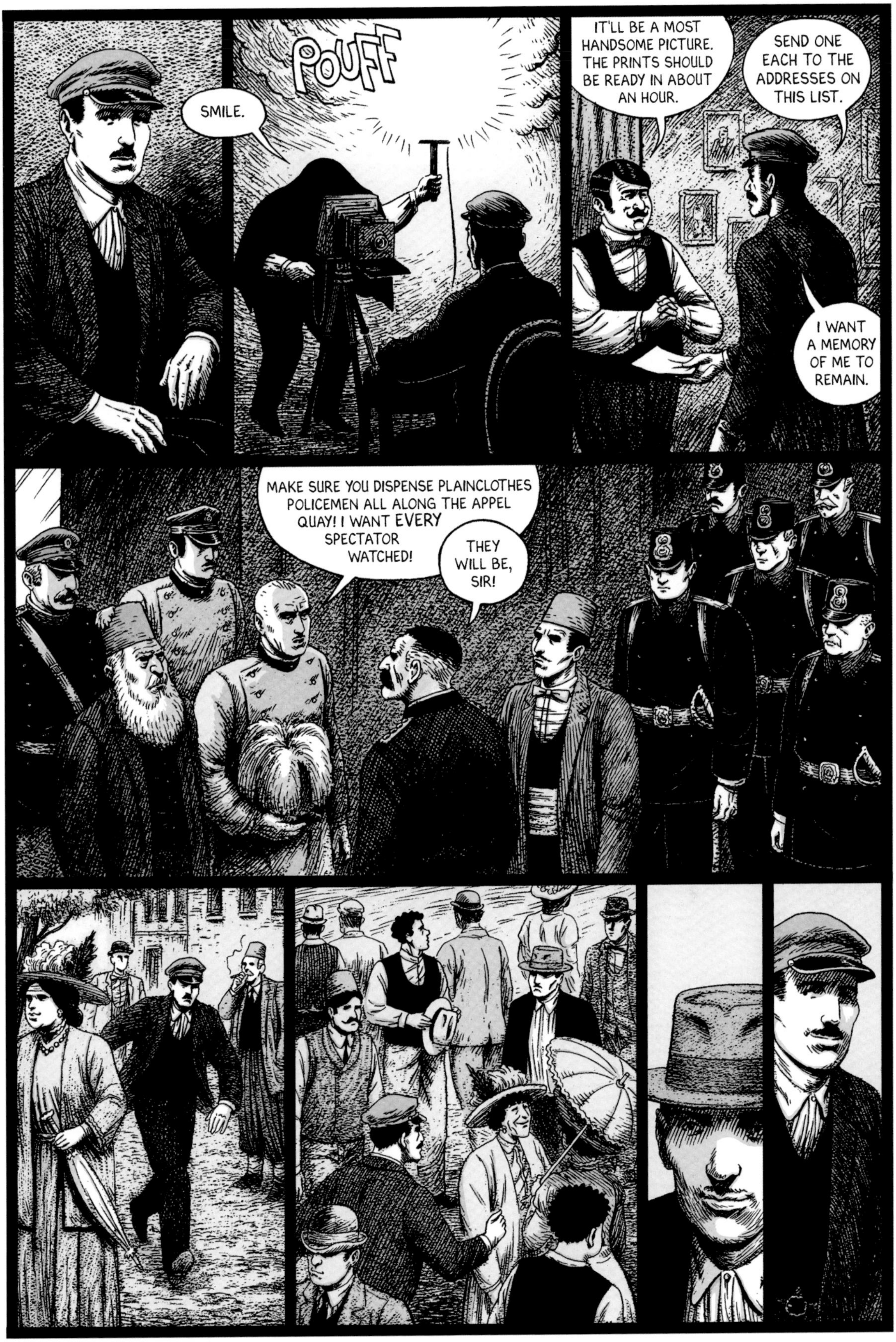
SMILE.
POUFF
IT'LL BE A MOST HANDSOME PICTURE. THE PRINTS SHOULD BE READY IN ABOUT AN HOUR.
SEND ONE EACH TO THE ADDRESSES ON THIS LIST.
I WANT A MEMORY OF ME TO REMAIN.
MAKE SURE YOU DISPENSE PLAINCLOTHES POLICEMEN ALL ALONG THE APPEL QUAY! I WANT EVERY SPECTATOR WATCHED!
THEY WILL BE, SIR!

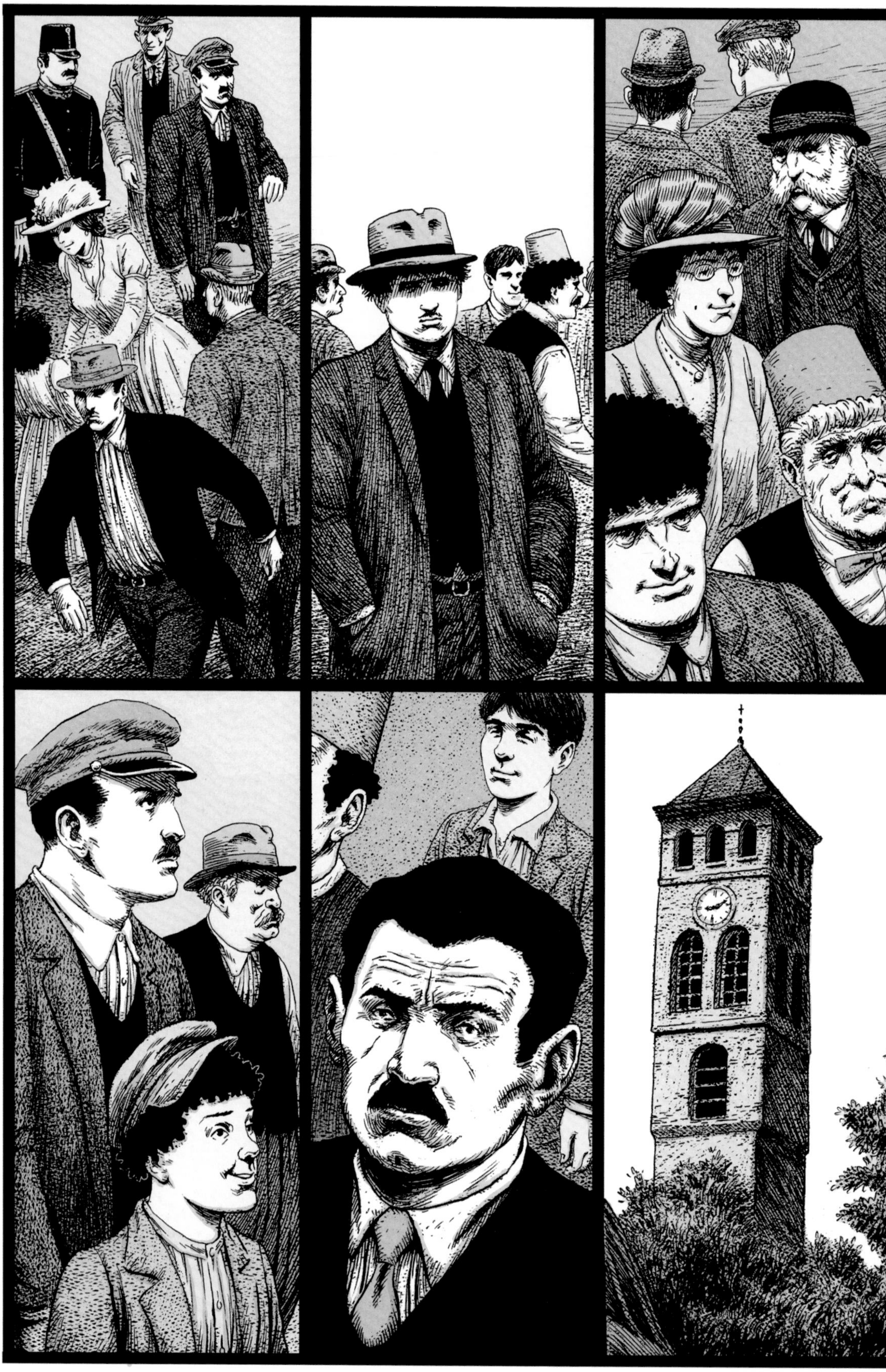

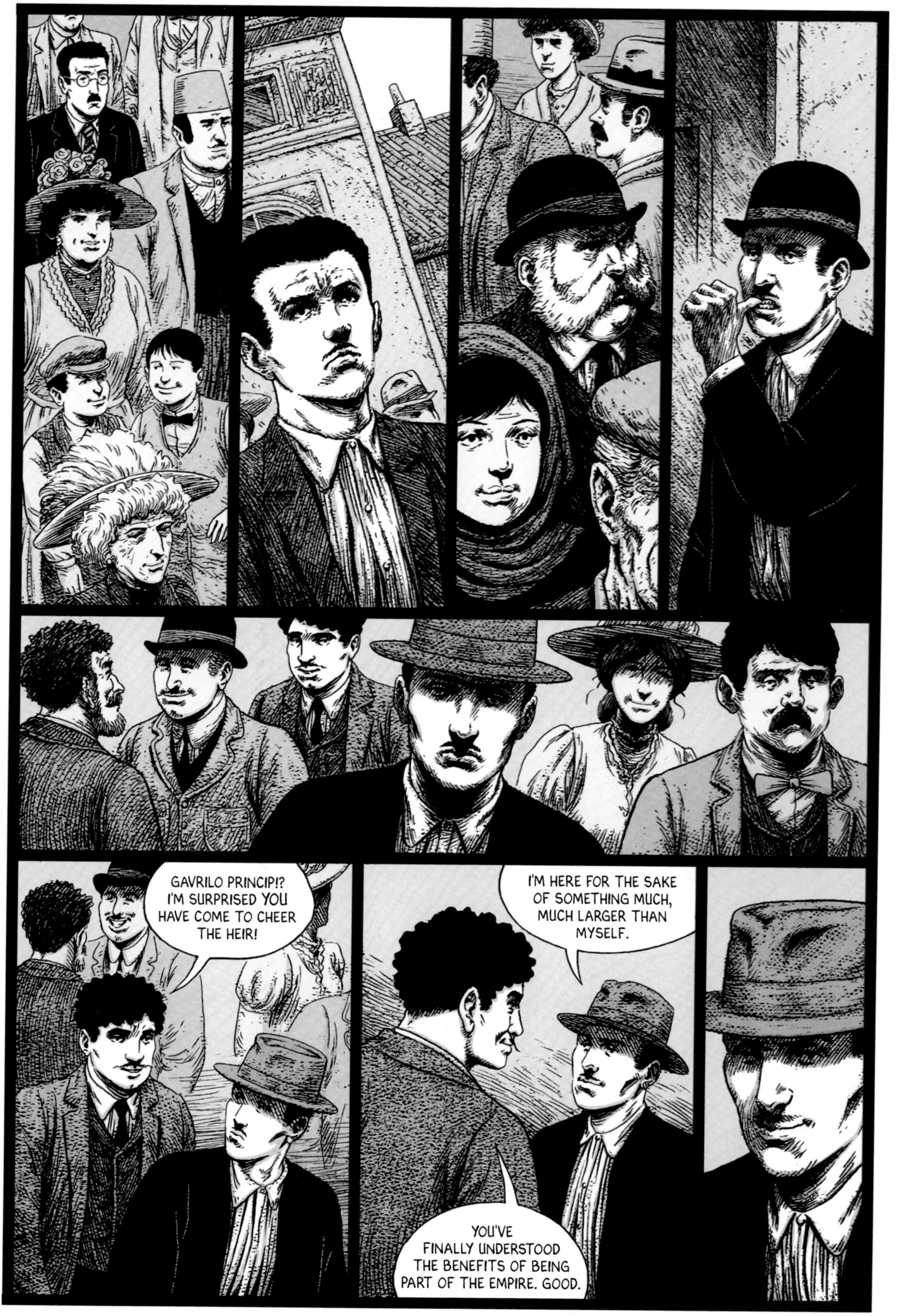
GAVRILO PRINCIP!? I'M SURPRISED YOU HAVE COME TO CHEER THE HEIR!
YOU'VE FINALLY UNDERSTOOD THE BENEFITS OF BEING PART OF THE EMPIRE. GOOD.
I'M HERE FOR THE SAKE OF SOMETHING MUCH, MUCH LARGER THAN MYSELF.

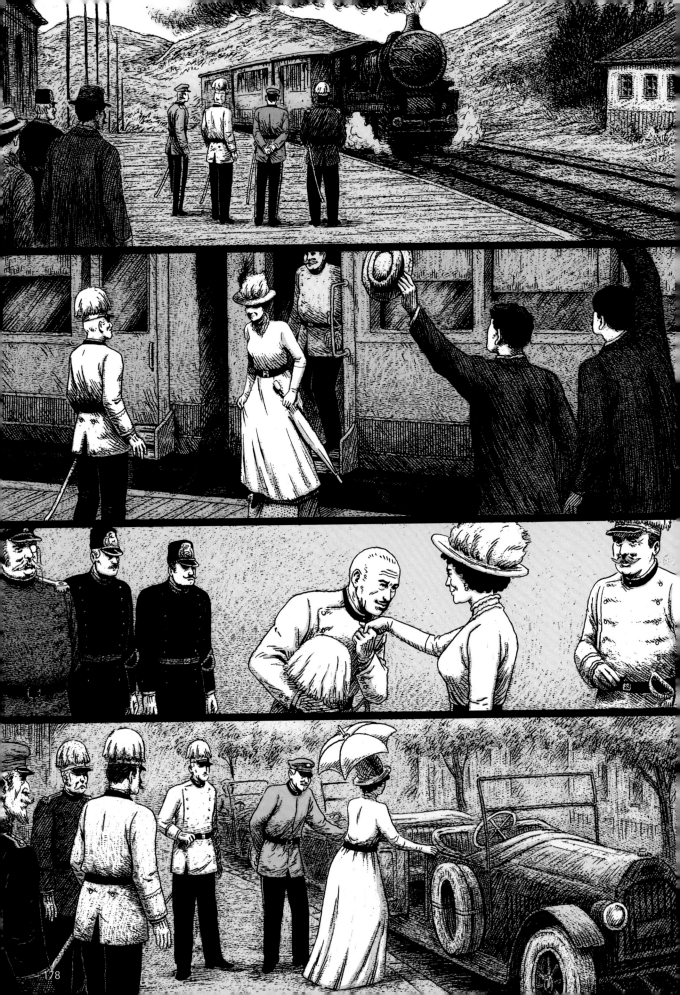

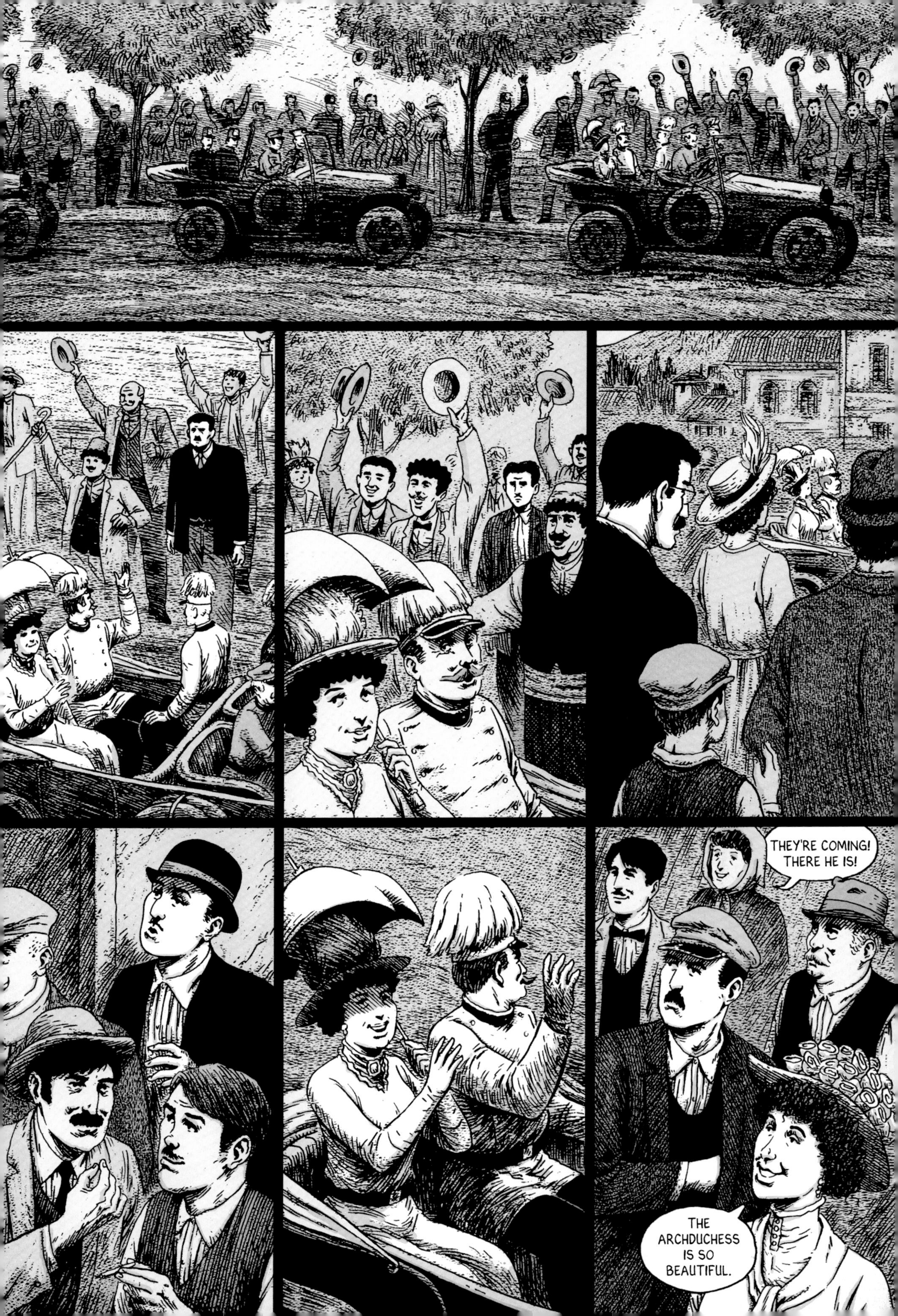
THEY'RE COMING! THERE HE IS!
THE ARCHDUCHESS IS SO BEAUTIFUL.

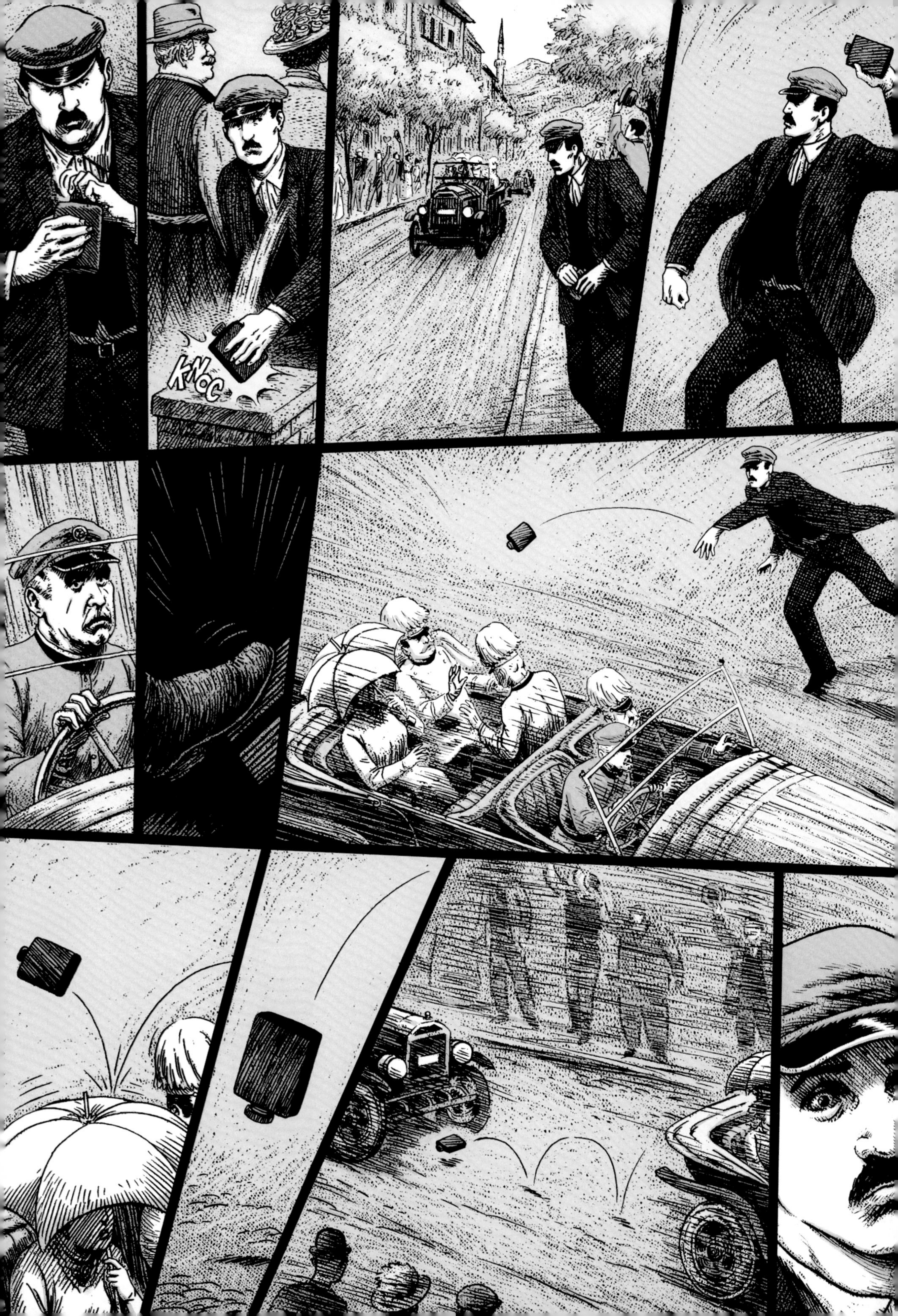
KNOC

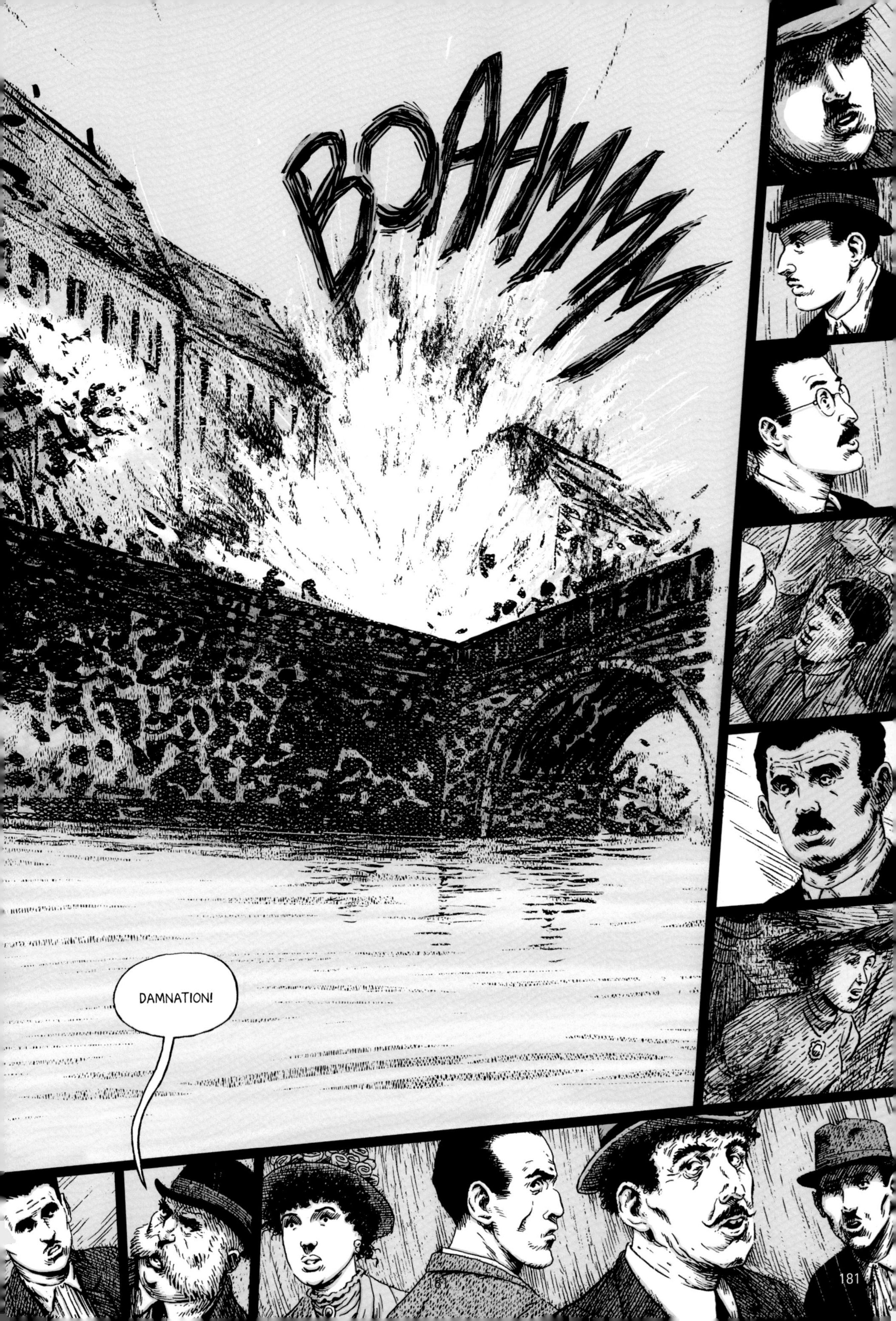
BOAAMMM
DAMNATION!

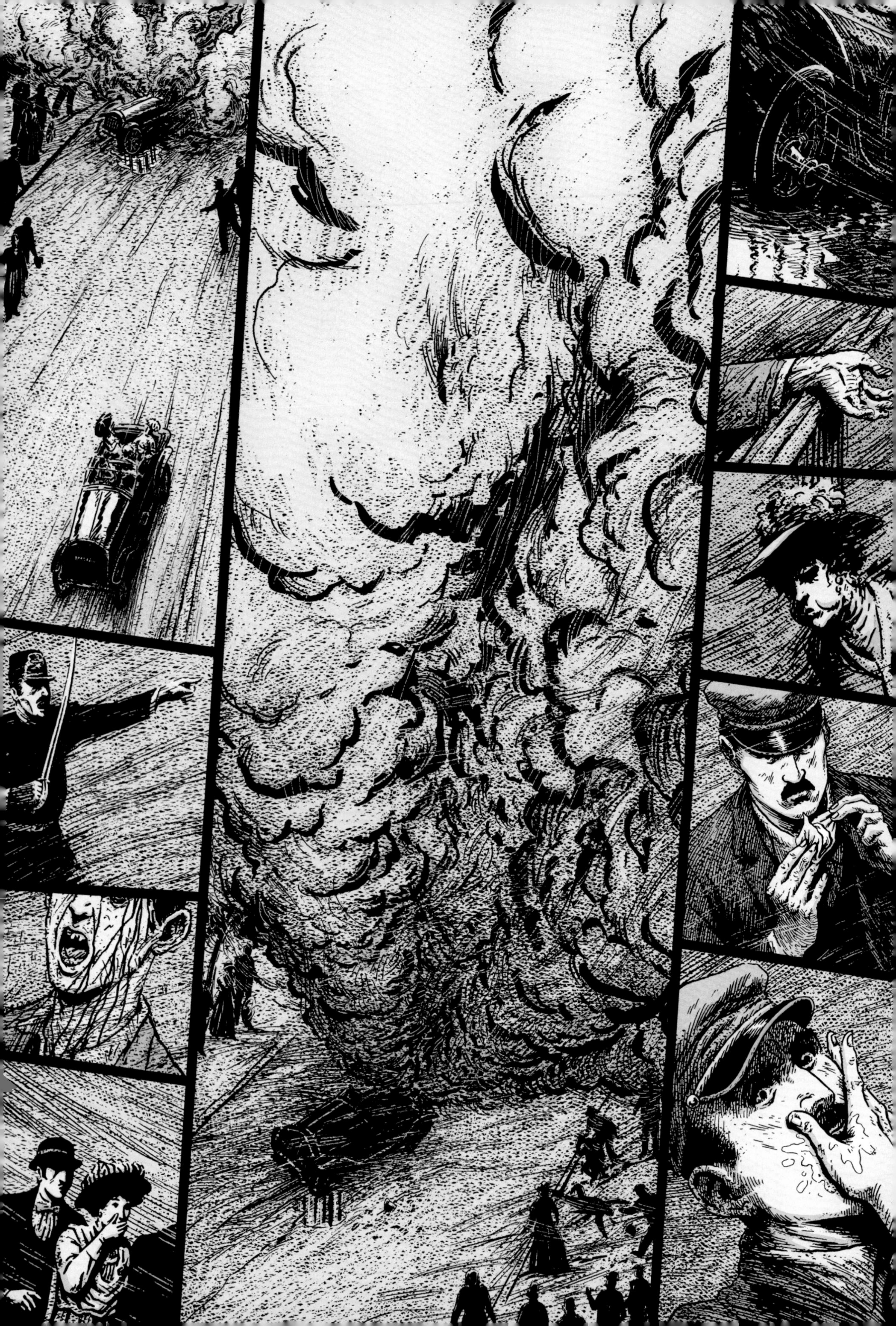

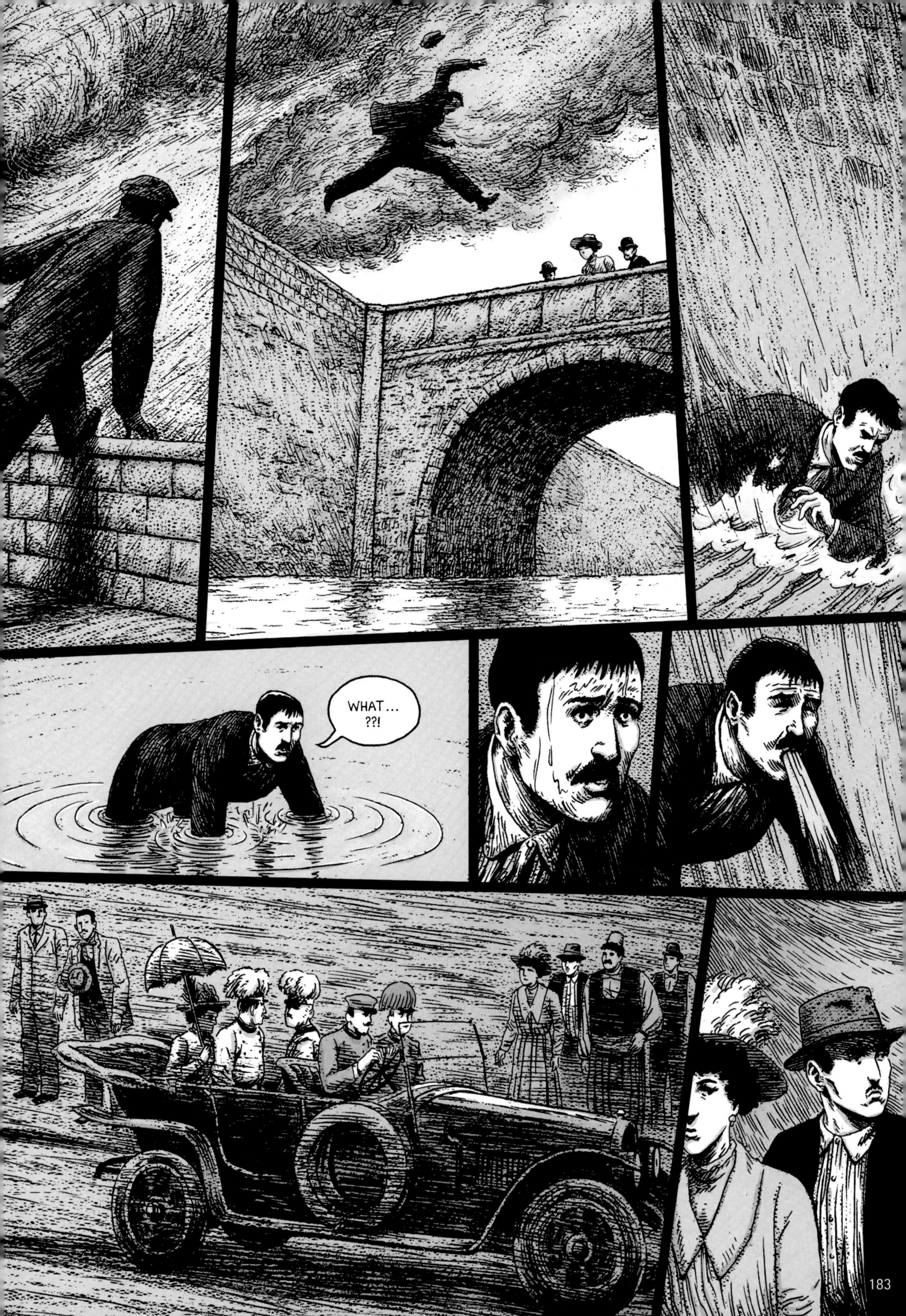
WHAT...
??!

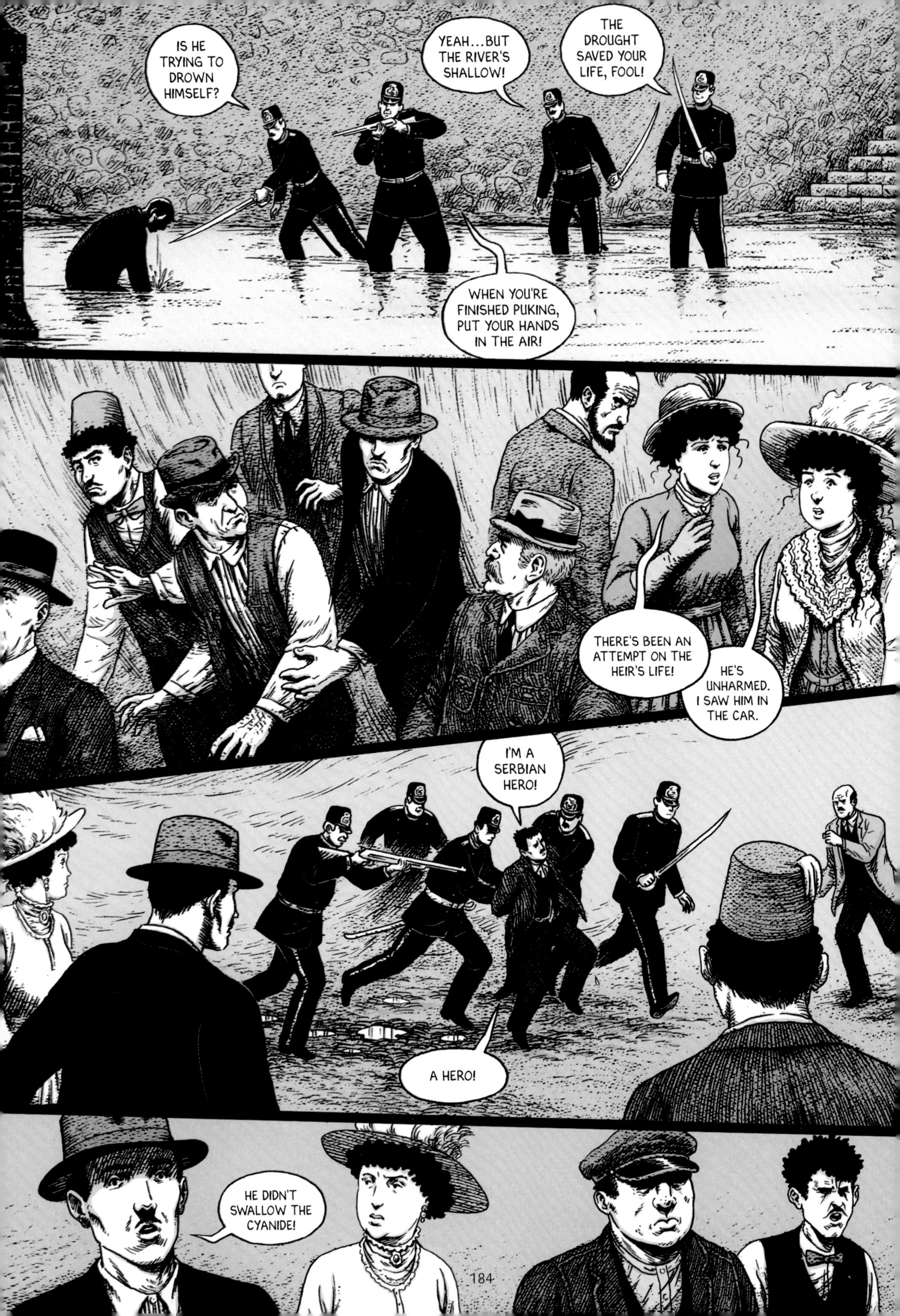
IS HE TRYING TO DROWN HIMSELF?
YEAH...BUT THE RIVER'S SHALLOW!
THE DROUGHT SAVED YOUR LIFE, FOOL!
WHEN YOU'RE FINISHED PUKING, PUT YOUR HANDS IN THE AIR!
THERE'S BEEN AN ATTEMPT ON THE HEIR'S LIFE!
HE'S UNHARMED. I SAW HIM IN THE CAR.
I'M A SERBIAN HERO!
A HERO!
HE DIDN'T SWALLOW THE CYANIDE!

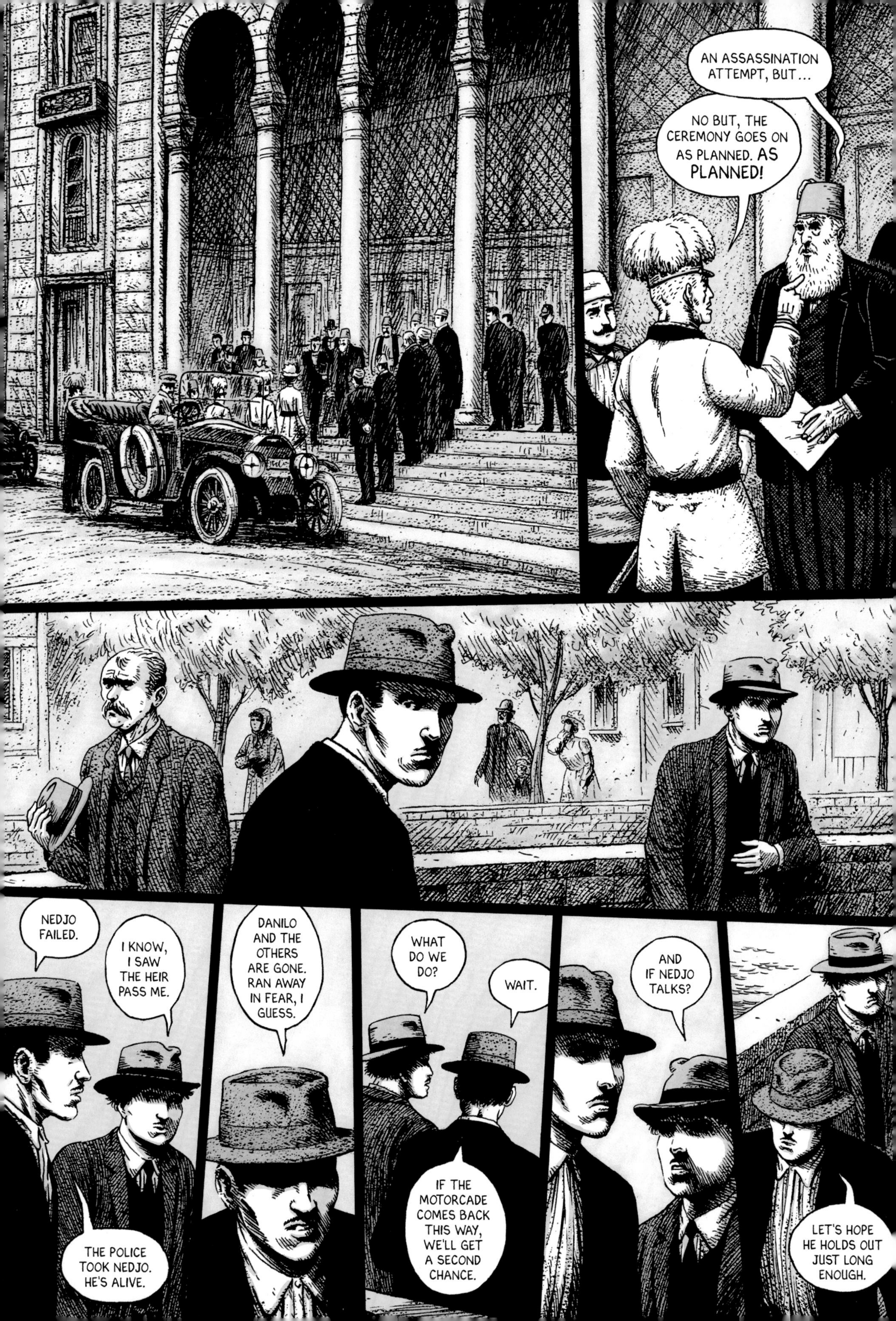
AN ASSASSINATION ATTEMPT, BUT...
NO BUT, THE CEREMONY GOES ON AS PLANNED. AS PLANNED!
NEDJO FAILED.
I KNOW, I SAW THE HEIR PASS ME.
THE POLICE TOOK NEDJO. HE'S ALIVE.
DANILO AND THE OTHERS ARE GONE. RAN AWAY IN FEAR, I GUESS.
WHAT DO WE DO?
WAIT.
IF THE MOTORCADE COMES BACK THIS WAY, WE'LL GET A SECOND CHANCE.
AND IF NEDJO TALKS?
LET'S HOPE HE HOLDS OUT JUST LONG ENOUGH.

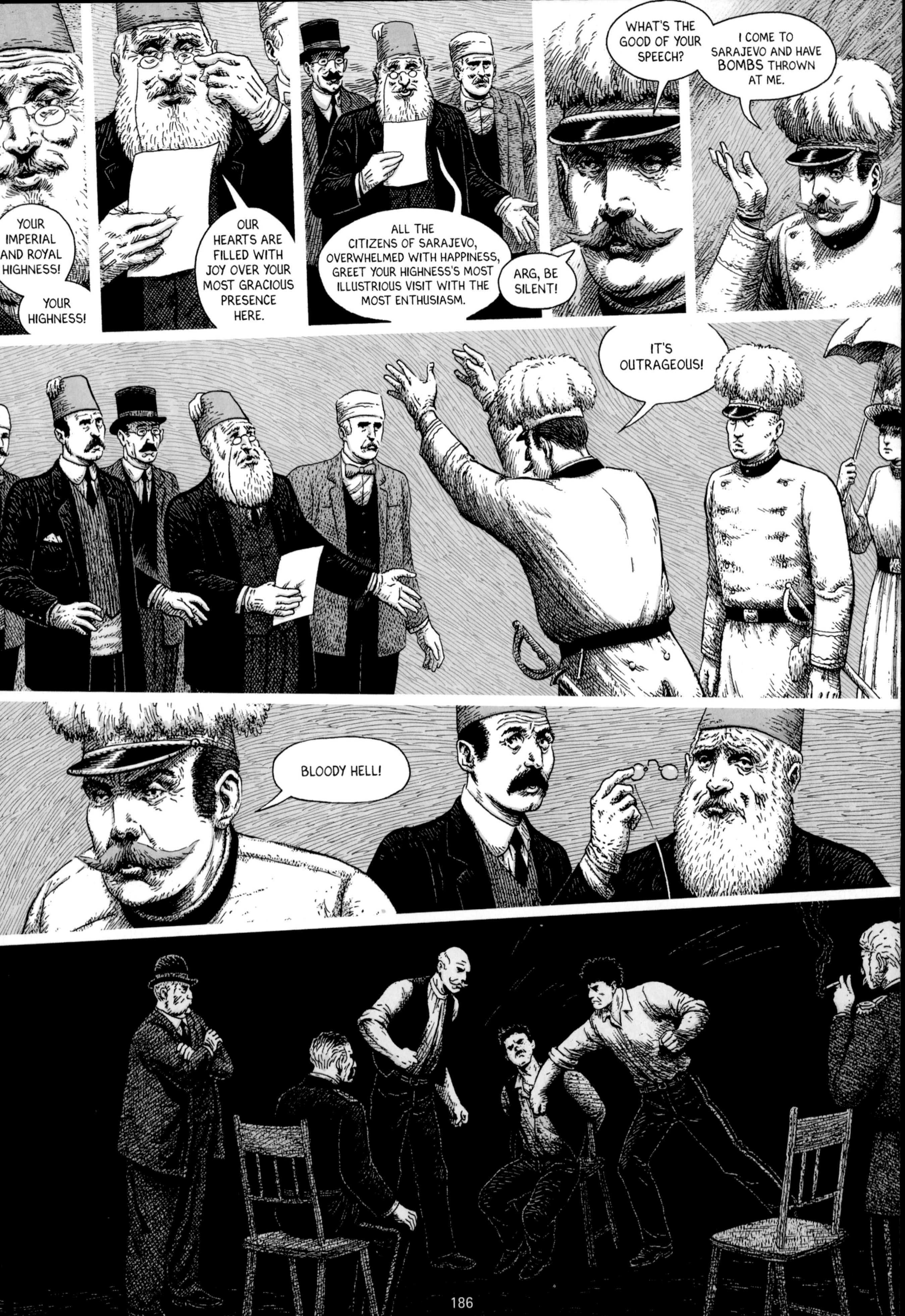
YOUR IMPERIAL AND ROYAL HIGHNESS!
YOUR HIGHNESS!
OUR HEARTS ARE FILLED WITH JOY OVER YOUR MOST GRACIOUS PRESENCE HERE.
ALL THE CITIZENS OF SARAJEVO, OVERWHELMED WITH HAPPINESS, GREET YOUR HIGHNESS'S MOST ILLUSTRIOUS VISIT WITH THE MOST ENTHUSIASM.
ARG, BE SILENT!
WHAT'S THE GOOD OF YOUR SPEECH?
I COME TO SARAJEVO AND HAVE BOMBS THROWN AT ME.
IT'S OUTRAGEOUS!
BLOODY HELL!

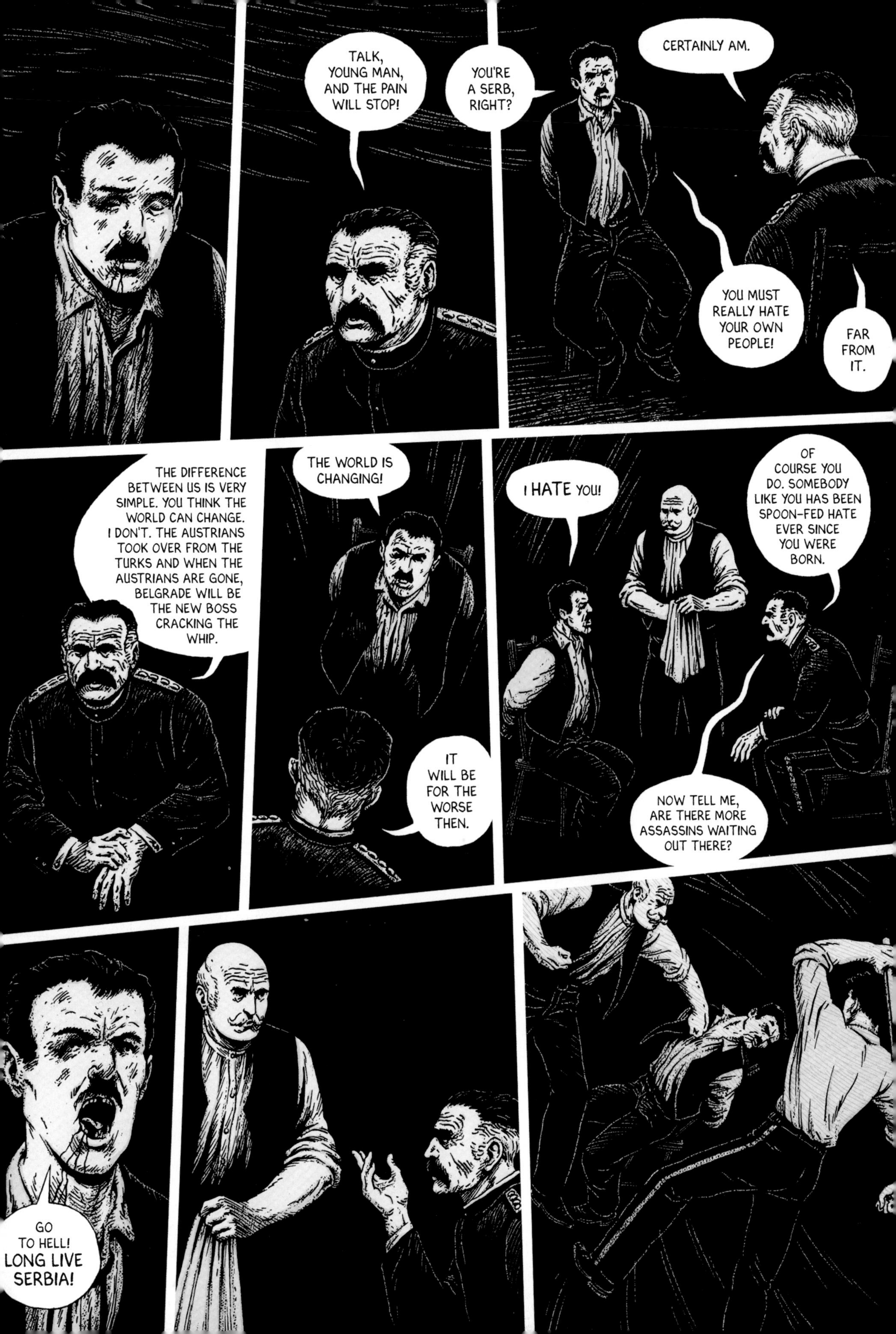
TALK, YOUNG MAN, AND THE PAIN WILL STOP!
YOU'RE A SERB, RIGHT?
CERTAINLY AM.
YOU MUST REALLY HATE YOUR OWN PEOPLE!
FAR FROM IT.
THE DIFFERENCE BETWEEN US IS VERY SIMPLE. YOU THINK THE WORLD CAN CHANGE. I DON'T. THE AUSTRIANS TOOK OVER FROM THE TURKS AND WHEN THE AUSTRIANS ARE GONE, BELGRADE WILL BE THE NEW BOSS CRACKING THE WHIP.
THE WORLD IS CHANGING!
IT WILL BE FOR THE WORSE THEN.
I HATE YOU!
OF COURSE YOU DO. SOMEBODY LIKE YOU HAS BEEN SPOON-FED HATE EVER SINCE YOU WERE BORN.
NOW TELL ME, ARE THERE MORE ASSASSINS WAITING OUT THERE?
GO TO HELL! LONG LIVE SERBIA!

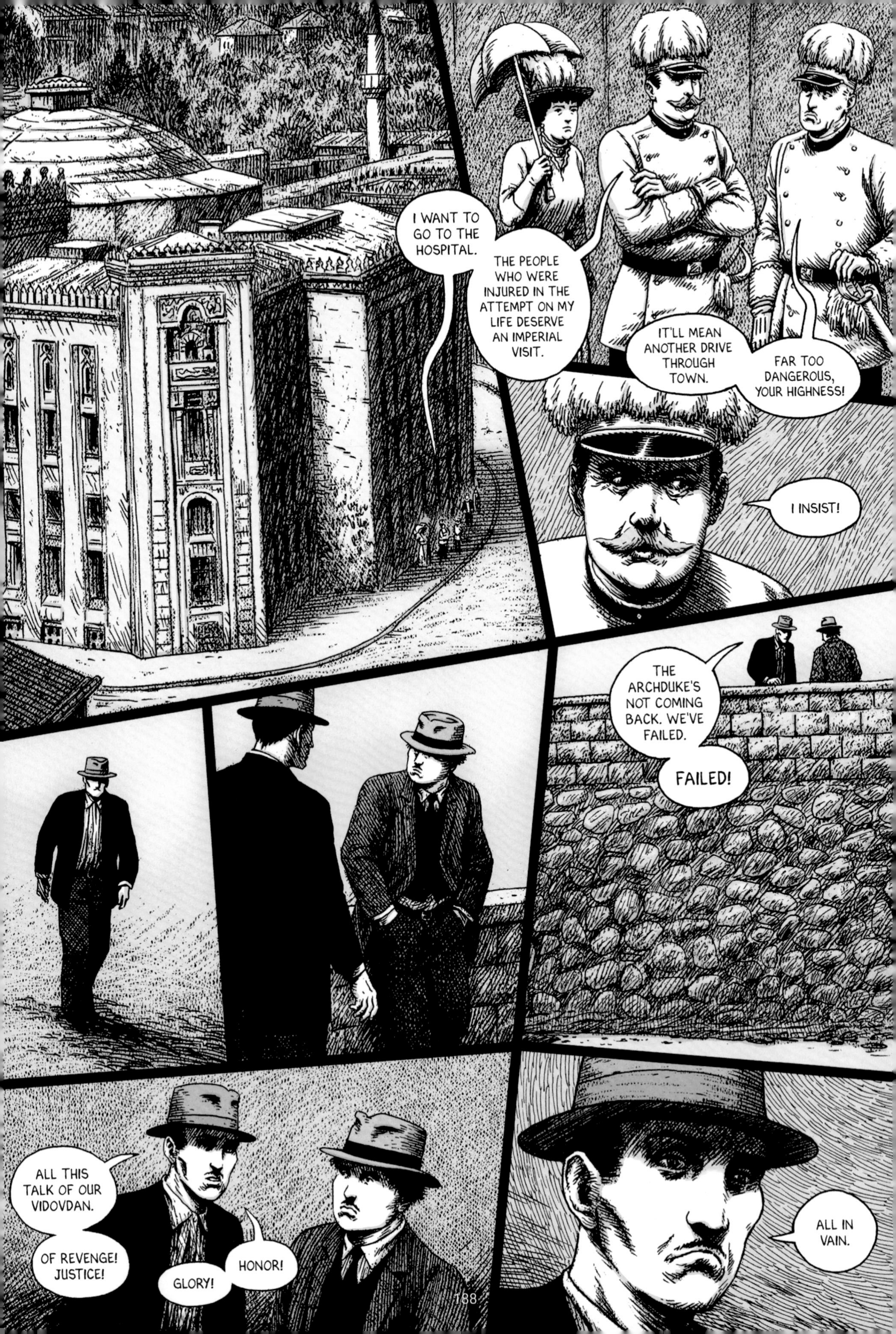
I WANT TO GO TO THE HOSPITAL.
THE PEOPLE WHO WERE INJURED IN THE ATTEMPT ON MY LIFE DESERVE AN IMPERIAL VISIT.
IT'LL MEAN ANOTHER DRIVE THROUGH TOWN.
FAR TOO DANGEROUS, YOUR HIGHNESS!
I INSIST!
THE ARCHDUKE'S NOT COMING BACK. WE'VE FAILED.
FAILED!
ALL THIS TALK OF OUR VIDOVDAN.
OF REVENGE! JUSTICE!
GLORY!
HONOR!
ALL IN VAIN.

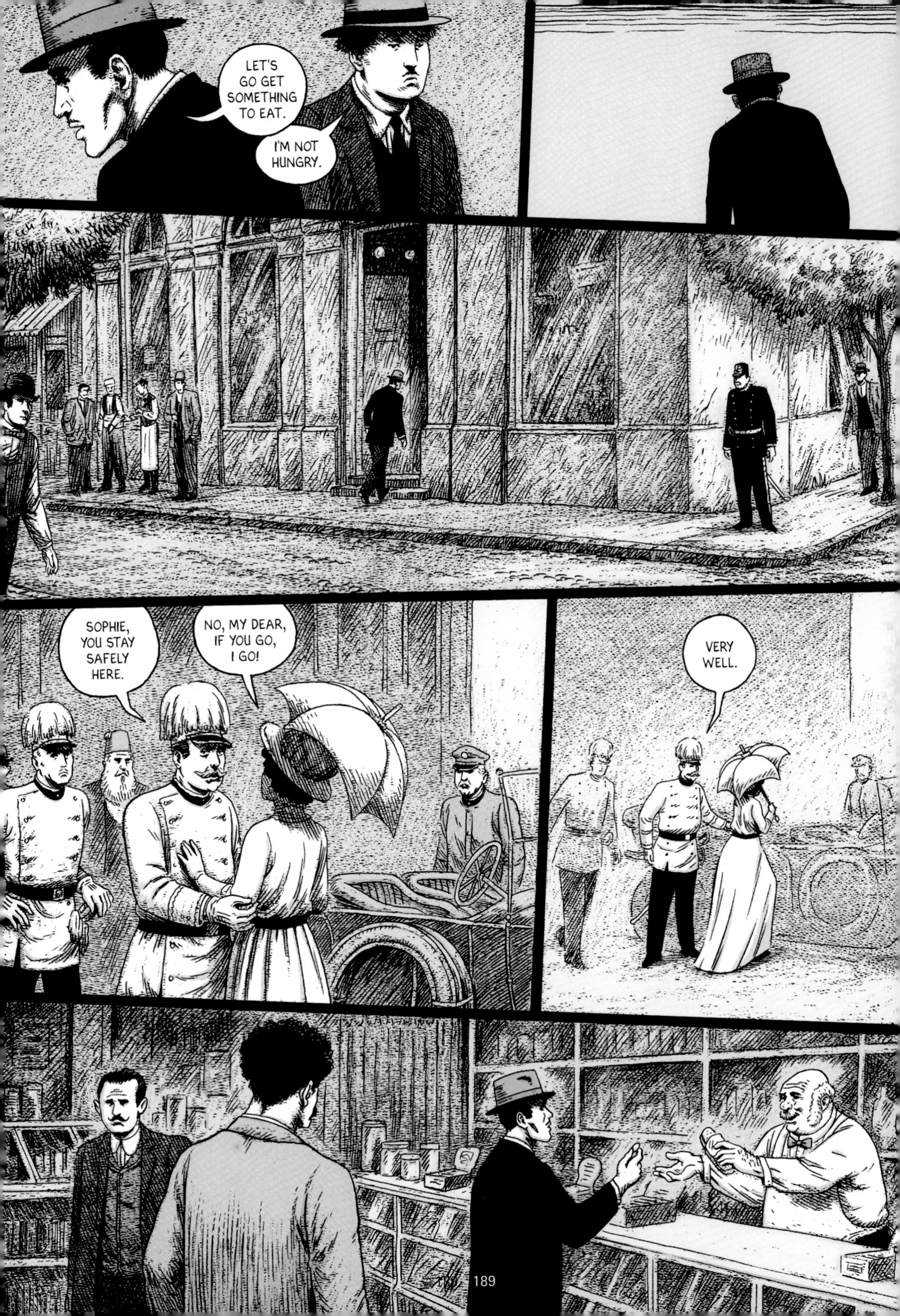
LET'S GO GET SOMETHING TO EAT.
I'M NOT HUNGRY.
SOPHIE, YOU STAY SAFELY HERE.
NO, MY DEAR, IF YOU GO, I GO!
VERY WELL.

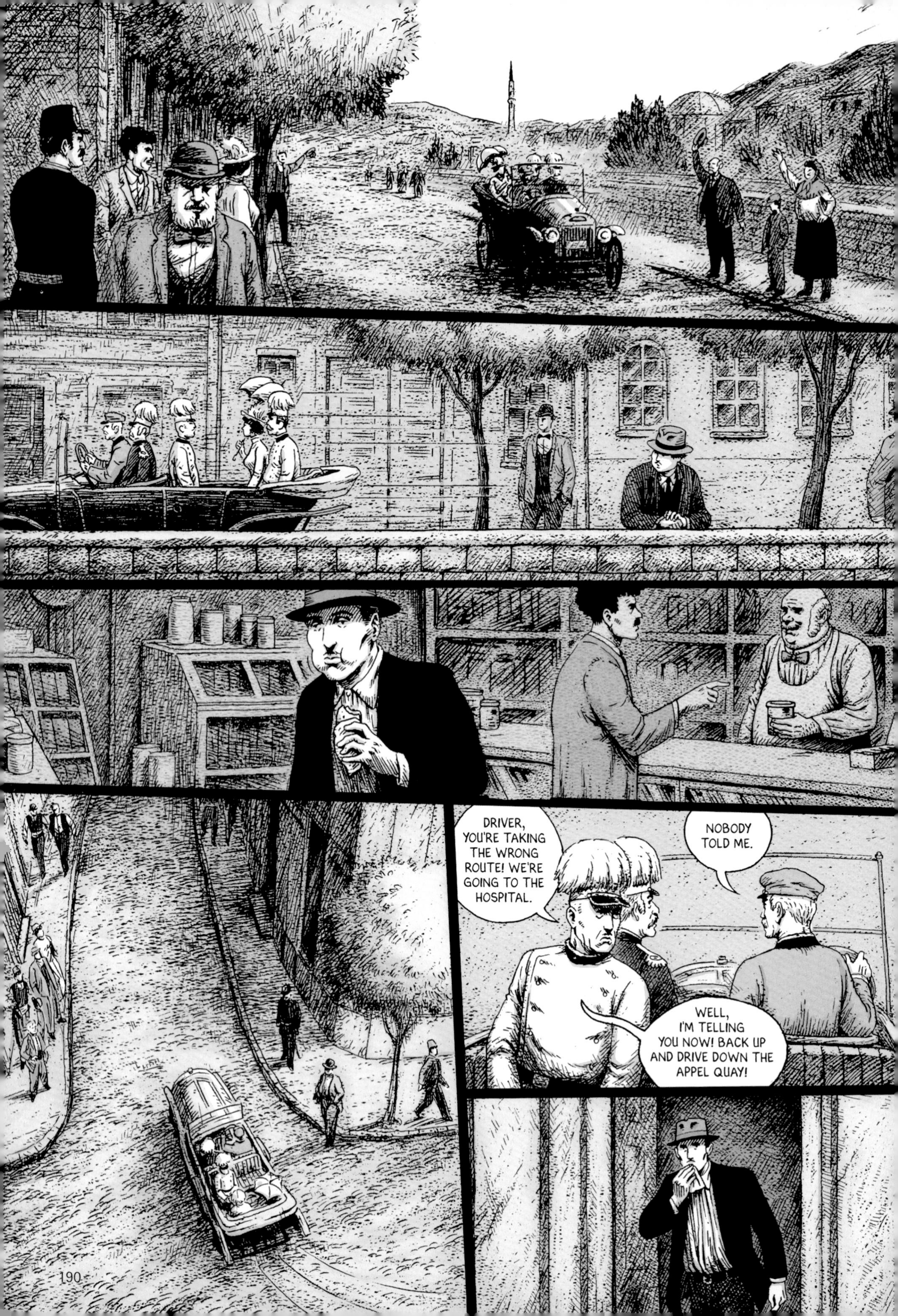
DRIVER, YOU'RE TAKING THE WRONG ROUTE! WE'RE GOING TO THE HOSPITAL.
NOBODY TOLD ME.
WELL, I'M TELLING YOU NOW! BACK UP AND DRIVE DOWN THE APPEL QUAY!

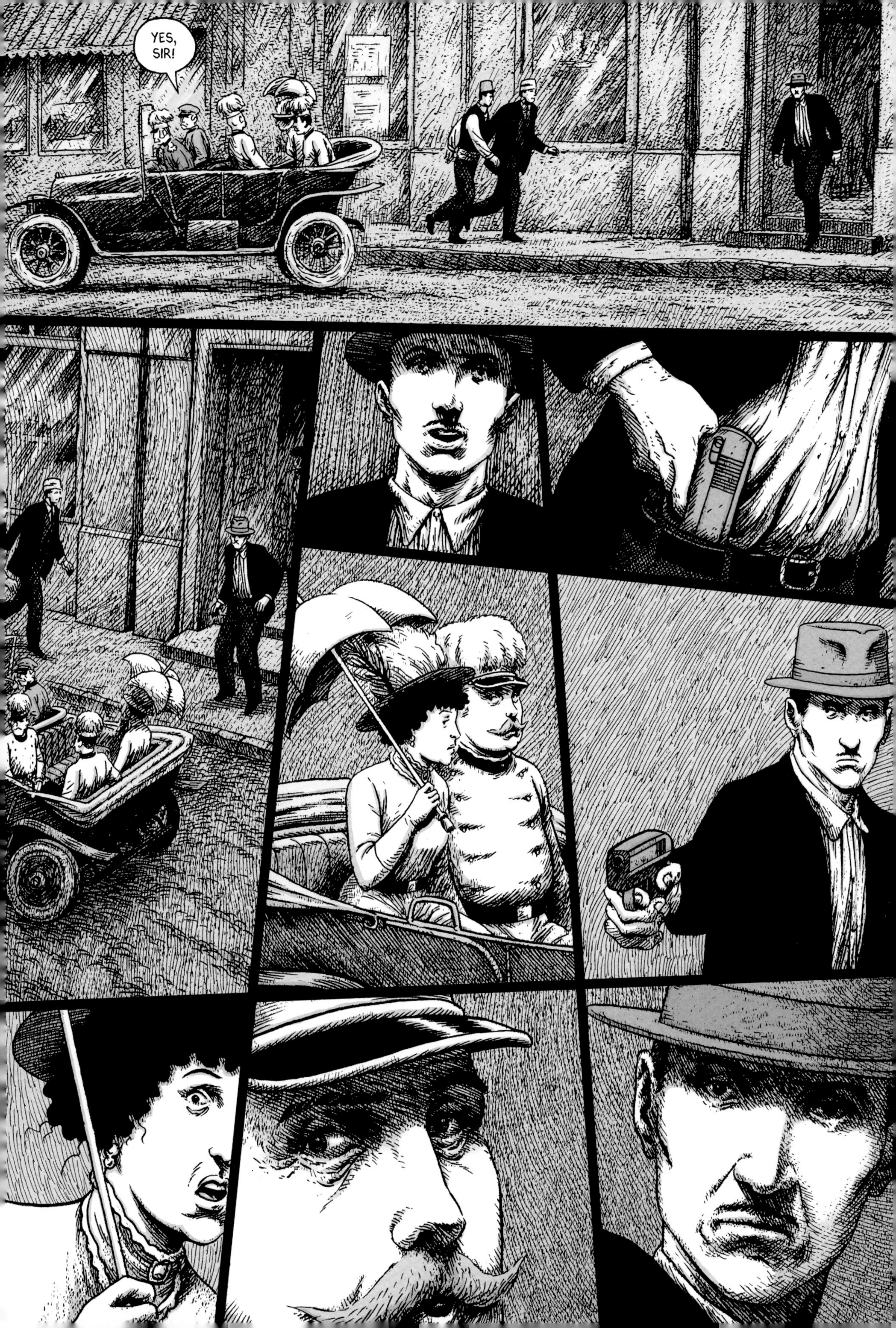
YES, SIR!

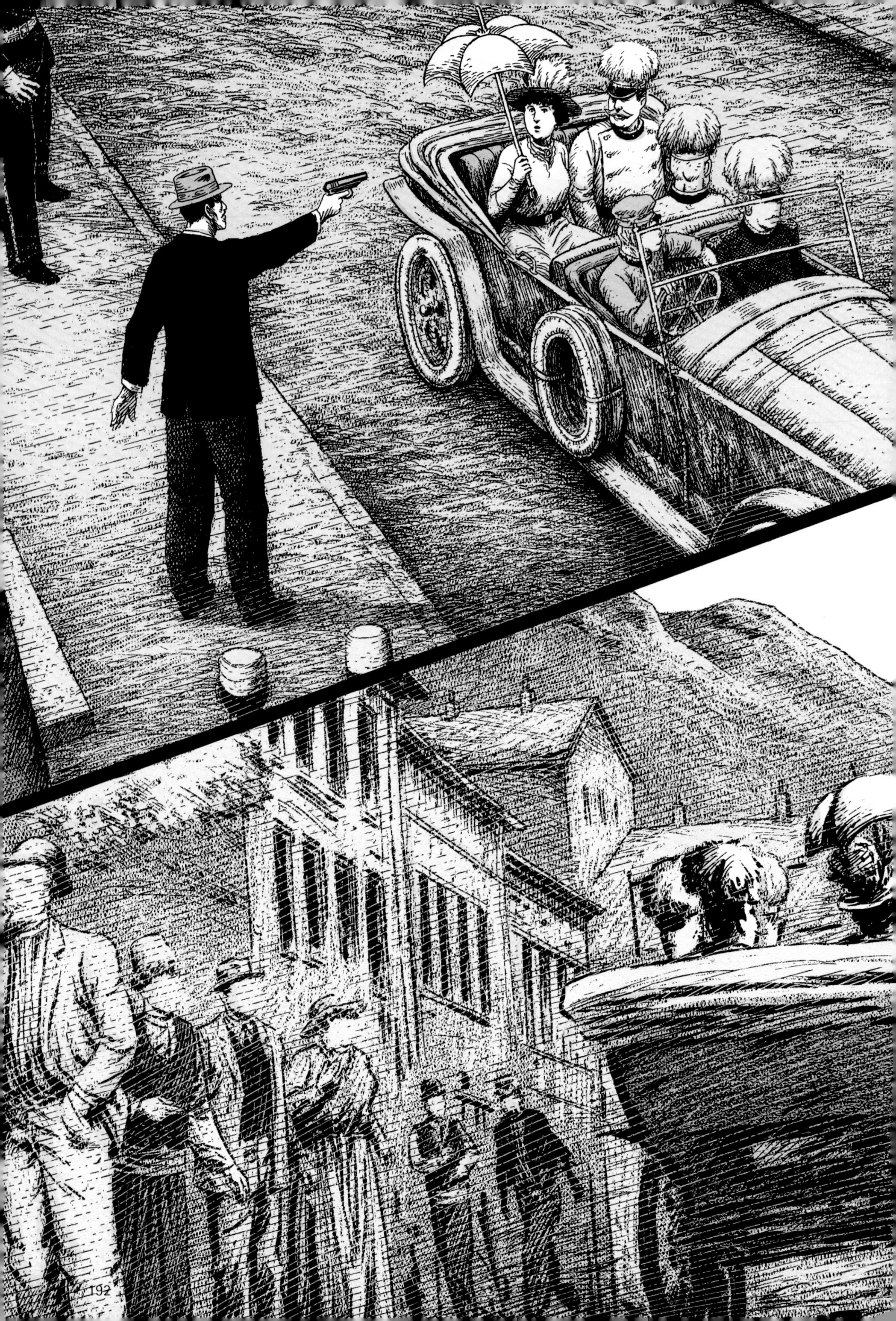

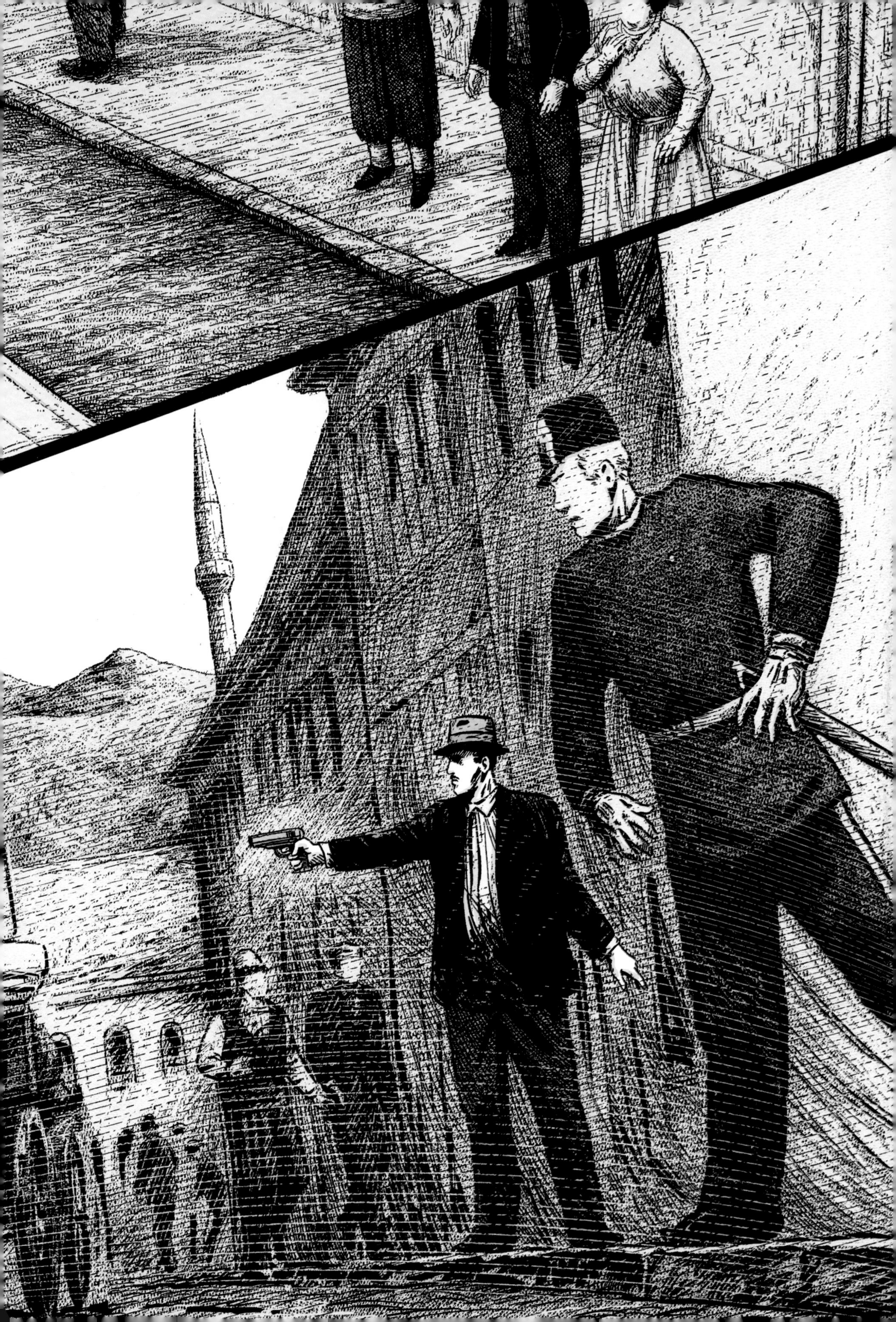

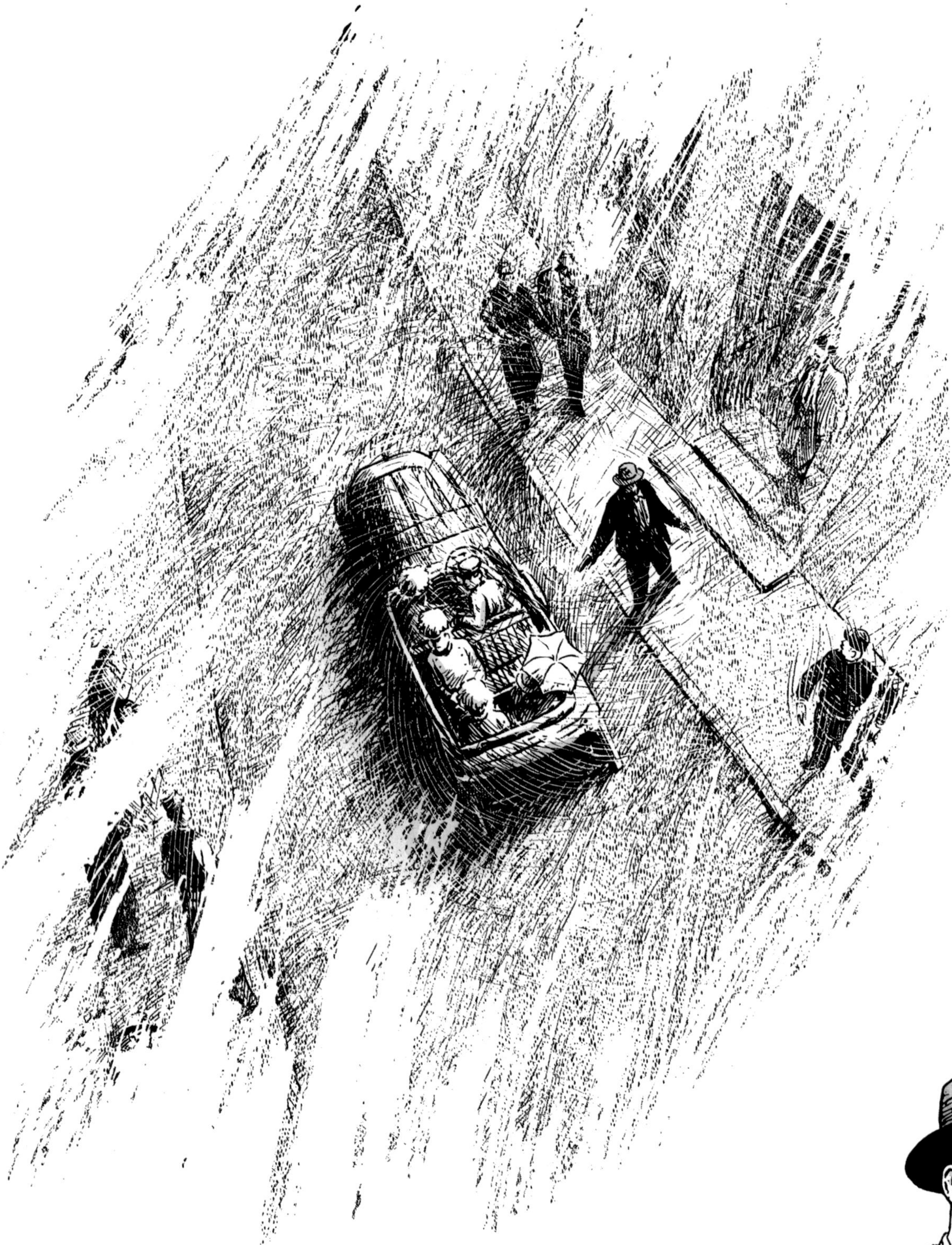

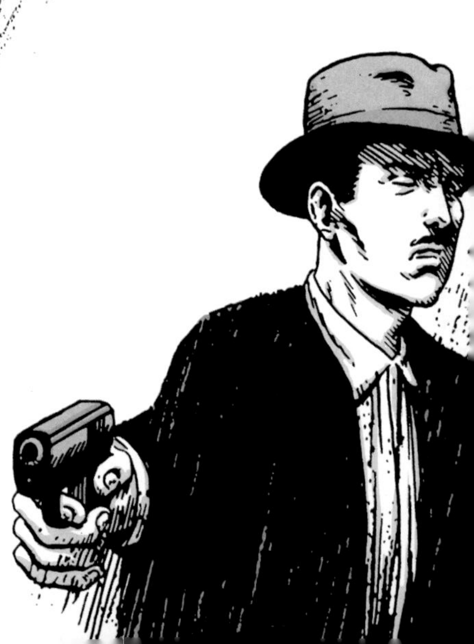

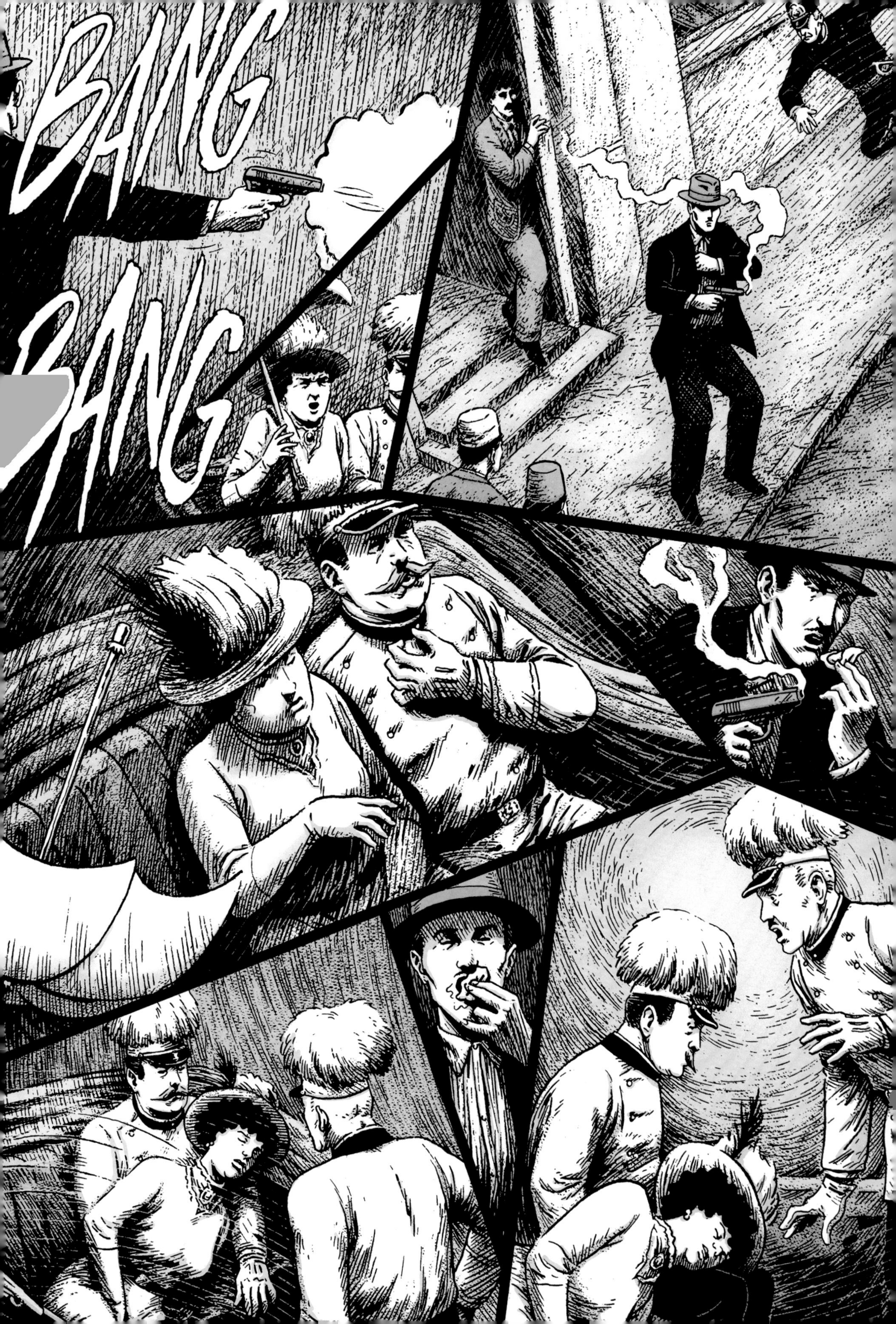
BANG
BANG

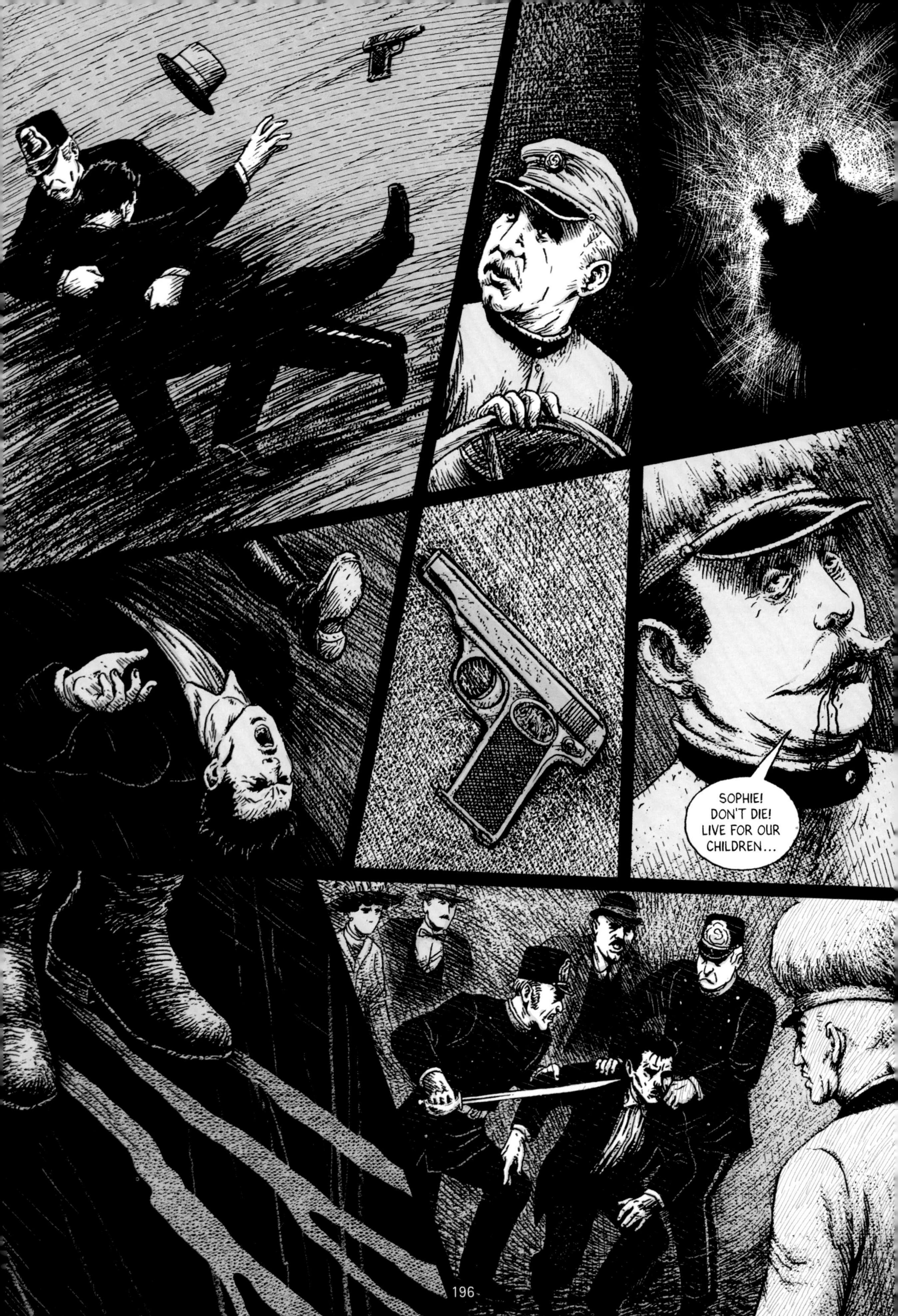
SOPHIE!
DON'T DIE!
LIVE FOR OUR
CHILDREN...

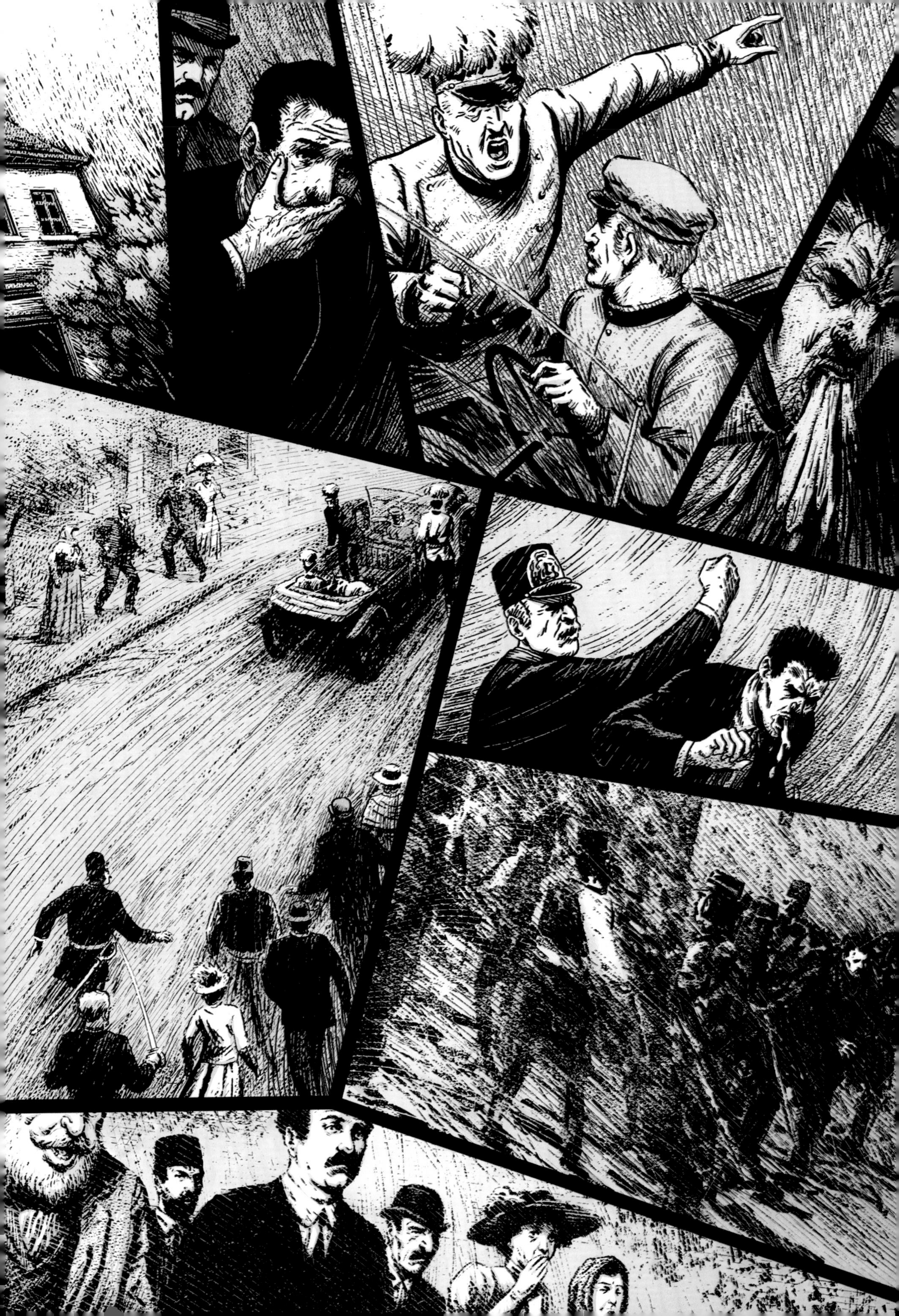

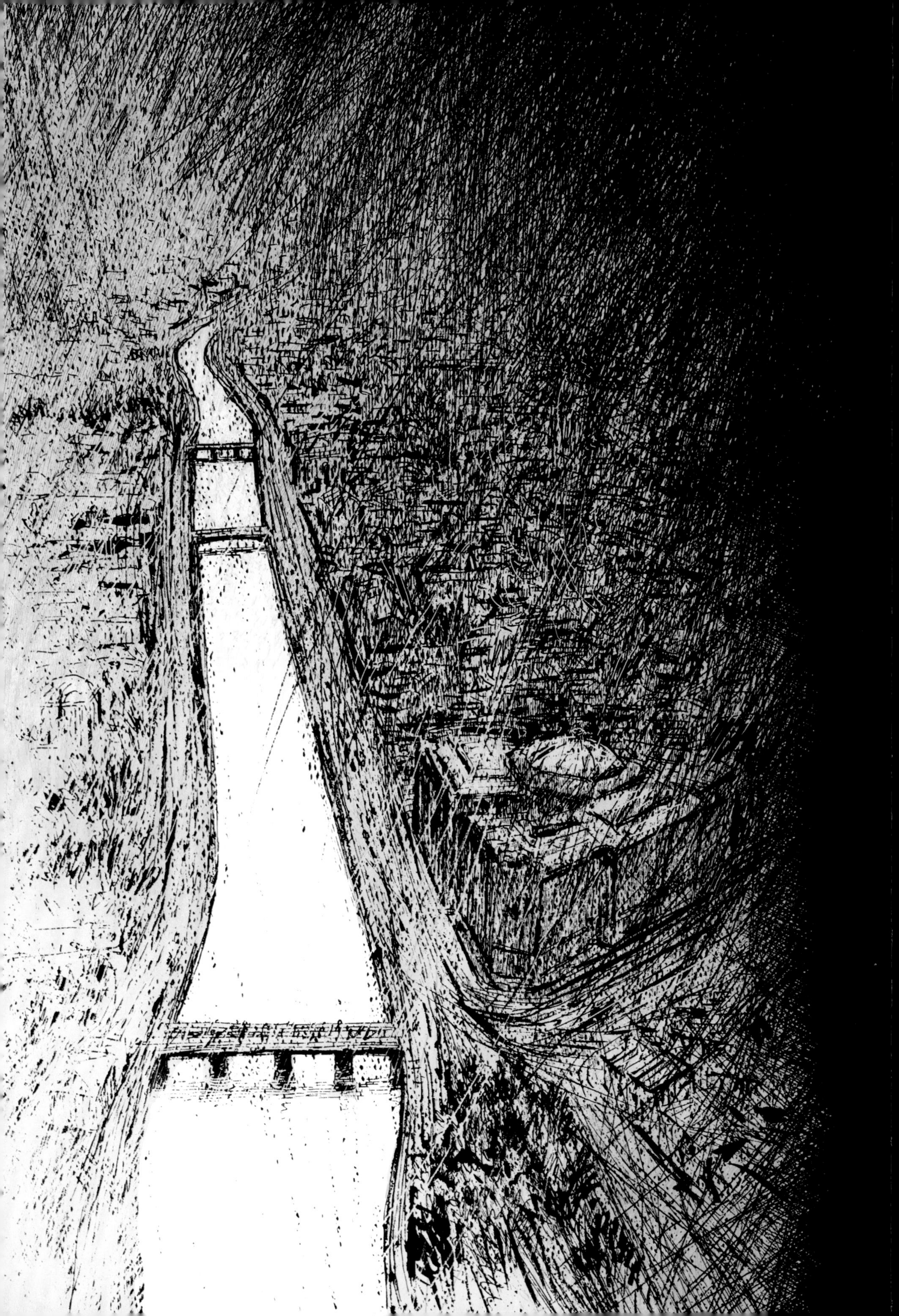

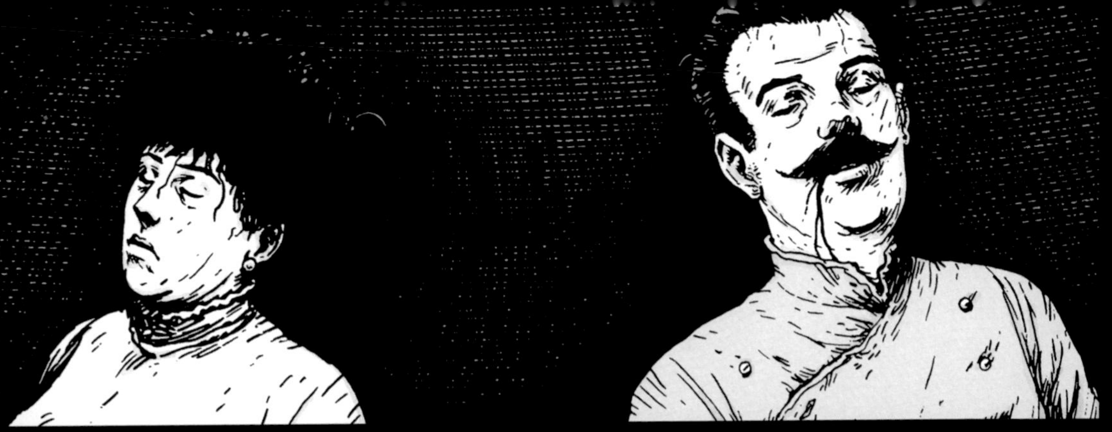

UPON THE ARRIVAL OF THE ARCHDUKE'S CAR AT THE GOVERNOR'S RESIDENCE, SOPHIE WAS FOUND TO BE DEAD. FRANZ FERDINAND PERISHED A FEW MINUTES LATER.

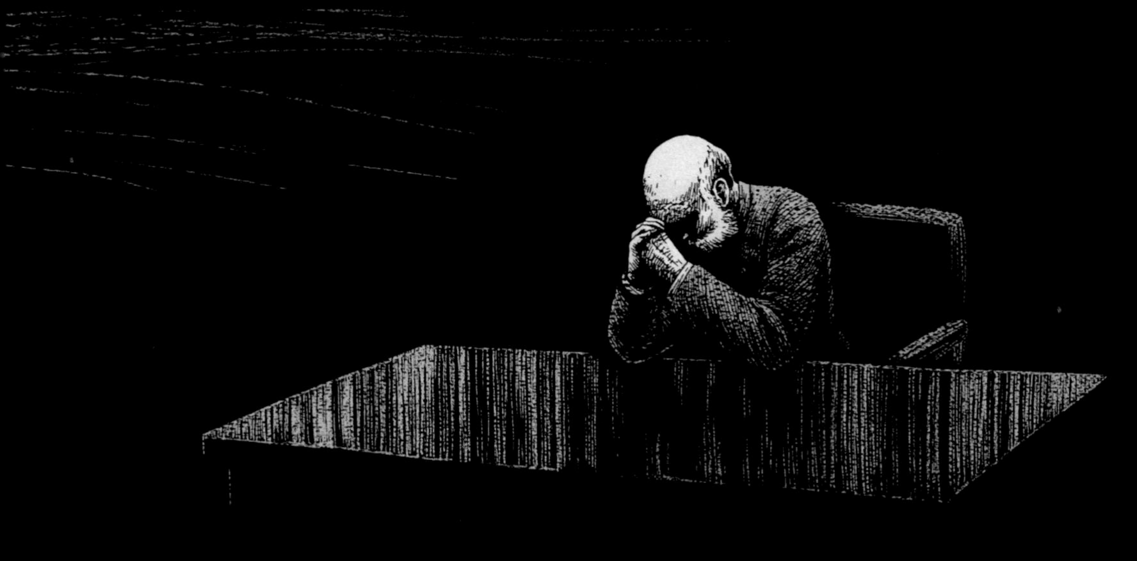

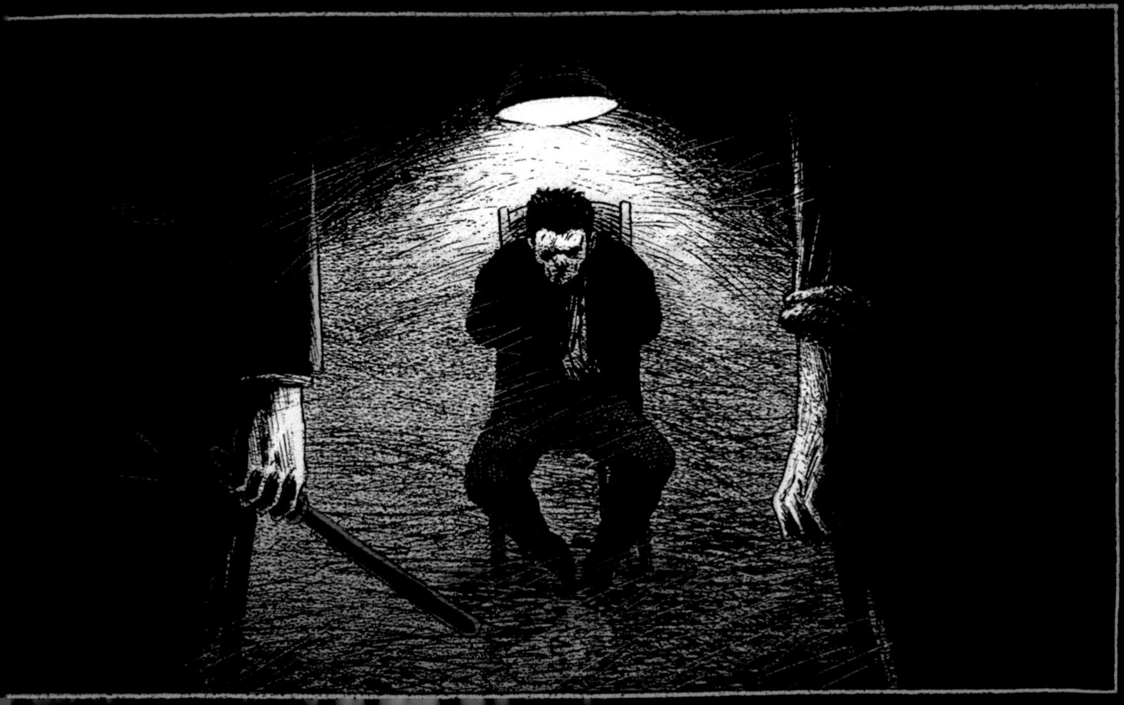

AUSTRIAN POLICE SOON FOUND OUT THAT GAVRILO PRINCIP HAD STAYED WITH DANILO ILIĆ IN THE TIME LEADING UP TO THE ASSASSINATION.

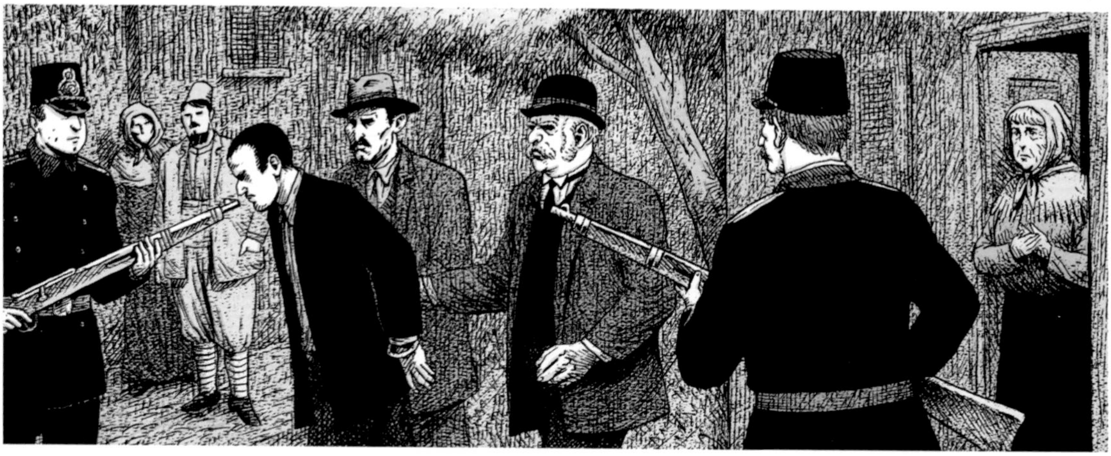

DURING INTERROGATION, ILIĆ ADMITTED TO BEING PART OF THE PLOT TO ASSASSINATE FRANZ FERDINAND AND NOT ONLY GAVE THE POLICE THE NAMES OF TRIFKO GRABEŽ, MUHAMED MEHMEDBAŠIĆ, CVJETKO POPOVIĆ, THE ČUBRILOVIĆ BROTHERS, AND MIŠKO JOVANOVIĆ BUT ALSO REVEALED THE CONNECTION TO THE BLACK HAND.

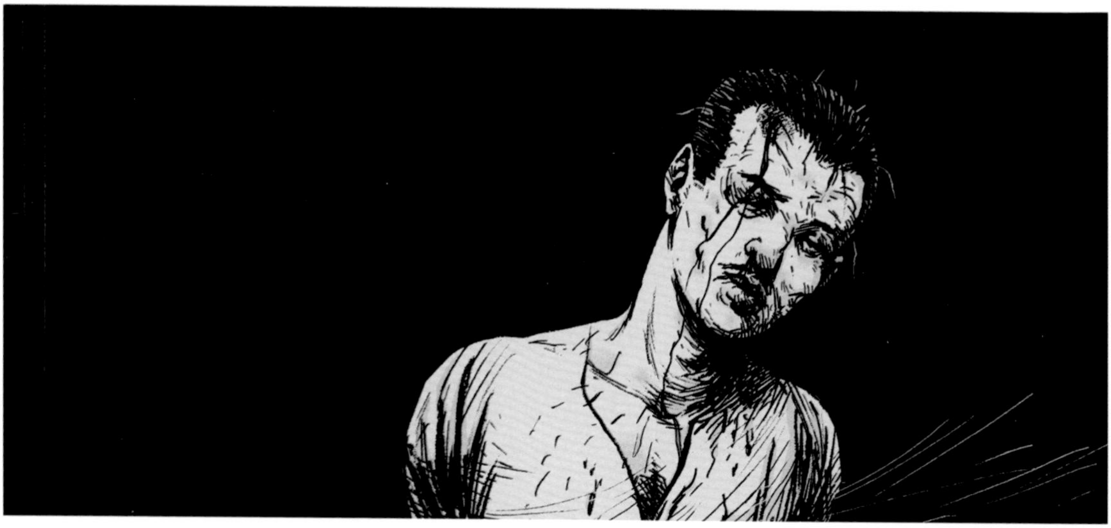

ALL THE CONSPIRATORS WERE ARRESTED, EXCEPT MUHAMED MEHMEDBAŠIĆ, WHO MANAGED TO ESCAPE TO MONTENEGRO.

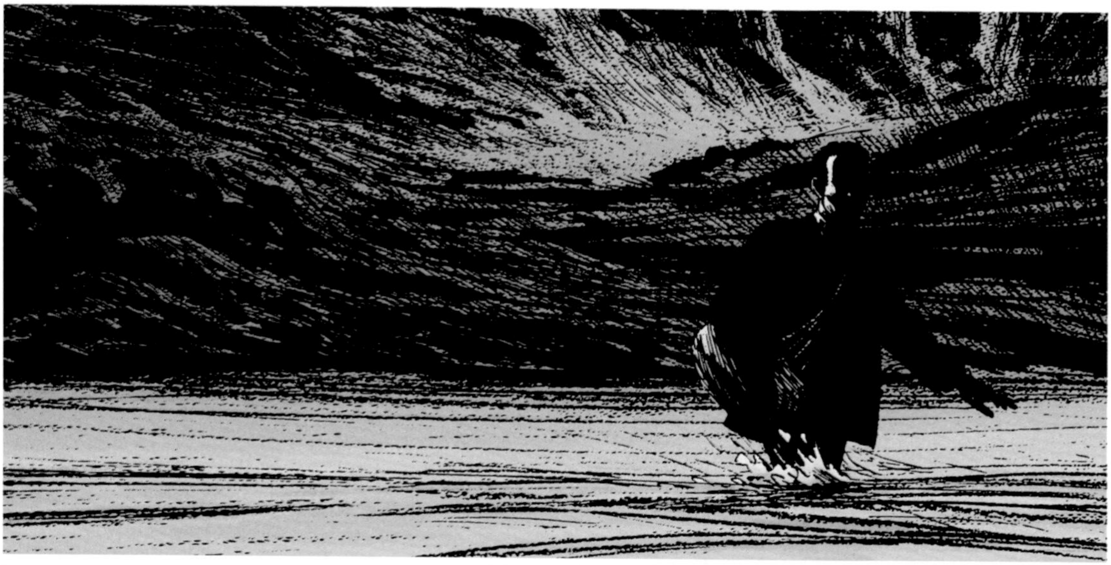

SCHÖNBRUNN PALACE, VIENNA

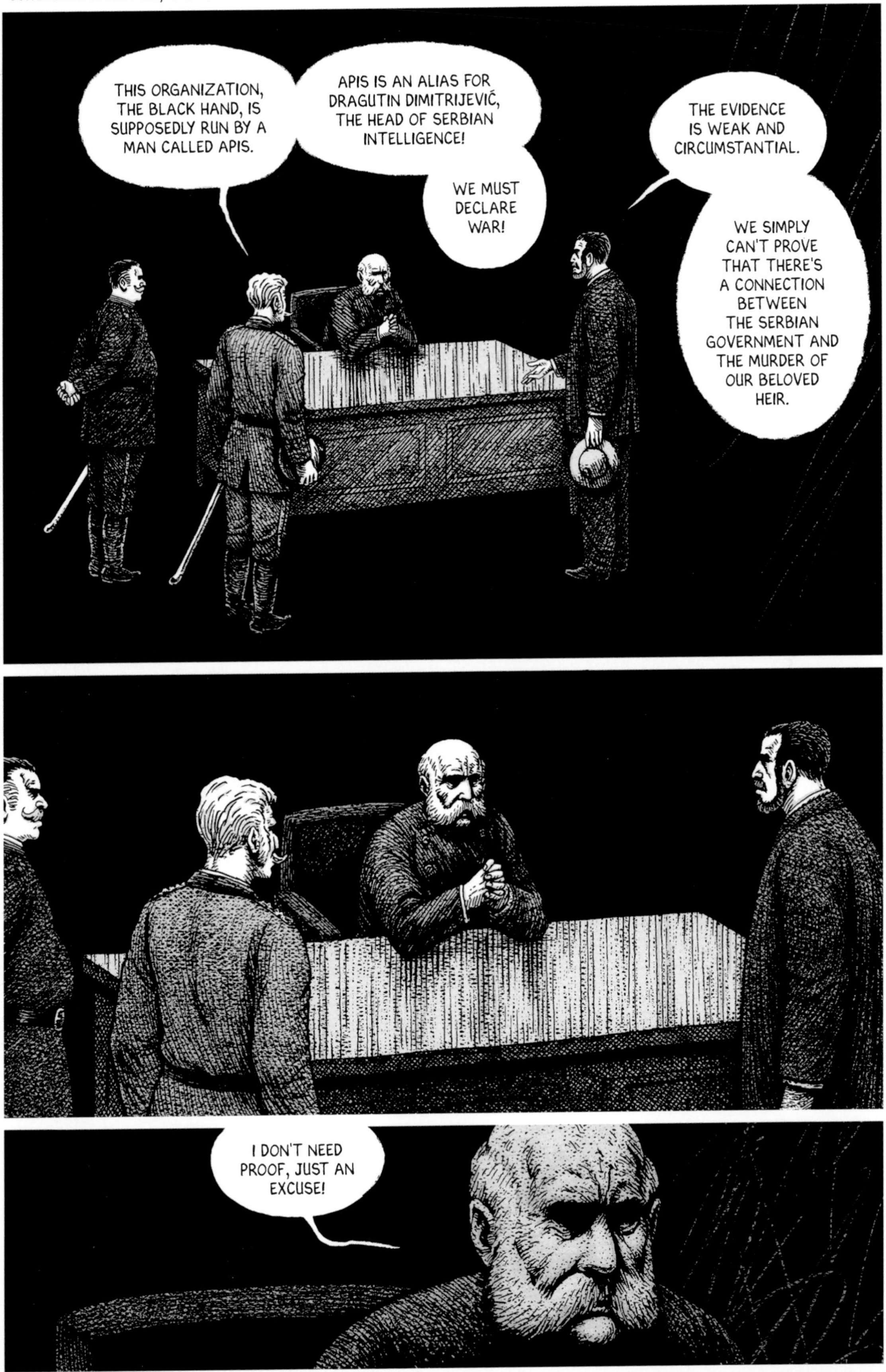

THIS ORGANIZATION, THE BLACK HAND, IS SUPPOSEDLY RUN BY A MAN CALLED APIS.
APIS IS AN ALIAS FOR DRAGUTIN DIMITRIJEVIĆ, THE HEAD OF SERBIAN INTELLIGENCE!
WE MUST DECLARE WAR!
THE EVIDENCE IS WEAK AND CIRCUMSTANTIAL.
WE SIMPLY CAN'T PROVE THAT THERE'S A CONNECTION BETWEEN THE SERBIAN GOVERNMENT AND THE MURDER OF OUR BELOVED HEIR.
I DON'T NEED PROOF, JUST AN EXCUSE!

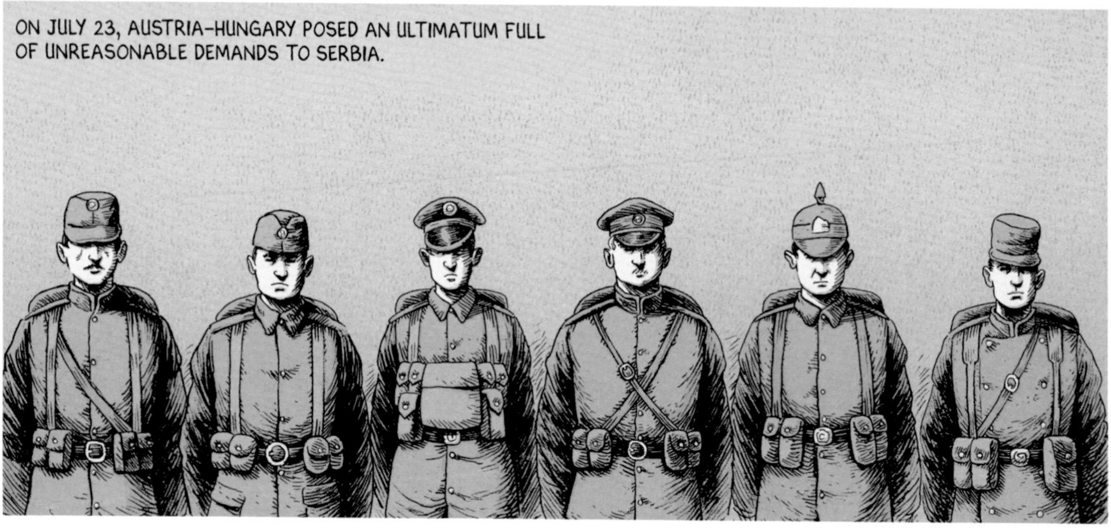
ON JULY 23, AUSTRIA-HUNGARY POSED AN ULTIMATUM FULL OF UNREASONABLE DEMANDS TO SERBIA.

THE GOVERNMENT IN BELGRADE TRIED TO ACCOMMODATE EMPEROR FRANZ JOSEPH AS BEST IT COULD WITHOUT LOSING FACE BUT TO NO AVAIL.

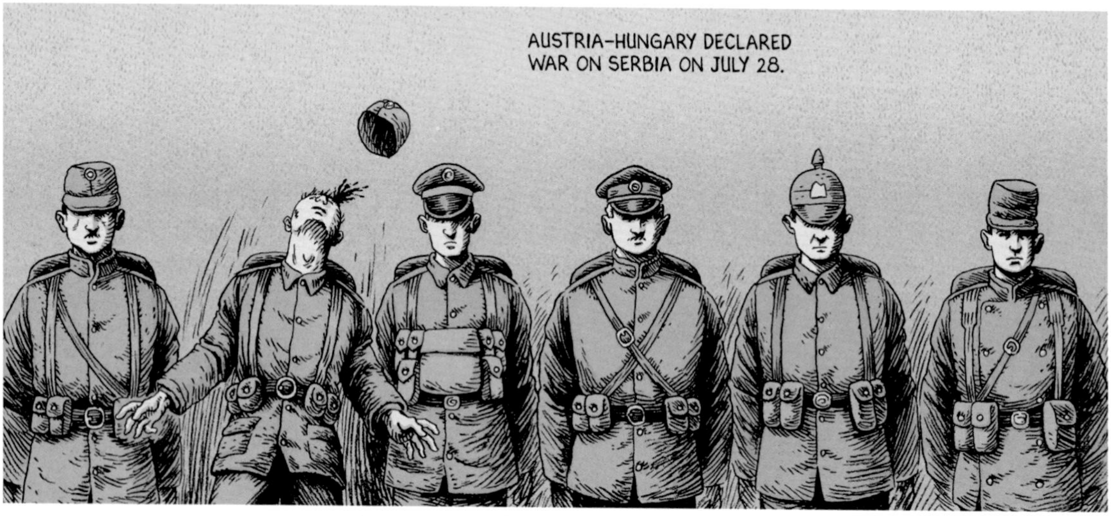
AUSTRIA-HUNGARY DECLARED WAR ON SERBIA ON JULY 28.

THE CZAR IMMEDIATELY SIGNED AN ORDER FOR GENERAL MOBILIZATION OF THE RUSSIAN ARMY.

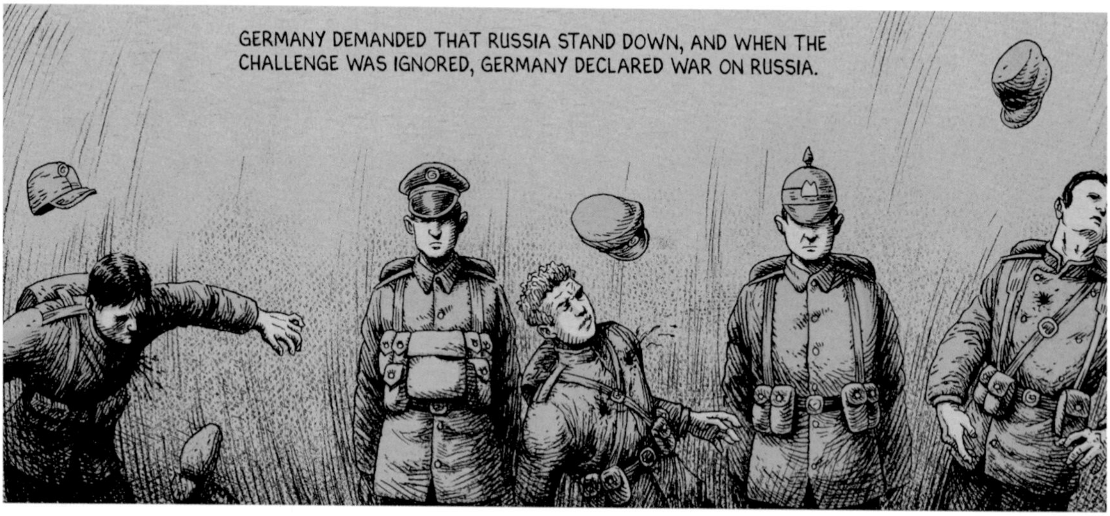
GERMANY DEMANDED THAT RUSSIA STAND DOWN, AND WHEN THE CHALLENGE WAS IGNORED, GERMANY DECLARED WAR ON RUSSIA.

TWO DAYS LATER, THE GERMANS ALSO DECLARED WAR ON FRANCE, AND THE GERMAN ARMY ENTERED FRENCH SOIL THROUGH BELGIUM.

THE VIOLATION OF NEUTRAL BELGIUM COMPELLED BRITAIN TO DECLARE WAR ON GERMANY.

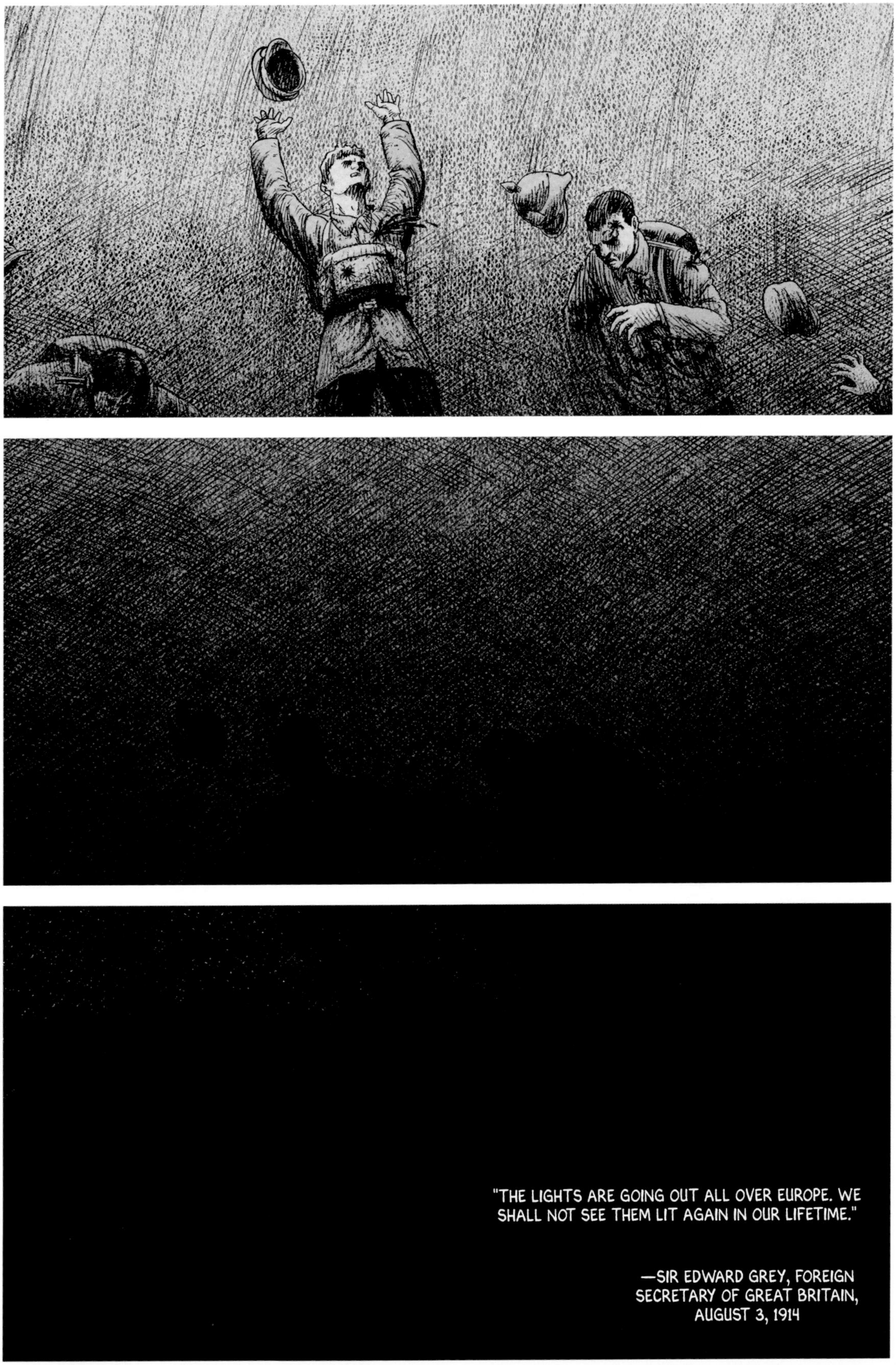
"THE LIGHTS ARE GOING OUT ALL OVER EUROPE. WE SHALL NOT SEE THEM LIT AGAIN IN OUR LIFETIME."
—SIR EDWARD GREY, FOREIGN SECRETARY OF GREAT BRITAIN, AUGUST 3, 1914

COLES

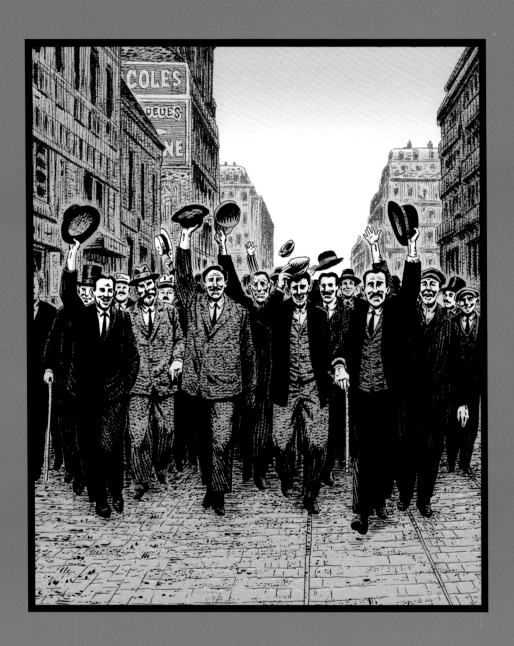

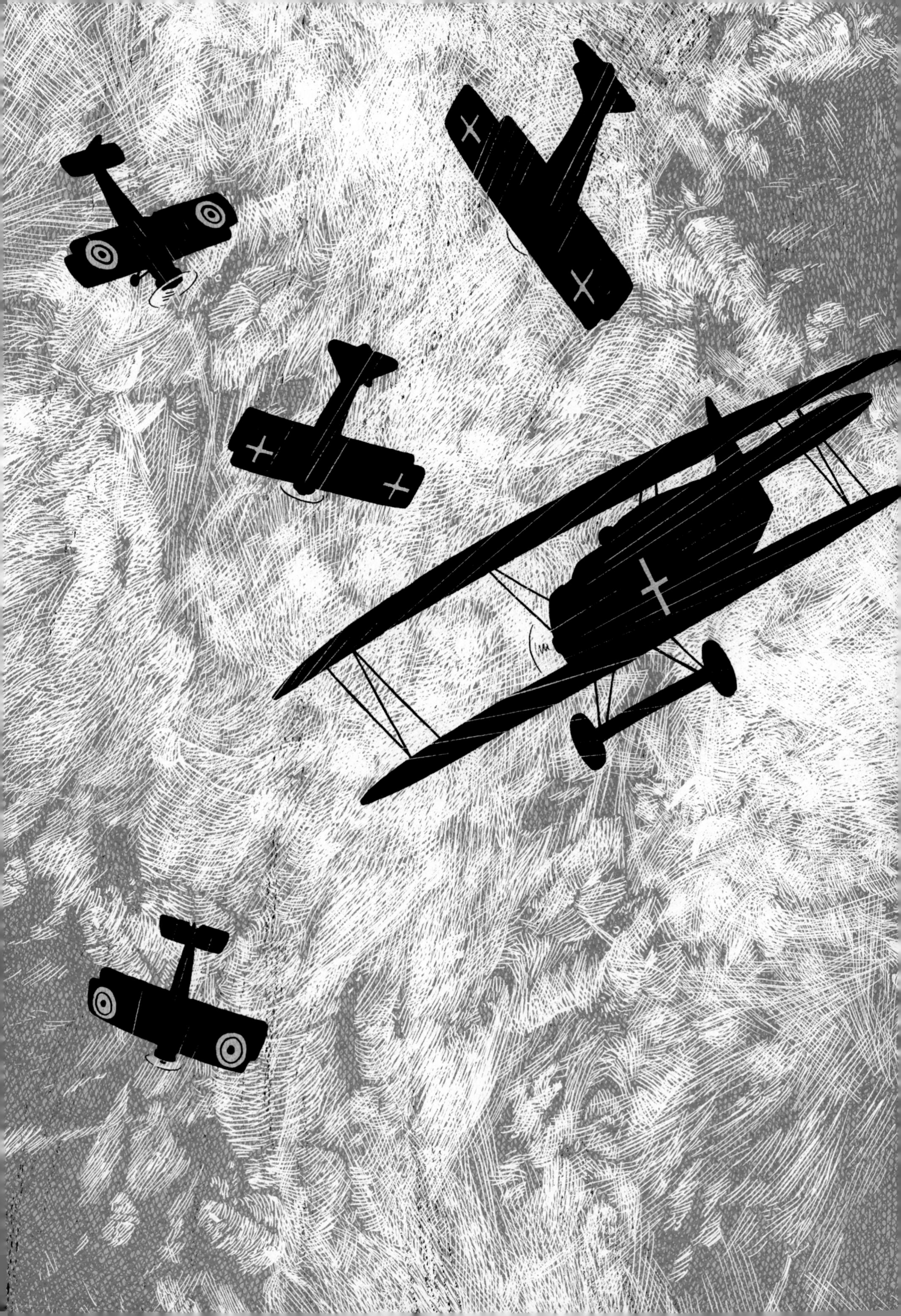

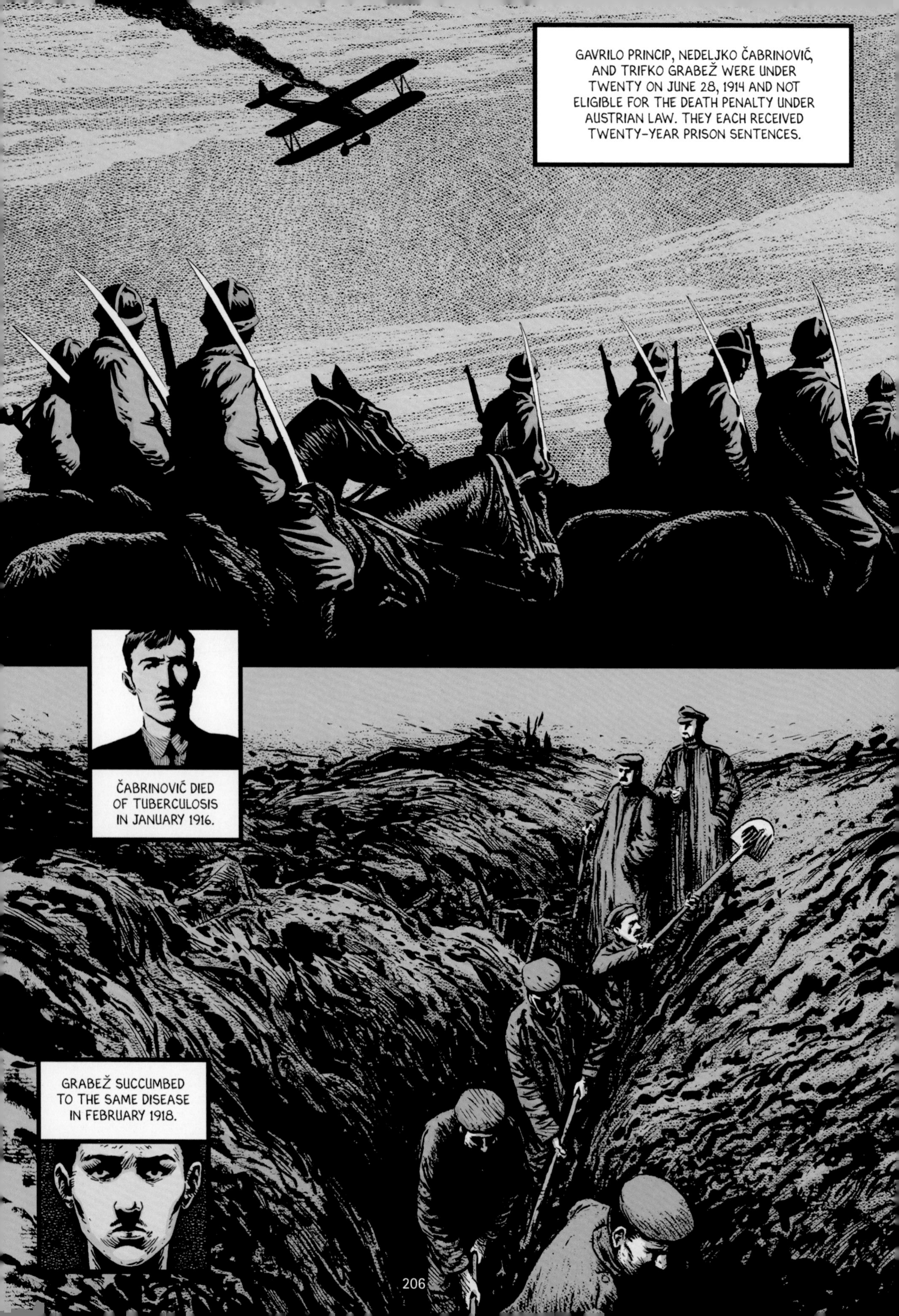
GAVRILO PRINCIP, NEDELJKO ČABRINOVIĆ, AND TRIFKO GRABEŽ WERE UNDER TWENTY ON JUNE 28, 1914 AND NOT ELIGIBLE FOR THE DEATH PENALTY UNDER AUSTRIAN LAW. THEY EACH RECEIVED TWENTY-YEAR PRISON SENTENCES.
ČABRINOVIĆ DIED OF TUBERCULOSIS IN JANUARY 1916.
GRABEŽ SUCCUMBED TO THE SAME DISEASE IN FEBRUARY 1918.

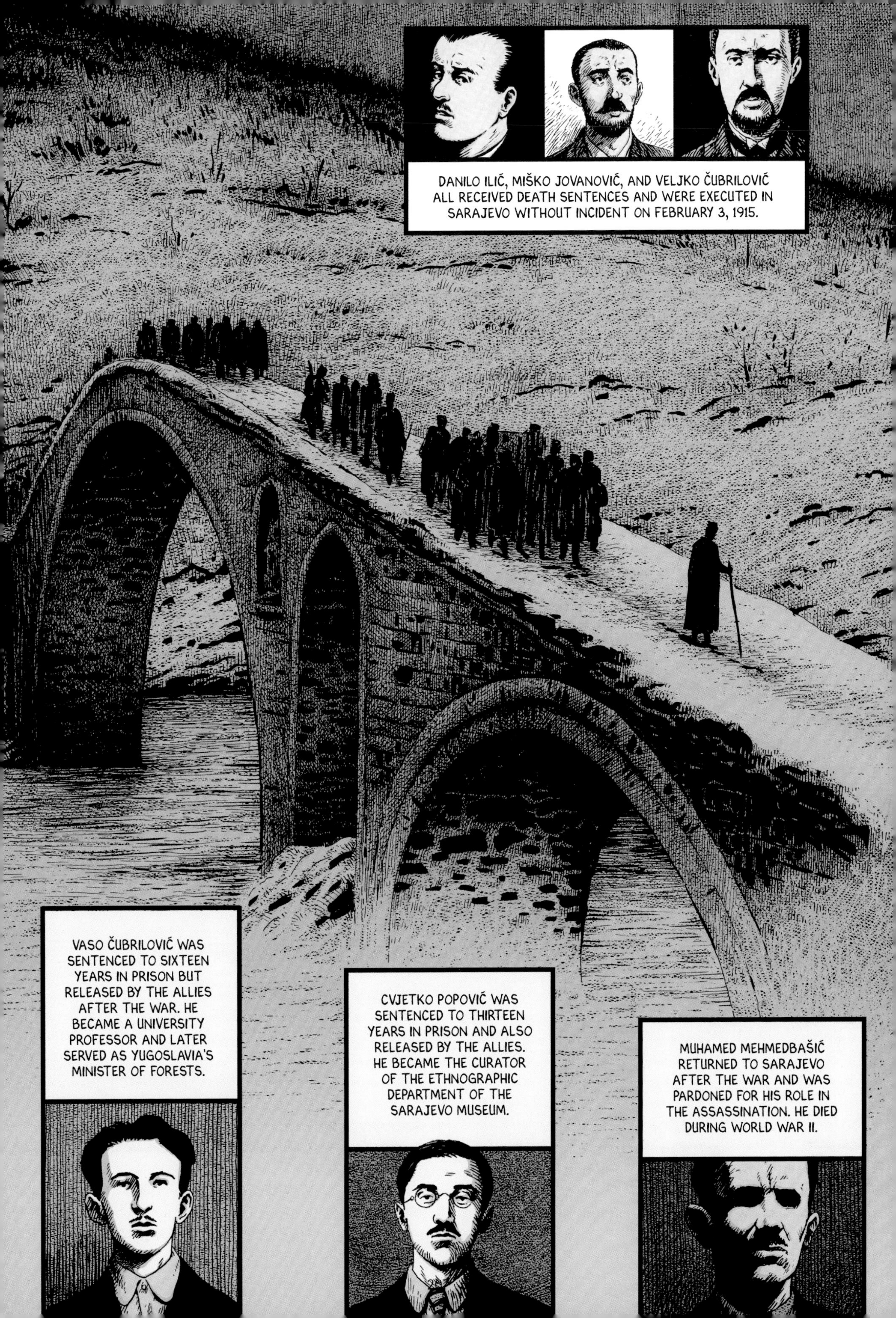
DANILO ILIĆ, MIŠKO JOVANOVIĆ, AND VELJKO ČUBRILOVIĆ ALL RECEIVED DEATH SENTENCES AND WERE EXECUTED IN SARAJEVO WITHOUT INCIDENT ON FEBRUARY 3, 1915.
VASO ČUBRILOVIĆ WAS SENTENCED TO SIXTEEN YEARS IN PRISON BUT RELEASED BY THE ALLIES AFTER THE WAR. HE BECAME A UNIVERSITY PROFESSOR AND LATER SERVED AS YUGOSLAVIA'S MINISTER OF FORESTS.
CVJETKO POPOVIĆ WAS SENTENCED TO THIRTEEN YEARS IN PRISON AND ALSO RELEASED BY THE ALLIES. HE BECAME THE CURATOR OF THE ETHNOGRAPHIC DEPARTMENT OF THE SARAJEVO MUSEUM.
MUHAMED MEHMEDBAŠIĆ RETURNED TO SARAJEVO AFTER THE WAR AND WAS PARDONED FOR HIS ROLE IN THE ASSASSINATION. HE DIED DURING WORLD WAR II.

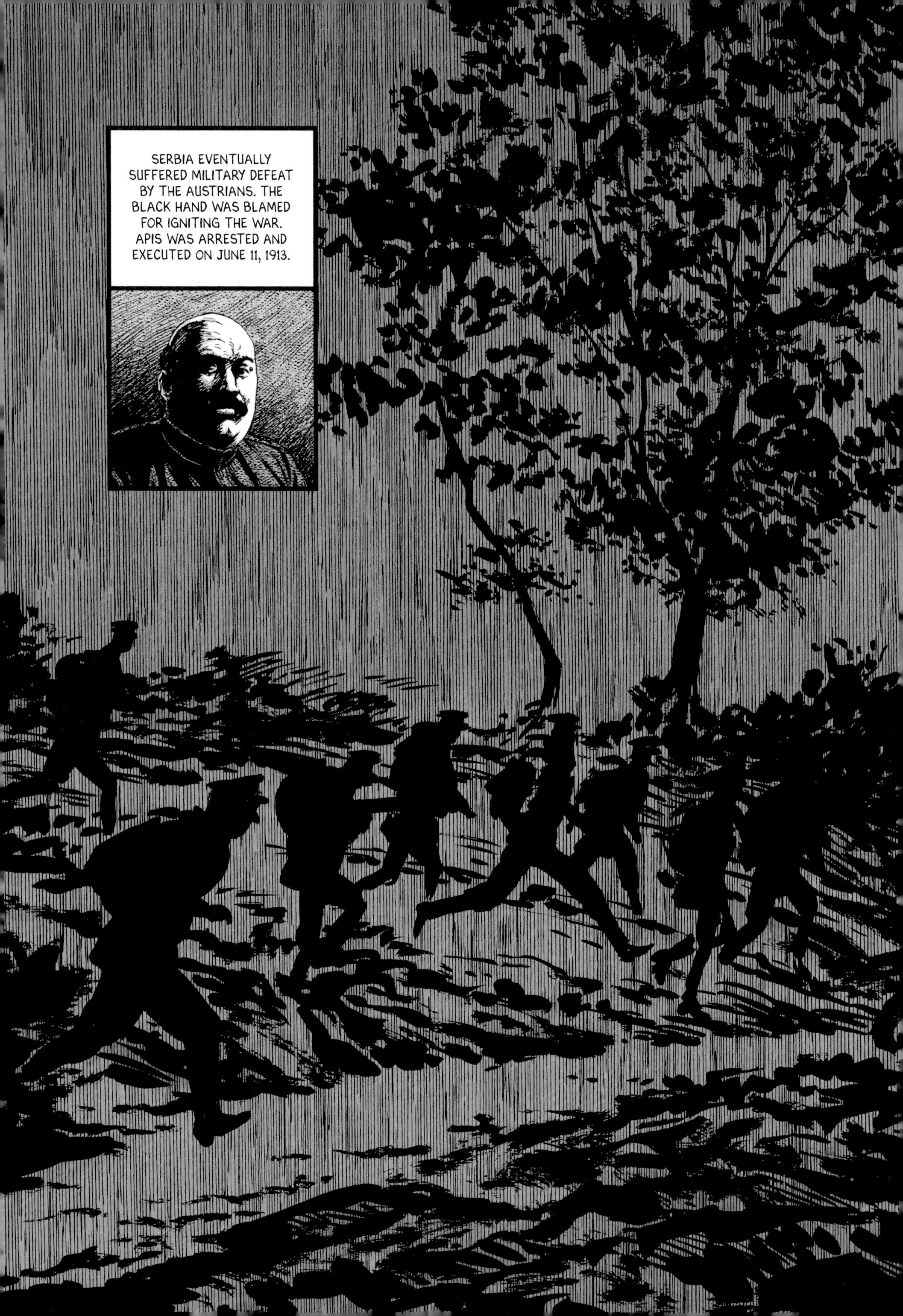
SERBIA EVENTUALLY SUFFERED MILITARY DEFEAT BY THE AUSTRIANS. THE BLACK HAND WAS BLAMED FOR IGNITING THE WAR. APIS WAS ARRESTED AND EXECUTED ON JUNE 11, 1913.

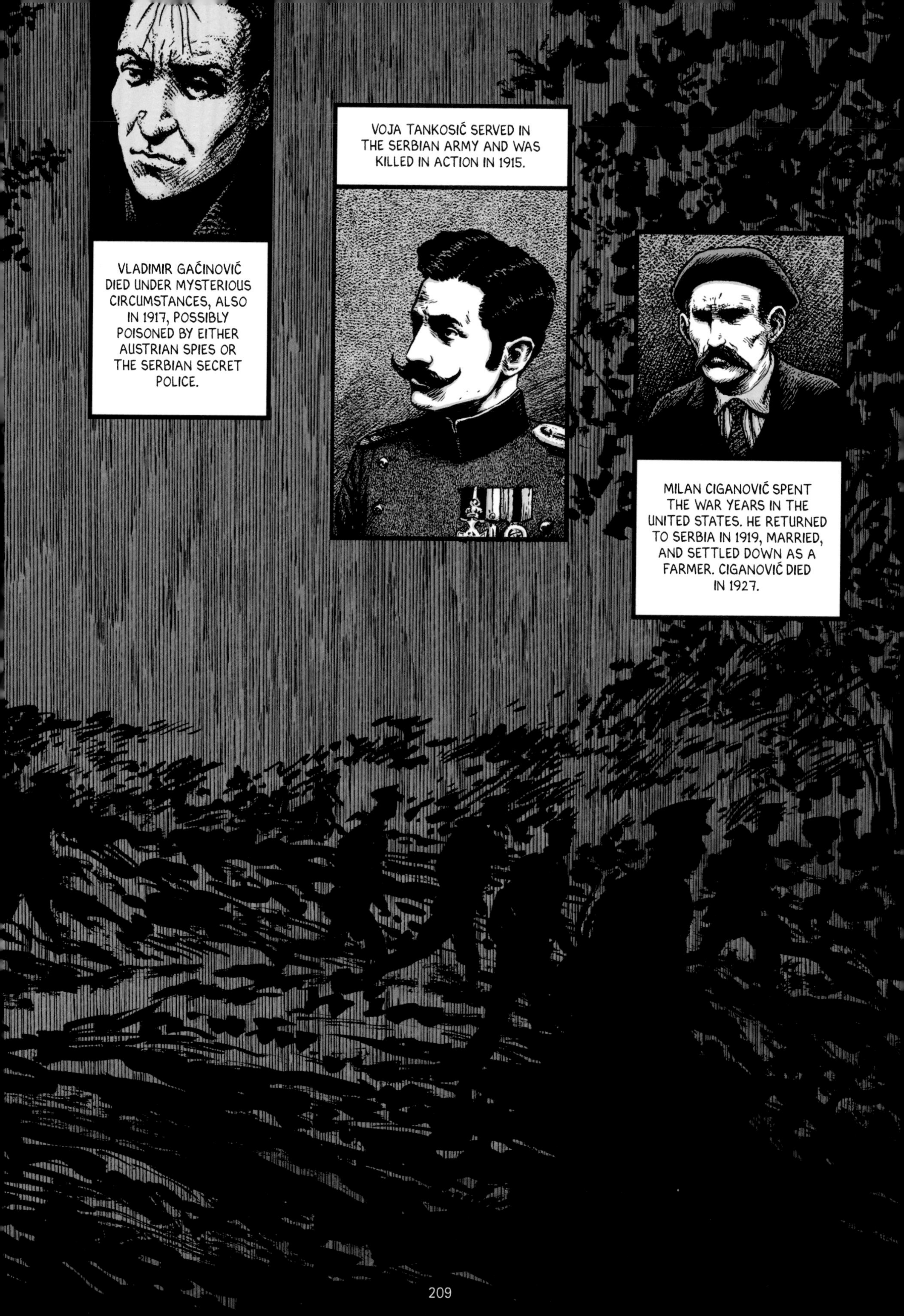
VLADIMIR GAČINOVIĆ DIED UNDER MYSTERIOUS CIRCUMSTANCES, ALSO IN 1917, POSSIBLY POISONED BY EITHER AUSTRIAN SPIES OR THE SERBIAN SECRET POLICE.
VOJA TANKOSIĆ SERVED IN THE SERBIAN ARMY AND WAS KILLED IN ACTION IN 1915.
MILAN CIGANOVIĆ SPENT THE WAR YEARS IN THE UNITED STATES. HE RETURNED TO SERBIA IN 1919, MARRIED, AND SETTLED DOWN AS A FARMER. CIGANOVIĆ DIED IN 1927.

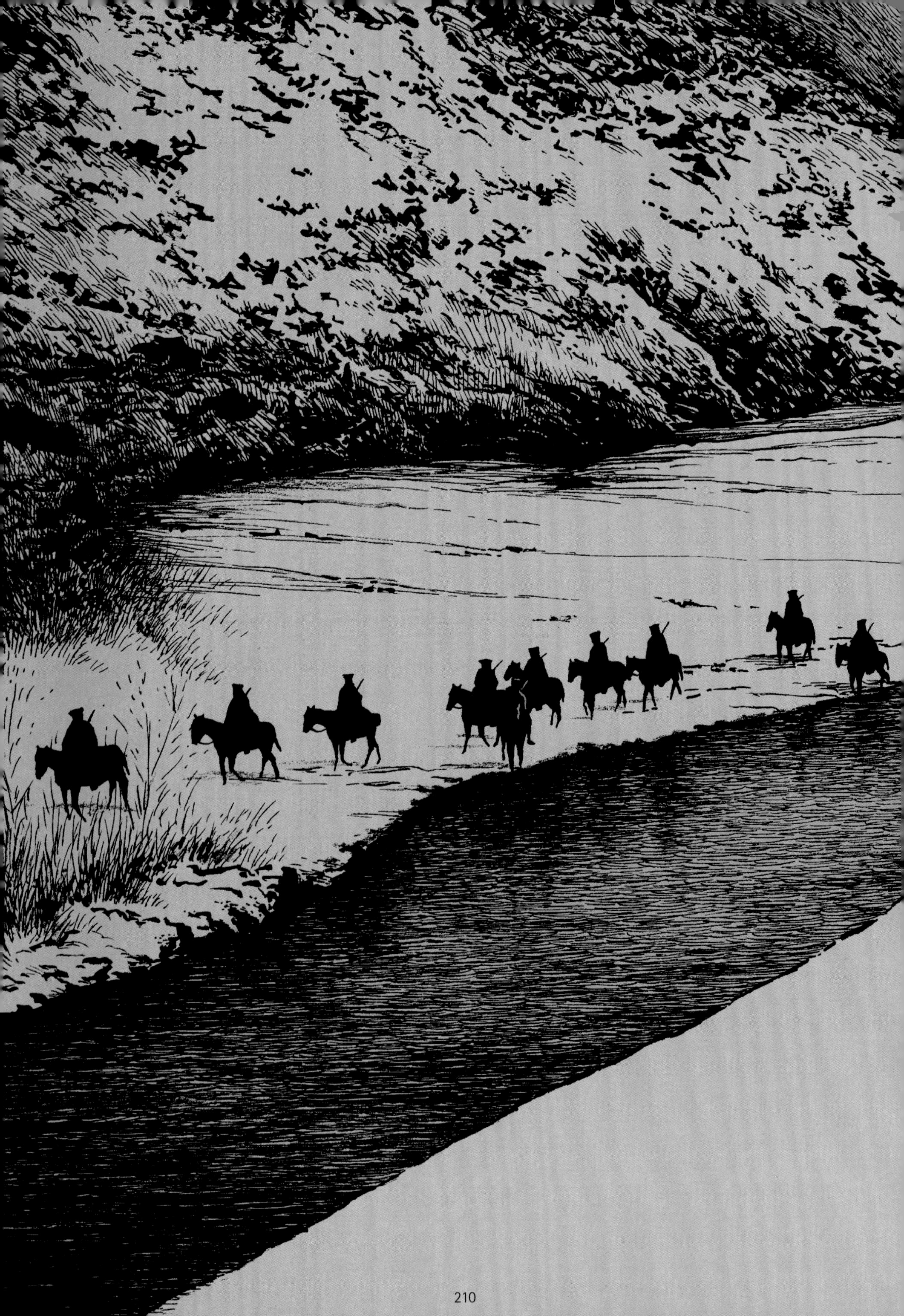

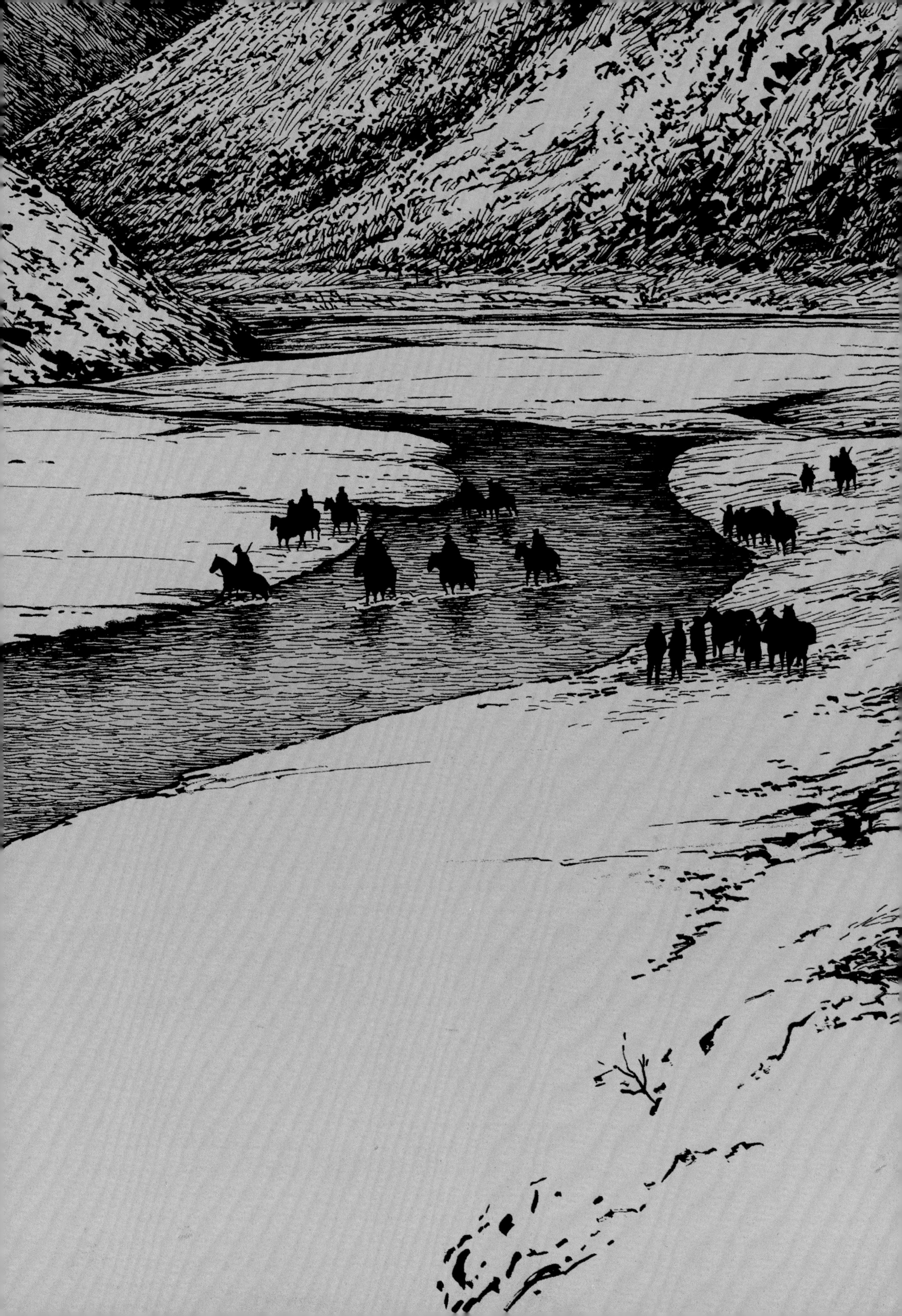

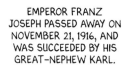

EMPEROR FRANZ JOSEPH PASSED AWAY ON NOVEMBER 21, 1916, AND WAS SUCCEEDED BY HIS GREAT-NEPHEW KARL.

OSKAR POTIOREK LED THE UNSUCCESSFUL FIRST AUSTRIAN INVASION OF SERBIA AND WAS FORCED INTO RETIREMENT AFTERWARDS. HE DIED IN 1933.

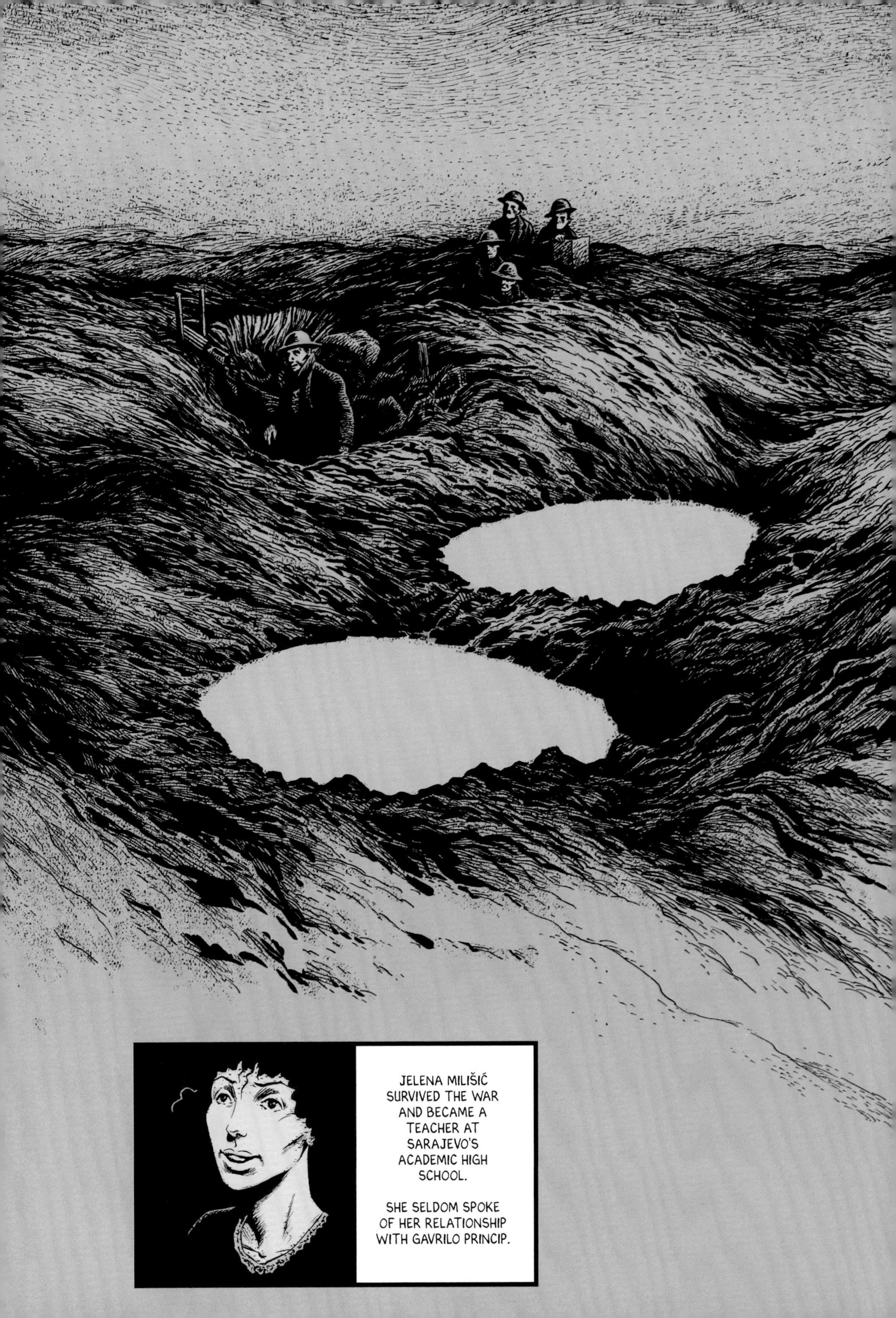
JELENA MILIŠIĆ SURVIVED THE WAR AND BECAME A TEACHER AT SARAJEVO'S ACADEMIC HIGH SCHOOL.
SHE SELDOM SPOKE OF HER RELATIONSHIP WITH GAVRILO PRINCIP.

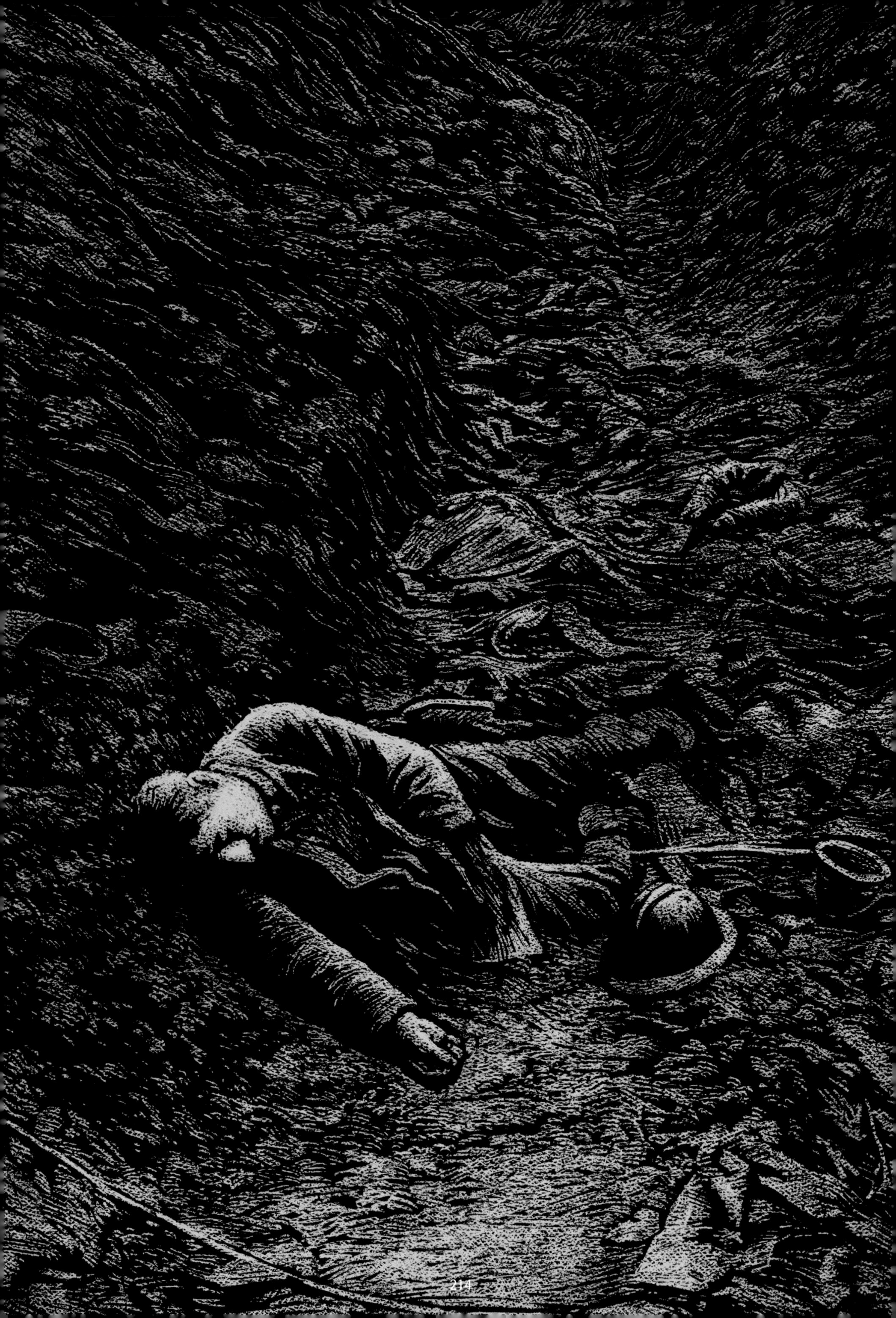

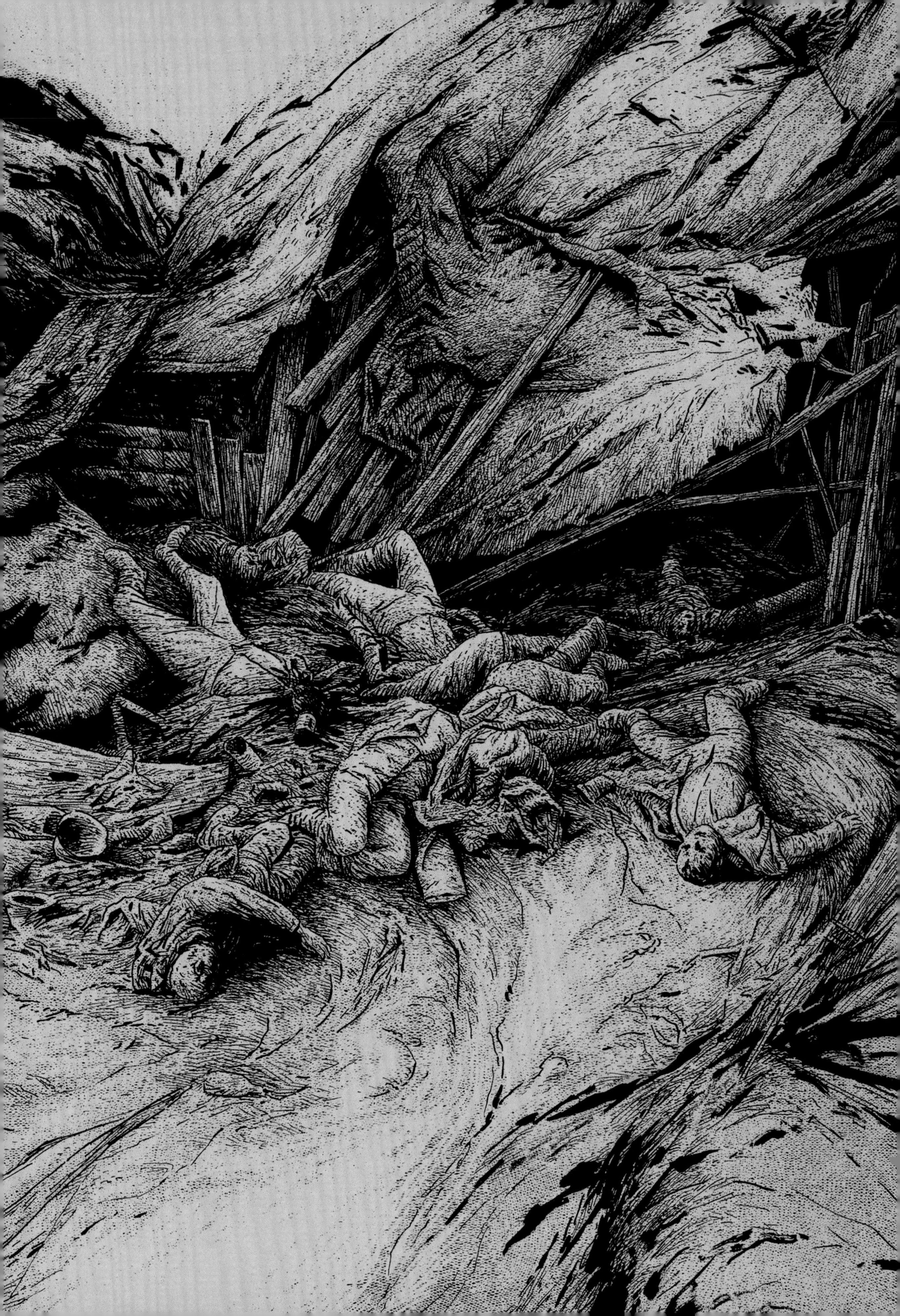

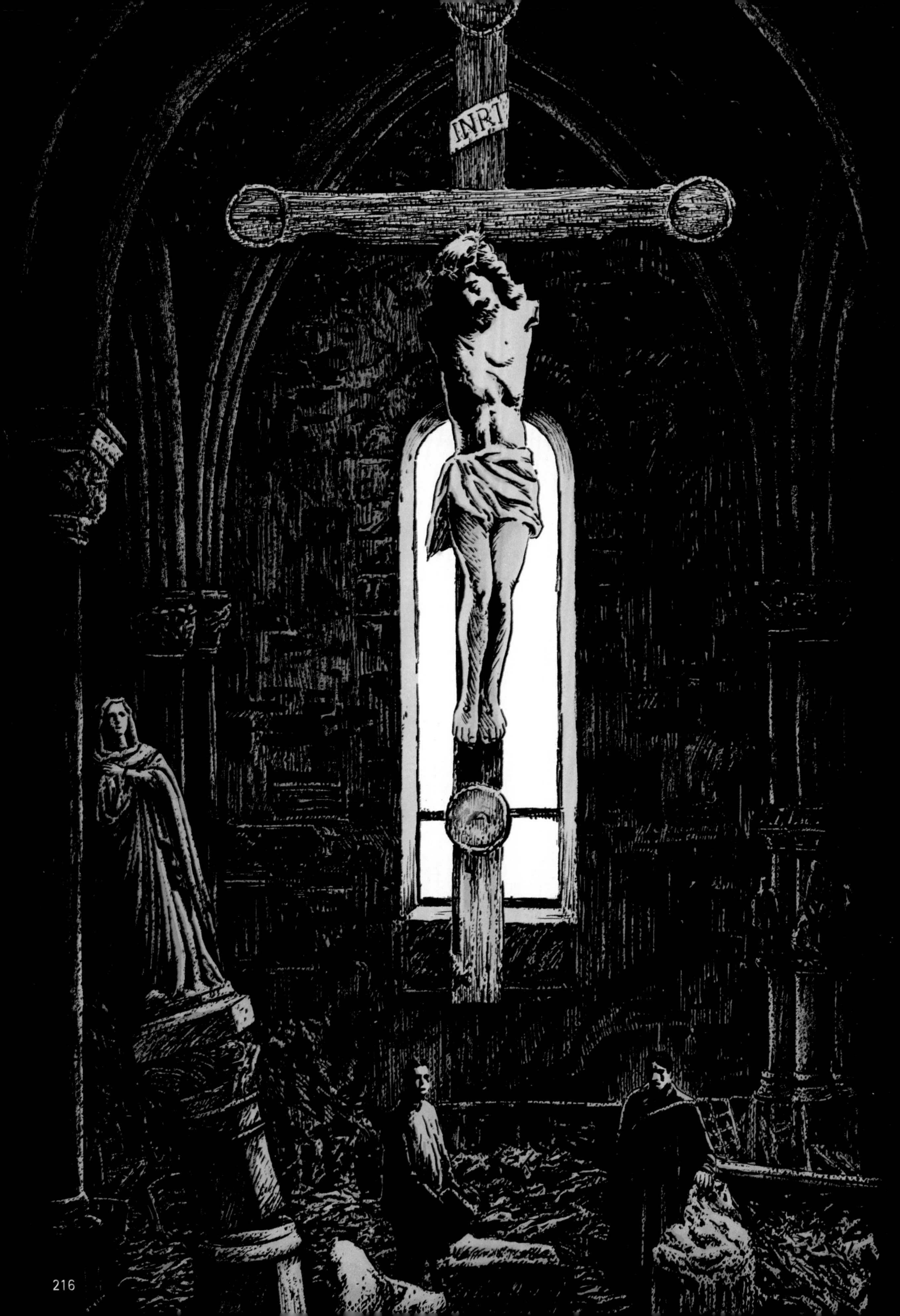
INRI

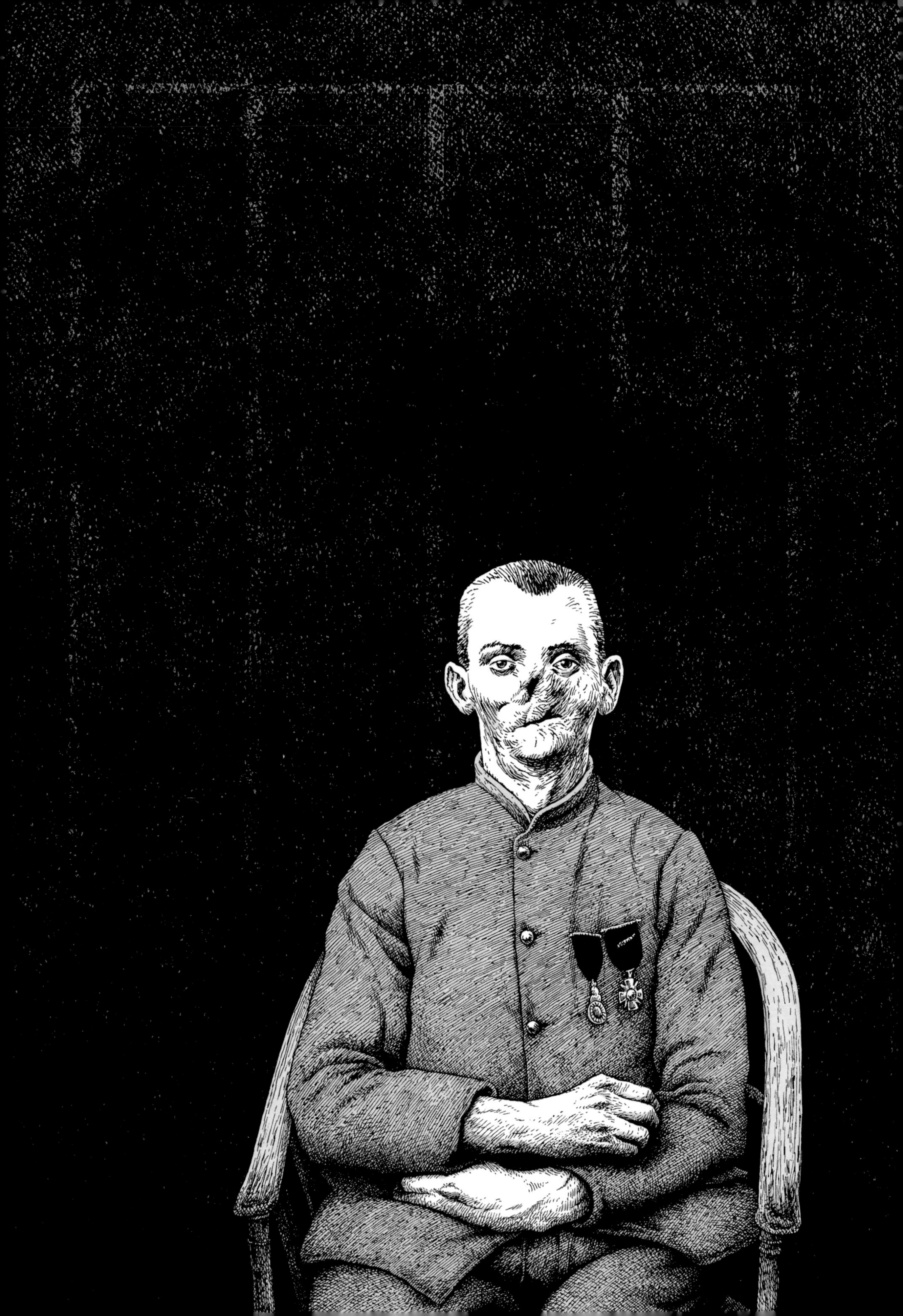

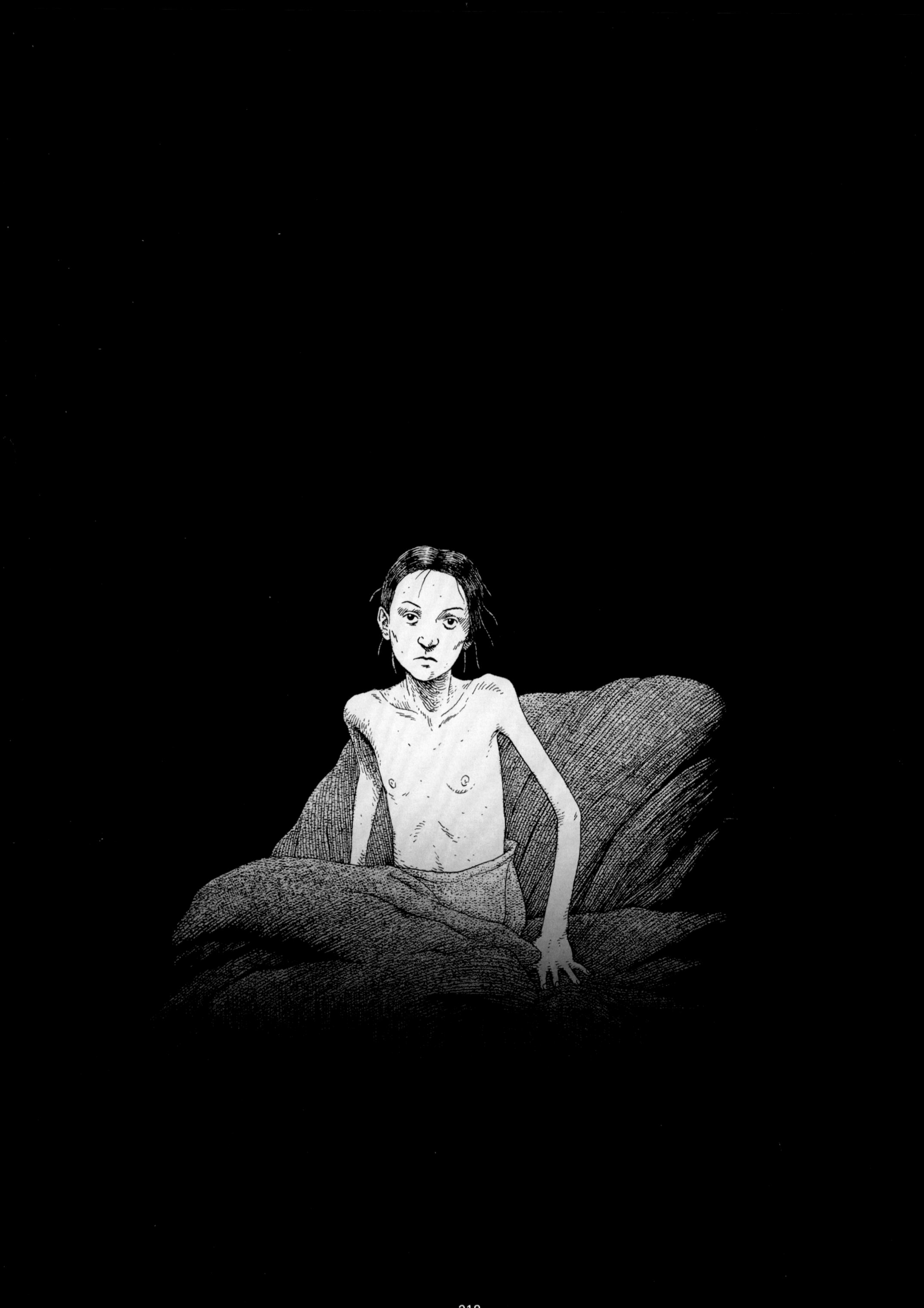

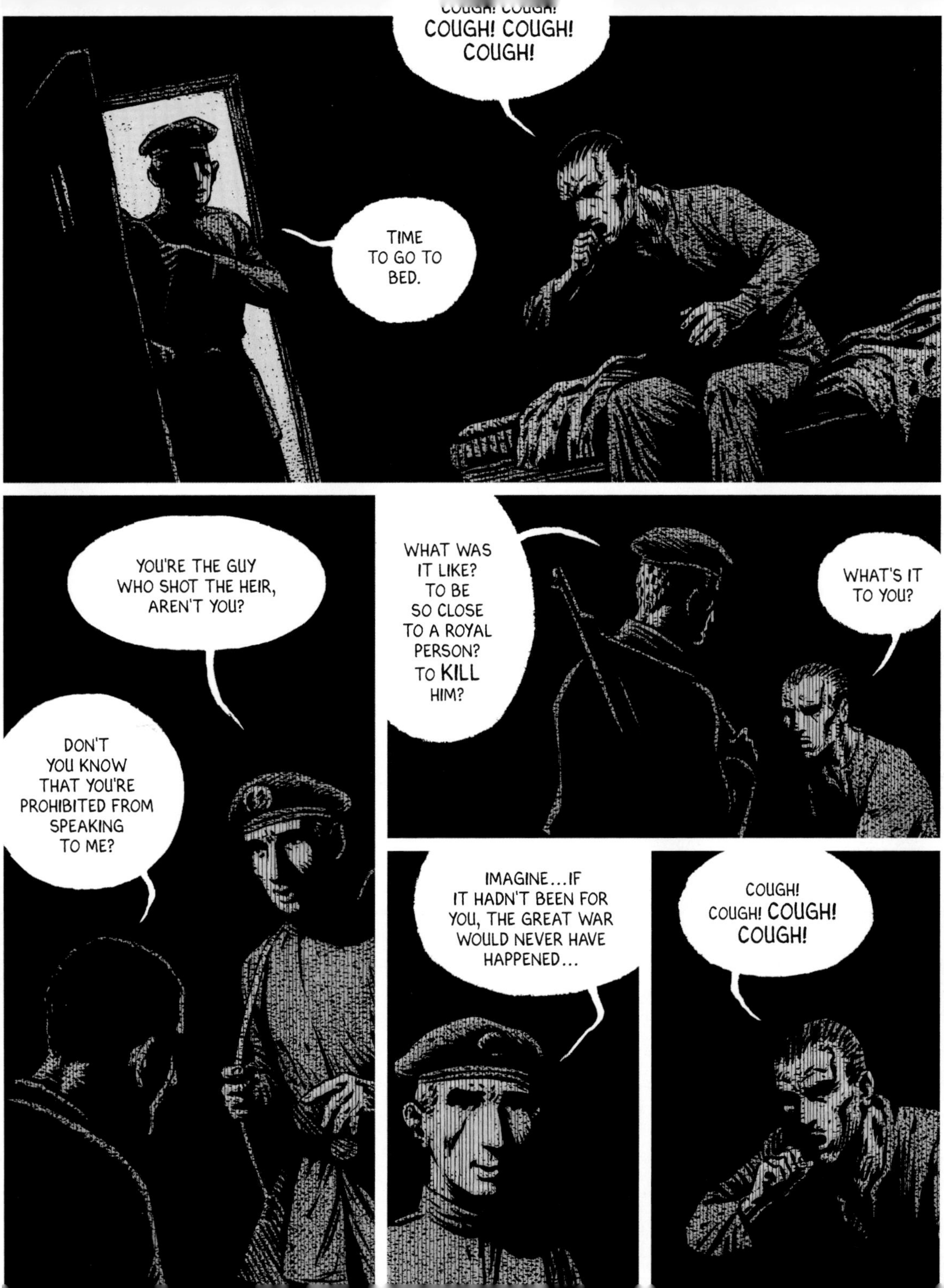
COUGH! COUGH! COUGH!
TIME TO GO TO BED.
YOU'RE THE GUY WHO SHOT THE HEIR, AREN'T YOU?
DON'T YOU KNOW THAT YOU'RE PROHIBITED FROM SPEAKING TO ME?
WHAT WAS IT LIKE? TO BE SO CLOSE TO A ROYAL PERSON? TO KILL HIM?
WHAT'S IT TO YOU?
IMAGINE...IF IT HADN'T BEEN FOR YOU, THE GREAT WAR WOULD NEVER HAVE HAPPENED...
COUGH! COUGH! COUGH! COUGH!

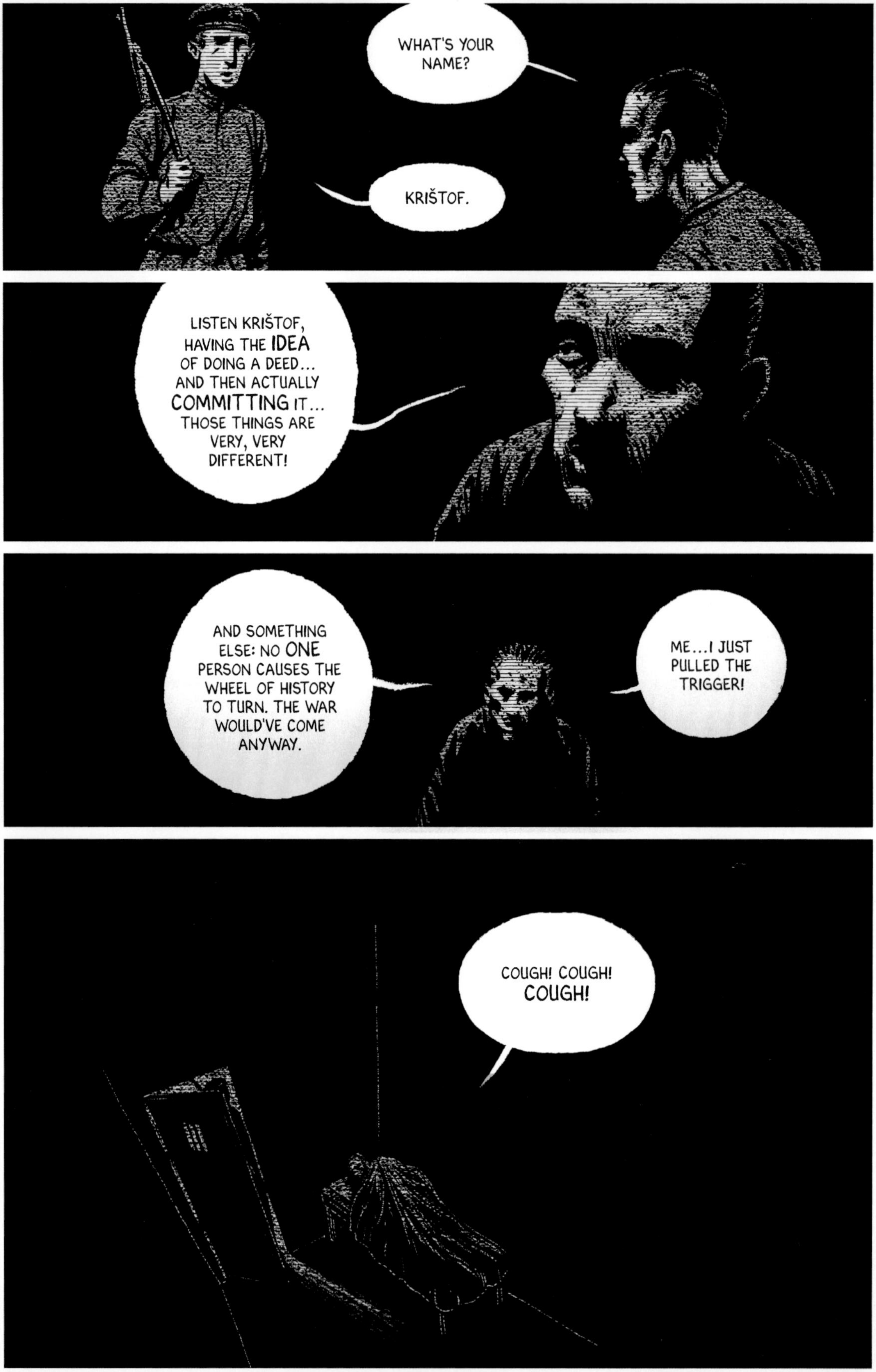
WHAT'S YOUR NAME?
KRIŠTOF.
LISTEN KRIŠTOF, HAVING THE IDEA OF DOING A DEED... AND THEN ACTUALLY COMMITTING IT... THOSE THINGS ARE VERY, VERY DIFFERENT!
AND SOMETHING ELSE: NO ONE PERSON CAUSES THE WHEEL OF HISTORY TO TURN. THE WAR WOULD'VE COME ANYWAY.
ME...I JUST PULLED THE TRIGGER!
COUGH! COUGH! COUGH!

ON APRIL 28, 1918, GAVRILO PRINCIP DIED IN THE TEREZIN PRISON CAMP, PARTLY OF TUBERCULOSIS, PARTLY OF MALTREATMENT.

HE WEIGHED EIGHTY-EIGHT POUNDS.

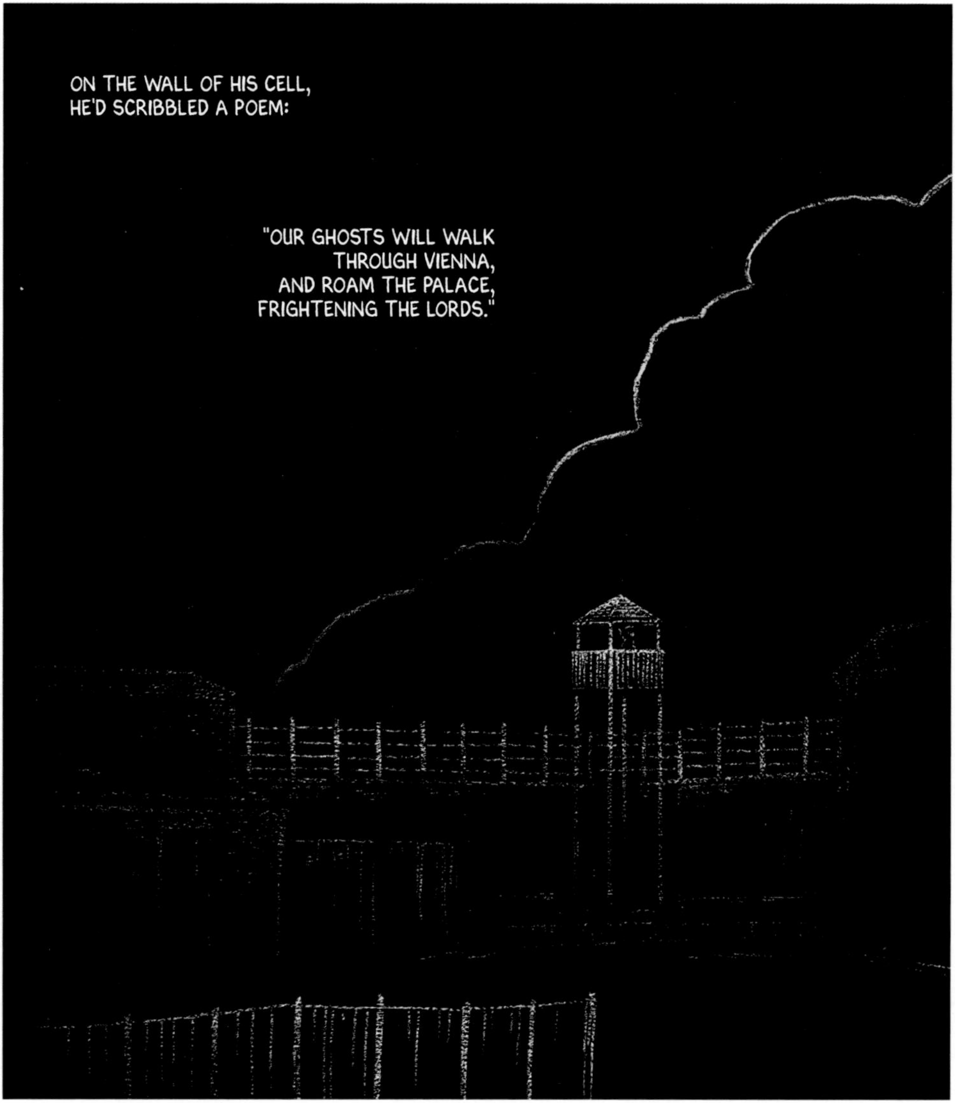
ON THE WALL OF HIS CELL, HE'D SCRIBBLED A POEM:
"OUR GHOSTS WILL WALK THROUGH VIENNA, AND ROAM THE PALACE, FRIGHTENING THE LORDS."

GAVRILO'S REMAINS WERE EVENTUALLY BURIED IN THE ORTHODOX CEMETARY IN SARAJEVO.

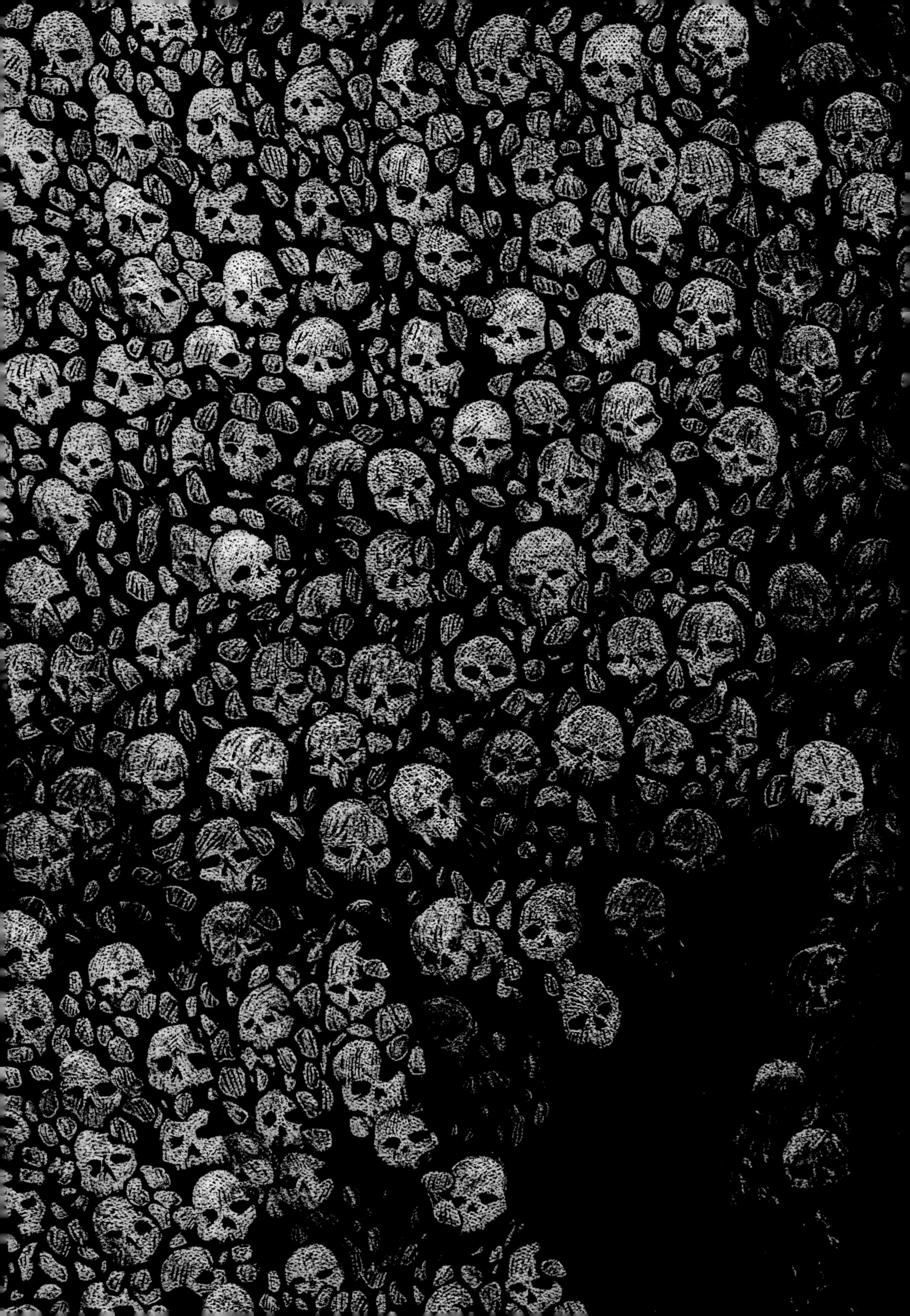

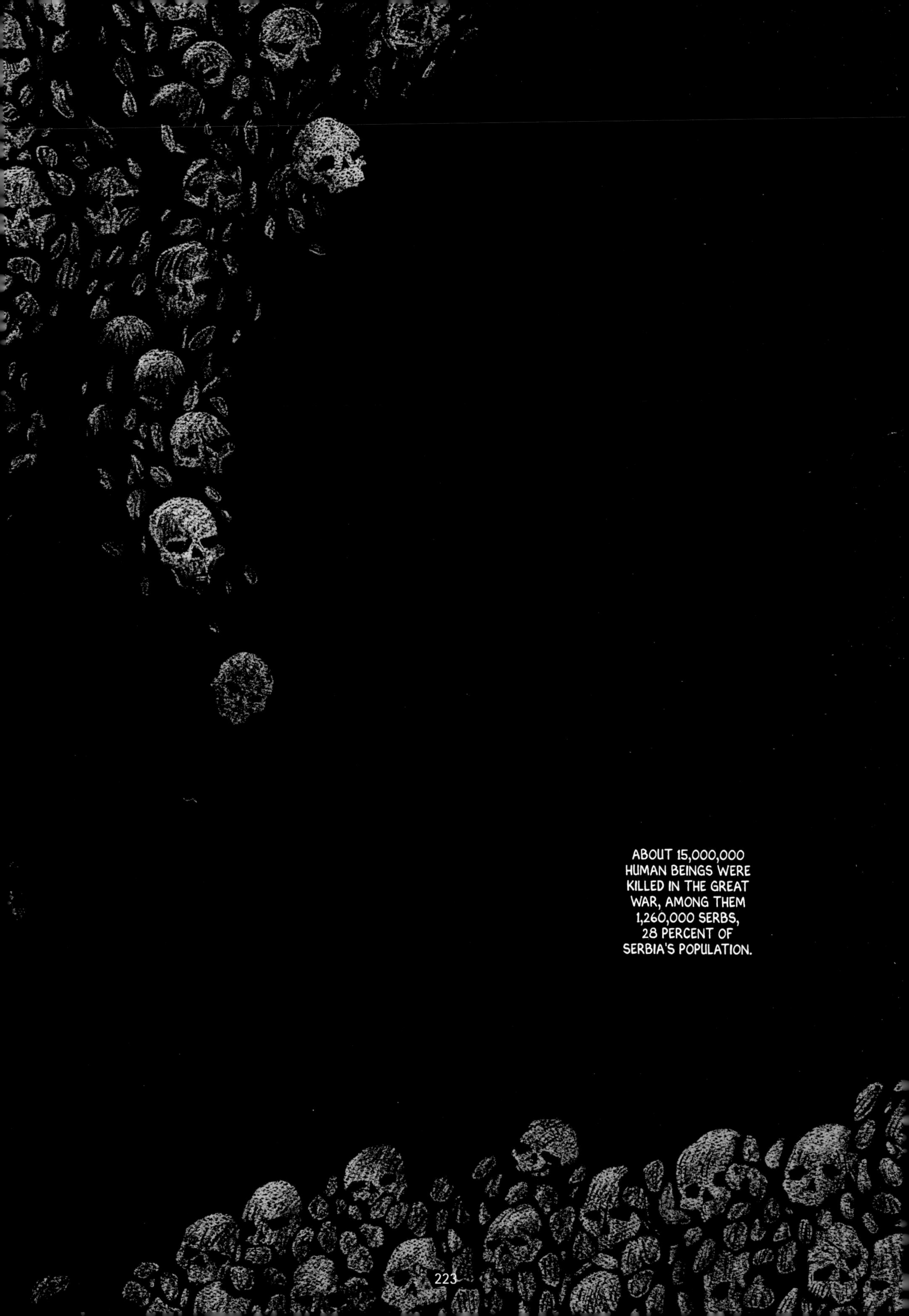
ABOUT 15,000,000 HUMAN BEINGS WERE KILLED IN THE GREAT WAR, AMONG THEM 1,260,000 SERBS, 28 PERCENT OF SERBIA'S POPULATION.

AFTER THE WAR, GAVRILO WAS HAILED AS THE HERO OF THE NEWLY FORMED STATE OF YUGOSLAVIA, WHICH INCLUDED SERBIA AND BOSNIA-HERZEGOVINA. HE WAS REVERED AS THE "ANNUNCIATOR OF LIBERTY" FOR INSTIGATING THE RELEASE FROM AUSTRIAN YOKE.

AUSTRIA
HUNGARY
ROMANIA
YUGOSLAVIA
BULGARIA
ALBANIA
GREECE
TURKEY

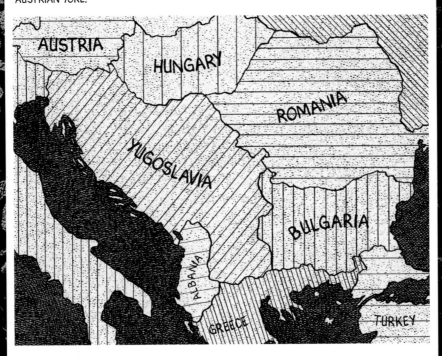

AS A CELEBRATION OF HIS DEED, TWO EMBOSSED FOOTPRINTS WERE PLACED ON THE SPOT OF THE SIDEWALK IN FRONT OF SCHILLER'S DELICATESSEN FROM WHERE GAVRILO FIRED THE FATAL SHOTS AT FRANZ FERDINAND AND SOPHIE.

AFTER THE COLLAPSE OF YUGOSLAVIA IN THE EARLY
1990S, THE FOOTPRINTS WERE REMOVED. THEY
WERE NOT PRESENT ON MAY 27, 1992, THE DAY OF
THE SO-CALLED "BREADLINE MASSACRE," WHEN
SERBIAN MILITARY FORCES SHELLED THE MARKET IN
SARAJEVO, LOCATED JUST A FEW BLOCKS AWAY.

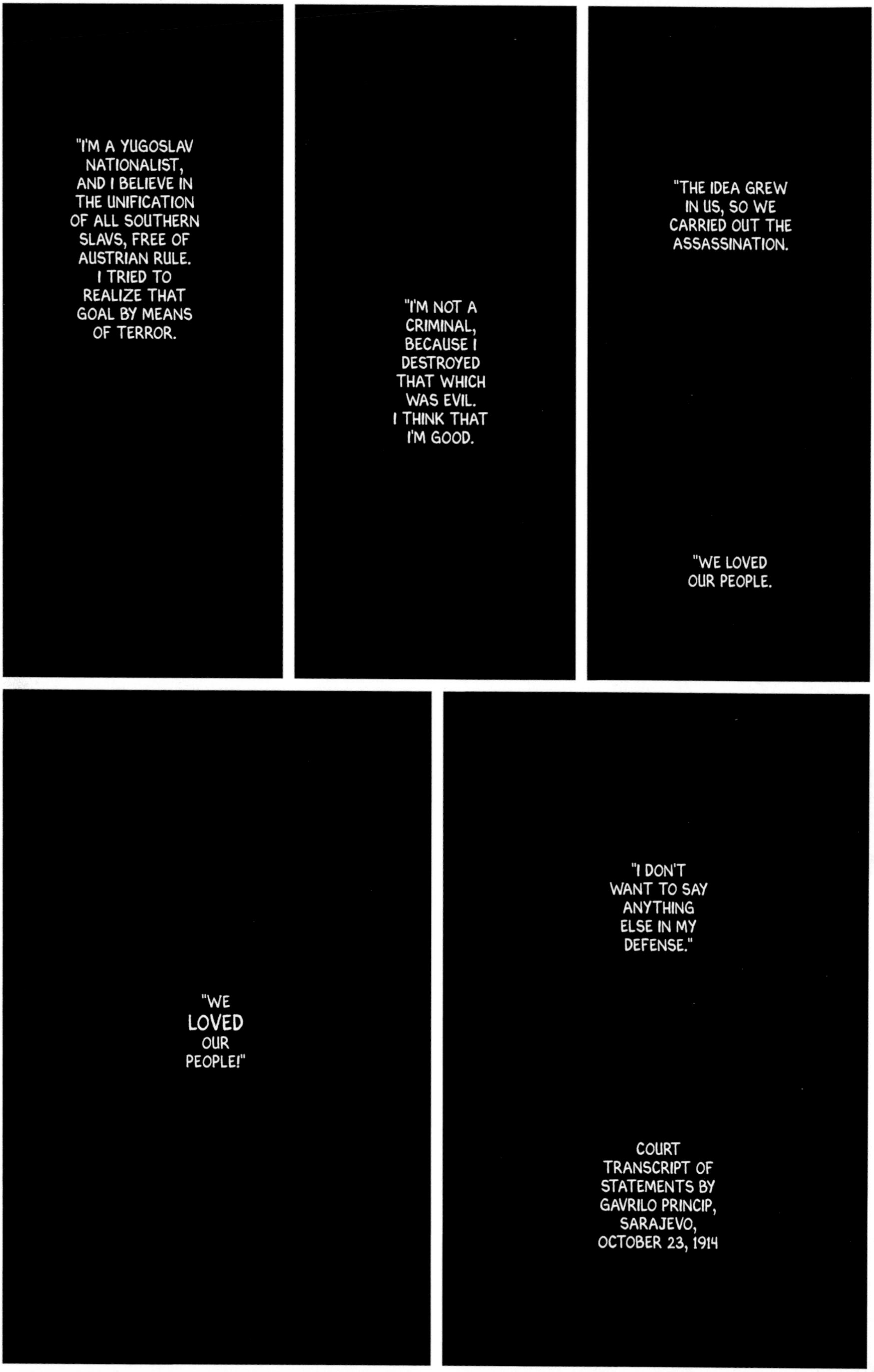
"I'M A YUGOSLAV NATIONALIST, AND I BELIEVE IN THE UNIFICATION OF ALL SOUTHERN SLAVS, FREE OF AUSTRIAN RULE. I TRIED TO REALIZE THAT GOAL BY MEANS OF TERROR.
"I'M NOT A CRIMINAL, BECAUSE I DESTROYED THAT WHICH WAS EVIL. I THINK THAT I'M GOOD.
"THE IDEA GREW IN US, SO WE CARRIED OUT THE ASSASSINATION.
"WE LOVED OUR PEOPLE.
"WE LOVED OUR PEOPLE!"
"I DON'T WANT TO SAY ANYTHING ELSE IN MY DEFENSE."
COURT TRANSCRIPT OF STATEMENTS BY GAVRILO PRINCIP, SARAJEVO, OCTOBER 23, 1914

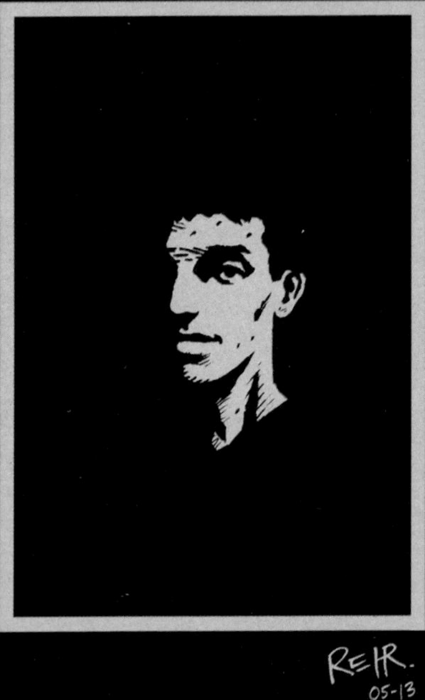
REHR.
05-13